MW00605807

Plane of the Godless
Book 1

By Peter Hartz

Plane of the Godless, Book 1
Copyright © 2019 Peter Hartz | ISBN-13: 978-0-578-46601-9
Author: Peter Hartz
Edited and proofread by the author.

All rights reserved. No part of this publication may be reproduced, distributed, or transmitted in any form or by any means, including photocopying, recording, or other electronic or mechanical methods, without the prior written permission of the author, except in the case of brief quotations embodied in critical reviews and certain other noncommercial uses permitted by copyright law.

This is an original work, conceived of and written entirely by the author. All characters depicted in this work are fictitious. Any resemblance to real persons, living, dead, undead, or resurrected, is purely coincidental. Names, characters, places, brands, media, and incidents are either the product of the author's imagination, or are used fictitiously. The author acknowledges the trademarked status and trademark owners of various products referenced in this work of fiction, which have been used without permission. The publication/use of these trademarks is not authorized, associated with, or sponsored by the trademark owners.

DEDICATION

This book is dedicated to my wife Kristen
And my daughter Addison
Who bring the sunlight to my life
And the colors to my world.

ACKNOWLEDGMENTS

Loads of thanks to the people who have supported and encouraged me on this long journey in addition to my wife and family: Luke Trombley, for coming up with the series title; Jay Woodard, the best boss I've ever had, bar none; our very good friends Scott and Shelley Paulsen, Shelley's sister Heidi, and Shelley's college roommate Physicist Dr. Angie Foudray; and last but not least the team of Phil Rustad, author of Dart, Alamo North Dakota, and Judge's Choice, and his editor Patricia Morris, an amazing person, both of whose advice and support was so amazing and so appreciated.

FORWARD

This story is the result of ten years of my spare time being obsessively devoted (or maybe 'committed' is a better word) to my first serious writing project. Ten long years of finding even a few minutes of my spare time, obsessing over the details, trying to not obsess over the details (and failing), trying to write an outline because everyone said that's how you do it (and failing), and ten years of my characters either laughing at me or basically ignoring me every time I tried to impose at least some sense of direction and order on them.

I had all these good ideas on where I wanted the story to go, and the characters simply told their stories the way they wanted them to be instead. As a result, I ended up pretty much writing this entire series 'stream of consciousness'. The result is that this story at the end of the word-slinging is almost nothing like how it started out. I think that is hilarious. I think the story is great now, and my original ideas would have probably produced something much less than I think it is. Oh well.

The world can be a terrible place. Even when evil is not involved, there is pain, suffering, and loss. One of the lessons I have been working to teach my daughter something I read on the Internet somewhere: while life isn't fair, it's still good. This story is how I would make the world a better place if I had the chance; how I would push back against all the negativity in the world if I could.

This work is also entirely mine. I had no budget to spend on unimportant little things like paying for professional editing, proofreading, or layout. I had to do it all myself. So, while I have spent a lot of hours working to extirpate every possible typo I could find, I bet someone somewhere someday will find at least one, and probably a lot more. And for that, I apologize. I hope that you will be forgiving if you do find something in the book that is less than perfect, and that you can enjoy the story without any little errors I made getting in the way.

"And now, on to the show." Strap in. I hope you have as much fun reading this as I had writing it...

PROLOGUE

The guard had come to his cell and told Koren that his mother and his sister had checked in at the jail and were waiting to see him. His heart, so heavy since the whole incident began, lightened up slightly, but it was really hard to get very happy about anything. The nightmare seemed to never end. He was certain that if he just tried hard enough, he would wake up, and all this would be just a bad dream. It was getting harder and harder to believe that's all it was, though. The arrest, the charges, the trial, the guilty verdict; all of it was a horrific experience he was trying desperately to forget, or wish away.

"Don't move." The statement had been abrupt, shocking him out of his reverie in the small bus stop shelter. He had turned towards the voice, and his blood had run cold. Two white police officers were there, one at either opening, trapping him in the bus shelter, guns drawn. And they were staring at him with cold, hating eyes. It was bad enough being a young African American man in an inner city, but he had to take the bus down to the community college, then from there to his full-time job where he tried to earn enough money to stay in school and out of trouble.

"Yes officer? What can I do for you?" He hoped the fear hadn't shown through, but he wasn't very good at hiding his emotions.

"You're under arrest. Turn around, and put your hands on the glass. Do it now!"

His shoulder still hurt all this time later where the officer who cuffed him had wrenched his arm around behind him, eliciting a yelp of pain and an instinctive physical reaction that had only made the officers mad. With bellows of "Stop resisting," he had been forced down onto the concrete sidewalk where the officers had painfully forced him into submission as they finished cuffing him. When they lifted him up off the cold sidewalk, he was bleeding from above his eye and the side of his face.

"Oops, looks like you shouldn't have done that, should you?" No

1

sympathy there. The scars had mostly faded in the year or so since he was accused of killing someone he'd never met, or even heard of.

The prosecutor had argued that he was a flight risk because he had family in other states, Florida in particular, and bail had been denied. The overworked public defender had not seemed to be very effective, and Koren had wondered if she had really believed his repeated statements that he was innocent. Never mind that he'd had an airtight alibi. The prosecutor had torn that apart with conjecture and hearsay and legal maneuvering. His lawyer had fought valiantly against the destruction of his only defense, but she hadn't succeeded. His mother believed that he was innocent, and he thought his sister still did, but neither of them was on the jury that had unanimously found him guilty. He was immediately remanded into custody, and now that he was convicted, he was a guest of the county until sentencing.

Guilty. He was found guilty of second-degree murder, and some other charges that seem to have been added simply to prove that he was an awful person. How was this possible? Even just the sight of blood made him queasy. The only time he'd ever been in a fight, he'd gotten beaten up pretty badly, and hadn't even landed a single punch. He sat in the holding cell by himself, dressed in a jail jumpsuit, resigned to never seeing the sun as a free man again. The prosecutor had made the news with the guilty verdict. A new prosecutor, the assistant county attorney had made a lot of speeches and statements to the press about "cleaning the scum off our streets", "justice for victims", and other things that made the news. In private, he was, in Koren's opinion, just a rich white man trying to make a name for himself at Koren's expense.

It was overwhelming, and incredibly unfair. He knew he hadn't done what they said. Why didn't anyone listen to him? The thought of spending the rest of his life in prison for something he knew he didn't do was overwhelming.

He went with the guard and sat down in the chair on his side of the glass while trying to smile. He picked up the phone handset, and his mother did the same. A moment later he was speaking with his mother, then later his sister.

* * *

"We still can't believe that that you were convicted," his sister said. "The prosecutor seemed to have it in for you, and your public defender didn't seem to be able to do very much."

"I know, but she is so nice. She tried really hard to do something, but there wasn't much she could do. I mean, the policemen that testified seemed to know everything, and they convinced the jury that I was guilty. I mean, I never knew her, I didn't even know who she was; I don't think I have ever seen her before in my life." Koren shook his head as his spirit seemed to crumble and tears came. "How did this happen to me? Why? I tried so hard to stay out of trouble! I didn't do this! I didn't do this..." His voice trailed off as he broke down entirely, sobbing, with his arms on the small ledge in front of him and his head on them as tears flowed from his eyes.

"Honey, come on, honey, you can get through this," Martha, his mother said as soon as she could take the handset from her daughter and get it up to her mouth. "Koren, honey, talk to me. You can get through this."

"Koren! Pick up the phone!" she said a little louder. She finally got to him to lift his head, and her heart broke at the look of utter devastation on his face. She desperately wanted to take him in her arms, hold him tight, and make everything alright again. But this time, she couldn't even touch him. It hurt. It hurt so much that her own tears fell as her willpower failed her in trying to hide what this had done to her.

"You believe me, don't you mom? You believe I didn't do this?" Koren begged. Her faith in him was the last lifeline, the last tie to the outside world he had. None of his friends had even tried to contact him since his arrest, and the rest of his family all had turned their backs on him. Everyone except his mother and his sister Aisha had stayed away, abandoning him to the hellish nightmare he was going through.

"Honey, Koren, I know you. I know the boy I raised. I am proud of you, of the young man I raised. I never, not for a single moment, believed that you might even think about harming someone, especially a woman. You, of all my children, are the most incapable of doing anything remotely like this. I don't understand why God is allowing this to happen to you. I pray every day to God that you will be pulled out of this and returned to me. No matter what anyone else has said or will ever say, I will NEVER believe that you could do this!"

Aisha nodded at their mother's words. She had grown up doting on her younger brother. They were only sixteen months apart, and had been very close since their father had died of heart disease nearly seven years ago. They had grown closer and had bonded in the aftermath of Troy's death, as their mother had struggled to make ends meet until the life insurance money had come through. Even then it had been nearly a year until some new sense of normal had come to their lives.

Koren's heart rose at his mother's unwavering support. He put his hand up on the glass, and his mother and sister both put their hands on their side of the glass, showing their support for their brother and their belief that he was wrongly-convicted.

The all-too-brief meeting eventually had to end, and the family was further separated once more as Martha and Aisha reluctantly had to leave the jail, and Koren was, with great reluctance and a returning sense of overwhelming dread, led back to his jail to the interminable wait of the next few days until his scheduled sentencing hearing on Monday.

CHAPTER 1

He released his concentration slowly and carefully, feeling the energies subside as he listened to the familiar sound of his success, and opened his eyes. In front of him was the gate he called, shimmering blue-black depths with white glows skittering across the surface, making the familiar but indefinable sounds of every gate he had ever seen. He sat for a moment to catch his breath, and pondered his life, and the path it had taken, once again. He was a long way from home, if a home he ever had. The gate stood as all the others had, taller than he was, reaching down to lay across the ground here under the trees. The open sky before had given way to the edge of the almost-forest in front of him now, and as he had walked, the pull inside had told him he was almost where he needed to be.

Now he lifted himself up from his knees and stretched. Calling a gate was always tiring, even now after so many times, more so when he must rely on his Patron for where the gate would lead. It was weariness not of body, but of some inexplicable way, like the times he had been brutally injured, or fought to exhaustion, and had taken weeks to fully regain his strength. The pull was stronger now, leading him through the gate, and he paused to consider cursing his fate. It was not worth the effort, he finally thought with an old familiar gallows humor. Why should the tide curse the shore upon which it stops? It just is the way of it.

Taking a deep breath as he always did before entering a gate, he stepped forward, stepping over the bottom and into the oval-shaped... thing in front of him.

* * *

The pain she was in would be over soon, she knew. They hadn't told her what would happen when they started, but she could see it in their eyes. The punishment they had been inflicting on her for the last – she'd lost all track of time a while ago – however long had nearly broken her and left her a mass of sobbing human wreckage, but she had retreated deep inside herself, to that silent, comforting place she had found after the accident that had nearly killed her those years ago. There she remained, while the men who had found their way into the cottage, and taken her here earlier in the night, acted like the animals they were. She had no chance to grab her glasses from the bedside table before she was punched and beaten into submission, her hands tied behind her with a short piece of rope brought along for the purpose. Then outside, into the big, black Suburban SUV she hadn't heard come into the yard.

None had offered clues as they had dragged her out of the secluded cottage, into the SUV, and out into the nearby woods, where, in their words, the fun had begun those hours ago. What little she had been wearing to bed on that warm late summer night had been cut away after she had been tied up. The beating that had commenced, because it was supposed to look that way. The one who told her that was almost apologetic. Almost. Whatever he had felt inside about what he was involved in, whatever guilt and shred of conscience that had flared in that moment, had been thrust aside by other thoughts as he carried out his part of their planned event.

The trip from the cottage took them deeper into the woods, their vehicle following a dirt trail they seemed to know. Stopping at a small foot path, pulling her out, dragging her up to a small clearing, throwing her to the ground. Retying her hands and feet. Then it began.

They beat her when she fought them, kicking and punching her. Then after the will to fight back had been replaced by pain, one tried to take crude liberties with her body, only to be thwarted by her resumed struggles. One continued to swim into and out of her vision, frustration clearly written all over his face but mixed with something else she couldn't quite define. Nothing personal, he said, just business. The look on his face said it was more than that to him, mixing business with his pleasure, but she did believe him, in a way. It wasn't about her, really. He was just paid to do what he was doing, regardless of who she turned out to be. His frustration was because she was winning: preventing them from taking from her that which she refused to surrender. They could, and did, beat her until near death, but when they attempted the other, somehow she found the strength to resist once more. After it became apparent to them that they could only have that sick prize after she was dead, they lost all will to add that to the insults and injuries visited on her. They knew that she would never surrender to them, without knowing where that strength came from.

She realized that her concentration was wavering, and her thoughts were wandering; a sign that she was very far gone. It would end soon, she realized, as visions of childhood, her past, her life began to flash before her eyes and her mental focus slowly left the mortal world behind. Blood loss, the pain of the broken bones and the horrible injuries, the eyes gone now from the knife, the voice that screaming had eroded to a hoarse gasp, all of it was slowly starting to fade. The darkness she could not see any more was slowly creeping over her now, easing away the pain. The coldness her body felt as her blood cooled and dried on her skin was fading away, replaced with a strange warmth that comforted her at last.

* * *

He stepped out of the gate into the darkest night, with the stars overhead obscured by the canopy of trees around him, and felt himself lose his balance for a moment as the world swooped around him like a drunkard. Almost as quickly as it came over him, the feeling ended, and he stopped where he was to make sure his balance would not betray him again, wondering briefly if it was from being in need of rest. Then he stayed stock still, listening cautiously to the sounds the night air brought to him. He clearly heard the sound of the gate just behind him; almost like water pouring quietly over rock, but somehow unnaturally so. He looked around as well, the special vision both his parents had bequeathed to him making everything seem almost as bright as day. Harsh experience had taught its lessons well: be aware of your surroundings before you act. He left the gate open behind him, in case he had to return through it and ready some weapon or some other thing he might need. The crossbow in his hands was cocked and loaded - ready if needed. Not wanting to expend the energy needed to make himself not seen, he simply waited a moment.

It was good he had, he realized, as the sounds of laughter came to him. Those voices spoke in a language he didn't immediately recognize, which was not really surprising. But not recognizing the words spoken was not the same thing as not recognizing the tone in which they were said, and his mouth tightened. The pulling feeling inside started up again, gaining in strength, and he knew what it demanded. His patron called for him again. He sighed as he realized that this place would not let him rest, either. He would make payment to his debt again, he knew.

The low, strangely watery sound from the gate behind him faded away to nothingness as he ended the spell that created it. Then he did spend the effort to make himself unseen; an old, well-practiced task he accomplished almost without concentration, even as the effort took its small toll on him, further consuming that strength he drew upon for magic.

He checked his weapons, loosening the sword in its sheath, expecting it would be needed soon. He considered leaving the pack behind, but didn't know if he would need something out of it in a hurry or not, and decided to keep it on him. But he opened the cloak, securing it back with the cord sewn into it across the inside of the back, and checked the pouches and their contents at his waist in old familiar habit.

He stepped off then, walking silently through the night, and moved towards the noises the people made. As he got closer, he could hear another sound under it all – the hoarse, rasping breath of someone near death, and wondered what he would find. Closer now, as the lights they had drew him cautiously forward. He identified four humans from the different voices, and a fifth was slowly expiring. He had little faith in mankind, and expected nothing better of them than what he could picture was happening close at hand: four had taken another out to a place where they could do their work, and not be interrupted.

Closer now, he went around one last tree, silent as the night and invisible as a breeze, and what he saw made his stomach turn over. The four men were dressed strangely, and all held some kind of black metal tube that made some strange light out of a flared end. The lights were all directed down to the ground, at a person they were gathered around. Anger flared inside himself as he realized that the fifth person was a human woman; naked, beaten almost to the point you could not tell her gender, and badly injured with blood coming from her face, her eyes, and many other places on her body; hands and feet tied, she had been the object of their entertainment for quite some time this night.

His eyes wandered around the small encampment, taking in the strange things he saw there. His gaze moved to the things the men held, looking for weapons they might use against him. One had some kind of knife that had blood on it– that he could identify easily enough. In the hand of another, he saw some kind of thing made of shiny yet dark metal that protruded out of the top of his closed fist, but he could not perceive what it might be. The one who held it seemed to treat it carefully, pointing it low and to the side, so it might be some kind of weapon. He would make sure that it was no threat to him, even if he didn't recognize it.

The pull inside welled up stronger within his chest now, and he had no qualms about what it called him to do, even as he realized that the woman had ceased breathing and crossed over to the other side. No matter; he would deal with that in a moment. First, though…

* * *

"Ok, she's gone. Let's make it look good. Pick up what we don't want left behind, and then we get out of here." Jack, the one she had recognized as being in charge, spoke in a focused tone of voice, directing the group with concise, simple commands. Another job completed, another big payday coming. He had just turned to his portion of the work, when a solid low thwonk and a hoarse gasp behind him caused his head to snap around, along with the light from the flashlight in his hand.

Bill had dropped his flashlight and his pistol, and was pinned against the tree behind where he had stood by what looked like the feathered end of a homemade arrow shaft sticking out of the upper right part of his chest, holding him against the thick pine trunk behind him even as blood oozed out around the gruesome injury. He coughed and wheezed. From the arrow's position on his chest, Jack knew it was through Bill's lung. Jack finished turning, and reached inside his jacket, drawing the handgun from the shoulder holster. The specialist standing over the body stared blankly at Bill, shocked into a frozen silence at the sudden violence visited on one of his current business partners out of the black woods with no warning.

Aaron took one look at Bill, and whipped out his own handgun. He quickly calculated where the arrow could have come from, and turned the flashlight in that direction. A former Army Ranger and combat veteran, he was the least shocked and paralyzed by what had happened, falling into a combat crouch with a grip on both the pistol and the flashlight with the speed and ease of long training and practice.

It didn't matter. The specialist made a sound, and Aaron turned that way just in time to see a knife of some kind flash across the specialist's throat, the arm reaching from behind him. He went down holding the spurting wound, and Aaron still couldn't see who killed him. But he suddenly did see a silvery-red flash of metal as that same now-bloody knife was thrown impossibly fast towards him. Then everything went black as awareness fled and the world crashed down on him.

Everything seemed to slow down as Jack watched. The knife that had slashed open the specialist's throat seemed to flash out of the darkness, thrown so hard it appeared in Aaron's left eye as if by magic, burying the blade completely up to the handle. As Jack's horror grew, Aaron seemed to stiffen, and fell backwards like a rock, hitting the ground like a dead weight. Pinned to the tree, Bill seemed to gasp one last time, then sagged, snapping off the arrow in the tree as he fell to the ground, obviously dead as well.

Jack looked wildly around, seeing a ruined throat and the bloody mess the specialist became in death, trying to see where the knife thrower was, and suddenly took a hurried step backwards as someone appeared out of thin air right in front of him. The uneven ground betrayed him, and he dropped his gun and flashlight as his arms flailed for balance. The man in front of him reached out with his right hand and grabbed a fistful of Jack's coat, preventing him from falling. Two eyes looked him over contemptuously as Jack reached up instinctively and grabbed the wrist holding him. He tried to break the grip, but the man's strength was enormous. He felt himself lifted off the ground easily, which terrified him. The shorter, slender man in front of him should not have been able to lift his entire 200 plus pounds with both hands, let alone just one. Holding the wrist with both hands desperately, Jack wondering who the hell this man was, and where he had been when the sounds the woman had made had silenced the noises of the deep woods around them in the hours before her death.

He opened his mouth to speak, but the man didn't give him any time for questions. Instead, he held up his left hand, fingers straight up, with the back of his fingers towards Jack. Then, with a quiet, curious sound, his fingers seemed to ripple, and suddenly there were bone-white claws extending from his fingers and thumb, each a good 6 inches long. His mouth fell open as rational thought left him to hyperventilate, his fear spiking to an impossible level that overwhelmed his mind, and he turned back to the man's face in front of him.

The man showed his teeth in a ghastly caricature of a grin that conveyed mostly disgust, tilted his head to one side, and Jack swayed as the man extended his right arm to full extension out from his body without Jack's feet touching the ground. Before he could wonder about that, the clawed left hand disappeared back behind the man and out of Jack's sight, and he was pulled suddenly back in. A huge pain blossomed, and he realized that the clawed hand had stabbed deeply into his chest. His breath froze as the pain in his chest burned hotter than the sun and his lungs suddenly stopped working. The world spun crazily as the pain roared completely over him. His last sight was the contempt for him in the grey man's expression as his vision grew dim, and then the world went away.

* * *

The simple mind-spell he had cast shielded him from the gore of the man's death at his hand, and that which had sprayed and splattered and splashed on it fell to the ground. Giltreas dropped the dead body contemptuously, stooping to carefully wipe the blood off his hands on the man's strange clothing. Then he retracted his father's legacy, hiding the claws from sight as if they didn't exist. The front of the man's chest was torn out, as if a huge creature had ripped him open. He reached down and picked up the black metal tube that the light emanated from, and looked it over curiously. It was the length of his forearm, but thinner than his wrist, well made, smooth and perfectly round with a texture engraved in the metal making it easier to grip. The end the light came from flared wider slightly, another piece of the strange metal. The light itself, shown through a clear material, was brighter than he should safely look directly at. But then the tugging inside reminded him that his work was not done. The pull was stronger now, and he let it lead him over to the dead woman. He went down on his knees, cutting the ropes that bound her with a small knife from behind his back, and looking at her wounds wearily. He knew then that she was the reason he had been... pulled here. This would take a lot of him. Sending a silent plea inside to his patron for assistance, he sighed as the pull pulsed inside him again, confirming and insistent.

He pulled off his pack now, then his cloak as well, setting them aside for the moment. Then he went around and gathered up the metal light rods and placed them on the ground to light up the still form in front of him, instead of spending more strength to call up his own light. That complete, he knelt on the forest floor next to her and took a deep breath, centering himself. Reaching inside himself, he summoned the arcane arts that he knew so well, calling forth his Physicker Sight to see the extent of her injuries.

There was almost no part of her skin that was unwounded. Old scars covered parts of her face and neck, and more of the same covered her from stomach to almost above her knees. Internally, she had much scarring, and very low on her stomach, voids showed where parts of her guts had been removed under still more scars, possibly by intent. She had suffered much in her life, and it seemed no one had been able to find a healer they could afford or they could barter with to ease that suffering.

He reached into a pouch at his hip, and drew out a small bottle. Unstopping it, he poured the entire contents into her mouth, and it disappeared into her tongue and the tissue of her mouth as if absorbed. He replaced it in the pouch, and poured yet another into her mouth. His Sight told him that no more was needed on that front. He paused a moment to put the now empty bottles back into the pouch, then closed his eyes.

He began the healing meditation of mind magic, hoping that on this plane the healing arts would come easy. Some planes he had visited were very hard places indeed to do such things. He opened his eyes, and watched as a glow, white at first, then, as his concentration built and his focus sharpened, a brilliant pure emerald green, emanated from his hands. A part of his thoughts were pleased that the mind magic worked so easily here. At first dim, the green light grew very quickly grew to glowing brilliance as he drew more energy from the plane around him. Then he lowered his hands over the dead woman on the ground in front of him. As the green glow came in contact with her, it flared intensely, so bright that it was almost hard to see through, and bright enough to cast light upon the woods around him. As he slowly swept his hands above her silent, not-breathing form, the green glow reached into her, healing broken bones, closing wounds and torn tissue, erasing scars, and healing bruises, eliminating any physical trace of what had happened to her before in her life.

Her body began to change with gathering speed as his drawing pulled more energy in to him to pass to her. The green glow emanating from his hands seemed to penetrate completely through her to the ground below, where the plants and grasses seemed to become brighter and stronger and grow a little bit as well. The pull inside him began to pulse in time with the healing green light from his hands, and he was drawn further and deeper into the work as it demanded more from him to heal this woman he had never met, and he felt his patron's approval of his efforts. His eyes closed once more, and the trance took over, moving his hands now without conscious thought. The power grew, coming from the earth and sky and everywhere around, until her entire body was obscured from sight by the intense, brilliant emerald light that now seemed to be coming from her as well, accompanied by a roaring sound a waterfall or a high wind might have made. Then suddenly the moment passed, the need ended, the light and sound disappeared, and it was over.

He opened his eyes and looked down, wondering who she was, and what made her so important to his patron, or anyone else who could request such a boon from his patron, as he paused to catch his breath after his work. The skin was whole. The story of what happened to her before he arrived, written in her blood and wounds, had been erased as if it never occurred. All that remained to tell the tale was the bloodstains left beneath her. Many times past had he performed the healing mind magic, but never on one so grievously wounded such as she, and he doubted that it could all be done away with. Seems that such thoughts had no roots.

His Sight told him that one small thing remained before the last, and he reached into another pouch at his hip by feel alone, taking out and unstopping a small bottle with an almost clear liquid in it. Gently pulling up each of her eyelids, he carefully poured some of the liquid into each, and watched as the cloudiness and haze of those now-healed eyes quickly disappeared. The bottle was stoppered and then disappeared back into the pouch whence it came from.

Now for the hardest part.

He closed his eyes, his lips moving in murmured, reverent prayer to his patron. Then he called forth his strength in another way. Soon he felt the response to his calling as a rushing sound filled his ears and a red glow tinted everything he saw in front of him. Very quickly again, the strength grew in his grasp until he felt it flowing through him like a roaring flame, pulsing in time to his heartbeat. He felt his patron's will join with his, augmenting and directing it, raising it to a level he had never attempted to achieve on his own. It was time. He opened his eyes, and reached out to lower one hand over her heart, and another to almost touch her forehead. Then he took a deep breath and released the red energy, letting it course out of him and into her, directing it deep inside the dead woman in front of him as it sought out that part of her that no longer held life.

A quiet gasp rewarded him as the dead body began to breathe again. The call to his patron worked. That intangible thing that was the difference between a dead body and a living creature sprang into existence, and she lived again. He was exhausted by the efforts he had put out to call the gate, conceal himself, fight, then heal and call the woman on the ground in front of him back across the veil. Never having been granted the time to recover from his last adventure before being drawn to this wood, he paused to catch his breath for a moment. He carefully watched her breathe, then took up his cloak and spread it carefully over her now perfect form to grant her some modesty, pulling the hood over one shoulder and under her head to cushion her gently. Then he sat back and waited, feeling the red pulse inside himself recede rapidly away to nothingness as his patron's will depart. He should have felt satisfaction knowing that his latest task was completed so quickly, but it was overshadowed by the aching exhaustion he felt. Now he could simply rest, and wait for her to awaken.

CHAPTER 2

Awareness came to her slowly. She felt strange. She wasn't sure where she was, and for the moment, had no memory of how she got wherever she was. But it was completely dark and - oh, her eyes were closed. She opened them, expecting not to be able to see without either glasses or contacts, but her breath caught in her throat as everything snapped into clear, sharp, perfect focus: the trees, even the stars above, and much brighter than she would have expected, too...

She heard the soft sigh of a breath let out, and her head snapped to the side. She started when she saw him. She was lying on the ground, a small circle of stones surrounding a low fire on the ground between them. And he was like no one she had ever seen. His skin was greyish white, as was his long, braided hair, lying over one shoulder to lay down the side of his chest. When he turned to look at her, his eyes in the firelight seemed to be an amber color she had never seen nor even heard of before. His face was long and lean, but elegant and handsome. He was clean-shaven and clean, and dressed in strange clothing. He looked tired, but he smiled at her.

Her mind spun as thoughts rushed through her head. Who was he? Had he saved her? What happened to... she lifted herself slightly, turning her head, and she choked as she saw one lying in front of a tree with an arrow sticking out of his chest. Another was on the ground staring vacantly up into the night sky, with his throat slashed open. A third lay on his back with a gruesome wound to his eye. And the fourth, the leader of these animals, with his chest torn and ripped open, laying haphazardly like he was thrown there by a careless child. She gasped as fear washed over her. She tried to sit up, but the world spun, and a gentle hand gripped her shoulder, steadying her. Confusion warred with fear inside of her, but obviously he meant her no harm, or he would have killed her when she was unconscious. The fear subsided as rational thought returned somewhat. It was obvious he had

15

killed her four attackers. More confusion welled up again.

"I don't understand. What happened? Who are you?" Her voice started up almost of its own volition as she pulled herself to a sitting position and arranged the strange soft cloak that was covering her to protect her modesty, putting out questions one after the other, until he held up a hand to say wait. Then he reached into his pouch – pouch? She suddenly noticed that he was dressed very strangely, in addition to his strange hair, skin and eyes. Almost like a monk, or what? And what was he doing?

Giltreas pulled out the components for the spell that would give him her language and let them communicate. The short chant came to him easily, and he activated the spell. The familiar draining feeling of a casting tired him a little more, letting him know the spell was succeeding. As the spell completed, the magical energy grew inside him much faster and way stronger than was usual, and a strange buzzing noise came to him, things he had never felt or heard when shaping and casting spells before. He realized that the air around him was vibrating, getting louder as the energy built up from casting the spell. The buzzing noise changed to a noise like a rushing river, and grew louder as the energy from the spell built up, roaring in his ears. He had never encountered this phenomenon before, and hesitated. He considered what to do for an instant, but when no other choice present itself, and having come this far, he reached out towards her to cast and complete the spell, touching her hand, hoping that whatever happened would be within his power to set aright later.

She gasped as a tiny jolt of electricity shot through her. A roaring noise instantly filled the air, very quickly growing louder and higher in pitch. When the roar grew intolerably loud, a huge white flash seemed to come from everywhere, making the woods brighter than daylight before blinding her. A stupendous concussion of sound accompanied the flash of light, leaving her ears ringing and spots before her eyes even as the force of the blast knocked her back to the ground and rolled her over twice.

She ended up on her stomach looking away from him where the force had tossed her like a rag doll, and as she picked up her head she saw that the white energy had mostly faded away to nothingness. She could still vaguely see its outline, almost like a wave, much taller than she was, racing away from the small clearing in an ever-expanding circle across the ground in all directions. As it passed trees, plants and every living thing, it seemed to flow right through them, temporarily making them translucent with white energy, almost like she was looking at an X-ray of the plants it passed, before it moved further on. She lost sight of it in the woods, but could catch a glimpse as she could see it sometimes between the trees, moving across clearings and up and over small hills. The ground and the plants in its path seemed to glow white for a moment as it made contact with them then moved past, then it slowly faded away as the wave moved on at high speed.

When her mind could focus again, she looked around the camp at the devastation the explosion had caused. The fire had been blown out. Everything, including the dead bodies that could be moved, had been pushed outwards, away from the center of the blast. Astonished and stunned, she looked back, and saw that the blast had spent its main force on the grey man. He was lying on his side several feet from where he had been before, with his mouth open and eyes shut. He was bleeding from his nose, mouth, eyes and ears. He was still, but every now and then would twitch like something was shocking him, and was obviously very badly hurt. She wasn't sure who he was or what he had done to cause the explosion, but he had killed her four assailants before they could finish her. As such, she would help him now if possible. She owed him that.

She stood as quickly as her trembling muscles would allow, then walked over on shaky legs to where the cloak had fallen. She picked it up and settled it over her shoulders, drawing its comfortable softness and gentle warmth around her, pulling the thick tie around her and knotting it off, and then walked over to the stranger.

She bent over him, and gently worked to pull him over onto his back. His head lolled in such a way that she knew he was at least unconscious, if not worse. She reached out and turned his face towards her so she could check him over more, and noticed huge hole between his ear and temple, extending up towards the top of his head. A good amount of his scalp was missing and his skull showed through the gap, broken and dislodged, with some part missing. The ghastly wound was pouring blood out into his grey hair, turning it bright red in the light from the flashlights gathered around and the campfire. Feeling sick to her stomach at the gruesome injury, she felt for his pulse, but couldn't really tell if it was there or not. Dismayed, not knowing what to do to save him, she froze, trying to think of something as she watched the blood seep now more slowly out of him. Looking around, she saw nothing around that could be used staunch the flow, and looked back to his wound, feeling helpless and sick with worry and fear for him.

And was shocked at what she saw. In just the seconds she had looked away and back again, the blood flow had slowed considerably, and was pooling in place, filling in the wound in defiance of gravity and several other immutable science lessons from college. Almost immediately, a green light began to glow at the site of the injury as the blood loss stopped entirely, and the pool of blood forming on the side of his head started to pulse, first so faintly that she was not even sure she was seeing it, until it was obviously there. She reached out and put her fingers to his throat, checking his pulse and dreading what she would find, when to her surprise, it was strong and steady, not the weak beating of someone whose injury placed him so close to death, a far cry from what she had found just moments before.

As she watched the pulsing green glow in amazement, she slowly realized that the blood was filling in the wound, taking the place of missing tissue and bone; then it began to change color. The sight of it stunned her. What was she witnessing here? In a short time, the ghastly wound closed up, healed completely. Even the hair that had been lost grew back, flowing down his head until it matched the rest of his hair in length and fullness. Then the glow moved slowly over his head and down his body. When it reached his feet, it seemed to fade into the darkness, and it was gone.

She realized at that moment that she had been hyperventilating, and forced herself to take a slow, deep breath. The man in front of her continued to breathe, but didn't seem to be moving around at all. He must be unconscious, or something, but he almost seemed to be sleeping. She decided. She couldn't just leave him here, so…

She looked around, and didn't see any vehicles, but that didn't mean much. She remembered being driven here in a Suburban or something like it, so it must be around here somewhere. The leader had been driving the SUV that brought them all here deep in the woods, so she picked up one of the flashlights that had illuminated her, and walked, as gently as her bare feet would let her on the ground in the trees, over to where he lay.

She flashed the light over his still form to see if she could spot where his keys might be. And turned away instantly, her stomach heaving as she saw the huge wound in his chest. There was nothing in her to come up, but her stomach valiant gave it a go anyways, wracking her body with the attempt to empty itself. The effort left her weakened temporarily, driving her to her knees in front of his bloody corpse. She squeezed her eyes shut hard, then reached out to move her hand across the damp ground until it touched his arm.

Keeping her eyes closed, she moved her hand around until she found his hand, then she moved it past his hand to his body. So far so good. Working her hand into his front pocket on that side of his body, she found some change, but no keys. Taking a deep breath, she turned her head until she could only see his feet from the corner of her eyes, then scooted around him until she could get to his other front pocket. Nothing. Where…? He had been wearing a light jacket. Must be in there. She turned her head slowly, sweeping her eyes up his legs, until she could just barely make out the bottom of the jacket. It was laying open on the ground, probably when… don't go there, she told herself. Just get the damned keys.

She closed her eyes and felt around where the jacket should have been, and reached into the pocket. Success! Pulling the keychain out, she opened her eyes to look at it, and immediately regretted it as her eyes were pulled to the ruin of his chest again. She gasped, clamping her eyes tightly shut, and turned away. Her stomach roiled again, but it knew it was empty, so didn't engage in any more futile acts.

She stood, turning away from the corpse as she did so, and looked around. Not seeing anything resembling a large black SUV, and her mind ran over the thought - of course the bad guys drive a BLACK SUV, and the largest they can find – must be compensating for something, she thought in dark humor. The thought conjured up something dark and cold inside her, and she shivered in the warm air. Pulling the cloak around herself more tightly, she held the key fob up over her head and pushed the unlock button.

A chirping sound came to her, and she turned, walking carefully over the forest floor and then the path she found. She followed the path for a few minutes, chirping the remote from time to time to confirm her direction, and found the truck around a bend in the path, down on the main dirt road. Opening the driver's door, she got in, started it up, and carefully drove it back up the path to the small clearing, barely clearing the trees on either side, and jouncing over the uneven path as she crept up to where the grey man lay.

* * *

He allowed himself a small celebration as he contemplated the furtherance of his plans. Another step completed, and an annoyance removed from his path as well. The call had come in just about twenty minutes ago.

"Sir, the first of those two problems is resolved, and the second will also be resolved soon. Unless there are issues, this is the only time we will talk."

God, he loved professionals, he thought with a contented sigh. He took a sip of the cognac that he saved for just certain special occasions. Expensive as hell, and oh, so fine. One down, one more to go, probably tomorrow. Now he could move his plan forward without having to fight with her over it. Yes, all was right with the world.

CHAPTER 3

She stood at the end of the bed watching him breathe, and her mind swirled with endless questions. Where had he come from? Who was he? Why was he dressed that way? And what the hell happened when he touched her? Her ears still rang slightly, almost an hour later, from the sound and force of the concussion. Her thoughts went back, playing quickly over everything that happened, like a movie in fast-forward. Trying to get his unconscious form into the Suburban, then getting him up into a fireman's carry and laying him in back. Looking over the small clearing, and picking up bits of torn pajamas, everything of hers she could find. Trying to remember the moments from when she got to the clearing to when she saw him kneeling beside her. Grabbing his strange pack and even stranger-looking crossbow and setting them in the back of the Suburban next to him. Then, the drive carefully through the woods with her lights off while being able to see adequately in the darkness.

Her memories after she woke up were mostly a blur now, her mind in a tangled whirl of half-formed thoughts and concepts that seemed to start to form, then where swept away by the currents of her emotions. She started to pull the cloak tighter around herself for a moment as she stood over the bed, then she forced herself to stop. She wanted to get into her own clothes. With one last glance at the sleeping or unconscious form on the cottage's guest bed, she turned and padded silently across the hardwood floor out of the room, pulled the door most of the way closed behind her, and went over to the master bedroom.

It had taken her less time than she thought it would to get his still form into the Suburban, lug his pack to the back of the vehicle, drive back to the house, and put him into a fireman's carry again so she could lug him up the steps and deposit his still but breathing form on the bed in the guest room. She had pulled off his strange boots, setting them aside, then looked him over once more. Every bit of her mind was on the task at hand, and her sense of focus was totally on getting this person, whoever he was, inside and safe. She should have been more tired. Must be the adrenalin still coursing through her. She should be hungry too, considering. She'd deal with that later.

His strange appearance struck an odd chord inside her. The rings on his fingers, one on each hand, whose stones seemed to catch the light and reflect more of it back. A necklace of some sort with a black, diamond-like stone on it in a strange, ornate setting around his neck. Thick, wide, matching bracelets were on his wrists, extending up his arms a small ways. Some sort of... something around his waist. And a belt with pouches and purses attached to it. Pants of a strange design. A shirt that looked more like a tunic of some kind.

And the weapons. She found several knives that would fit well in one hand, and couldn't have failed to noticed the large, long-handled sword (a sword? had she fallen down a rabbit hole or something?!?) on a belt at his left hip back in the clearing. That she had taken off him when she tried to lay him down gently in the back of the Suburban. It lay against the chair in the bedroom, clustered around with the few other things of his she pulled off him in her attempt to make him more comfortable while he slept.

Everything about him was different somehow. Like nothing she had ever seen in real life, but possibly a movie or something. Not overly ornate, or flashy, not very plain or very rough, but somewhere in between. Serviceable clothing that looked to be well-made, but of fabrics and cloths that seemed made by hand, and stitched together one piece at a time. Nothing on him was worn out, but it all looked... worn in, or gently used – that was the best term she could think of. And it all seemed to go together as if purchased from the same place, she thought, then wondered where that thought had come from. Some costume shop or something?

There were rings on a few of his fingers; one a plain gold band, a few others with stones set in simple settings. One, however, was of a very ornate design, set with a black stone that, from the corner of her eye as she looked away, seemed to have a very faint glow deep inside. The necklace around his neck had a pendant on it that seemed to be difficult to look at directly, almost like it didn't want to be seen. Each time she leaned forward to get a better look at it in the light from the hallway fixture, her mind wandered to a different subject. She shook her head as if to clear it, and decided to talk to him later about it.

The belt around his waist came off, pouches and all, and she set that aside on the small bedside table, easily in reach and view. Didn't want him to think she had stolen from him; she'd seen his handiwork in the clearing, but shied away from that thought just as quickly as it had come to her. She even pulled the cloak off herself and set it over the back of the chair, confident enough that he stayed asleep or in whatever state he was the whole time, and that he wouldn't see her.

That had been earlier. Now, though, with whomever he was taken care of, she backed out of the room, turned off the light, and closed the door part way. She left the light on in the hallway so that when he woke up, he would be able to see around him.

She walked back to the master bedroom at the end of the hall, and turned on the light. She glanced at the clock on the dresser as she reached inside, noting that it was nearly two in the morning as she pulled out some under things and started to pull them on, not really looking at what she was doing as her hands followed a familiar ritual, her mind far away on the earlier events of the last few hours. The underwear was too large, so she reached into the drawer again, thinking that some of her clothing from before her latest weight-loss effort must still be in the drawer, and pulled out some that she thought would fit her better, remembering the few pounds she had already lost, and how much more she still wanted to lose to get to her goal. She tried to put the next pair of underwear on, but they were also too big. Then she noticed something about herself, and stood there stunned for a moment, before going quickly into the master bathroom. Flipping on the light by feel, she looked at herself in the huge mirror over the double sinks in shock and disbelief. Then the world swam before her eyes, and she had to lean heavily on the counter top in front of her, looking down away then pressing her eyes tightly shut, hiding from the site that greeted her in the mirror. When the room stopped shimmying around, she looked up again. And gasped again at what she saw.

Someone she had not seen in many years looked back at her. The image was much younger than her forty-seven years. The thinning, greying hair was gone, with and in its place was original reddish-brown locks, rich and full. And long. Not more than three hours ago, it had been cut very short because it would not grow right anymore, in the cutest bob cut that she could get to hide the thinning patches on top. The skin on her face was smooth and flawless, without the crow's feet at the corners of her eyes, or the age marks that had started to take up residence there. The wrinkles on her neck were gone. Her skin everywhere she looked was smooth and flawless, better than she had ever seen it, she realized. The moles and other blemishes on her face and neck were gone. Her body, her arms, her hands, everything was incredible. But that wasn't the biggest thing.

All the scars from the accident years ago that nearly killed her, and the seemingly endless surgeries that had put her back together as best as could be with modern medicine, were completely gone. Erased, as if they had never been there before. Her nose was straight and unbroken. The ears were level once more. The eyes were as well. The room spun again, and she sat down on the floor on her naked backside – hard. She sat there, and closed her eyes, trying to catch her breath. When she could look around and the room stayed put, she pulled herself to her feet once more, realizing that she was feeling youthful strength and flexibility for the first time in many years. Decades. And looked back in the mirror once more.

The form and figure looking back at her looked like a supermodel. Or maybe an Olympic athlete, like she always planned to be in college, and almost was in high school before the accident. The extra weight that she always wanted to lose was nowhere in sight. What she saw was toned, defined muscle under smooth, flawless skin. She looked at the back of her left hand, and that surgical scar was gone as well, where the cyst had been removed some years back. Or the winding scars on her legs where that dang horse had thrown her off onto the barbed wire fence. The almost-faded scar on the right side of her forehead where her little brother had hit her with the toy truck that required eleven stitches when she was nine. Every bit of skin she could see was perfect and flawless, without scars, nicks, pock marks, age marks, wounds, blemishes, moles, or any imperfections at all. An almost hysterical part of her mind threatened to giggle when the thought came to her: she looked touched up, like a digital photograph after someone spent hours in Photoshop or something. But it was real, she realized in wonder. Even her breasts were smaller and perfect, without that middle-aged sag that she'd come to accept. She looked like a teenager again. But she was forty-seven, she reminded herself. Wasn't she? Incredible.

She wasn't sure how long she looked at herself before turning away, turning her mind away from the impossible to the practical. She had started the day probably fifty pounds heavier. Which meant that there was nothing in the entire cottage that would fit her now, except the robe hanging in the bathroom. It quickly served to cover her up, and the giddy hysteria seemed to bubble back up inside again, threatening to come out as she realized that it almost wrapped around her twice and covered her down to above her ankles.

With the requirements of modesty and decency met, she walked quietly out of her bedroom, down to the guest room where she assured herself her guest was still sleeping as she placed the cloak over the back of the chair. Then she walked out into the main room of the luxurious cottage. She looked around, and felt a sudden need to sit on out on the porch as a silent whisper of faint memory from last night came to her, and in discomfort, hurried out the front door, closing it quietly, and settled into a chair back away from the light near the door. Dave would be here later this morning. He would know what to do, if anyone did.

But deep inside in the silent reaches of her soul, she doubted that things would ever be the same again. What had happened? And what was going to happen to her and everyone that depended on her because of it? No answers came to her, and she stared off into the night, deeply troubled.

CHAPTER 4

Dave pulled off the main road and onto the dirt path, where he stopped and got out to open the gate, worried about his older sister. He hadn't slept well at all last night, which wasn't like him. He woke up several times to bad dreams, first of someone torturing first Michelle, then moving on to him, while he was powerless to stop it. He finally woke up at just after five in the morning, and decided to get an early start on the two hour trip to the cottage to bring her dogs up for her week away. He continued on up the path, leaving the gate open as he usually did when he visited the cottage. When it was just her, he insisted she close the gate, however.

Dave adored Michelle, and was so worried about her health lately. He knew Michelle hadn't been honest with him when she said she was fine, but couldn't bring himself to push her for the truth. Too many years looking up to her, first as his big sister, then as a survivor of that horrible accident the summer she graduated from high school, and on to everything else leading up to her role as his boss. She went through so many reconstructive surgeries because of that drunken truck driver who had also smoked a lot of weed that morning all those years ago. Then she spent months in physical therapy, telling everyone she was fine in that same tone of voice she always used when he thought she was trying to convince herself the most. It all had taken its toll on her, but she survived, and even recovered. She learned to walk again, then to run. And had never stopped since.

And through it all, came an inner strength that was incredible, awesome to behold. By sheer force of will, she could accomplish the impossible. And she set out to prove it by putting herself through college, while saving as much money as she could for the future.

Then after she graduated with top honors with an MBA from Carlson School of Management at the University of Minnesota, she moved on to become a business woman. She started her own company with the settlement money from the accident, and made it successful. She grew it through careful decisions and well-planned strategic acquisitions, both here in the States and two in the UK, but underneath it all, it was still the same data services company that was well led and managed, just larger. She had even hired him after he completed his time in the Marine Corps and gone to school on the GI Bill for a Masters' Degree in Data Security. In the last few years, she had hired a few experienced upper managers to delegate more and more of the day to day operations to, and slowly began to step back, telling others she wanted to enjoy life while she was still young.

But when her health began to change, and the obvious changes to her appearance got worse in the last six months, he had overcome that younger-brother awe enough to ask her what was going on. And when she told him it was nothing to worry about, she knew he saw the lie in what she said. He had heard it enough in the long months of recovery. But her eyes begged him not to push it, and he hadn't. Not with her.

He did, however, have a long conversation with one of her doctors, in the best interests of her company. Dave was Michelle's Medical Power Of Attorney, as well as a member of her immediate family and part owner of the same firm she started up, and the doctor had spilled the beans. He cared too much for his patient and longtime friend, not to mention her whole family, to hold out for long.

Cervical cancer. Third stage. It had spread, metastasizing into her lungs and elsewhere. Inoperable for the most part. It was moving really slowly, however, and was responding to the latest in chemotherapy. The odds were better than fifty-fifty that she would recover. After surgery had yanked out another bunch of parts of her she no longer needed where the cancer had started, and radiation treatments had their way with others, of course.

He knew that the odds were not that great. But he still let it go. Especially when he noticed her quiet planning taking effect to transition more and more of her duties and responsibilities to trusted associates and subordinates. He would be there for her, as any good brother would, no matter what. And in any capacity she wanted. She deserved that from him.

But the dreams last night had left him nearly terrified. There had never been even so much as a hint of threat against her recently. Everyone she worked with respected her greatly, because she did so much to help other succeed. Sure, there was the usual whack-job that threatened anyone, especially a woman, in a powerful position, but nothing recent came to mind.

Her health had made him want to take care of her, so after some careful searching, he put in a purchase offer on a luxury cottage in the woods, a place out of the way and mostly off the grid that she could use as a refuge when she needed a break.

He had been prepared to pay for it out of his share of the fortune from the success of the company, but she hadn't argued, and signed the expense approval herself before he presented it to the CFO and the board. She was hard-headed, but eminently pragmatic. And she trusted her brother. If he said she needed some place to get away to, she didn't argue. Too many other issues and tasks, that she could do something about, needed her attention to fight over something so important to him.

But if something happened to her at the cottage that supposedly only the most trusted family members knew about, then there was a problem. No one else outside the inner circle even knew that it existed, let alone where it was. Which spoke volumes.

He had pulled off the secluded highway onto the private, curving, heavily shrouded road in the early morning light. Then he glanced once more in his rear-view mirror as he pulled away. The road behind him wound back and forth beyond the gate, and at this point he couldn't even see the highway. Which is how he wanted it when he set out to find this place for her.

The trip up the secluded, winding driveway seemed to take forever, and he wanted to go faster, but it was narrow, and he wouldn't do anyone any good if he hit something, like one of the huge pines growing right next to the dirt path. It was also not in the best condition, either, he reflected as he slowed down close to the end of the drive. He came around the last turn into the clearing where the cottage had been built, where he saw a big black Suburban parked right next to the front porch.

He pulled in and stopped behind the SUV, deliberately blocking it in, and a chill ran down his spine as he took it in. No license plate, with a temporary tag in the back window the only proof that it was registered to someone. Dark tinted windows. Nothing else on it identified where it came from. It certainly didn't belong here. He would have to check the VIN with accounting to see if it belonged to the company or not. But that could wait until later.

He glanced across the clearing to the garage, and saw his sister's expensive Italian sedan inside through the open garage door where it should be. His mind touched briefly on the memory of when she leased it just a month before, but then he returned to the task at hand. He eased open the door on his as quietly as he could, and carefully pulled out the heavy Glock pistol from the shoulder holster inside the light jacket he always wore when carrying. Then he stepped as silently as he could around the Suburban, to make sure it was empty. He opened the front passenger door, and noticed the keys were in the ignition. Closing that, he pulled the back passenger door open as silently as he could, and covered and cleared the inside of the big vehicle. Nothing appeared in the shape of a person, or big enough to hide one, and he turned, pushing the door shut slowly, and crept up to the stairs, glad that the builders had done such a fine job of putting the whole cottage and porch together that he was able to make almost no noise. Then at the top of the steps, he heard something.

It was quiet, and barely carried to him, but he heard it clearly: the sound of a woman clearing her throat; almost an "eh-hem". He turned towards the source of the sound, half raising the pistol, but not pointing it at anything yet, and saw someone sitting on a chair close to the house, back in the early morning shadows.

"You're not gonna need that, Davey D. Seriously." Her voice carried to him clearly, even though it was an almost-whisper.

"Why's that? Who are you? Where's my sister? I see her car. Where is she?" he said, his voice almost as quiet. He didn't change his ready stance, just turned to face her more completely. He was confused. Who was she? The voice tugged at his memory, but he couldn't place it. It was like he had heard it once, a long time ago.

"Things are so strange, Davey D. I don't know what has happened. And I have no idea what to do next." The quiet voice came to him again, and he paused. Only his sister ever called him that, and only when she was trying to send a message to him that only he would hear. No one else even knew about the nickname anymore. But the voice didn't match anyone he currently knew. He just couldn't place it.

"Who are you? Where's…" He paused as she stood, and he could see her a little better as she stepped slowly forward. She was wearing… what? Just a robe, wrapped and belted around herself? He thought he recognized it from the cottage. What in God's name is going on here?!? Then she slowly stood and walked towards him, both hands cautiously out away from her sides.

"Don't wanna get shot, Davey D. But things are strange, so let's both take it slow, ok?" She stepped fully into the early morning light, and he stared at her face, trying to remember where he'd…

"Oh my GOD!! Michelle? Wha..?" He gasped, as he couldn't believe what he was seeing. She looked like she was eighteen years old again! Or…

"Something happened to me last night. Something…" she broke off as a sob came over her, and her face crumpled as emotion overwhelmed even her formidable self-control at last. Davey holstered the weapon as fast as he could, then reached out to wrap her in his arms, and he simply held her as she collapsed into his arms and cried.

* * *

It had been a strange hour for him, Dave reflected. Not as strange as what his sister had gone through, though. She's shown him where every scar had been before on her face, neck, arms, legs, back, and any other place she could while maintaining her modesty, and he still couldn't believe it. Only the fact that he had grown up with that face had enabled him to believe her. Then she told him what she could remember happened to her in the woods, and cried again in his arms. He felt powerless to ease her pain as she shook and sobbed, but then the storm passed. She described the stranger she had awoken to, and the strange clothing he had been wearing. The archaic cloak she had been wearing when she woke up that had obviously come from him, the tunic, the pants, the boots. The belt, with the pouches on it, and the weapons. The jewelry: rings, bracelets, a necklace with a stone of some kind that seemed to glow when you saw it out of the corner of your eye. He looked at her in disbelief, but followed her to the guest room door and peeked in on the man sleeping there. She went in further, and checked his breathing, then shook her head as she came out and closed the door part way again, as if in disbelief herself.

Then they had sat in the family room down the hall from the guest room, across from the kitchen, and talked for another hour. He eventually learned that she was wearing the oversized robe because nothing fit her anymore. She had lost every bit of extra weight she had, and didn't have anything remotely close to her size in the cottage. Her skin was a perfect, flawless olive, reflecting their half-Italian ancestry, and her hair seemed to glow as well. Then she carefully lifted her legs, and he received another shock. More hair. He knew that she had gone and had most of her body hair permanently removed at a laser skin clinic when she had the chance and the money. Better than shaving, she'd said at the time. But it had grown back that night. Then he pointed out that her chipped tooth seemed to have been fixed as well, and she hurried to the hall mirror to see, and made another discovery.

Her teeth were… different. She opened her mouth, and the bridgework and reconstruction of her teeth and mouth on the right side had disappeared – in its place were real teeth. The whitening she had done seemed to have been altered. They were now more of a natural ivory, no longer the pure white she had been so proud of. And every filling in her mouth seemed to have disappeared, along with the chip that had been there on the upper front tooth, a souvenir from slipping while climbing over a chain link fence when she was eleven. Her teeth were… perfectly natural, along with everything else about her.

She'd come back to the couch with a stunned expression on her face. "What could do this to me? This is almost like a dream or something!" The shock and awe in her voice was almost amusing to him, and he let her think about it for a while.

"Hey, where's Sadie and Abby? You brought them with you when you came up here, right?" Her gaze turned on him almost like an interrogation. He stayed at her house sometimes when she was away so that her furry companions could be cared for. She strongly disliked the thought of leaving them at a kennel in the care of someone she didn't know.

"Crap. I forgot. They're out in the 4Runner. Want me to bring them in?" He leaned forward on the couch to stand, and she nodded.

"I really need them. Can you go get them for me?" She asked in a voice that was small and vulnerable as she looked at him. His heart melted as he looked at her, trying to understand everything she was going through, and failing completely.

He stood, bent over her and gave her a quick hug, then walked softly across the polished hardwood floor to the door. Whatever had happened to her, Dave reflected as he walked down the steps outside and went over to the SUV he came in, had thrown her life completely upside down. Now what the hell did she, and he, do about it? Would things be the same? He opened the back door to his vehicle and reached in to lift the little dog Abby into his arms, then held her in one arm as he gave Sadie's leash a gentle tug, then unclipped it. The bigger dog, still lean and beautiful in her red cedar-colored coat and white paws and tip of her tail, looked up at him and thumped her tail from her spot on the back seat of the midsize vehicle. But she didn't get up, and he smiled almost sadly. Sadie had been trained so well. But she was showing her age. The grey on the muzzle, and the mellowing as she slowed down a little more each year. She was approaching ten years old now; probably a senior citizen for a lean, athletic, once-graceful sixty-pound Labrador/Golden Retriever/surprise mix.

"Sadie, come. Let's go, girl. Michelle is here." Sadie stood at the command, stretched her front and back legs one at a time to her full length as best she could in the vehicle, then hopped slowly and carefully out to the ground.

Abby wriggled in his arms briefly, trying to get down, so he set her on her paws, and she shook all seventeen pounds of herself before strutting over to the side on the grass and relieving herself. Sadie followed suit, and soon enough they both loped up the steps to wait beside the long-familiar door, looking back at him as he came up behind them.

"Wait," he said as he opened the door, and they both sat and waited until he had stepped through, just like they had been trained to do by Michelle. He held the door open and said quietly "all done", and they ran in past him.

He caught up to them in the living room, seeing Abby wriggling in Michelle's lap. Sadie wagged her tail so hard that her back half moved with it, her head on Michelle's knee. She wrapped her arms around Abby, hugging her close, and sobbed briefly. Then she sat back, stroking the happy little dog in her lap as it settled down to the attention. Sadie just lay down on the rug and laid her head on Michelle's foot, her tail moving slowly.

Dave sat back down across from her in the love seat. "So what do you want to do now? I am not sure where to go from here." He stared down at his feet, running a hand through his thinning hair.

She took a deep breath and closed her eyes, her mind racing. "Obviously, we have to figure out who tried to have me killed. I don't know how to go about doing that. I also don't know what I am going to do about my appearance. No one is going to believe that I am me. I don't even know if I believe it myself." Her hand slowly stroked Abby's back as the little dog soaked up the attention. Dave looked over and smiled at the sight, and then his face returned to its previous frown.

"Well, I think we should hang out here for a couple days and see what happens. You took the entire week off. That buys us some time to figure this out. For now, you are simply a cousin who came here for a little vacation and got here too late to save you. Dang, that sounds weird." He looked over at her, a question in his eyes. "What do you think?"

"We have to figure out what's going on with the grey man in the other room, too. Where does he fit into all this? He obviously killed my attackers before they could do me in, and then did something to me to make me this way. I want to have a chance to talk to him and find out what happened." She shuddered briefly, and Abby sat up to look back over her shoulder at Michelle, who saw the look and smiled again, running her hands down Abby's back once more.

"Yes, Abby, I won't stop petting you. You are the center of the world, after all..." The smile was wavering, but it was there. Somewhat. Dave was somewhat relieved to see it at all at this point.

Dave came to a decision, and turned to her. "I think I should call Allie and get her up here. If someone came after you, she might be next. Until we get this sorted out, I want her safe."

"Of course. I should have thought of that. Get her moving as soon as possible," she said quietly.

He pulled out his cell phone, and called his house. His wife answered, and said "You got there ok?"

"Yeah, I am all safe and sound up here. I think I will be here until tomorrow. I think I need to decompress a little myself, get away from the circus for a little while," he replied, hoping she remembered.

Her breath caught in her throat, and her mind raced. As the business had gotten more successful, Dave had decided that they needed some code words that they slip into conversation on the phone in case of emergencies. The phones could be tapped, or there could be bugs in the house for someone to listen in. She had thought it somewhat silly then. Now, she wasn't laughing inside. Decompress was a code word. It meant that bad things were in motion. Circus meant that things were happening fast. She racked her brain for the proper response, and then remembered what would fit her situation.

"Well, as long as you're back in time for your honey-do list, I can relate." Relate was a response saying she would be joining him as soon as she could get out the door.

"Glad you understand my need to escape the rat-race, honey. See you tomorrow. Call if you need me." Escape meant no one was in immediate danger, but action was required, and soon.

"I will. See you when you get back. Love you," came her automatic closing statement, as she already was thinking about what she would need to take to the cottage.

"Love you too, hon. Bye." He hung up the phone, then turned back to Michelle. "She's on her way as soon as possible," he said.

She just smiled gently. He had told Michelle about the code words, and made her memorize them as well. His time in the U.S. Marine Corps had left their mark on him; he was prepared.

A comfortable silence fell over the family room of the cottage. Sadie stood and stretched, then walked across the cottage to the kitchen where the water bowl was located. Abby, who didn't like to be separated from her good buddy, hopped down from Michelle's lap and followed. Shortly the sounds of two dogs drinking from the same bowl could be heard coming from the kitchen.

Michelle slowly lay down on the couch. "I'm so worn out. Everything that has happened to me has drained me, and I didn't sleep at all last night since. Let me just nap a bit here until our guest wakes up." She started to curl up on the couch, but Dave stood, and walked over to her. He reached under her with both arms, and lifted her up, holding her close. She laid her head on his shoulder as he carried her to the master bedroom, and she reached down to pull the covers back so he could set her right into the bed.

"You sleep good, big sister. I won't let anything happen to you. I love you." He bent down and kissed her forehead, but she was already asleep. He tucked her in, and walked quietly out of the room. The door he left open slightly, so the dogs could come in and get to the pet bed laid out for them at the foot of the king-size bed Michelle was asleep in. Then he went to the kitchen and removed both dog's collars, a practice that Michelle had gotten into so their tags wouldn't wake her up in the middle of the night. She was somewhat of a light sleeper, and the dogs loved to sleep in their bed. There was even a blanket over it that Abby could snuggle under. She would sleep on the bed under the covers if Michelle would let her, but she didn't get to do that very often. Abby was a restless bed companion.

He set the collars on the counter as quietly as possible, and then went along the outer wall in every room, checking and locking all the windows and doors. Then he went out the front door to make sure his ride in the yard was locked and secured.

He walked over to the attached garage and searched it thoroughly to make sure no one was inside either the car or any place else, even pulling out his flashlight and shining it up into the rafters. There was nothing blocking his sight lines up into the high ceiling, and very little clutter around to hide behind, so it didn't take long to clear the area. He walked back out, and opened the keypad, entering the code that would activate the garage door opener, and lower the steel door to the closed position. Then he went around the outside of the building, checking things out. He even opened the black Suburban and checked it over quickly to make sure no one else was inside, and then he took the keys he found still in the ignition and locked it. He also checked and locked his 4Runner.

Satisfied that everything was secure at the moment, he went in the main door and locked it.

Once that was completed, he stood for a moment, taking a moment to try to mentally catch up on everything that seemed to have happened, while looking at the interior of the cottage without really seeing it.

CHAPTER 5

Michelle awoke completely with a suddenness that was unusual for her. As she got older, she seemed to swim more slowly back up to consciousness. She lay there a moment with her eyes closed, blissfully enjoying comforts of the warm bed and soft sheets as her mind drifted from thought to thought. Then she remembered everything that had happened since last night and opened her eyes in shock.

The ceiling flashed into crystal clear focus instantly above her. Everything seemed to be sharp and clear to her sight. She held up her hand a foot in front of her face, and her eyes seemed to change focus from far to near instantly as well. She sat up in bed, and swung her feet over to the edge to get up. The oversized robe she was wearing seemed to hang off her everywhere. It had fit just a day ago, though. It was all so surreal.

She stood, and went into the bathroom to relieve herself, stopping only a moment to look in disbelief at the image staring back at her in the mirror. She almost smiled at the shocked look on that other, much younger image staring out at her. She wrapped the robe around herself tightly to protect her modesty as she left the bathroom and turned out the light. She looked over at Sadie and Abby's bed, and saw Sadie, but Abby had wandered off. Wondering where she went, Michelle turned and looked on the bed, but she wasn't there. Not under the bed either. With a glance at the clock that read almost eleven in the morning, she went out into the hallway. She had slept for less than an hour, but felt refreshed as if she had been asleep the whole night, which made her wonder. She hadn't slept at all last night. She walked silently throughout the cottage, peeking into every little corner and nook that Abby liked to curl up in.

Abby wasn't in the living room on the couches. Dave was, though, snoring lightly with his stocking feet up on the long sofa. She smiled gently at her protector, and then turned to continue the search. Not in the kitchen.

Starting to grow concerned, she opened Dave's bedroom, and peeked inside, but Abby wasn't there. Where could Abby have gotten off to? A sudden thought and a small fear occurred to her, and she turned back to the hall. Her bare feet stepping almost silently on the hardwood floor, she peeked in the door to the guest room.

Abby was on the bed. And the occupant was awake, looking at the little dog cuddled up against his side with her head on his stomach. She was relieved to see that his hand was slowly stroking her back, and he had a smile on his face. Noticing her, he turned his head, and smiled at her.

"Good day, my lady. Are you well?" His voice was soft, and gentle. Those amber eyes seemed to be warm and welcoming in the mid-day sun light coming through the windows.

His speech was very formal and almost archaic, but there was no trace of accent to him. She realized that she was staring at him, and started.

"Yes, I am feeling very good. How are you feeling?" She answered almost automatically, and then shook herself internally. Get a grip!

"I am somewhat tired from yesterday's events, but in due time I will recover. It will be a while before I am able to defend myself adequately against foes of significance, but I am fit enough and whole." She flinched at the reminder of what had happened just hours before, and he slowly raised himself to a sitting position and swung his legs off the side of the bed, trying not to disturb the dog, who decided now was a good time to get even more attention from her new best friend. Standing and stretching, she wagged her stubby little tail furiously and walked across the bed next to him. Then she climbed into his lap, put her paws up on his chest, and started trying to thoroughly wash his face.

"Abby! Stop that! Sheesh! I'm so sorry…" She started to step forward to pull the little dog away, but he merely smiled and allowed it to continue.

"What a wonderful little animal. Does she belong here? She must have come into the room whilst I slept, because I woke to her warmth at my side. Truly a comforting little sprite." He petted Abby fondly, and then grinned up at Michelle. He did hold her gently so the wiggling little dog couldn't continue to clean him, though, Michelle noticed with a small smile.

"She's my dog. Her and Sadie, the other one. The other one is a little better behaved, and knows not to climb up on the furniture without permission." She tried, and failed, to glare at her small companion.

"Are you hungry? There is plenty of food if you like. Dave made it up here, and probably is getting hungry, too." She hid a smile behind her hand.

"I could break my fast, certainly. I must step outside to relieve myself, however. Which way is the back house? I do not recall seeing the lay of this place before awakening here." His question could have been in jest, but she realized with a shock that he was completely serious. He sat up and turned, lowering his feet to the floor.

"Uhm,", she said, completely off guard, "Let me get Dave and he can explain that to you. Wait here a moment. Abby, behave yourself! Sheesh!" Michelle looked at the little dog moving to curl up in the stranger's lap, and shook her head as she turned to walk down the hall. She noticed out of the corner of her eye as she left the room that he tried to reach for his boots while not disturbing the now-curled-up dog in his lap.

She walked in the direction of the sitting room, turned the corner into the sitting area, and Dave spoke up.

"I've been trying to figure out who could have done this, and the list is pretty short. As in, non-existent." he said, turning towards her with a worried look on his face.

"Well, forget about that for the moment. Our guest is awake, and you need to show him how the indoor plumbing works. He was asking the way to the back house to relieve himself." She stared at him, willing him to behave himself. Dave's sense of humor ran from crude to borderline insulting when he was fully on his game, a product of his time in the Marines, probably, and it could be a little hard to take. She had seen the results of their guest's handiwork, and didn't want Dave to be the object of a repeat demonstration.

Dave was a little too worried for his usual dashing repartee today, it seemed. "Sure. Introduce me?"

"Yeah, come on." Walking back to the guest room, she stepped through the open door, with Dave following her.

"This is my brother David. Dave, this is… uh, I don't think I ever got your name." She frowned as she suddenly realized she had forgotten her manners.

The guest stood, and stepped over to them. His slight but formal bow, out of place in anyone else, was elegant and simple, and seemed completely consistent with his appearance.

"I am Giltreas Orzasch. Of late, a traveler, and sometime tinkerer." The formal self-introduction was also consistent. Michelle had the strangest sense that she was back in time several hundred years, or possibly at the Renaissance Festival or something. "It is a pleasure to meet you, Lord David." He held out his right hand, and Dave automatically reached his out in response. His surprise was evident when Giltreas clasped forearms with him, but he recovered quickly enough to return the gesture.

"I can see that your ways and customs are different here, My Lord. But that will have to wait. Can you show me to the back house? I have need to relieve myself."

"Uhm, it's just Dave. Follow me. I will show you to the bathroom." The look on Dave's face was one of confusion and uncertainty.

"A bath room? One does not normally relieve one's self in the bath, good sir. Perhaps you are jesting?" There was a gentle, knowing smile on

Giltreas' face, as if he expected Dave to yell "Gotcha" or some such thing.

"Uhm, no, that would be bad. Here, let me show you what I am talking about." He opened the door to the bathroom as Michelle wandered off to the kitchen. She would cook breakfast, she decided. Having something to distract her at the moment sounded like a good idea.

Dave led the way into the spacious bathroom, and indicated the toilet beyond the sink. "Around here, it is customary to use a toilet to relieve one's self. Most have a cover, and all have a seat. If you need to leave… something solid behind, you put the seat down, and sit down. There is paper typically nearby to wipe yourself with." Giltreas blushed slightly at the intimate conversation as Dave showed how everything worked. "If you are leaving water behind, lift the seat and go. When you are finished, lower the seat and lid. There is a handle usually on the tank," Dave said, pointing to a silver lever on the side, "that you push down on then release to flush the bowl with. Sometimes it may take a couple times to get everything down, but that's ok. Wait until the sound of water refilling the tank to end, and you can flush again." He flushed the toilet to show how it worked.

"When you are done with that, wash your hands in the sink, with soap. You lift the lever on top of the faucet, move it left or right for hot or cold, and push it back down to shut it off. And be careful; the hot water is hot enough to burn." He demonstrated the control, and pushed down on the pump on top of the soap bottle to show how it worked. "There are towels on the rod here by the door that you can use to dry your hands. Also, it is customary to lock the door when you are in here, and to put the seat and lid down when you are done. Otherwise the dogs will drink out of the toilet, and that could make them sick." He showed how to lock the door, then unlock it again. "I'll explain public bathrooms later."

"Any questions?" he asked, turning back to Giltreas, to see an amazed look on his face.

"I detect no unseemly odor. Where does the waste go? Certainly it does not simply pour out under the house?" Giltreas seemed impressed at the idea of indoor plumbing.

"Actually, no. There is a pipe under the house that connects to a larger pipe under the road. That leads to a water treatment plant in the nearby town. There are small houses and cabins like this one all along here that are connected to the system. The clean water in the faucets comes from there in a different set of pipes as well." Dave was careful to answer the questions, but he was simultaneously trying not to stare at the same time. Someone who had never heard of indoor plumbing? Wow. This will be interesting.

"I'll leave you to it then. Come out to the kitchen when you are finished. Holler if you have any questions." Dave turned to leave, and Giltreas locked the door behind him.

Sometime later, Giltreas walked in to the kitchen, sniffing appreciatively at the smells coming from the stove. Dave noticed him, and turned with a smile.

"Did everything come out ok?" He asked innocently.

Michelle turned and socked him lightly on the nearest shoulder with her fist. "Knock it off, you. Behave yourself."

Dave winced in mock pain. "Oww! You meanie! Quit hitting me, or I'll tell mom!" He rubbed his shoulder, carrying the joke further.

"Everything is well. Thank you for your concern." Michelle looked at Giltreas a little weirdly after that, but said nothing, turning back to the stove.

"Hope you like eggs, bacon, and hash browns? We are a little traditional here, and I am in the mood for breakfast food." She asked over her shoulder.

"Whatever you are serving, My Lady, will be my pleasure to consume. The smells are heavenly. Do you feast like this every day?" Awake and rested, his smile was quite warm and very charismatic.

"This is pretty much normal for everyone around here. Some people like fruit, some like oatmeal, there is a lot of variation. We are the only culture in the world that generally eats different foods for breakfast than any other meal. A peculiarity of our way of life, I suppose." She realized she was rambling a bit again, and picked up a heavy frying pan and held it over counter where the plates were set out, dishing a helping of scrambled eggs with cheese onto each of the three plates resting on the tiled surface, then some bacon from the same pan.

Setting the now empty pan back on the stove, she turned off the flames under both pans, and lifted the second one over to the plates as well, scooping out a helping of hash brown potatoes onto each one. That pan went back on the stove with a clang, and she pulled the oven mitt off her left hand, grabbing two plates and handed one to Giltreas.

"Have a seat at the table. Do you want orange juice, coffee, water, or milk?"

"What would you suggest, My Lady?" It was a graceful question for someone who seemed so out of place.

"I usually have orange juice. That barbarian over there," she said, pointing to her brother, "usually has coffee."

"With cream and sugar," the barbarian in question said cheerfully as he stirred the contents of a large mug with a small spoon. Lifting it to his mouth, he took a gulp, then swallowed. "Ahh. My morning pick-me-up," he said with a smile, drinking again.

"I should like to try both." He took his plate over to the table on the small woven mat that had some utensils set out on it already, and then stepped back to the counter. She handed him a mug of coffee, which he set next to his plate. Then he stood and waited.

She glanced at him, and said, "Have a seat. Dig in before it gets cold."

"My Lady, it would be unseemly for me to sit before the lady of the house, and before my host," he said graciously.

She hid a smile as she said, "We don't stand on formality around here. Please, have a seat. I'll be there in just a moment." She reached up to a cupboard door that she opened, and pulled out a pair of glasses. Setting them on the counter, she opened the refrigerator next to the stove, and reached in to pull out a tall square container that seemed to be made of brightly-covered stiff paper, poured juice for them both, then put it back into the cold. Then she carried them over to the table, setting one in front of her plate and the other in front of his.

CHAPTER 6

Giltreas tried not to stare at everything in the room like a poor country peasant in town for the first time, but it was difficult. The room he had awoken to had been… interesting. Large and spacious, with large windows that covered a most of the wall beside the bed that let in light through a soft white covering, seemingly of the finest woven cloth, with some kind of ripple pattern that ran from side to side.

The bed itself was smooth and flat, but soft and comfortable nonetheless, and covered in the finest bedding he had ever laid down upon. Warm, soft blankets made of a flawless expanse of smooth cotton had been pulled over him, and his head had lain upon pillows the like of which he had never seen. The lush comfort had pulled at him, beckoning him to sleep longer. And the floor must have cost a king's ransom. Some kind of wood, incredibly smooth and polished to a finish of which the finest elvish craftsmen would have been jealous. If it weren't for the workmanship that deliberately produced an edge along every plank, it would have been difficult to see where one finely-finished piece of wood ended, and another began.

The walls were perfectly smooth as well, adorned in some hue close to the color of the summer leaves of a tree, and the wood bordering the walls at the floor and around the doorways, along with the doors themselves, had been colored a spotless white. The doors were ornately and expertly carved, with a simple recessed square pattern repeating itself six times, three from top to bottom, and two from side to side.

The furnishings in the room were equally of high quality. The headboard, footboard, side table, and dresser along the wall facing the end of the bed had all been of the same beautiful wood, another he could not recognize, and all of the highest construction the likes of which he had not seen in recent memory. Finished to the same tone in a way that subtly brought out the grain without emphasizing it too much, the warm tone and color had been polished to a sheen that fairly glowed to him.

But that had been just the start. When his hosts had come to check on him, their strange attire had pulled at him. They seemed to enjoy rich colors. The robe she wore was a deep burgundy, plush and rich and soft, and luxurious to see. His pants had been a deep blue, cut in a fit and style he had never seen before. His shirt was cut from a smooth cloth made in a gentle green and white pattern that went both across and up and down, forming squares and rectangles, and it buttoned up with pearly white buttons that matched the ones at his cuffs. Under the fine shirt at his neck one could see another shirt of a solid green color that matched the outer shirt.

His hair was fine and brown, as were his eyes. He wore a beard unlike any Giltreas had ever seen before. His cheeks and neck were clean shaven, as was his upper lip. But his chin was covered in a very short, well-groomed affair that was speckled with grey in amongst the brown.

He inquired about where to relieve himself, and was surprised, almost shocked at the result. Surely his hosts were wealthy nobility, to afford a home such as this. A bath-room, indeed. White, elegant constructions, smooth and glassy in finish, with lavish woods everywhere and square, smooth, warm stones under foot, cut square and polished to a deep shine, and set in place with equally impressive skills. He tried not to stare and let his mouth fall open as things were demonstrated to him. Powerfully skilled mages must have done much of the building of this place; of that, he was most certain. Or perhaps dwarvish craftsmen. That would explain much.

When finished with his morning ritual, he had opened the door, and followed the smells to the kitchen, only to find the Lady of the house herself cooking for them all. He kept silent, but was all along expecting servants to come from somewhere to take over for her. A woman of her obvious breeding and high social standing should not be doing such menial work herself. It was unseemly. But as he watched, she completed her tasks with a practiced ease that told him she was more than comfortable where she was.

Giltreas had known a few nobles such as her: the independent kind that prided themselves on being able to do many things that others of their standing would have found beneath them. They usually had other ideas that were equally outrageous to their fellows as well. Nobles were too important, and too busy, to have their time taken up with the labors best left to servants. They were meant to have their every need taken care of, because that was the way of it since time immemorial.

Giltreas personally found the whole argument tedious and quite boring. Nobility was overrated. Not that he would ever admit he felt that way. His heritage and upbringing had served to wash out any awe he might have of others, and left him with a cynical eye that his cousin had poked him about every chance she got. But he knew better than to insult the proper sensibilities of the effete, over-pampered nobility he came upon. And was, sometimes, directed by his patron to dispatch. Upon those occasions, he wasted not the words nor the breath necessary to put forth such 'blasphemous' ideas, but got on to the business at hand with all skill and dispatch. Which was just as well. The wolf did not commune with the hare he was to prey upon, after all.

The morning meal was quickly consumed, and was every bit as fine as the sights and smells of it had promised. The orange juice was a delight. Coffee after the meal was not really something he enjoyed, but he consumed it dutifully, with generous helpings of both cream and sugar to make it more palatable. Still, the aroma was enticing. He supposed he could get to enjoy it eventually. It seemed to give him some extra energy, which bore some thinking upon.

The man, David, cleaned up the kitchen, rinsing the dishes in a sink somewhat similar to that in the bath room, with water coming out of a silvery pipe that sprang up from the back of the sink. He then placed the dishes into a white cabinet under the counter, and swung the door back up to close it off from view.

Dave poured himself another cup of coffee, needing the pickup the caffeine was providing, before he followed Michelle and Giltreas back out to the sitting area. Glancing at his watch, he estimated that his wife should be arriving soon – and just as he sat down, Sadie woofed a warning or greeting: she heard a car.

* * *

Allison turned around the corner, and almost stopped the car where it was as she took in the sight of the black Suburban parked in the yard. Then remembering the code words in the phone conversation earlier, she pulled into the yard and parked. Getting out, she grabbed her purse, slung it over one her head and one shoulder. She closed the driver's door, and opened the back door. She lifted the small black and white dog down, holding on to his leash so he wouldn't run off into the woods like last time. He pulled at her with all his twenty-three pounds in that direction, but she just held him back while she grabbed her purse and swung the door shut.

Max led her over to some grass in front of the porch, and relieved himself. Then he looked up as the door opened, and started barking. "Max, knock it off!" An exercise in futility, she knew, but she could wish, anyways.

Dave came out of the door, and she stopped a moment to read his expression, trying to get clues to see if she needed to be on her guard. Her hand was in her purse, closed around the grip of her trusty Glock 10mm pistol. For a normal trip up to the cottage, she would have left it behind, but she wanted it nearby in case it was needed, since she had no idea what had happened. She hoped to God it wasn't needed.

Dave smiled at her and met her at the base of the stairs with a hug. "What's going on? Who owns the Suburban? What – ?"

He cut her off, saying "Come in the house. Someone took a run at Michelle, but thanks to a new friend, she is ok. Better than ok." His words gave her more questions than answers, but she followed him inside.

And stopped to stare at two people, whom at first glance she was certain she had never met, who were sitting on the couch and loveseat.

The man was dressed strangely, and Allie unknowingly had the same thought Michelle did the first time she saw him; that he was in the Renaissance Festival. It was going on right now, she remembered. Then she realized that her mind was wandering. 'Focus,' she told herself. She looked at the other person, a young woman, who looked barely twenty, wearing the robe Allie knew belonged to her older sister-in-law. And the young woman looked perfect, like she just stepped out of a fashion magazine or something. But there was something about her that tugged at Allie, something familiar. The woman looked so similar to a younger version of... Then, in a rush, it came to her.

"Oh... my... God..." Allie's mouth dropped open, and she stood there stunned. "Michelle?!?"

"Yeah, Allie, it's me. Apparently our friend here has found something Ponce de Leon looked for several centuries ago." Michelle tried to make it sound relaxed, or calm, or anything rational. It was nothing of the sort.

"I did only what I was called to do, my lady. My Patron played a part, I suspect. However, I do not know what has caused such a transformation of such... completeness. Whatever it is about, I am certain we will know if He wants us to." The newcomer's speech was soft, and gentle, but with a nearly perfect accent. Nearly.

"You say about the same way that Michelle does." Allie knew she was drifting a bit, and tried to center herself.

"I am not surprised. The Learn Language spell I cast in the night of last is not perfect. I can only learn that way what she knows and how she says it, not the best way to say everything, and not always what it means. I do not seem to have any gaps in my speech so far that you are unable to understand, however, so I suspect for that reason, and others, that Michelle is quite learned and educated," he stated calmly, then tried to not be uncomfortable as the three of them stared at him in shock.

"What is it that has stunned you so?" Giltreas asked calmly.

Michelle was the first to speak up. "Is magic what happened to me to change me so much? I mean, I don't even recognize myself. I never remember looking this good before, except maybe before the accident."

"Of a certainty it was magic, and some few different ways, my lady. After I dispatched the four brigands that had beset themselves upon you, I then turned myself to the task of bringing you back. I cured the poisons in your body, and cured the sickness which had grown throughout you, with potions. I healed you of your wounds (which seems to have erased all your old scars and injuries as well, not an unusual thing to happen) with mind magic, and cured the blindness they inflicted upon you with another potion. Then with my patron's help, I revived you with cleric skill. You had passed over just as I made it to the small clearing you were in." He took a breath, and noticed that they were staring at him more intensely. "Have you not healers that can do such as this available to you?"

Michelle's head was reeling. Did he really say revive, as in resurrect? That she was... DEAD? No way. Never in a million years. Her mind slammed the door hard on that thought, walled it off, bricked over the wall, and ran screaming (figuratively anyways) away from it.

"No, we don't have people who can do magic like that here. There is no such thing here as magic. Wait, is that what happened when you did something at the end to cause that huge explosion?" Things began to make a strange, impossible sense.

"I cast a spell to learn your language, so we might speak with each other, yes. The spell must have worked, because we are speaking, but I remember nothing else until waking up with your small companion laying her head upon my side in that room's bed. How did I get there? Did I walk? I don't think my strength was that used up that I wouldn't remember doing so, but stranger things have happened. What is this explosion you speak of?" His turn to be confused, he supposed.

"I started asking you questions, and you put a hand up to stop me. Then you reached into a pouch at your left hip, pulled out something, and chanted a few words. Whatever was in your hand glowed briefly, then it disappeared, and a buzzing sound started to come from you. After a moment, you reached out to me and touched me, which caused a bright white light and huge boom. I was thrown away from you, and you had some kind of injury on the right side of your head, like it exploded. I could even see that parts of your skull were missing, and you were bleeding badly. But as I watched, the blood filled in the wound, and turned to skin and bone. Even the hair that was destroyed by the blast grew back. You didn't wake up, though.

"I drove the Suburban those... men... had come here in, back through the trees up to the clearing, picked you up and laid you in back, drove back to the cottage, and carried you into the house. I got you onto the bed, tried to make you comfortable, and left you there to sleep. You were breathing normally, and you had a strong pulse, so it looked like you were going to be ok. I couldn't find any sign of the wound on your head, so I hoped everything was alright.

"Dave showed up here with Sadie and Abby, and I let him peek in at you for a moment, just so he could know I was telling the truth –"

"I never doubted you, sis." Dave interjected.

"– I know that, but you had to look; I would have – then I waited for you to wake up. The rest you know from there."

Giltreas was silent for a moment. Lady Michelle's description of the event when he cast the spell was not unlike what happens when a spell fails or is turned by another caster or spell, but when that happens, the spell does not succeed. He had never seen otherwise. In this case, however, it succeeded.

<Stranger and stranger. I have my wonders to this.> He said softly out loud in Elvish, his mother's tongue.

<How do you mean?>

He turned to look at Michelle in astonishment.

<You speak the High Elvish tongue?> he asked her in that same language.

<Apparently I do, sir.> The formal address was straight out of his childhood lessons, and he contemplated for a moment. Then, on a whim, he spoke in another language back to her.

<The stones say this fire burns deep with mystery.>

<I see those stones clearly.> She seemed almost amused. And yet, stunned, of course.

In the language of his father, he spoke again. <What do you make of this?>

She seemed to consider for a moment, then spoke slowly and carefully, for this language was hard on the human throat. <I have no thoughts of clarity.>

Allie and Dave watched this exchange in almost awe, having no idea what was said. Dave was about to ask what was going on, when Michelle spoke again. 'Must be getting slow in my old age,' he thought with an internal smile.

<This is French. Do you understand this?> She asked him.

<Yes, I do.>

<How about Spanish?> Hmmm.

<Certainly.> The tone of his response reflected the humor in his eyes.

<But perhaps not Japanese?> She asked in the language that she had learned only recently to further her business needs.

<Perhaps I do.> His smile grew larger.

Now in English, she asked "Did you learn those languages before? Or did your spell do this?"

"It must have been the spell, because I have never heard the like of them before. What races of beings speak in those tongues?"

"Those are human languages. Humans are the only beings we know that we can speak with, that have spoken language." His question was strange to her, and bent her thinking slowly in a new direction, but before she could think her way to the question slowly forming in the back of her mind, he spoke up.

"It appears that the spell did something unexpected. Instead of my learning your first language, the spell taught me all languages you know. And you seem to have learned languages from me, a first that I have never heard of afore. My mage teacher told me how the spell works, and what it cannot do, and this is certainly something unexpected. I wonder if anything else happened because of it."

"Well, there was this one thing…" Michelle went on to describe the white wall of energy that raced out in all directions from the small clearing, and heading up into the sky, come to think of it, and its effect on everything it passed through.

Giltreas blinked at the description. He had no idea what that effect was, but it must have been caused by the spell, or whatever caused it to detonate. Would every spell cause the same thing to happen again? Magic was an important, significant part of his set of skills. If it did not work normally here, he needed to know, and right now. He would need to know what of his skills he could depend on. He stood. "Will you accompany me outside? I must discover if magic will work reliably here for me or not."

Everyone else stood as well, and Dave led the way to the door and out onto the porch.

Giltreas took up the rear, and stopped in astonishment when he reached the top of the porch staircase. "What are those…things?" A huge, shiny black metal… thing sat there in the yard. And there were other… things… in the yard as well, similar, but different in forms and colors – a dark grey one similar in shape, and a smaller green one.

"Those are…" Allie stopped a moment. Should she say it? "…horseless carriages. We have several names for them, depending on…" She stopped.

He stepped down, and reached out, touching the big black one on its sleek flank. Then he turned away, and walked further into the yard. What they were could wait. He needed to find the answer to more important questions first.

Allie heard Max bark behind her, and then he whined. He wanted out, since everyone else was outside. He didn't like being left alone away from Allison, for all his bluster. "Shhh, Maxie, its ok. I'll be right back."

Giltreas stopped. What to cast? Mayhap a simple illusion to start? The cantrip came easily to him, and he released the spell.

A huge horse appeared in the yard, Cailio, the charger of his swordsman mentor. It pawed the ground with a thud, and snorted. He dismissed the spell. The horse tossed its head as if to say good morrow, then disappeared.

What more complicated spell next? Shape change.

Dave, Allie, and Michelle watched in wonder as Giltreas changed into a huge black, fur-winged wolf, looking most of five feet tall at the shoulder. He took a step, flapped his wings, and glided a moment a few feet, then turned back. Dave found himself looking at the ground under the shape Giltreas had changed into. The shadow cast by the sun in the clear blue afternoon sky was the same as the form gliding in for a landing between them and the trees.

He dissipated the spell, changing from the Harrower Wolf back to his normal form, then looked around. A target?

"David, do you have a target I might abuse? I wish to cast another spell."

* * *

He paused from reading his newspaper, and looked at his watch. The last distraction from his plan should now be removed. All that was left now was cleaning up.

His wife noticed his smile as he glanced at his wrist, and smiled one of her own as she asked, "What are you thinking about, dear? Something from work?"

"Nothing, honey. Just checking the time, and it occurred to me that we haven't gone out for a great steak recently. Up for a jaunt downtown?" He looked over at her, his smile still, and wondered not for the first time what such a beautiful, wonderful woman was doing with him.

"Hmmm. I think I can squeeze that into my busy schedule…"

CHAPTER 7

The late morning sunlight had moved on to early afternoon, with the warm sun slowly shifting overhead towards the west. The leaves on the trees, and the needles on the pines, rustled in the light breeze, adding a gentle undercurrent of comfort to the warmth of a September day in northern Minnesota. A sparrow landed on the porch railing, and Dave's eyes followed it as it looked at the people sitting there. Then it flitted off, leaving the four as it had found them, alone with their thoughts.

Dave, Allie, Michelle, and Giltreas sat in the comfortable chairs on the porch that faced the main yard of the cottage and the cars parked there, and enjoying some ice cold lemonade that Michelle had made early yesterday after arriving straight from work. Each had their mind on something different, but every face shared the same distant gaze as they contemplated recent events.

Allie kept glancing at Michelle out of the corner of her eye. Wow. Whatever had changed her had really done the works. Michelle looked perfect, and part of Allie wanted to be jealous. The rational part of her brain kept intruding into her thoughts though, trying to convince her that Michelle's life had been so very hard, and she deserved some good things to happen to her. But that didn't stop Allie from wanting what had happened to Michelle to happen to her, and for a very personal reason.

For reasons different than Michelle, Allison and Dave were unable to have children. It was a constant sorrow in the back of her mind, a loss that she had never been able to completely come to peace over. She was from a somewhat large family, and had four brothers and sisters, two of each. The fourth child, and the last girl, her parents had stopped pestering her years ago to have kids, when they realized that it would never happen, and the whole thing caused Allie to cry herself to sleep. Not as much anymore, but it still happened from time to time. Dave was there for her, though. He held her as the storms came, and the tears fell. He shed plenty as well, not only for himself, but because he knew the depth of her pain, her loss, her grief.

But now, Michelle had been transformed, and everything that had been wrong with her had been erased as if by magic. Then Allie caught her thoughts, and snorted internally at her choice of words. 'As if by magic' could be replaced, and had been, by simply, 'by magic.'

Allison had barely gotten to the cottage, and had not even been told everything that had happened to Michelle, who the grey stranger was and what his role was in things, when he had needed to go outside to test his magical skills.

She winced again internally as her deeply ingrained natural skepticism in anything to do with magic and the paranormal had been ripped out of her completely, and replaced with... something else, she didn't know what. The mind of the pragmatic Marine she had been when she met Dave in the U.S. Marine Corps couldn't tolerate things that weren't grounded firmly in reality. Now, though, her thoughts were adrift, her comfortable world of what she could understand with her five senses, and her expectations for that world to follow the laws it had always adhered to, picked up like a child's toy, and kicked across the room and out the window. Firmly grounded reality was suddenly an expanse of metaphoric sand that shifted and moved under her as she tried to find her internal balance once again. She had no fear that her mind might crack, because if that was going to happen, it would have in Iraq. No, she wanted to understand how the world had changed, and where she fit with those changes.

But most of all, she wanted what happened to Michelle to happen to her, so that she might try again to become a mother. In the end, beyond her deep enduring love for Dave, nothing much else really mattered to her. She was 34, some six years younger than David, and still in the prime of her life, but time for motherhood was moving on for her.

As she thought about it, she cataloged her physical inventory, and was not too upset over what she had. She might find five pounds to lose if she looked very hard, but she was dedicated to keeping herself in as good a condition as possible. She ran three miles, three times a week, and her times weren't too bad. She kept up with her Aikido daily, an art she had settled on after getting out of the Corps. And she went to the range diligently, every other weekend, firing off a box of fifty shells, to keep her aim and her focus sharp.

In between that, she worked as a volunteer at a nursing home, helping care for the residents there who had a range of issues from simple old age to advanced Alzheimer's, Parkinson's, dementia, and every possible physical ailment that getting older treated everyone to eventually. All in all, she was, if not exactly happy, satisfied that she was taking good care of herself, and doing good, positive things in the lives of others. But she wanted more. She ached, yearned, and dreamed of becoming a mother.

* * *

Dave wondered how he was going to keep Michelle, and now that he thought about it, Allison safe. Someone had gotten to Michelle, and they had nearly taken her from him forever. Like everyone else around him, he never thought that violence would be directed at him or his family. They lived in a relatively quiet neighborhood with very little crime. They stayed out of certain parts of the metropolitan area of Minneapolis and Saint Paul. But if someone could get to Michelle here at a remote cottage in the middle of the woods that no one was supposed to know about, no place in the world was safe. He knew that his thoughts were getting paranoid, but he couldn't help it in the face of a threat he couldn't confront, and didn't have any information about.

'Thank God for Giltreas,' he thought to himself again. 'If he hadn't come along when he did, Shelly would be dead. I owe him more than I can ever repay. But I intend to try.' Grimly, he made a silent promise that whoever had done this would pay.

He glanced left again at Giltreas, sitting in the chair next to him. He was staring out at something only his eyes could see; his face completely unreadable. Who, or what, was he? Where did he learn how to do what he did to save Michelle, change her, heal her, so completely that she was unrecognizable, and then do what he did in the yard just a short time ago? And would he teach Dave?

'More importantly, could he teach me? Is it something I can learn?' Skills like that would definitely come in handy when he started on the trail of his target. The shape-change alone was incredible, but what Giltreas had done to his target board had been sheer, incredible exhilaration. Giltreas had described it as a simple spell, but that 'simple spell' had destroyed the entire upper target. 'Casting a magic stone', he called it. Whatever it was, it had hit the heavy sheet of plywood with enough force to shatter it, throwing pieces in an arc some fifteen to thirty feet in all directions from the sawhorse it was bolted to.

But all special abilities aside, he still needed to protect Michelle and Allison. And he had no idea how to do that and still track down whoever started this, and end it. Permanently. But he would figure it out. Nobody takes a run at his loved ones. Ever. He supposed he was turning 'to the dark side', but didn't much care. Family mattered. Not much else really did, when it came right down to it. Only family mattered.

* * *

Michelle sat and thought through what she knew. Giltreas could make magic; cast magic spells. That point had been driven home, as preposterous as it seemed on the surface. Her transformation, as miraculous as it seemed, had a simple explanation. For whatever reason, Giltreas did it.

That wasn't the hard part. Oh no. Not at all. Huh-uhh. The hard part? That would be figuring out how to get back to her life, looking like someone else. How did she prove that she was the real McCoy? How would she make anyone believe her? Everyone knew her scarred and damaged visage. No one knew what she looked like underneath that damage. And now that it was wiped away, and this new, reborn appearance had been… thrown on her, what did she do? She had nearly fourteen hundred people depending on her to run the company she had founded and grown to its present state. She looked, and to be honest, physically felt, nineteen years old.

A laugh escaped her, and she quickly smothered it, turning it into a cough, as she contemplated her senior staff taking one look at the gorgeous teenager barely out of high school she had become in the big meeting room across from her office, and calmly walking out to call security.

But a more serious look appeared on her face as she considered what had happened to her last night.

The memories were fragmented, obviously because she had drifted in and out of consciousness, but the last thing she remembered before waking up and finding her world-view shredded, was that she warmed up at the last moment, before a deep darkness fell on her. She shuddered internally, trying to hide her distress from those around her, but it got through anyways, and she felt a hand on her shoulder.

* * *

Giltreas was assured that his skills at magic were at hand, and available to him should need arise. His sight was drawn to the strange metal carriages in the yard several feet from him, and then he forced himself to look away as he tried to gather his thoughts.

Obviously, these humans had things and machines and devices he had never encountered before, nor heard of, or even contemplated could exist. 'Horseless carriage' was an interesting name, but without a horse, or oxen, how were they moved? And their strange appearance, right down to the wheels under them, glinted strangely in his thoughts, much more so than the building behind, below, and above him. Everything was different here. Almost like a fantastical story told to young children before the last of the day had past and sleep came upon them. The explanations to Giltreas about the horseless carriages had been confusing, but he thought he had grasped enough to understand. They were machines crafted to carry people and their things great distances, and burned something similar to swamp gas in liquid form. Strange, indeed.

He wondered again, but only briefly, why his patron had sent him here. Was his work completed? He felt more rested now than he had in recent times; his physical and magical strength had recovered completely with a speed that left him wondering many things. Was this a result of this new plane he found himself upon? Or something his patron had done? Was it permanent? Some gifts his patron laid upon him were permanent, while others were not. And all things could be changed, he knew. Angering his patron was a sure way to have those gifts turned against him quickly, with horrifying result. It was a lesson learned through pain and blood; his patron was not to be trifled with.

He heard a laugh next to him, sounding strained, as the woman he had saved tried to cover it with a cough, and he reached out to gently touch her shoulder. Her eyes were drawn to him, and he could see the emotions roiling behind, the turmoil she suffered. He knew not the source of her unrested spirit, but he recognized his hand in her present state, and his heart went out to her. Rarely was he granted chance at caring; such was the demands of his patron. Now, his caring had harmed someone, an unthinkable thought. Still, he knew he could give more, and what he had, he gave fully and readily, radiating comfort and warmth towards her.

* * *

Michelle blinked as she looked into Giltreas' eyes, feeling positive emotions flow from him at her. The turmoil insider her calmed, and she knew that whatever happened, she would figure out what to do. She always had.

She turned to David, and asked, "What now? What do you want to do?"

The conversation started up. Dave rose to the occasion.

"I am going to figure out who did this, and... resolve it," he stated grimly, then paused in astonishment as another voice spoke softly.

"I would lend you my skills in full measure, Lord David, to aid you at your task, if you would have me. What was done to Lady Michelle was monstrous. Such who would do thusly deserves truly a response appropriate." Giltreas spoke softly, but there was no mistaking what he was saying, and Dave smiled in response.

"I accept completely. And please, do not call me Lord. This country has no nobility. We are all commoners, I suppose. Although Michelle is just a little more noble than the rest of us." She turned at his teasing voice, and surprised everyone, herself most of all, by sticking out her tongue, something she hadn't done to her Davey since they were both very young.

"The only problem I have is, I have to find a way to keep Michelle and Allison safe, while you and I go after them. I don't want anyone coming in behind me and trying to take either of them out while I am looking elsewhere. And I don't want to have to worry about them." David finished softly.

"I have a suggestion, if I may be so bold." Giltreas spoke hesitantly. He wasn't sure if it was his place to speak up, and he was still processing David's statement that they were all commoners. Truly?

"Any help you offer would be greatly appreciated." Dave said, turning towards Giltreas, as did Michelle and Allison.

"My mother would welcome them in her house, and keep them safe."

CHAPTER 8

It was decided with very little argument, because Dave wouldn't have any, and Michelle decided that since she was on vacation, she should get well and truly away. The lone voice of dissent was Allison.

"I can take care of myself," she declared, as if that ended the discussion.

"That's not the point, honey," Dave rejoined patiently. "I know you can, you know you can, Michelle knows you can, hell, even those drunken morons outside Kieran's last month might know it pretty well by now, too. But you aren't bullet-proof, and enough guys with a good plan would be able to get to you, and you know it. One bullet would mess up everything for me real quick. Sure, if they get close enough, or you know they're coming, then I don't have to worry. But if they surprise you, it's over. And I am not going to lose you." His voice turned grim at the last moment, and she shuddered inside. She knew it would have killed him to lose Michelle, and Allison knew it would be just as bad, if not worse, if she was killed. He had told her so before.

"I still think I could be a help here. Besides, I don't know anyone there. Wherever it is." One last token effort, she decided.

It was Michelle that turned the decision for Dave, by not playing fair. "I want you there. I don't want to be alone in a strange place. I want a familiar face to talk to, that I know I can trust. No offense, Giltreas. But I don't know anyone there. I don't want to go by myself." Giltreas nodded his acknowledgement that he was not offended. Then he had to hide his smile as Michelle kept talking.

"What if I talk Giltreas into doing to you what he did to me? Healing me? I know that you have always wanted to have kids, like I used to. What if he is able to make that happen?" Her voice finished softly, gently, as she turned to look more completely at Allison, her sister-in-law.

Allison turned her face away as the tears suddenly overwhelmed her and the thoughts she had had earlier roared through her brain, wiping every other thought away. She reached out to Dave, and held his hand as her eyes closed involuntarily against the searing pain.

Giltreas sat in silent astonishment at Allison's response to the gentle words. He called up his Physicker Sight, and looked at Allison more carefully, and was dismayed. Poisons in small amounts laced her body, including the center of womanhood low in her belly. Other injuries and scars laced that same area, inside and out. There was also a sickness in her, mild, so not glowing brightly at all, but slowly it would spread, and while not deadly, would make her joints and bones ache in a number of years. His sight told him that remedying everything would be a simple task for someone like him, and even for a beginner in their first season studying the arts. Did no one here have any healers that could fix such simple things? He kept silent, however. This was not his argument to make, no matter how much he agreed with it, but he still hoped it would come to pass. He wanted a clear path, with as few companions as possible, when he went to war. It was his way.

Giltreas had already decided to pursue the wrong-doers who had set those foul now-dead men on Michelle's trail. He often was allowed to right such wrongs, unless it was counter to his patron's wishes or if his skills were needed elsewhere. He would work alone, as he preferred, if need be, but too many things told him that this world was like no other (the strange clothing his current companions wore, the craftsmanship of the house he awoke in, and those incredibly strange "horseless carriages" setting there in his sight proved that to him by sight alone), that he knew he would need a guide.

Giltreas would have chosen David, if given a voice, and asked the others to remove themselves to safety while he worked. He had no concern about the gender of a companion, to be sure. It was simple intuition that told him David would be the most help in his task to right a wrong. As the thought occurred to him, he felt a reassuring pulse in his chest as his patron confirmed his choice of companion for this quest, and the choice to pursue such retribution, as well.

That David decided much the same thing reassured him. David would make a worthwhile companion, after Giltreas assessed his skills to see how much help he would be when words end and action begins. The way David carried himself spoke scrolls to him, though. The man at one time was a warrior, and seemed to have kept himself in readiness. He would be a worthwhile sword-mate as well, Giltreas decided. Now to resolve the rest of the situation and the safety of David's loved ones. Giltreas would have felt much the same way in pursuit of unknown foes through strange pathways, as this plane promised to be. Turnabout to be, he needn't have worried so much, as Allison turned her tear-streaked visage upon him.

"Could you really fix me? Really?" The desperation in her voice tugged at him, and his emotions welled up inside.

"Of a certainty, my – Allison. T'would be a simple thing, really. And an honor to do so for you." David's face turned towards him now, unshed tears in his astonished eyes, and the Physicker Sight confirmed that David's needs should be addressed with his magic skills as well. "David, I would gladly do said same for you. Verily, I would do such for sweet Sadie and little Abby, for they both have the need as well, such wonderful companions they are. Max has no such need, being so young, and in perfect health."

* * *

Dave's heart overflowed as he turned to pull Allison from her seat into his lap, and they both held each other tightly as tears ran down their faces like rain. He had no idea what he needed, but if Giltreas was offering, he would gladly, and humbly, accept. Giltreas' presence here was a gift from whatever God or Gods there were, he decided. While not a terribly religious person, he held his simple spiritual beliefs close to his heart. Then he pulled back from Allison, and looked her in the eye.

"Will you go with Michelle, for all our sakes, and be safe while Giltreas and I run this down? I promise that you will not have to stay there any longer than necessary. I will give you anything you want when you get back." His eyes pleaded with her to say yes.

"Anything for you, my love. Anything," she said, giving in. She buried her face into his shoulder again, and while the tears didn't overflow again, she sat there silently as a last few coursed down her cheeks.

"But you have to promise to come back to me. You once said you would die if you lost me. I feel the same way about you." She grabbed his shoulders and nearly shook him in the intensity of her demand. "Promise me!"

"I promise." He said it quietly, but with the same intensity, then wrapped his arms around his wife, and pulled her close for a moment.

Giltreas chose that moment to inject himself into the conversation. "I will promise as well, Allison, that I will do everything to bring him to you at the end of our task," he spoke with grim intensity as he looked her in the eye.

Allison glanced at Michelle once, then nodded at Giltreas. Then Giltreas spoke once more.

"Come, my companions. Let us attend to these needs now, that we may move on to the less pleasant endeavors, the sooner to have them completed," Giltreas said as he rose, and walked to the door back into the cottage, pausing to see if they followed, then opened the door and stepped inside.

The others stepped inside, to see him kneel down to Sadie, pet her gently, then murmur something.

A light flared red, then another yellow, a third green, and then a fourth blue. He seemed to hesitate for a moment, then a fifth light, this one white, flashed briefly.

Sadie stood, shook herself, and stretched all of her sixty-five pounds. Michelle was astonished, as the grey had disappeared from Sadie's muzzle even as the stiffness disappeared from her legs. She looked like a young dog in the prime of her life, not the grand old dame she had become over time. She wagged her tail fiercely, and licked Giltreas' face, even as everyone heard a new voice coming from where Giltreas knelt on the floor. It was a strange voice that seemed to be coming from Sadie, not Giltreas.

"Thank you," was all it said.

"You are most welcome, sweet Sadie." Sadie wagged again, licked Giltreas' hand once more, then turned and bounded over to Michelle.

"Pack mother! I am well and young again! We must play!" Sadie stood on her hind legs, and licked Michelle's face as she bent down in open-mouthed astonishment. She turned to Giltreas, as shocked as anyone else in the room, except for Giltreas, who had a gentle smile on his face. "Wha...!?!"

It is always a boon to be able to render your companions speechless, he decided. A simple, but wonderful, pleasure in life.

"I cast animal-speak upon her. You can hear the words of her thoughts, and she yours. It lasts but a short while, I am afraid, but a small gift I can give you for your years of faithfulness to such a splendid companion." He turned and knelt down, then the same first four bright flashes of light flowed from him to Abby, and she wiggled into his lap, licking furiously. He took the thanks stoically, and then set her on the floor, standing to wait.

"Shall we complete our work here upon you?" he said as he turned to Allison and Dave.

"Play now! No work!" Sadie bounded over to Giltreas, and the voice coming from her had a certain childish tone to it.

"Sadie, we can play later," Michelle smiled, wondering how long this would last.

"Sadie wait. You see. We play; much fun," as she hopped up on the couch, then laid down, head up, tail thumping into the cushion fiercely.

"Sadie, off the... never mind." Michelle turned to Giltreas with a smile, and asked, "How long until that wears off? Not that I don't mind, but..."

"Some small part of time. It never lasts very long. Those who work with animal companions will use such in time of need when alerted to danger, or how they were injured, or while training them up to their role." Giltreas returned with a smile of his own, obviously enjoying his prank. Then he turned and faced Dave and Allison.

Allison's world was rapidly changing around her, and she felt herself tensing inside, bracing for some unknown that seemed to be rushing towards her at great speed.

Giltreas sensed her apprehension, and reached out to place his hand on her arm. "Gather your peace, my friend. This will be pleasant for you. And, gather your clothing about you. It may get looser of a sudden." Comprehension dawned, and she giggled as she grabbed the waistband of her jeans with both hands. Dave, who had also been struck by a case of the sillies, grabbed his jeans with both hands. "Fire away, Giltreas."

Allison's world seemed to slow down as Giltreas murmured something, and the first of the colored flashes began. The lights jumped from the hand Giltreas held out towards them, and flashed over her as quick as she could count to two. Everything she saw suddenly changed color as each of the spells washed over her. Almost every part of her body tingled, and incredibly, every part of her body suddenly felt different. As the last flash of light washed over her, her vision suddenly changed as everything went out of focus, and as the world sped back up to normal, she realized she could no longer see.

She closed her eyes, and heard Dave next to her say "Crap! Contact lenses," and start laughing out loud. Then Allison joined in the laughter as she realized what had happened. She no longer had any use for the contact lenses she wore every day, because whatever Giltreas had done restored her vision. The effect of wearing her contact lens prescription was now the same as if she had a wrong prescription in that was much too strong.

"Michelle, can you take us to a mirror? I need to get these bleepin' contacts out before I go blind." Michelle stepped forward, and grabbed Allison's hand, then Dave's as well.

Michelle looked at Giltreas over her shoulder as she began to pull the two towards the hallway where the bathroom door was located. "Do you know what contact lenses are?" When he shook his head 'no', she continued, "Well, you might want to see this, then. Come on."

Giltreas watched in fascination as both Allison and Dave washed their hands carefully before sticking their fingers gently in each eye one at a time, pulling out something for which he had no description. Dave turned where he was, and held it out to Giltreas. When he put out his hand, Dave deposited the thing that had been in his eye on Giltreas' upturned palm, and turned back to the mirror to remove one from his other eye.

"What is it?" he asked, fascinated, as he looked closely at the tiny, soft, curving, slightly tinted see-through thing in his hand, touching it with a finger.

"It is something people can put in their eye to correct their vision if they can't see very well. Each person needs a different strength, depending on how bad their eyes are. Most people have different ones for each eye. If your eyesight is good, wearing contact lenses will make your vision worse,"

Dave said as he removed the second one, and looked around. Unbelievable. He could see perfectly without lenses now.

Giltreas looked up in surprise as Dave described what he was looking at.

"I have never heard of such a thing like this before," he said, faintly in awe of what he was learning.

Allison's breath caught in her throat as she looked in the mirror after getting her now-unneeded contacts out of her eyes, and into the small garbage can under the sink. While her transformation was not as dramatic and incredible as Michelle's had been, she still could see the difference plainly. Small, almost invisible scars from teenage acne, spots from sun damage, anything at all that had made her less than perfect, all were now either muted significantly, or washed away completely. Her change was not as complete as Michelle's, either: where Michelle now looked as if she were a living example of digital photo retouching, Allison now looked as if a professional had spent a long time on doing her makeup. The rest of her that she could see, such as her arms and neck, was lean, sleek, and toned. Wow. While she had carried very little extra weight before, the result of a rigorous and diligent exercise regimen, she now looked, where she could see, like the finished product she had always worked towards.

Allison turned to Giltreas and said, "Where are you from that you have never seen a car, or contact lenses? What is it like where you are from?"

Dave winced internally; leave it to Allie to cut right to the chase. Someone else might have some tact, and not asked such a forward question. Allison was a classic U.S. Marine, though. She determined her objective, and let nothing deter her from getting to it. Just like when she pursued him when they met in Iraq.

He stared intently at the mirror in front of him, astonished at the sudden changes. He looked... different somehow. Softer skin, no crows-feet around his eyes, even skin tone, it was all so amazing.

"I was born in the Forest Kingdom of Akkesh," Giltreas answered absently, still fascinated by the lens in front of him. Then he looked up, holding out his palm, with the lens on it. "Have you not heard of it?"

Dave plucked the lens from his palm, and stepped on the pedal to the garbage can, then dropped the lens in. "Nope. I have never heard of it before. How did you get here?"

Michelle cut in then from the doorway, saying "I think we should have this conversation in the living room, instead of the bathroom. Let's move out there."

Ushering the three others out of the bathroom, she led the way down the hallway to the big room across from the dining area, and waved the others to sit down. She sat on the couch, and waved Giltreas to sit next to her, as Dave and Allison sat in the loveseat. When everyone was settled, she indicated that Giltreas could continue. Sadie chose at that moment to try to jump into her lap. She grunted, and shifted the reddish/golden dog around until they were both comfortable.

"The Forest Kingdom of Akkesh is on my home plane. From there, the Queen of the Elven Throne rules the Elvish kingdom, various human kingdoms, as well as some of the Dwarvish mountain keeps to the west that choose to be attached to her rule. Several other planes of humans also swear fealty to Her Majesty, as a symbol of their respect for the benevolence and wisdom of the Throne, and Her willingness to keep them away from harm, and support them in times of need," Giltreas spoke softly, his voice adequate for them to hear clearly. "It is in her kingdom that I propose we bring Michelle and Allison to while we seek the evil doors and render unto them their due justice."

Allison was the first to open her mouth at the fantastic statement. "How do we get there? And, Elvish kingdom? Dwarvish mountains? We don't have any elves or dwarves here on Earth. Never have. They are myths, or legends, or something."

Giltreas was surprised at her statement. "There are neither elves nor dwarves here? What is this Earth you speak of?"

"Earth is what we call this world, this planet, that we all live on," Michelle said, trying to pull together in her mind what was going on. So many pieces were still missing, though.

Dave spoke up, then. "How do you travel to there? How did you get here, for that matter?" he asked.

"I am adept at calling up gates that will take a traveler between planes, or any place I have been or can distance-see on the same plane, although calling gates to traverse between planes is harder, and takes more strength," Giltreas said in that same, soft voice. "There are other ways to get to places I have not visited, as well."

"These gates, are they big enough to send that black truck in the yard through?"

Michelle and Allison suddenly turned to Dave, and Allison spoke up, "What are you thinking?"

"I think that we need to hide the Suburban. And Giltreas said he dealt with the ones that attacked Michelle. I think we may need to clean that up, and send the bodies through the gate as well. Someone is going to come looking for them, and the Suburban. Eventually, we can return it to the rightful owner, if we figure out that they didn't have a part in this. But for now, I think we need to take some steps, along with getting you two to someplace where I don't have to worry about you. Can we send the truck through a gate to your world – your plane? Will that cause any problems?" Dave said, turning to Giltreas.

"I can make it so the gate will suffice. As to problems with it, some might be curious, and others might be fearful," he shrugged. "I care not for their concerns. Many travel through the Kingdom on their way to other places, and other planes even, having many strange things and devices with them. Certainly the dwarves will make unusual devices from time to time. I will vouchsafe for the watching of the thing, and the four whom I dealt with. The Queen will be willing to lend us locked cells aplenty for them, so they will not wander off, nor cause problems amongst the people of the Forest Kingdom."

That got him a very strange look from the others, and he wondered where it came from. "It would be better if they were to walk there. I have no desire to heft dead bodies, nor any interest in the stench a corpse will cast about. I will revive them, much like I revived Michelle after her ordeal."

Shocked silence ruled for a moment as the three stared at him, and in the stillness, Sadie's voice was heard from where she sat on Michelle's lap, turning and raising her head to look up at her. "Sadie and Abby and Max go outside now."

It didn't really register at first, as Michelle turned to Sadie and started stroking her head and neck. Sadie shuffled her front feet from her seated position, and the voice was heard coming from the dog again. "Sadie and Abby and Max go outside now."

Michelle blinked, and turned to Giltreas with a wry grin. "I could get used to this. How long will the spell last again?"

Giltreas thought about it, then reached out with his senses to see if the spell showed any signs of ending. He blinked in surprise as what he detected registered. "I think it may not end," he said, his tone of voice conveying his confused feelings to them.

"Sadie and Abby and Max go outside right now. Abby needs." Sadie's voice was a little more urgent this time as she jumped down and took a step towards the door, turning to look back at Michelle.

Michelle stood, and walked over to the door and leashed Max before letting the three dogs out, as the three other people followed her outside. Max pulled her along, and jumped off the three steps of the porch, something Michelle had seen the young dog do many times. Abby followed, jumping out and hitting the ground running, and headed over to the bushes at the edge of the walkway. Sadie took the steps in one hop as well, the much taller dog making the move with a youthful grace and athleticism she had not shown for a few years. She squatted in the grass just beyond the paved sidewalk, and as she relieved herself, an "Ahhhh..." was heard from her. Max finished his business, going both, but Abby was still going. It was apparent from the quantity of solid matter coming from her that the spells from earlier had helped her out considerably.

Michelle turned to where Giltreas leaned against the porch railing post, and said "What do you mean, it may not end. Is that supposed to happen?"

Dave moved over to let Allison get closer to hear the explanation as well, as Giltreas spoke up. "There is a certain tell that will show when a temporary spell will end; a waning of the energy from the casting of the spell is evident. When the energy from the casting has faded away, the effect of the spell itself ends. I sense no energy from the casting still in Sadie, which would mean the spell has ended, and yet we still hear Sadie's voice. This has not happened to a spell I have cast before. It takes the strength and will of a Mid God or nearly so to make such spells permanent, something I most certainly am not. I must think upon this." His focus turned inwards, and Michelle turned back to the dogs, making sure they stayed in the yard, letting him think as her mind raced. What do you do with a talking dog?

Dave moved down the stairs, over to the black SUV, and opened the front passenger door. He had already noticed that there were no plates on the vehicle, and a temporary tag was taped up in the back window, as if it was just purchased new. There was nothing telling on the temporary tag, though. Now he opened the glove box, and pulled out a sheaf of papers folded up in an envelope, and started going through them.

And what he saw caused him to nearly drop them. He then put them back together, put them back in the glove box, closed it up, and slammed the door in a hurry. He then walked around the front of the Suburban quickly, and said "We have to get this thing out of here as soon as possible. Get your stuff together; we have to leave as soon as we deal with the situation in the woods."

Giltreas, Michelle and Allison all turned at the urgency in his voice. "Who owns it? What did you find out?" Michelle voiced the concern first.

"It is registered to a company I haven't heard of before, but the address is in Bethesda, Maryland. My instincts tell me they might be a defense contractor. Which means it is most likely lo-jacked. It also means that someone in the government may be behind this. We have to get this situation cleaned up before someone comes looking for it. We have to get you and Allison to safety right now. We probably should take the dogs, too. Allison, get the dogs into my SUV, and get them situated. I don't know how long we will be gone, and I don't know any other way to see to them without bringing them along. Get all their stuff ready to move. Giltreas, is it ok if we bring them along?"

Dave turned to the grey man, who simply nodded, then said, "They will be welcomed. Companion animals are respected and cared for."

Dave nodded, and then turned back. "Michelle, can you show us back to the clearing? We need to get on this right away. Also, Giltreas, if you are going to revive them, I will need to get some things out of my car." He turned to the slender man, and asked, "Will we be able to make a couple trips? I want to get them out of here right away, but I will need to get them supplies, clothes, food for the dogs, and anything else they might need."

"Certainly I see no reason why not." Giltreas smiled inwardly at the snap of command in Dave's voice and the quick succession of tasks thought out and presented so efficiently. The human would make a good companion, to be sure. He took charge in a dangerous situation, and showed no hesitation or fear. Giltreas did not understand everything that was going on, but for now, the need to act took him, and he took a step forward, but then turned towards the cottage. "I must retrieve my pack and my things from the room. I will return momentarily."

Dave waved him on, and went to his own SUV. Opening the back, he lifted the top on his ever-present tool box, and pulled out a mostly full pack of long wire ties. He wanted something to cuff the bastards with, and this would do nicely. A strong nylon rope he always carried with him was next. This would work. He moved back as Allison came out the cottage door with an armful of stuff she deposited in the back of the SUV. He glanced at what she deposited, and mentally took inventory of what was there, and what he might need to bring later.

Food for Sadie and Abby was already there; he had topped off the food bins for both of them before coming up. Allison brought supplies for Max from her car, and dropped it all in the back of the 4Runner. Dave opened the bin for Max, glanced inside, and closed it again. He estimated that all three dogs probably had food enough for a month or more in the sealed plastic bins that he and Michelle favored for storing food. The grey bins themselves were square, and had a circular lid on them with a rubber gasket that enabled them to be air and water tight, and kept the smell of the food contained; a must for a cottage in the woods with the wildlife around. Michelle had bought all three nearly a year ago, and had given the third one to Allison when Max was just a year old.

Food bowls of plastic, and water bowls of stainless steel. Six-foot black nylon leashes for each dog, along with longer variable-length spring-return leads that let the dogs roam out to sixteen feet on walks. A stack of blankets for the dogs to sleep on; Max usually had no problem sharing with his canine cousins.

Allison deposited her bug-out pack on the next trip from her car. He knew it would have a few days' worth of clothing and other personal supplies in it she might need, a survival knife and sharpening kit, along with a cleaning kit and quite a bit of ammo for her Glock. He really wasn't sure how much, but it was probably three extended-round clips, and a couple boxes. No more than two hundred rounds. The shoulder holster she preferred was most likely in there as well. That was where she deviated from her Marine Corps training – no hip holster for her. She was more of a boy scout than he was, he grinned to himself. She had told him when she made up the pack that it was something she never expected to use, but it was like insurance – you inevitably needed it if you didn't have it, and she felt better knowing it was there.

It also contained a trio of two-way dual-band amateur radios with spare batteries. Michelle, Allison, and Dave all had their amateur radio license, something Allison had pestered them about until they gave in. Dave smiled as he thought to himself, 'She's more of a geek than I am, too.'

He stepped back from the bumper of the SUV as Allison dropped another load of stuff in it, and at a glance from her, confirmed she was done, closed it up tight. They both turned as the cottage door opened, and stopped in surprise.

Giltreas returned out the cottage door, and Allison and Dave both gawked at him momentarily. He had his sword at his left hip, and all the things Michelle had pulled off to let him sleep the night before were back in their place. A medium-sized, worn leather pack was on his back as well.

Dave shook himself, then spoke up, "Giltreas, is it a problem taking both the black one and the dark grey one with us? We have too many people to ride in just the black one, if you are going to revive the four others."

"It will be no problem, David. It will certainly cause stares, but no one will openly challenge you. We should be able to get to the royal palace, and leave them out in the carriage area near the stables," Giltreas said, as he wondered to himself what was going to happen next.

Dave nodded to himself, then spoke up. "Allison, drive mine, take Michelle, and get the dogs into the back seat. Then you lead the way to the clearing, where we pick up our travelling companions. Giltreas, you can ride with me," he said, as he led the way around to the passenger side of the big black Chevrolet. "Are you comfortable with putting your pack in the back of the grey one?" At the answering nod, he continued "Your sword can go in the front seat with you, with the hilt pointing up towards you." Did he really just say sword? Really?

Giltreas followed, putting his pack through the open door in the back grey carriage to one side, then walked over to forward-most door Dave opened for him on the right hand side of the black carriage. He detached the sword and sheath from his belt and put the sword in first, then he climbed in himself. A handle fixed just inside the door towards the window in front was well suited to pull himself in, as was the narrow platform just below the door.

David was just getting in himself. He then reached to his left, and pulled a strap over his shoulder to his right hip, showing it to Giltreas. "Grab that buckle, and do the same. This will help protect you if things get bumpy."

Once Giltreas was secured, Dave turned the key waiting in the ignition, and started up the machine.

Giltreas looked in wonder at the sound and slight trembling sensation coming from the black "horseless carriage." Interesting.

He watched in fascination as Dave pushed with his right foot on some sort of pad sticking up from floor below his feet, then used his right hand to pull a stalk mounted just behind the wheel towards him and down. He reached out to grasp the handle in front of him to steady himself as Dave turned the wheel slowly while looking over his shoulder, backing the carriage up some ways from the house to allow the smaller grey machine room to maneuver, pointing the carriage at the back of the yard.

The other carriage continued to move backwards with them, two white lights glowing on the back of the carriage, then three red lights appeared, one on either side, and one higher up in the center. The grey carriage stopped, and the white lights went away as it started to move away from them, towards the back of the yard.

Dave moved the stalk behind the wheel down further from where it was. With both hands on the wheel, the carriage moved again, forward this time, following Michelle, Allison and the three dogs in Dave's carriage as she led the way towards the woods behind the cottage. They proceeded slowly over the somewhat uneven ground, but the bumps did not seem all that bad to Giltreas. Certainly better than most carriages and wagons he had ridden in before.

The path through the woods was unfamiliar to Giltreas, and it appeared, to Dave as well. Michelle led the way confidently, though, with the red lights appearing only when she slowed to maneuver over a particularly difficult patch of ground, or a narrow spot between two trees.

Quickly enough, Michelle turned and stopped at the base of a low hill. David stopped his carriage as well, and pushed the stalk behind the wheel up to the starting position. He then turned something on the trunk leading to the wheel, and the sound and vibration stopped. He looked towards Giltreas, and reached down with his right hand to push on a red part of the thing the strap had connected to. This released the strap that crossed his body, and caught it with his right hand. He then let it retract, transferred it with his left, and set it aside just behind the door. He then lifted his left hand to the door, grasping and pulling a handle which opened the door, all the while watching to see what Giltreas would do.

Giltreas mimicked the actions, retracting the strap, and opened the door to get out.

He stood, then stepped around the door, and pushed it shut.

Dave stepped forward to the front of the Suburban, and waited for Giltreas. Then they walked together to where Michelle and Allison were waiting.

Michelle was speaking to Allison, saying "I don't think you want to go up there until things are a little more cleaned up. I nearly lost my lunch last night, and I could barely see what was around me in the dark. It is pretty gruesome. No offense, Giltreas," she said, turning towards him as they walked up to the women.

"None taken, I assure you, Michelle. At best, death is not a pleasant companion." He sketched a half bow to her, with a wry smile on his face that conveyed understanding and apology both.

Allison, however, did exactly what Dave expected – she led the way up the hill with a toss of her head that said volumes.

Dave knew his wife had been in a few firefights in Iraq, when her convoys up from Kuwait to Bagdad had been ambushed. He had heard later from some friends of his in one convoy that she had kept her cool, and returned fire with her M16A4 rifle. The insurgents had tossed grenades and smoke bombs at them to cover their approach. No one knew if anyone hit anything, but she never stopped firing at targets that kept appearing and disappearing through the dust and smoke surrounding the road, all the while carefully conserving ammunition. After the insurgents had broken off the attack and ran, she had advanced with the others to secure the forward approaches to their position, and to make sure that no one was still planning to attack. She gained the respect of her fellow Marines that day, and it was not the only time since. Dave expected her not to be affected by what he expected to see up the small hill.

Allison was the first to move into the small clearing, her pistol out. Dave was reminded again that she always went armed, he reflected as he walked in behind her. Michelle hung back, not wanting to go and see the scene again.

Giltreas walked up casually, then looked at Dave as he finished surveying the scene, then turned to look at him with respect.

"All four were armed with pistols, and you took them out with just knives and a bow, it looks like. From the look of it, they were caught by surprise, and didn't even have time to react, or prepare." The look of respect he gave Giltreas made him uncomfortable. He was not one to brag; there was no need, when one's actions were the only message one should need to send.

"Fortune shone down upon me, David." He turned away.

Dave snorted, but turned himself back to the task at hand. "How will you do this? What steps will you take?"

Giltreas stepped forward, and started talking. "Before calling on my Patron to help me revive them, I must heal that which caused their deaths, else they simply slip back across the veil once more. Then with the assistance of my Patron, I shall call up the strength, form it to my will, release it upon them, and bring them back to this side once more."

Dave nodded. "Makes sense. Before you bring them back, I want to secure them, and make sure they have nothing they can use to get away or start up trouble again."

"Wise of you," he said, and turned to the task at hand.

The one next lying next to the tree that had been killed by the crossbow bolt was first. He pulled the broken shaft out from where it was sticking out of the man's chest, and lifted the corpse with very little difficulty, carrying it over to a clear area between the one with his chest torn open and the one with his throat cut. He then lifted the one with the slashed throat, setting him in the row as well.

With all of the dead lined up in a row, he stood at their heads, closed his eyes and lifted his arms, palms up.

With a suddenness that shocked Allison and Dave, a rushing sound came from Giltreas at the same time a greenish light flashed from him to the four dead men on the ground. Allison gasped as she saw the wounds simply disappear as the green light from Giltreas flashed over the bodies. They were still dead, though.

Dave just stared for a moment, until Giltreas gave a quiet cough. He looked up at the grey man in front of him, and said "I gotta learn that someday. Do you think you could teach me?"

Giltreas blinked, then thought about it. He had never trained a student before, but the idea of teaching this human man was not unpleasant. "Certainly, David. I would be honored to see what you can learn from me."

"I will take you up on that," Dave said as he pulled something out of his back pocket. Rolling each of the dead men over onto their fronts, he gathered their hands behind them, and a long white cord of some kind was looped over each wrist and through each other, binding their hands behind their backs with a "zzzzzippp" sound he had never heard before. Then Giltreas laughed as Dave used the rope he brought along. It was a devious idea that had never occurred to him, and he wholeheartedly approved, intending to use it himself should he have the need.

When he had finished tying them up, he searched their pockets, and under their outer clothing around each one's chest and under their arms, making a pile of their possessions.

Each of them had a similar device made of dark metal that Dave seemed to disassemble, then set aside carefully. "What are those?"

"Those are weapons. We call them guns or firearms. Very dangerous. They can kill a man easily from considerable distance with one shot." He reached under his coat to under his left arm with his right hand, and pulled out another one similar to what he had pulled from each dead man. He did something with his, and a long and thin portion of it fell out into his hand. He then worked a piece of it that seemed to slide along the top, releasing a small brass-colored bit with a rounded end on it, before he handed it to Giltreas.

"It fires a small projectile at very high speed, and will continue to fire as fast as you can pull the trigger until it is empty. What I handed you is called a clip. It holds rounds that are fired. As each round is fired, the gun reloads itself with a new round, ready to be fired again. That magazine holds 15 rounds. When the last round is fired, the slide on the top will lock back like it is right now. You drop the current magazine, put in a new magazine, push a lever to release the slide, and it is ready to be fired again." He handed the now-empty gun to Giltreas, taking the magazine back.

Giltreas took it carefully, looking it over, as Dave spoke again. "There are some safety tips you need to know. First, always assume a gun is loaded and ready to fire even if you emptied it yourself; even then, it is wise to be very careful. Second, do not point a gun at anyone unless you intend to shoot them. Third, never put your finger on the trigger until you are ready to fire. That is where the bullet comes out," he added, as Giltreas felt the end of the barrel. He handed the gun back to Dave, and smiled.

"We must trade knowledge, my friend. I will teach you what I can of magic, and you will teach me of your fire arms. But, on to what we must do. Shall we revive these miscreants and be on our way?"

Dave's smile went away quickly. He nodded, acknowledging and agreeing to the trade then looked loaded his gun, sliding the magazine home, and released the slide to chamber a round. "Go ahead. I'm ready."

Allison nodded, holding her gun with both hands, finger off the trigger, with the gun pointed to the ground. "I'm ready, too. Let's do this."

Giltreas closed his eyes, and briefly wondered if he was doing the right thing. He had no desire to carry dead bodies, even in such a magnificent carriage as what he had rode in back to this clearing, but he had no signal from his patron... never mind, there it was. Very well. His patron must have plans for these worthless brigands. He hoped whatever it was that it would be was painful for them. Very painful, and not short-lived.

The magical energy rose more quickly this time than it ever had before. A small part of him wondered if it was because he would be attempting to revive four dead, one after another, but his concentration didn't waver, and he focused his attention on the first of the dead forms before him

To the watching Dave and Allison, it seemed as if Giltreas was suddenly glowing, bathed in a red light from an unknown source that seemed to cling to him like a mist. Then Giltreas raised his arm towards the bodies on the ground, and the red light jumped from Giltreas to the first of the four. But it didn't stop there. The red glow seemed to congeal on the body, and then it gathered itself and flowed to the one next to the first, until it had lit all four dead bodies, in less time than it took to draw a breath.

Then something happened.

First one gasped, then another, then another, until all four were breathing. Allison realized that she had been holding her breath, and let it out. Damn! Neat trick! She hadn't realized she spoke out loud until Giltreas turned and smiled at her. "I want to learn magic, too. Not sure what I have to trade, though."

Giltreas merely smiled at her. "I will be glad to teach you what I can, Allison."

Then the body on the ground that breathed first, shifted and groaned. Soon enough, all four were awake, squirming and struggling to get free, and blinking against the bright midday sun that filtered through the trees above into the small clearing, while trying to figure out where they were and what was happening.

Dave had left them lying on their faces when he secured their hands behind them. Now he spoke up, the conversational tone of his voice completely at odds with the words he spoke. A shiver ghosted down Allison's back. She had never heard him like that before, but she agreed with it. The Modern Warrior she had met in Bagdad was back with a vengeance. The thought raised her adrenalin and keyed her up.

"I see you have all rejoined the living. Literally. Let me make something clear. You attacked my sister. Bad choice. I happily would have left you dead, but I need to cover up what you did for now until I can figure out who ordered this. Explaining dead bodies is a bit of a challenge around here. The one that killed you in the first place brought you back from the dead so we don't have to carry your corpses. You can walk to wherever we stash you.

"If any one of you object to what is happening, though, someone will kill you again, and your friends will carry you. And this time, I won't ask him nicely if he will bring you back again." The conversational tone in his voice was a surprise to Giltreas, but his words were not, not that he objected to them. The impact of what he said and how he said it, however, was profound. One did not spare niceties with these types. He walked in front of the four to where they could look up and see him, crossed his arms in front of him, and glared at them. He said nothing, however. He had no reason to waste words on dirt.

"So, a couple of more things before we get started. If you value your worthless lives, you will not move unless I or someone other than you four say so, or I will start hacking off fingers and/or toes. If you don't follow direction very well, I will start to hack off larger, unnecessary body parts. If you talk out of turn, I will pull out your tongue and cut it off. Do you understand?" He never raised his voice, or forced any words out.

All four froze in fear as heads nodded in quick, spastic jerks.

"I have gone through everything on you, and taken it all. Your hands are wire-tied behind you, and you should look at your feet before we go. Then we are going to take a trip to where my friend is from, where we will leave you in a dark little hole to rot until we decide what to do with you. Who knows? They may even feed you once in a while, if you behave. But from now on, you will do exactly what I or anyone else says, or things get ugly.

Do you understand?"

Four heads nodded again in fear.

CHAPTER 9

Jack was still disoriented. He was not sure what was happening. The last thing he remembered was the grey man lifting him off the ground with only one hand, and then his world went dark. He knew what the plan was, and how things were supposed to turn out. This was so far from the plan that it was laughable. He glanced at the others on the ground next to him, and heard the fear they all felt in their shallow, rapid breathing.

Then the grey man reached down, and lifted him easily off the ground and stood him on his feet in the clearing in the sunlight that filtered through the treetops above them. He guessed that it was somewhere around midafternoon, but he couldn't see his watch. From the feel of his wrist, he was no longer wearing it anyways. He glanced around, and saw another woman – Allison, Dave's wife, he guessed. She was holding what looked like a Glock, and from the look of it, she really knew how to use it. The totally blank expression on her face scared him more, for no readily apparent reason. Who were these people? He had been incredibly sloppy, badly underestimating them, not even bothering to check out their backgrounds to see if they were a threat. Apparently that was a fatal mistake. Then things got worse as another woman stepped in front of his field of vision, dressed in a bath robe.

"Hi. Remember me? I know I look a little different now…" He stared at her, then comprehension dawned. Michelle Wilhelm! What –

Her hand came out of nowhere, and pain shot through him as the edge of her hand connected with his throat, and he suddenly found himself unable to draw a breath as the strike momentarily paralyzed him. Gasping, he realized that he was on his knees, choking.

A green light flashed over Jack, and he could breathe again. He looked up just in time to see Michelle twist out of Dave's grip, and kick out to Jack's right, connecting with the now-standing specialist's groin area, and he winced as the hit went home dead-center. Then the grey man lifted his hand, and Michelle seemed to levitate up from the ground until she was a good foot above the ground, floating back away from the four bound men.

"Kajzhtaka zhemfik donameck, sondemm?" The words were in a language Jack had never heard before, and they were so utterly foreign he had no idea where it came from.

Michelle glared at him a moment, then nodded, the fight going out of her. But as she was lowered to the ground next to Allison, her next glance at Jack said volumes: this is not over, not by a long shot. Jack winced internally. From his briefings, he never guessed that Michelle was capable of even a hint of physical violence. This whole situation just got worse by the moment. If they had not surprised her so completely, things could have gone very differently. Of course, she looked insanely different now, and incredibly hot, and he could not even guess as to the cause. Then realization dawned, and he looked at the grey man, and swallowed hard. For some reason, the thought that he had somehow changed... restored the Wilhelm woman in this way scared him even more. What was he capable of? What wasn't he capable of? No limits came to mind, and that was the worst of all.

Another green light flashed, and the imported specialist stopped dry-heaving and writhing on the ground in pain. Dave stood him up next, and he continued to shake in fear, breathing harshly.

Aaron was stood up next, and squinted in the light. He turned to look around, and Jack saw that his eye, where the thrown knife that had killed him had struck, was milky white. Apparently, his eye was not completely repaired. Jack also noticed that Aaron's earlier fear had subsided, and seemed to slowly be replaced with something else that Jack couldn't quite put his finger on.

Bill was the last to be stood up, and then they were marched down the small path to where the Suburban was parked, along with another SUV that Jack recognized from his obviously incomplete briefing files as belonging to the second target, Dave – a late model Toyota 4Runner. The rope that stretched between all of their right ankles made walking a bit of a challenge as it dragged on the ground and occasionally caught on something. It was just short enough that the four had to walk close together to be able to move. Smart. There was no way they could run with their hands tied behind their backs and tied together like that. His estimation of Dave's intelligence and capabilities went way up. He was almost glad he didn't have to go up against him.

The way Dave and Allison handled themselves seemed to indicate that they were both former military, and had at least some combat experience. Dave had obviously seen his share, but Allison was way more deadly than he expected. If he lived through this... what a stupid thought. He realized with a start that he had no control over what happened to him from this point on, and where he was going. He almost lost control of his bladder at the thought.

The back door on the Suburban was opened, and the four of them were forced into the back seat, stacked one almost on top of the next. It was not comfortable, but no one asked his opinion. He looked around, and saw that the Suburban had been picked clean of any potential weapon or tool they could use for escape, before he remembered that he and his team had done precisely that before they picked up Michelle and brought her out here.

The grey man stepped into the front passenger seat, after setting his sword and pack on the floor in front of him. He strapped himself in, then turned to watch them silently.

Dave opened the back of his 4Runner, and then set the garbage bag containing bloodstained coat Jack had once worn and all the belongings from the four attackers in the back. He wanted those items (especially the weapons, but the cell phones, too) in a different vehicle so that they couldn't be used to free themselves. He took a moment to remove the batteries from the four cell phones, rendering them, he hoped, completely inert.

He then turned to Michelle, who was in the driver's seat, and said "I'm not sure where we will be going to open this gate, but keep your eyes open, ok?"

She just nodded, no smile on her face.

He got into the Suburban, and turned to see Giltreas mumble something, and he looked at Giltreas in surprise as the other reached out his hand. Without thinking, he took it, and as he did, a slight shiver went up his arm. Then Giltreas spoke up.

"Can you understand me now? If so, answer me back in the same tongue." The language was new, the same as what he spoke to Michelle in back at the small clearing. Surprised, he nodded, and said "I do understand."

"In order to sow confusion amongst your enemies, we must travel some distance away from here before opening the gate. I wish to make it seem that these animals accomplished their goal before leaving, and then disappeared. Do you know a secluded place much like this that would be appropriate for calling a gate?"

Jack listened in surprise as Dave also seemed to know the language the grey man spoke, and even answered back in it, leaving Jack with even more questions about the capabilities and experiences of his one-time targets. The conversation continued as Dave backed up the Suburban, turned it around, and drove back to the cottage. The 4Runner followed as they passed the cottage, took the long driveway out then went back out to the main road.

Giltreas looked around in awe as the carriage exited the wooded area and paused. The road in front of them was a smooth, flawless white/grey expanse that was wide enough to allow two such vehicles to move side by side. It went as far as could be seen in both directions, flowing with the low rise and fall of the ground, and was painted with a solid white stripe closest to them, a line of dashes down the middle in that same white, and a yellow line was on the far side. Beyond that, a low depression down from the road lay, with another road still beyond. And on both sides and in between was an expanse of green grass that seemed to be well maintained. The trees of the forest they had been in stretched onwards in both directions on both sides of the fantastical road, following as it curved out of site in either direction.

Dave looked to his left, and waited as some few others similar to this amazing carriage passed them at great speed. A small, low, red one, with only two doors, a white one nearly as big, and two others, one with only one door on each side, and an open area with things he didn't recognize stacked in the back, tied down with rope. Then the black Suburban pulled out, and accelerated with surprising ease until it matched the pace other carriages had held. He turned, glancing at the four men behind him, and looked back to see Dave's carriage behind them, keeping pace. He noticed that the roadway on the far side held carriages of all different shapes, colors and sizes heading beyond them the other way. One very large carriage even pulled a huge box on wheels, making a tremendous roar as it passed.

They followed the road some short while, possibly more than a quarter of an hour Giltreas guessed, when both carriages moved over to the left side, and Giltreas watched both the world around them and the men behind him.

As Giltreas observed, they slowed, and crossed the depression in between the two road ways on a higher path of dirt and rock, turning towards the roadway that headed the other direction. After a brief wait to allow other carriages to pass, a time that was clear afforded itself, and both carriages crossed the amazing roadway onto another dirt path on the opposite side of the double roadway.

They headed down the slight incline from the hard road into the trees once again, following the dirt path as it lead this way and that until Giltreas could no longer see the roadway again, and pulled into a clearing deeper in the woods.

Giltreas stepped out, noting with satisfaction that the path ended here in a clearing some thirty paces across and to the side. More than large enough. He turned, walked over Dave's door, and to his surprise, the window moved down. His thoughts moved back to the matter at hand quickly. Questions could wait until the current situation was settled.

"I will open the gate. I will walk through to ascertain if it is safe and where I expect to be. I will step back through, and wave for you to go if it is clear. On the other side, move forward so that Allison and Michelle may follow in the next carriage, but do not move much beyond until I come through and dismiss the gate. We will then follow the roadway to the city," Giltreas finished, all the while speaking in the new language.

"Very well. Whenever you are ready," Dave returned in the same language, then asked, "What language are we speaking?"

"This is the tongue of my mother's race." Giltreas turned to the other carriage, and walked up to the door on Michelle's side. The window once again moved down, and Sadie stuck her head out before Michelle could pull her back inside, her front paws on the back of the seat Michelle was sitting in. The same explanation was given then he walked around to the other side.

Allison rolled her window down, and watched as Giltreas murmured something, then a light warmth briefly flowed through her. Then Giltreas held out his hand. She took it carefully, and another sensation went through her as Giltreas spoke.

"Do you understand me, Allison? Answer back in the same tongue, if you please." The soft look on his face was surprisingly gentle as he spoke words that were both new to her and understood at the same time.

Realization dawned, and she smiled as she spoke up, "Of a certainty. Was that a spell?"

Giltreas smiled at her. "Yes. You have learned the language of my mother's race. You will need it where we travel, as no one I have ever met afore has knowledge of your tongue."

Allison thought about it, and then asked, "Are you going to help the four fools like that?"

Giltreas shook his head with a smile at her characterization. "I see no reason to. Others will learn their language in the same manner. They, however, can learn new languages as a child would do so, since they have shown that they cannot act properly around civilized adults. This will prevent or at least slow them from gaining comrades that might assist them with further mayhem."

Allison's laugh was echoed by Michelle. Sadie, surprisingly, woofed once as well, then laid her head back down on the back seat of the 4Runner.

Everyone in both cars watched as Giltreas walked to the front of the vehicles and took several more steps. Then he stopped with his back to them, and held out his arms away from his body with his hands forward as if inviting embrace. Had they seen his face, they would have observed that his eyes were closed. The hair on the backs of everyone's neck stood up as a strange, electrical sensation washed over them: Giltreas was drawing in a huge amount of energy as he concentrated.

The engines in Suburban and the 4Runner both struggled for a moment as if the vehicles were running hard, or towing a heavy load, then they went back to a normal idle as the draw ended.

Giltreas was deep in spell-trance, completely focused upon the gate he was calling, and how to make it wider and taller. He had done such a thing before, when transporting a wagon and team of eight oxen, which actually required a larger gate than the one he was forming in his mind. He was also picturing both ends of the tunnel between the gate, and where he wanted the other end located in relation to the Elvish city that was home to the Queen of the Forest. Too close to the city walls, and it would be perceived as a threat. Too far away, and the travel would be more difficult; he knew not how well the ground was, and how well these metal and glass carriages could traverse difficult ground. They seemed capable enough, but one could not judge such things carelessly when time was of the essence. He settled on the distance beyond a bowshot, and released the spell to complete.

With a suddenness that was shocking to see, the gate appeared in front of Giltreas, wavered for an instant, then stabilized, right in front of the eyes of the seven people in the two trucks. The three dogs, however, missed it entirely. The somewhat oval-shaped gate touched the ground, and was wider and taller than either SUV, with room to spare for a person to walk along side through it if they wanted.

Giltreas had a moment to wonder about why he was not drained from the calling, then dismissed the thought. His patron's work again, he shrugged to himself. Then he stepped forward, and walked through the gate, disappearing from view.

A moment later, he returned, and waved at Dave, who shifted into gear, and the big SUV moved forward and into the gate.

CHAPTER 10

Human cities in non-industrial societies throughout time and across every material plane shared some commonalities of design: high curtain walls of rock and stone, very wide areas cleared around a city so that an invading army could not find cover and resources to use in a siege, and so that the attackers could be seen well in advance and, if not completely prepare, at least close the gates and keep them out.

Forest-dwelling elves tended to take a different approach to building large settlements and cities. Preferring locations deep inside vast forests, they adapted the trees and brush that normally grow there to help form perimeter markers, build living quarters and homes, and provide protection from the sun above, and the rains and snows of inclement weather as well. The great city of the Elvish Queen of the Forest was no exception.

Built into a vast forested area in the heart of the Elvish kingdom in a bend on the shore of a huge river that meandered through the forest and a thousand leagues south to the sea, the city was home to nearly twenty thousand beings; mostly elves, but some humans and dwarves lived there full time, as well. And it covered an area some three to four leagues across, in roughly a circle.

Elvish rangers and clerics had started the city some seven hundred years before, at the coronation of the new Queen in honor of her reign. Sturdy oak trees were planted closely in rows to form walls, and as they grew, they were carefully tended so that they could still flourish despite their proximity to one another. The in between spaces were filled with thorny hard bushes, which were then encouraged to grow thick and wild, providing a measure of security to the inhabitants of the vast city. The oaks anchoring the walls were close enough together that when the big trees had matured, a guard could walk through the trees above ground around the entire wall. And the whole of the trees and bushes making up the walls were magically enhanced to make them resistant to fire.

The north side of the city was right against the big river that provided water to the inhabitants, as well as boats to move food and goods to and fro. The gates at the south, east, and west sides of the city were anchored to stone columns erected by Dwarvish craftsmen who leant their talents to the city as a gift to the young new Queen. The massive doors were from human craftsmen who built them out of the wood of ironwood trees, found in the far east of the realm across the great sea to the far west. Dwarvish skills enabled the massive doors to be moved by a single guardsman, despite being the weight of many men.

Structures in the city were built of the wood of trees carefully selected in the vast nearby forest, so that the overall health of the forest was not damaged, but enhanced. Some trees were moved aside in the new city walls to make for better pathways and roads through the city, and to give some form to the layout of the buildings.

The road to the city was paved with smooth, cut cobblestones, and was wide enough for two freight wagons to pass each other with much room to spare. The trees to either side of the road had been cleared back some ten paces, allowing traffic to pull off to the side of the road for whatever reason they might have.

The city's security was seen to by the small groups of guards that patrolled the forest surrounding the walls day and night, as far out as many as five leagues.

Goltamas always liked guard tower duty. One stood on the upper branches in the tallest oak tree just to the side of the gate at your station, and looked out upon the road leading up to the gate below. The view was clear nearly four hundred paces. For the last several hundred years, the kingdom was at peace. Those who would harm travelers had been cleared from the neighboring forests nearly twenty leagues in all directions.

The quiet duty of the west wall guard post was a welcome respite, especially on a day as special as this. The warm sun shown down out of the clear midday late summer sky, gently warming everything it touched as it filtered through the forest canopy above. A warm, gentle breeze flowed over the city and its inhabitants from the southwest. In a few more moons, that wind would come down from the north, bringing cold, snow, and ice as the days grew shorter and the nights colder and longer.

But for today, it was pleasant. Almost nothing of interest ever happened. Goltamas had fought in border clashes with the neighboring races that were less than charitable towards his kingdom. He'd had enough violence in his long service to the crown and the Queen to wish to avoid any further contest.

Unlike young Tarkhan standing next to him. Tarkhan was new to the guard group. He was a diligent student of arms and tactics, and showed much promise on the field. He was also a standout with a bow, particularly good with the weapon all elves learned to use since childhood. Unfortunately, he was also inflicted with what Goltamas' instructor long ago had called "the disease of youth." Young, and eager to prove himself, he required an older hand at his side until he was properly seasoned. He viewed gate guard duty with the importance it deserved, however, which kept him diligent and attentive to his duty. He would have been sent to guard the market, or something less desirable and less important, if he had not shown the proper attitude towards his role.

Guard duty at every post was always in pairs. Guards on duty were not supposed to hold their position if a serious threat to the city presented itself. They were supposed to observe until the threat was known and understood, then one was to go and report to the lieutenant or captain on duty so that a proper response could be mustered. And if one was injured, the other had the duty to escape and report.

Now, Tarkhan coughed quietly, a signal to Goltamas. Tarkhan's attention was focused on some happening at least three hundred paces out from the city gate. Goltamas looked where Tarkhan was staring, and saw a Traveler's Gate standing there.

It was much wider and taller than such a gate would need to be if a single traveler was coming through, or even a line of men in single file, making Goltamas step over to Tarkhan's side. Placing a hand on the young man's shoulder, he waited to observe what was happening before dispatching the young guardsman to report.

As the two watched, a single figure stepped through the gate, stopping to look around carefully. After a moment, the figure went back through the gate again. Goltamas took in a breath, waiting to see what would happen. And was totally unprepared for what he saw next.

A large black, shiny metal… thing, on strange black wheels, emerged, rolling forward several paces, then stopped. It was as wide as a large freight wagon, and looked to be nearly as long. It had a long forward section, followed by what looked like a nearly upright, slightly curved piece of glass that one could almost see through. Goltamas and Tarkhan had never seen anything like it. Tarkhan was about to comment, when a second, slightly smaller shiny metal thing similar to the first rolled out of the gate. Then as they watched, the same person they had spotted first through the gate came back through. Neither guard could see who it was, as he immediately turned back towards the gate. He raised one hand, and the gate disappeared. Then he turned, walked past the two things towards the gate, and the two strange contraptions followed, and Goltamas finally got a clear look at the stranger on foot.

"Well. This will get interesting. Tarkhan, go tell the captain of the guard that Giltreas has returned," Goltamas said, with a slight smile.

"Yes sir. Who is Giltreas? I have heard the name before, but no one ever talked about him very much." Tarkhan's curiosity was evident on his face.

"Go now. We can talk later, young one. You will probably hear about him later, anyways. Some voices will certainly not be silent." The tone of voice was dismissive without being oppressive, and Tarkhan left, knowing not to press his question further. As he started on his way, he heard Goltamas behind him say, "Ask for someone to relieve me, and come back up when you are done. I will greet Giltreas when he gets here."

"Yes, Guardsman," was the respectful reply.

* * *

Giltreas walked up the gently climbing road at an even pace, glancing over his shoulder from time to time to make sure the two carriages were following; they maintained their distance from him and each other, and a part of his mind thought briefly that the weather was much the same in both places. Then he put that thought aside. He knew he would have to approach the walls and the west gate carefully, so as to not cause alarm. It was for that same reason he walked in front, instead of riding inside, that those guarding the city might see him and hopefully recognize him, or at least his peaceful intent. He glanced around, taking in the warmth of the midday sun that shown down on the open roadway, and the open grasses growing beside it. Once he had thought that road to be a marvel. Now, having seen the perfectly smooth, painted roadways that the humans built for their carriages, he was saddened at this road's replacement in his mind as an accomplishment to be lauded.

But his mind was also in turmoil. Something strange had happened to him, and seemed to be continuing. He never would have guessed in all his years that he could revive four dead corpses in that manner in such a short time. The strength to attempt such a thing should have been beyond him, or any other mortal being. Yet he accomplished it without being taxed overmuch. Such an ill-advised feat might have killed him once before. His patron seemed to direct and support him to do things he would never have attempted before, and had never heard of being done by a mortal of any race. His eyes narrowed as his thoughts went to his patron. He thought he heard a distant, gently mocking laughter of an almost-familiar voice in his head, but it disappeared almost as fast, and he sighed internally. It would never do to accuse his patron of such things as wandered through his thoughts at the now. He had endured severe chastisement before for lesser transgressions.

He walked up to within twenty paces of the gate, and called out. "A traveler seeks entrance. Might my companions and I enter?" The two carriages stopped another ten paces behind him, and he heard their strange rumbling cease as the drivers stopped their 'motors', whatever those were.

A familiar voice answered him gruffly. "What business do you have here in the City?"

He smiled. "I wish to visit family, and ensconce some brigands into the gentle hands of the Queen's jailer. I also have some travelers with me that seek refuge. I wish to ask the Queen for her Royal protection for them. I must present myself to the Queen. And I wish to see my mother. I might also engage in drunken revelry with old friends, brawling with old enemies, and carousing with old lovers. If time permits, of course."

The gate swung open, and Goltamas, his first guard instructor, stepped out at the head of a group of guardsmen, some of whom he recognized, and others he did not.

Goltamas stepped up to Giltreas, and held out his right arm. Giltreas grasped arms with him, then Goltamas swept him up in a hug. Stepping back, he spoke up. "What are these strange things that follow you? And where are these others you speak of?"

Giltreas turned, and waved, beckoning.

Dave opened his door, and stepped out. The Suburban was pointed slightly to the left, and he walked around to the front. With a slight head bow, he spoke to the guardsman at the head of the small group.

"I am Dave. I would like to get the four miscreants out before they cause any troubles. Would some of your men assist me?"

Goltamas waved, and four of the elvish guardsmen in his group stepped forward. Dave walked around to the right side of the machine, and pulled on the door handle, opening it. He then reached in, and pulled the first one out.

The guardsmen laughed as they saw his hands bound behind him and the rope around his ankle leading to the next one that Dave was pulling out.

All four were standing in a line looking at the strange beings in front of them. Jack's heart sunk further as he realized that he had no idea where he was anymore. The gate they had traveled through had been like nothing he had ever seen. When the front of the Suburban had touched the gate, a light had flashed towards them in a slight burst of noise, and in a blink of an eye, they were all here, wherever they were. Everything seemed different, as if they were in a different forest, with an old cobblestone road that led up to a city walled in trees and thorn bushes. Now, these men in front of them, dressed in some strange leather armor with metal pieces sown on, were laughing at him and his team. And the worst of it was, they were definitely not human. He slumped, looking down. He had no clue how he would even get back home, if he would ever be free again. And he was definitely not among anyone he could befriend, if the greeting the guardsman in front gave the grey man was any indication. Then Giltreas did something, and all the guards seemed to glow white for a moment, and Giltreas spoke again in that same language.

One by one the guards came and touched his bare skin; some on his hands, others on his face and neck. He didn't dare resist; he had no idea what would happen if he did. He also didn't speak, as he sunk further into a deep depression. One of the others, Aaron, however, didn't seem to have the same restraint.

"What are you doing, you freaks?" He snarled out, obviously not really concerned about his future. Then again, if he was the sort that was, Jack reflected, he probably wouldn't be here in the first place.

The lead guardsman who had touched Jack turned and spoke. "Giltreas cast a spell upon us so that we could learn your language. I would watch your tongue, human. We could keep it cut out of your foul mouth, and put it back only when we have questions for you. You are not amongst any friendly beings here, and we do not take kindly to brigands. You have no value to us. I suggest you find it inside yourself not to anger us."

Dave spoke up then. "These four attacked my sister. They are very dangerous, by the standards of my home. I would not trust them at all. That is why I have trussed them up like that. I would not remove their bindings until they are safely behind bars."

"Fuck you, asshole. You were next, you know," Aaron spat out at Dave, and Jack winced.

The Elvish guardsmen gasped. The translation of Aaron's first statement the guardsmen could understand was not something to be said in the company of civilized beings. And the threat was clear enough, coming after Dave's statement of what they did. It also confirmed their guilt, not that confirmation would be difficult to attain, once the Queen started asking the four some difficult questions under a compel-truth spell.

Dave simply shook his head, otherwise ignoring the statement, and Goltamas looked at the human again with respect. He then turned to Giltreas.

"Is there anyone else in your party? Let us meet them," he invited.

Giltreas waved once more, this time to the smaller grey carriage, and the doors on that one opened.

Allison stepped out first, and her appearance was taken in, but then Michelle stepped out, closed her door, and walked calmly around to where Allison had stopped at the front of that carriage. Then they both walked up to Dave. As she passed the men standing in a line with their backs to her, Michelle took the opportunity to punch Aaron once in the kidney hard enough to knock him off his feet and leave him on his knees gasping for breath in pain. She smiled sweetly at him, but didn't say a word. Allison stopped to stare at the man on the ground in front of her as Michelle moved on to Dave's side.

The guardsmen were taken aback that the slender, stunningly beautiful, regal human would do such a thing. Or that she even could with such ease and composure.

The guards of the forest city saw many humans, including human women, as they passed through the gates on their way to their business. Many of the human women they had met in passing had struck them as rough, self-sufficient types who might be capable of such a thing, but this was quite a bit beyond their experience. She held herself with a grace and presence that seemed to command respect from everyone around them; obviously a noble woman of some kind. But her readiness to administer retribution, with a smile that appeared genuine but couldn't have been, stunned them. Her actions were totally at odds with what they expected from her appearance.

Allison only smiled grimly at the man Michelle had hit. He looked up in pain when she stopped in front of him, then tried to move back from the look on her face. She simply nodded to him, and walked on, wrestling with her internal turmoil. She looked up again at the men that Giltreas was talking to, and her turmoil got worse. They definitely weren't human. The eyes were different, in a way that was hard to define. But they shared that same eye color as Giltreas; a deep, rich amber that seemed both totally alien and yet so intelligent.

That they were of the same race as Giltreas was not in doubt, but there were differences. Where Giltreas' skin color was a uniform grey, almost stone-like in tone and color, the guardsmen's skin color was a pleasant greenish-grey color that somehow looked right on them, and made Allison think about the green of the woods and grasses of the forest around them. But they shared the same slender build. And where Giltreas moved with a certain feline grace, almost like a jaguar or mountain lion, these men had a certain movement that struck her as more deliberate. While their movements were less flowing than Giltreas, they still moved with an inhuman grace. They reminded her of a yoga instructor she once had, she suddenly realized.

Michelle stopped beside Dave as he spoke up in the elvish tongue. "This is my sister, Michelle. And this is my mate, Allison." The introductions were short, and to the point.

Goltamas bowed briefly to the two, and said, "I bid you both welcome, Ladies. Come inside with us while we bring your brigands before the Queen. She will wish to ascertain their deeds for herself. If they are guilty, we will hold them until their fate is decided."

"Eventually, I think I might want to bring them back to our world, if I think we can get them dealt with properly there. If not, I might consider leaving them here permanently. We will have to see what works the best for you, us, and them," Dave said carefully in English, so that the four would hear him.

Goltamas shrugged, and said, also in English, "Most brigands are simply killed, and their remains fed to the hogs, or something worse. But if you wish a different fate for them, or should Michelle, I am certain that the Queen will be understanding of your desire. Come." He waved them forward. "Bring your carriages while my men walk these four to a place fitting of their stature."

"Goltamas, would you like to ride with us? It would be easier to have you show us where to park them." Dave had a slight grin on his face, knowing that the chance might be the first, and possibly last, time the guardsman might have to ride in a vehicle like that.

Goltamas considered, and then nodded. "I would be honored to ride with you. I will direct you to the stables. There should be adequate space there, and it is somewhat near the palace."

Goltamas walked up to the first of the two amazing metal things that the new humans had arrived in at the city gate, his mind drinking in the unique site. It was adorned in a black as deep as any night, but its surface held a polished, mirror-like finish that bespoke to him of Dwarvish skill and sorcery. There were windows of glass set along the top of the carriage, inset back from the outer surface a bit. He thought it was glass, because he could see through it somewhat, but the glass was darkened somehow, as if to prevent clear sight to the inside. He reached out, and the side of the carriage was cool, and felt like metal, but with a smooth surface that must have taken great skill and many hours at the forge to hone and polish. And he had no idea how the color had been applied. He looked lower at the wheels, and was just as amazed at them. Metal surrounded by a black material which he could not remember seeing before, with many sigils and patterns on the surface rising up slightly; to Goltamas' eyes, they must be letters of some kind, but in a language he had never seen before.

Giltreas walked up beside Goltamas and pulled on a handle set to one side of the door. The handle moved slightly with the motion of his arm, and then with a low clunk, the entire side of the carriage opened the way he had seen before.

Goltamas got in, after unbuckling the sword strapped to his left hip, gawking at the smooth tan leather and the sheer sight of the inside of the "carriage". This was like nothing he had ever seen before, and his wonder and amazement grew. 'I must congratulate that old dwarf next time I see him. This is an amazing war wagon,' Goltamas thought to himself as he settled into the most comfortable chair he had ever been in, or possibly ever seen. The luxury of it was almost… unsettling for a hardened soldier used to so much less. Giltreas pushed the front passenger door closed, and got into the vehicle in the second row of seats. Goltamas looked around in amazement, and saw that there was a light on the ceiling of the carriage, which went out when David pulled the door shut.

Dave started up the Suburban again, and looked back as Giltreas seated himself in the back seat. He heard his 4Runner start up behind them, and then shifted the Suburban into drive, waving to Goltamas to direct him.

Goltamas was an old soldier, and counted himself as seasoned and worldly. He had been in many battles, and seen many places, but this whole experience was astounding. As he pointed, the human in the seat next to him gently turned the wheel in the direction of his hand, did something with his feet, and the shiny black carriage seemed to move like an extension of his will. He turned to look over his shoulder, then noticed a mirror attached to the outside of the door he had entered into, and leaned forward to look to see the second carriage following along behind in the reflection.

The city streets were wide, and well paved with smooth cobblestones, bordered with small strips of green grasses or bushes, as befitted a seat of government. The buildings on each side and everywhere that Dave could see were a strange combination of wood and stone. Whereas the corners of the structures were usually stone, the walls seemed to be almost grown in place out of the ground, giving the appearance of trees that grew together to form walls and roofs. He marveled at it all as he worked his way down streets, past buildings that had signs above them indicating merchants, taverns, inns, and other functions, as well as homes and other dwellings. Doors looked sturdy, and windows were bordered by shutters that were open during the day. Awnings of wood were over every door and window to provide some protection from the sun, rain, and snow.

And everywhere he looked, there were people. He recognized more elvish kind, as well as humans, and what he thought were dwarves, some with beards, some without, but all of those were built like wrestlers, wide and low, with powerful shoulders. The tallest of them would only come up to mid-chest on him, though. And everyone stared open mouthed at what went by them. But the looks from the dwarves were something else. It was almost envy, or something else, and a few looked downright unhappy or angry. But no one seemed interested in stopping the odd looking and sounding caravan as it made its way through town at a walking pace.

Dave had no problems maneuvering the big vehicle where Goltamas indicated, and it appeared that Allison had no trouble either, as he monitored her progress behind them. Of course, as a logistics and transportation specialist, she was trained to drive just about everything the US Marine Corps had to offer in any conditions, including tanks in non-combat situations. This would be simple for her.

It seemed like they had travelled about a mile or so deep into the city when he saw the stables. The main building seemed to be nearly fifty yards wide, possibly just as deep, and had a paddock in front of it that was just as wide, and probably twenty yards front to back, with a fence made of sturdy poles that extended up to the height of a man, with spacing in between to allow people to climb up. The gate itself was wide enough to allow the

Suburban to drive through and then some when both panels were opened. He looked behind the 4Runner, and noticed that the four thugs were no longer back there. He glanced at Goltamas, who saw where he was looking and shrugged.

"They have been taken to the Hall of Law, to be locked in cells until such time as they are called before the Queen. She will ask them of their crimes, and compel the truth from them, to judge them against your and your sister's accusations."

"I think I will need to help your guards out. The restraints I put on their wrists will be very hard to cut loose without the right tool," Dave supplied.

"We can go there when we have put these carriages under guard." Goltamas didn't seem that concerned.

"I will be taking the grey one behind us back when Giltreas and I leave. I will need it to get around on our... plane."

Giltreas spoke up then. "We must speak with the Queen, and I must present myself, as her subject. I wish as well to spend some time with my mother. I have not seen her in quite some time." His quiet voice carried in the vehicle clearly, and Goltamas merely nodded.

* * *

"Sir, can you come over here for a moment?"

"Sure. What is it?"

"Sir, unit 2376 is unreachable."

"Which one is that?"

"The file on it says that it is on some assignment with a special unit somewhere. The notes are code-word classified eyes-only."

"Hmmm. Can you think of a reason why it might be unreachable?"

"Several. These monitoring packages don't work all that well. Lowest bidder, and all that."

He looked over the shoulder at his subordinate's workstation, then shrugged mentally.

"Log it. Probably just a fault of some kind."

CHAPTER 11

The wait to see the Elvish Queen was shorter than Dave expected. By his watch, they sat in padded wooden chairs in a small room for only twenty minutes or so. The door opened, and someone said something to Giltreas, who was seated next to the door. He stood, and when they looked at him, he nodded his head towards the door, and then he walked ahead of them down a corridor.

Dave contemplated recent events again as he followed Giltreas down the hall. The Hall of Law had been interesting, as had been the head jailer. He had brought a small wire cutter with him, and once the four were placed in what were obviously jail cells, he had told them to back up to the bars, where he had cut the wire ties from their wrists. Dave had explained the reasons why they were being incarcerated, and trying to explain how potentially dangerous they were, and while the guardsmen had listened carefully, Dave had the impression that they didn't believe him. Giltreas had then cast that same Learn Language spell on the head jailer and all the guardsmen on duty at the time, and they had touched Dave to learn the language he shared with the prisoners. Then he had followed Giltreas back to the stables, where Michelle and Allison had shifted the contents of the two SUVs so that what was going back with Dave was in the 4Runner, and what was staying was in the Suburban. The dogs had been leashed, brought out of the 4Runner, and allowed to attend to any business they had with the grass bordering the paddock area. Dave had moved the bag of personal effects from the four fools, as Allison had dubbed them, into the back of the Suburban. Then they had all gone to the Hall of the Queen, where they had waited in a small room off the main throne room until the queen had sent a guardsman for them.

A short walk later, they stood just outside a wide, arched doorway that had two elves dressed in impressive armor and armed with staffs that were topped with what looked like short, three-bladed spear heads.

Giltreas turned to them and spoke in low tones. "You are newcomers to the kingdom, and are not expected to know the proper methods of speech and presentation. Do not copy my behavior, as my standing here is different than the norm, and some might take offense. Instead, be yourselves. That will offend almost no one." Something in his voice made Dave wonder what Giltreas was thinking, but the other continued before he could ask questions.

"Once inside the hall, advance no further than the beginning of the red mats, and wait there until summoned. I will vouchsafe for you to the queen, and you will then be called forward. A small bow of the head is sufficient for Her Majesty. She does not stand for much in the way of ceremony." He sketched a brief head bow as he spoke, and nodded as they indicated they understood.

Giltreas turned, squared his shoulders, and walked through the entryway to the hall of Elvish Monarchy.

Dave stepped aside and allowed the two women to decide who should go first. Allison gave a brief motion with her hand, sending Michelle, with Sadie and Abby on leash and in heel position, to follow Giltreas. She then stepped in herself, Max at her side, and matched herself to Michelle's deliberate pace, with Dave bringing up the rear.

Dave glanced around once, taking in the beings that populated the hall, and the hall itself. Stained-glass windows lined the walls, letting in multi-colored light, depicting scenes one would expect to see in a royal building: kings and queens all seated in the same hall on a low dais, with a somewhat unprepossessing throne as their seat, presiding over courts, with colorfully dressed people standing in front of the throne. The walls themselves were a combination of stone columns and thick, well-cut logs that had been smoothed to an almost glassy finish. The floor was made of dark blue-grey stones, set smoothly and level across the entire room. Dave guessed that the room itself was no more than sixty feet deep, and maybe thirty feed across, with a vaulted ceiling that might top twenty five feet at its peak.

His gaze turned to the throne at the head of the room, where the same dais depicted in the stained glass windows was located. The red mat Giltreas told them about extended some twenty feet from the dais towards the entryway, and was about ten feet wide. It extended up the steps up to in front of the throne. The dais itself was maybe twenty feet wide, allowing people to walk around it, and fifteen feet deep. The top of the dais was only three steps above the regular floor, with a simple but well-made and heavy-looking throne made of solid wood sitting in the middle of the dais. Several guards lined the walls on either side of the dais, and two more stood just behind the throne, along with four men and two women in what Dave thought of as fancy dress duds, and all of them the same race as the guards

– elves, Dave told himself. Then he glanced at the queen.

She had a simple circlet on her head woven of white and yellow gold, with a single black-red jewel set in it at the front that was nearly as big as his thumb. She was dressed in a shimmering gown of simple design that was of a deep, intense, crystalline green color. She had deep sage-green hair, grey-green skin, and large green eyes that swept over the newcomers curiously, taking in their strange clothing and mannerisms as they approached.

Michelle stopped two feet from the edge of the red mat, and simply waited calmly. Allison stopped next to her, with Dave behind them both. Sadie and Max immediately sat on their haunches. Abby flopped down into a frog-sprawl, her little stubby tail wagging as she looked around.

Giltreas had walked further on, half way across the red mat towards the dais.

"Our loyal subject Giltreas has returned." The queen spoke in clear, distinct Elvish that carried everywhere in the hall as she looked down on the man in front of her without expression.

Giltreas bowed from the waist elegantly, with his hands sweeping out and to the sides, then back in as he straightened up again.

"Yes, Your Majesty." Giltreas' voice easily carried to everyone as well. Dave decided it must be a trick of the architecture.

One of the brightly-dressed males standing beside and just behind the queen bent down to whisper in her ear, but she waved him away. He stood up stiffly, and seemed to glare at Giltreas.

"Still not wasting words, I see." The queen's quiet statement could have been a condemnation, but it was something much gentler.

Giltreas shrugged, a simple gesture that conveyed more than one emotion. "I will of certainty when necessity calls for it, Your Majesty." The queen quirked a smile at the inconsistent statement.

"And I see you have brought us human guests. What do you say of them?"

"The two women request the sanctuary and protection of the crown. One is in danger from her own people, and the other could be as well. The man is brother to one, and husband to the other."

The one who glared at Giltreas earlier stepped forward and spoke, somewhat angrily. "Why should The Crown extend protection to humans? Why would not their own people protect them?" The queen placed her hand on the man's arm, silencing him. She turned, and with a look, sent him back to where he had stood. When she was sure he had himself under control, she turned back to Giltreas.

"My seneschal does not speak for me, but he asks a question I would also ask. I do not wish to bring strife to my kingdom, so I would know what enemies they have, and if they would hunt for them here amongst my subjects." Her question was calm and not unexpected. "I have also been informed that four men, named as brigands by Giltreas, have been placed into my jail, with not much explanation as to their crimes. I would have an understanding of this situation." Giltreas turned and waved Dave forward.

He stepped calmly up to stand next to Giltreas, and bowed respectfully to the woman on the throne the way Giltreas showed them earlier.

"My name is David. The four men in your jail attacked my sister. Giltreas interceded, and reversed what had been done. They did not act on their own. Someone directed them, or more likely, hired them to do this. I need to place them somewhere where those brigands will not be able to harm anyone else, or report to their master of their failure and capture, until I have been able to find out who is behind this, and end the threat to my family. I cannot do that while my sister and my mate are someplace where they are not safe. I do not know who is involved in trying to kill Michelle, so I don't know who to protect her from." Dave took a breath, and let it out.

"I see. Are there no guardsmen on your plane that could protect her?" The question could have been condescending or even derogatory; instead it was simply curious.

"We have weapons, arms, that could kill them from a great distance, and I would not be able to stop weapons like that from a truly determined and skilled killer. It is safest if no one knows where they are."

The queen considered for a moment. "Would you permit a spell of truth-seeking and compulsion to be cast upon you? I have certain responsibilities to my subjects. I must know if there is a danger to them before granting sanctuary to your family."

It was Dave's turn to think. "Would this spell be permanent?"

She smiled. "No. It would be dispelled, or would fade, after some few moments. Indeed, the laws of the Deus Magus do not allow such a spell to become permanent."

"I agree, then." Dave nodded to her, a gesture that seemed to convey trust and acceptance to her, and she smiled again. Then she turned and nodded to a guardsman at the edge of the dais.

The guardsman bowed to the queen, then walked towards the human. "There is nothing to fear, human. This spell causes no harm." He reached into a small pouch at his belt, and pulled out something that looked like flower petals. He crushed them in his fist, then opened his hand, palm up, at eye level. His mouth opened, and spoke words Dave did not understand. The petals in his hand glowed until they disappeared as if they had not been there, and glow grew to encompass the guardsman's hand up to his wrist. He then reached out and touched Dave on his forehead.

A strange feeling came over him. It was almost like inhaling a little nitrous oxide at the dentist before having his teeth worked on.

The guardsman looked at Dave critically, then turned and nodded at the queen, before stepping aside.

The queen then spoke up. "Is your true name David?"

"It is. I am also called Dave, which is a shorted version of David. You may call me either."

"Very well, David. Have you or anyone in your family engaged in any evil act that has caused you to flee from justice to my House?"

"No, Your Majesty. Those who sought to kill my sister were the evil-doers."

"Are the companion animals your family travels with any danger to harm anyone needlessly?"

"No, Your Majesty," he said. "But I must say, they will defend themselves or their human people if someone seeks to harm them or their humans. They are extremely loyal, but have also had much in the way of social interaction and acclimation to being around people. If they are left alone or treated with kindness and respect, they will return such actions with the same. The two older ones, Sadie and Abby, are well-trained. Max, the black one, has not had much training yet. But we are working on it. They will not soil or water indoors."

"Is my realm in any danger from anyone on your plane by granting sanctuary to the women of your family?"

"I don't see how it could be, your Majesty. As far as I know, no one on my plane knows how to get here, and no one even knows that this plane exists."

"Certainly mages on your plane could trace the pathway to here to find them? That is no simple task, but most more-learned mages would be capable of such a thing."

"There is no real magic on my plane. As far as I know, there never has been. There are no mages. Only stage magicians that use sleight-of-hand and tricks to convince people that they can do magic. But no one is capable of doing anything at all like I have seen Giltreas do."

Her mouth opened wide at that statement. "No magic? None? Magic is the birthright of every human, elf, and dwarf everywhere! The Gods gifted the races with magic. Every human can do at least some simple spells to defend themselves, heal, cure sickness or poison, or cure blindness. Yet you say that no one where you are from has ever been able to do this?"

"That is correct, Your Majesty."

Her eyes were wide with shock now. "But why? How is this even possible?" She turned to look at her advisors that stood next to her throne. Their faces betrayed their own stunned amazement. She glanced at Giltreas, who merely shrugged, conveying that he was confirming David's statement, along with the absurdity of it all.

Michelle, however, had been looking at the seneschal at that particular moment, and his own face showed shock, and something else. Possibly...

fear? Why would he be afraid of this?

The queen didn't seem to notice. She turned back to David, and struggled to think of how to proceed. Humans with no knowledge of magic? But they possess weapons that could kill from a great distance? Still, she needed assurance that there was no danger to her people.

"Is there any way you can think of that someone from your plane might be able to bring harm or strife to this plane?"

Dave thought for a moment, and could not come up with any way for that to happen. "None, Your Majesty. I can think of no way that anyone there could even get here. I will not be able to get back here without Giltreas' assistance once we leave and begin hunting for who is responsible."

The queen considered for a moment, and could not come up with any other questions she needed asked in this manner, so she waved the guardsman forward. He stepped up, and cancelled the spell.

"I am satisfied that you are not evil-doers yourself, fleeing justice, and that your enemies would not be able to bring harm and strife to my plane and my kingdom. Therefore, I grant sanctuary to... which are your names?" She inclined her head towards the two women who were standing with the dogs.

"I am Michelle, Your Majesty. And this is Allison." Allison bowed to the queen when her name was spoken.

"Very well. I grant sanctuary, protection, and the hospitality of my home to David, Michelle, Allison, and their animal companions, in the name of The Crown, and of my House."

Michelle spoke up then. "On behalf of Allison and David and myself, I thank you very much for your kindness and hospitality." She inclined her head in what became a brief, respectful bow.

"You are welcome. I would also like to meet your companions as well," the queen said, as she smiled down on the three dogs. Allison looked down at Max, and smiled. For once, the irrepressible little dog seemed to be calm and quiet. That was subject to change without notice, however. She looked up and said, "I would be happy to introduce you to Max, your Majesty, and I am sure Michelle would be glad to do the same with Sadie and Abby as well."

The Queen then motioned them back, and aside. As they stepped away, David noticed that additional guards were entering the throne room, and taking up position along the walls, and in front of the dais where the throne was located.

When the guardsman who had cast the truth-speak spell on Dave turned to the queen and nodded, she spoke up again.

"Bring in the four brigands for questioning."

* * *

Jack knew something was up when the guards approached his cell again. He couldn't believe the construction of the prison around them. The iron bars were more than two inches thick, and were set deeply into solid rock. The door swung inward, and was locked by a huge iron bar that was secured with a thick chain and hasp. When he tried to touch the chain, he received a shock that forced him to let go of it. Somehow the chain was electrified, but he had no idea how it was done; no wires were present.

Now one of the guards spoke to him again, and in English. "Extend your arms through the bars together. You will be restrained for the visit with Her Majesty the Queen."

He did as he was told, since the head jailer was watching carefully. Jack studiously tried to avoid eye contact with the huge... being. It wasn't hard, given the differences in their height.

Standing easily all of eight feet tall and then some, with massive shoulders, hugely muscular arms, and looking like he could break Jack in half with a single one of his incredible fists, the Minotaur was... words failed Jack. He was bare-footed, with only a loin cloth around his waist, and he was holding the biggest two-headed hammer Jack had ever seen like it was a twig leaning over one shoulder. The expression on the bull-shaped face was heavily laced with equal parts contempt and an eagerness that chilled him to his core. It was almost like the being near a fighter who just waited for the opening bell to tear into his opponent. The sight of the incredible being really drove home the situation he was in. He wanted to curse and swear, but was terrified of even opening his mouth near the impossible creature.

When they had first been brought down through the guard room and down the stairs, someone had cast the same learn-language spell on the Minotaur, and Jack had flinched when that massive hand had reached for him. But all he wanted was contact with Jack's hand, and then a moment later, he spoke to all four of them as they were herded into the main room below ground where the cells were located.

"I am Karonashkk. I keep Her Majesty's jails. Do nothing to make me angry. You wouldn't enjoy that as much as I would."

The specialist had swallowed and mumbled a prayer in his own language. Bill had just stood there in terror. Jack had swallowed in fear, and tried to keep from losing control of either his stomach or his bladder.

Aaron had spat on him and mouthed a curse. Karonashkk had merely lifted Aaron with his free hand, walked towards the cell door which suddenly seemed to open on its own as he approached, and thrown the much smaller human form through the air and against the back wall with a thud. Aaron lay on the floor wheezing and trying to catch his breath from the impact, shrugging the now painful shoulder that had hit the wall first and shaking his head to try to clear the fog that had suddenly appeared.

The guards laughed at Aaron. He glared back when he could. The Minotaur had walked over to the man crumpled against the back wall of the enclosure, and spoke again.

"I will be glad to teach you humility, and respect for your betters, worm, should you need the lesson. If you think of escaping, I will hunt you down. If you hurt one of the guards, or anyone else, I will beat you senseless. If you wish to test yourself against me, ask nicely. I will be glad to show you that you are wrong. I am the keeper because no one can stand against me."

"I would listen to him if I were you, human," Giltreas added then. "He has been studying and learning the warrior ways for nearly four hundred turnings of the seasons. Before that he was a gladiator by choice in the far eastern reaches. No one has ever bested him, nor even come close."

Dave cut the zip-ties that bound the other three after Jack had been unbound. The rope had been removed by the guards when they reached the jail hallway.

Jack turned his focus to the guard who finished securing him, then told him to step back to the back wall. He complied meekly, wondering where this sniveling coward he suddenly became had come from. Had it been there all the time? Was he simply an opportunistic bully who finally realized that he was no longer a threat?

Bill and the specialist were secured just as easily. Aaron fought his jailers until Karonashkk had set down his war hammer, enter the cell, and pinned his face against the wall, wrenched his arms behind him, and held him there easily until the bonds were set on him. Then the Minotaur had dragged him along by his wrists as he lead the procession to just outside what seemed, from the small glimpse he got through the archway ahead on the right, like a huge room.

Then Jack heard a woman's voice speaking in the same tongue as the… elves? He had no idea what it said, but something about it seemed to make him want to hide. Then the guards ushered them through the archway.

* * *

He sat back after ordering, and looked happily at his wife. She noticed his look, and smiled back at him.

"You are really in a good mood tonight, honey. What has you feeling this good?"

"You make me happy."

She made an "aww" sound at him, and smiled wider. "I hope you still feel that way after you see the credit card bills from my shopping trip yesterday."

He winced theatrically, and mopped his forehead in faux worry. "Am I going to have to get a job washing dishes here to cover it?"

"Maybe. We'll see."

"You are such a troublemaker. Why do I ever put up with you?"

"I thought you loved me?" She pouted at him.
"That must be it."

* * *

"One of our team leaders never checked in."
"Which one?"
"Special operations lead 317, sir."
That produced a disgusted grimace. "That one is the most unreliable S.O.B. out of them all. Not sure why he is still an asset." He thought for a moment.

"Uhm, sir, what do you want me to do? Follow the procedure and notify Op Central?"

He thought for a moment more, then said "Screw him. I am tired of his games and problems. File the report. He can deal with the fall-out. He better not be in a bar somewhere drunk this time. I am certainly not covering his ass anymore. While you're at it, contact Tech Ops and ask them to pull his cell's location. If the info is not back by the time you file the report, note that the request has been made and will be appended to the report later."

"Yes sir." He nodded internally. He was glad to be finally throwing that glorified thug under whatever bus was coming to run him down with this latest stunt. He liked his world orderly, and was happy when everything more or less was in place. 317 had never shown any interest in his requests to behave and fall in line, he thought to himself as he called up the secure email program, then the proper form to send the request to Tech Ops, and filled it in before sending it. He then opened the appropriate report, and worked his way through filling it out in his browser.

He was most of the way through some fifteen minutes later when he got an email back from Tech Ops. Opening it up, he read that the cell phone in question was not on the grid. The response included a short list of reasons why: destroyed, battery removed, under water for more than an hour. He added the Tech Ops response to the report with a link to the file should the recipient wish to read it themselves, and sent it off to his leader for approval and forwarding.

CHAPTER 12

Allison watched as the four men who had attacked Michelle were lead into the throne room, and wasn't sure if she wanted, or would need, her gun in the next few minutes. The second guard station they had gone through to get to the throne room had requested that all weapons be left in their care. She and Dave had both unloaded and deposited their firearms in the basket placed in front of them, with Michelle putting a small folding knife in with her pistol; then Dave had asked them not to touch them. He added his Gerber multi-tool next to the guns. The basket had then been carried gingerly back to behind a wall, and set on a shelf up and out of the way, as Dave had watched. He then nodded, and led the way back to the guard station, ignoring the indecipherable looks the guard was giving him. Allison had merely waited patiently.

Now she wished she still had it, but wasn't too worried. She was trained and capable of handling herself. And that huge Minotaur with the massive sledge hammer looked capable, too. Wait, what? Minotaur? She did a double-take. Yep. She was well and truly down the rabbit hole for sure now. A laugh threatened to break free from her control, and she closed her eyes and took a deep breath. Her memories of learning to be iron-willed in Marine boot camp, and all the years of study before that, came back to her, and she found her inner balance. She opened her eyes and watched as one of the four, the one that had threatened Dave earlier at the city gates, struggled to get free from the Minotaur, and almost succeeded. She saw Dave out of the corner of her eye as he leaned forward onto the balls of his feet, ready for action, and realized that she had also focused herself, standing loose with her hands at her sides, but ready. Oddly, Michelle didn't move, but seemed to be the most poised of the three. The sense Allison read from Michelle was... a sword held at the ready. She blinked as the thought made her lose focus for a moment, and as her eyes narrowed at

Michelle in thought, it happened.

Aaron laughed inside as he suddenly twisted sideways and kicked around and up behind him, connecting with the huge animal that held him and breaking free of his grip at last. His hands were behind him, but that was not an issue. Rolling backwards onto his back, then his shoulders, he passed his wrists behind him and around his legs, and he rolled back upright, gained his balance, and Started Something.

Guards standing by the other prisoners reached out and dragged them back, forcing them to their knees as Aaron moved forward to make his play. Sadie suddenly stood and barked once, her hackles fully up, her head low as the sound escaped her, the usually gentle dog suddenly reminding Allison of the wolves of her distant ancestry with shocking clarity.

Jack wondered what good it would do Aaron if he did get free. There was no way to get back to their world. The thought depressed him further, and he almost looked down, but couldn't pry himself away, like a front row seat to a train wreck in slow motion.

Dave watched in surprise as the one broke free, wincing as a flying foot connected with Karonashkk's elbow and it bent at an impossible angle, obviously injured. The huge being was shocked at the sudden impact, and was a moment too slow to get moving and try to slow down or stop the crazed human in front of him. He saw off ahead that the guards had closed up in front of the throne with amazing speed; now some twenty spears pointed out in a defensive position protecting the queen, but the guards didn't advance. Their role was to defend the Queen. It was the job of the other guards spread throughout the room to end the threat. The other guards began to close in, but before they could, Allison was in the middle of the room standing between Aaron and the queen.

Max and Abby stumbled over themselves and each other as they tried to hide from the sudden tumult behind their humans, tangling the leashes attached to their collars around the human legs they were now behind. Oddly enough, Sadie had to be restrained from advancing on Aaron. She had never shown that sort of protectiveness before, and Michelle looked down in astonishment as she heard the words "hurter" and "protect" come from her oldest canine companion.

Aaron looked at the smaller woman in front of him, and he smiled. It was not a nice smile, filled with hate and rage. But it faltered for a slight moment when he realized that she had no expression on her face whatsoever. It was like she was totally… empty of emotion. That should have been a warning, but he was not quite sane anymore. The way he died, then was brought back to life, but with only one functioning eye, had severed what little connection to reality he'd had left. Seeing all the elves, the strange place they had been brought to, and the huge Minotaur, and having said monster toss him around as if he was a balled-up piece of paper, had broken something deep in his mind, and the control his training in the Army Special Forces instilled in him had mostly left for some far-away locale. His conscious mind had stepped back from control, and the Berserker Rage consumed him, waiting for the right opening. He bared his teeth at the woman – after he beat her down, he would take her right here, as was the right of every conqueror.

Dave started to step forward, but Allison, who was turned most of the way away from him and most likely couldn't even see him, waved him back. She then flicked a look to him even as she moved into Aaron's path, and what he saw made him frightened for her. He'd seen that look before, after she had come back from the convoy mission that had been ambushed. She had locked out all emotion, as she had been trained. He finished his step forward, ready to engage, but then he stopped. He fervently hoped that she wouldn't do something she would regret later.

Aaron swung the chains on his wrist at her, trying to use it as a weapon, as the queen she had only just met behind her gasped audibly. The guards didn't know what to do, having never seen someone else, especially a human and a woman at that, step in between the queen and danger. Certainly someone who had been granted the protection of the Crown and the Queen's own house should not be where she was. She should have been kept behind them, as their honor-bound duty was to protect her, not the other way around. They were already reacting, but a moment too slow, when he struck out at her. But it was over before they could get there to subdue him.

The chain went past her as she suddenly spun away from the swing on one foot, twisting her body out of the path of the swinging chain, and she pivoted onto the other foot as she used the momentum of avoiding the chain to bring her other leg sweeping up, leaning into the motion to put her full weight and power behind the strike, and her foot connected with the side of his jaw and head. The powerful kick knocked him completely off his feet, out cold as he spun like a dropped toy to hit the floor some few feet further back where he started, in front of the huge red-skinned jailer.

Dave winced at the results as his wife flawlessly performed the same spinning back kick that he had been on the receiving end of many times during their sparring and training sessions. He knew that he was no real match for the nearly two decades of additional martial arts training she had had since very early childhood, but the speed and effectiveness of that single strike still stunned him for a moment, driving home just how deadly she could be when she was not holding back. He was lucky she had been holding back all these years, he decided. And those three idiot wanna-be gangsters outside Kieran's Irish Pub that late Saturday evening awhile back were abundantly lucky to be alive at all, he realized with an internally shudder.

Allison watched the body on the floor for a moment, satisfying herself that he was still breathing but unconscious and therefore no longer a threat, then she turned to the throne, and bowed to the queen, a motion that Dave recognized from the dojo.

"I apologize, Your Majesty," she said, with her head still bowed but her eyes up. Then she straightened, and walked back to where Dave and Michelle stood. Both came forward and pulled her into an embrace, while the rest of the guards looked at her in surprise, then back to the body on the floor. Sadie jumped up and licked Allison's face, and a satisfied "good" came from her. Dave and Michelle both felt the tension in her slowly release as her emotions calmed down and her breathing slowed as she regain her center once again. She had to get her anger on a shorter leash, she thought to herself. Losing control like that fell under the heading of Not Good At All. Sensei Davis would be disappointed in her.

Karonashkk looked down at the body at his feet in astonishment. He had never seen the like before, and no idea how the human woman had done it, but her method was clearly effective. He winced as his injured arm flared in pain, and then turned to Giltreas as the other approached.

Giltreas had a strange smile on his face as he looked up at his oldest friend. "Where did you find these humans, Treya?"

Giltreas shrugged, smiling at the private name the huge being had given him all those years ago, and cast a short healing spell on the injury, then looked up again. "I am not sure where I was. I was lead there by my patron."

Karonashkk flexed his arm, and smiled down at his friend. "You are a good healer. You could always live in one of the temples and help the humans out."

Giltreas laughed softly at his friend's predictable statement. Karonashkk had been trying to get Giltreas to leave his Path and follow something more… gentle ever since he first heard of it. He was concerned about the cost that Giltreas would pay later in life, in the dark of night. Giltreas sighed internally even as he smiled at his one-time mentor and trainer. Karonashkk would never understand, or even believe, that Giltreas had been chosen, nor that he had unwillingly acquiesced to do what he now did for his Patron.

Minotaurs had very little regard for the Gods, with good reason. They were a long-lived race, and reproduced slowly, and his race had suffered greatly during the War of the Gods. It had been all of six thousand years and more since that disaster had nearly ended the entire race, and the clan leaders still counted all the Minotaur peoples at barely thirteen thousand.

When Giltreas had been pulled away from his mentorship to begin training for his Patron, Karonashkk had urged him to ignore the call, but Giltreas had accepted his fate with resignation. His explanation to his friend had been received with much skepticism, but had been accepted as the reason Giltreas believed he was supposed to go. He had never accepted it as a truth, however. And he made it his quest to turn his friend and protégé back to a gentler path. Karonashkk had often tried to enlist him into the guards, to place himself in the role of protector, where he would find opportunities enough to test his mettle against the wit and whim of evil. The huge Minotaur believed that one always had a choice, and that Giltreas had simply never made a different one when he had the chance. Karonashkk respected the choice Giltreas made, and his right to choose. But he also believed one could always change one's mind.

Giltreas smiled up at his old friend and patted him on the arm with a soft smile, then turned away to stand with David, Allison, and Michelle.

He was no more certain than any other in the throne room what Allison had done, except, perhaps, Michelle and David, he realized. They didn't seem surprised that Allison had prevailed. Giltreas had never seen such a move before. It was almost that her response to his attack had been the move of two dancers, practiced long and hard. It certainly showed that she was well trained in... something. He turned to look at the throne, and his eyes lingered on one of the three chained humans remaining in the room. The man Giltreas seemed to think was their erstwhile leader looked upon Allison with a combination of fear and... something else. Giltreas snorted internally. Fear he could understand. Every intelligent being faced fear at least once. He was not sure what else he was seeing in the man's eyes, though. Something certainly foreign to Giltreas' own makeup.

* * *

Jack looked at Allison like she had a second head. He had never imagined that she could do something like that. The pressures on his mind bore down further, and he sank deeper into a black depression as despair seemed to color everything around him. He revised his estimation of her considerably upwards, as he had with the other two. He had thought 'taking them out' would be such a simple task. Proof that he was completely wrong hammered at him. And his spirit broke a little more under the strain.

CHAPTER 13

His friends always thought he was a little off. He had wandered through his freshman year of high school almost in a trance, distracted by the thoughts running through his head. He had spent so many hours of his life playing games, reading fantasy books, and watching anything that had to do with magic. He even talked some friends into playing magical roleplaying games when he was younger. Most never had much interest, but Daniel had enjoyed immersing himself in a world where powerful mages cast spells and used psychic abilities to change the world around them.

He always felt like if he just concentrated harder, bear down more, and applied every bit and more of his willpower, he could move things with his mind, just like the characters in a book, or like a movie.

Now, laying on his bed propped up on his pillows in his room, he read a favorite passage in the worn-out copy of his favorite book again, and at the pivotal moment, when the good blacksmith reached out his hand, and broke through to use his mind to call his sword to his hand, and fight off the evil knight, who was shocked by the sudden reappearance of his foe's weapon from the grass where it had fallen. Daniel's pulse soared with the adrenalin that rushed through his blood as he wished so hard that he could do it himself. He reached out his hand towards the desk at the foot of his bed and 'pulled' with all his will, when he suddenly felt something different as he imagined the pen on the desk lifting up and flying to his grasp. A surge of power flowed through him, and the pen flew straight at his head. With a yelp, he threw both hands up in front of his face, the book flying across the room and out of sight somewhere. The pen shot towards him, the tip stabbing into his hand in a sudden flash of pain. He shook his hand instinctively, and the pen flew away from where it had temporarily stuck, and he stared at the hole in the palm of his hand. Then the unreal nature of what had just happened hit him. He had actually levitated something with just his mind, from across the room! More than that, he had thrown it with so much force, it had stuck into his hand!

Then the pain registered, and with it the realization that blood was dripping from the wound. He wrapped his other hand over the injury, and tried to will the pain away. Another surge of power went through him and down his arms to his hands, and with a tingling sensation, the pain suddenly disappeared. He slowly lowered his other hand, and looked where the wound had been. It was gone. Then so was he, as the room swam, his vision tunneled, and for the first time in his life, Daniel fainted.

* * *

The room was small, dark, and permeated with the smell of stale sweat and fear. The door leading out of the room to the rest of the building was solid wood, and didn't have a knob on the inside, only a keyhole. A small door was set at an adult's eye level in the door, and also opened outwards. The walls, floor and ceiling were solid oak planks, set tightly together to not allow any light through. A small light fixture was in the middle of the ceiling, with a single bare bulb in it. There was no light switch to turn the light on and off inside the room.

She had been thrown into the room late last night, after a long trip tied up and blindfolded in the back of a produce truck. She had no idea how much time had passed since she had been tossed into the dank, smelly room. She also had no idea what time of day or night it was, since there was no view of the outside to see the sun, or any other indicator. The light from the ceiling was joined with the light from under the door; neither had gone out since she arrived.

As she sat huddled in fear and pain in the almost empty room, her thoughts wandered back to her family and her life at home. Her mother, father, and younger brother had all been on holiday in Sebastopol, the Ukrainian city on the Black Sea. She had gone down to the hotel gift store to look for something for her mother for her birthday. She wanted to get a nice card, and possibly a flower. Her father had winked at her when she asked to leave the room briefly, and ushered her out almost before her mother could object. Now, she wished that she hadn't gone.

She never got a good look at the strange man that had come up behind her suddenly, and he had clamped his hand over her mouth before she could even make a sound. Before she knew it, she had been pulled into the back room, through a door out into the alley, and tossed into the back of a waiting van before slamming the door, where the man who took her and another man tied her hands, put a blind fold and gag on her, while a third one had drove the van away.

A short time later, some hands had flipped her over onto her face and stomach. She shrieked in fear, but the gag prevented the sound from carrying outside the moving vehicle. Hands pulled her clothes down, and she suddenly felt a sharp pain in her rear end, and then the hands shoved her away, leaving her sobbing in fear as she pulled at her clothing, covering herself once more. Soon after that, her mind began to feel hazy and strange. As she lay in a drugged stupor, and a part of her mind tried to make sense of what was happening to her, she barely noticed as hands grabbed her again and pulled her out of the van.

Much later her mind slowly began to clear, and with that clarity, came terror. She seemed to be in a tightly restricted area, and from the sound and motion, she had to be in some kind of truck that was in motion. She had no idea where she was, and where she was going. Worse, she had no clue how much time had passed since she was abducted. At several points many hours in between, the truck had stopped, someone had come to feed her and let her out in the woods along the road to relieve herself. She thought about running into those woods to try to escape, but she was never alone. A man, dressed in workman's clothing, was always within arm's reach, and her legs were chained together, allowing her to shuffle, but never to run.

She tried everything her desperate young mind could think of. She begged and pleaded to be set free. She told the man that her father was an important man in the government (which was true, but she really didn't know much more than that, as he never spoke of what he did), and that he could find her and would come and kill them all. She promised him all her savings and any money she could get from her parents to buy her freedom. She tried attacking him in her frustration and tears, but he was so much bigger and stronger than her, and he seemed to know just what she was thinking. He just restrained her while he laughed, then tied her hands behind her back once again, put the blind-fold back in place, and threw her back into the specially constructed room behind the false wall at the front of the cargo area of the truck. The next time they stopped, she started up again, with the same results. The third time they stopped, he threatened to beat her unless she behaved. When she opened her mouth to yell at him, he simply slapped her across the face hard enough to knock her off her feet. After that, she could only cry at the nightmare she was in.

She guessed that nearly four days had passed before she was blindfolded and gagged this time, and pulled from the back of the truck that had carried her away from her family for so long, frightened beyond rational thought, crying and shaking from fear and the harsh conditions, and weak from inactivity and being in the nearly lightless and restrictive compartment specially built for smuggling people across borders throughout eastern Europe.

She heard voices talking, laughing, and at one point thought she recognized a few words in Russian, but the accent was strange. Then someone said "Da," and a new voice spoke to her. She was dragged into a building, through some doorways, down a flight of stairs, and thrown into a room, where her blind fold and gag were removed, along with the chains on her legs and the rope used to tie her arms together at the wrists. She tried to struggle, but was unceremoniously thrown against the wall, hitting her head hard enough in the impact to see stars.

In heavily accented Ukrainian, he told her that there was a chamber pot in the corner for her to use, and that he would be back in the morning to begin her training. Then he walked out of the room, and she heard the solid sound of a heavy lock securing the door.

She looked around, tears running down her face, desperate to do anything to escape or do something to get free, but the light from the small fixture on the high ceiling told the story. She was in a room barely three meters by four meters. There was a crude bed with a lumpy mattress on it pushed into the corner of the wall opposite the door. She saw the chamber pot in the back corner opposite the bed, and shivered at the phone book next to it with some of the pages torn out, its intended use obvious to her. The door and floor looked to be made of solid, heavy planks, and the walls and ceiling were chipped plaster covered by stained and faded paint. She walked over to the bed, and despite the stale smell to the coarse blanket, her exhaustion and fear made her climb onto it and sit with her back against the corner so she could watch the door, crying constantly.

Her name was Svetlana, and she was a long way from home. She was only fifteen years old.

After the crying stopped, she relived again what had happened as her subconscious mind tried to process the events so different than anything she had ever experienced.

Through the long, sleepless night in the dank room, she wondered what her parents and her younger brother Mykola were going through. She knew her family loved her, and she loved them completely.

She had once been lost in a store for hours when she was only six years old, and when she was finally found, both her parents wept and held her tight. She had been terrified, even though nothing bad had happened – she had simply gotten separated from her mother and father during a shopping trip for new clothes for the family.

Since then, she had always tried to stay close to them, knowing that as long as they were close, she was safe. But as she got a little older, she stepped a little further away, testing the limits of that feeling of safety. Nothing ever happened to her, so she still felt safe.

This time, she didn't leave the hotel, confident that her parents were just two floors up in their room. And her father's pride and trust in her had left her feeling a confidence that was now long gone, a distant, misleading memory.

The door opened, and the same man from the previous night came into the room.

"Stand up when I come into the room," he growled at her.

She started crying again, and asked through her tears, "What do you want from me?"

"You will learn your place! Stand up!" He shouted at her.

"My father will find me, and he will kill you! There is no place in Ukraine that you can hide from him!" She screamed at him even as she slowly and fearfully climbed to her feet, shuffled a half step away from the bed, and stood there shaking.

He just laughed. "I don't care who your father is. And what makes you think you are in Ukraine anymore?"

"Where am I?" she asked, shaking further and fearful of the answer.

"You are in Georgia. Your father will never find you here. And if he does, I will kill him myself." Her captor then told her in heavily-accented Ukrainian that he was going to force her into her new life as a prostitute using the most crude, unimaginably barbaric methods of which she had ever heard. But first, he demanded to know if she had ever lain with a boy or man before. Her horrified negative response brought a look to his face that only the most generous would ever mistake for a smile, and his response froze her in her place.

"Good. Your first time will be worth much, much more. Very good."

Sexual slavery was one of those crimes that most people shook their head at, and then looked the other way. What could one do? The bad men had guns, and would fight to protect their "business". He seemed fearless, unconcerned at her plight, and confident that she would do what he said. Then he used the knife that seemed to materialize in his hand as he slashed, ripped, and tore her clothing from her, then he beat her, slapping and punching at her, holding her down while her screams and sobs at the pain went unanswered. When he was done with her, he stood and stomped out of the room, slamming and locking the door behind him as she lay in despair on the bed in the room.

Some hours later, the door to her cell opened, and she shivered in fear. The huge man stalked into the small, dark, dank, sparsely furnished room, and told her to stand up. When she flinched away and cried out in fear, huddling in the corner of the bed and didn't respond, he began to bellow at her again. Svetlana suddenly looked up at him, and a new emotion came over her. Everything she had gone through in the last four days raced through her mind, and a new emotion welled up uncontrollably from deep inside her soul. For the first time in her young life, she was consumed with an unfamiliar emotion: rage. She gritted and bared her teeth at him, and a sound that could have been made by an angry predator came from her as she growled at him a guttural sound that had no language, only emotion. He just stood there and laughed mockingly at her, having seen it all before, knowing that he would break her, or she would die, just like all the others.

Then he paused, for something new, something different, something he had never seen or heard of before, was happening.

Svetlana suddenly felt something; something warm, then hot, flowed over and through her, like a fierce wind from the south in summer time. She embraced it's suddenly-energizing comfort, and felt a sudden answering current deep inside herself that welled up and joined the feeling coming to her from everywhere around her. She suddenly had an image in her head that she had seen once in a book when she was in school, and it almost felt natural to want to be that image, to want that image to be her, and her whole body shook heavily as she embraced the rage, the hot wind, the deep current inside, and the image all at once.

Alozar had been doing this a long while. He knew everything that could happen, and how to deal with it. The stock had always been broken or discarded in the end. Sometimes, both happened to the same cow. But this time, it was not going to be that simple.

The image of the slim, young, beautiful, naked, defenseless girl in front of him seemed to shimmer, and he found himself frozen and transfixed as the entirety of her eyes suddenly glowed red. Then her bared teeth changed, flashing into fangs, and the guttural growl started high like a puppy, but then it grew deeper. He gaped in shock, but whatever was happening to the girl in front of him didn't seem to be stopping with just her eyes.

The pale skin he could see in the dim light suddenly changed to a scaly blackish green, and her shape grew and changed rapidly even while he watched. Then with an almost audible snap, the transformation was complete, having taken only a second or maybe even less. Alozar stepped back suddenly and let out a high-pitched scream like a little girl at the top of his lungs, as the form on the bed stood up on the floor in front of the bed. Where there had been a small teen girl, was now a huge, muscled, winged, tailed, fanged, clawed nightmare from the darkest pit of hell, standing so tall that the horns on its head nearly scraped the ceiling. Terror swept over him as he realized he was trapped in a locked room with an impossible creature that growled and glared at him for the briefest of moments, yet a minute part of his mind admired the sleek, otherworldly form in front of him, a graceful and symmetrical form that was a perfect apex predator, like the admiration a person might have for a full grown lion or tiger.

The blackish and greenish scaled form in front of him crouched slightly, spread its arms, and with them it's impossibly huge leathery wings, and leaped at him. Needle-tipped claws on its feet ripped into his skin first as the massive form crashed into him, smashing him to the wall then down to the hard floor with a thud, and the fanged snout below those impossible glowing red eyes snarled in his face as razor-sharp talons from its fore-limbs tore into his chest.

Those huge fangs ripped out his throat as the massive weight pinned him to the floor, then those impossibly strong arms proceeded to rip his body apart piece by piece. As pain the like of which he had never known before overwhelmed him, and darkness began to close in, the weight on what was left of his body went away. He heard a snarling breathing, then rapid footfalls as the thing that ripped his life away turned and yanked open the door somehow, then ran out into the hallway. Even as his consciousness slowly fled, he heard it sniff the air as it paused outside the door, and with a snort, it ran off. Then blackness crashed down on him and he felt himself dissolve in nothingness forever.

Down the hall in the room used as a kitchen, three men, the other owners of the brothel, laughed at the muffled scream they had heard – it wasn't the first time, and wouldn't be the last, one of their playthings screamed. They shared crude comments about the new girl's fate, and calmly went back to breakfast, talking and joking amongst them. A dull thud made them pause, then less than a minute later, they heard pounding footsteps rapidly approaching.

Before they could react, the door shattered with a huge booming crash, and pieces of wood showering the room. Reflexively, their eyes snapped to the impossible event, and a huge dark form with glowing red eyes, black-green scaly skin over massive rippling muscles, sharp horns on its head, and leathery wings on its back, charged through the shattering door and into the room, roaring like an enraged bear. It didn't even slow as it looked around, spied the men sitting at the table who gawked at it in frozen amazement, disbelief and complete fear, and it's path altered to where only moments before they had joked about the fate of their newest acquisition.

It was over almost as soon as it had begun, then the heavy thudding footfalls continued up the stairway past the kitchen and through the door at the top of the steps to the alley behind the illegal brothel, where a huge winged form took flight into the dark evening sky.

* * *

"Oh God," Koren moaned. "Help me!"

It was Saturday afternoon, and his sentencing hearing was now only two days away. The days seemed to all turn into mud together. There was none of his previous daily milestones of school and his part time job to help him keep track of the ebb and flow of the days and weeks. Lately, though, he couldn't avoid counting down to the day he would learn how long his freedom would be taken from him for something he knew he didn't do.

He was totally unprepared for what happened next. A slight wind began to blow, and he thought heard the sound of a wolf howling way far off in the distance, followed by other wolves answering faintly. The smell of trees and the woods suddenly came to him, and with a minor crescendo in the sound of the wind, a person, a tall woman dressed in leathers and boots, appeared before him. The winds died down, and in the silence that remained, he was certain he could hear the pounding of his heart.

"What is it you wish of me, mortal?" The sound of her voice was unlike anything he had ever heard before, with an almost bell-like clarity and a harshness that seemed to convey steel and challenge all at once.

"Wh... who are you? How did you get in here?" The shock of her appearance had paralyzed his whole body slightly, and his voice was no more than a strained whisper. He could hear his pulse pounding in his head in the almost supernatural silence that covered the small holding cell.

"I am Diana the Huntress. I heard your cry to the Gods, mortal. Calm yourself. If you are an innocent, you have naught to fear from me. I hunt wrongdoers, and bring them to justice. I come and go as I wish on any mortal plane, when one such as you calls me." She spoke with a calm confidence that was almost overwhelming, but his pulse slowed as he realized that someone had answered his call. Maybe this would be alright after all.

Diana looked around the small cell he was held in, and frowned. "For what reason are you held in this cage, human? What did you do for your fellow mortals constrain you like this? And what is your name, mortal child?"

"I am Koren Daniel Davis. Most people call me Koren. The police and the prosecutor think I killed someone. I have already been found guilty. In a couple days, I am being sentenced for something I didn't do. I will probably spend the rest of my life in prison for this shit." The last word came out in a harsh grunt. He was almost overwhelmed just talking about it, but made it through without tearing up again. Almost.

Her eyes bored into him, and he could almost feel something sifting through his mind as the memories of his entire life flashed before his eyes. He could only hold still and wait, unable to move or speak as the being in front of him went through his mind looking at everything she could find.

At last she was done, and he had no idea how much time had passed as he stared into those green eyes, transfixed by his experiences. She looked at him once again, and snorted in disgust.

"You are certainly guilty of harming no one. Indeed, you are a good person, the likes of which should be lauded. And just as clearly, this 'prosecutor' seems to not have bothered with finding the truth. He chose to ignore your explanations and press for your guilt. And your advocate could do little to protect you. I find this all distasteful." The last five words were spoken with an emphasis that reassured him. Maybe this would work out after all.

"I must deal with this injustice that is about to be visited upon you, young Koren. I would be remiss in my oaths and my honor if I were to allow this to go forward. From what I have seen, you will momentarily be taken into this courtroom, where that judge will decide how long you will be locked up. I will not let this happen." The sound of wolves howling faintly came to him once again.

"I will give them but a moment to do the thing that true justice would accept. If they do not, then I shall deal with the situation as I see fit. Do you accept my intervening in your justice, Koren Daniel Davis?" The last sentence came out almost like a ritualistic chant, and he nodded firmly.

"I have done nothing wrong. I accept." With that, she vanished, but he heard her voice in his head.

"I will wait until the moment is right. Fear not. You will not be imprisoned for this thing you did not do."

* * *

Here and there around the world, a few strange events happened. There was no predictable pattern to the events, and most were not witnessed. The few witnesses seemed to look away, their minds denying the impossible events, locking away the memories from consciousness, and tried to go on with their lives as if nothing happened. But something had. And as their subconscious minds wrestled with events so alien to their version of reality, denial set in in an attempt at protecting their sanity. A blissful yet uneasy calm settled over their conscious thoughts once again, filled with the mundane aspects of their normal lives. For the moment.

CHAPTER 14

The queen looked over the three remaining men in front of her. The fourth had been bound hand and foot, and returned to the city jail cell, under heavy guard, after his wounds had been seen to. She was as shocked as anyone else witnessing the altercation and Allison's deft response to the mayhem which occurred, but a part of her was also secretly pleased. The events clarified her thoughts nicely: Allison had only been reacting to the situation. The human man had initiated everything, which spoke scrolls to what path she would follow. Allison also clearly seemed to be protecting her, in spite of her guardsmen, who were between the queen and the human brigand.

The remaining three had been forced to the floor. Their legs were also bound, preventing a repeat of the action that had driven away her calm and inner peace. Then they were stood up. The head guard had stepped forward and cast truth-speak on them. Now all that remained was for the queen to ascertain what these three's intentions were, and what to do with them.

Giltreas approached the throne, and spoke quietly. "Your Majesty, these humans all speak a tongue I have not encountered before. I would offer my services to cast Learn Language for you to be able to speak with them. I would humbly submit that you finish the spell with Allison or Michelle."

She looked at him for a moment, then nodded for him to continue. He cast the spell on her, then she looked to the two women. Deciding between them, she spoke out.

"Allison, would you approach me? I wish to complete the Learn Language spell with you." The head guardsman stiffened for a moment, but held his tongue. He clearly was not happy with the thought of a human capable of such violence near his liege, but was wise enough to not argue.

Allison saw the guard's reaction, but nodded to the queen, and walked slowly towards the throne, her hands down calmly at her sides. She was not certain, but felt that she should not step onto the raised dais that supported the throne, and stopped there.

The queen stood, and approached the edge of the dais as Allison stood there. Then she calmly held out her hand to Allison, who took it briefly. She felt nothing, but the queen certainly did, because she started, as if lightly shocked. She then dropped Allison's hand, and turned to take her place on the throne again. Allison calmly returned to the side of the room where Dave and Michelle stood, and waited to see what would happen next.

The queen gathered her thoughts, then spoke in English to the three bound men standing before her. "Which of you is the leader, or was it that unpleasant being that was removed earlier?"

She was met with silence. "Will no one speak for you?"

Bill spoke up. "I don't have to say anything. I know my rights." The others nodded, and she cocked her head.

"This is my realm. You have no rights here but what I grant you. If you will not speak, then I will deal with you as I see fit. Is that your decision?"

They nodded at her, mute once more, and she sighed internally. "Very well. You shall remain in my jail until such time as one of you decides to speak for you all, or all of you decide to speak for yourselves. Guards, return them to the Minotaur. We shall see if your tongues are loosed in seven days."

They stared at her in dismay until they were led from the room.

The queen turned back to Allison, Michelle, and David. "The action of one of them undertook in my throne room, and their unwillingness to speak, have said all I need know for the moment. Perhaps later their tongues find themselves loosed," she said in Elvish. "I find in your favor, in the absence of any dissent from those you accuse. It will take much to change my mind, especially since David has answered under spell for you three."

She then turned to Giltreas and spoke fondly. "Step forward, my faithful subject." Giltreas readily obeyed the command.

"You shall be my eyes and ears amongst these humans. I wish to know of them many things. Why do they dress so differently? Act so unseemly? My guardsmen speak of an amazing black war wagon that is in my stables, and a smaller one that David is said to own. They love their companion animals, as do rational peoples anywhere, so I can see much to their character in that stead. But I wish to know more. Go with them with my blessing, Giltreas."

He bowed, and said, "As you wish, Your Majesty."

With that, she stood, and walked to the back of the throne room, to a door covered by a tapestry. As the cloth was pulled aside, she turned back, and said, "Come to me, my son, and bring your companions. I wish to speak with them and you, and get to know my guests better."

With that, she turned, and walked out, and the fabric covering the doorway fell back to cover it again.

Dave, Michelle, and Allison all turned to Giltreas in surprise, and he blushed lightly. "Yes, I am the son of the Elvish Queen of the Wood." He turned away slightly in embarrassment.

Allison spoke up tentatively. "Does that make you... a prince, or something?"

"I hold no noble title or dignities. That is the way of it as a bastard child. It matters not to me. I wish not to speak of it."

Michelle nodded her head. "Then we won't bother you with questions." She glanced at Dave and Allison to her right, and they nodded back to her. Sadie, on the other hand, pulled herself over to Giltreas and licked his hand, wagging her tail as she looked up at him. From her smile, she had her own opinion of him, no matter his protestations. "Good-noble-person." He laughed, and petted her on the head.

"Sadie, you are a queen amongst dogs." He bent down and hugged her close for a moment, petting Max and Abby as well as they pulled forward to get in on the attention, then stood. "We must be off to the Queen's antechamber. She wishes a private audience with us all. This way."

* * *

Daniel picked up the phone, and called his best friend and neighbor next door, trembling with excitement as the pen slowly spun in midair at his prompting.

Jimmy picked up the phone after seeing the caller ID. "Hello?"

"You gotta come over here!   Quick! You're not gonna believe this!"

Jimmy responded, "Ok, be there as quick as I can." he hung up, and turned to head to the door.

"I'm going to Daniel's house, mom!" He yelled as he made his way to the door.

"Wait!" She poked her head out of the kitchen and stopped him with a yell.

He nodded. "Are your chores done?"

"Yes, mom," he said impatiently, shifting from foot to foot. He had been waiting for Daniel to call all day, and the urgent tone in his voice agitated Daniel, as usual.

"If I check and you haven't done them completely, you and I will talk later."

"They're done, Mom. Can I go?"

She nodded. Sixteen was such an impatient age. "Be home before dinner. Your father will be home soon. We're having meatloaf tonight."

"Ok, mom, sounds good. Bye!" and he was out the door.

Moments later, Daniel opened the back door below the deck on the lower level of his house where his bedroom was. "You gotta come see this!"

He pulled his friend into his room, and shut the door.

Pushing Jimmy onto the bed, he stepped back. "You see that pen on the desk?" Jimmy nodded, wondering what was up as he looked at it, then jolted upright as it lifted off the desk, and hovered in midair as if on a string or something. Then it moved over to Daniel's hand.

"How the heck are you doing that?" He asked in amazement, as he at the pen floating in front of him in midair. "I don't see any strings or anything!"

"I am doing it with my mind! I can't believe this! And you know what else I can do?"

Jimmy gaped at his friend. "What?!?"

"I can heal myself! Watch this…" Daniel held up his hand as if to wave, concentrated, and the pen flew up, then into his left hand in a sharp motion, breaking the skin again. Daniel pulled the pen out of his hand, and it started to bleed. Daniel showed it to Jimmy, who was shocked at what he was seeing.

Daniel closed his eyes and touched that current inside himself once again; only this time, he felt an answering current from everything around him, connecting with him deep inside. Reaching out with his mind, he pulled that current into him, and opened his eyes as he covered the wound from the pen with his other hand, willing the energy to heal him. As he concentrated, he suddenly saw the wound glow briefly. Then he focused again on what he was trying to do.

As both boys watched in amazement, a green light emanated from Daniel's right hand, and the shallow wound in his left hand from the pen disappeared as if it had never been there before.

"Isn't that incredible?" Daniel crowed to his friend.

Jimmy shook off his shock, and looked at his longtime friend with new eyes. "Can you heal others?"

Daniel thought about it for a moment, and shook his head. "I don't know. I just found out I could do this earlier today. I haven't tried."

Jimmy stood up. "Will you try to heal me?"

Confusion flashed across Daniel's face. "What do you need me to heal? There's nothing wrong with you, is there?"

"Well," Jimmy returned, "That's easy enough to do. Jab me with that pen. Or a pin or something."

"I can't do that to you!" Daniel pulled back, aghast at the idea of harming anyone, let alone his friend.

"I can do it. Here. I have to know if you can do this." There was a note in Jimmy's voice that Daniel suddenly recognized. Desperate longing. And in a flash, he understood.

Grimly determined, he stood. "I can't hurt you. But if you can, I will try to heal you."

Jimmy looked around, and reached over to Daniel's bulletin board. Pulling off a pin, he took a deep breath, and slashed the back of his hand, hoping it didn't hurt too much. It did, though.

Daniel nodded, and looked at the cut on Jimmy's hand, trying to bring up the sight he saw just before he healed himself, and there it was. A not-so-faint green glow was coming from the new wound. As Daniel held on to this new vision, he looked his friend over, and saw several other areas that glowed green as well. All the other areas that glowed had a greenish sheen that was nearly grey, with only a hint of color in them, and Daniel understood. They were old injuries that had mostly healed, but had left their mark behind.

"Did you break your arm at one point? It looks like the bone cracked or something."

Jimmy gasped. "That happened before we moved here. I fell off my bike when I was seven. I had a cast on for like eight weeks. How do you know that?"

"I seem to have this way of seeing that shows me old and new injuries. I see a few on you. They are grey-green, barely green at all. The cut on your hand is very green, but it is not that bright, probably because it is not very serious."

Daniel reached for the current deep inside, and channeled it into his hand. The greenish glow grew, and he moved his hand over the cut Jimmy had just made.

Jimmy felt a brief, electrical tingle, and when it went away, he looked at his hand. The wound was gone. He started to pull away, but Daniel wasn't finished. He grabbed Jimmy's wrist with his right hand, and directed the current out his left hand as he passed moved over Jimmy's left arm, where the old wound quickly disappeared.

"Does that feel better? The glow there is gone." He didn't stop there, though. He suddenly looked at Jimmy's head, and saw something else – a bluish glow behind his eyes. Daniel suddenly connected that with why Jimmy wore glasses all the time. He spoke softly to his friend. "Take off your glasses, Jimmy."

Jimmy jolted as if someone had stuck his finger in a light socket, then quickly took his glasses off. Only a few feet away, Daniel was suddenly out of focus. Jimmy's vision was pretty bad.

Daniel focused on the current, and moved his hand over Jimmy's face and eyes, but the greenish glow did not make the blue glow from Jimmy's eyes go away.

"Nothing happened. Was something supposed to happen?" Jimmy asked anxiously.

"Hmmm. Your eyes glow blue, but your cut and your arm and

everything else glowed green. I wonder…" He thought about it, and then looked at his hand. He tried to change the glow from his hand to blue, thinking that fixing vision must be different than fixing injuries, and his hand suddenly emanated a brilliant sapphire blue. Smiling now, he moved it over Jimmy's forehead, his friend's eyes so wide he could see white around the entire iris in each. He held his hand there while directing the blue glow into his friend's head and eyes. The matching blue glow from Jimmy's eyes faded slowly, then went away entirely.

"Oh my God!" Jimmy looked around, then at his hands, then leaned over to look out the window. "Danny! I can see perfectly! What did you do? Sorry, Daniel! What did you do?"

"I think I fixed your eyes. Wait a moment, let me fix everything else I see on you."

Jimmy waited as Daniel pulled the current into himself, shaped it, and, in a flash of insight, reached out to Jimmy to shake his hand.

Jimmy took his hand, and as quickly as he could, he willed the green energy to flow throughout Jimmy's body, and watched as it erased every area that glowed green. In the blink of an eye, every grey-green glow in Jimmy went out.

Daniel stepped back, held the vision a moment longer, and nodded when he didn't see anything else that needed work. It was getting much faster and easier each time he did it, he noted. Then he looked Jimmy in the eye. "When does your dad get home from work?"

Jimmy nodded, then looked at his watch, amazed that he could see, stunned at everything that had just happened, and tried to hold his elation in check at the possibilities that rushed through his mind.

"In the next half hour. Can you do it?"

Daniel seemed to straighten, looking suddenly much more mature and, somehow, maybe just a bit taller. "I want to find out."

Jimmy nodded, and they silently walked out of the house together.

Daniel looked around at the neighborhood as they started the two-block walk back to Jimmy's house. The sights and sounds of the suburban environment around them suddenly pulled at his focus. Everything looked the same, yet somehow different. The sidewalk seemed more dull and drab than usual, but the grass, trees and bushes arranged against houses and along property lines all looked more alive than ever before, as if the color had been artificially turned up in a photo editing program. A bright red cardinal flew past him, a splash of brilliant color against his field of vision, and he seemed to be able to watch every pump of its wings as it dipped then pushed hard to soar up and out of sight into the trees lining the street. A cat hid behind a bush a few doors down the way, its yellow eyes following their path and making contact with his briefly as they went by. And the sounds came to him much clearer, as well. A warm, light breeze was blowing under a clear blue sky just visible through breaks in the leaves of the trees overhead, rustling everything in its path.

"Do you think you can do it, Daniel?" Jimmy asked with quiet anxiety as they walked down the street and around the corner towards Jimmy's house.

"I think I can. I was able to heal everything wrong with you, and some of it was much older than your dad's injury, right?" Daniel's voice was low, but confident. "I will give it a shot. I have to try."

Jimmy was so grateful his friend was willing to attempt to heal his dad that he had to hold back tears.

"Why do you think you can do this all of a sudden?" The question was fairly simple, but Daniel didn't have the answer.

"I have no idea. I was just reading my favorite book, you know the one, and I reached out to the pen on my desk. I could suddenly feel it as if it were in my hand, and when I tried to pull it towards me, it flew so fast it stuck into my hand. When it fell off, I saw it was bleeding. I was so shocked by this that I tried to make the pain go away, and when it did, the hole the pen made went with it." Daniel relayed the story quietly, as if others were listening.

Jimmy had no idea what to think about what had happened to his best friend. He could only think about what he so desperately wanted Daniel to do. One thing was obvious, though. If he was able to do it, Jimmy would never be able to pay him back for it. That much he knew for certain.

They turned the corner to Jimmy's street, and saw that the minivan was already in the driveway. Jimmy's dad must have gotten home early, as he was rolling his wheelchair heading down to the mailbox at the end of the driveway to get the mail.

As they got within ten feet of where Jimmy's father was getting the mail out of the mailbox, Daniel turned on his special vision, and looked at Paul, Jimmy's dad. He was so shocked at how much damage he saw that he nearly stopped walking.

The car accident three years earlier had nearly killed Paul, and had left him paralyzed from the waist down. It was a week that Daniel was certain he would never forget any of it. Even now, the moment that Jimmy had called him in tears to tell him his father might die was still crystal clear. Daniel had told tell his mother what happened, and she had instantly swung into action. Together Daniel and his mother had taken care of everything else while Jimmy's mother spent every moment she could at the hospital, waiting for her husband to wake up, and pestering every doctor she could for any scrap of information. Jimmy had stayed with Daniel in his room, and had cried himself to sleep next to Daniel, wondering if his father would still be alive in the morning, while Daniel hugged his friend, tears running down his own face.

The recovery had been slow, with weeks spent in the intensive care unit, which turned into months in physical therapy. But Paul had worked incredibly hard to get back everything he could, and nearly fifteen months later, he had returned to his job for a local television station, managing their computers and technology.

Daniel's mind returned to the present as he surveyed what he could see in his friend's father. Damaged nerves, broken vertebra that had never fully healed, atrophied muscles everywhere below the injury; the damage was extensive. The worst of it, and obviously central to everything: Paul's spinal cord was completely severed in his low back where the broken vertebrae had been surgically fused together.

But it wasn't just the injuries from the accident. A lifetime of other injuries, seen to Daniel through his special vision, was evident to him in the man in the wheel chair. Most of them glowed a faint, grey-green color, like Jimmy's arm. A broken shoulder that had left a faint glow, a knee that had been torn up in high school football decades before; anything that Paul had ever suffered was visible to Daniel's sight. There was almost no place in him that didn't seem to have been hurt at one point or another.

Paul, Jimmy's dad, looked over as the boys walked up to him, then grinned in amusement as his son's friend Daniel offered his hand in a handshake, something that had never happened before. "Hello, Daniel, it's good to see you again." As he looked into Daniel's eyes, he reached out to shake the young man's hand, and suddenly, a very warm, comforting feeling shot up his arm, into his body, and roared through him from the top of his head down to his toes. Daniel concentrated at changing as much as possible as quickly as he could, knowing that he might only have one chance to do this if Paul pulled free of his grip before he was finished. Time seemed to slow down during his moment of hyper-focus as he pulled from that current of energy deep inside him and all around them, changed it to the purest green color he could think of, and literally flooded it into the form in front of him as fast as possible, seeing the entire being as one container he needed to fill as quickly as possible.

Paul instinctively tried to pull his hand back, but Daniel's surprisingly strong grip held him fast for a few more moments before letting go. He looked at Daniel's hand in surprise, and thought he saw a faint glow for a moment, but when he blinked, it wasn't there.

Jimmy turned to Daniel, and asked, "Did it work?"

Daniel looked at Paul with his vision, and saw that every old injury was gone – erased, as if it had never existed. The spinal fusion had been reversed, and every vertebra looked perfect. The spinal cord had been reattached. Even muscles that had atrophied away were now toned and strong. He nodded.

Jimmy turned back to his dad, and Paul was stunned to see tears coursing down his son's face. Concerned, he started to reach out, but

Jimmy threw himself into his father's lap, wrapping his arms around his father's shoulders, and sobbed.

Then he realized something. He could feel Jimmy's weight against his legs. His mind froze. Then his hand reached out, around Jimmy, who felt the movement. Jimmy quickly stood up and stepped back. Paul touched his leg. And for the first time since that horrible day, could feel his hand on his own leg. Tears suddenly welled up in Paul's eyes, and he gasped, sobbing himself. Jimmy had gotten himself somewhat under control again saw the tears on his father's face, and lost it once more.

"What happened? Daniel? Did you do this? I felt something when we shook hands. What was that?" His voice sounded almost watery as he tried to make words get through his suddenly overwhelming emotions.

"I don't know how to explain it, Mr. Bretton. I just... I can heal. Can you stand up? I... erased everything wrong with you." Paul just looked at the young man with incredulous eyes, his mind trying desperately to process what had happened, and what he was feeling.

"I don't know. Wow. This is incredible. Wait a minute." He closed his eyes, took a deep breath as a more tears made their way down his face, and held it for a ten count. Then he opened his eyes. His hands were almost robotic, locking the brakes on the chair in well-practiced habit. He then reached down to lift each foot up with his hands to flip the foot rests up and out of the way. He looked down at the cement pavement of his driveway in front of him without really seeing it.

Then, steeling himself, he leaned forward, and stood unassisted for the first time in three long, impossibly hard years. He looked down at the ground, suddenly further away than it had been in a long time, and the enormity of what had happened overwhelmed him. He sat down suddenly, grateful the chair was still there, then leaned all the way back, sagging against the back rest.

Jimmy stepped quickly up to his father's side, and went down to his knees. "Dad! Are you ok?"

"This is so overwhelming! What happened?"

Jimmy stepped around to the front of the chair, and pulled his dad to his feet.

Paul looked around, and saw Daniel standing there with an incredible smile on his face that seemed to reach all the way past his ears to his hairline, as if he had just gotten the greatest gift in the world.

Paul swayed a bit as his balance slowly returned after so long, and as his stability returned, so did his tears. "Oh my god. OH MY GOD!" Sobbing in happiness, he swept the two boys into an embrace, and cried as he hadn't before since finding out that he would never walk again. Then he laughed through the tears.

Emotions so strong were overwhelming the three, when suddenly they heard something from the open garage door.

All three turned to look towards the source of the sound. Marie Bretton had come out to see what was taking so long, only to see her brave, emotionally strong, incredible husband, standing. On his own. Actually hugging their son and his friend Daniel so hard, their feet were off the ground. She lost her balance, and sat down hard on the cement just inside the garage door.

"Oh crap! Mom!!"

"Honey!!"

"Mrs. Bretton!"

CHAPTER 15

The hallway that Giltreas took them down was different than what they had been in before, and led to a stairway that climbed to a second level. A short hallway after the stairs led to a doorway covered in a heavy drape that had two guards with lances taller than themselves stationed outside it.

Giltreas stopped outside the door, and spoke to the guards. "My mother has requested my presence and that of my friends."

The guard on the right looked them over for a moment, taking in Dave and Allison's strange clothing, and Michelle's robe, then his eyes went to the three dogs accompanying the humans. Sadie had sat when Michelle stopped, but Abby stood looking up at the two strangers before her, wagging her tail so hard that her entire posterior went with it. Max, on the other hand, wagged his tail fiercely at the end of his leash, standing on his hind legs as he tried to get close enough to meet and greet what was obviously two new friends that he could play with. Abby, while less enthusiastic than Max, nonetheless tried to engage the two for some play as she went into play stance, her tail wagging.

Sadie looked over at Max, and woofed once. The sound of the word "Sit!" came from her, and Max looked at her in astonishment, then plopped down to sit as directed. His stub of a tail continued to move, though.

The guards laughed and nodded. The spells they used to augment their senses in their role guarding their queen showed no evil or ill intent in any of these two- or four-footed beings in front of them. The one on the right turned and spoke quietly into the room behind the curtain, then nodded and held the drape aside, motioning them inside.

Giltreas moved forward calmly and confidently, and the rest of the group tried to act as if they knew what they were doing.

The room beyond the doorway was different than they expected. The outer wall of the room was just to the left of the hallway, and it appeared that the hall continued onwards a few feet before opening to the main room on the right. A wall had been laid to cut off the line of sight into the room for anyone standing in the doorway.

They turned the corner, and were in a comfortable sitting room, with chairs and couches arranged into a cozy area around a low table in between. The queen looked up as they entered, and stood, walking over to embrace her son. She had changed from the courtly raiment she had worn in the throne room, and instead was in a more comfortable dress, with stockings on her feet to give her some warmth on the polished wood floor.

The walls and ceiling were also of a rich wood finished in a warm brown, and burnished to a smooth finish that did not reflect much light. Here and there tapestries were hung to break up the sound, displaying scenes and images from the world around them. Windows opened to look out at the city, and towards a wide river flowing past in the distance at the edge of the town.

The greeting lasted a few moments, and the queen turned to the rest of them. Michelle bowed slightly, but the queen waved her hand in a dismissing gesture.

"I have no need of such courtesies here in my private quarters, and I seem to see that you are unused to employing them. Come, sit with me, and we shall talk." Then she broke off and looked down at Sadie as the reddish-golden dog came over to the end of her leash and sat in front of her, wagging her tail up at the elvish woman, a smile on her doggy face.

"And who are you, my grand dame? What a splendid creature you are!" She bent down to let Sadie smell her hand, then passed it down the side of Sadie's neck in greeting, clearly comfortable with animals, or at least dogs.

"Pretty lady nice. Sadie likes you."

The queen laughed, and turned to her son. "I didn't sense you cast Animal Speak. Your skills are getting better, my son."

Giltreas shook his head. "I cast it some time ago this morning. It has not abated as expected. See for yourself."

She gave Giltreas a confused look, and then turned back to the dog she was petting. The detect magic spell was as natural as breathing to her, one of the earliest spells a person with any skill at magic learns, and she murmured the incantation almost automatically. Then she focused on the dog in front of her, and gasped.

"What does this mean? The spell is permanent?"

Giltreas shrugged. "Apparently so. If not, I cannot ascertain when it will fade."

"But only a Mid-God should be able to do such a thing. This is shocking. My son, have you ascended to Deus?"

A shocked look passed over Giltreas' face, and he turned his focus inward to think about the question. "I do not know. It certainly did not occur to me that I might have. I have had no opportunity to ask any God if that is a truth, at any means."

"We must ascertain this." A determined look crossed her face, but before she could do or say anything else, she was stopped by a single quiet word from her son.

"Why?"

The quiet word, spoken calmly and neither defensive or accusatory, caught her by surprise. As she thought about it, she could not come up with a reason other than personal pride.

"Do you wish to know?" Her eyes searched his. She had always been challenged to understand what was in the mind of her quiet, different son. His sire had been a mystery, but he was always more so. Normal patterns of behavior and expected responses were few and far between when he had been young, and without knowing it, he had taxed every one of his care givers, an enigma that few could understand.

"It would change nothing about me that is worth to know, Mother. I find contentment in that which I am." He spoke the words surprisingly without the rancor and bitterness she might have expected from someone forced into what he was required to do by his Patron. That thought was followed by another, and she wondered if what had been demanded of him, and what he had done to meet those demands, had bent his mind after such a long time. But his smile was gentle, soft, and warm. Nothing showed her that he was injured in the mind at all, and she sighed. He was right. Knowing would not change what mattered about him.

"Forgive a mother's pride in her son," she said with a gentle smile, as she turned to the others where they sat. "I welcome you to my home, and my city."

Michelle smiled back. "Thank you. It is peaceful here," she said as she looked out a window that overlooked the city, and towards a wide river at the city's edge.

The sounds of a modern city she was used to were all missing – the cars, trucks, and busses, the sounds of people walking, the occasional airplane overhead. And even more, the smells of a city – the dust, exhaust, and, sometimes, the smells of the sewer system underneath that was often so hard to get away from in some parts of downtown. Instead, the sound of the wind through trees, people, horses, oxen and other animals walking and lowing, and the fresh smells of nature – trees, grasses, and even the distant smell of water carried from the river to the room.

The central building housing the queen and her seat of government was the highest building in the city. The floor they were on seemed to be probably thirty feet above ground level, and the view seemed to indicate that every other building was no more than two floors, with possibly an attic here and there. Even buildings of commerce, inns, and the royal stables were all lower than the manor they were in.

Michelle turned back as the queen spoke to her. "You have had such an ordeal. How are you fairing?"

She thought about it before speaking. "I am all right, I guess. The biggest difference is how much my appearance has been changed. I don't know that I can go back to my old life. No one will be able to recognize me. I certainly can't go back to my company and attempt to continue running it. Everything seems so surreal. I have never really looked like this before, even when I was young. Giltreas erased a lifetime of scars and old injuries that I suffered over the last thirty-plus years. Now I don't know what to do with myself. I am certain that I do not understand why this has happened. And I do not have any idea what to do and where to go with my life from here." She said it quietly, with very little emotion, but even Giltreas was troubled by this.

"Michelle, I do not know what to say. I was directed by my Patron to do what I have done, but if my actions have caused you harm, I deeply apologize. Your condition before what those men did to you, along with what you said about your plane not having any magic, nor any race other than humans, tells me that most humans have never experienced this before. I fear that my helping you has done you no favors." The look on Giltreas' face plainly identified his inner conflict, but Michelle shook her head emphatically as she turned to face him.

"It is okay, Giltreas. You have no reason to apologize. As you said, you were directed to do this. I deeply appreciate what you've done for me. I just don't know where to go from here. My path forward will be very different than my path before, I am guessing." She smiled at him. "Life is an adventure to be lived and not just experienced, right?"

Dave twitched as her last sentence struck a familiar chord in his memory. She had leaned on that philosophy as change after change had thrown her entire life and the goals of her teen years out of reach, as she adapted to her challenges, and made new goals.

A brief, small, tremulous smile found its way onto Giltreas' countenance as he acknowledged her statement, but his internal discord continued to fester. Magic had always been an accepted part of his life, and as much as he had used magic in the service of his patron, he had also used it to heal and help others whenever he was free to do so. But here, with this woman, was evidence plain that his successful attempt to help, even at his Patron's request and, even, His urging, had caused harm. What did it mean when a good act caused harm?

Giltreas continued to contemplate the thoughts running through the back of his mind as he listened to the conversation continue around him, no sign of the inner turmoil that roiled through him.

The queen picked up on something that caught her attention earlier in what Michelle had said. "You said you run a... company? What do you mean by that? I have no knowledge of this."

Michelle thought for a moment. "Do you have merchants here? People and groups of people that buy things and sell them to others?"

"Yes, we call them merchant houses. You run a merchant house?" The queen's question came from her confusion. While her opinion of the capable young human woman in front of her let her believe that she could do anything that her mind was set upon, merchanting was sometimes and even often not the most honorable business, and many times, larger merchant houses were suspected of supporting piracy, and possibly brigandry as well. She and her advisors were unsure of the exact relationship between the larger houses and the annoyances that caused so much trouble, but they felt, indeed almost sensed, its existence. Often they tried to extirpate it from one region of the seas, only to have those they removed be replaced by others. There was no simple answer to this vexing problem. It was simply too expensive to ship things by magical gates, as the number of mages that could cast such powerful spell was limited. Even those that could cast it and keep it open long enough to move any number of freight wagons through it could not do it regularly, as it was simply too taxing of a mage's magical strength and reserves of energy.

Michelle thought for a moment, sensing the distaste with which the queen held such enterprises and the people who were involved in them.

"Where we are from, we refer to a merchant house as a company. A company may have one or more things that it does. Some make things to sell; those we call manufacturers, as they manufacture things. Some buy from manufactures and resell them to other companies or directly to people who use them. Those are wholesalers and retailers. Still others do things, perform services, for companies and individual people. My company provides services to other companies."

The queen thought a moment, then asked another question. "What services does your company perform?"

"Most companies have a huge amount of information that they need or want to keep track of. My company provides ways to store and organize that information, to bring it up as needed, and to perform research on it. We also keep it safe from those who shouldn't see it. We make it available when the owner of that information wants to see it, add to it, change it, or get rid of it." Michelle spoke calmly, as if such a thing were commonplace.

Seeing the quiet, almost proprietary air that Michelle spoke with when describing the... 'company' she was involved in made the queen pause. It was somewhat of a minor shock that merchant houses would pay someone else to house their records and the like. No one had ever thought of doing such a thing in any of the realms she protected. It also confused her.

"That is... interesting. I never would have thought of forming merchant house -- or company as you call it? -- to do such a thing. Moving information around must be cumbersome and challenging." Her mind held an image of a wagon with a huge load of papers and books being pulled through the city streets, followed by a retinue of men with swords and spears to protect it.

Michelle smiled internally. This was an interesting challenge to her – to describe modern information technology concepts to someone from a pre-industrial society, let alone a pre-information-age society.

"We have things, devices, that are capable of storing much information and displaying it when needed." Michelle turned to Allison, who reached into her pocket and removed her phone, handing it over to Michelle with a small smile of her own.

"No signal here, I suppose," she said with a chuckle.

Michelle nodded, then stood and walked over to the queen, turning on the phone as she did.

"This is just a small one. Others are much larger, and can hold a lot more information," she said as she called up the Kindle electronic book reader application Allison used to read from. Opening it, she turned the screen to the queen, who gasped.

"What is this?!" she said in hushed, awed tones.

"This is a book reader. You have scrolls? That is close to what we call a book. This device, called a smartphone, can store hundreds or even thousands of them. Ally has a few dozen that she keeps in here to read when she has free time." She held the phone in her left hand, and showed the queen how to turn pages by touching the screen on one side or the other. Then she went to the library page, and showed that there were several books stored on the phone, and each one had its own text, and a unique cover page and picture.

Overwhelmed by the small thing in front of her, she closed her eyes for a moment, then blinked up at Michelle in awe. "And this is what you do? You store books for companies?" Her confusion grew.

"Not exactly. The words in a book we call information, but information could be many different things. One company that makes things might have the plans on how to make those things, instructions on how to use them and maintain them, other information on who has bought them, how much it costs to make them, how much they make selling them, and so on." The queen's eye started to glaze over just a bit as new concepts came at her so quickly.

"So you run a company that stores information for other companies. I think I understand that a little better now, even if it will take me some time to make much more sense of it," she added with a small smile as she regained some of her internal balance.

"Well, yes I run it, that's true; however, I started the company myself many years ago, and have been growing it ever since. Right now it is in two different countries, and expanding as customers demand more from us."

"How many persons does your company employ?"

"Ahh, I think the number is just over one thousand two hundred now. We acquired another company last fall, and have integrated them into what we do, adding another two hundred or so. Dave, here," she nodded at her brother, "is the head of the part of the company that deals directly with the devices that store and move the information."

The queen and Giltreas were both shocked. This unassuming human woman in front of them ran a merchant house which employed over a thousand beings? The queen paused to consider for a moment, and decided she wasn't sure if that was more surprising, or if it was that Michelle had built it herself. She detected no falsehood in the woman, though, and her brother and his mate showed no signs of unease at her statements that would indicate a falsehood on her part.

Giltreas had known that Michelle was a woman of some substance and achievement, but that large of a merchant house was almost unheard of. Rarely would one find a merchant house of more than some few hundreds, with possibly only one he could recall possibly approaching a thousand. Even the standing city guard was barely two thousand, out of a city of twenty-three thousand beings of all races – mostly elves, but some humans lived there, and fewer yet dwarves from the mountains to the west.

The conversation turned to more practical matters as the humans continued to process the events of the last day, and Giltreas and his mother the queen continued to consider the strange humans in front of them.

"Mother, I will need to assist David in bringing things that Michelle and Allison will wish to have with them while they stay here, as well as things and food the dogs will require. Will it be acceptable for me to open gates here inside the royal quarters to accomplish this?"

Michelle started to speak up, "Your Majesty—"

"You must call me by my name, Delara. I have no need for such formality in any setting other than the throne room," the queen interrupted with a smile and some humility. "I have no need of people to constantly remind me that I am a ruler. It keeps me from communing with others."

"Delara, we don't wish to be a burden or cause problems. I have no idea how long we will have to stay here, or how many times Dave and Giltreas will be coming here while they are looking," Michelle said quietly.

The queen's facial expression was gentle and kind. "You should have no fear of being a burden. I cannot imagine that any such as yourselves would be vexing. And as for my son coming to visit you, and by extension, me, on a regular basis: I welcome the chance to see him more often. If keeping you close to me in my living place gives me that gift, I cannot see it as a burden, but as a gift. You would be granting me a boon by staying here."

Allison smiled, and even Michelle felt better about that. But the Queen's next question drew her up short in thought.

"Do you not have responsibilities to your merchant house that you must attend to? Will those responsibilities languish unattended while you are here gossiping with me? And Allison, what of the needs on your time?"

Allison turned to look at Michelle, and saw that she was considering the question, so she spoke up. "Dave is such a good provider that I don't need to work. I have no real responsibilities. I volunteer my time to help others, but I am not required to be anywhere. And I can disappear like this for a few months before someone gets concerned. I travel a lot with my free time. I might need to call someone in a few weeks so that they don't worry about me."

Delara pondered Allison's statement as she thought about someone having no need to work on a daily basis to feed and clothe themselves. Her thoughts turned to the idle nobles of some of the southern human kingdoms, but decided that the comparison of those indolents to Allison didn't seem to fit, when Michelle interrupted her musings.

"I have been planning for a transition to new leadership at the company for some time. Some time ago, I was told I had a disease inside me that was slowly killing me, so I set everything up for Dave to take over the company. I will write a letter to my lawyer telling him to transition everything to Dave for the duration while I am away. He already has plans for Dave to take over eventually. This will simply put them into play for the short term." Michelle turned to look at Dave while she said the last sentence, and smiled at the shock on his face as he realized that he was her hand-picked successor – something he had clearly not expected.

"Are you sure I am a good choice, sis? I don't have your touch, experience, anything. And you were the one that built everything. Would the department heads follow my direction?"

She smiled at him. "You have been there every step of the way for the last, what, seven years, since you got back from college after your time in the Marines. Everyone respects you. Your leadership during the China hacker war cemented your role in the company, and proved that you are someone who will do anything to support their people. You are the only real choice I have; the only person that I trust with everything I – WE built."

"What about Steven?" Dave said, sounding like someone who was looking for reassurance.

"Steven is a good financial guy, but not a very good leader. He just doesn't get how to treat subordinates with respect. He believes they work for him. You know that your people don't work for you, but that you work for them. And you have managed somehow to get all your leadership people under you to realize that, and emulate your methods with their people." She shook her head. "Steven will not advance any further until he realizes that. I sent him off to that seminar on Servant Leadership last year. His only feedback to me when he came back was 'Well, that was interesting.' He just didn't get it."

Allison had stopped perfectly still, and was staring at Michelle in shock, when Michelle turned to look at her. "What is it, Allie?"

"You're sick? What, cancer?"

"I did have cancer, yes. Now, I doubt it. Giltreas, do I still have it? Or did you erase that, too, along with twenty five years of aging?"

Giltreas looked her in the eye, and saw the wish, the yearning in her, but at the same time, the dread that it might not be true.

"It is true, Michelle. I have healed everything that was wrong with you. You need have no fear of what was before. It is gone from you now."

Her head tipped forward as her eyes closed, and a tremulous sigh escaped her as her fears for her health were suddenly, and completely, eradicated. Then she looked up at Allison again.

"Why didn't you say anything?" Allison sounded hurt, Michelle realized, and with good reason.

"I told myself I didn't want you to worry. I suppose that was at least partially true, but I think it was more than that. I didn't want you to feel like you had to spend every waking minute with me for the remainder of my time. You have your own life. I didn't want to take you from it."

"Don't you think that I would want to make that decision for myself? I don't work, I volunteer. I could walk away from all of that today and not regret it, if it meant spending all that time with you instead." The quiet voice conveyed that she was upset without hammering it home.

Michelle gazed at the younger woman, and realized her mistake. She had worked hard at learning never to make decisions for her employees; here, she had done so with a dear member of her family, and her brother's wife, at that. "I apologize. I wasn't thinking about how you'd feel about it. I am really sorry I upset you. And you're right, you deserved the chance to make the decision for yourself about how you spend your time."

"Well, next time you're gonna die of something terrible, don't do it again." The words were light, but the emotion behind it was anything but, and Michelle pulled Allison close for a one-armed hug for a moment, then sat back on the couch next to her again.

"I promise." Michelle smiled at her. Then she turned to David.

"You don't seem very surprised. How long have you known?"

"That you have, or should I say had, cancer? A long time; almost from the beginning. I bullied your doctor when I started to suspect something. He understood what was at stake, and he cares about you, so it didn't take much arm-twisting." Then his tone grew serious. "Don't you ever keep something that serious from me again, young lady. I'm your brother. We are the only family we have left." He tried to glare at her, but failed.

"Wow, I seem to have made the same mistake twice. Imagine that." She smiled. "Well, all's well that ends well, right?"

The tone of voice was both contrite and repressive at the same time – clearly, she wanted to drop the subject.

"I have been thinking about it, and Allison and I will need regular supply runs. I am going to need clothing, too, but that is more problematic, since I don't have anything that will fit me," she continued

Delara spoke up. "I shall provide anything you require that I am able. You are my guests. Michelle, Allison, what I have that you need you are welcome to."

"Thank you, Delara. We will not abuse your generosity." Allison nodded in agreement.

"But we will also need things for the dogs that you most likely will not have. Kennels for them to stay in, food, dog beds, you know." Dave nodded. He would get all that, and Giltreas would help him get it here.

Sadie looked up from where she lay on the floor as the conversation turned to her and her canine family members. She stood, and stretched, then shook herself, making the metal tags on her collar clatter, then sat looking up at Michelle. "Hungry. You feed now?"

Allison looked down at Sadie. "I don't know if I will ever get used to that. It is pretty neat, though. Dave, we left everything for them in the 4Runner. Can you go get it?"

Dave stood, and Giltreas did as well. "Mother, we shall return momentarily."

CHAPTER 16

Gnezy slowed the car as he approached the police tape stretched across the street at the corner. The call on the police radio had been vague, but clear enough in one regard: an investigator was needed at an address in the old commercial district downtown.

A uniformed officer lifted the tape as he recognized the senior detective in the city's homicide division, waving him under. He pulled further down the block to where the rest of the cars were gathered like cows around a watering trough. He looked further down the street, and saw another tape line closing that end of the street, with two cars parked on either side of the street, and the officers out standing guard to prevent anyone from getting too close to the crime scene.

He got out and stretched, looking up at the three-story brick building that had once been a small factory. He had no idea what the building had been built for originally, but it looked all of its one hundred plus years old. The rest of the buildings up and down the street were similar. Most had been converted to house business offices. He reached back into the car to grab his coffee, then thought better of it, leaving the now-cold drink where it was.

He turned and walked towards the steps, pulling his coat aside to show the badge clipped to his belt at the uniformed officer standing guard at the door.

She nodded unhappily at him, and led him inside, talking to him as she went. "It looks like the basement housed an illegal brothel."

"Why do you think it is a brothel?" He asked as he indicated that she should lead him into the building.

"The officer who arrived here first discovered a number of young women in rooms locked from the outside. The rooms contain only a bed and a chamber pot." He grimaced and nodded in agreement.

135

"That does seem to fit with a brothel. Are the victims, the girls, still here? And why was a homicide investigator called in?" he asked, as they went through a doorway that led to a staircase heading down.

She glanced at him as she turned the corner onto the stairs, and he saw in the light coming from the overhead fluorescent fixture that her face was a green that seemed more pronounced than the light could account for.

"The victims, the girls, were all transported to hospital. Most were hysterical, but some were catatonic. As to why you were called in, I think you should look for yourself." Her tone of voice was not something usually used with a person of Gnezy's rank and seniority, but he ignored the lack of respect when he realized that she was close to losing control of herself. He merely grunted and followed her down the twenty or so steps until they turned the corner and found themselves in a lobby that was probably five meters by eight meters, with a modern, solid steel door mounted in the wall at the end to the left, along with a video camera and phone. The door was open at the moment, and another officer stood there, a pasty sheen covering his complexion and the evidence of his lost lunch speckling his once-spotless uniform pants and shoes.

The doorway opened to a small enclosed area with another door opposite the first. Four video surveillance cameras were mounted in each of the corners near the ceiling. It was obvious from the construction of the room that this was a man-trap security room, designed to contain anyone who got past the first door. Usually only one door would be opened at any given moment, controlling access to what was beyond the second door. Both were propped open now, though, and the police officer pointed wordlessly down the hallway before turning resolutely back to look towards the exit, clearly turning his back to what was down there in an effort to not think about it.

Gnezy walked down the wide hallway, taking in the windowless doors set at regular intervals, some of which were opened, others closed. None of the purported occupants were in sight, however, and he continued on towards the opposite end of the hall.

As he got closer, the first thing he noticed was that there was no door in the doorway. The second thing he noticed was that the doorway had been smashed open as if a raging bull had run through it. The shattered remnants of the door frame and the door itself lay scattered across the floor to the far wall. But as he stepped around the remains of the breakfast the officer at the other end of the hallway had deposited on the floor and into the room, the fate of the door was not what caught his attention and pulled at the bitter coffee in his gut.

The room was a gory mess straight out of one of those American horror films that his daughter loved to watch with her friends. The room looked as if a bomb had gone off, throwing parts of the unfortunate occupants everywhere. Ripped and torn chunks of human remains were strewn everywhere, and blood covered everything in sight. Even the ceiling, he realized as he looked the room over, trying, with some success, to keep his suddenly unruly stomach under control.

Taking in the furnishings, he realized that it was a kitchen, with appliances and counters on the right wall and opposite wall, and a table and chairs set up to the left.

He couldn't tell how many people had started out in the room at first. Then a gruesome thought came to him, and he counted four heads. Looking across the room, he saw another door that opened to a set of stairs leading upwards, and bloody foot prints leading out that way. Whomever, or whatever, had done this had fled that way, he realized. Then the overwhelming stench of guts, blood and flesh began to overcome him, and he stepped back into the hallway.

The smell wasn't much better there, but it lessened enough to let him look around, and he noticed that one of the opened doors part way back down the hall was barely hanging on its hinges. He walked back and looked into the room, and found another body, this one in only marginally better shape than the remains in the kitchen behind him. He pulled out his flashlight, and looked the body over, noting the injuries that had killed the big man.

The story written in the carnage in front of him seemed to indicate that the man had been ripped apart by a huge animal – possibly a tiger or a bear. That made him pause and he looked around the room.

There was no evidence that the room had housed a wild animal of the sort that could have done this, but there was something of interest on the floor in front of the bed.

He pulled out a pair of surgical gloves, and held up the remnants of what looked like clothing. A teen girl, he decided. The clothing had been slashed and ripped up into an unusable state, probably by the poor dead soul on the floor in front of the bed.

What had happened at first seemed obvious enough to him. The man had taken liberties with a teenage girl, probably a kidnap victim. But he was interrupted while he was still in the room, and met his probably well-deserved end. Gnezy went through the pockets of the pants, and found another piece of the puzzle.

Ukrainian currency, not Georgian. The girl was not from around here. He wondered where she was now, and if the creature that had killed the man had carried her off. There was certainly enough blood in here as well for a second victim, he guessed. Not that he was any good at that. Better leave that to the techs that would be coming to document the scene.

He stepped carefully back out of the room, making sure not to step on any 'evidence' on the floor, just as the first of the crime scene techs came through the door.

"Senior Investigator. What do we have here? Smells bad enough. Dead body?" The man's face was grim and serious, and Gnezy appreciated the professionalism the man showed.

"There is a dead body in this room here, and four more in the kitchen at the end of the hall. Also, there are bloody footsteps heading up the back staircase at the other end of the kitchen. I would like to get images of the footprints from that trail as soon as possible."

"Certainly. Any guesses as to who did this?"

Gnezy snorted. "More like what. The kitchen is a mess, but it looks like it started in here. The body in this room seems to have been attacked by a tiger or a bear or something big, strong, and very angry. Whatever it is, I am fairly convinced that it is not here now, though. We will need someone to open every door down here, and see if the first sweep missed anyone. I will coordinate with the officer in charge upstairs while the rest of your team gets here and gets to work."

The technician's eyes got wide at the thought that a wild animal was the perpetrator, and he swallowed. He had noticed the uniformed patrolman he saw earlier that had obviously vomited on himself, but had thought that the man simply had a weak stomach. Now, he wasn't so sure.

"How bad is the kitchen?"

"It is worse than any nightmare on this Earth. If I was a religious man, I might compare it to hell."

* * *

Gnezy retraced his steps back up to the ground level, and found the senior officer on the scene.

"Has anyone looked in the alley behind the building? It looks like whoever did this went out that way."

The officer nodded. "We secured the alley, but haven't let anyone go back there yet. I can have someone take you around to it. The building next door has a hallway that runs straight back there."

"Good. I will take a look, and then come back around to here."

The senior officer waved one of his subordinates over, and directed him to take the investigator around back.

The back of the building housing the horrors within looked almost normal to Gnezy's eyes, until he looked closer. Bloody footprints led down the short stairway from the back door, skipping some in hurried flight, and led away from the back door to the center of the enclosed alley between the industrial buildings, where they turned and ran away from the building. While he would have expected the footsteps to have less blood the further away from the scene, these seemed to leave just as much behind, if not more. Additionally, there were drops of blood in between and all around the footsteps, and it made Gnezy suddenly realize that the body running away had to be covered in blood, and it had dripped off as they fled. As the feet left blood behind, more flowed down off the body to replenish what was behind on the pavement.

The steps seemed to get further apart, probably because the body was running and gaining speed, he thought to himself, when they abruptly ended. Did the body get into a car? Or something else? That wouldn't explain why the blood drops continued without the footprints, though. Then he bent over and looked at the footprints in front of him. And noticed something else.

"What do you see, Senior Inspector?" The younger officer spoke up when he saw the suddenly intense evaluation the Inspector was giving to the footsteps.

Gnezy straightened up, and turned to the officer, waving him forward to look for himself.

"Tell me what you see." He always took the chance to mentor others, but this time he wanted to see if his thoughts were validated, as well.

"Hmmm." The younger man looked closer at the bloody print in front of him. "No shoes or boots. This person was barefoot. The feet are somewhat strangely shaped, too. And, what is this in front of the toes of the print? What are those? Gouges in the pavement?"

"Yes, indeed they are. What does that say to you?"

Zenadine straightened up, a shocked expression on his face. "Claws?" he asked incredulously.

"I would agree with you if it was not so preposterous. What kind of man runs around barefoot, and has claws that can cut into asphalt like that?" The Senior Inspector was at a loss for words.

Zenadine realized that the question was rhetorical, and remained silent as they both stared at the impossible evidence in front of them both that should not exist.

The senior officer from around front of the building found them that way moments later, and approached the two men. "Senior Inspector? There is someone from the Ukrainian Interior Ministry out front. He would like to speak with you." Then he glanced down at the prints himself.

"Hmmm. Barefoot. Wait, are those claw marks?"

CHAPTER 17

After bringing up the duffle bags and packs that were in the 4Runner, Dave made a mental list of what he needed to bring back right away for Allison and Michelle, and a second list of what they would want on a regular basis. Queen Delara assured them that most of their needs would be taken care of – food, a place to sleep, clothing if they wanted it. Michelle took her up on the offer of clothing, since nothing she had would fit her anymore. Allison wanted her own clothes, and some other things, such as books to read, some clothing to work out in, and a few other things.

Michelle put down food for Sadie and Abby, and Allison did the same for Max. Delara watched in happy amusement as the dogs did some tricks for the after-meal treat they all received. She was amazed the hand signals that Sadie responded to, and had to try it herself. Abby knew some hand signals as well, though not as many. Max, on the other hand, knew several, and even knew a few tricks that Sadie didn't.

Michelle watched in amazement as Max stood on his hind legs, then waved his paw at Allison. "When did you teach him that one?"

"He kinda started doing that on his own. I just marked it with a word, and added a hand signal. He is easy to train, when he isn't flying around the room barking his silly head off," Allison said as she petted Max's head and back.

When they were ready, Dave and Giltreas said their goodbyes to the Queen, Michelle, and Allison. Dave's goodbye with Allison was a private moment involving a long hug, and a whispered conversation as the others looked away and talked quietly to give them their space.

At the last moment, Dave asked Allison what she wanted done with her pistol, still with the guards outside the throne room.

"I'm not sure. I don't know if I will need it here or not, but it is comforting to know that it is nearby. I would like to have it close in case it is needed. I would also like to keep in practice once a week. Delara, is it a problem if I keep my weapon nearby? And fire it once in a while to keep my skills up?" Allison turned to the queen, who nodded.

"You may keep your weapons with you in your quarters, on your person, or whatever you chose. What manner of weapon is a pistol?" Her interest was more than just a passing thought.

Dave smiled to himself as Allison tried to think about how to answer the question.

"The closest I can think of is a crossbow? Do you have those here?" she asked.

"Yes, we have crossbows. They are heavy, slow to fire, hard to reload, and generally not used much because of those reasons, excepting for guard duty where they can be loaded and set aside for need. Eventually, they need to be restrung, though, and that is challenging as well."

"Well, think of it as a very small crossbow that can fire as quickly as you can pull the trigger. It fires a very small bullet the size of the end of your finger. I can show you, if you like." Allison responded.

"I would be interested in seeing you fire it. It might be fun to see what I can do, if it is alright with you." Delara said, and glanced at Giltreas as he smiled. "What, my son, do you forget my own training before I ascended the throne?"

"Not at all, Mother. I remember fondly you teaching me to use bow and staff. It was a long time before I could equal your skill. I seem to remember your challenges with sword, however," and she laughed.

"Yes, sword was something I could never get the handle of. Unlike yourself." He simply bowed in response.

Allison turned to Dave and said, "Can you bring me a few boxes of ammunition for my Glock and my cleaning kit, and maybe a few spare sets of ear and eye protection? I want to stay in form, after all."

"All right. Anything else?"

"I'm certain there will be more as we think of it, but for now.. Thanks, sweetie!" She smiled brightly at him.

Dave and Giltreas walked down to the stables again, this time to leave the elvish city for Michelle's cottage in the woods. The walk was in silence, but Giltreas could tell that Dave was unhappy, possibly about leaving his life-mate behind. He reached out and patted Dave on the shoulder, causing Dave to look over and produce a wan smile.

"I know they will be safe, but I will miss them," he said quietly as their footsteps sounded in the stone and wood hallway.

"I will bring us back here many times that you might not miss them much."

"I appreciate it a lot. And I appreciate everything else you have done. Michelle is just as important to me as Allison."

Giltreas nodded, and turned the conversation to the matter at hand.

"Where will you begin your search for the man who set those brigands on your family?"

"The only place they could have learned about that cottage is at the company. That is the only place that connects Michelle to it. Someone we hired said something, or knows something. The problem is, everyone we hired has been carefully screened. We have strict rules that can't be avoided, since we have some significant government contracts. Everyone has been investigated by the FBI, a branch of the Federal government. That is the only way we qualify to work for the government in data services."

Giltreas turned that thought over in his mind, working through the strange words and their different meanings, until he was pretty sure he understood what had been said. Then he spoke up.

"Mayhap not your government did this? You did say that the black horseless carriage was connected somehow to them."

"Yes, I did. And it certainly looks that way. The government knows everything, or can figure out what they don't know pretty easily. But that doesn't make any sense. Why would someone in the government want Michelle dead? What is the point? None of this adds up." He paused, thinking about it, then continued. "Of course, there are enough assholes and sleaze-balls in the government that it makes the most sense to look there. The real question is why. And that is something we may never know."

"We will find the answers together, Good David. And we will punish the guilty. If you are unable to do so because of your laws, I shall step into the gap and do what needs to be done. The wrong has been undone, but it must also be righted." The resolute sound of Giltreas' words penetrated to the very depths of his heart, and he put his hand on Giltreas shoulder in silent thanks.

* * *

He had always maintained his innocence to the other inmates, much to their amusement. Three years into a life sentence for child molestation and murder, his story had never changed. It didn't seem to matter to the inmates, the guards, or even his lawyer; all of them seemed to think he was guilty. Since well before the conviction, they had given him the impression that they were just going through the motions. But his mother had always stood by him, and his sisters. His father had abandoned him "to your fate, and may you rot in hell, you little bastard." The words had hurt, as had the betrayal that his father showed. His mother divorced his father shortly after he said that to her youngest child, also feeling the betrayal and sense of abandonment that her son so obviously felt.

Ironically, the parents of the child he was supposed to have molested and killed had never believed that it was him. The father had written him a letter telling him that they were still looking for the real killer, but no one believed them either. The press didn't want to talk to them, convinced that the prosecutor had gotten it right. The prosecutor believed that he couldn't have made a mistake, and refused to talk to the parents of the little six year old boy after the trial.

During the trial, the state prosecutor had tried to convince the parents of the victim that he had the right man, but they never accepted it. They even tried to convince the prosecutor that this stranger, whom they and their precious little boy had never met, didn't do it. But without any proof, just their feelings that he wasn't the right man, their arguments fell on deaf ears, getting the response of "I told you not to talk to him. He is like all the others, just lying to save his skin, and only sorry he got caught."

Now, he knew that his time on this earth was most likely over. He normally had been kept in the part of the prison reserved for sexual offenders, but a guard he had never met before who took him to the showers in a part of the prison he had never seen seemed to know what he was doing. And all of it spelled doom to one Craig Sanderson.

The three other men in the shower area all looked at him like he was the main course at a feast in their honor. He tried to ignore them while simultaneously keeping them all in sight, but Craig could feel the tension, the anticipation in their movements. This was not going to end well for someone.

He closed his eyes as the hot water flowed over him, and thought about surrendering to the inevitable. He was never getting out. His family would be better off without him. Maybe they could sue the prison system after his death, and get something back for all this nastiness he had been dropped into.

He still had no idea how or why the police had connected him to the crime. He was nowhere near where the child had been killed when it happened. He KNEW he had nothing to do with it, as sure as he knew that the sun rose in the east. His lawyer called it all circumstantial evidence, nothing concrete in it, the jury should see right through it, etcetera. They made it sound like it was routine and that he would have him out of jail and acquitted in time for dinner.

Only it hadn't happened that way. The prosecutor seemed to be able to anticipate every move the defense team made, and what he couldn't get disallowed, he undermined. The state's legal warrior was skilled and experienced, and it showed. Every trick in the book was pulled to make the case stick, to make the jury see him as the ultimate personification of evil. And after nearly two days of deliberation, it had worked.

The despair turned to anger now as he thought about everything that had been taken from him, and a low growl escaped through clenched teeth. He turned towards the wall, and the rage took him completely. A fist suddenly much more massive than he expected, covered in coarse, black hair, smashed into the wall in front of him.

"Holy shit! What the…" He turned at the sound, and growled at the three huge naked men he was trapped in the shower with. They looked at him with fear, not with the loathing they had first shown him. He took a step forward, and his gait felt strange. He looked down, and saw the form of a huge silverback gorilla where his normally lean frame should have been, and looked up again.

The three men had not seen the change, so they had no idea where their intended victim had gotten off to, nor how they suddenly came to be trapped in an enclosed, locked room with a massive, enraged primate that could easily tear them apart if they made any sudden moves.

The huge fangs it bared at them made one wet himself in fear. He knew that gorillas were many times stronger than men, and this was going to end badly if they made any threatening gestures towards it.

Then it roared at them, a sound so loud in the enclosed place that their ears nearly bled. Deafened, the one pulled at the other two as he sunk down into a posture of submission on his knees, covering his head with his arms. The other two did the same, praying suddenly to a God they hadn't thought about since childhood.

The guard at the security station monitoring the cameras noticed that a different prisoner was in the general population shower, and wondered where he had come from. Then he stiffened in sudden realization as he recognized Craig Sanderson from the sequestered part of the prison. How the hell had he gotten into the general population area? Who had put him there? He did recognize the three inmates in the shower with him, however, and knew that something was going down. He reached over for the phone, and hit the emergency button. Whatever Sanderson did, it was not the role of the guards to have him mistreated like this.

The emergency signal went out to the ear piece of every radio-equipped guard, and to every speaker in the secured areas that prisoners didn't have access to. The guard that had brought Sanderson to his little meeting with God stiffened suddenly, then cursed under his breath as he heard the alert tone. He had lost a child to a drunk driver that had never been caught, and felt that the parents of Sanderson's victim deserved a little closure. He had no real knowledge of the case, but just wanted, in his own twisted sense of right and wrong, to get a little justice for the parents. So he had arranged a little church session for Sanderson, but now it seemed that the jig was up. He sighed, and then unlocked the door to the shower to retrieve the inmate before things got too far out of hand. He had the door partially opened when it was smashed open the rest of the way, and a massive form stalked out on its knuckles and roared at him.

He recognized the thing in front of him, and lost control of his bodily functions as he fell back against the wall opposite the door to the shower facility. He slid down to a sitting position, and then shied away in fear as the form came over and roared at him, making his ears ring. Then a massive hand reached out and effortlessly lifted the nearly two hundred pound guard off the floor by his uniform shirt, and threw him down the hallway, only to lope after him as he slid across the hard surface.

The guard at the monitor station looked back into the shower area, and saw only the three prisoners from general in the monitor. And they didn't look too good. But where had Sanderson gone? He switched to the camera in the hallway outside the shower just in time to see a guard slide down the hallway on his back and crash head first into the solid steel door at the end. Then his breath froze in his throat as the massive form of an adult gorilla strode into view of the camera, obviously enraged. Where the actual EFF had that come from!?!

The phone up to his ear suddenly spoke to him, and he nearly dropped it in shock, unable to take his eyes off the screen.

"What is the emergency? Hello? Talk to me! What is going on?"

"Sir, are you near a monitor station?"

"Yes! What are you seeing?"

"Camera 309, sir. I…"

The voice on the other end paused, then… "Holy Mother of God! Where did that gorilla come from? What the hell is going on?!"

Craig Sanderson slowly pulled his rage back inside himself, and felt his form change back as he got it under control.

He looked down at the guard in front of him, and glared at him. He saw the frightened eyes looking up at him, and it only made him madder. He bent down closed, and through clenched teeth, said "What, the fact that I am locked up for life for something I didn't do wasn't enough for you, you had to go and sign me up for some extra-curricular activity with your three friends back there?"

He reached down and hauled the stunned, terrified guard back up to his feet and slammed him back against the wall behind him with both fists, bringing a hoarse gasp from the man.

"How many times do I have to tell the whole damned world that I DIDN'T DO IT?!" The last came out as a roar, and he changed into the gorilla form again in a flash.

The guard writhed in his grip, terrified almost beyond words, and tried to speak, but it only came out as a wheeze.

"Please, I have a wife and kids! I…"

The angry beast threw him down the hallway again, and he felt his form shift again as his mind focused on a different image this time.

The guard came to a rest on his seat, with his back against the wall, and friction prevented him from slamming into the doorway this time. So he was looking straight at the gorilla when it changed into a Siberian tiger, which locked eyes with him and slowly started pacing down the hallway towards him.

Every step was one closer to his death; he just knew that he was going to visit his dead child soon. At least the agony of his loss would end with his death, he was sure of. But it wasn't enough to take him away from where he was now.

He turned away and curled into a ball as the fear consumed him at last making him a broken, sobbing wreck, screaming "I'm sorry!" at the top of his lungs over and over again.

The officers watching on the monitor were stunned and paralyzed at what they were seeing. It simply did not make any sense. How did a man change into a gorilla, then a tiger? How was this possible? Their minds responded in different ways, mostly along the lines of trying to deny what they had witnessed. The events they watched they were completely unable to process that they were so outside their world view and experience. They could be forgiven for that.

The tiger got close enough for the screaming guard to feel the hot breath on his cheek, when it suddenly turned away. This was not the person that had harmed him. He didn't know how, but other than a bad decision on taking things into his own hand, the guard was basically a good person; one who had suffered a horrible loss of his own that had torn at his soul, Craig realized, as he changed back to human form.

Craig sat down against the wall, and waited to see what would happen next. He saw movement out of the corner of his eye, and turned to see one of the three men from the shower peeking around the open door.

Delmar had never been so terrified in his life as when he was confronted with the gorilla in the shower. It had left, and he had heard some words screamed in the hallway, and saw the guard thrown past the door in his way down the hall, followed by a huge tiger walking by. Once the guard started screaming, he knew that something really bad was going to happen to the guard, but the screaming went on and on, and nothing happened. Getting his courage up, he tiptoed to the door, and peeked around.

He took in the guard curled up in a ball on the floor against the door, and the child killer (or, maybe he wasn't, if he hadn't killed the guard) squatting against the wall nearby. He looked up at Delmar, and smiled at him, making Delmar nearly piss himself again at the look in the other inmate's eye.

Delmar knew that he was looking in the face of death if he made even one wrong move. He didn't doubt for a moment that the other prisoner had changed into a gorilla, then a tiger, as terrifying and wrong as those thoughts were, and he wanted no part of any of that.

The doorway at the other end of the hall opened, and several guards in full riot gear made their way slowly into the hall. They took in the screaming guard, the naked inmate next to him down in a catcher's stance leaning against the wall, and the open door to the shower. Then a face peeked around the open door, and the lead guard waved that prisoner back into the shower. The prisoner quickly complied, even pulling the door most of the way shut.

None of the guards entering the hallway had withessed what the guards monitoring the security cameras had seen, so they started down the hallway confidently; ready to pound the inmate into submission if necessary.

"Lay down on the floor and put your arms and legs out wide! Do it now! Do it…"

Craig decided at the shouts of the guard that he was done being cowed into submission. He stood. He smiled. He changed form again.

The guards stopped moving forward, and more than one of the four lost control of his bodily functions as the inmate in front of them stood, smiled, and in a flash turned into a massive brown bear. The bear looked down at them from where its head touched the nearly nine foot tall ceiling, and growled loudly at them. Then it dropped down to all fours, and shuffled forward.

The four guards in front backed up slowly against the closed door behind them. One reached behind them to try the door handle, but the door opened into the hall they presently occupied, and the weight of the four terrified men against it held it shut as tight as if it were still locked.

The bear stopped about ten feet from the now terrified guards, and as it stood up it changed back into the form of the inmate. Then he spoke to them.

"I didn't do what I am in prison for. And I will not be abused by anyone ever again. You can take me back to my cell, but if one of you lays a hand on me, or tries anything at all, I will rip you all into bloody little pieces. Do you understand me?"

The quiet tone of voice, and the sound of absolute confidence in it, came through loud and clear. The guard in front nodded, then held up his hand as the inmate tried to walk past them. "Wait!"

"WHAT!?" he thundered at them, and the sergeant flinched.

"You're naked! You need something to wear! You can't go out there like that!" it came out in a rush, nearly unintelligible, and he tried to get his point across before he was sure to be ripped to shreds.

Craig suddenly looked down at himself, then leaned up against the wall. "Fine. I'll wait here."

"We can take care of that. Can one of us see to the other guard? Is he hurt?"

"He might have a few bruises. I tossed him around some. I think he is not in the best of moods right now. You might want to get him to a shrink.

I hear they have some around here somewhere." It was a joke; he had steadfastly and adamantly refused to see one to help with his supposed 'mental disorder', knowing that he was innocent of what had put him in prison in the first place.

"What did he do? Why did you...?" The lead guard had no words as he looked at the other end of the hallway where two of his men had reached the tortured soul on the floor, and tried to calm him.

"My cell is in the sex-offender wing. I take it I am not there now?" A shake of the lead guard's head confirmed what he suspected.

"I think those three men in that shower were supposed to administer an attitude adjustment to me because of the crime I didn't commit." The grim tone of voice brought the lead guard's attention back to the naked inmate in front of him. As he looked at the naked man in front of him who had just moments before shown such extraordinary, unheard-of abilities, his innate skepticism must have shown on his face.

The inmate turned to look him in the eye. "I'm in here for life. No chance of parole, in a state without the death penalty. Don't you think that if I had done it, I would not have held back? I could have shredded those inmates, that guard, and your entire team. Don't believe that I couldn't. But in spite of this bullshit I am in the middle of, I still believe that all life is sacred and has value. I couldn't have harmed that child. I could no more have killed that guard than I could have ripped those inmates apart. As much as I might want to because of my current situation, I can't, not if I want to be able to live with myself, regardless of where I am." He turned and looked at the prison around them, and his gesturing hand took in the place he was locked up inside. The flat tone of his voice and the pain on his face showed the hellish nightmare he couldn't wake up from that had lasted nearly four years since he had been arrested for something he knew he didn't do.

The guard had heard many stories over the years from prisoners; too many to count. Almost every prisoner spouted that he was innocent. He must have been framed. The prosecutor had it out for him. The police framed him. Someone else did it; it wasn't him. But this was different.

Here was a person fully capable of destroying everyone and everything in his path, or even just walking out untouched if he wanted, and he chose not to. The thought of just standing here next to him both terrified and exhilarated him to the point that he was a little short of breath. Maybe this one was telling the truth. But it wasn't his job to change anything, or even to care. It was his job to preserve the way things were, the order of things created by the justice system, whatever its flaws.

"Well, there is nothing I can do about your situation. But I can get you back to where you belong – I mean, where you are assigned to be. I am certain that the recordings of this are going to get out, and you will have a lot of unhappy company soon. They are going to want to know how you did that. Hell, I want to know, myself, even if it is just to know if anyone else is capable of doing it." His thoughts flashed back moments ago to the form of the huge, terrifying bear. He suddenly realized that he had wet himself in the moment, and he flushed in embarrassment. But he tried to go on gamely.

"Let's get you something to wear, and get you back there," he said, as more guards started to appear, along with a medical team for the guard who had finally screamed himself hoarse.

Craig turned and nodded at the guard on the floor that was now rocking back and forth, eyes shut tight, teeth clenched hard, a low continuous moan coming from him with every breath. "He needs a lot of help. Something else is buried deep inside, and it is eating him away. I took my anger out on him, sure, but something made him think doing this to me was ok."

The lead guard turned in surprise as the compassionate statement reached his ears. The other guards that had just arrived had apparently been told that something had happened, but everything was under control at the moment, and they needed to listen to the sergeant of the guard on scene.

The sergeant took the coverall, socks and undergarment the guard behind him held out, and handed it to the inmate, who put everything on, followed by the slippers.

Craig wondered at the changes inside him that allowed him to change shape like that. It felt so natural that it didn't bother him; it was like he could have always done that, if he'd just known how. He was exhilarated at the thought, like he could fly or something. Hmmm. His mind was on other things as the guards led him back to his cell in the sex-offender ward. The sergeant of the guard walked amiably beside him, ushering him through doors and hallways. He didn't say anything, as he contemplated the huge change deep inside.

The last doorway he was led to was the entry to his cell. The sergeant wanted to say something to the young man in front of him, but had no idea what would be ok, or even received. The look the inmate gave him acknowledged that, but also held a raft of other emotions. The anger was still there, but was joined by despair, frustration, and some other feelings too complex for sergeant of the prison guard to understand. One emotion the sergeant clearly recognized, though: an overwhelming sense of loss. For a moment, the inmate and the guard just looked into each other's eyes, and while they did, some connection was made between them. Then it abruptly disappeared as the inmate turned away, and walked into his cell.

The clang of the door closing seemed to echo down the hallway for much longer than usual to the guards, as each one independently came to the same question: was the locked door keeping the inmate in, or keeping others out? And would it really keep him in if he wanted out?

Craig turned at the last minute and spoke through the door to the sergeant, who was walking away slowly. "Hey, I want to speak with my lawyer, and the prosecutor for my case. Can you see if that is possible?"

The sergeant turned back and responded, "I don't see why not, at least in the case of your lawyer. I am certain you will need to speak with him anyways, once more people see the security camera footage of your recent adventure. The prosecutor is another matter. I can put the request through channels, and he might be more convinced of coming if he learns about your ability. Or maybe even less. I will pass it up."

"Thanks. I appreciate it." The words clearly carried the anger and frustration Craig felt to the sergeant, and he winced internally. The more he contemplated what had just happened, and considered the overall ramifications, he became more and more convinced that the younger man locked up in the cell didn't belong there. But by the same token, he was glad it wasn't his job to make that determination. He squared his shoulders, and walked on to face whatever storm was about to blow into his life.

CHAPTER 18

The gate returned Giltreas and Dave to the same clearing as before. The drive back to the cottage was quiet as both men contemplated the new experiences that they had both stumbled into. This time, with no prisoners behind him to keep his attention on, Giltreas looked around absently at this strange plane that Dave called home, not really focusing on what he was seeing as he considered the strange actions of his Patron in recent memory. He was a very sharp, well-trained, skilled tool that was applied to solve problems that had a clear and precise nature. What he was now doing was in some ways quite far outside what he had ever been called upon to do, but the warm, gentle pulse he felt in his chest at the thought affirmed that the notice from his Patron had been clear: he was doing what his Patron wanted.

Dave likewise spent the few minutes contemplating everything he needed to do so Giltreas would be able to blend in and be able to be effective in the search for whoever had ordered Michelle's murder. It was a tall order. With no state identification card, he could not prove that he was in the country legally, let alone that he was from the planet. He snorted internally at that thought. Dave was convinced that Giltreas was not human. On the one hand, his mother was the elvish queen of a place that humanity here on Earth had no idea existed. But even if he had status as a noble, there was no way to prove his existence. If Giltreas was picked up by any local, state, or Federal authority, Dave had no idea how it would play out. He was in the country illegally, certainly. He almost smiled as he considered whether or not he was on the planet illegally, as well.

The train of thought was cut off abruptly as he made the turn onto the dirt road that led to the cottage. He turned to Giltreas and spoke.

"We have to get on the road right away. I need to get to the office and get you an ID card so you can come with me to work Monday. We will have tomorrow to plan and think about what to do, but right now, I am at a loss. I guess we will have to just see what happens when I get back to the office and everyone else is there. That one said I was supposed to be next, so if the first one we are looking for is someone there, they will be surprised to see me. We will have to keep our eyes open to see if we spot anyone not expecting me.

"In the meantime, we will have to get a load of things back to the ladies at the elvish city. Will you be able to open a gate from anywhere, such as inside my house? Or will we have to come back here to go there?" The question came out with a slight bit of apprehension, as the inconvenience of a lengthy trip across the state would make the logistics of Michelle and Allison staying in Queen Delara's household.~~

"I will see when we get there, but there should be no need to come back here. I am able to call a gate from most any place I find myself, and I can send a gate to any place I can remember." It wasn't only places that he remembered, he thought to himself, but that was a story for another time.

"Good," Dave replied. "We have a lot to do before Monday to get you ready for being in the corporate world. Clothes, changing your image somewhat, things like that. I was thinking that I would present you as being a new recruit for my program. That would let me get you a badge with full access to everywhere." He saw the confusion on his passenger's face, and sighed internally. "I have a lot of things to explain to you, as well. I think that we will go directly to the office after we get to town, so I can answer all your questions, and get you acclimated. The place should be empty. We'll cover as much as we can, but if you run into anything, feel free to ask any questions that come to mind. I think we might want to stick with my language, English, and anything sensitive we will have to talk about in a private room."

Giltreas nodded. This world was strange. He would need as much guidance as possible to make sure he didn't draw attention to himself. A question presented itself to him, and he gave voice to it.

"Shall I cut my hair? I am guessing from your appearance that most men will not wear long hair. I am certain to be unusual enough that I want to do what I can to not be a wolf amongst the sheep."

Dave nodded. "I'm glad you asked. I wasn't sure how to bring that up, as lots of people are very attached to how they look."

Giltreas shrugged. "It is only hair. From time to time, I am pressed to a task that requires me to change my appearance. It will grow back, unless I like the new countenance I see, then I will maintain it a while."

"Most men in a corporate environment like our company wear their hair short. There is no requirement to do so, but it is easier to keep clean and neat. I know someone who can cut and style it for you. We will have to go shopping for clothes today, as well. We will have to get you a lot of stuff to wear. A nice suit, slacks, jeans, shirts, shoes, stuff to wear underneath, and so on. It will be getting colder soon, so you will need some cold weather stuff, too."

He thought for a moment more, then glanced over at his passenger. "Do you plan on carrying weapons at the office?"

Giltreas thought about the question, and what it implied. "Mayhap a single blade, easily concealed, would suffice. Is that an issue?"

"I don't think so. We have metal detectors at the entrance that most visitors have to go through, but you won't be a visitor. Another benefit of bringing you in on a Saturday – we can get the orientation process completed without anyone else seeing and asking questions."

Giltreas wasn't sure what orientation meant. The definition of the word brought to him by the Learn Language spell made little sense. Some parts were confusing, and he didn't see how which way he was looking would make much sense in terms of fitting in. Were there some things he was supposed to look away from? That did not match what was said earlier about access to everything. Instead of asking questions now that might be answered by waiting, he simply shrugged.

"I will be guided by you, then, my friend," he smiled gently.

Dave saw the smile, and smiled back. "We will get you completely inside, then we can start digging." The smile turned much more predatory. "And when we find something, we will have work to do."

"Agreed."

* * *

The senior inspector walked around to the front of the building, staying away from the back stairway where evidence had yet to be processed, and the blood cleaned up. His stomach, usually quite robust, had decided that, given the circumstances, it would be just as happy as the rest of him if it never had to see, or smell, any of what was inside that place again.

The man standing patiently outside the front door near the officer stationed there turned as he approached.

"Senior Inspector. I am Borysko Yevtukh." He held out his hand, and the inspector took it in surprise.

"What can I do for the Special Group Alpha, Mister Yevtukh?" The question came out much calmer than Gnezy would have expected.

Yevtukh winced internally. He should have expected a senior inspector in Georgia's national police agency to recognize him. Well, what's done is done.

"I am following the trail of a produce truck that apparently dropped someone off at this address within the last day or so."

Gnezy gave the man standing next to him a hard look. "Why is your government taking such a close interest in something that happened in my country?"

Borysko looked down briefly, and decided that honesty was required here. He was in a different country, and had no official support from his government.

The clerk had been looking at the main door when the girl had been snatched, but the sound of the back door slamming alerted her that something was wrong. She had turned, and immediately noticed that the young girl that had been looking at greeting cards near the back of the store wasn't there anymore. She put it together with the strange man that had been standing around making her nervous rather quickly, and called the police.

Within minutes, the police had arrived, and quickly after that, security camera footage had confirmed that the girl had been grabbed bodily by the big man in the farmer's coverall, tossed in a van in the back alley, and had been driven away.

While talking to his wife in their hotel room above the gift shop, Borysko had a sudden feeling of dread wash over him. His wife saw all color drain from his face, and put her hand to her mouth in fear.

Borysko turned and ran for the door, shouting, "Lock the door and call the police! Something has happened!" The door slammed behind him before he could say anything else, and within minutes, he was down in the gift shop, arriving just as the occupants of the first police car that just arrived finished walking across the hotel lobby and into the small shop.

Most times, police officers would have not allowed the father of a potentially missing minor to have any involvement in the investigation, but Borysko Yevtukh was a high-ranking officer in the Special Group Alpha, the special police forces of Ukraine dedicated to, among other things, fighting organized crime. It was impossible to exclude him from seeing the security camera footage, or anything else.

A single phone call to his superiors had been all that Borysko had needed to secure permission to go after the kidnappers himself, with a unit under his command mobilized to follow as quickly as they could assemble.

Within several hours, they were on the trail. Traffic camera footage had allowed them to follow the path the produce truck took, but they were unable to overtake, being forced to rely on officers at the central headquarters to review what was coming in from the national traffic coordination center. Several times during those first two days, they thought that the truck was going to get entangled in the road blocks, sober driver checkpoints, and anything else they could come up with that would allow local police units to intercept the truck and get the girl back, but somehow the driver magically detoured around everything they tried.

After the fifth near miss, an enraged Borysko had told his boss to investigate everyone in the traffic center, to see if they had any ties to organized crime or a criminal record, but nothing had come up. Regular updates to the background checks they were required to undergo when starting the position ensured that no one was working the other side of the street.

Then the unthinkable happened. The truck left the country. They weren't sure how, but it was possible that they paid off the border guard in advance who just waved them through. The truth was much simpler, though. He worked a predictable, regular shift. The slavers had made an effort to always send their truck through at the times when the same guard was on duty, and familiarity with the driver and what he was hauling had caused his attention to detail to wane. Had he figured out that all the previous trips the truck took through that international checkpoint were designed to put the guards at ease, he might have been more vigilant, but the 'special cargo' the truck had carried lately had only been on the last two trips, long after the guards were convinced that the nice older farmer delivering produce was on the up and up.

For the most part, he was, too. He owned a farm, and sold that produce at farmers markets in Georgia. No one really asked him why he would travel an extra three days to sell his product, but if they had, he would have told them they paid more in Georgia for his somewhat exotic cargo. Which was also true. It just so happened that he had an arrangement with a distant cousin to earn some extra money that his farming business desperately needed.

The rest of his team had turned back reluctantly at the border, wishing they could continue. Yevtukh understood their feelings. They would be quite far out of their jurisdiction. One or two vowed to come with, until he ordered them to return. The going was slower after that, but he got lucky a couple times. Once at a petrol station, where he told the clerk that the truck had backed into his car, and another time at a restaurant where the truck had delivered a small load of squash and green beans.

He knew that he had fallen much too far behind to just continue rushing onwards, so he had stopped just over the border, and called his supervisor. Several senior members of the special police force for fighting organized crime had convened a hurried ad-hoc meeting, with Borysko involved by cell phone. He had listened patiently while several people dredged up the latest intelligence information they had on movements of the kidnappers and slavers that had been seen, and the pattern and information they had so far matched one particular group, a Georgian crime group known for kidnapping young girls, and forcing them into prostitution. There were a few other possible places that they might go, but for the most part, almost all of the girls ended up in an illegal brothel in Tbilisi, the capital of Georgia. With a whispered prayer to God above, he continued on the trail, hoping it was the right one.

The trail had led him here. He wasn't sure how far behind his daughter's kidnappers he was, but was certain that it was no more than 24 hours. Seeing the police presence, his intuition told him that something might have happened here concerning his daughter.

Now he turned the Georgian inspector, and said, "My daughter was kidnapped four days ago in Sebastopol. I think she may have been brought here."

Gnezy couldn't keep the wince from his face. "Can you identify what she was wearing?"

"What do you mean?" Fear gripped him; fear, and something else only a father of a teenage daughter might recognize.

"We found some clothing a teenage girl must have been wearing, given its size and styling. There is no sign of the girl, however," he added hastily as the light in the Ukrainian's eyes suddenly blazed.

Borysko sighed. "Yes, I should be able to." He tried to keep his emotions in check, but the fear was winning.

The ripped and torn clothing in the evidence bags handed to him by the Georgian inspector was definitely what his daughter had been wearing four days ago when he'd seen her last. He looked up at Gnezy, and his worry and concern threatened to overwhelm him. "I am almost certain it is hers. You say she is not here? What happened? Why are all these police officers here?"

Gnezy paused, considering his next move carefully. Borysko Yevtukh was a father whose daughter had been in the crime scene at some point, this was true, but he was also one of the most respected law enforcement specialists in the entire region. If anyone could make sense of what had happened here, it might be the middle-aged Ukrainian in front of him.

That last thought drove his thinking, and he found himself speaking before he knew it. "Come with me. We have no idea what happened. I think that we may never really know. I must warn you, though; the scene is a house of horrors. I have never seen anything like this before. Never seen anything this… bad."

As Borysko looked at the other man, he saw revulsion in his eyes, and suddenly wondered if that greyish-green sheen had been there all along, or if it had shown up as the man spoke. He had no idea what to think about that, but nodded his head. His daughter, his beloved Svetlana, named for his own dear grandmother on his mother's side, had been here. Steel filled him as he knew he could endure anything to find her, and he had a career of seeing crime scenes and witnessing first-hand the horrors man could inflict on his fellow man behind him. That, and his complete professionalism and experience, would get him though what he was about to see – would get him through to find his little girl. He knew this as well as he knew his own name.

He was wrong. It was indescribable. The first room he was taken to, where his Svetlana's clothing had been found, was bad enough. The destroyed remains of what had once been a big, strong, young man lay strewn on the floor in front of the crude bed, and blood had sprayed everywhere. The most was on the floor under the... parts, but it was everywhere and on everything, even the ceiling. But the most horrific assault on his senses was the smell of blood, flesh, gore, and the contents of the dead man's intestines.

Borysko was pale and shaking as he backed out of the room, and a tiny, detached part of his mind was inanely happy about not stepping in anything... bad.

Gnezy looked at the other man, and waited for him to recover his composure. When Borysko looked up at him, he said, "You do not have to see the rest, if you wish. It is up to you."

Borysko shook his head. "I must know. I can get through this. I must, for..."

Gnezy merely nodded. He had two daughters, who would be a few years younger than the missing girl must be, based on the size of the clothing they had found and Borysko had identified.

He turned, and walked further down the long hallway. Borysko noticed the smashed-in doorway, and it made him wonder. Then he looked down at the floor, and for the first time, noticed the bloody footprints leading down the hall from the room.

They had obviously not been made by anyone wearing shoes, and his breath caught in his throat as he realized that whatever had torn apart the criminal in the other room must have made them.

He bent down and studied them, and was very surprised when he realized that they were very unusual. If it was a tiger or bear or some other predator, the print in front of him would not look this way. They were almost man-shaped, but there was a pattern to the blood left behind that made Borysko think of snake scales, or something similar. But the most shocking thing about the imprint was the gouge marks in the floor at the front of the print.

It was hard to notice in the subdued lighting of the environment, but once looked at in the proper angle, he could tell that they were there. The claws had to be razor sharp to dig into the hardwood floor like that, and there was blood left in the indentations. They were also laid out similar to the position of human toes, with the furthest-forward indentation on the inside, and the rest slanting out and back towards the outside of the foot.

He grimaced at the puzzle the bloody tracks represented, then stood, following the Georgian Senior Inspector further down the hallway to the smashed-open door. Gnezy paused, warning Borysko with his eyes that this was going to be bad, and he took a deep breath to steady himself. He immediately regretted it. The smell was unbelievably worse here. He held his breath as he stepped into the room and glanced around.

His professionalism warred with the contents of his stomach, each trying to assert itself as the pinnacle that demanded the most attention. For the moment, his professionalism was winning, but he knew that his guts would win if he stuck around too long. A brief glance around the room, and his eyes locked onto something that his mind could process. Tracks, identical to the strange ones in the hallway, led beyond the slaughter to another door that was hanging half off its hinges, exposing a stairway that also had bloody prints from the mystery being on it. The light in the stairwell to indicate that it led directly to the outdoors, and he glanced at Gnezy, who simply said, "We can take the other way around."

Borysko nodded, and stepped around the puddle of someone else's lunch that he only now just noticed on the floor outside the kitchen that was now a small pocket of hell.

He knew that he would not shed a tear for the animals that had kidnapped his daughter, and wondered secretly inside what had done this. Nothing came to mind.

Just as the Georgian officers before him, he had no idea what had turned the illegal business into a slaughter house, then left those impossible, bloody, clawed footprints everywhere and in the narrow back alley behind the building. Gnezy pointed out how the footprints ended, but the drops of blood continued for a few meters beyond, getting more spread out the further away from the end of the prints, and the evidence did not spur any great insights of his own.

"I can think of nothing and no one that be able to have done this. Certainly, nothing comes to mind. I can contact my department back in Ukraine to see if anyone else has heard about this, if you wish."

"I need to confer with my superiors before doing so, but I expect that this will not present a problem. I have no idea how to explain any of this, either. I suspect that we never will be able to do so with any success," Gnezy offered, and his sincerity came across clearly in the slowly alley darkening as the sun set in the west.

CHAPTER 19

Most police calls, even ones where a body was discovered, are somewhat similar, and yet there are elements that are completely different to each one. No murder was exactly the same. Whether the method of death, the scene, the surroundings, the amount of blood and gore; no two were the same in that regard. But there was always a body. Once in a while, there were some living people there, either those that lived at the location, family members or friends, or a possible perpetrator or perpetrators. But as always, the deceased would never be able to tell what had truly happened.

Officer Danielle Corrigan had been to several crime scenes involving a deceased victim over the nearly twelve years she had spent with the Chicago Police Department. It went with the territory in a metropolitan area with one of the highest per-capita murder rates in the country. Her partner, however, had graduated from the Chicago Police and Firefighter Academy barely three months ago.

Danielle was rather fond of her partner, in a strictly professional way. He was a great young man, a former Military Police enlisted man from the Air Force. By his own previous admission to her privately, he had never seen a dead body. She could see on his face as he drove up to the scene in the late afternoon sun that he was a little pale.

"You gonna be ok, Mike?"

He kinda smiled back at her. "I can get through it. No worries." She wasn't sure if she believed him, but that was ok. He would survive.

Danielle thought back over the call as they turned down the last street. Someone called in to report the sound of gunshots in a quiet part of town. A person, possibly male, was seen running away from the house afterwards. Whoever had called it in said they looked into the house, and saw blood and a body in the kitchen. But they didn't want to get involved, so they said they weren't going to wait for the police.

She pulled up and stopped, the emergency lights on the top of their patrol car dancing off the neighborhood houses and trees in the late summer midday sun, and they stepped out, making their way up the walk. On the off chance that whoever may have done this was still in the area, they both had their hands near their still-holstered side arms.

Clearing the house had been relatively straight forward, after confirming that the person was in fact dead. The officers came back to the kitchen, and called in an update to the dispatcher, who said the crime-scene technicians were on their way, along with a detective to start the investigation.

The deceased was laying on the tile floor next to the table just outside of the main portion of the kitchen, with a counter-top separating the appliances and sink from the rest of the area. The thirty-something Caucasian male was laying on his back, obviously dead with what appeared to be three gunshot wounds to the chest. His short hair, well groomed appearance, and dress shirt and slacks indicated someone who worked in a white-collar profession. There were no signs of struggle anywhere.

Danielle was looking around to see about the crime scene, when a slight movement caught her eye.

Standing quickly, her weapon just seemed to teleport to her hand, and she faced the form she saw standing in front of the stove, on the far side of the counter that bordered the cooking area of the kitchen.

"Don't move! Hands up! Come forward!" The commands came easy, and Officer Mike Dunphy stepped to the side to bracket the person while also keeping Danielle's field of fire clear. The figure's hands went up, but his face was not clearly visible in the darkened kitchen. Danielle had a sense of a male, probably the same age as the victim, and seemed to be dressed similarly.

"What happened?" The voice sounded muffled and confused, as if the person was standing behind a thick cloth or curtain.

"Sir, you need to step forward into the light. Do it now."

The figure looked at her, then stepped tentatively forward – passing through the counter on his way into the lighted area next to the body on the floor. And as he passed into the lighted area near the table, Danielle gasped as she got a good look at him.

The person that had just walked through the counter top and cabinets was a perfect match for the man on the floor, which made Danielle's mind start to skitter like a deer on an icy lake.

The figure looked down at the body on the floor, and a gasping sob came from him. He suddenly blurred slightly, and the officers both inhaled sharply as the figure became indistinct to the point that they could see through him.

"Oh no! Sandra! My children!" He fell to his knees next to his body, and sobbed uncontrollably.

Shock froze Danielle, but Mike somehow shook himself free of the paralysis they both found themselves under, and holstered his gun as he knelt on the floor next to the... man? Ghost?

"Sir, is that... are you... uhh..."

"Yes, that's me. I... I must be dead." The sound came out barely audible, in between sobs.

"Do you remember what happened?" Danielle almost laughed hysterically at her partner's question, but kept her wits under control.

The man started to speak, when they all heard footsteps coming down the short hallway from the front door.

Brad Dennisov had been a detective and investigator for several years in the Chicago PD, long enough to know that he should never believe he'd seen everything because that was when the next shocking thing would pop up and remind him of his insignificance in the grand scheme of things.

But when he turned the corner to the kitchen, he was initially confused. Why were these two uniformed officers letting a civilian contaminate the crime scene?

"What's going on here? Who is this man, and why..." He broke off when the man looked up with tears in his eyes, and shimmered, appearing to go somewhat insubstantial and see-through. Shock froze him in place at the impossible happening.

"Sir," the younger male officer spoke up, "It appears that this is the ghost of the man who was killed here tonight." The tone of his voice was somewhere between strangled by stress, and hysterical.

Brad looked over to the man kneeling next to the corpse, noting that other than the bloody gunshot wounds on the dead man's torso, the two were dead ringers for each other. Then he winced internally at the sick pun he had just unintentionally thought.

"Is that true, sir?" Brad's voice was calm and gentle, the voice of someone used to dealing with distraught relatives on the worst day of their lives – when they had just lost, or even, God forbid, witnessed the death of, a beloved family member or friend.

"Yes. I remember now. He shot me, and then he ran out the back door."

"Wait, let me try something." The senior female officer pulled out her smart phone, then held it up sideways. "Recording video. I want to see..." She trailed off as she did something on her phone, and nodded a few moments later. "We can record him and what he says."

"Good idea, officer." Brad turned back to the ghost. "Can you tell us what happened? Who did this?"

"Yes. It was my younger brother. He wanted money from me he claimed that I owed him. I have no idea what he was talking about. I don't owe him any money. I don't think my wife Sandra owes him anything, either. I make… crap. This is impossible." A hoarse sob came from him again. "I made good money. I have never been in debt; well, other than the mortgage, the cars, that sort of thing." He took a deep breath, and seemed to shimmer again, before disappearing completely for a few seconds. Then he came back, seemingly more substantial, as he took in a deep breath and held it before letting it go.

"Do you know why I am still here? Have you ever seen this happen before?" His pleading eyes bored into Brad.

"No, sir, I haven't. I am really glad you are, so we can solve who did this, and make it right." Brad took a breath in as the totally impossible situation slowly became a little more normal, whatever that was. "Can you tell us your name, and the name of the person that shot you?"

"My name is Henry Allen Tomlinson. My younger brother, James David Tomlinson, killed me. He had a gun. I can remember it better and better now."

All four of them gasped as the air shimmered in the middle of the room, and a smaller image of the room appeared to float in midair in the room. As everyone watched, the body on the floor of the image disappeared, and the scene was clear and the sound of Henry coming home to find his younger brother standing in the kitchen was crisp and clear, like watching it on television.

The officers watched as Henry stood to view the scene of his death with bitter eyes. Danielle had turned her smart phone to the new scene, and watched on the screen as it recorded the video and audio of the entire event, culminating with the three gunshots. Then James bent down and picked up his spent cartridges, hissing as the hot brass from the just-fired cartridges burned his fingers as he put them in the pocket of his light jacket. He then turned, and the scene zoomed into his face and paused, giving a completely clear, well-lit view of the man that had coldly just gunned down his brother, before the scene continued on as James turned and ran out the back door beyond the kitchen table. Then the scene disappeared.

Brad had tried to hide his astonishment as the murder was replayed for him. He turned to the female officer, and asked, "Did your phone record that? Can you check that it is in there?"

"It was on the screen, so I assume it was recorded. I will check. Gimme a second…"

A few minutes later, she looked up, and nodded. "It's all in there, in full 1080p High-Definition glory, especially the clear view of his face at the end. We got the bastard." She said it quietly, turning to the ghost of Henry at the last sentence. "Sorry."

"Don't be. He wasn't always, but things changed when he dropped out of college. I haven't even seen him in a number of years. I didn't know he was back in town."

It was silent in the house for a few minutes, until Officer Corrigan's radio broke in on their thoughts.

"The wife is out front with her kids. What do you want to do?"

Henry looked up suddenly, and hope clearly burned in his intense gaze as he spoke up. "Can I seen them? Please? I don't know how much longer I can stay here like this. Please?"

Danielle considered for a moment, then turned to Brad. "It's your call, but…"

The detective only had to think for a moment what he would have wanted. The situation was anything but normal, so…

"Let her in alone at first. She can go back out for the children once the situation is under control. Close the front window drapes first. I don't want anyone else to see what is happening in here. And let's keep her in the front of the house away from this. I don't want her to see him like this."

Henry managed to sob his thanks out, and stood waiting for what was to happen.

Danielle waved Officer Dunphy towards the front room, where he headed to close the room off, and turned to the ghost now standing a few steps closer to the front of the house.

A woman's voice was heard as the man's wife made her way into the house. "Hank? Why are all those police cars out front? Is everything ok? Henry?"

Henry moved into the front room as he went to his wife.

"Honey, stop there, please."

Sandra stopped as her husband stepped into the well-lit family room. Then her hand flew to her mouth as he seemed to become somewhat invisible and insubstantial for just a moment.

"What is going on!?!" Her voice held both equal parts panic and fear. "Why are all these police officers here? Are you ok? What happened to you just now?"

"Honey, my dearest love," tears started to flow down his face like rain now as emotion overwhelmed him, "Jim came here tonight, demanded that I pay him money of some kind, then shot me three times. I think I am dead." His voice broke as he stood there sobbing, but he couldn't look away from his wife's eyes.

Her gasp as she listened to what her husband said tore at the hearts of the three listening police officers. It wasn't the first time the detective and the senior patrol officer had worked a crime scene where a loved one had died. But from there, this situation obviously diverged, the rookie cop thought to himself. The woman, the wife of the victim, looked at the ghost of her husband in white-faced shock and anguish. Her hands flew to her face as everyone could see her world come completely apart in front of her eyes.

Henry reached out reflexively to comfort the woman who had become the center of his heart and soul nearly two decades before, but his insubstantial hands and arms passed through her, and his anguish was plain to see on his face as he sobbed out, "Oh God, help me! What do I do now?"

Almost as soon as his words were spoken, everything changed again.

* * *

The neighbors outside had gathered across the street, held there by the police tape strung across the yard and street that cordoned off the house. They had watched when the mother had driven up, and gotten out to talk to the officers guarding the perimeter of what was obviously a crime scene. Rumors of gunshots had spread amongst the waiting crowd of neighbors, and most waiting there were filled with dread of what would be known soon. This was a good family in a good neighborhood. Things like this didn't happen anywhere near here.

The wife had been allowed inside, while the kids stayed in the car, fear plain to see on everyone's face.

It was not more than a minute or two later that someone gasped and pointed across at the front picture window now shielded by curtains a police officer had drawn moments before.

As everyone watched, it seemed that a warm, white glow started to come from the inside of the house. And with that light, a feeling seemed to slowly reach out to them. A sense of peace, and calm, and stillness seemed to wash away their fears and concerns. A short time later, an officer near the waiting family car heard something on his radio, and opened the door to escort the scared young boy and girl to the house. As the front door opened to admit them, that glowing white light spilled out to illuminate the yard and the face of the officer who had just finished bringing the children up to the door. As the people watched, his face was transfixed by what he saw, and a warm, soft expression crossed his face. It was still there long after the door had closed and he turned back to the street.

CHAPTER 20

The ride to the home David shared with Allison had been an eye-opening experience for Giltreas, filled with strange and wondrous sights unlike anything else he had ever seen. From time to time, he had found himself glancing at David as he drive the carriage they rode in, in hopes of seeing... anything that might have shown Giltreas that David was as impressed and in awe of the things Giltreas was seeing for the first time, but it became apparent to him that David was a true child of this place, and the things that amazed Giltreas held no glamour for the human.

As the road stretched out in front of them, and time moved on, the pace itself that they held on their travel was, in itself, a wonder. Faster than the fleetest horse, it was still slower than some of the magical beasts he had encountered. But the carriage they rode in held to its pace so effortlessly, with simple movements by the hands and feet of the one driving it; that was a wonder in itself. At one point, some many leagues into their journey, David had pulled off the long stretch of road to stop for what he called 'gas'. Apparently it was some liquid that the carriage consumed to give it the strength to carry them onwards. A few some minutes outside of a strange building, and they were away again. If coin had changed hands to pay for the 'gas', Giltreas had no knowledge of such a transaction.

A short time later and further down the road, David had glanced at a blue sign as they verily flew past it on their way, and had spoken up.

"Are you getting hungry again? I am thinking of getting some food."

It had been a long afternoon, and the sun was beginning to ebb lower to the west, past the broken strands of trees and the occasional building that broke the sight to the horizon, and Giltreas had discovered that he was, indeed, open to sustenance.

"Yes, I could eat again."

"Ok, good. There is a McDonalds off the next exit. We can hit the drive-through, and get some burgers or something. Beef ok with you?"

"Certainly. I can contribute some small funds if you so desire."

"Nah, that's not necessary. As long as you are here on this world, you are my guest, and I will pay for whatever you need." The words had been quiet, but Giltreas heard the tone of voice clearly. "It is the least I can do, after what you have done for, well, all three of us."

"If you are of a mind to provide for me, then in the near, I shall accept. However, should things change, or should you wish it, I can provide for myself and for us. Simply ask, and I shall step forward."

* * *

David glanced at Giltreas, and smiled. It had become much clearer to him that Giltreas was an honorable being. As that thought echoed in his mind, he suddenly wondered if it was appropriate to refer to Giltreas as a man. Was that a human term, or was it race-neutral?

"Giltreas, I have a question. Do the different races, such as the elves and dwarves, use the terms Man and Woman for humans alone, or are they used by all for referring to adult males and females?"

Giltreas pondered the question briefly, and ascertained some of the thoughts behind it before responding. "Yes, all higher races refer to male and female adults as men and women. If they speak of such in their own race, then no appellation is necessary. However, elves will state human male or female, and such is true with other higher races."

"How many other higher races are there?"

"Humans you know of, and elves and dwarves as well. There are Halfling, Yeti, several races of Giants, Minotaur, Centaur, and several races of Demons, but those keep mainly to themselves. Demons are peaceful with other higher beings, but shun contact because other races find them difficult to tolerate. They rarely venture onto planes where the other higher races make their settlements, and then only to trade. I believe that they are as much uncomfortable with other beings not of their kind, as well, but I have never had the moment to ask.

"Minotaur and Centaur tend to stay by themselves, but will interact with other races. Giants tend to be intemperate, and make poor neighbors. The Gods keep peace between the races, as does the Throne of the Elves, but there can be problems from time to time between any of the races. Rarely do they end in war, but it has happened. Human tribes will sometimes ask for the throne to help solve conflicts and disputes, something that is unique to them. Most other races do not have issues dealing with their brothers and sisters of their kind, just others."

David was quiet and thoughtful for a while, considering what Giltreas said. Then he turned the carriage off the long road, or 'freeway', as he called it, and pulled up to another strange building.

'Drive through' was an interesting experience. A board behind the building held words and pictures describing the foods they had available, but none of it was familiar to Giltreas. He simply waved his hand gracefully to David, indicating that whatever David chose for them was acceptable. Words were exchanged between David and a voice that spoke from the tall board, and they pulled forward around the trail to the first of two small windows, where David handed the young girl inside a piece of paper covered in green and black designs. She handed him back some different pieces of paper, and some jingling coins, which he put into a bin in between the two front seats.

David pulled up to the second small window, and another young person handed him two cups with strange lids on them, and a small white bag that smelled interesting. David then moved the carriage to a part of the paved area behind the building, where they talked about restaurants, fast food, money, and other such topics while eating.

The food was interesting. A 'quarter pounder with cheese' sandwich, some 'French fries' in a paper holder, and a 'coke'. All words describing foods he had never encountered. It was, for the most part, good. The sandwich was hot, with onions, pickles, cheese, and sauces of some kind on it. The 'French fries' were hotter, and salty. The 'coke', on the other hand, was fascinating. It was sweet and yet had an almost bitter bite to it, and it was very cold. David said it was because it had ice cubes in it when asked. Giltreas also felt something in it that subtly raised his strength slightly, which worried him. The thing in it was similar to what was in the 'coffee', but was different somehow, possibly in the mixing. His Senses told him that there were tiny traces of different poisons in it, confirming the feelings it gave him. Not much, to be sure, but enough to explain the sweetness and the strength it fed him. It would not do to take in too much of it; one could become dependent on such things, and he knew he would never encounter it on any other plane, so dependence was a crutch he could ill afford.

Back on the road after their repast, the conversation ebbed and flowed as topics came and went, but for the most part, it was silent in the carriage, until David spoke up in a serious tone.

"We will need to get you some different clothing to wear, so you will fit in." Giltreas nodded. Everywhere he had looked here on this plane, the mode of dress was similar to what David and Allison wore.

"I also want to take you to the office, and get you familiar with a number of things; the layout, the stuff you will see, get you a security badge and how security works, and such. It is Saturday, so it will be mostly empty, except a few people on my team that monitor things on the weekends. By the time we get through shopping for you, it will be later, so the place will be mostly empty."

Giltreas nodded his approval, to David's obvious relief. He would not be able to assist David in the quest to run to ground the evil ones which had beset Michelle if everyone was instantly drawn to him because of his appearance.

A few hours of travel to a huge, sprawling town led them to a place of many stores, which David called a "shopping mall". Indeed, many people seemed to inhabit the place, with many small and some large stores everywhere, all brightly lit, some with music coming out of them. Giltreas was trying to process everything that had happened to him. As time stretched onwards, David quickly had them to a couple different stores for the clothing Giltreas would need. Trying on clothing was interesting. David chose the items, and Giltreas had gone into a little room where he had put them on. The first few items had been challenging, until he learned the general way that things worked. He was not above asking some questions, in his mother's tongue, through the seemingly flimsy door that shielded his modesty (not that he was bothered by such things) to get some specifics on this or that. After that, things had gone much quicker. David had told him not to use magic to alter the garments to fit, because if they didn't purchase an item he tried on, it would have been a problem to put it back with the label not matching the cut and fit of the garment.

The first store had provided a trove of clothing to wear – several pants, some of the "blue jeans" like David wore, and some others somewhat more formal, along with several shirts, under shirts, small things called boxers to wear under his outer clothing, along with stockings and a couple different pairs of shoes and one very fine pair of black leather boots.

The second store had been a much different place. A "business suit" was, as explained to him by David, worn for formal occasions. It was very different than anything he had ever seen before, but he had to admit that the look was fascinating. More shirts to accompany the suit, some items of fine silk with a somewhat strange name called neck ties, and new shoes and stockings completed the look. The image staring back at him in the huge mirrors reminded him of some of the richer merchants dressed in their finest who made their way to the Elvish City for an audience with the Queen from time to time, but this was much more refined, with minute seams and stitching, and tightly woven cloth so fine he was shocked at its richness. When he asked the helper in the store what manner of cloth it was, he was nearly stunned speechless that it was, indeed, wool. Certainly wool much finer than anything his mother's people had ever put forth.

Giltreas expressed concern to David at the cost of all this, but David merely shrugged and waved off the question with a quiet, "I can easily afford this. No big deal."

So Giltreas had acquiesced, becoming the owner of a lot of new clothing. And some footwear the likes of which he had never word nor even seen before; similar, however, to what David wore.

The bigger experience of the trip, however, had been the city they had driven into. It was huge, bigger than anything he had ever seen before. Even the massive Dwarven city deep under the mountain gave much to this place.

The road had gotten wider at one point, and there were many more carriages on it. Buildings some but a single level, some other much taller, became much more common along the way. At one point, they had passed a building with many carriages outside it parked in rows where many looked very similar except for the colors they were painted. David had explained that it was a store where people bought carriages; a 'car dealer' it was called.

There were still many trees to be seen, but in between the trees, were many buildings. Giltreas had the impression that he was seeing only a very small portion of the city around him, a thought confirmed when asked of David. All of which made him feel small, somehow.

They made good time, getting to the house that David shared with Allison, where he was shown to a guest room he was to stay in while he was here on this plane. He changed to some of the "casual" clothes David had procured for him, and also put on new shoes and socks. Once attired, he cast mend on the clothing to both clean it and tailor it to his form, making it all much more comfortable.

From there, a quick trip to a nearby store where a young woman with bright red nails cut and "styled" his hair for him, an interesting experience to be sure.

But it was the small journey into the heart of the city that evening that confirmed for Giltreas that these humans were wondrously capable.

As long as he had lived in his short life, he had never imaged buildings so incredibly tall and majestic. Shimmering in the setting sun, sheathed entirely in glass, they stretched upwards for a long ways. Even the building they went into was immense by any standard Giltreas could think of. David drove the carriage alongside of the building and down a sloping area behind a low wall. He stopped at a black box that was attached to a stand that sprouted up from the gray stone alongside the paved carriage way. He held something up to the small box, then touched some of the raised things that studded the front. Each one he pressed in caused a beep, and the door at the bottom of the way folded aside. David set the carriage in motion again, and they drove through the door, turning to the left to avoid running into a solid-looking stone wall. Giltreas looked behind them as the carriage cleared the threshold, to see what manner of men had moved the door, and were pulling it closed upon their passing, but could see nothing.

The parking area stretched to what Giltreas estimated was the far end of the building itself. There were but a few carriages there at the moment, of all different colors and shapes. David found a spot close to a glass door, pulled in, and shut off the vehicle. He seemed to think for a moment, as if considering what to say next. He seemed to have some trepidation on what he wanted to do, possibly worried about what Giltreas would say. He smiled.

"You must speak your mind. If subterfuge is necessary, I am not offended by such."

David smiled slightly as he turned to look at Giltreas. "I would like to introduce you as Gil Owens. Your name alone would make you stick out, along with your appearance." Giltreas nodded once in response.

"I am comfortable with this. Gil Owens it is. We mustn't alert the prey we seek before he is truly in our jaws." Giltreas smiled broader. "Would not be the first time such a path was undertaken. I shall think of myself as Gil Owens from henceforth, to make the ruse more natural."

"Well, Gil, let's get going. I have the perfect role for you as a cover for what we will be accomplishing," David said.

'Gil' merely cocked his head in question.

David shrugged. "I am a United States Marine. Well, not on active duty anymore. It is a branch of the military, somewhat similar to the Guardsmen of your home city. Every so often, I bring in men or women who used to serve in the military to our company, and put them through a couple years of training in Information Technology. It doesn't matter if they have any experience or not, I pay for the training and their salary while they are learning. If they chose to leave the company, they are welcome to. I get the satisfaction of getting them into a well-paying career. If they chose to stay, we find a place for them. It is my way of supporting my fellow veterans. Some of them have had some pretty significant injuries, and worry about finding work and building a career because of it. For the most part, they don't have any problems with finding a job after they are done here. With two years of experience and a host of training and the certifications that come with it, along with their military service and experience, they are highly sought after employees. By us, especially. It also gives me an extremely loyal team I can depend on."

Giltreas was impressed. "And you will pass me off to them in that capacity?"

David hesitated. "Not exactly. Let me explain." He thought for a moment, and then seemed to come to a decision.

"The people on that team, my team, will know that you are not a past member of our military. If I present you as having served in the military, they will want to ask a lot of questions, and when you are unable to answer them, they will see through any attempt to hide things from them. So I will have to bring them in on what is going on. At least a little. They are all very loyal to me and to Michelle, but still, I am not sure how much I want to tell them. Which could also be a problem. Trust cuts both ways. In order for me to have their trust, I have to be worthy of it. Hiding things from them would undermine that. Since new people on my team do not really interact with anyone else while they are still training, it won't be an issue with anyone else."

"I can see that. There is only one solution, my friend. Tell them everything, and ask them not to tell anyone outside of your... team. If necessary, I can prove anything you wish of me to establish the situation as needed."

David thought about it for a few brief moments, then nodded. "I will call a meeting with them Monday to discuss what is going on." He seemed to be settled on that issue, then.

"Ok, Gil. Let's go get you into the program."

* * *

It was some time after David and Giltreas had left them that Michelle and Allison heard a polite cough outside the door to the suite the queen had set aside for them. Max barked once, but Sadie just sniffed, then said, "Queen person." She did wag her tail, though. Abby and Max walked over to the doorway and wagged their stubby little tails, waiting impatiently as Allison walked over to the door and opened it.

Delara stood there, politely waiting for an invitation to enter, which was quickly given in the form of a waved hand and a slight head bow.

The elfin woman bent down and petted Abby and Max, who had both come to the door to greet the visitor. Sadie stood, stretched, and walked over with a happy wag of her tail to get her due attention.

"I am most impressed with your animal companions," she said.

"In what way?" Michelle spoke up from where she had just stood up in front of the comfortable couch against the wall just inside the door of the suite.

"They are calm around those they have not met," she responded, bending down to pat Sadie on the head. "That is unusual for dogs around the city. They also showed much restraint in the throne room." Sadie sat next to where Delara stood, and pressed her shoulder into the queen's leg as she gazed up and wagged her tail.

"Pet me more, nice Queen person? I like you." Delara chuckled and petted Sadie down over the top of her head and down to her shoulders as Sadie just continued to wag at her.

"They have had quite a bit of training to be socialized like that. They have a long way to go, if we really wanted to take them that far, but for the most part, they are good dogs," Allison said with quiet satisfaction in her voice. Dog training was something she really enjoyed. She had taken Sadie and then Abby through training for Michelle, and had been working with her own dog Max for over a year.

Delara smiled in surprise. "I hadn't realized that one could train dogs to that extent. For the most part, they are viewed as scavengers that live near the higher races and feed off their leavings. Some farmers and others seem to have taken them as pets, though," she frowned as she thought about it, and both Michelle and Allison nodded as the light seemed to come on in Delara's mind.

"Humans where we are from have built bonds with dogs for centuries. We have formed mutually beneficial partnerships with them for at least five thousand years, if the archeological records are accurate. I wouldn't be surprised if it went back much longer than that." Allison said.

"Interesting. What do humans use dogs for?" Delara seemed fascinated by the subject, then laughed as she sat down on one of the comfortable couches that adorned the outer room in the suite that she had provided for them, only to have Abby jump up and climb into her lap.

Michelle started to rise from the couch across from where Delara was sitting, consternation clearly across her face. "Abby! Get down! I'm so sorry. She is normally not that bad."

Delara waved her off, petting the little dog gently as Abby looked up at her and wagged the stub of her tail happily at the attention. "She is a comforting little companion. I am not dismayed."

She laughed again as Max tried to climb into her lap, and even Sadie got into the act as she wandered over to the queen, tail wagging. "Pet me too!"

"Would that I have one more hand, sweet companion!" Sadie simply stood next to her, and dropped her head onto Delara's knee, wagging her tail as she gazed up at her 'new best friend'.

Allison smiled, shaking her head. "If you never want to be alone, get a dog. Sheesh!"

Delara laughed. "We do not have such familiar companions here. My seneschal was against allowing your companions into the throne room, but I could not insult Giltreas' companions by refusing them entry. I was pleasantly surprised that they did not soil the floor. Then they did not bark and carry on, even when those foul men were brought in." She shook her head and frowned as the topic took a darker turn.

"I do not understand what motivates humans sometimes. To be paid to visit such despicable injury upon one such as you, Michelle, goes counter to everything I try to teach all those whom I serve as queen. Clearly, there is a dearth of compassionate service to educate those who would think in such ways where you are from. Why would the Gods not work to prevent such atrocities from taking root in the minds and hearts of others?" Delara was clearly troubled at the thought that the humans Michelle and David and Allison lived with were capable of such things, and even more so that the Gods allowed humans to get to the point that they would be capable of such things.

Michelle thought about it a while. The statements that Delara just made clearly brought up many questions, and answered almost none. It was readily apparent to her that Delara, and these Gods she spoke of, were doing things for mortals here and elsewhere that they were clearly not doing for the humans of Michelle's world.

She ventured a question. "Gods are supposed to take an active role in the lives of mortals? We have not seen any evidence of that happening except for a single one that was supposed to have lived among us some two thousand years ago."

Delara was shocked. "I could not imagine a plane without the direct influence of the Gods on the lives of those that live there. Two thousand full seasons?" Her eyes were wide at the impossible statement. Then her breath caught in her throat, and she gasped, stunned at the thought that suddenly occurred to her. Her eyes were impossibly wide as she looked from Michelle to Allison, and then back to Michelle.

Allison suddenly leaned forward where she was seated on the comfortable couch next to Michelle, her eyes intent. "What is it? What?"

Delara's eyes focused on Allison, and she found herself struggling to breathe for a moment. Then she shook herself.

"There have been myths and legends about a plane of Godless humans, who were so lost that the Gods abandoned them to their own means." Delara's hushed tone was barely audible in the still, silent room. "An uprising of evil swept away all those that served the Gods, and a great tower was built by humans to show their might in the face of the Gods, who wanted nothing more than to guide them and help them grow along the Great Path. It is said that they turned away from magic in all its forms even as they turned away from the Gods and their benevolent guidance. It is told that the Gods then set up a wall to prevent magic from being used. That wall also prevented anyone from using magic to open a gate to that plane. Without the Elvish crown to mediate and without the Gods to prevent such destruction, the humans there engaged in wars that destroyed all life."

A heavy silence fell on the room as the weight of the queen's statement swept over Allison and Michelle.

Delara suddenly stood to pace as she thought deeply about what had happened. Deep in thought, she didn't notice when Max suddenly started following her around the room. Each time she stopped, her left hand crossed over to rest in her elbow as her right hand cupped her downturned face, he stopped, sitting a few feet behind her and looking up as if he was waiting for something from her. When she walked forward again, he followed behind her, continuously looking up at her as if she had food or his favorite toy.

She turned suddenly in mid stride to say something to Michelle and Allison, and was startled to see Max suddenly sit right in front of her, and stare up at her. She was so shocked that she forgot what she was about to say.

Allison had watched Max intently as he followed the elvish queen, not worried that he would harm her, or she would harm him – he was quite agile and athletic, and could get out of the way in a hurry if need be. She was more interested in what he was doing, because his behavior was somewhat unusual. He almost never followed anyone around like that, not that she could remember.

Delara stared down in surprise at the little dog, and suddenly smiled as he wagged his stubby little tail at her from a seated position. To Allison and Michelle, it was clearly a case of him offering behaviors to see what would get him what he wanted from the person in front of him, but Delara had never seen anything like it before, and was charmed by it.

Bending down, she petted the little dog, and he came out of his sitting position boisterously, standing up on his hind feet and putting his forepaws on her now-horizontal thigh as he stretched up to lick her face and wag fiercely at her. Delara laughed, and murmured something to herself, smiling suddenly up at the two human women.

Allison cleared her throat, and spoke up. "Is everything ok? Is he bothering you?" She leaned forward on the couch, clearly intending to come to her aid if Max's affection was not well received, but she just laughed again.

"He is a most wonderful little spirit. How large will he get when he has stopped growing?" Her hands petted the little black dog as he reveled in the attention.

Allison smiled, and sat back. To her, people should establish their own relationship with companion animals, and she wouldn't interfere unless they were uncomfortable, or if the animal, be it a cat, dog, horse, or anything else, looked unhappy, uncomfortable, or if they looked like they were bothering the person. Since the elvish queen seemed to be enjoying the attention, she decided to wait and see what happened next.

She didn't have long to wait, as Sadie stood, stretched, wagged her tail, and trotted over to bump her head into the queen's shoulder from one side, as little Abby, all 16 pounds of her, also got into the act, worming her way in between Max and his new best friend, and all but climbed into her arms.

"Yes, Little One, I shall give you some attention as well. She is even smaller. Will she be as big as Max when they are finished growing?"

Allison smiled. "Actually, they have both stopped growing. They are as large as they will be, unless we stop taking good care of them and they get fat. Max is almost four years old, but Abby is almost ten years old. Sadie is the oldest of the three, she is just over eleven years old." Sadie turned and wagged at Allison as she heard her name, but then turned back to Delara, and from her they heard, "Sadie need love too. Pet Sadie?"

Michelle grunted out a laugh. "Sadie, you are so shameless."

Sadie turned to her human, and said, "What is shameless? Is Sadie bad?" Her tail stopped wagging briefly, and she dipped her head slightly, clearly thinking that she had upset her person.

"Never mind, Sadie. You're a great dog. Good girl." Michelle's voice conveyed some slight regret at possibly causing her beautiful red-gold faithful companion some discomfort.

Michelle turned to see Delara stand up with Max and Abby in each arm, and she crossed to the couch next to Allison and sat down with both dogs in her lap. Sadie followed, and "Sadie up too?" was heard.

"Yes, good Sadie. Come up." She patted the couch next to her, and Sadie clamored up onto the tough fabric, lying down in her side with the top of her head pressing against the outside of Delara's thigh.

"I was thinking that you must come from the Plane of the Godless, but if that was so, then you would be evil. We have always been taught that the Godless must be so, but I do not believe that evil, godless ones could have such wonderful companions as these. I am disturbed by what I have been taught seemingly at odds to what I observe. May I ask someone to join us so that I might learn more about this?"

"Of course. I am curious as to what is going on here as well." Michelle waved a hand in invitation to her, and Delara closed her eyes. When she opened them again, she spoke quietly, but the sound of her voice seemed to resonate around the room in a strange way.

"Anaradelle, I humbly call you to ask a question. Will you come to me now?"

Silence swept over the room as they waited, then a voice that seemed to be filled with the sound water flowing in a gentle creek answered out of thin air. "Of course, your Majesty."

The air seemed to shimmer in front of them in an open area of the room, and suddenly a being stood there in front of them. The woman in front of them seemed to be clothed in a pure white robe, with white skin and hair, delicate features. Her eyes were as blue as the summer sky at noon, but there was a depth in them that said the being in front of them was old in a way that words could not convey. Allison suddenly felt very small, as if she stood on the edge of a vast canyon that dwarfed them into insignificance.

Anaradelle inclined her head in greeting to the elvish woman in front of her, and her smile grew very wide as she took in the three dogs all vying for attention in or very near her lap. But then her eyes swept over the two human women in the room, and her breath seemed to catch in her throat.

She turned back to Delara, and asked in that same gentle voice, "Who are your friends? I do not believe I have met them before. Their souls are unfamiliar to me."

Michelle and Allison kept quiet at the astonishing being in front of them. To them, it seemed as if they were smaller and less real in her incredible presence.

Delara spoke up. "This is Allison, and that is Michelle. I believe them to be of the Plane of the Godless Ones."

Anaradelle's hand flew to her suddenly wide-open mouth, and her eyes were huge as she took an involuntary step back. "The Plane of the Godless Ones? Truly?" The sounds was barely a whisper. Then she seemed to shake herself.

Warily, she looked them over much more carefully, and a slight flash of light seemed to come from her. To Allison, it was as if someone had taken a photo with a flash, but to Michelle, it was as if she and Allison had suddenly been covered in many different colors of light, then it abruptly vanished as quickly as it had appeared.

"What was that? What did you do to us?" Michelle spoke up firmly, leaning forward in her sitting position as if preparing to stand.

Anaradelle seemed to relax after the light had faded. "My apologies to you, Michelle, and you, Allison. But I needed to know if I was in harm's way. I am clearly not, but I can understand if you were surprised. I meant no offense."

Michelle seemed to be mollified at the moment, and sat back with her arms crossed in a closed position that indicated she felt a need to guard herself. Allison looked over and noted the change in body language of her sister-in-law, and her closest confidant and friend, and realized something had happened that she missed completely.

"What happened? What did you see?"

"Anaradelle here cast some kind of spell that made us both light up like a Christmas tree for a moment. I have no idea what she did, but it seemed a bit impolite to do something like that without asking." The look she gave to the newcomer in the room, regardless of how she came to be there, or the unusual presence she seemed to have, said she was not happy with the woman in white.

Delara spoke up. "It is not wise to take umbrage with a Goddess." The look she favored on Michelle was not happy.

Allison's eyes got very wide and her mouth fell open at the word Goddess, but no one seemed to notice.

Anaradelle lifted her hand in a placating gesture towards Michelle, while looking gently on Delara.

"She is right, my child. It was improper to do what I did." Nodding her head towards Michelle and Allison, her face was more serious. "I beg your favor. One must never offer insult to those who do not court it upon themselves."

Michelle lowered her head slightly and nodded, still watching the strange woman in their midst. Allison simply shrugged and said, "Ok by me. No harm, no foul," which caused Anaradelle to look at her with mirth in her timeless eyes.

"Oh, what a wonderful saying," the glowing goddess said, laughing lightly. "I must remember that. 'No harm, no foul,' indeed."

Michelle laughed as she gave Allison a quick look. Even Delara smiled widely.

Anaradelle looked back to Michelle, and her eyes narrowed. "I sense no taint of evil, nor evil intent, that clings to either of you, but with you, there is something that seems... I know not what." She seemed to pause as if considering what she was experiencing. Then her eyes lit up in shock and surprise, and she turned to Delara.

"I must take leave of you all now, Your Majesty," she said simply, then just vanished without a sound.

CHAPTER 21

David's plan for Giltreas came apart pretty much before he could even put it into motion.

After walking over to the end of the area where David parked his carriage, he had pushed a small shiny bump mounted on the wall in a metal plate, next to the word 'up'. The bump lit up, and a few minutes later, one of the recessed metal walls on either side of the small metal plate slid open to reveal a small room with metal walls somehow painted to look like wood. A metal handle at about waist height was attached around the back and side walls, offering a place to hold on to. David waved Gil (as he now was thinking of himself) into the elevator, and pushed another raised bump, the upper most of three, next to the number 2. The doors closed after a few moments, and as Gil wondered what would happen next, the entire little room started to lift. He looked up in surprise as he felt the motion for a few minutes, but David seemed lost in his own thoughts. A soft, pleasant tone sounded, the motion stopped, and the doors opened. David walked out a small ways, followed by Gil, then stopped, mouth opened for a moment as the sounds of several people cheering came to them both. He then closed his mouth, shook his head, and walked forward. Gil heard him mutter what sounded like, "Great; this will be fun."

Gil frowned slightly at the tone of David's voice, and then he glanced where the other man was looking. The huge room was bordered on two adjoining sides with many windows that stretched upwards to the ceiling, where a circular window showed the darkening sky. Two upper floors were in evidence across the remaining two sides of the room, with walls and doors set into them, back away from the glass half-wall that followed the forward edge of the upper floors. A wall of glass ran from one side of the room to the other, with a desk in the center, and two unusual-looking doors of some kind on either side, the left of which seemed to be opened at the moment. Behind the desk was a man in what appeared to be a uniform. But that was not where David's gaze was fixed.

A huge rock wall dominated the left side of the equally huge room they were in, just inside the glass wall by the desk. The irregular, natural-looking surface stretched up to near the ceiling, which was quite high up above them indeed. The wall itself was reds and oranges and yellows, and had dark grey, brown, and black things stuck to it in locations that seemed to indicate hand and footholds.

Three dark blue ropes stretched from atop the wall where they seemed to be connected to round white things mounted to the beams in the ceiling. They stretched down the wall itself, where they were attached to three men on the wall. Two were at the top looking over the edge, and the other was half way up. Gil was shocked to see that the one still climbing up seemed to be missing most of both of his legs.

As Gil watched in amazement, the legless man climbed up using his arms alone, a feat of strength that made him nod his head in acknowledgement the man's determination and fortitude. He was half way up the center of the wall, with the positions on either side taken up by the two men standing at the top of the wall cheering their companion on.

David, followed by Gil, walked forward while watching the man still ascending. With each pull of the man's heavily muscled arms, he lifted himself using nothing more than brute force, holding himself with one hand while the other reached up for the next hand hold. His pace was not quick, but his movements were deliberate, and seemed carefully planned out. As he reached the top, the two humans at the top let out a huge "OOH RAH, MARINE!" Their hands rose above them in victory as their voices boomed across the room. The last climber pulled himself over and onto the ledge, turning to sit on the edge as he basked in the cheers and clapping that filled the huge room with clamor. Gil was incredibly impressed as he realized that the man had done his feat without the aid of any magic whatsoever.

Gil turned to look at David, only to see his companion and Michelle's brother clapping and hollering as loud as the rest of the people gathered round the wall as he walked forward towards the group of men and women, a sense of pride and awe across his face.

The two humans on either side clapped the last climber on the back hard enough to push him over the ledge, and he held on to the strap that lowered him back to the ground with one hand as the other showed his middle finger back up at the top two people who had just pushed him off. They laughed, then as the saw their friend was lowering himself hand over hand down the wall ok, first one then the other turned their backs to the wall, crouched into a sitting position, and pushed off backwards, coming down to the floor just after the first one had landed. He then pulled himself back into a chair that had wheels on it.

David walked forward to where the man sat in his chair, a huge smile on his face. The other people gathered around him helped remove first the strap that had lowered him back down, which was quickly attached to a point on the wall, then the safety harness that was wrapped around his lower torso and the stumps of his legs, which were missing below the middle of his thighs.

As Gil approached, he realized that he had rarely seen such massive upper-body muscles outside of a smithy. The short-sleeved shirt he wore proudly proclaimed "Property of the USMC."

He didn't see David approach until he heard a voice saying, "Well, now I have seen it all. Good job, Nate. That was incredible."

The smile on Nate's dark-skinned face seemed to freeze for a moment, and he turned to look up at David, only to see David's outstretched hand. He reached out and shook hands with David, and then the smile grew more natural once again.

"I told you I would do it eventually. Not going to let something like a little wall stop me after all that," Nate said, his voice deep and rich.

"Yeah, I know. I knew you were stubborn enough to do it eventually. I'm just glad I was here to see it."

A shouted "GO!" interrupted them, and David looked around to see three more people starting to climb the wall. This time, it was two women and a man, and the man was not in the lead. Nate turned the chair to watch, and laughed.

The woman in the center seemed almost to be a spider as she rapidly ascended the wall. The other woman, on her right side, was only a little behind. The man, however, was only half way up as the other two made it over the top.

"Woo hood!! Air Force whoops Army again!" the first woman to the top let out, and everyone laughed, including the man on the wall, which caused him to lose his grip and head back to the floor as more laugher crashed over everyone. The women jumped off, descending to the ground, and the one that had climbed the center of the wall removed her safety line, handed it to the next person, and hugged the man who didn't make it to the top. He returned the hug, picking her up and swinging her around as she shrieked in laughter.

David looked around, seeming to count how many people were at the wall, and he shrugged. "Well, I see everyone is here. What is this, a climbing party?"

Another man stepped over to David, and spoke up. "We were all at Mark's house to watch the Vikings game, and Nate said he could climb it. We decided that there was no time like the present, and we all came down after the Vikings lost. Again."

"Well, does anyone have any place they need to be?" David looked around, and saw that the serious tone to his voice had everyone on the floor's attention. No one seemed eager to leave, so he nodded. "Team meeting in 15 minutes in the third floor tech training room. We have some stuff to talk about, and I need to introduce everyone to a new team member."

The looks Gil got from his place at the front of the room as everyone filed in were curious, but he was relieved to see that they were not openly hostile. The room was interesting. There were steps up both sides of the room to four different levels, each with seats for six people, and a narrow table that stretched completely across to each aisle in front of the rows of seats. A white cloth was suspended from the ceiling against the front wall in front a white glossy panel that stretched from one side of the wall to the other, and started at waist height to extend up above his head. A low table and chair next to one side of the screen. It was, Gil decided, a very well built room for teaching. He wondered how much his old mage trainer would have appreciated it.

The last one in shut the door, and David waited until the stragglers had found their seats. Nate had parked his wheeled chair next to one of the tables on the lowest level. Gil called up his Physicker sight, and was aghast at what he saw in the bodies of the people in the room.

Old injuries that had not been properly attended to were liberally scattered across nearly every physical form in front of him, including the two women who had climbed the wall. One person was missing an eye. One was missing some of his manhood and parts of his guts.

Nate's injuries were the worst, however. The forces that had wreaked such havoc on him had left their mark, but had not dimmed his spirit in any way, as evidenced by his triumph over the wall a short time ago. Still, Gil winced inside as his sight showed him the extent of the man's injuries. Part of an ear was missing, and the eye on that side, while clearly still his own, could not see. Two fingers on that same side's hand were gone. There was what appeared to be metal bits and pieces embedded in his lower back, and his spine was severed in two places in his lower back. Gil was shocked that the man was smiling at all, let alone climbing a wall like he had just witnessed. The pain he appeared to be in just sitting there in his chair would have overwhelmed many a lesser being. Gil was about to stand and respond to what his sight showed him, when David walked to the door and closed the blind on the window next to it, then spoke up.

"Ok, we have an issue. Someone made a run at Michelle last night." The place went deadly silent at the statement, and a low murmur started up. David held up his hand, and instantly, silence reigned once again. Everyone in that room deeply respected and appreciated Michelle, as it was hers and David's company that was giving them so much, in terms of training, skills, experience, and a career. To everyone in that room, including David, someone making a run at her was the same as if they had made a run at all of them, and they were all combat veterans. It bonded them together closer than family, and they gladly included Michelle in that, though she had never served. David always wondered if it was because of how she had overcome all her own personal challenges in the injuries she had faced, a state familiar to them all in the friends, family, and fellow members of the teams of which they had been part.

"Gil here intervened. She is safe and unharmed. Gil has offered to help find out who was involved, and help deal with them. I need Gil to look like he is a member of the team, even though he has never served in any branch of our military. I don't know much about where he is from, but I have been there, and I am convinced that he is trustworthy." A hand shot up, and several more as several people in the room looked at Gil, then back to David. Some continued to stare at Gil, however, as if trying to see what secrets he might be hiding.

"Yes, Phil."

Phil spoke up, clearly not happy with what he was hearing. "Are you sure Gil is not involved?"

"Yes, I am sure. Gil took care of the four men who were. It's complicated."

Phil spoke up again. "What do you mean, 'it's complicated'? Who is he? Where did he come from? How did he take care of four men?" The questions came quickly, and some nodded in agreement at the questions being asked.

David glanced at Gil, a look that was not necessarily worried, but it showed Gil that David was getting in over his head. He leaned forward slightly and started to open his mouth in an offer to speak up, but David simply shook his head and looked back at the men and women in front of him.

"Gil is not from anyplace nearby. He has some rather impressive skills that I have never seen before," David said, and Phil spoke up again.

"You're telling me he took out, what, four men by himself, last night? What kind of skills? What are you hiding? What aren't you telling us?" Phil had been an investigator in the Army, and it showed as he focused in right away on the fact that David was being a little indirect in his statements. His eyes leveled back on Giltreas, and the look was not favorable. "How did you do it? What never-before seen skills helped you do all this?"

David simply looked over at Gil, and Gil stood up. He strode to the front of the room, crossed his arms, and spoke just loudly enough to be heard by everyone. "Magic."

Disbelieving laughter came back to him from most of the occupants of the room as it became apparent that his statement was not well received.

Gil smiled internally, wondering if he had some of the bard's showman in him. Probably, he decided.

Phil didn't laugh or show much of a response. He merely looked over the person standing at the head of the training room carefully. He was dressed in a pair of normal shoes, jeans, and a shirt, all clothing that would fit in anywhere. His hair was cut very short, and other than the greyish color of his skin and hair, he appeared to be very non-descript. He held up his hand to the people around and behind him, asking for silence.

"Prove it." The two words echoed into the silence.

Gil looked over at David, who simply shrugged a nod back at him. Then he looked back at Phil. "Are you prepared for the consequences of your words?"

Phil just sat back and waved a hand at Gil. "I trust Dave. I don't know you. What magic could you do that would impress me? What could anyone do? Magic is nothing more than sleight of hand. Parlor tricks to confuse kids and the gullible. Don't get me wrong; I am as impressed as anyone when they pull off a particularly well-executed trick. But I have never seen anything miraculous in it. And certainly nothing that would help someone take care of four adult men."

"Very well." Gil waved his hand, and suddenly it was totally quiet in the training room, except for the sounds of the huge winged grey/black wolf that Gil changed into, as it looked back at Phil, then around the room at the other suddenly frozen men and women in the room. The wolf walked over in front of Nate, then shook itself and sat down, cocking its head as if to see how the man would respond. Nate swallowed as the huge form stared him straight in the eye for just a moment. Then it stood, and Gil was standing there once again. He held out his hand to Nate, who stared at it as if it were a snake. Then he blinked, and took the proffered hand. And just like that, his whole world changed.

David saw the four colored flashes of light, and suddenly, Nate was completely, utterly whole again. Every injury and amputation was erased, as if it had never happened. Giltreas held onto the hand of the now-restored human as Nate's eyes became impossibly wide, and his dark-skinned complexion paled.

Then, suddenly, into the silence, Nate felt himself pulled upright out of the chair, and he nearly fell as he realized he was standing on his own two bare feet. He looked down, still desperately holding the hand that had pulled him up, and nearly choked out a laugh as he saw the pants he was wearing, carefully cut to cover up the disfigured stumps his legs had once been, barely extended to just above his knees.

He looked back at Gil with incredulous eyes that suddenly started to fill with tears. As he started to sob and his knees threatened to give out under the emotional weight they were abruptly not strong enough to carry, Gil wrapped his arms around the larger man, and hugged him tight. Nate simply returned the hug, and wept on Gil's shoulder.

The rest of the room was as silent as a funeral where the deceased had suddenly sat up in his coffin and asked for a beer. And none of those eyes were dry as they witnessed the restoration of the strongest, the most wounded, and the most deserving of them all.

Then Gil released the man, who stood somewhat unsteadily, unsure of what to do next, still staring at his feet through eyes filled with tears.

Phil felt the pillars of his life suddenly washed away by a tsunami of emotions. He was a man of science, of logic, of the physical world. While not an atheist, he was the next best thing; someone who believed that if there was a god, that being didn't care about this world or anyone in it. He had been looking at 'Gil Owens' when the shape change had happened, and he held his breath as the most impossibly huge wolf he had ever seen appeared where Gil had been the moment before. Stranger still, the massive form had huge, furry wings that seemed not out of place one bit. Then the wolf was gone, and if that had been all, he was prepared to believe in the man's claim of "magic". But it wasn't all.

He had acted as the team's counsellor, big brother, father figure, and shoulder to cry on since he had come to Michelle and Dave's company several years before. His US Army training in criminal investigation had made data security an excellent career for him, and he had applied himself with the same intense focus that had aided him so well in his military career.

All of his experience and training had allowed him to focus on what mattered, and eliminate what didn't. That made him a creature entirely of the physical world – what he could see, feel, and evaluate. Every event, every bit of the physical world around him, every action; all of it could be identified, classified, ordered, and processed. Everything had rules that had to be followed. Gravity produced a measurable effect. Bullets did specific damage. Bombs wreaked havoc on the human form; the more damage, the less chance of complete recovery and the greater chance of permanent marks and scars left behind to tell the story of where the person had been and what had been done to him.

But what he had just witnessed defied logic. It defied classification. It defied the brain's ability to be processed and put neatly into the context of past experience and training. Legs simply did not instantly reappear completely whole some years after being destroyed by a roadside improvised explosive device. The ability to walk did not simply come back as if it had never left, not after shrapnel had severed the spinal cord in the back in two places.

Phil felt himself begin to shake as his mind rebelled against what he had just seen. The blood drained from his face, and his eyes tried to cross as his vision tunneled and the colors of the room around him washed away to grey, then black and white. He closed his eyes and pulled in a huge breath, letting it out slowly, then did it again. And again.

Nearly seven deep breaths later, he felt himself coming back from the brink of passing out, and slowly opened his eyes. He was looking down at his hands as they gripped the front edge of the narrow table in front of the seat he was occupying, and noticed that his knuckles were white. That led him to realize that he was gripping the table so hard that his fingers, hands, and arms all throbbed from the effort. He struggled to loosen his grip and disengage his hands from the desk, all the while the sound of someone laboring to breathe rasped in his ears. He swallowed, and the breathing sound stopped momentarily, but it returned a moment later when he took a breath, and he shook his head, trying to clear it.

His left hand suddenly released its death lock, and he tried to pry the fingers of his right hand off of the desk before it, too, suddenly let go. He fell against the chair back and sat there nearly hyperventilating, staring at his hands as the color slowly returned to them, his mind blank and occupied with only his hands. Then the memory of what just happened came back to him, and the hands clenched into fists.

David looked over the shocked people in the room, and every one of them was struggling with what had happened. He looked back at the most incredible person he had ever known. Staff Sergeant Nathan James Beloit, USMC, Retired, had always had a certain serene composure about him that others were always amazed by once they got to know him. The being inside the body that had been in the fire and brimstone of war had moved beyond the hurt and pain, the paralysis, and the amputations, to see that life was still worth living, that challenges were still there to overcome (like the rock climbing wall earlier) and that there was a lot of life left to live, and not just to exist in.

But now, that serenity was gone, and it was replaced by something else: the look of a child that had just been given everything he had ever asked Santa Claus for, for every year, all at the same time. The amazed smile looked out of place with the tears streaming down his face. Or, maybe it didn't. It was ok with David either way.

He looked back at Gil, and the grey man's smile was tinged with a bit of sadness. David thought it through, trying to figure out why Gil was sad, and something astonishing occurred to him: Gil was a deeply compassionate person, and the pain in Nate had cried out to him to be put to right. It was almost impossible for Gil to ignore the state of the extraordinary man in front of him, so he had acted. And that sadness was from Gil knowing all the suffering that Nate had endured for years before he could encounter Gil and be made whole again.

David wondered what the impact would be from the change, because Nate was not exactly an unknown. Highly decorated for valor and courage under fire, he had served three tours in Iraq and two more in Afghanistan, the last of which had nearly killed him. He spoke regularly to returning wounded vets at the Veterans' Administration Hospital in town, a true inspiration to those who had lost so much, and was due to speak there again in a few weeks. That next time would be a trip.

David's attention returned to Gil, and the other had simply stepped back from the prominent position at the head of the room as those who had witnessed his incredible, reality-defying act of compassion and power. David snorted inside as he thought that people had already forgotten about the Harrower Wolf that had appeared in front of them mere moments before.

Several minutes later, David realized he could tell who seemed to have recovered their internal balance: as they found their psychological footing again, their eyes were inevitably drawn to stare at Gil. He didn't seem offended by the attention, merely smiling warmly and gently at each new pair of eyes that locked onto him. Ironically (or maybe not), the last to look at Gil again was Phil. Appropriately, however, he was the first to break the silence.

"THz..." He coughed as his voice sounded hoarse and dry, then laughed, sounding somewhat shrill and unsteady, but it was a laugh after all.

"That was some 'magic trick', Gil!" The room erupted into laugher at the incredible statement, and even Gil chuckled a bit.

Phil continued on. "Ok, I think we can accept certain things as true now. Nate, you ok, buddy?"

Nate looked up at the sound of his name, and that smile beamed so bright that people suddenly felt a little blinded by it.

"Hush, DUH?!?!? Why wouldn't I be? I feel INCREDIBLE!" The last word boomed out over everyone, and the laugher started up from everyone again. Then Nate shocked his audience by leaping up and doing a complete backwards flip, landing again where he had stood with his clenched fists over his head in an athlete's victory pose. The move was perfect.

"Alright, calm down, Marine. We need the floor intact. And the ceiling as well, come to think of it." Dave wasn't sure who had said it, but it set off everyone again.

But then the moment turned serious as the retired Marine turned to Gil, and his next words shocked everyone into a silence that hovered over the room like a cloud.

"If you go there, I will follow you to hell."

Gil smiled slightly and briefly, and answered. "I have no wish to go back there. And it would not be seemly for you to follow me anywhere. I have no desire for servants or thralls. And you have a life to live here."

David spoke up then. "Nate, you need time to process what has happened. Hell, I think we all do. I'm not sure if Phil there will be ok for a while, so we need to look after each other and make sure that everyone is alright."

"And, the rest of you lot could use, though not as much, what I have done for good Nate here," Gil added quietly. "I can see that most of you have old wounds and such. I would be honored to cast the spells that would restore you all."

The quiet statement took everyone by surprise, and not a sound was heard as the entire group held its collective breath. Then the woman who had so quickly climbed the wall earlier spoke up, her voice hoarse with emotion, and almost silent as a whisper.

"You would do that for us? Really? You don't even know us!" Heads nodded as she continued. "What do you want in exchange for this?"

Gil glanced at her as he answered the woman. "Truly, I desire nothing. Tis a task I am happy to bear for those who protect the weak from the strong." A single, vast, singing pulse flashed through his entire being as his patron endorsed his actions, much to his surprise. But he kept any indication of such off his countenance, and continued. "Indeed, it is an obligation that you all are due for the service you have so selflessly given to others. If David or I should need some small thing while we find and follow the trail to the evil doers, I would hope that you would be willing to assist, but I would never demand a thing from you in exchange for doing what I feel is right. To do so would go against my own sense of honor."

Heads nodded now, and some eager smiles were seen around the nearly dozen men and women in the closed off training room.

A member of the in-house security team making his way around the building that evening had just walked past the closed training room door on his way to his next check point. He knew David's training team was inside, as he had been at the front desk next to where the climbing wall was situated in the main lobby, and had seen them all file into the elevators for the brief trip up to the next floor and into the room they now occupied just off the rotunda. He had watched on the security monitors as they entered the room, and the door had closed behind the last one. There were no security cameras or microphones in the training rooms, because of the sensitive nature of some of the meetings that were held there with representatives of defense contractors and those private corporations that wanted secrecy and non-disclosure agreements and the like. Everyone on the security team had been briefed that certain things were not to be talked about, even amongst other security guards.

Unlike most companies who contracted out for private security teams, Dave had insisted that the security team members be full employees, with benefits. His feelings were well known on the issue. He felt that people how contracted out roles like security and maintenance were abrogating their moral responsibilities to those that worked around them. He also felt that full time employees could be counted on to go above and beyond when the circumstances required it, and his belief in that had been affirmed more than a few times over the years since the new facility had opened and the business had grown. Those same employees had shown loyalty to Michelle and Dave over the years, and had seen that loyalty returned in full.

Carl had been with the company since before the building opened, and had always wondered if he was dreaming. The security role paid quite a bit more than the same job at other companies, and his wife appreciated the benefits, especially the company medical insurance plan, a lot. They were both getting older, and with age came the variety of ailments and indignities that an aging body graced its owner with.

It was a rewarding role. He was an Army veteran back in the day, and he appreciated immensely the efforts David expended in trying, and succeeding, to get recent veterans the job training and experience they needed to have long and successful careers. All were eligible for the GI Bill, but the spots on David's team were a coveted prize that were the envy of anyone not lucky enough to get picked. Carl knew that the program couldn't be cheap, but David did it anyways, with Michelle's blessing. She took almost as much satisfaction out of it as David did. And David got the joy of doing something to help his brother and sister veterans.

Now he paused suddenly as he thought he saw colored lights out of the corner of his eye coming from behind the closed blind in the window to the training room. Turning, he saw nothing out of the ordinary, shrugged, and kept walking along the path to the next waypoint, humming softly to himself. He presented the access card on the lanyard to the card reader at the next door in front of him, opened it, and went through and on his way.

CHAPTER 22

The guards came early Monday morning. He was cuffed and chained, not brutally, but not gently, either. His wrists ached where the normally too-tight handcuffs held him as they led him into the courtroom. He walked over to the defense table and stood by his attorney, and the bailiffs didn't bother to unchain him.

The judge banged his gavel, and talking stopped. Other preliminaries followed, but Koren didn't pay much attention. The judge then turned to him, and spoke.

"Do you have anything to say before we get to the victim impact statements, Mr. Davis?"

He nodded. "Yes, Your Honor. I do. I did not do this."

The judge seemed to sigh, then nodded. "Unremorseful to the last. Very well —"

What the judge was about to say was drowned out by the very loud sound of wolves howling. Koren winced as the sound assaulted his ears, but he had been almost expecting something. To the others who'd been there for the sentencing, the shock was near total. But it paled in comparison to what happened next.

With a rush of wind that carried with it the smells of woods and vegetation, Diana appeared. Only this time, five very large wolves with varying shades of dark grey to midnight black fur appeared with her. The wolves looked around, then stood or sat closely at their mistress's feet, but their eyes continued to wander from person to person in the courtroom warily.

The crowd of people in the courtroom watching the proceedings gasped initially, and one person let out a soft scream that cut off abruptly. The silence that followed was broken only by the breathing of the wolves that seemed to gather around the woman in brown leathers and boots. It was almost like the gallery was holding its breath, waiting for the next apparition to appear.

She stood in the middle of the courtroom, between the judge and the defense and prosecution tables. And she stared at the judge, without saying a word. The judge stared back at her, too astonished to speak, frozen in place. Then she turned, and glanced at Koren before glaring at the prosecutor. He stared back transfixed, and Koren realized she was sifting through the prosecutor's memories like she had his a few days ago. Then, after a few moments, she snarled at him.

"You WORM! You KNOW of this child's innocence, but you wish to put lock him away in a cage for the rest of his life because you do not like the color of HIS SKIN!" The outrage in her voice couldn't be missed, and she glared at him, jutting her head towards him slightly. Her hands were clenched into fists at her sides as her entire body radiated her opinion of his part in the whole proceeding. "I shall return to you shortly, you dog!"

The proclamation of Koren's innocence from the woman brought a gasping cry from Koren's mother Martha, seated behind the defense table, as his sister wrapped her arms around her mother's shoulders to comforting the now sobbing woman as her own tears began to fall.

The prosecutor surged to his feet in anger, but what he was about to say was drowned out by the sudden tumult that overwhelmed the room as everyone started to speak at once. Then he shrank back into his chair as one of the huge wolves at this strange woman's feet stood and growled loudly at him, lips drawn back in a snarl that clearly indicated how the wolf felt, which prompted the other four to stand with the first and lent voice of their opinion to that of their brother. He shrank back into his chair as far as he could as he eyed the wolves that stood less than ten feet away fearfully.

The judge banged his gavel over and over, trying to shout down the noise and bring order to his courtroom once again, while trying to process what was happening.

Diana turned to the judge at the noise, and waved her hand back behind her at the crowd. A cold wind washed over them, silencing them except for the soft crying of a now-hopeful mother and sister.

The Honorable William Hastings pointed his gavel at the woman that had appeared in his courtroom, and spoke up sternly. "Just who do you think you are, young woman? What right do you have to interrupt my courtroom like this?"

She looked at him for a moment, and he stared transfixed as she looked inside him. Then she nodded once, and spoke.

"I am the Goddess Diana. Mortals have oft called me Diana the Huntress. I am here in the cause of justice, at the invitation of young Koren Daniel Davis. I have searched his memories, and can find no evidence that he is guilty of what that worm," she inclined her head towards the prosecutor's table briefly, "has accused. I will ensure justice for the young human."

The judge gaped at her briefly, then harrumphed. "He has been found guilty by a jury of his peers of murdering a young woman. That is all I need to mete out justice as required of me by our laws."

"Tell me, you who would sit in judgment. Do your laws deserve higher place than the true justice of the Gods and Goddesses? Do you wish me to believe thus of you?"

"This is a human court of law! I will not have these proceedings disrupted by anyone." He waved his gavel at the three guards that had been staring blankly at the woman and the wolves that had just appeared in the court room. One saw the judge waving furiously at them, and nudged the others.

They all glanced at the Judge Hastings, and then at each other. With a shrug, they started forward, clearly intending to do something to return control of the room to the judge, while one spoke quietly into his radio to try to bring some help to deal with… whatever was happening. They didn't get very far. The wolves stood up on all fours, and seemed to draw closer to the woman. But even that wasn't necessary.

"Touch me at your peril, mortals. I will entertain no such actions that would impede me upon the just path I am meant to follow." The words were clear, but the voice that spoke them sent chills down the spine of everyone in the room. She spoke with a hollow, rasping sound that was low and intense with something approaching menace, and the guards were terrified at the sensations that it conveyed to them. The woman seemed to be nearly eight feet tall all of a sudden, and her form glowed with a white light that seemed to draw the eye of almost everyone in the room. Almost.

Two of the police officers in the gallery couldn't look at the light. And the prosecutor turned his face away, closing his eyes tightly, trying to shut out the intense light that seemed to sear straight down inside him all the way to his soul. He shuddered as his fists clenched tight enough for his nails to leave an impression in his palms. Then the light faded somewhat, and everyone seemed to let out the breath they had been holding all at once.

The judge tried once more to gain control of the proceedings. "What evidence do you have that might indicate this person is innocent? How did you get in here anyways? What kind of trick is this?"

Diana stared at him silently for a moment, her eyes leaving Judge Hastings feeling uncomfortable and defensive. Then she turned to the defense table.

"Young Koren Daniel Davis, attend me." She spoke the words as a command that could not be ignored.

Koren turned and tried to shrug off the hands of the bailiff holding him back, without much success. Another walked quickly to the table to restrain him, but She acted first.

Fists now unclenched, she raised her hands, and the three big, burly uniformed men were lifted up in the air, then as everyone watched in shock, they drifted back away from the table and were dropped by the door as they struggled against the invisible hands that held them easily on their short, moving experience. The act caused more gasps of surprise and fear, this time from everyone including Koren.

Now unrestrained by the guards that no longer seemed interested in doing so, Koren walked over and stood in front of the woman. Her presence seemed to make him seem small and insignificant, but hope still burned inside him that this might turn out ok. He stopped three feet in front of the Goddess, and squared his shoulders, looking her confidently in the eye.

Diana nodded in approval, then she turned to the prosecutor with a sour eye. "Name the victim. I shall call her forth from The House Between Worlds, and she will have her time to speak her truth."

Donald Collins swallowed as his mind raced. What if she could do this? His whole career was teetering on the brink. She was right earlier when she said that he did in fact know that the defendant was innocent. He knew a lot more than that, actually. And that was the whole problem. He decided to not say anything at all. He tried to glare back at her, but that fell away as he couldn't meet her eyes for more than a second. But he didn't dare say a word.

Diana seemed to expect that Collins was going to keep his mouth shut. She turned to the spectators, and said, "Who among you will speak the name of the dead? Who speaks for her?"

An older woman and man stood, obviously struggling with emotion and pain as they held each other's hand tightly. The man spoke up. "We do. Her name is –"

"STOP! What is this!?! I object!" Collins stood at his table, a look of desperation and fear plainly across his features.

"Worm, I do not give you leave to interrupt me! It is not time for justice to attend to your misdeeds. Sit down, cur, afore my wolves put you in your place, or worse!" He sank back down reluctantly, and started to hyperventilate slightly. This was not going to go well. Not well at all.

Nancy McCrae, the mother of the dead young woman, spoke up this time. "Her name is Belinda Nancy McCrae." The bravery of a wounded parent carried her through her statement, but the pain of losing her only child overwhelmed her once more, and tears poured out of her tightly closed eyes like raindrops as she turned to bury herself in her husband's arms, sobbing. It was too much. Why did this happen to her baby? Sobs prevented her from hearing the gasps of the spectators once more, but she felt another hand on her shoulder that didn't belong to her husband, David.

Then she heard a voice that she thought she would never hear again. "Momma?" It was soft, but it cut through her pain like bright sunshine into shadows. Her breath caught in her throat, and she opened her eyes as she turned towards the source of that single spoken word. Then she reached out to wrap both arms around her daughter, miraculously standing there next to her, clad in a pure white robe that almost seemed to glow, with a warm, incredible smile on her youthful face.

Her father looked at her in astonishment as tears flowed from his eyes. Then as she looked up at him, she smiled, reached out, and pulled him to her in a fierce hug for a few moments. Then letting go and stepping back, she spoke to both of them together.

"I have to go set something straight. Don't go anywhere." Then she turned and walked towards the front of the courtroom, the white robe glowing bright enough to illuminate the dark places in the room.

Diana reached her hand out to Belinda, and the young woman took it, allowing herself to be drawn to the center of the open area between the judge's bench and the prosecution and defense tables.

Diana spoke up in a voice that seemed to contain the wind and the ground all at once.

"Child, do you remember what happened to you that ended your life?" The question was gentle, but stern and implacable all at once.

"Yes, I do." Resolve hardened her response, and she looked at the Goddess with steel in her eyes.

"Did this young man, Koren Daniel Davis, have anything to do with what happened to you?" A gasp went up from the gallery of spectators, as the question was asked. She turned to look at the young man sitting transfixed at the defense table. His eyes were as wide as saucers as he looked at the young woman he might spend the rest of his life in prison for, standing calmly in the room for all to see. Silence followed for a brief moment, then –

"No, he did not. I have never seen him before in my life. He was not there when I was killed."

Diana turned to the judge, and spoke up. "You who would sit in judgment of your fellow humans, does this assure you of this young man's innocence?"

The judge didn't hear what was said at first, as his attention was entirely on the face of the young woman in front of him clad only in white from her neck to her bare feet. It was a face he was certain he would never forget, even before her visitation to his courtroom. Then he realized that the goddess had addressed him, and he turned to her once again.

He was struck, suddenly, by the deep green of her eyes. In some ways, she looked young and wild, but in other, more subtle ways, her gaze was as old as the deepest forests anywhere in the world. Then he cleared his throat, and said, "I beg your pardon. Could you please repeat that?"

"I ask you again, does this assure you of this young man's innocence?" The question was clear, but the tone of voice made the words into a statement, and he frowned.

"Well, if he didn't kill her, then who did?"

Diana turned to Belinda standing beside her, and inclined her head towards the mortal, who looked back at her with sudden anger in her eyes. "Speak, my child. I will not allow any harm to come to you or your family. On this you can trust."

She nodded, and then turned to the judge. What she said next rocked the court room and everyone in it to their souls.

"Well, for one thing, he is white, not African American. He is, or was, my boyfriend, my fiancé. His father is a police officer. We were having an argument in our apartment, and he got upset. He wanted me to stop hanging out with my friends; he called them whores and dykes. He slapped me when I refused, so I hit him back, as hard as I could. It knocked him down. When he got up, he picked up a kitchen chair and hit me with it as hard as he could. He killed me. I don't know that it was intentional. I left my body as I died, and heard and saw him swearing in fear and frustration."

The judge nodded slightly, and then spoke up. "Do you see the person in this courtroom?"

Belinda turned and looked over everyone in the room, then shook her head.

"Nope, I don't see him here, Your Honor. But I do see his father." Her eyes narrowed as she stared hard at one of the two police officers that couldn't look at the light of the Goddess earlier.

Officer Paul Smith wrenched his eyes away from the impossible sight of his son's dead girlfriend that had suddenly appeared in the courtroom, and became aware that every eye in the room was looking right at him.

His son Tristan had called him late one night and told him that a bad accident had happened, and Belinda wasn't breathing. He'd raced over to Tristan's apartment in his squad car, only to find out that the girl he'd thought of as a future daughter was dead. He had called his sergeant, which had set a huge series of events in motion. The sergeant had said that this was not going to be a problem, because the prosecutor "owed him one".

The cover-up began with another officer being told that the perpetrator was a young black man. One young man matching the description had been conveniently found waiting at the bus stop near the apartment building that night, and had been arrested on the spot.

It had all snowballed from there. An innocent young man, and from all accounts an outstanding student with a bright future in front of him, had been convicted largely on very thin circumstantial evidence. The middle-aged, experienced prosecuting attorney had known all the tricks, as if he was a seasoned veteran decades older.

The small group of officers who knew about the cover-up had simply sat back and watched, making all the right noises at all the right times. Those who didn't know about it seemed to think that the young African-American man was guilty, simply because he couldn't account for where he was. His claims that he had been with a white girlfriend had only served to further his guilt when the supposed girlfriend couldn't be found.

Unknown to most of the people in the room, an officer, one Officer Paul Smith, actually, had gotten to her and convinced her that she should disappear for some time. Given that she had a minor drug arrest in the past, she had needed very little convincing.

"Or else you will find yourself on trial with him..."

It had been enough to send her out of state to live with an aunt and uncle for quite a while. She had been so terrified that she refused to come back, and her parents had covered up where she was to the investigator the public defender had assigned to look for her.

Which all led up to now. What was supposed to be a neatly wrapped up case seemed to be coming apart faster than anyone could even take a breath. They were so close! Now, a 'Goddess' (which, given how she had arrived and what she had done in the short time since, probably actually was) had turned everything upside down, and the, whatever she was, was staring right at him, her eyes hot with hatred and barely suppressed rage. Then she moved.

"I loved your son! I would have married him! We had been together so long, since junior high! You were even family to me! But then he started using meth, and everything went to hell. He became violent. I told you he was having problems, but you and your wife just looked at me like I was crazy. Well, who's crazy now? HUH?!?"

It all came out in a rush as she stalked over to Paul and got right in his face, screaming at the top of her lungs as he flinched back from her in fear, anger, and self-loathing. But she wasn't nearly finished.

"Where did you find this poor young man? What did he do to you or anyone else to ever deserve this?" The volume of her voice overrode everything else in the court room, except, strangely enough, the sobbing of Belinda's parents and Koren's mother and sister. Everyone else in the room was too shocked at what was happening, and seemed to be frozen in their seats.

Belinda reached out with both hands, and easily hefted the much larger police officer off his feet by his body-armor vest. Then she turned and threw him over the rows of spectator's benches to land hard and very painfully on the floor in front of the Goddess, sliding the last few feet to stop right in front of the wolves. The ones with the very bright eyes, and very big teeth. The ones that were now only inches from his face. A chorus of snarls washed away all rational thought as the huge animals just stared into his eyes, snarling, as he gasped in pain from the hard landing that he had just taken. Something trickled out of the corner of his mouth, and he wiped at it, only to see his own blood on the back of his hand.

Gasps, and more than a few screams, had escaped every mouth in that courtroom as the otherworldly strength of the dead girl registered, and people scrambled to get out of her way as she walked slowly back towards the front of the court room.

The Goddess Diana looked down at the police officer with a mix of loathing and disgust, and with a seemingly negligent wave of her hand, sent a wave of green light flashing over him. In an instant his pain was gone, but the fear remained, and he realized when he could breathe again that he had both soiled and wet himself.

Diana turned to her wolves, and spoke in a language no one recognized, which prompted two of them to suddenly disappear.

"Now we wait as my children hunt the one whose actions have brought us to this place today." The words seemed to echo differently in the suddenly silent room.

No more than five minutes had passed before something happened again, and during that time, Paul was certain that every eye in the room was looking at him. He didn't know if the pained, disgusted looks the spectators in the gallery were casting his way were the result of the grotesque smells that were coming from him or from what he had been accused of, but he decided it didn't matter, whatever the reason.

With a shimmer and a rush of air, the wolves returned, but with someone that Paul, Belinda, and Belinda's parents recognized very well.

A terrified Tristan was in half crouched, with his arms up, his face turned away, his eyes squeezed shut, and a scream was coming from his mouth. Then, when he had run out of air and nothing happened to him, he opened his eye, only to see his father laying on the floor, with three more of the huge wolves that had suddenly appeared at his job standing over him.

Then he heard a sound behind him and turned towards it. All the color drained from his face as he saw who was there. "Oh, no! Belinda!"

The sight of her drove him to his knees, and he scrubbed at his face, hoping that what he was seeing would go away when he opened them again, but also wishing with all his might that the vision of his dead fiancé would still be there.

Tears coursed down from his eyes as he looked at the face of the only girl he had ever loved, that he had so carelessly killed in a meth-fueled rage nearly a year ago. His shoulders hunched over, and he sobbed loudly, his pain like a lance through the heart to those that watched.

Belinda looked at him, astonished. She could see that he was completely clean and sober, and was clean shaven and dressed rather nicely, two things that had been missing in their final months before that last moment they had shared together. Then tears started to course down her face as she felt his pain, the emptiness, the utter desolation and lack of joy anywhere inside his mind or soul. He regretted everything so completely, she realized. He must have gotten sober, gotten off the meth after that night.

Belinda's time in The House Between Worlds had been difficult, as she tried to come to terms with what she had lost, and at whose hands she had lost it all. She would have been able to go to one of the window rooms to look in on the friends and family she had left behind, but it had not been all that long ago in relative terms, and she wasn't ready.

She had not forgiven Tristan, convinced that he was unrepentant, and she was resentful that he had been allowed to go on with living, even if he had, as she believed, been arrested for her murder.

But when Diana's presence had come to her, and told her that an innocent young man had been arrested, tried, and convicted of her murder, her rage at Tristan had grown. She believed all along that Tristan had not been remorseful even the tiniest bit, and had gladly gone along with the conspiracy that had allowed him to get away with ending her mortal life.

She had let some of that rage out earlier when she had found the supernatural strength inside her that let her throw Tristan's father some fifteen feet through the air as easily as if he was a paper airplane.

Now, as she looked at the only boy, the only man, she had ever loved, she realized that he was in enormous pain inside. He looked like he hadn't slept well in a long time, with bags under his eyes and a gaunt look on his face from weight loss she hadn't noticed before. He was a tortured soul, twisted and wracked with pain that he had been barely holding inside.

For Tristan, the sight of the one person in his entire life, more than ever, that he had loved more than life itself, had ripped open the wounds that had never really healed, and he broke apart mentally and emotionally, sobbing on the floor while repeating her name over and over. His mind, already suffering from the enormous pressures put on it since Belinda's death at his hands, snapped. His last vestiges of intelligence that he had been barely holding on to with the last of his mental strength suddenly slipped between his fingers like water, and rushed away into the dark corners of his mind, taking with it all rational thought.

Diana looked down at the remorseful mortal, gauging his suffering. She looked into his soul, and saw that he was dying deep inside. There were memories of the time after Belinda had died at his hand, where entire days had passed while he waited to be arrested and sent to prison, a fate he longed for, ached for. He couldn't go on with his life anymore, she could see. He was barely eating enough to stay functional. The old life he'd known, full of things she didn't understand from this strange plane, had ceased to have any meaning to him when the realization of what he had done had hit him hard enough to cause physical pain.

Belinda reached Tristan's side, and knelt down where he was curled up, rocking back and forth in the fetal position on the floor, his hands clenched into fists that were held tightly over his eyes. She had never seen him like this before, and it shocked her. She reached out, and grasped his wrists, trying to pull his hands away from his eyes, calling his name softly.

"Tristan, honey, look at me. Tristan, come on, look at me. It's ok. I'm here, baby. Look at me." After what seemed like hours but was in reality only a few minutes, the sound of her voice and the feel of her hands on him, pulling at him gently but firmly, reached deeply into his psyche past the walls and doors his consciousness had retreated behind, to finally register. The sound and feel of her pulled at him, but he resisted. The pain was so great back there, out in the world. And he didn't deserve redemption, that much was clear. Better to end it all in here. Better to stay here for all time. He knew he was hiding away, and that staying there would be the end of him, and he didn't care.

But the sound of that voice that he loved so much, and the feel of her hands that he missed so completely, had caused something to flare in the darkness of his retreat. Hope suddenly appeared somewhere deep off in the distance, like a single match lit in the darkness of endless night, a long ways away. He turned away from it, not wanting to believe it was real. It couldn't be real, and even if it was, hope was for those that deserved it.

But hope sometimes is a thing that will not be denied. And as Belinda called his name over and over, and gently caressed his hands and face, wiping away his tears, that tiny flickering light slowly grew, and with it, presence of mind slowly returned.

Paul stared at the... whatever she was... that had been the little neighborhood girl he and his wife had welcomed into their family all those years ago. When Tristan had called him, and told him to come over, Paul had heard the tears in his only child's voice, and feared that the worst had happened. He told Tristan not to do anything, not to call anyone, and just wait for him to show up.

His protective instincts had flared into life when he saw what had happened, and that irrational instinct to protect his child had overridden his duty to uphold the law and do the right thing. Now, he saw that he had failed to protect his son from the one thing that no one could: himself. And Paul was ashamed.

Diana turned to the judge, and just stared, with one eyebrow raised. He was so completely focused on the scene on his courtroom floor that he didn't notice her gaze at first. When he finally did, he almost jerked out of his chair. As his eyes met those of the incredible being that had so turned his courtroom upside down this day, he knew what she expected, demanded, required of him. He cleared his throat, and banged his gavel for attention.

Most of the eyes in the court room turned to him, including the white-faced prosecutor, the astonished public defender, and the eyes of the young man who had, until today, expected to spend the rest of his life in prison for something he didn't do. The judge paused, looking into those eyes of the young man that the justice system had nearly condemned to life in prison unfairly, and a part of him wilted inside. How could the system get it so wrong? How could he have missed... whatever had been missed in this case, and allow this young man to be found guilty? He glanced at the prosecutor, and saw... something on the man's face, and in an instant, he knew what the prosecutor knew: Koren Daniel Davis was innocent. Completely, utterly, innocent. Judge Hastings fought the sudden urge to empty the contents of his stomach onto the bench in front of him. The prosecutor knew! That rotten, horrible bastard!

He put that thought aside to be processed later, and cleared his throat again.

"Given the extraordinary circumstances of this hearing, I am vacating with prejudice all convictions, and declaring the defendant free to go. The bench will refuse to hear any motions to retry this case against the defendant, and will hold in contempt any prosecuting attorney should they attempt to do so. That is all." He banged his gavel once again, and looked back into the eyes of the Goddess once more.

She looked back at him with a twinkle in her eye, and she smiled at him. A wave of warmth and happiness flowed through him briefly, and he smiled back, only to frown once more as the weight of the proceedings intruded again.

Koren stepped back, bumping into the defense table, stunned at the sudden turn of events. Then he turned as he heard voices behind him, and was barely able to brace himself before his mother, a hefty woman, crashed into him, wrapped her arms around him and squeezed him so hard he couldn't breathe. Her tears soaked into his orange jumpsuit as she held her son tight, thanking God over and over, when she felt a presence beside her.

Martha Davis turned, and gasped as the Goddess Diana looked into her eyes, and smiled. A hand went to her shoulder, and the sensation of the touch washed through her.

"Thank you for freeing my Koren! Thank you!" She flung her arms around the Goddess, who laughed lightly, a sound that conjured the feeling of a gentle breeze on a warm summer's day, hugging the mortal woman back.

"You are welcome, mortal." A nod of her head accompanied the statement, then she turned away, back to face the now white-faced police officer still lying on the floor, propped up on an elbow.

"Your crimes are many in this happening, human. You are a guard of the city, yes?" At his short nod, she spoke again, her voice harsh and unforgiving. "You have failed at your duty to protect the innocent. Worse still, you have caused an innocent to be punished for the misdeeds of another. You also failed as a father, since you tried to shield your son from the consequences of his actions, something no one has a right to do for anyone. Your deeds speak of a man without honor, and one neither fit to keep laws of humans or Gods, nor fit to be a father. A child of such a man cannot be expected to uphold the precepts of honor as required of all men and women. And yet, I sense in your child a burning desire for what is right and good to be upheld."

Diana glanced down at where Belinda and Tristan huddled on the floor, his head in her lap as his eyes remained tightly squeezed shut. She held on to him while gently caressing his face, whispering to him, trying to pull him back from deep inside where he had shuttered himself, while he muttered and moaned, rocking back and forth.

It was obvious that Tristan Smith was hurting, but those in the court room found it difficult to have any sympathy for him because of the act of violence which ended Belinda's young life. Belinda's actions confused the thoughts of those that might try to condemn him in their own thoughts, however. Her obvious concern for her killer greatly complicated things in the eyes and hearts and minds of the spectators.

Paul Smith looked over at his son, and realized that he couldn't protect his only child from what was happening to him now. His son was broken and alone, trapped deep inside his mind where only his demons roamed, howling and tearing at his soul. He tried to reach out to Tristan, but a look from both Diana and Belinda stopped him cold.

Diana turned to the judge, and spoke once more. "Do your laws condemn the deeds of this oath breaker? Or must I mete out Justice of mine own to right the scales?"

"He has broken several laws, and will be held accountable. Bailiffs, take the officer into custody." The iron-cast voice of the judge broke into Paul's thoughts, and he stiffened in fear. He started to rise, but a wolf saw the action, and its head snapped towards him, its body going completely still while a low growl heralded bared teeth. He sank back to the floor, and waited for someone to come and get him, fearful of what would happen should he resist.

Diana watched the proceedings with skepticism plainly on her face. It was clear that she had her doubts about what would happen to the officer. She turned to the judge, and spoke once again.

"I shall watch over what happens to that mortal. Should I be dissatisfied with what happens to him, I will return and deal more directly with this brigand."

Paul's face went white as he heard the cold anger in the Goddess's strange voice, and he shuddered. Any thoughts of fighting the charges he guessed would be coming at him evaporated as he slumped down, wishing he could disappear.

Cuffing the officer's hands behind him and relieving him of his utility belt and other accessories took moments, and he was lifted up to his feet and walked back to the holding area behind the courtroom, all the while looking over his shoulder at his only child.

Diana turned once more back to the prosecutor, and her glare could have frozen the sun. Donald Collins stared back, trying and failing to muster any resistance to what was coming.

"What do you have to say for yourself, mortal?"

"I... ash..." Nothing came to mind that would make what happened here any better, and Donald suddenly came to the conclusion that saying nothing would probably be the only way to not make things worse. His mouth closed almost with a snap, and he simply glared at the supernatural being in front of him.

Diana reached out one hand, palm uppermost, and curled the fingers in a motion that seemed to be pulling gently at something unseen. As she completed the motion, the image of a private conference room appeared to float in midair above her hands. It was small at first, but at a motion from Diana's hand, it grew until it was near life-sized, becoming three-dimensional and true to life, as gasps came from almost everyone in the room at the impossible happening in front of their very eyes. Koren had the almost whimsical thought that it was a good thing the high ceiling in the room they were in was so high, or the scene the Goddess was displaying wouldn't have been able to fit. As it was, everyone in the room leaned in towards the conjured image.

The conference room in the floating conjuration was well furnished. The main table was dark cherry wood with a finish that was polished to a glassy finish, and big enough to seat at least ten comfortably along both sides. Two men sat at the table near one end, frozen in time. Koren realized that one was the prosecutor, but he didn't recognize the other.

The judge did, though. It was Mark Gadsden, the county attorney, the man Collins reported to. With a slight gesture, the conjured scene came to life.

"So you think that you will be able to get a conviction in the Belinda McCrae case?" Gadsden was asking Collins. The younger man nodded in response, a smile on his face.

"Yes, no problem. The work my assistant Kellen did is top shelf. He is going to make a good prosecutor someday. No, I don't foresee any difficulties. One more little gang-banger druggie off the streets. That's always a good thing." Collins laughed, a sound that was anything but pleasant, given the context.

Gadsden shook his head. "You really don't like them that much, do you?"

"Not really. What difference does it make? I wish all those little pieces of shit would just go back to Africa. Leave this country to those who deserve it. Hell, they can't even learn to speak proper English!"

A shocked silence descended on the courtroom as the scene paused. Collins looked around wildly, desperate to be any place but here. He surged out of his chair, and started to make a break for it, but someone stopped him in his tracks.

Ariana Wilmington had grown up in a very affluent suburb, the child of a doctor father and a lawyer mother. Her parents had been so very proud of her when she announced that she was going to law school, and wanted to be a defense attorney. And that pride only grew when she took a role in the public defender's office. Ariana had been taught from a very young age that honor and integrity mattered the most in a society where laws didn't really prevent crime. Laws only dealt with punishing the guilty, and sometimes, in rare cases, provided some restitution to the victims. In many cases, though, victims could never be made whole again.

Now, the slender young woman stood, and as Collins made his break to run out of the room, she stepped up, and put the lessons of her latest fitness regimen to work, a hard right cross catching the bigger, older man in motion squarely on the left side of his jaw. The impact snapped his head back around, turning his whole body with as he fell to the floor, unconscious.

"Wow! Man that hurt!" Ariana shook her hand as the pain welled up, and held it tightly with her right hand. Still holding her injured hand, the young public defender suddenly realized what had happened, and turned beet red. Turning to face the judge, she tried to think of what to say.

"Uh, Your Honor... I... hum..."

The judge looked at her in astonishment. What else could possibly happen to totally break down the decorum in court today? The day was getting stranger and stranger. What the hell did he do now?

"Young lady, what did you just do? Is it your place to stop him?" The anger in his voice was slightly tempered by the memory that Collins had been about to flee the courtroom after being revealed to be a racist who most likely knew he was prosecuting someone who was innocent. He tried to focus on the violent act in front of him, and deal with that while he tried to determine what he needed to do to regain control of the room.

"I apologize to the court, Your Honor. I realize that my actions were incredibly wrong and inappropriate. I was just so angry when I heard what he said to his boss, that – there is no excuse for my behavior. Again, I apologize." Ariana was blushing so hard that her entire upper body felt like it was going to burst into flames. She ducked her head, unable to meet the gaze of the angry jurist in front of her, and then winced as the pain continued to get worse.

Her boxing instructor had told her that hitting someone without a glove would probably break her hand if she wasn't careful on choosing where to land her punch. He was right, she thought now. She most certainly broke something in her hand. And probably, she just broke her career, too. All that work for nothing. What had she been thinking? Well, she could always go to her mother's firm and practice there, if she didn't get disbarred.

The Goddess had been looking at the older man laid out unmoving on the floor from the single punch of the young woman now holding her hand, when she let out a laugh.

What Judge Hastings was about to say was forgotten when that sound broke in on his thoughts. He looked over at the... was she really was a Goddess after all? Was everything he'd ever been taught about religion and faith just simply... wrong?

He looked over at Ariana Wilmington, then back to the laughing woman that had appeared and turned his court upside down. Diana stared down at the unconscious prosecutor while she laughed a moment more, and then turned to Ariana.

"Mortal child, you are simply delicious. One punch. Amazing!" Then she noticed that the young woman's hand was hurt, and waved the woman towards her, calling up her Physicked Sight to see what had happened.

The people in the gallery looking at the Goddess were shocked when her green eyes suddenly glowed a bright light that washed her eyes completely white. Diana looked at the woman's hand, and with another careless wave of her own hand, another flash of green light healed the broken hand. She then placed her hand on the mortal woman's shoulder, and nodded.

"Well done, my child. You have served the cause of justice this day. I consider you worthy." The ring of steel in the voice took Ariana's breath away for a moment, and all she could do was nod in reply. Then when her voice returned, she spoke quietly to herself.

"I just hope I don't get in too much trouble for that." Diana heard the words, and raised one eyebrow. The realization that this young girl that had impressed her so much with her willingness to do the right thing might get her in trouble came to her, and she turned back to the judge.

"I consider this girl's actions to be above reproach. Do not oppose me in this," she warned, and the judge nodded to acknowledge that he had heard the statement, but frowned just the same.

"Diana, there must be decorum in a court of law. We cannot have people getting physically violent with others in this room, no matter how much they might deserve it. The law is clear in this. What am I supposed to do? The precedent that ignoring this sets is not right. She must be held accountable for her actions. The laws are established to make this country a fair and just place for everyone."

Donald Collins groaned from his place on the floor as consciousness slowly returned. His jaw hurt for some reason, then it all came back to him and he realized that the public defender had stepped in front of him on his way out the door, and he woke up on the floor. She must have punched him, or something. He opened his eyes, and the first thing he saw in front of him across the floor was Belinda McCrae with Tristan Smith's head still in her lap, still keening softly to himself as his body rocked back and forth.

Belinda looked up at the sudden movement, and her eyes narrowed as she saw another member of the conspiracy that had almost sent an innocent young man to prison for her own murder. He looked away first as the look in her eyes registered, remembering how easily she had thrown the police officer through the air.

Diana looked down at the now-awakening man, and with a nod, sent her wolves forward to prevent him from escaping her again. Not that it would have mattered in the end. She had gained enough knowledge of him while sifting through his memories that she could find him with just a thought now. Then she turned to the judge once more.

"I care not for the laws you mortals have written. Indeed, the results of those laws almost punished an innocent for the crimes of another. This young woman has stood for my cause, for justice. That she should come to harm so selflessly doing so places her in great esteem in my eyes." Ariana sucked in a breath as that statement rocked her to her core, but before she could respond, the Goddess continued to speak. "My faith in your doing the right thing is shallow. I shall have one of my wolves protect her. She shall not be harmed for this."

"Diana, this is not necessary. I must be held accountable, or our entire system of laws breaks down." The words came out quietly, but with a conviction that impressed the Goddess and the judge.

"Nonetheless, I am not accountable to the laws of mortals. You are something special, child. You are what the humans have oft called a Paladin. Gods and Goddesses have blessed and protected your kind since time immemorial. It is our sworn duty to do so. I will brook no arguments in this." The last sentence came out sternly, with a hint of warning in the words that was not lost on Ariana.

"But how will I explain a wolf following me... oh my..."

The wolf that would be her protector stepped forward, and shimmered slightly, then in its place stood what appeared to be a young woman, but in armor and a cloak. A sword hung at her left hip, and a smaller blade on her right. The woman's hair, a pastiche of reds and blacks, matched the fur of the wolf that she had been before, and her eyes were a distinct red-amber color. But the thing that Ariana noticed most was that the young woman standing in front of her was incredibly beautiful, in an exotic, almost wolfish way.

The gaze she turned on Ariana almost made her shiver with its intensity as she coolly assessed the young lawyer. Then she nodded once, and spoke. "I am called Zestrilla, Mistress. I shall be by your side always, to protect you and keep you in the Goddess's cause. I am greatly honored to serve you, Human Paladin. What shall I call you?"

Ariana blinked. An old story about rabbit holes came to mind, and a hysterical laugh threatened to escape her control. When she was under as much control as she thought she was going to get, she spoke up, her voice more level than she thought it would be.

"I am Ariana Wilmington. You can call me Ariana or Ari, whichever you prefer."

Zestrilla bowed her head briefly, her strange eyes never leaving Ariana's face. "I shall call you Ari then, mistress. When it is appropriate." She looked around, her eyes taking in the strangeness of a world she which had never seen before, and frowned slightly.

"You must tell me of this plane, Ari, and what you do. I must learn what I need to know to protect you."

Diana turned back to the sprawled figure on the floor in front of her. Collins was still shaking his head slightly, trying to clear the last of the cobwebs from it from the single punch that had knocked him down so easily.

"And now, I come to you. What shall I do with you, worm? You are an evil, poisonous, lower being, much akin to a pig that would eat anything it finds under its snout. The father of that poor soul at least had a motive that was easily understood even in its wrongness: the need to protect his progeny. You jest and jape about the pain you cause others. You find joy in others' suffering. These are not the traits of an honorable man. I have gazed into your soul, and found only decay, rot, and evil. Truth and honor matter not at all to you. You only wish to attain fame and fortune, and will sacrifice anyone and anything that gets in your way. What have you to say of your sins?"

Donald Collins, an eloquent, very intelligent, highly educated man, found something to say.

"Fuck you!" Then he grimaced as the stupidity of what he just did and said registered, as her eyes narrowed. Then she lifted her left hand, and he rose off the floor with it, in the grip of the same unseen force that had moved the police officers earlier. But while they had only squirmed in discomfort, he writhed in agony as the vice-like grip tightened around him, squeezing the breath and life out of him, making it impossible to breathe, let alone speak.

"I would expect no less from an evil-doer of your black-hearted ilk." The words came out cold enough to freeze fire, and more than one person, including the judge and the public defender, gasped out loud at the overpowering tone in Diana's voice.

"I must find a punishment suitable to your evil. Since you are so hateful towards those whose skin color does not match yours, I condemn you to be what you hate. And to suffer for it greatly. My children, attend to my will!"

The four remaining wolves sprang up, and leaped one at a time at the dangling man, vanishing inside him. Diana loosened her invisible grip slightly, and his ability to breathe suddenly returned. A shriek escaped his mouth, then another, and as the people in the court room watched in an almost horrified fascination, his skin slowly darkened to a nearly black hue as he struggled against the torture he was being subjected to.

Then it was over, as quickly as it began. The wolves exited his form, as they landed lightly on the floor and padded silently over to the Goddess, sitting at her feet. And they all seemed to have the same satisfied smirk on their wolfish faces.

Collins became aware that everyone in the room was staring at him like he was an alien from another planet. He looked down at his hands, and an anguished cry escaped him as he fell to his knees. He started rubbing his hands together franticly, as if to wipe away the dark color his hands had changed to. Tears began to flow down his face as he realized that his worst nightmare fell far short of what had happened to him here. Then he looked up at the angry Goddess, and held both hands out to her in a desperate plea.

"Please! Change me back! Change me back!"

"I will not. You must learn the value of all your fellow humans, not just those that you share the color of your skin. You will remain this way until I am satisfied that you have learned the lessons you must know to help your fellow mortals. This is my judgment. Summon me if you wish, and I will consider whether or not you have grown beyond your ignorance and childishness. Lie to me, and I shall make your torment complete. And never-ending. You will learn, and you will grow. Or you will remain this way until the end of your days, however many or few you might have left in front of you."

She stared down at him as the horror of his existence washed over him, and he collapsed to the floor weeping uncontrollably while trying to rub every part of his exposed skin in hopes that the darkness put there by the deity would wipe away; a forlorn, impossible hope that was rapidly becoming an unfulfillable, futile wish. The unthinkable had happened: he became what he despised and hated the most, and his mind was collapsing inwards on itself as it tried to process what was happening to him.

She turned to where Belinda and Tristan were on the floor, and inclined her head towards the young woman.

"Have you considered your choice?"

"Yes, Goddess. I choose this. He needs me, and I miss my family."

"I must take something from you, then."

Belinda smiled. "I don't need much, just my family. I will be ok without it."

The Goddess nodded in approval, and returned the smile more widely. "You are indeed a most cherished child, Belinda Nancy McCrae. Keep it. You may have need of it. And you have shown that you deserve it. It is my gift to you, for the pain you have endured this time away from your loved ones."

The room suddenly seemed slightly warmer as the blessing registered in the minds of the watching mortals in the courtroom gallery.

Diana turned to the mortals in the room, and seemed to stand up straighter. While she didn't seem to actually grow any taller, everything around her seemed suddenly smaller, and less significant as she revealed her presence fully in the presence of those watching the extraordinary events unfolding in front of them.

"I return to Belinda Nancy McCrae her life on this mortal plane."

A gasping sob was heard from Belinda's mother, and her father staggered backwards to sit heavily down into the seat behind him, overwhelmed at what he was hearing. Belinda didn't even look up at the pronouncement. The glowing white robe she wore abruptly changed into jeans and a shirt, and sandals appeared on her feet.

But the Goddess Diana was not finished.

"Do you wish for this mortal to be punished for what he has done to you?" The gallery seemed to almost hold its breath to see what the response would be.

"No! I love him! And I know now that this is destroying him inside. I think he has been punishing himself enough. I will work to bring him back to me, to help him heal. And when he has recovered, I will teach him everything I have learned from The House Between Worlds." She looked down as she gently caressed his head and hair, a look of pure love on her face.

Diana nodded her approval, then turned and looked at Judge Hastings once more. "I will leave him in her care alone. This is the judgment of Diana. Should he be healed enough to resume his life, he shall have my leave to do so. Should he pass beyond, I will carry him to The House Between Worlds myself, where he shall finish his recovery, and go on to another life, just like any other mortal.

"Belinda Nancy McCrae will call upon me to ensure that my will and judgment holds sway amongst you and your kind." The tone of the Goddess's voice, and the odd ringing tone that seemed to penetrate into the minds of everyone listening to the pronouncement, made any argument seem less than pointless. No one wanted to stand against this extraordinary being; this...Goddess.

Belinda's mother and father, now weeping with joy, joined their daughter, kneeling on the floor next to the young man that had taken her from him once before.

Belinda looked up at her parents, tears falling from her own eyes.

"I'm home, Momma and Daddy! I missed you so much! I have so much to tell you! Together we will help Tristan heal. I know we can do it. He didn't mean to hurt me. He is off the drugs now. I can see that inside him. He will never touch them again. He will recover." The tears flowed harder from all three as they embraced over the nearly comatose young man, accepting any price that brought their only child, their beloved Belinda back to them.

Nancy and David McCrae turned to Diana, and she spoke once more, her voice almost obscured by the tears that fell now like rain.

"Thank you for bringing my daughter back, Goddess. We can never repay this. Thank you!"

Diana seemed to shrug. "The call of justice must be answered. You owe me nothing whatsoever for doing that which is right. Be well, parents of Belinda. I must be elsewhere."

With that, her four wolves still in lupine form threw their heads back and howled in a wild and woodsy chorus, then one by one they vanished, until the Goddess herself disappeared in a rustle of wind and the scent of the forest and the earth, leaving behind a completely silent room except for the sounds of the prosecutor's sobbing, and the moans of the near-catatonic young man with his head in the lap of the only person that he ever truly loved, and that he was certain, back then in better times at least, was the only person that had ever truly loved him for who he was.

CHAPTER 23

"Daddy! Daddy!" Derrick turned at the sound of his four year old daughter's happy voice and thumping footsteps as she ran into the kitchen from the back yard. Katie had a huge smile on her face as she ran at him and jumped, expecting her father, as he had so many times in the past, to catch her and sweep her up into a big hug.

"What is it, Katie McGee?"

"Daddy! That's not my name!"

"Oh? What's your name then, my little girl?"

With a big grin, she leaned back in his arms and said, "My name is Kathleen Corinne Hanson."

"Well, Kathleen Corinne Hanson, what's up?" His smile was nearly big enough to reach from ear to ear at his wonderful daughter's sparkling personality. He was certain she got it from his wife.

"Daddy, there's a new big white horsey with a funny pointy thing on his head in with the other horses. And he's really pretty!" Her eyes gleamed like it was Christmas morning. "Is he for me?"

Derrick Hanson had no idea what she was talking about. A new horse?

"Are you sure, honey? A new horse?"

"Yes, Daddy, yes! Come see!" She scrambled down from his arms and grabbed his hand with both of hers, pulling him towards the back yard and the paddock and the barn.

He was still wondering what was going on when his daughter pulled him by the hand around the corner. The sight in front of him nearly caused him to trip, but he caught his balance and allowed himself to be pulled further along towards the fenced in corral where the riding horses were out in the sun and breeze. He was certain that his mouth was gaping wide open in shock.

His first thought was that one of the neighbors was playing a trick on him in some way. The thing he was seeing couldn't be real. Unicorns didn't exist, right?

It – he – was good sized, with delicate features, fine musculature, and a head and face that was almost like an Arabian, but there was something different about his eyes as he stood still, looking over the other occupants of the paddock. And he was the brightest white Derrick had ever seen. Then the newcomer turned to look at him, and the intelligence in its eyes was a stunning thing.

Kathleen pulled him up to the fence, and said, "See? Isn't he pretty? Can I ride him? Please?"

Derrick stood there leaning on the fence for a moment as he and the newcomer looked at each other. Then the pure white creature walked over to the two humans, and the strangest thing happened. He heard a voice coming from the huge white creature in front of him.

He shook his head as the strange words coming from the unicorn came to him. The lips and mouth moved in time with the sounds he was making, but Derrick didn't understand a thing the big creature was saying. He shook his head again as it cocked its head at him, then a shuffling sigh seemed to escape that deep chest. It walked over to the fence where he was standing, then stopped, in arms reach. The unicorn chanted something, and then seemed to glow a delicate blue for a moment. Then, quicker than he could react, it swung its head towards him, coming in contact with his face for the briefest of moments, before he backed away again.

Then the day got even stranger.

"Do you understand me now, human?"

His vision swam for a moment, and his grip on the top rail of the fence tightened for a moment as he tried to keep his balance.

"Daddy! The horsey talked!" Katie's voice was filled with wonder and glee, as her eyes stared wide open at the huge white form in front of her.

"Daddy! I can talk! I can talk! HEE HAW!!!" The white horse capered around in front of him as he made his shocked-sounding declaration, then he stuck his head down and forward as he bellowed out the braying sound of a donkey at full volume. It was an impressive imitation. "I just love human children. Don't you? Of course you do; you had her. Wait, you didn't steal her from anyone, did you? She doesn't really look all that much like you…"

"You be nice to my daddy! He didn't steal me from anyone! He's my daddy!" Katie's indignation came through loud and clear as she wrapped her arms around his waist and held on tight.

"It's ok, Katie. It's ok. He didn't mean it. Did you?" He glared at the unicorn in front of him with an edge of anger, but still with that underlying disbelief that this was really happening. He reached down and pulled her arms away from the lock they had around his waist and picked her up. She turned her head into him, burying her face into his neck for a moment, then turned to look at the white figure in front of her, her face mashed up against his as she held on to his neck tightly.

"There it is. I see the resemblance now. My sorrow for having upset you both." The unicorn turned his head down and away slightly, looking at them from his left eye. It was, Derrick decided, a pose devoid of any real remorse.

"Wow. You're a real piece of work." Disgust flooded through him as he realized that the unicorn was mocking him and his daughter both.

"Oh, cast your anger elsewhere, human. I am above such petty emotions." He snorted, then turned to look at the horses behind him. Then he turned back as Derrick spoke.

"Where did you come from? What are you doing here? Do you have a name I should call you?" His brain started working again, barely, as he sought to figure out the conundrum he was confronted with.

"Where did I come from? Most unicorns have a father unicorn and a mother unicorn. Do I need to explain that part of it to you? You had her, after all. I think. I only have your word for it, I suppose, but you look quite honest. I guess I can take your word for it that you understand such things." The tone of voice was gently mocking and slightly derisive, but with an edge of true humor in it. Derrick began to understand that the being in front of him enjoyed the verbal fencing he was trying to engage Derrick in.

He turned to his daughter, and said, "Will you run and get mommy, and tell her to bring the camcorder out?"

"Ok, Daddy! You wait right here, mister white pointy headed horsey. I'm going to get my mommy!"

She scampered down out of his arms, and ran off towards the house as fast as she could.

Derrick turned back to the unicorn as it came closer to the fence. He started to open his mouth again, but the beast beat him to it.

"I scented the odor of fine mares. It is intoxicating to me. It called me from across the planes. Are any of them in season, perhaps? Might I have some time to express my appreciation for their form, grace, and beauty?" The eager look in his eye reminded Derrick of a teenager full of lust for his first girlfriend, and he almost laughed. Then he remembered what the unicorn wanted to do, and ground his mental heel down on the sensation before it escaped.

"I would really prefer that you not... indulge yourself in that sort of thing. Most of these horses are not mine. I board them here for others who don't have a place of their own to keep them. That would be against the agreement I have with their owners, and besides, I don't want my family to see that."

"Ah yes, your little Katie is a sweet child, but much too young to be observing the finer points of my techniques. I understand. Perhaps, though, we might be able to work something out for a later date, after you have had a chance to discuss my... needs and desires... with the owners you mentioned? Please?"

The yearning in the unicorn's eyes was a palpable thing, and he sighed internally. Deciding to redirect the entire conversation in a different direction, he thought of a different question to ask.

"We have never seen anything like you before. We certainly have never heard of an animal such as yourself being able to talk. Where do you come from, and how did you get here? What should I call you, anyways? Do you have a name for yourself?"

The unicorn drew himself up to his full height, and proudly arched his neck as he spoke. "I am known far and wide as Llellondryn! Mares of all species tremble at the mere sight of me! But never in fear!" He reared up and bellowed an equine call at the sky, then his front hooves came down to the ground with a loud thud.

"As to how I got here, I opened a gate across the planes and walked through. Where are we, by the way? What plane is this? Which God holds sway over this place?" Llellondryn looked around for the first time, and took in the farm implements and vehicles that dotted the grounds of Derrick's horse farm operation. "And what are those things?"

The huge form seemed to shift his weight onto his back legs, then he performed a prodigious leap that cleared the fence easily, landing with another, louder thud before trotting off towards the pickup truck and horse trailer parked near the garage.

Derrick gaped at the impossible act that the unicorn seemed to carry out almost nonchalantly before hurrying along after to try to prevent any mayhem that might occur. Although, he thought to himself, what he might be able to do to stop the impossible creature from anything escaped his thoughts at the moment. But Llellondryn seemed to content himself with just looking at the truck and trailer in front of him intently, circling around to the far side away from the house as Derrick tried to keep the pure white being in his sight.

Then he heard the back door close, and his wife's voice came to him. "Honey, what did you want me to bring the camcorder for? Katie said something about a white horse with a funny point on his head, but..." Her voice trailed off as Llellondryn came around from the other side of the trailer, but at least she had the presence of mind to whip the camcorder up, turn it on, and start recording.

Llellondryn, for his part, stopped cold at the sight of Derrick's wife. He stood stock still for a moment, just staring at the woman holding the camcorder in front of her as she looked back equally in awe over the top of what she held in her hands. Then he shook himself, and walked slowly towards her. What happened next caused her to nearly drop the expensive electronic device she held so carefully in her hands.

"My Lady, you are a vision of beauty and perfection. I am awed to be in your presence. Even in your peasant raiment, you are obviously blessed by the gods themselves. What are you doing with a bum like this on a farm? You could be holding court in the Elven Queen's city, taking your just due from worshippers that would come far and wide to simply behold your incredible features and your radiant beauty."

Shock did not really come close to what Miranda was feeling, a small part deep inside her decided. Later, she was amazed that her hands were so steady that she didn't miss any part of that statement the unicorn laid on her. It was too much. She started laughing.

"Derrick, where did this... what is..." *gasp* "Oh my. Oh my." She found she couldn't form any rational sentences.

Derrick laughed at seeing his wonderful wife so taken aback. He turned to Llellondryn and put his hand on the unicorn's shoulder. "I see you have a fine appreciation for what really matters. Flatterer."

Llellondryn turned to the human. "What? Too much? She is really fine, I must say. You must have had to hit her over the head and run off with her before she woke up to get her to like you. Did you get her with child before she knew what happened so she would stay with you? Or, it must have been gold. Did you buy her affections? Pay some huge dowry to her father? Or perhaps rescue her from a dragon? I don't see you as the knightly sort, so that couldn't really be it. You look kind of... well, not up to THAT task, I must say."

"Hey, that's not very nice. She chose ME! I was just lucky she even liked me!" Indignation warred with laughter, but mirth was winning. It was just too funny. Derrick had a good sense of humor about himself. He knew he would never win any contests, but his ability to laugh at just about anything, and not let problems upset him, had won her heart his junior year of college.

He glanced happily at Miranda, remembering the stunning beauty his roommate had introduced him to at that student mixer nearly ten years ago. The green eyes and dark brown hair framed a face that was perfect, with a soft skin tone and fine bone structure that would make a supermodel blush. The rest of her was just as perfect. She was a three sport athlete in high school and attended college on a full-ride athletic scholarship. He was still astonished to this day that they were so incredibly compatible on so many levels. He definitely married up.

"My lady, I am Llellondryn, and I am at your service." He bowed his head low and bent on elegant leg in a dashing pose for a moment, then looked up at her. "Do you wish to go for a ride? I promise to be gentle for your first time. Of course, the second time, I make no such promise…"

"Hey, that's my wife, you animal. Be nice." The look on Llellondryn's equine face turned from one of lust to one of contrition pretty fast.

"I was just casting a joke. Don't get your tail in thorns." He turned back and trotted off to the paddock.

"I suppose I must return to those that appreciate my company and the refinements of life and love that I have to offer," they heard as he headed away from them. As he neared the fence, he executed another prodigious leap that carried him easily over the fence and back inside.

His wife looked over at Derrick as Katie spoke up. "I told you he was a pointy head." Llellondryn snorted as if he had heard that, which he probably did, Derrick decided. Horses have sensitive hearing; there was no telling if Llellondryn could hear even better than that. Probably.

Miranda put one hand on her daughter's shoulder while the other held the still-recording camcorder. "Hon, what was that? Did that really just happen?"

"You saw it. Heck, you recorded it. We can watch it back to confirm it really did."

She turned the camcorder in her hand, and then stopped the recording, closing the screen. Then she spoke up.

"What do you think would happen if we put that up on YouTube?" She laughed at the shudder that seemed to come over him. Then Llellondryn's voice carried to them from the paddock.

"What is YouTube?"

CHAPTER 24

It had been almost two weeks since he had gotten the call that the Michelle situation had been handled and the David situation would be resolved shortly. Since then, nothing seemed to be going right. David had shown up back at work the following Monday as if nothing had happened, and he brought in a new member for his "team". He hoped that he had not let anything show on his face when David held a company-wide meeting to talk about Michelle taking a leave of absence. He also stated during that same meeting that Michelle had temporarily transferred her control and duties to David while she was away, something she apparently had set up a while ago.

He had smiled and nodded like everyone else, as if it was a good idea, when inside he thought it was anything but. Michelle and David both refused to take advantage of the lucrative government contract business that was just waiting to be exploited. It would have made everyone rich. Well, richer, he thought to himself. The upper management and execs were all getting bonuses every year that were significantly higher than the industry standard, and that trickled down to the workers at every level, as well, not that it should have. He firmly believed that workers should be just happy to have a job with such a wonderful company. The benefits, including the health insurance plans, the more than generous 4.01(k) matching policy, and everything else, were extravagant.

His careful suggestions that the benefits be trimmed back to further profitability, and thereby enrich the executives and higher-ups, had been jerked hard to a cold stop. It was almost like Michelle and David were running a charity for the middle class here! But the look on Michelle's face had been clear enough as she stated to him that they all had enough money, and that the company was not built on the work of the "leadership group", but on the efforts of the front-line employees. Even the private security teams that patrolled the building here in the U.S. and the building in Ireland, and manned the front desk and the surveillance monitoring station, including the off-site team that managed the remote security monitoring center, were included in this foolishness, which he internally found to be ridiculous. Everyone knew that you didn't build wealth by sharing your profits with everyone under you. But, the look on both David and Michelle's face indicated that the subject was closed.

A few weeks later, Michelle had all but ordered him to go off to that new-age joke masquerading as 'leadership training.' Inwardly, he had laughed his whole time there, all the while nodding at the appropriate places, and saying all the right things. But it was clear that whoever thought up this bunch of crap had their heads up their collective asses. 'Servant Leadership?' Really? You serve the needs of those who report to you? Not hardly. More like not ever. The employees needed to just follow direction. If they weren't capable of it, they could easily be replaced. Hell, the HR department got resumes by the basket full every time an ad was run.

He was not sure how they did it, but Michelle, and then David when her brother had come on board, had built this piddling little company into the darling of the local business community. It didn't make any sense to him. Empowerment? What the hell does that really mean? Employee engagement? If they weren't engaged by themselves, they needed to be reminded that they were here to work. And all those amenities were wastes of space, including that eye-sore of a climbing wall all those gung-ho veterans swarmed over all the time like beetles on a massive mound of feces.

When he got back from the new-age, incense-snorting, campfire sing-along calling itself leadership training, he almost gave away his real opinion when she asked him how it went. It had been a huge waste of his time and the company's money. But when he opened his mouth, the look on her face said that she believed all that crap, so he had said nothing about his true feelings. Instead, he mouthed something about that it was interesting, and he would have to think about it. Or something similar to that. He didn't really remember what had come out. But she hadn't seemed that upset by his response. She had just nodded knowingly, as if that was the expected result. It should be. All that stuff would need a lot of syrup to be poured on it to make it go down easier.

But all that left him with a problem. He desperately wanted the company to expand into providing services for the Federal government. And he knew, because his friends in high places (as he liked to think of them) had told him all about their plans. It would bring in money by the truckload, something that would have enriched everyone, down to Michelle's precious janitorial staff. But when he tried to bring that point up to justify his position, always respectfully, of course, she had shot him down. There was no way, she'd said, she would allow the technologies that had been developed by their incredibly bright programmers and mathematicians to be used by 'them'.

And when that NSA contractor had committed treason in releasing all that highly secretive and classified information to those reporters, it had solidified both hers and David's resolve to never do business with 'them,' while the sounds coming from his government contacts seemed to grow more insistent and strident.

That's when someone had whispered an idea in his ear. If Michelle and David were both out of the picture, he would be in effective legal control of the company. If such an amazing coincidence were to occur, would he sign on the line and let the government in? What a dumb question. All he could think about was the millions of dollars that would line his own accounts when he nodded firmly. That had set the plans in motion. All he had to do was get the tracker onto her Maserati, and tell them when she was planning on going to that cottage that David and Michelle both believed no one else knew about.

His eyes had narrowed when they told him about it, and he wondered if they had used company funds to build it. In fact, that had been one avenue his special friends had asked him to investigate surreptitiously. Even though it was a privately held company, a case could be made for embezzlement if they had siphoned off corporate funds to build something like that and they later registered the deed in their own names. In the end, it would be dicey to take that all the way to court, but in the meantime, both Michelle and David could be arrested and charged with embezzling from their own company. That would transfer their corporate authority to him for the duration of the investigation.

The problem was, none of it would stick, because it was a privately held corporation. Michelle and David controlled over ninety percent of the company by their direct ownership. And while he had been granted a small percentage of the company, and the highest level outside the two siblings, it amounted to almost nothing. Employee stock ownership programs were notorious. The shares issued had no real, tangible value, and while laws tried to prevent some abuses, there was very little employees could do, short of taking the company to court, which guaranteed that said employee would get a glow-in-the-dark target painted on their forehead, and a sign taped to their back that said 'Kick me (to the curb)' on their back.

The stock program at Michelle and David's company was limited to executives. The rest of the employees all received direct bonuses and retirement fund matches, which in his mind, was only slightly above downright dumb. It meant that the employees couldn't get uppity and make inappropriate demands, like he had seen elsewhere all too often with plans like that.

And now, things were at a stalemate. Obviously, David knew that someone had tried to deal with Michelle. She had signed her control and duties over to David, and gone on an extended leave of absence. She had announced it on a conference call to upper management the following Wednesday. While her voice had sounded a little different, it was clearly her on the phone. Then, she had hung up, and David had taken over. And he'd seen all his plans get tossed in the trash.

He'd called his friends to ask what came next, but they had put him on ice. They'd seemed surprised at his information, and for the first time, had seemed indecisive and unsure of their next move. Apparently things hadn't gone as planned, and they didn't know what to do next. But David seemed to have some plans of his own.

It was a subtle thing, but the special team David had assembled from his fellow military veterans seemed to close ranks around David and the new guy that had just joined them. That wasn't unusual. He had tried for a couple years to get more information from David about how he ran the team, and such. But David had simply told him that it really wasn't any of his business, since he had nothing to do with HR, and HR reported up through David. So, new members came on all the time, as other members left for greener pastures as they completed their year of training and their first year of real work. Another waste of company funds that could have gone to better causes, in his opinion, but no one asked him. And he wasn't about to chase that goose. David could be downright scary at times, probably because of his military experience.

His thoughts turned to the new team member. His appearance was a little unusual, like he never got out in the sun. His eye color was also unusual – a vivid amber color that he couldn't remember seeing in anyone else. And his hair was a uniform grey color, almost the same as his skin. He couldn't remember ever seeing anyone that looked remotely like the new guy previously. Where does David find these bozos?

When the new guy, Gil something, looked him in the eye, it was almost like looking at his wise old grandmother. It was almost like looking into a deep pool, or having Gil look through him all the way deep into his darkest secrets. The effect was somewhat disconcerting, but if he hadn't been trying to maneuver his way into a better position in charge of the company on at least a temporary basis, it wouldn't have upset him. As it was, he needed to try to keep his calm. Some things were going right. Michelle was somewhere off being detained by that team, and David...

Why wasn't David on ice with Michelle somewhere? How had that team not gotten them both? He had been assured that the team sent out to help with the situation was some of the very best, and had never failed to complete its objective. From what he had been able to deduce during the meetings to plan the moves, they were supposed to grab Michelle, secure her, and 'take her off the board'. David was supposed to then be intercepted when he went to join his sister at the cottage. Then Allison was supposed to join her husband and sister-in-law. He thought they would be held out of contact for no more than a month, which should have been sufficient to him.

With no one around to oppose him, as the number three person in the company, he would have been free, after two weeks or so, to sign off on the contract he was so eager to get for them.

He turned to look out his corner office window as he thought his way through things once again. Where had the plans gone wrong? It obviously had, because David showed up that Monday morning, and had promptly taken over. David had been in charge before, and no one batted an eye when he came in and announced that Michelle was on an extended and well-deserved vacation. They had been concerned, because all the little peons and minions loved her like some ancient nature goddess from whom all good things flowed. He snorted inside at that. She was just a lucky bitch who used every ridiculous advantage she had to try to wheedle her way into any opening, no matter how small or inappropriate.

His father had always told him that some people are destined to be in charge of the great unwashed masses of mindless sheep that made up the vast majority of the population. His family was old money, he was proud to repeatedly say, and were above all the rabble that wandered aimlessly through life making more squalling brats to play in the mud at their day care centers while their parents both went off to dead end jobs that never gave them the opportunity to advance their careers, their finances, or their children's futures. His future was assured, though. His family's money would see to that.

So when someone approached him about a meeting with a U.S. Senator about a serious issue with which he could provide assistance, he didn't hesitate. He was appalled at what the Senator told him about what was really going on in MDST, and wanted to help with the situation any way he could.

The Senator and his aide had laid it all out in front of him. Michelle was using a new cryptographic technology that they would not let the agencies of the U.S. government have access to. As far as anyone was able to tell, it was an entirely new cryptographic technique that the NSA had not been able to break. They couldn't even figure out how it worked, let alone decrypt it. And while it had only been detected on the private links between the two data centers the company had here in Ireland, they assured him that it was only a matter of time before Michelle and David decided to sell it on the open market.

After all, with that traitor NSA contractor leaking everything that he could about the NSA's forays into encryption in the last few weeks, which they were only doing to make sure we were all safe from terrorists, something the NSA couldn't touch would be worth billions on the open market. That would occur to Michelle and David eventually, and it was a temptation way too big for anyone to refuse. Everyone was human, after all, and everyone had a price. The new technique had to be brought into the NSA so that it could be analyzed and worked with until it was safe for release into the commercial market.

But Michelle in particular had shown such contempt for the government people that had come to visit with her last year that she had actually ordered them off her property after refusing to even discuss the idea. She had assured them that she had no intention of ever making the technology available to anyone else, but no one anywhere had believed her one bit. Everyone was out for themselves, and she was no different. All these altruistic things that the company did just simply had to be a cover for darker ulterior motives, in the eyes of the NSA.

So he had agreed to the plan. He had walked away from that meeting with a smile on his face. This was his chance to get to the top, and he was committed all the way. Everything was accounted for, and nothing would be left to chance.

But when David had shown up for work, he had been shocked. He'd called the contact number for the team leader, but that had gone directly to an announcement that there was no voicemail on the line, and hung up on him. His call to the Senator's aide had also been met with a wall. The man had said he would convey the message that David had returned, and someone would get back to him. But no one had gotten in touch with him since, and he wondered what was really happening over there.

At first, he had assumed that someone was looking into what happened, and that the opportunity had just been missed to grab David. He'd heard nothing about Allison, and he had no idea what was happening with her. That wasn't surprising, as she had no official role in her brother's company. She did have enough card access to get to the non-technical areas of the facility, he'd been shocked to learn when he started, and she came and went whenever she wanted, wandering in at random times to meet with David in his office, or sometimes to have lunch with him or his team of combat veterans in the free company cafeteria. He was certain that they were getting it on in the office with the door locked and the blinds shut, but he'd never been able to catch them at it. Truthfully, he didn't want to. She was, frankly, smoking hot, in his opinion, and while it would be nice to see her in the midst of a nooner, he had no interest in seeing David in a hedonistic pursuit.

But now, he decided to push the issue a little bit. There were legal documents that needed signing, and it was a wedge he could leverage to try to get more information on what was going on. So he requested a meeting with David for some point this week to get things rolling in that direction. He would get results, he was certain. It was only a question of being careful, subtle, and asking the right questions. And he was good at that.

CHAPTER 25

Her mind wandered as she ran, covering her route while she considered everything that had happened to her in the previous three weeks. The sounds of the footfalls behind her brought her back into the present moment as she smiled at the sound. Some were still straining somewhat, but in the last few weeks, every city guardsman that had decided to take up the offer to train with Allison had made progress in their conditioning. She looked over her shoulder, and spoke up in the Elven tongue.

"Three more times around the city, and we'll call it a day." A mixture of good-natured groans and laughter answered her as they heard the joke in her voice. They knew by now that she would not push herself that far. Her regular route carried her for what she guessed was about five miles. Three more laps would put that at more than twelve miles, and that was more than she wanted to do unless she was training for a marathon or some other event.

The Elven guards ran in their boots, something she was prepared to be upset about, until she examined a pair for herself. Each set of boots was hand-crafted to the owner's specific feet in a labor of love with which she was incredibly impressed. There were proper arch supports in them, and soft soles that cushioned and supported the wearer's feet almost as well as her running shoes. They ran in tunics and leggings, the standard wear for when they were in training. During colder times, they would add a cloak or heavier outer coat that would provide additional warmth.

One of the guardswomen had approached her after her first morning run, asking her what she was doing running all around the city in that way. When she explained the conditioning regimen she maintained, the elven woman had nodded. Word of her exploit in the throne room had made it near and far across the city in the usual way that rumors seemed to travel, and was the talk of the various races in the taverns and merchant counting rooms.

Some merchants had inquired respectfully if she was available to serve as protection for their caravans to the other cities around the continent, but she had turned down the offers of work that came her way. As long as the strike team that had attacked Michelle was still in the Queen's jail cells, she would be close by. She knew what they were capable of, and had tried to impress that knowledge on Karonashkk, the Minotaur jailer. She wasn't certain she was succeeding at first, but the eight and a half foot tall red-skinned being had listened carefully to everything she had said, and had asked thoughtful questions, gravely made careful notes on a parchment scroll to make sure he had everything down.

Karonashkk had asked her to spar with one of his Elven guards, to better understand what the strangely dressed humans in his care were capable of. It hadn't been much of a contest. Allison had trained in various martial arts since she was four years old, starting with Aikido, then moving on to Krav Maga at age twelve, the art developed by the Israeli Defense Force for its Special Forces soldiers. She had added some Japanese kenpō and Kenjutsu for a few years, mainly to get some weapons training and experience, and then moved on to Taekwondo and found that she enjoyed it immensely. At thirty-five years old, she had been studying the fighting arts for over thirty years, and it showed as she went through the guardsmen and women like they were practice dummies. Even unarmed against those holding swords and spears, she had been able to stay unscathed, dealing out quite a bit of damage in the process.

It was a strange feeling to not be holding back in any way in training and demonstrations. A mage had been asked to oversee the training to heal any injuries that might happen. Expecting to have to attend to the brash human female who had been delusional enough to think she would survive against trained Elven guards dedicated to the defense of the Queen and the capital city, several of whom were centuries older than her and had been training for many decades longer than she had been alive, instead he had been forced to heal an ever-growing litany of injuries to those same guardsmen.

Yintarin, the Dwarvish mage, had looked at her in awe after two men with real swords had set on her, only to see her easily overcome the odds and put both senior guards down without getting injured herself. Astonishment had made Karonashkk speechless for a time, followed by consternation as the ramifications of what the four men in his jail could be capable of raced through the Minotaur's brain.

Karonashkk and Allison had several minutes of conversation over the fallen guardsmen as the mage attended to their wounds, as the other Elven guardsmen listened, still in shock to what they had witnessed.

Allison's mind returned to the present as the cavalcade approached the guard barracks. She slowed down to a walk, continuing to move as she checked her pulse in her neck, feeling pleased as the rate slowed quickly. Somehow, the spell that Giltreas had cast on her at Michelle's cottage had also returned her to the height of her physical conditioning, and had stripped away what little extra weight she had been carrying.

The sight of her abdomen that evening had been a pleasant revelation, as the much-coveted six-pack she'd had in the Marines was back, along with the muscle definition of the highly-trained athlete and modern warrior of her younger days across her upper body and her legs. Michelle had given her a mock gasp, hand dramatically over her mouth, as she stood in her sports bra and panties, which had earned her sister-in-law an upturned hand with her middle and adjacent fingers flashed at the older woman (who looked nothing of the sort anymore), with the phrase, "read between the lines," and a wide, happy smile accompanying it.

She frowned as she contemplated the dilemma that Michelle faced. Her husband's sister seemed to have lost most of her appetite now, and didn't really sleep anymore, either. Most nights she wandered the huge building the Elven queen had said was their home as long as they wanted and needed it.

Whatever had happened to Michelle seemed to have transformed more than just her appearance. Allison had spoken with the Dwarven mage about it, and he was at a loss to explain what had occurred. He asked to examine Michelle, and Michelle had agreed after considering the request briefly. But the mage had not uncovered anything that might explain the situation. The results of the few spells he had cast, explaining that they were just to determine if anything was wrong, had led to more questions than answers.

Michelle and Allison had talked about MDST, the company she owned with Allison's husband, and her concerns about where the company would go from here. Michelle thought it was becoming more and more evident that she would not be returning to her previous leadership role as CEO, given how different she looked. Allison was not as sure. Most people exhibited more mental flexibility than Michelle was prepared to accept, but that was probably because Michelle herself was the subject to which they would have to adapt their thinking. Allison had no real helpful ideas on how Michelle could encourage that flexibility into her subordinates, however.

The weekly visits from Dave and Giltreas, or Gil Owens, as he wanted to be called for the duration of his time helping Dave pursue Michelle's attackers, had kept them up to date in the search for Michelle's enemy, and had also brought whatever was needed by the women in their unwanted vacation. The dogs had adjusted well, with kennels set up in the women's quarters, their regular food and water bowls, and all the food, treats, and other supplies the three canines would need.

Sadie's "voice" had not gone away, something that had both shocked and amused Yintarin to no end. In studying what had happened to the happy, friendly dog, he had discovered something else about Sadie's new-found voice; the listener heard her speak in their native language, and when they spoke to Sadie in that same language, she understood them as easily as if they had been speaking in English, the only language the big reddish-golden dog had ever been exposed to. Like everything that had happened to Michelle, he had no explanation for what had happened to Michelle's canine companion.

Yintarin had approached Giltreas on one of the frequent trips to Delara's home, and had asked politely if the dwarf could help discover why the magic spells Giltreas had cast on Michelle and Sadie had such inexplicable results, but the son of the queen had not been interested. Yintarin had bowed respectfully, and stated the offer would still be there should Giltreas change his decision.

Later, Yintarin and Allison had spoken briefly about what was different about the effects the spells Giltreas had cast on Michelle. Allie had nodded her understanding that things were different than what the mage had expected, both in the changes that had been done to Michelle's appearance, and the fact that the Animal Speak spell cast on Sadie should have faded away a long time ago.

Yintarin was quite adamant that the Animal Speak spell never lasted more than several minutes, and had even demonstrated the spell, and its duration, on a horse in the paddock next to the Suburban. The demonstration also highlighted another difference in the two spells: Sadie was much more eloquent than the horse had been. Where the horse had spoken in an almost childish speech pattern, using simple words and short sentences and phrases, Sadie's statements were much more like what one would expect of an adult, with more fully formed sentences. Sometimes Sadie fell back on more broken diction, but that seemed to be more of when she didn't want to make the effort, than any lack of ability.

As time went on, and the spell gave no indication that it would end any time soon, Sadie's ability to speak grew, along with her vocabulary. Which wasn't always a good thing. Allison's time in the Marines had added a lot of salt and spice to her own vocabulary when she was less than thrilled, and she found herself having to censor what came out of her mouth constantly, especially after the first time Sadie dropped the crude expletive for defecation along with an f-bomb in casual conversation.

Sadie fell into the role of interpreter, of a sort, between the women and the other two dogs. It was surprisingly effective to tell Sadie to make Max stop barking all the time, or to tell Abby to stop licking anything, everything, and everybody she came in contact with. And Sadie was not shy about telling Michelle and Allison when any of the three needed to go outside to relieve themselves. Which brought up another "teachable moment," as Allison explained that "Abby needs to go take a shit" was not really an appropriate way of expressing that particular biological function. Of course, the statement lost a lot of its edge because Michelle was trying really hard, and failing miserably, not to laugh uproariously at what her bigger, older dog had said.

The response from Sadie brought Michelle over to explain that "Go fuck yourself," no matter how cheerfully offered, was really not polite, either, and while it was a useful statement, it needed to be reserved for moments that really deserved the very aggressive sentiment. Sadie's pithy statement brought Allison to tears trying not to laugh. The usage was right, but Michelle had been at a loss to have to explain what the word meant to the listening Delara; apparently the Elven language did not have an equivalent, all-purpose word that could be used in so many different ways. The young queen just laughed when the intended meaning behind the offensive word was conveyed, saying that there were worse things in the world than a cursing dog.

Allison stopped walking, and started to fall into some Tai Chi exercises, walking the guards through the forms as she herself used them to stretch and cool down after the run. She was impressed with the elven guards that had dedicated themselves to physical betterment at her hand, and while she tried to resist the urge to fall into Marine drill instructor mode, she enjoyed the challenge of seeing how far the elves could be pushed.

It was probably a result of the racial differences between humans and elves, along with the fact that the youngest of the elven guards was past to seventy years (full turnings of the season, as they referred to it) old that gave her charges more psychological grace and balance than humans of a similar point in their development.

Elves lived extraordinarily long lives, by anyone's standards. Karonashkk had explained that Minotaurs lived about twelve to thirteen hundred years, dwarves lived to somewhere around seven hundred, halflings lived about three hundred, and humans of this place lived somewhere around two hundred years old. Which brought up the question of how long was a year, or a full season's turning.

Allison was mildly interested to hear the explanation: a full turning was 365 days, with every fourth turning having one extra day. The discovery that an additional day was required came from a female dwarf mage named Domilla some few millennia ago who had studied the sun, the moon, and the stars. Domilla had invented the math necessary to calculate the length of the year. There was a calendar of sorts in use, but it had almost no correlation to the Julian calendar in use on Allison's home plane.

There were twelve months in the calendar, but that was where the similarities ended. A month was made up of six weeks, and each week was five days long. Each day was referred to simply as first-day, second-day, and so on. Weeks and months were also referred to by their numeric position in the calendar as well. Years were counted up from the beginning of the calendar. It was year 2563 in that calendar. At the end of the year, there was a week that was not part of any month. It occurred at the spring equinox every year, to celebrate the end of winter. The extra day every fourth year was added to those five days of celebration and general relaxation with family and friends.

The Tai Chi took nearly a half hour, and at the end of that time, the sweating and tired guards of the city bid their new trainer a good day, and wandered off to freshen up. Allison headed back to the quarters she shared with Michelle, two little dogs, and one obnoxious, nearly-hyperactive, attention-challenged, much-loved, foul-mouthed red-gold dog.

CHAPTER 26

Steven Williams walked into David's office with the slight smile he presented to the world that he always assumed people thought was pleasant. He pulled the door shut behind him to begin the meeting he had called, and walked forward to the huge desk set in the corner between the floor-to-ceiling windows that made up two walls of the corner office. The large, well-appointed room was on the third floor of the data center building, with an expansive view of other downtown buildings and a parking ramp. Not for the first time, Steven looked around the room, noting the memorabilia from David's military career, and the items that depicted his hobbies and interests.

A veritable shrine to the Minnesota Vikings dominated one corner, with a signed game-worn Kevin Williams jersey in a glass showcase hanging on the wall. Another section of the wall showed pictures of David in Marine combat fatigues with a group of men and women in front of a huge vehicle, with rifles slung casually across in front of their body armor, with their helmets and sun glasses in place to block out the mid-day sun.

Steven's reverie was interrupted by a strange tingling sensation, and the sense that someone was behind him. He turned reflexively, but there was no one there, and he suppressed an internal shiver that seemed to come from out of nowhere. When he turned back to David, he thought he saw a strange look on the other man's face for a moment, but it was gone so quickly that he wasn't sure what he saw, or even if it was his imagination playing tricks on him. The memory of the strange sensation seemed to twinge at that moment for some reason, but he put it behind him as he walked up and placed his portfolio on the near edge of the desk, selected a chair, and sat down.

"Well, Steve, you called this meeting, what's up?" David smiled at Steven, and internally, the Chief Financial Officer seethed. He had made it plain several times to David that his name was Steven, not Steve, or Steve-O, or Stevie, or anything else. But he shrugged aside the old irritation, and pasted his usual smile on his face.

"Well, there are a number of things that I would like to speak with Michelle about. Do you know when she will be returning?" It came out completely innocently, sounding as if Steven was a concerned employee with legitimate business with the owner of the company he worked for, he was pleased to note.

"Well, her doctor has told her that she needed to get more rest. I think that is what she is doing. I am her legal power of attorney for the business, and her brother. Is there something you need to talk to her about that you cannot discuss with me?" David said it pleasantly enough, but inside he was certain this was the person he was looking for.

In the past four weeks since Michelle had been attacked, David's team had quietly begun to notice everything going on around them. Phil had been leading and coordinating the efforts. His sixteen years of experience as an Army criminal investigator had come in handy in ruling out potential suspects. Slowly, they had eliminated everyone else inside the company, after a lot of careful, surreptitious and detailed work. Of course, the discussion the night 'Gil Owens' had been introduced to the team had been lively, to say the least.

It was amazing to see the results of the spells that Giltreas had cast that night. His explanations of what he had done had been picked apart and dissected by Phil and several others who were incredibly curious about the impossible abilities that Giltreas so took for granted. While Giltreas had not been able to provide answers to every question, it was evident to everyone in that room that he was not trying to hide anything related to his abilities, and magic in general, from the team. He later told David that he believed that establishing trust with the team was as important as David said it would be.

There were some questions that he had bluntly stated he would not answer, including those about some of his past experiences using magic, saying that his Patron would not be pleased were he to speak about them. He had expected more pushback on those issues, but he was surprised that the first time he made that statement he was met with knowing nods and grim faces. He had asked why they were accepting of his polite but pointed refusal to answer, but Phil had spoken for the group when he said they respected that he couldn't talk about everything, and that everyone in the room most likely had been in situations that they were unable to talk about. It was the nature of being in the service of a state or nation.

Magic, Gil had explained, were thought of as two groups of skills: spells and enchantments. Casting spells started with four cardinal spells: heal, mend, wound, and rend. Heal and wound were spells that affected living things, just like mend and rend were spells that affected things that were not living, such as things made from metals, stone, or wood. Children were taught the four cardinal spells, and how well and how easily they were able to learn and cast them indicated how far their abilities would go, and how much they should be trained in the future as they grew to adulthood.

Spells could be cast in a variety of ways. The easiest was through the use of parts of plants, which were called makings, which were gathered in hand in the appropriate amounts and ratios, then were consumed by the magical force that caused the spell to happen, while the spell caster concentrated on the act the spell was meant to accomplish. This is the first form of magic learned, because some of the power needed to cast the spell is taken from the makings used to form and shape the spell. Mages call this plant magic. There were hundreds of spells that could be cast in this way, and the most powerful spells known were plant spells.

The time a spell caster needed to wait between casting spells started out very long, and diminished as the caster became more adept at the various spells they use regularly. New spells usually would require significant time to recover before casting any other spells, simply because of the demands a new, unknown spell made on the magical strength of the caster.

Potions are similar to plant magic, in that parts of plants are used to make potions. A kettle or pot is filled with the right amount of the purest of waters found, which is then heated. Plant makings are added in the right amounts, and then the pot is infused with magical force to bind the spell. The resulting magical potion is then used immediately if needed, or portioned out into small bottles that hold enough for a full dose. Mages know of only a very few potions: cure poison, cure sickness, cure wounds, and cure blindness are the most common, although the opposites could be created: poison, make sick, wound, and blindness. Potions provide the ability to use magic very quickly without using magic strength, such as while fighting.

After learning spells with makings, there were other forms. Runic magic involved carving a rune or runes into something permanent, such as wood, stone, or metal. The rune spell caster infused the work with magical force to set the spell in place and define what the spell would do. A word was also bound to the work. The result was called a rune mark, or mark. Then, to cast the spell, one needed to simply infuse the rune mark with magic force, and say in their mind the bound word when the mark had absorbed enough magical force to complete the effect. Runic magic was helpful because the mark maker only had to learn the spell, then infuse it into an object with a runic mark carved into it. Once completed, the mark could be used over and over by anyone capable of putting enough magical force into it and speaking the bound word.

Wand magic involved binding a spell or spells into a wand, and binding enough magical strength into the wand to cast the spells a number of times. A word was also bound into the wand for each spell that was bound to it, to serve as a release word to cast the spell. Spells could be bound to a staff, as well, but such enchantments of a large object required much greater skill and power on the part of the maker, although spells bound to staves could be cast many more times, as the larger objects could hold much more magical strength. Once the magical force in the wand or staff was used up, a mage could recharge it, even if he or she didn't know the spells or the bound words of those spells.

Enchanting is the skill of binding a spell to something, such as weapons, armor, clothing, jewelry, a door, a rock, or any non-living object the mage desired. Most mages could enchant things with spells, but such enchantments were not permanent. Permanent enchantments required enormous skill and magical power to make the effect permanent, and caused the mage to have to spend many days or weeks recovering from the effort. A God or Goddess could make such permanent enchantments, but rarely did so, for reasons they did not share with mortals.

Enchantments could be either an effects or spells. Effects could make someone stronger or give them the ability to see in the dark or heal the wearer much faster than normal. Enchantment spells could be cast repeatedly until the magical strength in the object was used up. Once that happened, a spell could be cast to restore the magical strength in the object if it was enchanted permanently. An object other than a wand or staff could only be enchanted with a single effect or spell.

Every adult and child of every higher race had some ability with magic, and was able to cast the healing spell to some extent. Beyond that, abilities varied widely. It seemed that the children that could hold their concentration the longest were the ones that would be able to do the most with their magical abilities, but the ability to draw upon the 'strength' that was the source that powered spells also varied much as well.

All children could draw from the magical strength from inside themselves, which then took some time to replenish just like getting tired required sleep to restore the body's physical strength. The source and amount of magical strength that a caster had available to them acted to limit their ability to cast spells – when the strength you used was depleted, you could cast no more until that strength replenished, which usually took most of the day or night.

Some beings were able to draw from the strength in the living things around them. A very rare and precious few were able to draw from the very fabric of magic itself without harming themselves. The fabric of magic was a seemingly endless well of strength.

Once in a great while there were those few that could draw from magic without needing to be taught. For those with that rarest of abilities, instruction in mage arts was limited to expanding the spells they were able to cast, and to make sure they could recognize when they pushed even their formidable skills close to their limits. Such beings could be of any higher race, and were exceedingly rare, so much so that they were heralded when discovered. Giltreas had not heard of one being discovered in hundreds of years, and no one knew what gave them their ability.

When a magic spell is learned and cast for the first time, the caster must use a lot of makings for the spell, and will only produce a small effect that will affect a single being. The caster must also touch the being to cast the spell. As greater experience with the spell is achieved, less of the makings will be required, and the effect will be greater. Some casters will eventually be able to cast spells without any makings, using simply magical strength to make the spell.

Once that is achieved, the caster will attempt to cast the spell over a distance, without touching the being to cast the spell on them. This will once again require the caster to use a lot of makings, as the casting is much harder. Again, the skill of the caster will increase until the distance involved is significant, and the makings required is once more eliminated. Then, the caster will attempt to cast the spell over two people close together, requiring many makings again, with minimal effect. Over time, most mage spells can be used with maximum effect over a distance to the most number of beings, who could be further and further apart. Mages who bring their skill with a given spell to this level are said to have mastered that particular spell. This process may take years, or longer. It is for this reason that spell casters from shorter-lived races such as humans will focus on few spells to master, while learning many other spells with much lower skill, and requiring greater makings.

There were some spells, two in particular, that were of great interest to the team: detect magic, and dispel magic. Detecting magic was a simple spell that required almost no makings and no strength. The skill and strength needed to dispel a magical spell needed to be greater than that of the caster who cast the spell in the first place. Dispelling enchantments was next to impossible. Because of the high level of ability and strength needed to cast them in the first place, very few casters equaled the skills of those that were capable of making enchantments in the first place.

Several hundred years before Giltreas was born, a very old Halfling mage of exceptional ability discovered how to craft a spell that cast other spells, such as the spell that Giltreas used on the team. That spell cast a cure poison spell, followed immediately by a cure disease spell, followed by a healing spell, and finished with a cure blindness spell. This spell required the caster to master the spells to be cast by the casting spell. The effect was great, but the cost was higher to the caster than the combined cost of casting the spells separately. Casters who could cast such a casting spell were prized, especially those who could do so while fighting.

What Giltreas did not share was the speculation that has been talked about in the Elven Mage Council: that a spell-caster that can cast all the spells they know, and a great many of the known spells, at the greatest effect from the greatest distance and affecting the most beings, may have ascended to Deus, or low-god. He personally did not believe in such things, although the arguments in favor were compelling. The one argument he found most significant was that the time to master spells to the highest level was very long, and that most mortal lives would end before any such ascension could take place. He was adept at many forms and spells of magic, and he did not believe that he had become a low-god. The thought was laughable to him.

CHAPTER 27

David returned to the present as he realized that Giltreas had successfully cast the spell to compel Steven to be truthful and forthcoming with what David asked him without Steven knowing, and the CFO had no idea what was about to happen in David's office behind closed doors.

Steven walked over and took a chair in front of the small conference table as David walked over to join him, sitting in his customary spot with his back to the windows.

"What's up, Steve? You didn't mention what you wanted to talk about in the meeting request. Is it something related to the budget for next year?"

Steven smiled outwardly, but inside the old familiar irritation arose at David's inappropriate familiarity. It was more difficult to suppress this time, though. Since his plans had come so far apart, and he had no idea where to go from here, he was a little off balance inside.

"Well, no. Actually, there are several things I wanted to discuss with you and Michelle. More with Michelle, since she is CEO. When do you expect her to return?" A strange feeling was beginning to make its presence known inside his head. It was almost like a pressure, or a minor headache, and he wondered if he was getting sick again. These late summer colds seemed to drag on forever.

David seemed to frown slightly, as if annoyed by the question. "Steve, you and I talked about this with you in the past, after the announcement that Michelle was on leave. I am the acting CEO. I am fully aware of everything that Michelle knows, and if I have a question, I can get in contact with her to ask. What is it that you need to talk to her about that you can't discuss with me? Why are you so insistent on speaking with her?"

The pressure increased as Steven tried to think about how best to respond to the question without giving away his real agenda, but he responded to the question almost as if someone else was controlling him.

"I need to know what happened to her at the cottage, and why they didn't get you at the same time."

Oh shit. Why did he just blurt that out? His face turned bright red as he tried to reign in his emotions and regain control, but the pressure inside his head increased, and started to cause some pain as he resisted whatever was influencing him.

"So you were behind the attack on Michelle?" The question came out flat, almost emotionless.

"Yes. I needed her and you out of the way so I could take this company in the direction it is supposed to go." What is happening to him? It was becoming surreal. Why was he just opening his guts this way?

"What did you think was going to happen to Michelle and me?" The tone in David's voice took on an almost menacing edge to it as David's face transformed slightly, and Steven felt the blood beginning to drain from his face at what he was revealing.

"The team was supposed to take you and Michelle to a secluded location, and hold you there for several weeks until I was able to sign some contracts with the government..." The narration of what Steven believed was supposed to happen just seemed to flow out of his mouth, even while he tried to stop himself.

David looked at the slightly smaller man sitting across from him in his office as his mind raced. It was obvious that someone had misled Steven about what the team was supposed to do, and he tried to connect what Steven was told with what Michelle and Giltreas said actually happened. He suddenly realized something, and his eyes focused on the CFO, the trusted member of the inner circle who had just proven that he was out for himself, and damn the cost to anyone that got in his way.

"You are a total fool, you know that, right?" The statement came out calmly without any emotion at all.

The rhetorical question confused Steven enough that the pressure didn't force him to blurt out whatever was in his mind. All he could do was gape at the younger man.

"The four animals you set on Michelle beat her to the point of death, and tried to rape her all the while. It is obvious that whoever you have been conniving with has lied to you about what they were going to do to her. One of them told me I was supposed to be next. I can only imagine what their plans were for Allison if they hadn't been intercepted." That same calm, emotionless voice suddenly caused Steven to lose control of his bladder slightly, before he clamped down completely, and he flushed as he felt the slight wetness in his pants.

The differences between what he was told by the Senator and his aide and by David shook him badly. He was a fool. Something else was going on here, but he couldn't wrap his mind around it.

Then a question occurred to him, and he said it before he could stop himself. "Is Michelle still alive? Where is she? What hospital is she in?"

David nodded once. "In all the years that you have worked here, that is the first thing I have ever heard you say that was not about yourself or your responsibilities."

"Well, where is she?"

"Why should I tell you anything?" David shot back. "You just tried to have her and I killed so you could take over our company."

"I have to have them try again! I have to get control so I can take this company in the direction it is meant to go! You have to tell me!" Horror at what he just said made Steven quake inside. What was really happening here? Why was he so forthcoming with his true thoughts?

David was utterly shocked at the depravity of the human-shaped thing sitting across from him.

"Let me explain some things to you, you little piece of shit." The first real anger flashed across David's face as his voice slowly grew louder, and his prodigious self-control began to slip. "First of all, this is Michelle's company. It is privately owned. She owns it. She built it from the ground up. She decides what is right for it, and what isn't. I am also part owner, and her legally-established successor. Which means that should she not be available, like she is right now, then I decide what is right for it, and what isn't. I am her legal power of attorney, just like she is mine. That means that I am legally able to act in her stead, and she in mine. Between the two of us, we own ninety-eight percent of the company. The one point two percent that you own isn't worth a fart in a tornado unless we decide otherwise.

"Second, you don't set direction and policy for this company. Michelle and I do. If you don't like what we are doing, you are free, within the limits of the non-compete and non-disclosure agreements you signed when you started here, to go away and do something else. I really wish you had just gone away instead of pulling this shit, because now I have to clean up the mess that you made.

"What in the hell made you think that you have any right whatsoever to decide this company, that Michelle built from the ground up by herself, should do anything? Your job was to manage the finances. Nothing more!" David's self-control was nearly gone as his hands gripped the arms of the chair so tightly his knuckles were white, and he half rose out of the seat while leaning forward part-way across the table. Then he forced himself to take a deep breath and sit back down, his face flushed with emotion.

Steven cringed in the expensive chair as David bellowed out the last two words so loudly that his ears rang, all the while wondering what had caused him to just spill his guts like this. He was about to speak up, when David beat him to it.

"I am really glad you came to me today, Stevie." The sarcasm was so thick, one could almost walk across it. "You are now going to tell everything you know about whom you are working with, and what you know about their plans. Speak up loud and clear so the mic on the web cam can hear you and get everything recorded, and so that the people on the other end can understand exactly what is going on. But before you do, Phil is going to come in and take over the questioning." The door to the office opened, and Steven's eyes darted to the left at the sudden intrusion. But any hope of escaping out the suddenly open door was dashed as he saw several members of David's team standing there, with angry expressions on their faces. He shrunk down even further as he realized he had no way out of the situation he was in.

Phil stepped into the office, and stared down at the pathetic little man looking up at him with fear plainly on his face. He knew intellectually that Gil's skillset was formidable, but the Compel Truth spell amazed him. If only he'd had that at his disposal back in his role as an Army criminal investigator, his life, and his work load, would have been so much simpler.

The entire team had been watching and listening to the feed from the webcam on David's desk from the outer office, where it was also being streamed to several other PCs for recording, both here and at the London data center. From there, it was being encrypted and stored at other locations around Europe, in case it was needed later. David was right, Phil knew, when he postulated that the Federal government was involved. That was the only organization with the reach and the capability to pull off what had had been done so far, and Steven's statement that a U.S. Senator was involved clearly finished all dissent on the topic.

While everyone liked and respected David, everyone loved Michelle. This was not going to be fun for Steven.

For the next hour or more, David and the entire team watched and listened to the main TV screen pulled from the nearby conference room to the main part of the administrative area outside David's office as Steven spilled his guts on everything he knew about the conspiracy.

Towards the end of the interrogation, Phil's trained investigative skills and instincts narrowed in on what Steven might have known about who might be behind the attack, and who was providing obviously very private information about Michelle's habits and when she would be at the cottage that no one outside David and Michelle and the contractors who built it for David should have known about. Unfortunately, Steven was such a credible fool that he never even thought to ask questions of his powerful benefactor that might have clued him in on what was really going on. The worst part of it for Steven was that the entire conversation was recorded, encrypted, and shipped offsite to parts unknown across the Internet.

Giltreas had been astonished by that capability, and what it meant in terms of proof later on of misdeeds, which led to his introduction to

PLANE OF THE GODLESS, BOOK 1

YouTube.com a week ago when the plans had been made for when they discovered whoever had been involved in the plot. David just chuckled and turned Gil loose on a computer the tech department set up just for Gil on the company network, and Gil had spent hours out of the day looking at all manner of videos from all over the world, his headphones on and his face glued to the screen in front of him. Everything from gardening to music to movies to combat footage was right there for him to view, and he soaked it up every chance he could.

Now he sat quietly in the back of David's office, having made himself unseen before David opened the door to let Steven in. And as the questioning went on, he grew more and more impressed with Phil as the human elegantly and delicately extracted every last thing that Steven knew, and pieced together things that Steven only slightly guessed at.

CHAPTER 28

Michelle was waiting impatiently in the throne room when Allison came in in a hurry. She had been sitting in the main room of the suite she was sharing with Michelle and the dogs when a guard had come up and told her that Michelle wanted her in the main room in the building as soon as possible. Now she hurried over to Michelle, speaking as soon as she saw her sister-in-law.

Michelle was dressed in a loose shirt and soft leather pants that she had borrowed from Delara, along with some sandals that had been found that would fit her. Personally, Allie thought that the queen had found someone to make them for Michelle, since they looked perfectly brand new, but Michelle just smiled and nodded when Allie suggested it to her.

Now, Michelle's face, which had been so serene in the last few days, was frowning. Clearly she was troubled about something, and Allie thought she also detected some anger, as well. The experiences she had had had had a profound effect on her, Allison decided, and not just physically.

"What is going... ahhh. A gate. Someone is coming to visit?" Allie shifted mental gears quickly as she saw the strange magical construct standing in the room, so similar to the first one she and the others had passed through to arrive in Delara's home.

"Not exactly." The response was grim, and Allison caught the undertone then. Michelle was more than a little angry, but she was a past master of concealing her emotions from most people. Allie knew her better, though.

"They found someone, then." The look on Allison's face suddenly matched that of the incredibly beautiful, amazingly young-looking woman standing next to her. A stray thought flashed through her mind as she recalled the miraculous transformation that Michelle had undergone at Giltreas' hand when he had brought her back to life.

The 'incident', as Michelle insisted on calling it, had changed everything for them all. David and Allison had been healed of everything wrong with them, including the need for glasses and contact lenses. Allison had been unable to conceive a child, something that Giltreas accredited to the minute traces of what he had called poisons he had found in her body, most of which was localized in what he referred to as her 'center of womanhood'. She felt and looked younger now, just like how she looked after she made it through Marine boot camp – in peak physical condition and full of energy and life. David had mentioned that he felt much the same way, since he had also been hit with the same spells that had fixed everything that was wrong with Allison.

But Michelle's transformation was complete. She was unrecognizable to anyone who hadn't known her in high school, before Fate had decided that she made a good target and crash test dummy. Nearly sixty extra pounds had been erased from her frame as if it had never existed, along with every scar, old wound, mole, every bit of flab and skin imperfection; you name it, Giltreas had made it all disappear with magic. But there were other changes, as well.

Michelle didn't seem to need sleep anymore. She also barely ate anything at all. And she didn't seem to miss either the sleep or the food. Allison had kept some small hope that the same would happen to her, but she was contented to not have to contemplate changes to herself of that magnitude. She worried about Michelle, though, and what impact those changes were having on her.

Allison had been studying magic when she wasn't working out with the guardsmen. The dwarven mage Yintarin had agreed to teach her, after warning her that she was much too old to start developing the concentration and focus necessary to advance very far. But he and she were both surprised at what she was capable of.

Yintarin also had been surprised at her physical abilities, but after a long discussion of martial arts, and how long she had been studying them, he was as surprised no more at either her physical abilities nor her single-minded pursuit of the mage arts and the progress she made. She had learned to focus all her attention on a task or goal many years before – she was just bringing that single-minded focus to bear on a new set of goals and aspirations.

Now both Michelle and Allison turned as Delara appeared dressed in her royal attire, with her small, understated crown of office in place on her head. She ascended to her throne on the dais, seated herself sedately and gracefully, then looked at the human women.

"Are you ready?" The short question came out gently, as she knew that Michelle was not at all pleased at who she was about to meet.

Michelle steeled herself and nodded. Four days before, David and

Giltreas had come through a portal to explain they had been unable to rule out Steven. With the mention of just his first name, everything clicked in Michelle's mind. It had to be. His attitude had always been borderline arrogant, but he had covered it well with his exceptional work in his role as Chief Financial Officer. Now, though, word had come just an hour earlier that, with the help of a convenient spell from Giltreas, Steven had spilled the beans, telling everything he knew, or thought he knew, about the attack on Michelle.

She was not at all surprised that Steven had thought the plan was a little different than what had actually happened. He was quite blind to some things, she had learned over the years of their professional relationship, especially things that contradicted what he 'knew' was true. The old adage came to mind: it is when you are convinced that something is true when it is actually wrong that you suffer the most.

The queen's guards finished taking their places around the room, and between the dais and where Giltreas had placed the gate. They had been assured that the man they were about to take into custody was no threat, but they were taking no chances. Experience was the best teacher. Michelle didn't mind the show of force. It would certainly cow Steven into acquiescence, a most desirable state.

Now a guard walked to the gate, and signaled that all was ready.

* * *

Steven stared blankly the strange apparition in front of him. The grey man had told him it was a gate to his home plane, whatever that meant. The shimmering, watery surface stood vertically in front of him, making a weird sound that he couldn't compare to anything he had ever heard before.

Giltreas had 'called' the gate as simply as anyone else made a phone call, waving his hand in a forward and upward motion that seemed to be connected to the manifestation of the thing now making a mockery of the physics that he had studied in college as an elective. Over to the side, David had been talking quietly to some of his team members. It appeared that half of them would be staying behind, while the other half went through to ensure that Steven was taken into custody without any issues. The one complication to their plans was Cora.

Steven's wife had shown up, intent on surprising her husband with a pleasant lunch at The Local, a nearby restaurant they both liked to frequent. Instead, she had been told that she would be accompanying her husband on a trip for a while. No one had had the courage to tell her what he had done, so he had been forced to tell her himself that he had caused a lot of problems, and was in a lot of trouble.

Cora was deeply in love and utterly devoted to her husband, and no matter how upset she was with him and what he had done, she couldn't be without him. Whatever happened to him, she vowed, she would be there at his side. The simple statement had humbled him and torn him apart mentally, shaming him to his very soul, and he had wept on her shoulder as she tried to rectify the two seemingly different people that inhabited the body of the man she married. It would take a lot of time for her to put the two together, and while she didn't forgive him for what he had done, she would be there beside him no matter what.

She had recognized that her husband's life was in David's hands, and she had taken him aside to quietly ask him to not kill Steven.

David had been shocked at the request, and it caused him to mentally take a step back and reevaluate his own state of mind towards Steven. He decided that he would defer the decision about what to do with Steven until later, but a small part of him knew that he couldn't take the other man's life, regardless of what Steven had done to Michelle or anyone else; he didn't want that on his own conscience.

David had simply said that she would have to accompany her husband, for her own safety. He didn't explain his reasons why, but she had guessed that Steven had been conspiring with someone who had convinced him to do something stupid. He meant well, but he was quite naive when it really came down to it. She had no interest in being the pawn of anyone who had been manipulating her husband, so she readily agreed.

Now, they waited, watching the strange thing for any sign. And it came.

A hand appeared and waved them forward in a 'come here' gesture that everyone recognized, extending out from the gate that hung in the outer administrative office area, and everyone who hadn't seen it before gasped involuntarily as the action drove home what Giltreas had said before: he used gates to travel to other planes of existence.

A short while after the hand disappeared, the first few team members went forward and followed David through the gate, wondering where they would appear on the other side.

Allison watched as David came through the gate, and he immediately stepped forward to clear the area where the others came through. He nodded at Allison, Michelle, then Delara, and stepped aside as Phil and Nate came through, followed by Christine. The three humans looked around in awe at the strange place and people they were seeing for the first time, then stepped aside.

Delara looked on with interest from her throne as the humans who were devoted to David and Michelle came through the gate. One man was of the same human group as David, but the second man had skin as dark as those from the land below the great desert, and the woman had the look of the far eastern tribes – almond skin and exotic eyes. All three moved with the grace of well-trained warriors, though, and she approved, even if her seneschal had not been happy, predictably, about allowing so many humans into her throne room. A patient smile had calmed him somewhat, though, and he had subsided. He had, though insisted on doubling the guards, something she thanked him for pleasantly. It was a wise decision, after all.

Michelle watched as Steven stepped through, then her hand went to her mouth as Cora followed, looking elegant and graceful as always, even in a situation as unfamiliar and fantastic as what she was currently caught up in. The understated dress suit she wore, suitable for the business world that she brushed up against from time to time in her role in the various charities she was involved in, was beautiful, a black and white floral print that was tailored to her figure without being inappropriate in any way.

Giltreas rounded out the group, closing the gate when he came through.

Cora looked around in astonishment as she emerged from the gate, and stepped forward as she had been told to by the strange grey-skinned and grey-haired man. The guards, dressed in what looked like costumes better found at the Renaissance Festival, all looked at her gravely, the seriousness of the situation etched into their green-skinned faces. She held gently to Steven's arm as she realized that her husband had truly made some monumentally foolish mistakes, and hoped that they would both get through it as unscathed as possible. Then she saw Allison standing next to a young human woman she didn't recognize, but who could be sought after for the cover of any fashion magazine in the world. Her flawless skin and almost ethereal beauty made Cora's breath catch in her throat, and Steven turned to look at what had caused his wife to be so startled. Shock made him freeze in place.

Whomever was standing next to Allison was, in a word, perfect. He had never seen someone of such unreal beauty. She seemed to glow from the inside. She had the same hair and eye color as Michelle, he thought blankly, but he simply could not identify who she was. Until she moved forward.

"Cora. It is so good to see you again. How are your parents? Still doing well, I hope?" Even the voice was unfamiliar to both Cora and Steven, but Phil was looking at her with his mouth open and his eyes so incredibly wide as she approached the slightly younger woman with her hands out.

"They are doing well. I apologize, you have the better of me. Have we met before?" The gracious tone was exactly perfect, a cultured, well-mannered example of class and breeding.

"I realize that I look a little different now. Trust me when I tell you I am more shocked than you are to be this way. It's me, Michelle," she stated, then waited to see if they recognized her or not.

Cora didn't. She simply hadn't spent enough time around her to pick up on the mannerisms that help provide non-verbal identification. Steven did. As did Phil.

The blood drained from Steven's face as he saw the results of Giltreas' handiwork for the first time, and up close.

Phil, on the other hand, was overjoyed. He had often looked at

Michelle's injuries with sadness, seeing the tale of her life's experiences written in pain and blood on her body, and in her eyes. He couldn't let her know that he had wished for any way to take away the suffering that fate had visited on the woman he admired so much.

Now, looking at her, he fought back the tears before they started to flow as he realized that everything he had ever wished for her had come true. She was beautiful, and perfect, and whole. Restored to her youth and beauty. No one deserved it more. Well, maybe Nate, he thought absently. He reached out to give his boss's sister a hug, a familiarity that was common in more private environs between Michelle and the team.

Which was when Allison acted. Steven was so wrapped up in staring at Michelle that he totally missed it when David's sister moved with all the speed and grace of the weapon she had become all those years ago. The edge of a hand scythed in to smash into his nose, and blood sprayed everywhere as it broke under the force of the strike. Her other hand punched straight out into his solar plexus, and he suddenly was gasping for breath and dripping blood everywhere as he bent forward, falling to his knees.

Allison stepped back, satisfied that the message she wanted to deliver was received by its intended recipient. Cora's sudden, shocked shriek split the air as she bent over her incapacitated husband, trying to staunch the flow of blood from his nose. Phil nodded once in understanding. Christine's hand flew to her mouth. She had always guessed that Allie was deadly, but the proof, and the extent, was a shock to her system that left her unbalanced. She had been on the fringes of combat, but had been spared from direct contact with the forces of war that had shaped and impacted the others on David's team. The look in the young Asian woman's eyes was difficult to fathom, and she turned to the human wreckage on the floor in surprise.

"How does that feel?" The question came out in a normal tone of voice, as if Allison was asking Steven how his day was going. But there was an underlying coldness to it that shocked Michelle, Phil, and Christine. Even Cora looked up in horror at the sound of death in Allison's voice. She had not had much contact with David's wife, seeing her at a few social company events once in a while. The younger woman that David had married had always struck her as a little rough around the edges, but a pleasant enough person who had a nice sense of style and a cat-like grace in the way she moved. Cora had never been able to pin down, however, what it was about Allie (as she insisted being called) that seemed to make her uncomfortable. The speed and efficiency with which she had pounded Steven to the floor stunned her, never having guessed that the other woman was capable of such violence at the drop of a hat.

Allison turned to Cora, and the older woman recoiled slightly. But before she could angrily denounce the damage to her beloved husband, Allison spoke up.

"I apologize that you had to see that, Cora. He had it coming for what he did to Michelle, and to us all by extension. We are here because he set four men on Michelle, who beat her to death and tried to rape her. It was only because Giltreas healed her and brought her back to life that she is here now. But because her appearance is so drastically changed, she can't go back to her life before. Steven did all this. Do you understand that? Your husband did this." The words came out quietly, but with a lot of anger behind them.

Cora covered her mouth with one hand, horror in her eyes. She always knew that Steven was ambitious, but never guessed that he was capable of anything like this. She crouched down again, and asked Steven, "Is this true? Did you do this?"

He was still gasping and holding his broken nose, and seemingly didn't hear her in his agony, so David spoke up.

"We recorded his confession of his part in all this. We know that he was being used by someone else, and we know he didn't really understand what they had planned for her. He thought she was just going to be kidnapped and held incommunicado, along with Allison and I, while he took over the company. The men that carried out the attack, though, definitely killed Michelle, according to Giltreas. And they tried to rape her, although somehow she was able to prevent that."

Michelle looked away and shook her head in denial at the latest statement of her death. She still didn't really believe it was possible for her to have died, let alone that Giltreas resurrected her. People weren't resurrected that way. It simply was not something her mind could process, and every time she was forced to confront it again, she shied away from it, throwing up a wall inside her mind that kept her from having to accept that it had happened.

She turned away, and stepped several feet towards the dais where the woman who had become her friend sat in her formal role as the Queen of the Elven Kingdom, glancing up at the older woman briefly, before turning away.

Delara looked at Michelle with sympathy, knowing how difficult her life had become. There was nothing she could do to help the human through it, though. One had to deal with what life dealt them by themselves in the depths of their own mind. No one could do it for them.

Allison looked down at Steven and Cora, deciding he had suffered enough for now. She pulled some herbs from a pouch at her hip, crushed them together, and cast a healing spell, something she had been working on for the last few weeks of her stay away from home. The spell succeeded, and she reached out and touched the man on the head that she had just pummeled. The green light flared from her hand, passing into him, and suddenly his nose was healed and the pain in his abdomen went away.

Cora gasped as the light flared from Allison's hand. That was not something she was capable of understanding; her world view had been shaken so much for one day that her mind simply turned in on itself, and she fainted. Steven only had a single moment to realize what was happening before he reached out and caught her before she fell and hit her head on the floor.

Michelle turned to Steven. He was holding his wife as he carefully lowered himself to a kneeling position, trying to support her and prevent her from getting hurt in her current state, when he suddenly felt Michelle's gaze on him. He looked up before realizing it, but then he turned away in shame.

"Oh no, you don't get to just look away and pretend that nothing happened." Michelle's words bit into him as the stinging tone they were delivered in registered. He still couldn't look up and meet her eyes as his wife slowly came to in his arms.

She looked up at him, blinking her eyes as she tried to clear her head. Allison knelt down next to her, and looked a question up at Giltreas as he stood behind the couple on the floor. Gil shook his head, conveying that there was nothing else wrong with her other than being badly shaken up. Then she spoke up.

"Cora, can you get up? We need to get you back on your feet, hon. Can you stand?"

Cora turned to David's sister, and for a moment, the look on her face showed that she still wasn't sure about the younger woman, but then she reached out to the proffered hand, and allowed Allison to pull her up to her feet. She was unsteady for a moment as she looked at the floor to maintain visual reference for her point of balance, but was able to stand unaided after a few minutes. She then turned to Allison, who was still supporting her hand and arm.

"Why did you attack Steven? And how were you able to fix him so easily?" The questions came out in a shocked tone that was still not entirely level and steady, and Allison smiled as Steven stood up behind his wife.

"I am sorry you had to witness that. I just couldn't sit back and let what he did go without a response, but he isn't the one behind all this. From what Dave told me, he was being used. He's an idiot, but there are bigger targets on the range." The flat hard tone of Allison's voice brought a shiver to everyone that heard it.

Cora still did not understand everything that had happened, and her mind was full of questions, but she had no idea where to begin putting her voice to them. But then she realized that Michelle was talking to her husband, and she stopped to listen to what was being said, to try to pick up more pieces of the puzzle her life had suddenly fallen into.

"Why did you think it was a good idea to do business with the NSA, or with any government agency for that matter? I really need to understand why you thought assault and kidnapping were legitimate tools of business. Where did you learn that? Your father? Did he put you up to this?"

Steven was at first contrite as he listened to Michelle's voice as she spoke calmly to him, but when she brought up his father, he bristled and stood up. "He didn't put me up to anything!"

"So all this was your own idea? Or did someone else whisper in your ear and tell you it was a good idea to have me and dragged out into the woods to be raped and beaten to death?"

David winced as her calm, even tone of voice registered, as if she was simply discussing a staffing question or the weather. He knew that she was more furious than he had ever seen before when that dispassionate tone of voice came out of her in situations where she should be anything but.

Steven opened his mouth to try to explain. "The Senator's aide said that you had developed something that threatened national security. It had to be brought under the control of the government so that it could be properly utilized in our national interests, and to make sure that it would not be used against us."

Michelle stood aghast at what Steven said. Did the man have any original thoughts in his head at all, or did he simply parrot what he had been told?

Cora had been listening carefully, trying to find any way to discredit the claims that Michelle, David and Allison were laying against Steven, when he all but confirmed everything they were saying. Then she heard her husband so blindly quote what had obviously been a line he was fed to justify whoever had used him to get to Michelle and her family, and her heart sank into her stomach. She'd always known her husband was a bit naïve, but she'd always thought of it as harmless, and even endearing.

It was part of what drew her to him so strongly back when they'd met in college – a sweet, innocent, harmless naivety that seemed to make him come across as younger than he really was. But now she saw how that same innocence had been used against her husband, and used to harm good people that Cora cared about. It was too much to handle, and tears came to her eyes as her emotions welled up.

Michelle seemed to know exactly what Cora was thinking as she turned back to the older woman, and held out her arms with a gentle expression on her face. Cora took to the offered sanctuary and held on to the woman who had suffered so much at her husband's hand while she struggled to contain her emotions and compose herself.

Allison turned to Steven, and he flinched back from her once more, fear written plainly on his face, but she simply gave him a lopsided look as she realized that he had been used as well. It was not in her makeup to apologize, but the short single nod of her head towards him seemed to be what he was going to get. He didn't trust himself to respond, though.

David happened to look up at the dais at that moment, and saw Delara sitting there silently on the Throne of the Elven Kingdom, simply observing. Her seneschal stood behind her right shoulder with an expression that could at best be described as bored, but something else lurked there, just below the surface.

David had asked Giltreas to open a gate to Delara's home so that he could brief Michelle in person some thirty minutes before they had come through, and Michelle had nodded her head silently to his news, not really surprised at who turned out to be the snake in the grass. But she had cautioned her brother to go easy on Steven, since he was definitely not the top bad guy in all this.

She also told him something she had observed in the older man: he was someone who believed the first version that someone brought to him, and had difficulty changing his mind when confronted with a new version, even when the facts clearly supported it. It was something that she'd quietly learned to work around, because he was a very good accountant and CFO.

But Michelle had unknowingly learned the same thing about Steven that Cora had known since shortly after she met him for the first time: he was shockingly naive inside. One or two simple statements here and there had been enough to clue her in. She'd always wondered how he had been able to get through college and get his MBA like that. Most people would have had it burned out before their first year of college life was over. Then she met his father at a company function, and it made more sense.

Steven worshipped the ground his father walked on. It was subtle, but it was clearly there. And his father encouraged it, all but demanding that he be given his rightful deference as head of their family, and as a very senior member of an older accounting firm that served Fortune 500 companies across the country. It was an approach that left very little room for original thought in a son that was totally dominated by the much stronger personality of his father. And while she could not detect any malice in the father, who seemed to be a good person, it had warped Steven's world in a slight but distinct way. Steven saw his father as successful and capable, who gave money to charities and helped people where he could.

But Paul, Steven's father, had one foible that had upset Michelle: he was an elitist snob. His support of the middle and lower classes only went so far, but those below him on the social strata needed to stay in their place: there was only so much room at the top, and those roles were already filled. His old-money family perpetuated the message from father to son, and Steven's two brothers seemed to be fully on board with the family message.

Now, though, Michelle's finely-honed ability to read people and summarize them, a skill that had come in handy in her role as a business owner building her company, put together a new picture of Steven, and with everything she now knew about him, she realized that he was in danger, as was Cora.

"Steven, you have really stepped in it. I think you were meant to be the fall guy for my murder, if you were to be left alive at all. It would neatly tie up the loose ends left by this stupid little stunt of theirs, and place the company into receivership that would enable the NSA to take what I wouldn't give them. More likely, you would simply be disappeared, and probably with Cora. With no one left to complain, the idiots who thought this up would have free rein to do whatever they wanted."

The words came out quietly, and David almost gasped out loud as the truth of her statement hit home. David stared at Steven for a moment before turning to Michelle.

"Well, in that case, what the hell do we do now?"

CHAPTER 29

The world had gotten a lot larger, and way more stranger, in an incredibly short amount of time, Daniel reflected. In the four weeks since he had healed Jimmy's father, he had been having the most incredible dreams.

The first night, he had dreamed that he was in a meadow on a hillside, surrounded by stately pine trees that were so thick he couldn't see through them. The entire open area was about the size of four football fields side by side. The grass slanted slightly down hill, and a small stream gurgled and bubbled through the center of the field.

As he stood staring at the beautiful place, he became aware of a figure walking out of the trees across field before heading towards him. He was plain looking, dressed in a flowing robe and sandals, and a simple walking staff of some type of wood was his only possession.

When he had gotten close enough, Daniel could make out a middle-aged man with almost black hair and eyes, and skin a middle shade of a man who spent a lot of time in the sunlight.

He had regarded Daniel seriously for a moment, while Daniel simply returned the look gravely. Then he smiled and spoke.

"Hello, Daniel. I am Sekur. It is time for your training to begin."

The time had flown after that. It felt like each night in his dreams he lived in the meadow for weeks at a time. And all the while, his instructor taught him things that greatly extended his abilities in magic. Sekur's ability and knowledge of magical arts seemed endless. And everything that was presented to him seemed to make sense in a way that he didn't understand. It was less like learning, and much more like remembering something that he had known once, but had forgotten. He progressed rapidly, and was astounded at what he was able to accomplish. He made mistakes, some of them horrific and painful, but his teacher also showed him how to undo the damage of his failures. It wasn't always easy, but he was up to the challenge. Most of the time.

Every morning he woke up, back in his bed in what he referred to as the real world, fully rested, as if he slept soundlessly, but his memories of the night before remained intact, and the skills and abilities he picked up while dreaming stayed with him.

Time seemed to fly while in that meadow. Day turned to night, and back to day again. While in the meadow, he was studying under Sekur's intense training and teaching. He worked around the clock, not taking a break to eat, sleep, or even to relieve himself. He didn't seem to have the need to. He had asked Sekur about it, but Sekur had told him that he had to figure it out in his spare time. He had spent a lot of time thinking about it, and decided that the training was entirely inside his mind, where the physical body's needs didn't come into play.

Daniel reflected what his instructor said in last night's session. He was told that he needed to go to a specific medical building in another city, and wait in the lobby until someone specific came in. Then he was to demonstrate what he had learned. Sekur had even shown him what the person looked like. Daniel recognized the man as a prominent football player on the Denver Broncos. While Daniel was a fan of the Arizona Cardinals and not the Broncos, he definitely respected the wide receiver's skills and abilities. The rookie had made a difference on a team that needed leaders, but a week ago had gone down with a season-ending, and possibly career-ending, injury to his knee, the same one he'd ripped up pretty badly on college, the local paper had said.

Now Daniel looked up as his subject hobbled in from the parking lot. He stood up and walked over to where the injured football player stood on his crutches, looking at the building directory.

"Darius Turraine?"

The man on crutches turned, smiling at the young man walking towards him. The fans meant everything to him, and he was happy to meet them wherever they sought him out. Inside, he was not happy about his injury, but that didn't matter at the moment. The young man was smiling at him, and holding out his hand.

"That's me. What's your name?"

"I am Daniel." Darius shook the young man's hand, and wondered at the strength of the teenager's grip.

"You have quite the grip, Daniel. You play ball?"

"Naw. I am more of a band geek, but I watch games whenever I can. Man, your knee got messed up, huh?"

Darius nodded. The hit had been clean, but he'd had his cleat planted, and the knee wasn't meant to move that way and not suffer.

"Yeah, I'm gonna go up and see this surgeon, and see if he can put my knee back together. Maybe get a few more years out of it before I have to hang it up and do something honest with my life. But if not, well, I got my degree, and I can always go back and study more." He said it with optimism, but inside it hurt to think that his dream of being a professional football player might be over almost as quick as it had begun.

Then he noticed something. Daniel's eyes seemed to glow slightly as he looked down Darius's body. Then the glow went away as he looked back up at Darius and smiled.

"I didn't know you had so many injuries. A plate in your leg, screws in your arm and your foot; wow, you've been pounded on pretty bad in your career."

Darius' mouth fell open. It was almost like Daniel could see everything he was describing. Now that the glow was gone from his eyes, he wasn't sure if it had been there or not.

"How do you know all that? You been following my career?"

"No, I can see it. I have some unusual abilities. It doesn't matter. What does matter, though, is I can fix it all. Everything. Like it never happened. And I can erase the evidence of those concussions you've had. Here."

Darius couldn't move back at all on the crutches, but it wouldn't have mattered one bit. Daniel didn't need to touch him to cast the spells. He didn't even have time to react before it happened.

He could only watch and wonder what was going on as the teenager raised his right hand, and first a red light flashed over him from that hand, then a yellow light, followed by a green light, then a blue light. Each one seemed to make his vision blur momentarily, but the blue one left him unable to see through his glasses. He pulled them off, and looked around to see everything clearly. Then he heard his foot hit something on the floor as he shuffled. He looked down to see a plate and several surgical screws on the floor next to him, and his mind swooned for a moment. He lost his balance and dropped the crutches before realizing that his knee didn't hurt. In fact, nothing did. Not even that low-level constant headache he never talked about. It was all gone. He glanced up to look at Daniel once more, and the teenager was just standing there, looking at him.

"What did you do to me?" The words came out strained, as if it was difficult to talk.

"I healed everything that was wrong with you. I also cast cure poison, cure sickness, and cure blindness to fix your eyes. It would suck if you weren't able to play anymore. You are going to have a great career." The words came out in a level tone of voice, as if Daniel was talking about the weather or something.

Darius heard a sound and turned to see his brother, Donald, coming in through the front door of the small medical office building.

Donald had followed his younger brother's career with pride and more than a little worry. He had seen the toll that the game was taking on his brother's body and, without admitting it to Darius, his mind. There were times that he wondered if it was worth the price that Darius would pay later. The plight of the older retired NFL players was big news right now, as the lawsuit they had filed against the league was the 'A' topic around the family when Darius wasn't there.

Donald had noticed things. Darius wasn't the same some days. It was obvious that a concussion he'd had in his sophomore year of college had had an impact on him. He was still great on the field, but off the field he'd had a few mental issues with his memory and his ability to process new ideas. It scared Donald to think that a twenty-four year old in the prime of his life was having those problems.

Secretly, Darius's older brother was happy when the latest injury happened. He selfishly hoped that Darius would get out of the NFL and not be taking the huge risks he ran with his future and his health. The family was not hurting financially, and Darius had already made millions the first two years of his rookie contract. He could get an injury settlement from the league, and never have to worry about his finances again. Donald was most impressed with how Darius had managed his money so far. He lived an almost Spartan existence, with almost everything going into investment accounts for the long term. He drove a seven year old Toyota Camry he had acquired used that had seen better days. He laughingly told Donald that his teammates had given him no end of grief about an early first-round draft pick showing up in a "beater", but he had turned the joke back on them when he asked them how much it cost to insure the AMGs, the Lamborghinis, and the Ferraris that they drove.

Donald stepped into the main lobby of the building, and frowned when he saw his brother standing in front of the building directory. His first thought was that Darius had forgotten the name of the clinic he was here to see, but he relaxed when he saw the teenager standing next to him. Then he noticed something else when Darius heard him come in, and turned towards him. Donald was completely stunned to see that Darius had tears running down his face. And the teenager had his right hand on Darius's far shoulder as his brother turned towards him. Then he noticed something else: Darius had dropped the crutches on the floor, and was standing up straight, almost as if –

"My knee doesn't hurt! Nothing hurts! And look at this!" Darius held something out towards Donald, as the older man came closer. And when Donald saw what it was, he stumbled slightly.

"Is that... did that come from... what is going on? How did this happen? Who are you?" The last was directed at Daniel, who smiled at Donald, and offered his hand.

"I'm Daniel. I healed Darius of everything that was wrong with him."

The teenager, Donald thought he was no more than seventeen, spoke with a quiet confidence that seemed totally at odds with the impossible statement he'd just made.

"What the fuck are you talking about? Get away from my brother, you nut-job!" Donald started to push Daniel away from Darius, but his brother grabbed his arm and stopped him. It wasn't that difficult, as Darius was almost ten years younger, and in the nearly perfect physical condition required to play in the NFL.

"Stop, Donald. He healed me. Look! I don't even need glasses anymore!" The joy in Darius's voice stopped him. He paused, and in the moment, Daniel spoke up again.

"Why don't you go in to the appointment, and see for yourself? I will wait here. Come see me when you are finished. Don't worry, I'll still be here when you get back."

Donald couldn't stop staring at Darius, and his mind stuttering to a halt as the unreal situation seemed to try to become real to him.

"Yeah, let's go, Darius. Leave this whacko. You have an appointment." Donald firmly grabbed his younger brother's upper arm and started to try to lead him towards the elevator, but Darius pulled free with a word.

"Wait." He bent down and picked up a handful of screws that seemed to be on the floor before grabbing both crutches in his left hand and stood. "Ok. Let's go. See you in a while, kid. If you're gone when I get back – "

"I won't be." The quiet words were inserted into the sentence.

" – then thanks, if for nothing else than fixing my eyes. Let's go, Donnie. Don't wanna be late for the doctor!" The cheerful tone of voice from Darius brought Donald up short. It was a sound that he hadn't heard from his brother in months, as the grind of training camp, pre-season games, and then the meat-grinder of the long regular season pounded down on his brother.

Nearly an hour later, Daniel was sitting in the comfortable, padded chair in the lobby, leaning back almost into a reclining position, with his eyes closed, when he heard someone coming out of the elevator. The footsteps came closer, then stopped in front of him. He knew it wasn't Darius, because the shoes had hard soles, Darius had been wearing athletic shoes, and the stride was different. His ears detected two other sets of feet coming along behind, though. One of them was Darius, which mean the other was Donald.

He opened his eyes, and smiled up at the man in the tie and the doctor's coat.

"Hi, Doctor. How are you today?"

"What the hell did you do to my patient?" Daniel was not prepared for the hostility in the doctor's voice, but in retrospect, it made sense. The doctor was not going to get paid for operating on Darius's knee. The realization made an entire new line of thought course through his brain that had to do with the economic impact of what he was capable. Sekur was right in preparing him the way he had; this was going to get messy. Not that he would do anything differently. He knew what his teacher wanted from him and the impact it would have, and frankly, he was glad to do it. It was overdue.

Now he looked up at the furious doctor standing in front of him, and stood abruptly. The motion was filled with a confidence that the doctor didn't expect from someone so young, but Daniel simply smiled inside.

"I healed him. It was simple, really. Here, let me look at you."

His back was to the windows, and the three older men were looking directly at him, when his eyes glowed brightly enough for the color of his eyes to be completely obscured by the light. His gaze swept over the slightly overweight man in front of him while the doctor stepped back in sudden consternation. What was happening here? Who was this teenager, and what was up with his eyes? In nearly twenty years as an orthopedic surgeon, he had never seen anything like it. He was speechless and mesmerized by the glow coming from those eyes in front of him, watching as they swept down his body, then back up. The glow went away when he looked the doctor in the eye again, a look of concern and compassion on his young face.

"Do you know you have prostate cancer? It doesn't really look that bad yet; probably not very aggressive. Also, you used to be a smoker some years ago. In a few years, you will have lung cancer, if I don't do anything about it now. Also, you have some pain in your left hip, and you had your ankle repaired some time ago. And, you're infertile, but not by choice. I can fix all of that. It won't take more than a moment, if you want."

"What are you talking about? Cancer? How do you know that I used to smoke? How can you do this?"

"Magic. I don't know how I can do it, but I know that I can. Look at Darius. Does he look like he needs surgery anymore? Or anything else, for that matter?"

The doctor was a man of science, and science demands proof in the form of repeated tests that reliably produce the same results, before belief can happen. The trained skeptic in him wanted to see it happen again, but the human wanted it more. He knew about the prostate cancer, and was facing the uncomfortable reality that he would have to have it taken out, along with some unknown level of his functionality in that area, but he was surprised by what Daniel had said about his lungs. He'd quit smoking more than twenty years before, at the end of med school.

The young man in front of him couldn't be more than a teenager. But there was something about his eyes, when they weren't glowing, that was, that drew the much older doctor in. It was almost as if the person in front of him was way older than he appeared. Those eyes watched him patiently, with a calm confidence that he rarely saw in competent surgeons older than himself.

He realized that he had simply been staring at the young boy in front of him for almost a minute, when Darius behind him spoke up, his voice almost shocking in the silence.

"Didn't I tell you, Doctor? There's something about him; like, in his eyes or something."

Donald had also been staring at the young man, wondering what it was about him that was so disconcerting. When his brother mentioned the boy's eyes, it all clicked, and he gasped almost silently.

Darius turned to his older brother, and asked, "What? What is it?"

"It's like looking at Grandpa Kevin. You know, like he could look right through you. He seemed like he had lived forever…" Donald spoke in a hushed tone, like he was in church, or at a funeral.

Darius nodded in surprise, realizing that the resemblance was uncanny. He remembered the surreal way that their grandfather had seemed to look at them as if every secret were written on their faces.

Daniel simply waited with a slight, content smile on his face that said he was comfortable with whatever happened. The truth was, the endless months and years he had spent in training with Sekur had changed him. He saw it in the mirror every morning he woke up from the sessions. He looked older somehow, as if he had lived a full life in the nights that he had spent training with Sekur in his dreams.

The training sessions had started out simple, with what Sekur called the Cardinal Spells, and moved on from there. After those were mastered, and fairly easily at that, Sekur had told him that they were going to find Daniel's limits. As the endless training sessions went on and on, seemingly months were compressed into every night's dreams, as days and nights were cycled through endlessly. And during those endless days, Daniel learned and mastered everything that Sekur had presented to him.

Simple spells were just that - simple. More advanced magical skills were introduced, and made part of Daniel's rapidly growing repertoire. Spells that seemed simple when first cast suddenly became complex as he learned to cast them over distances, then over multiple subjects first close up, then also at a distance. The ability to transport himself very far away would come in handy as he was called upon to do more and more tasks for Sekur, something he was happy to do in exchange for the training and skills he was learning.

Spells and magical abilities that had to be cast and used during combat had been a stressful and painful time, as the scenarios he was thrust into in the meadow became more complex and dangerous every night. He didn't always succeed, and in some cases, he thought he even might have died more than once. But he learned and got better. And he went on to master those skills and abilities as well, no matter how difficult or painful it was to do so. And the months went on and on.

When the subject of what Daniel would do with the skills he was learning from Sekur came up, Daniel was adamant about only doing things that benefitted others. He would not harm anyone, unless it was necessary to save someone else, or was clearly the right thing to do; but even then, it could only be after everything else had been tried first.

Sekur had agreed with a smile, saying that Daniel would be a force for good in the world, and would accomplish great things. He asked Daniel to remember two cardinal rules: if an act harmed no one, do it, and protect those who couldn't protect themselves. However, he cautioned Daniel that there would be times when Daniel would have to harm someone in the defense of someone else, or in the cause of doing what was good and right. He said that Daniel needed to not be paralyzed by indecision if those moments came up. Almost anything done wrong in the innocent pursuit of doing what was best could be set aright again with Daniel's magic skills, and Sekur was available to assist with what Daniel needed, so long as those actions served the Greater Good.

Daniel had listened gravely, understanding that sometimes one needed to make difficult decisions, and do hard-to-understand actions, or even impossible-to-understand actions, if that is what it took to do the right thing. He thought about the civics class he'd had the previous year in high school, where the teacher had talked about the choices a soldier needed to make to protect civilians: take a life to save a life. While the teacher had talked in terms that made it clear he thought that soldiers never needed to kill someone to protect someone else, Daniel had not agreed. He had read enough history, especially about the events surrounding World War II in which his grandfather had served, to know that sometimes people needed to be stopped permanently. When he had brought it up in class, the teacher had all but berated him for his views, saying that the Allies didn't try hard enough to find a solution to the "German Crisis," which made Daniel laugh out loud, and got him sent to the office.

Daniel explained that it was ludicrous to call World War II, a seminal event in human history that had cost billions of dollars and millions of lives, a Crisis. The principal had tried to tell Daniel to just agree with the teacher, but that didn't go over well, so he got Daniel to agree to keep his opinions to himself, do the work, and answer the questions from the material that was part of the class if he wanted to keep his 4.0 grade point average. Daniel agreed, but with the statement that he knew the teacher was wrong, which got a nod from the principal while he reiterated that Daniel better toe the line in the class.

Now he looked at the older man in front of him as the doctor started to speak again, listening intently.

"Prove to me that you can do this."

The smile on Daniel's face grew wide. This is what he was waiting for. He looked one more time, seeing a middle-aged man with the usual excess weight around his middle, maybe forty pounds or so. This would be interesting.

"Hold on to your pants, please." He spoke gently, waiting for the response he knew was coming.

"Excuse me?" The doctor was befuddled. Why did he need to hold on to his pants?

"Your pants are about to become much too big. You might want to hold on to them, so they don't fall down. That wouldn't be good."

The doctor's eyes got suddenly very wide, indeed, as he scrambled to grab his pants at his sides.

Daniel nodded, and then cast the spells again. First, cure poison, because poisons can cause sicknesses and injuries. Then, cure sickness, because sicknesses can cause injuries. Then he cast the healing spell, to erase injuries and the impact of poisons and sicknesses. Finally, cure blindness. Sekur had told Daniel that a healing spell didn't cure blindness; it only repaired most of the physical damage to the tissues of the eyes and the nerves. He explained to Daniel that it was because of how complex the ability to see really was.

The doctor watched as the upraised hand of the teenager flashed different colors, almost too fast for him to follow. Each time the light flashed from Daniel's hand, the doctor's vision washed out into that color for an instant, returning to normal for only a moment before the next spell hit him. After the fourth spell, he realized that his clothing didn't fit anymore. He had lost a lot of weight, and felt incredible. He also couldn't see through his glasses anymore, but he didn't dare reach up and take them off. Daniel simplified things by doing it for him instead, and he gazed in stunned amazement at the crystal clear world around him. It was real. He almost let go of his pants before he remembered that it was not a good idea, having suddenly lost more than six inches off his waist.

"Here," Daniel said quietly. Another spell was cast, and the doctor realized that he didn't need to hold his pants up anymore. He looked down at his now well-fitting clothing, then back up at the teenager in front of him, his mind stunned, and completely at a loss for words.

Donald stepped back in shock as he witnessed what Daniel did to the doctor, suddenly weak in the knees and nearly unable to stand up. He was lucky that his brother was there to catch him before he fell. Darius, too, was shocked by the transformation of the older gentleman in front of them. He looked years younger, a lean, handsome man of no more than thirty years of age, and Darius turned to the young man once again.

"How can you do this?" He spoke in a hushed tone, almost reverent, and Daniel turned to him and smiled.

"I have the ability, and I have been trained to do this. It is my task in this world to do this. I have to go now. I have to get home." An impish smile suddenly flashed over his young features. "Hey, if you think all that was neat, watch this!"

The three adults looked at Daniel in confusion, not understanding at first, but then something happened that drove home that they had been involved in an extraordinary event.

With a slight 'WHAP!' and a mild breeze of displaced air, the teenager that had turned their three lives upside down in such a short amount of time simply disappeared in front of their eyes.

CHAPTER 30

Svetlana hadn't had any idea where to go when she fled the death and destruction she'd left behind in the horrible building in Georgia. She couldn't stop and ask questions in her current state. Either she would have to stay in the gargoyle form, which was sure to be a bit... off-putting... to strangers, or change back to her human form, for which she didn't have any clothing. After avoiding people and populated areas for three days, she'd managed to steal enough things to wear to have at least a semblance of modesty, something she was grateful for after her ordeal. But she was very shy about approaching strangers. She didn't speak the native language of Georgia at all, and other than her native Ukrainian, she knew only a few words and sentences in Russian. She wasn't sure what help her native Ukrainian would be, but since she wasn't sure she would find anyone nearby that could speak it. So she became a homeless stray as she tried to find her way back home.

She'd eventually met some girls her own age on the streets of Tbilisi, when hunger had finally forced her back to the only city she knew was nearby. They accepted her as another runaway, not knowing anything about her other abilities. She helped them scrounge for food, and they banded together to fend off the boys living on the streets as they tried to survive. Most were barely literate, and had no idea how to get to Ukraine, a place that was a world away from where they were now.

She didn't dare go to the authorities, because she had killed those men. She wasn't sure if, as long as she stayed in human form, they could connect her to the crime. She also didn't believe that they would take proper care of her, based on the stories the one girl who spoke Ukrainian told about her own experiences with the police.

Svetlana knew she shouldn't stay with the girls, but she had no idea on what else to do, or how to get home. She decided to start hanging around the city library, to see if there was a way she could learn what she needed to know. First, though, she was trying to learn Georgian, so she could read the books there without assistance. Her new friends thought she was strange at first for wanting to hang out with books all the time, but gradually they accepted her strange obsession, after she repeatedly told them she just wanted to figure out how to get home in her miniscule Georgian language skills.

Some of the older girls turned tricks for money, prostituting themselves out for the money needed to buy food. One older girl suggested that Svetlana try it as a way to contribute, but the look Svetlana gave her made her blood run cold, and no one ever brought it up again. She contributed in other ways, though, some of which she was not proud of, but was nowhere near as bad as that other thing. She had killed several men for trying to get her to do that against her will. There was no force on earth, and no argument in any language, that would get her to accept it willingly.

So, her assistance to the group usually was as a lookout, watching for police as her friends "liberated" things from stores that they desperately needed. She had the pattern down, she thought. But not really, for the situation abruptly changed.

A huge, burly man in the uniform of the city police force surprised her where she stood on the corner, getting her hands cuffed behind her before she was able to even react. A special sweep had been set up to get the girls off the street and into the welfare system that might give them a chance at a normal life.

A flash of rage had overtaken her before she realized it, but she stepped on it quickly, squelching the change before it began. Broad daylight was not the best place for her to let that cat out of the bag, and she had gained a lot of control over it, and her anger issues, in the possible five or more weeks since what she was calling the 'incident'. She decided to play along for now, waiting for her chance to get away. But if the man tried anything at all with her that was like what had already been done to her, she knew wouldn't hold back. Pigs like that got what they deserved. Besides, the first form she learned to change into wasn't the only one she knew.

Perhaps an hour later, Svetlana was seated at the desk of the man that had caught her, as he started typing something on his computer. She was still in her handcuffs, but they were moved to the front so she could sit more comfortably.

The sergeant had already figured out that the girl in the mismatched, wrong-sized clothing didn't speak much Georgian. He had asked her several questions outside the car, before he transported her in the back of the car to the police station, along with two of the younger girls. One spoke more Russian and a little Ukrainian, but they were not able to talk about very much. Still, she was able to tell Svetlana not to give her real name, something she was already planning, in case someone would be able to connect her back to the incident at the brothel.

The killings of the men that ran the brothel had been big news on the streets. A few of the girls she ran with had been unfortunate enough to be brought to Tbilisi that way, and had been lucky to escape to the dubious safety of the streets, where groups of homeless kids preyed on everyone and anyone who could be taken down. The bigger homeless boys raped any girl unlucky enough to be separated from their regular group. Boys found alone and vulnerable were beaten, rarely to death, but the targets were left in a bad way.

Svetlana herself had been accosted by two boys in an alley sometime after midnight one of the first nights she'd been out on the streets of the city. She'd been forced to make sure they'd been unable to tell anyone about her. The new abilities she'd gained in her escape she kept secret from everyone she could, certain that she would be hunted down and killed if anyone knew. She would take a lot of people with her before she was ended, but certainly she would find herself in the next life if she wasn't careful.

The word had gotten out after the bodies of the two older homeless boys had been found: there was a vicious animal of some kind loose in the city. The wilder tales talked about a tiger or lion that had escaped from a nearby zoo, but no one really knew what was happening. Then word had gotten out about what had been found in the brothel, and speculation turned to the men there as the source of the wild animal. Something they had brought in as a pet, or more likely, to threaten the working girls there, had gotten away from them and killed them all for their troubles.

Svetlana had smiled inside at that last thought, even as she was repulsed by what she'd done to the men. The memory of that day woke her up frequently in the middle of the night as the horrifying ease at which she had been able to do that haunted her dreams. But they were mostly right: she'd been brought in as a pet, and had escaped their control and destroyed them. She lost no sleep over their deaths. But the act itself had been horrific to relive every night.

Now she looked up innocently at the police officer, and said nothing as he questioned her, first in Georgian, then Russian, and finally in fluent Ukrainian, which had startled her as she heard her native tongue again for the first time in who knew how long. He'd smiled somewhat, as if he'd won a prize by finding her native language, then the questioning had begun in earnest.

"What is your name, girl? What is a Ukrainian girl doing so far from home, and living on the streets with the rest of them?"

Almost against her will, she'd spoke up before she could stop herself, the draw to speak her own language for the first time in weeks so strong inside her.

"I was…" She stopped before she said too much. But it was an opening the sergeant had been waiting for.

"I know you are a long way from home. Don't you want to get back there? Isn't anyone looking for you? Your mother or father?" The warm, kind words seemed to seep into her, working their way past her walls, and pulled at her where she was hiding inside. She suddenly had the urge to tell him everything, but quickly stepped on that. Everything she knew would get her in deep trouble. They would never return her to her family if they knew what she had done, what she could do. She had been a voracious reader before her kidnapping, and some of the fictional stories she'd found so interesting had been about what happens to those that are different in the extreme. Still, there was something she could tell him.

"My name is Svetlana Yevtukh. I was kidnapped from the Ukraine over a month ago. I am fifteen years old; I don't really know what day it is now, so I can't tell you exactly how long ago it happened. And yes, I do want to go home. But I don't trust anyone."

The calm, quiet answer surprised the sergeant. His past experience with the street kids in his city told him he wouldn't get anywhere, but he had to try. His own daughter was almost ten years old, and it broke his heart to think about what was happening to these kids he saw every day. He always wished he could help them, but they had to give him something to work with. And this one just did.

He stared at her in shock for a moment, and then he reached for the phone on his desk. He punched in a few buttons, and spoke rapidly in Georgian to whoever answered the phone on the other end. She caught a few words here and there, including 'Ukrainian girl', 'missing,' and 'brothel'. Her fear spiked, and the urge to run, or to do something else 'more significant' to protect herself, was almost overpowering. But the knowledge that she could do that something 'more significant' helped her stay calm, and wait until the man was off the phone.

He turned to her and spoke again in Ukrainian. "Your father spent nearly a week looking for you in the city here before he was forced to return to the Ukraine. He left a message for you that he misses you dearly, and hoped that you would be found alive, safe, and unharmed. Which appears to have happened. He left a number to call when you were found. Would you like to call him and tell him you are ok?"

Numbly, not expecting anything like this to happen, she nodded, then held up her hands with the cuffs on them.

He smiled. "You're not going to run away from me, are you? I guess we can take these off you."

With that done, he pulled the phone over to her, and dialed a number written on a note from his desk drawer. Then he handed it to her. She put it to her ear, and heard it ring, her heart beginning to pound. Was this really happening? Then her father answered, and she knew it really was.

"Hello?"

"Daddy?" It came out in a strained whisper, but he heard it anyways.

"SVETA? Oh my lord, my little Sveta! I have missed you! Where are you? I will fly there today. Are you ok?" It was strange to hear her father trying to talk through his tears as he openly wept over the phone.

"Daddy, I'm ok. I got out of that place. I'm ok!" Now she was crying, tears coursing down her face. The sergeant didn't say a word, but pushed a box of facial tissues across the desk to her, and she smiled at him gratefully as she wiped at her eyes and face. "I don't know where I am. Talk to the policeman." She handed the phone back to the man, then pulled her knees up to her chest and rocked back and forth, trying to get control of her emotions.

The police officer spoke to her father for a while, discussing where they were, and how they would keep her safe until he could get there to pick her up. He handed the phone back to her, and she talked with her father some more. She asked if her mother and brother were there to talk to, but he said he was at work. But he was leaving as soon as he had arranged to fly to Tbilisi to get her. He told her that she would be safe with the police officers, and they would keep her in the station with them until he could get there. It was still mid-morning, so he expected to be able to get into Georgia that same day, and would be united with her by evening. Happy that she could suddenly see the end to the long nightmare her life had become, she was suddenly optimistic that things would be better soon.

They ended the call, and she smiled at the police officer, suddenly happy that he had caught her earlier that morning. He was caught off guard as the young girl bounced out of her chair and wrapped her arms around him in a big hug as she giggled.

* * *

Several hours later, Svetlana was bored out of her mind. She'd been staying in the station, with a nice police woman bringing her food and drinks to sustain her, surprised at how much the young girl was eating.

Officer Oksana Tsverdievna had been surprised when the girl was found. Everyone assumed that she had died on the streets somewhere, if she hadn't been killed outright by whatever had torn up the brothel and carried off elsewhere to be eaten, but her body had never been found. As time went on, no one expected her to turn up.

Now she sat and talked to the girl, trying to find out what had happened in the basement of that building she had been taken to, but Svetlana was, unsurprisingly, very tight-lipped about what she had gone through. Oksana assumed that it was because she had either not seen anything at all, or had seen too much, and didn't want to recall the painful memories. For that matter, everything about that experience had to have been painful. Being yanked away from your parents and brother and then driven for four days through three countries had to be traumatic.

Now she frowned as a police lieutenant stepped into the room and motioned her out for a moment.

He closed the door behind her, and spoke up. "You are needed down at the evidence locker." She frowned, unwilling to leave the girl alone, especially with the more senior police officer. Something about him had always left her feeling a little like she needed a shower, but there had never been anything specific for her to put her finger on. Since there was nothing specific that raised a flag to her, she nodded once. "I will be back in a moment. Don't let anyone in or out of this room, by order of the commissioner. Her father is a high-ranking member of the Ukrainian government, and is on his way here. His plane will land in less than thirty minutes, and expects to see her here."

After sufficient reassurances that the girl would be safe with him, she ducked her head into the room to explain that she was being called away, and would be back soon, before hurrying away to get the task completed as soon as possible.

Once she was around the corner, the police lieutenant nodded to himself once, and opened the door.

The girl was cute, that was sure. He sat down across from the table she sat at, picking at the remains of her food.

"Svetlana, isn't it? Can you tell me what happened at the brothel when you were brought there?"

"No." The one word response surprised him, and made him a little angry.

"You have to tell me what happened. Several men were killed there, dying painful deaths that shouldn't happen to anyone." He pressed slightly, leaning forward a bit to emphasize his position and trying to mentally dominate the young girl and force her to answer his questions.

"No, I don't. And I won't." The words came out calmly, as if spoken by someone talking about the weather.

"No you won't what?" More forcefully. He didn't understand why the girl in front of him wasn't being cowed into answering his questions. It was almost like she didn't care about him.

The truth was that Svetlana was on guard the moment she saw him. His attitude reminded her strongly of the first man she'd killed; that same sense of entitlement that didn't care about anyone that got in their way. She was not about to tell anyone what had happened, least of all anyone like that man. But she reached deep inside herself and touched that current of energy again, readying herself in case her special abilities were needed.

"I won't talk to you about it. Do you understand what I am saying? Stop talking to me. I have no intention of talking to anyone about that, least of all you." The tone of voice was more emotional now, but of the wrong kind of emotion, as far as the lieutenant was concerned. She was dismissing him, something he found intolerable. It was almost like she was treating him like something she'd scraped off her shoe.

He stood up, and slapped both his hands down on the table loudly, expecting to scare her. Then he started to bellow, "You better start talking, you –"

Something happened. Before his very eyes, the slender teenage girl disappeared in an instant, and a nightmare appeared, towering over him in the room. The glowing red eyes stared down at him out of that green-black face as he shrank back suddenly, and the horrifying visage jutted towards him with lightning speed. A clawed hand reached out and fastened onto his right wrist, not letting him go as she spoke to him in a deep voice that was filled with anger, hatred and the potential for violence.

"Or what? What are you going to do to me, you puny little turd?"

He tried to pull his hand free frantically, but the strength of the grip that held him was beyond anything he could imagine. He tried to reach for his gun, but it was on his right hip, the same side that was now held fast in the gargoyle's grip. The green-black scaly hand was both warm and cold on his skin, and he mewled in terror as the huge winged beast held him fast, slapping aside his left hand as he awkwardly tried to reach across his body and get to his gun.

"You really don't want to do that. As much as I want you to, you really don't want to."

He suddenly lost control of his bladder for just a moment as he realized that he was looking at the being that had shredded the slavers.

"Let me make it easy for you." He was suddenly free, and he fell back, having been trying to pull away with all his strength. "Go ahead, worm. Give me a reason to do it again."

The gargoyle was suddenly gone, and the young girl was back. She sat down primly, and resumed picking at her food. A part of his mind wondered where her clothing had gone when she'd been the other thing, but he couldn't voice the question, or anything else for that matter.

"Or don't. I don't care. But if you get in my face again, one of us will enjoy the result much less than the other." She stared up at him with a malevolence that was a physical thing in the room, hounding him, driving him to fight or flee.

She stood suddenly, slapping both palms down hard on the table in an exact mimicry of his earlier tactic, and he jumped nearly a foot into the air as the effect slammed into him.

"Get out of my face!"

He turned to go, and made it to the door just as it opened, and the young female patrol officer darted into the room.

"What are you doing in here? Didn't you hear me earlier? Svetlana, are you ok?"

She looked up at Oksana as the lieutenant bolted out of the room, a very slight odor she almost recognized following him as he fled.

"I'm fine." The words came out calm and relaxed, as the younger girl looked up at the policewoman with an innocent look on her face. She was about to say more, but there was a quiet cough behind her through the open door from the hallway.

She turned, and saw that the captain was beckoning her out into the hallway.

Svetlana had finished eating some time ago, and was just reading the paperback book someone   had found for her to help her spend the hours waiting until her father came for her. The door opened suddenly, and the young police woman came back into the room. She could tell that the officer was upset and trying to hide it, but wasn't succeeding.

She watched as the police woman tried to say something, but when she opened her mouth, nothing would come out. Her pale, drawn face showed her emotions clearly.

"What is it?" Svetlana was getting nervous.

Oksana couldn't say anything. Words wouldn't come out. Some of it was fear of what the young girl in front of her was capable of, but the rest of it was that she just couldn't process how the slim, slender young girl in front of her had done what she had just seen on the monitor in the security room when the captain had rolled back the recording for her.

The door was still open behind her, and she glanced nervously behind her where, just out of view from the room's occupants, the tactical team was forming up. She had argued against it, but procedure was clear when a possible threat existed inside the police station. Then she turned back around to Svetlana. She didn't think she was in any danger from the sweet young girl, but the scene on the monitor, in crystal clear full color, wouldn't get out of her mind's eye.

Svetlana looked around the room, to see if she could figure out why the woman was suddenly so nervous, and her breath caught in her throat when she saw it in the upper corner of the room. A video camera, with a red light on it. And it was pointing at her.

A bad word came out of her mouth as she came to her feet.

"Wait!" Oksana took a half step forward, with her hand out, palm forward, in the universal sign for stop.

"Why? So you can lock me up? You can't. No one can keep me here. I will survive just fine on the streets." The words came out tinged with frustration and more than a little despair.

"It doesn't have to be that way. Your father is coming. He will be here soon. We think he is no more than a ten minutes or so away. Just talk to me."

Uncertainty was plainly on Svetlana's face as she stood wondering what to do. But the situation changed suddenly when the police lieutenant that had accosted her in the room earlier burst back in, his service pistol in his hands. He shoved Oksana aside, and screamed "Don't move!" as he pointed the weapon at the girl.

The captain watching from the security room cursed suddenly as the annoying asshole disobeyed a direct order once again by thinking he was being a hero. He had been called to the room some time earlier when the tech watching the screen carefully had called him in a panic.

What had happened in the brothel last month became clear as he watched the small teenage girl transform into the huge green and black winged creature. The lieutenant had fled the room almost immediately after she had changed back, which said some interesting things about her. She could have easily ripped the man apart the same way she obviously had done to the men who had been involved in her ordeal, but she showed considerable restraint this time. That made her thoughts, and her motivations, much clearer to him.

The ability also explained how she was so calm in the face of getting detained by police during a sweep of homeless kids, a stressful ordeal for anyone. Now, he couldn't tear himself away to run to the room two floors up, convinced that he was going to see the idiot killed the same way. But something else happened instead.

Oksana stood up, and slowly moved to insert herself between the lieutenant and the girl, whatever form she was in, never taking her eyes off the wild-eyed man with the gun. She had never liked him, and was convinced that he used his family connections to get promoted and transferred to this station, for some reason. She had always wondered why he'd chosen the inner city to work. Now her mind raced as she considered the possibility of a connection to the slavers that kidnapped Svetlana, but she didn't have enough information to connect them.

Her eyes never left his as she stood, trying to keep herself between the gun and the girl, her hands up and out at shoulder level.

"Lieutenant, put the gun down. You know the regulations. You also have seen what she is capable of. Do you want to be the next one she deals with? She was calm and content for several hours, and never changed once until you bullied her. If you back her into a corner even with a gun, do you think you will do better than the four men did against her?" The words came out calmly, but a little louder to make sure that she was heard over the gasping almost-hyperventilating sound of his breath as he struggled to control himself.

Svetlana waited in her human form, head cocked as she watched to see what the two people in the room would do, but her heart was sinking as she realized that she had to leave as quickly as possible. There was no way she would be safe now that they knew what she was capable of. They obviously, from Oksana's statement just now, knew that she had killed those men. She had to separate herself and make sure that she was safe, and then try again some other way to get home to her family, if they would even take her back. She briefly wondered deep inside from time to time during the last weeks if her father and mother would still love her after what she had done, and what she had become.

But that was a different problem to be solved later. First she had to survive the current situation. She guessed that bullets wouldn't hurt her in her other form, because when she'd killed the two boys who tried to rape her, one had had a knife. He had tried to stab her after she changed shape, but the blade had skittered over her skin, and hadn't even left a mark. So she calmly waited to see how Oksana would fair against the asshole that had tried to force her to talk earlier. So far, it wasn't going good for the young woman.

"Get out of the way, you idiot! She is dangerous! Why are you protecting her? She killed my – " He broke off suddenly, face flushing as he almost said something that might get him in real trouble, and Svetlana's eyes narrowed at hearing his words. Her mind raced as she tried to figure out what he was about to say, then it occurred to her. He had been asking about what happened at the brothel, not to the two older boys she had killed trying to defend herself. She looked closer at him, trying to remember what the men looked like, but he didn't look anything like the first man, and she hadn't seen the faces of the other men long enough to remember them very well.

Oksana heard it, as well, and things suddenly began to make sense to her. All the little clues that had nagged at her subconscious for months came together, and unlike Svetlana, she had seen the faces of the men killed in their previous arrest photos passed around the station as the detectives tried to figure out how they died and what killed them. She knew the girl behind her had done it now, and she even knew why. But this new information helped clarify things considerably, as her orderly memory brought up the image of one of the men killed in the kitchen. He was a close match to the crazed lieutenant in front of her, and she nodded.

Organized crime existed everywhere. It was the bane of every police organization and honest citizen in every country everywhere. There had never been even a hint that the illegal brothel had existed in their city, let alone that it employed girls that were underage, all of whom had been kidnapped elsewhere and forced into the sex trade against their will. If they had a high-ranking family member on the force, and on the vice squad, like she suddenly remembered the lieutenant was, it would make their job much easier.

"Was he your cousin or your brother?" The question came out in a flat, unemotional voice, with only the tiniest inflection that gave away the smallest fraction what she was really feeling inside.

"He was my –" He broke off again. This was not going well. He knew that the video system also recorded audio, and he started to sweat as he dug himself in deeper.

Oksana nodded at the miniscule shred of confirmation. It didn't matter. Now that the investigators knew what to look for, they would find the connection.

The captain watching in the monitoring room swore in vile temper as he, too, put together the signs. He turned, grabbed a radio from one of the two technicians, and yelled at the other to keep him informed as he ran from the room, hoping he got there soon enough to prevent a bloodbath again, this time in his own station house.

The stalemate continued upstairs, with Oksana staying in between the gun and the girl, and the lieutenant trying to get a clear shot. Svetlana, for her part, simply glared at the man in front of her, letting her rage out through her eyes, which now glowed red even in the bright lights of the room and the glass windows on the wall. Oksana continued to try to talk the man out of his weapon, and Svetlana felt grateful that a police officer was trying so hard to protect her. But if the man shot Oksana down trying to get to her, she was going to do to him what she'd done to the others in that place. This time, though, she was going to try to leave him alive, and let him suffer. She'd had enough, she decided.

The captain burst out of the stairwell after running up the two flights of stairs, somewhat out of breath, but didn't stop, trying to get to the room before things went completely south. He almost made it.

The man suddenly changed tactics, and in a flash, the barrel of the gun flashed out, hitting Oksana's protector on the side of the head even as the technicians watching remotely watched in horror, convinced that everything was going straight to hell right in front of their eyes.

Snarling in triumph, he brought up the gun and opened fire in one smooth motion. The result was not what he was expecting.

Svetlana flashed into her stone gargoyle form and raised her arms to protect her face and eyes as the man emptied the gun into her body. The impacts drove her back somewhat, and stung, but when his gun was empty, she looked down and saw she wasn't bleeding. The bullets had smashed into her form, some staying there while the rest fell to the floor. Then she moved.

The captain got to the room and shouldered his way through the tactical response team that still didn't know what to do, even at the sound of the gunshots, making it into the room in time to see the girl, or the creature, whatever she was, fling the heavy wooden table into the wall. The windows there shattered at the impact, leaving a huge gaping hole where they once set, the cold fall air suddenly chilling everyone nearby.

With the table out of the way, Svetlana leaped forward, and ripped the now-empty and useless gun away from him with one hand as the other reached out to close around his throat. Massive muscles tensed as she heaved him off his feet, slamming him back into the wall behind him so hard that his world spun and the plaster behind him gave way. Then she bent down and roared in his face, a deep rumbling sound of elemental rage that carried to everyone nearby.

The captain made it into the room, and she turned to him, her eyes narrowing. She lowered the stunned lieutenant and turned to evaluate the new person in the room, to see if he was a threat, a rumbling growl escaping her with every breath.

"It's ok. I don't even have a weapon. Svetlana, your father will be here soon, and you can go home. It is ok. You will be ok."

The deep, guttural, gravelly voice that came out of her gargoyle form was deep and full of pain and anger as she responded.

"He will not want me anymore, after he sees what I have become, what I have done."

"You don't know that." The captain spoke in soothing tones, trying to calm the girl down. He had no more idea than anyone else how the young girl was able to do what she had done, but he had children of his own. He knew that she had been brought to the now-closed brothel, and had been there when the men were killed, but had no idea that she had done it. Now that he knew, he was horrified at what she'd had to do to save herself. Becoming this thing, and doing everything she'd had to do to live and survive, to get away, must have taken its toll on her.

"Why don't we wait together, and see? I have children, daughters of my own. I would be out of my mind with worry if my daughter was missing, and I would be so happy to have her back that I wouldn't care about anything else. I promise you, it will work out ok."

She shook her massive head as tears started up in her eyes. The man was so kind, but he was so wrong. He wasn't her father.

"It's true. But running out now will not solve anything. If your father won't take you back, I will take you in. It will work out. I promise."

"What about those men? What about him?" She motioned to the man on the floor, who was now just trying to clear his head and get back up to his feet.

In response, the captain reached slowly behind him, pulling out his handcuffs and showing them to her. "May I deal with him?"

She laughed through her tears, nodding at the captain. "Do you need help?" The giggle seemed totally incongruous, coming from the massive, fearsome form, and he smiled.

"Only if he moves. But, try not to damage him. We need him in one piece, so we can figure out what he knows about the criminals in this town."

"Tell him if he does not answer your questions completely, I will come back and eat him, piece by piece." She turned her head slightly away from the lieutenant and winked at the captain so the younger man couldn't see her eye. He got the message with a slight curling grin, which vanished almost as quickly as it had appeared.

She watched carefully while he handcuffed the man, who was still shaking his head to try to clear the ringing noise from his ears while the world still didn't want to stay still.

After the disgraced lieutenant had been handed off to the tactical team outside and the captain shut the door rudely in their faces, he turned to help Oksana up to her feet. It was while their eyes were elsewhere that she changed back again.

She glanced over at the young girl standing slumped with her hands down by her sides, the very picture of abject despair, and held out her own arms. "I will stay here as well. We will see what happens together. Is it ever cold in here. Can someone bring me a warm coat for her and I? Captain, would you need one?"

Svetlana swarmed into the woman's arms, holding on tightly, and Oksana winced as the girl's strength registered, and then looked down at her in surprise as she laughed once.

The teenager worked one arm free, and gestured behind her. A white light flashed from her hand, and the window was suddenly whole again, as was the table. At another gesture, the warmth returned to the room, as well.

The captain just stared at the young girl in utter amazement then looked at Oksana's equally wide eyes. Before he could stop himself, he blurted out, "Wow!"

Svetlana didn't let go of Oksana, but the policewoman thought she felt Svetlana's form start to shake. Worried that the girl was crying, she leaned back, only to realize the girl was laughing silently, a big silly grin on her face.

A laugh escaped her own throat as she spoke up, "Well, that was amazing. How are you able to do all that?"

It was silent in the room for a moment, but a much more sober Svetlana spoke up. "I don't really know. I do know that when things really started to get bad, I felt something I never felt before. I touched it, and now I can do lots of things. Not all of them are good. I still have nightmares about the bad ones. I feel bad about what happened to those men, but..." She trailed off, and the captain nodded.

"Don't feel bad about what happened to them, but about what the actions cost the good person that had to do it to survive." He was speaking carefully, trying to keep the girl from indicting herself for the crime. Then he realized something, and looked up at the camera. "Shut down the system in this room. Delete the files, on my authorization. This is critical."

The red light on the camera blinked three times then went out, and he nodded.

"Svetlana, nothing will happen to you. You are the daughter of a Significant Person in the Ukraine, and as such, it is my duty to make sure you get home safely. Nothing more. What happened to those men will not be determined, and that is how it will stay. Do you understand?"

She looked at him with wide eyes, grateful for his compassion, and nodded quickly.

"Thank you very much, Captain!"

"You are very welcome, child. It is the least I can do, and they had it coming. We discovered evidence of, well, let's just say not everyone made it out after they were taken there."

Svetlana shuddered, and tightened her arms around Oksana, causing a gasp of pain. "Sorry," she said, loosening her grip, but not letting go.

Svetlana's father Borysko Yevtukh bounded out of the cab and headed up the stairs, his mind an exulted whirl. His beloved Little Sveta was inside! She was so close! It had been almost five weeks since his shining, perfect daughter had been savagely ripped away from her family. The grief had been overwhelming to him, his wife, and his son. His wife had taken it especially hard; understandably. They had been especially close, mother and daughter. But he had kept the pain of his monumental loss inside, and used it to keep his focus on finding her.

The time he had spent in Georgia looking for his daughter had been frustrating in the extreme. Away from his home country, and the resources he took for granted there, he'd been worse than ineffective, flailing about without a clue as to what to do. He'd spoke with every police officer he could, including the captain of this precinct station, until he'd been certain he'd made a pest of himself. The captain assured him that he understood, and personally made arrangements for him to stay in a hotel at their expense, but the week he'd been there had been less than fruitful.

So, with a heavy heart, he'd returned home to the Ukraine, and a job he could barely do, all the while wondering if he'd see his little Sveta again. When he returned to Ukraine without their daughter, his wife had broken down, clearly believing they would not see their daughter again, but he never gave up hope. He never shed a tear, not even in private.

Now, with the phone call earlier today, the inky black darkness that had washed the colors out of his entire family's life seemed to vanish. His wife had been speechless in her joy and tears as he recounted the conversation, then she'd sunk to the floor, overcome with emotion. He'd held her long enough to make sure she was ok, then started making calls while he threw together a quick bag of clothing for his daughter and some things he would need for a quick flight, arranged by the Ukrainian Consulate in Tbilisi.

He was so close! His path carried him up the front steps of the building, and his trained eyes latched on to someone that was looking at him with a strange intensity. Then he saw the gun in the man's hand as he stood in Borysko's path to the front door.

A spike of pure torment slammed into him even as he thrust himself aside and down. Three more shots rang out, passing through the air where he had just stood, before the two officers standing outside waiting for him wrestled the gun away from the man and threw him bodily into the wall, temporarily stopping his efforts.

Borysko gasped in pain as he realized he was shot in the side. He didn't think it was serious, but it still hurt worse than anything else he had ever experienced. A small part of him thought he was lucky his assailant was such a terrible shot, but his mind was suddenly fixated on the sound of glass breaking above them in the building, followed by broken glass and what must have been the remains of a window frame raining down onto the sidewalk between him and the door. Then something else happened.

A huge winged form landed on the sidewalk between him and the man struggling with the two Georgian police officers. It was shaped roughly like a human, but it was a black-green color, covered in scaly skin, with two huge wings that sprouted from its upper back. And it was massive. It looked to be two meters tall or more, and from the side, the horrifying visage looked enraged. Through his pain, he realized that this is what had killed the men in the brothel where he'd gone when trying to find Svetlana those weeks ago.

The creature watched for an instant as the man who had shot him stared back in stunned paralysis, and then it threw back its head, opened its mouth, and roared, a sound that was so loud everyone's ears rang. In an instant, it stepped forward and grabbed the man that had shot Borysko, hoisting him easily up into the air. He was convinced that for some reason it was going to demonstrate what it had done to the men in the brothel, but instead, something else happened.

"Why did you shoot my father?!? WHY?" The sound of its voice was a deep rumbling bass that seemed to be made of stone, but then the words registered. ...father? Then that meant... was that Svetlana? Was SVETLANA the creature that killed those men? That would explain why they didn't find her or her body in that horrible place, but how did she become this? What happened to her?

Answers to those questions weren't forthcoming, but the answer to Svetlana's question was.

"He is Special Group Alpha! He killed my Chechen brothers, him and his kind!" The words came out between gasps of pain and fear as the shooter stared into the eyes of his death, certain that he would be joining his fellow freedom fighters.

"So I was taken to bring him here for you to shoot him?" The words came out flat, almost emotionless, but there was still that edge of elemental fury about them.

"You? Who are you?" Confusion warred with fear on the man's face as he wondered what this creature was. The question made no sense to him, at first. Then, everything changed.

The huge beast threw him to the sidewalk, where he landed hard on his back and hit his head, the wind knocked out of him, but somehow his line of sight stayed on the beast. And while he watched, it flashed into the form of the target's daughter. He was so stunned and frightened by the happening that he lost control of his bladder as the girl darted forward.

"He is my father! I am SVELTANA YEVTUKH! I was taken from my family weeks ago! And you shot him!" He flinched back as the sheer volume of the girl's magically enhanced voice impacted on his ears like a gunshot.

Borysko suddenly saw his daughter in front of him, and nothing mattered. He started to pull himself across the concrete to her, but the pain was making his vision cloudy. One of the officers was already on the radio demanding an ambulance to get him help, but that didn't matter. All that mattered was his little Sveta was here. The rest could wait, everything else in the entire universe could wait until later; like how she could do those things.

Svetlana flashed back to her gargoyle form again, and lifted the now screaming man off the concrete landing in front of the police station entrance, as her claws, harder than obsidian and razor sharp, dug into his skin through his leather jacket as she lifted him off the ground once again.

"So everything I have suffered these last weeks has all been so you could kill my father?" The face in front of him nodded yes frantically, and the man shrieked in pain as the talons tightened again, but the door burst open, and Borysko saw a man in the uniform of a city police captain come through them, running right up to his daughter, and hold his hands out to try to calm her down.

"It will be ok, Svetlana. Let him down. You got him. Don't let anything else be on your hands. Think of your father! He is right there! Go to him, and let us deal with this piece of garbage. Please!"

The face darted towards the captain then the massively muscled shoulders seemed to sag. The Chechen was thrust at the captain, and he caught the suddenly free man, forcing him to the ground and holding out his hand to the police officer next to him for handcuffs, which quickly appeared. He cuffed the man almost by muscle memory alone, watching father and daughter to see what happened next.

Svetlana stood with her back to her father for a moment, as if not daring to turn and see if it were really him, then she changed back to her human form, and looked fearfully over her shoulder, as if dreading what she would see.

But all she saw was her father laying on the cement steps, one hand covered in blood holding his lower side, the other reaching out to her, a look of yearning on his face, along with the utter desperation and the minute spark of hope of a man dying of thirst reaching for water.

Her world dissolved into tears as she ran to him, her beloved father, and he gasped in pain as she crashed into him, holding on to him tightly. He wrapped his free hand around her and pulled her tight to him, even as the pain made him light headed, and for a moment, they just held each other. Then she pulled back and gasped at the sight of blood leaking from him.

"Papa! You're shot! No! I thought he missed you! No!" she wailed, "I won't lose you again! Papa!"

"It's ok, Sveta. I love you. I'm not going anywhere. It hurts, but I think I will be ok."

Svetlana blinked away the tears, and suddenly her memories flashed back to that first night after she'd gotten free. A plain, non-descript man with a kindly smile had met her in a meadow, and offered to teach her how to "do more, so much more." But she'd been fearful, and it had been too soon after the incident, and her dreams had collapsed into nightmares, like so many times since. He'd appeared time and again, trying to help her through the worst of the horrors her mind threw at her night after night, but she'd never taken him up on his offer to teach her. Now she wished she had.

She suddenly heard the voice of that man from her dreams, and gasped at what he was saying. Then she reached inside to where she found the hot stream, taking some of it inside her, and shaping it into a green light, which flared out of her hands. She looked at her father, and at his wound, and the green light flashed from her to wash over her father from head to toe. It flared for several seconds as it connected father and daughter, then it pulled back to her hands.

Borysko gasped as the pain abruptly vanished. More questions for his amazing daughter came to him, but she stood and walked to the two police officers that had initially struggled with the Chechen man that had shot her father. Both were sore and hurt from the brief confrontation, but she didn't give them a moment to consider before the light flared from her hands, bathing them from head to toe in its healing energies. Then the light went away, and she spoke briefly.

"Thank you."

Before they could anything but stare at her, she turned and ran back to her father, who was now on his feet, and wrapped her arms around him, holding on for dear life.

He winced at her strength, and she lightened up her hold at his sound of pain. The green light flared from her again, and the rib she'd just cracked healed as if it were never injured. Then she looked up at her beloved father, and tears fell like rain. Her nightmare was almost over. She was almost back where she belonged, and if they weren't back in the Ukraine again, at least she was with family.

He looked down at her, a million questions burning through his brain. Thoughts of what she was capable of doing, both in healing his gunshot wound, to changing into that incredible form, danced and capered through his consciousness. He knew that he had finally found his beloved daughter again, and that he had to get her out of Georgia and back to the Ukraine as soon as possible. Everything else about her could wait. But time was against them, and he knew it. He had to get them moving, back into the car below, out to the waiting plane, and back to his home country, where he had the resources to protect her and keep her safe once more.

But the only thing that came out of his mouth was, "My beloved little Sveta! Oh how I have missed you, my girl!" And his sight blurred completely as his tears came at last, and the reunited father and daughter simply held each other in a city thousands of kilometers from home in the foreign country that had become the place they found one another again, both weeping as the reunion they both craved nearly more than life itself finally happened.

CHAPTER 31

Senator Robert Del Monico was a very important man. It said so on his door. He was a U.S. Senator. That made him important. And important men didn't waste any time on the fools and idiots that were always around, asking for things. So he'd been prepared to tell his secretary to tell the latest idiot that showed up at his Washington D.C. office looking for a meeting without an appointment to take a flying leap, when he paused.

"What did he say his name was again?"

"He said his name is David Wilhelm, sir." He paused as the name registered. Did Wilhelm know his connection to what had happened so far? Did he have any idea what was supposed to happen? The last thing Del Monico knew, the team leader on loan from the black-ops section of the Pentagon had reported that Michelle was dead, and they were set for stage two, waiting for David to show up. Since then, they'd heard exactly nothing. Now David Wilhelm was in his outer office, asking to speak with him privately. What the hell did he do now?

"I'm tied up at the moment. I have no idea when I will be available. If he wants to wait around, it may be hours. Tell him that." He held his breath as he waited to see what happened.

"He said he will be more than happy to wait, sir." The smooth voice of his very lovely secretary came back entirely professional and calm, a soothing presence on the other end of the line that he found he really appreciated at the moment.

"Thank you, Kira." He hung up, then stood suddenly to pace. A moment later, inspiration struck, and he picked up his cell phone, dialing a number in his contact list.

"What is it?" Her voice always grated on him, usually so full of impatience that seemed to be more pronounced in the last several weeks as their plan had come apart.

285

"He's in my office," he blurted out.

"Who's in your office? What the hell are you talking about?"

"David Wilhelm is in my office. He's here. What do I do?"

"He is in right now with you? Listening to you babble at me? You fucking idiot! What the hell is wrong with you?" Contempt lashed at him through the line, and he winced. He was a fucking U.S. Senator, not some stupid middle-school idiot that she could just bully into giving up his lunch-money! The thought died inside before it made it all the way out his mouth this time. Instead, something else almost as bad came out.

"No, you fucking bitch, he's out with my secretary, asking to see me, fuck you very much!" He returned her contempt on a platter with a side of disgust.

"Shut your mouth, you little shit. If it weren't for you screwing the pooch on this, we'd already have achieved what we wanted, and this whole situation would be on cruise-control heading off into the sunset. Instead we have no idea where they are, and what is going on. So here's what we're going to do. You are going to wait there, and I am going to send Arnold over. He will come up the back way into your office, and you will invite Wilhelm in. Geoff will wait outside in the hallway with the security team, and at the right time, you will call them in to your office. Arnold will 'witness' David attacking you, and Geoff and the security team will take him away. We can get this whole shit-pile back on track and still get what we want. But if you fuck this up, I swear I will feed you to my pigs. Got it?"

Sweat beaded on his forehead as he suddenly realized that he was about to be exposed to potential violence.

"But what if he actually attacks me? He has to know that someone made a play on his sister. He's a retired Marine. He could really fuck me up! I read his file, what we could get of it."

She laughed at him. "Why do you think Arnold is going to be there? Arnold can handle one stupid Marine. Arnold is a decorated retired Navy Seal, if you recall. You'll be fine. And who knows, if you get slapped around and live to tell about it, maybe you'll finally grow a set of balls and be worth a damn. Now wait for Arnold and the team, and get this right. Got it?" She seemed to be awfully fond of those last two words, he thought bitterly.

"I got it, you pathetic waste of organic material," he rejoined in a pleasant, conversational tone of voice. Then he signed off with a cheery, "G.F.Y, you P.O.S," certain she knew the reference, and hung up the phone.

David waited cheerfully, talking on the phone in the Elven tongue with Nate. He was certain he was being recorded, both video and audio, and hoped that the strange language was giving whoever was watching some severe fits. He occasionally smiled at the secretary, who smiled back in a perfectly professional way. Giltreas whispered in his ear that he heard someone enter the office beyond the secretary, and he heard some others moving up the hallway outside. From the sounds of them, they were heavily armed. David nodded with a smile again. It didn't matter. They weren't there to question the Honorable Senator from Missouri in his office. That would happen elsewhere. By the time they got into the office, the Senator, and whoever else was in there with him, would be long gone.

It had taken a lot of careful consideration and planning on how to pull this off. People on two planes had been alerted that morning that the plan was in motion. Everyone knew their role, not that it would be all that complicated unless things went wrong, but everything they could think of had been planned for. Nate had been a valued asset in that. He had a real knack for small-unit military tactics and strategies that were easily adapted to this situation, and had put together a simple but effective way to get what they wanted. Now if everyone and everything cooperated, no one would get hurt. And if someone didn't cooperate, well, Allison was standing by, at her request. She wanted to try out the healing spell she had been working on diligently. And if anyone got dead, Giltreas was at the ready as well.

It was just over fifteen minutes after David had first entered the lobby area of the senator's office when he looked up pleasantly as the secretary behind the big oak desk spoke his name.

"Mister Wilhelm? The Senator will see you now."

"Thank you," he responded as he stood, and walked to the door she held open for him. He paused just before the door, smiled at her again, and then proceeded through the door.

The door shut behind him, and he sensed the spell Giltreas cast on it, then again as a second one was cast on the other door into the room. No one would be getting through those doors any time soon.

"Senator? I am David Wilhelm. Perhaps you know who I am?" He walked over to the desk, pointedly ignoring the other man seated in one of the two chairs in front of it.

Arnold looked over the man in front of him with carefully hidden contempt. He was to wait until enough time had passed, a couple minutes, before he was supposed to rescue the Senator from this latest nut to grace the Senate Office Building on Capital Hill, something he was really looking forward to.

"I'm sorry; I don't believe we've met before. Am I supposed to know who you are?" The smooth voice hid his trepidation, and the Senator smiled his best public smile at the man that stood in the way of his ambitions. He took the hand that was offered in a brief handshake, then let it go, surprised at how much relief he felt when nothing happened. That was when something did, but it was not directed at him.

David's right hand flashed suddenly into a fist, and David pivoted to his left where Arnold was seated next to the desk, putting all his weight behind that fist, connecting with Arnold's jaw and stunning him temporarily. Then something else happened.

Another person simply appeared in the room, in the open area between the desk and the main door. He was unusual in his appearance, with grey hair, a greyish tinge to his skin, and mesmerizing amber-colored eyes. He murmured something, and a flash of light came from him, followed by something out of a bad science fiction movie.

A wall of what appeared to be glowing water seemed to form out of nowhere, standing there in his office. It was almost seven feet tall and four feet wide, with a raised edge that bordered it. It stood in midair a few inches above the floor, with an oval shape. The entire construct glowed and waivered slightly as it illuminated the corners of his office in the whitish light it threw into the room. He looked at it dumbly, wondering what it was, when the second man stepped aside, and four more men in military-style black clothing, boots, gloves and balaclavas stepped out of the strange thing into his office. They went over to Arnold, grabbed him by the arms, and two men pulled him into the thing, then came for the Senator. He started to scream, but it didn't matter. The grey man in the room murmured something else, and no noise came out of his mouth, even though it felt like he was screaming at the top of his lungs. Then the two remaining men grabbed him and, at a nod from David, pulled him with them into the strange thing standing in his office.

Arnold had always considered himself to be a tough, capable man. But he knew he was smart, too. That was why, when he suddenly found himself in a strange room after being pulled through whatever that was by the two masked men who had grabbed him in Del Monico's office, his eyes darted around to evaluate his surroundings. His heart sank as he realized he was now surrounded by seven men and women facing him all dressed in black, with balaclavas covering their faces. And every one of them held a pistol in their hands, pointed down at the ground. He shook his head once more to try to clear the effects of the punch, then was pulled along further away from the thing he had just emerged from, only to see the Senator he was supposed to be protecting pulled through the same, whatever it was, as well.

Del Monico felt his world spin crazily as he was suddenly not in his office anymore. The room they were in was strange, as if it was built on a movie set or something. He looked around when his balance returned, and was shocked at what he saw.

"What the fuck is the meaning of this?" He bellowed at the top of his lungs, but no sound came out again. Shit. How the hell did they silence him like that?

David nodded at the grey man, who waved his hand at Del Monico, and then spoke. "Ok, you can be heard again."

"What the fuck is the meaning of this shit?!" He was rewarded with the sound of his voice blasting out into the room, and cursed inside when he realized that it sounded strained and somewhat fearful. "When they figure out you have assaulted a U.S. Senator, and kidnapped me, no less, you will be lucky if you rot in jail for the rest of your pathetic lives!"

"So, you feel that the law is something that should be respected, then, Senator?" Something in David's voice should have warned him, but he had too much steam behind him to stop now.

"You're goddamn right, you stupid little fuck! Now bring me back to my office before things go bad for you!" He tried to shake himself free of the men holding his arms, but they were incredibly strong, and didn't seem to have any problem holding on to him.

"So, the fact that you chose to have a black-ops team attack my sister and kill her, then plan to wait around to kill me, then go and kill my wife, is how YOU respect the law?"

The anger in David's voice snapped him out of his bravado. He tried to say something, but instead his mouth just opened and closed like a fish out of water as he tried to figure out what to say next.

"Having trouble with telling the truth? Don't worry; we have a solution to that. In the meantime, I need you to have a seat in the chair behind you. We have the camera set up to record you while you are sitting down. That's the best angle, what with the lighting and all."

The two men holding him backed him up to the chair he hadn't noticed before, and forced him into it. Then the grey man walked up to him, and Del Monico shrank back from him as he realized that this man had done whatever had been done to get him out of his office and to... wherever they were now.

"Don't worry. We need you to be in one piece for this." David walked over and stood next to the chair he was being held in, and stood there for a moment looking down at the U.S. Senator, one of the most powerful elected officials in the entire country, an unreadable look on his face. Then his hips and shoulders twisted as his fist flashed out and connected with his nose, smashing it flat onto his face, in a stunningly powerful blow.

Del Monico shrieked in pain and shock as both hands flew to his face to hold his nose, which was now bleeding profusely.

"I thought you 'eeded 'e i' one 'iece!"

"Oh, I do. I just wanted you to experience a little pain and suffering, you tiny little pile of shit!" David's voice rose at the end, and the sheer volume and vitriol in it caused Del Monico to shy away from him in fear, to his own internal disgust. He started to sob as the pain and the situation threatened to overwhelm him.

"You think you can't be gotten to? You think you are protected? What are we all to you? Just pieces on a chess board that you can fuck with any time you want? Is that all we are to you?" David leaned down and thrust his head into the Senator's face, almost daring the man to hit him back, but Del Monico was off balance from the pain and badly terrified at what was happening.

Arnold was appalled at what was happening. The men that had captured them seemed to be entirely focused on the tableau unfolding at them, and he could only watch as David punched the Senator. He was completely outnumbered, in an unknown location, and unarmed, being guarded by several people who clearly had training, and just as clearly were committed to the path in front of them. There was nothing he could do about it, and he ground his teeth in frustration.

"I 'ink you 'roke 'y 'ose." The sentence came out in a miserable sob, and David nodded.

"Good. You deserve more. I should kill you for what you did to Michelle, and wanted to do to me and my wife. But instead, we have a different idea. You are going to tell us, in your own words, exactly what the fuck has been going on, and why. But first, Gil, if you would please?"

Giltreas looked at the pathetic human in front of him, and grimaced. This was the worst kind of man he could imagine: a coward who wanted to be a king. He cast the spell to heal the man, and the Senator looked up suddenly as the pain went away as if it had never happened. He looked down as he felt his nose, and it didn't hurt. Shock further wore away at his sanity as he looked up at the grey man in terror.

"What did you do? How did you do that?"

"It was but a simple healing spell. Most children learn it by their eighth summer." The contempt in the strange man's voice was a new thing; he hadn't heard anything like that since his older brother had stopped beating him up in middle school.

"And this will clean up the blood you have all over your clothing." Another flash of light enveloped him, and he looked down as the blood that had been soaking into his expensive suit, tie and dress shirt suddenly vanished, as well.

"And now, you will speak the truth, you pathetic little man." Another murmur, and he felt a tingling feeling in his brain for a moment.

Gil moved aside, as did the men standing beside the Senator. He looked around, and suddenly looked at the camera in terror.

"I won't tell you anything. This is wrong. I won't say a word. You have to bring me back to my office. Right now!"

David just smirked, and hit record on the expensive digital camcorder mounted on the tripod some six feet from the chair, and tightly focused on the Senator's face. The light from the nearby windows provided enough illumination to let the camcorder clearly capture the identity of the man sitting there.

"Tell me everything you know about what is going on with Michelle

Wilhelm, David Wilhelm, Allison Wilhelm, and MDST, the company owned by Michelle Wilhelm and David Wilhelm."

"I…" He fought it with a desperation and courage he didn't know he'd ever had, but in the end, the spell to compel truth Giltreas had cast on him was by far stronger than any mortal's will, and he found himself speaking uncontrollably.

Under Phil's skilled questioning, the entire horrifying story of abuse of power at the highest levels of the Government of the United States of America came out.

Arnold could only stare as what he was involved in, and the monster he worked for, was laid bare in front of him. He knew that his boss was ruthless and powerful, but even he'd had no idea what was really happening. All he'd been told was that there was a threat against the Senator's life. That was something he knew how to deal with. But this. This was something else. Something else entirely. He realized that he was grateful that the plan had been turned on his head before he had done something he would have regretted. And he was getting more than a little pissed off at how he had almost been used to do something in a plan that was so evil.

David tried to keep from vomiting all over the floor as the true story came out. For the most part, it was similar to what Steven had said, but the Senator knew a lot more, including the truth about what was supposed to happen to Michelle, David, and Allison. They were all to be killed. The blame was supposed to be placed on Steven, who would be arrested for the murders. When he was safely out of sight, he would never return; instead, he would be quietly killed and stuffed in an unmarked grave in a distant forest in Idaho, along with his wife.

With every officer of MDST, Inc. out of the way, a federal judge would be presented with a petition to place the company into receivership, in order to have its assets seized. Then the coveted cryptographic technology would be turned over to the NSA, who would do whatever they wanted with it. The Senator didn't know what the NSA wanted with it in the end. He didn't really care. All he cared about was getting the company into the NSA's hands. That would have triggered the transfer of millions of dollars from a black account in the NSA to a special account in a foreign bank to which only he had access.

But when David asked who else was involved, everyone who familiar with the U.S. Congress was shocked at the answer that came out.

Giltreas turned to Nate, and asked, "Who or what is the Minority Whip of the U.S. House of Representatives? What does that mean?"

CHAPTER 32

The four brigands, as Giltreas had labeled them, were led into the throne room for their next audience with the Queen, their hands and feet chained while they were still in their cells with locks that had been affixed by magical spells. Aaron, as his usual charming self, had not been able to stop screaming obscenities and curses at everyone around them, so a wizard had been called, and Aaron found himself on the receiving end of a silence spell cast on his head. He could scream at the top of his lungs, but when he realized he couldn't even hear himself, he had to fall back on glaring at everyone around him. He could hear them, he realized as they laughed at his state, but he couldn't make a sound.

A normal person, such as his three erstwhile companions, would normally be terrified at the display of magic so casually used against them. To Aaron, it was just another reason to hate everything about this stupid place. He was certain he would get his chance to kill every human and freak around him, starting with the huge red monstrosity that seemed to enjoy taunting him with its very presence. Sure, it never even looked at him unless it was going to smack him around, but he just knew it was rubbing it in that Aaron was in the cell and the red bull-headed freak was not.

Jack resolved himself to never getting home again. He expected he would die here, on this world, wherever it was, and would never be seen again by his family, which, come to think of it, was a fate he completely deserved. There was nothing left, but to accept his fate. A strange calm came over him as acceptance worked its way into his consciousness. He was ready to die. He just had some few moments left to ponder if there was any hope for an afterlife for a murderer like himself.

He looked around, and paled when he saw that Michelle (the new version, at any rate), David, and his wife Allison were also in the throne room, along with that strange grey-skinned and grey haired man that had so completely scared him and the others when they were resurrected. He also saw five humans that, from their clothing, had to have been part of Michelle and David's company. He had no idea who they were, but they appeared to be former military, including the one African American man, who seemed to be built like a body builder, or professional wrestler or something. They were, though, all armed. He could see pistols in holsters under their unzipped hoodies, when they moved. It was not readily evident, but he had been around armed people enough that it was obvious to him. David and Allison were also armed. He wondered why at first, but then realized that the show of force was for him and his team members. The thought wore at him a little more.

Jack shivered, not wanting to look Michelle, David, and Allison in the eye. It all seemed so pointless now – the money, the job, what he used to do. Funny – he realized he just referred to his old life in the past tense. 'I wonder what that means,' he thought to himself.

Then there was no more time to contemplate what was happening, as the four of them were stood in the center of the room, with easily thirty guards surrounding them, all with spears held pointing at them. If Aaron acted out now, it would not end pretty for the psychopath, he thought. Or for the rest of them, when it came down to it. It was strange how the thought of dying here didn't scare him, for some reason.

The head guardsman once more cast Compel Truth on the four, doubting that anything would come of it again, just as it had the first time these four miscreants had been presented to the Queen.

Once again, the Queen spoke up. "Which of you is the leader of this group?"

Jack suddenly found himself speaking before he could stop himself. "I am." He then looked down away from eye contact with the queen, suddenly ashamed of himself. His mind had undergone such a huge change in the last weeks in the jails in the Elven city, and he wondered if that was more the result of dying and being brought back to life, or if the situation itself was the bigger contributor. He didn't trust himself to decide which it was.

"Is it true what David has said, that you attacked and killed Michelle? And that this was a task given to you by someone else?"

Jack hesitated a moment, as if struggling with himself. The queen wondered if he was fighting the spell, but in reality, it was much simpler. He was coming apart inside, his mind slowly breaking down and losing touch with reality. He was so incredibly far from anything familiar, and was powerless to stop what would happen to him. He was among people that could compel him to answer truthfully any question they should ask. Somewhere deep inside, a small, frightened part of himself, untouched by the spell, suddenly desperately wanted to confess his sins, as if that might, if not save him, at least grant him some peace, and that part of him reached out and took control, and his mind coalesced enough to answer the questions put to him.

"Yes. It is all true." He suddenly said the words so calmly, that it surprised even him

"Why would you do such a thing? Is she a criminal that you were sent to dispatch? Had she committed some crime by your laws that called for such a punishment?"

"No, not that I know of, Your Majesty." He said it quietly, but the impact was loud.

"Then why?"

"Because I was paid to... to..." Even with his new determination to come clean, he still couldn't say 'because I was paid to kill her.' It just wouldn't come out.

"How much? How much were you paid to end the life of this young human woman? What is the life of a mortal human woman such as she worth on your plane?"

Jack spoke again. "Two million dollars for Michelle. Allison and David were worth an additional million dollars each. It was supposed to be split equally among the four of us."

The queen had no idea what a dollar was, and only a very limited idea of how many a million was. Such numbers were the purview of seers and magicians, who dealt in such abstract, unreal thoughts. The thought that someone would pay someone so many of something to kill other humans, was just not real to her. "Who paid you?" The question was short and demanded an answer.

"I don't know. I was contacted anonymously." That, at least, was to be expected.

"What was the end planned for her? For them?"

Michelle's hands tightened their grip in Allison's and Dave's hands. It was one thing to know she'd been harmed by these men. But hearing this somewhat calm, resigned recitation of everything, here and now, was almost like being assaulted again. Inside, a part of her was screaming over and over, 'I am not an animal to be butchered!', as tears started to run down her face. She turned away and buried her face behind Dave's shoulder as his emotions burned slowly inside.

Allison suddenly reached her hand up and wiped at his face, and he realized that he was also crying. Giltreas felt the emotion coming from the three humans, and reached out to place his near hand on Dave's other shoulder. Dave turned back as Jack started to speak again.

"We were supposed to leave her body in the woods behind her cottage, and then take care of David and Allison. It was supposed to look like David raped and killed the two women (to totally destroy his reputation), and then killed himself. The plan was for it to take several days to find them. By then, my employer would have accomplished whatever he set out to do."

"Is this what you are normally called on to do? To slaughter your fellow humans like so many mindless food animals?" The question came out harshly from the normally serene young queen, and it impacted in Jack's mind like an explosion.

Jack blinked harshly as the question washed over him, and his situation began to hammer at his sanity again. He started to hyperventilate, and the color washed away from his face. His mind started to spin as his thoughts raced through his brain, and the room washed out as his vision tunneled. He lowered his head slightly as he tried to spread his arms to catch his rapidly disappearing balance, but his hands were secured together in front of him. His mouth opened as if to speak, but it was his internal voice that screamed in sudden wordless agony into the silence in his mind as the last vestiges of sanity finally began to leave him.

The guards, not knowing his intentions, braced themselves at his sudden movement, not remembering which had tried to attack their queen the last time they were here, not that it mattered to them. All they knew was that these humans had proven themselves to be violent animals, and had killed one human and threatened to kill two others.

Jack felt his consciousness begin to leave him, when he felt a presence, and a gentle, musical voice spoke softly to him. "Calm yourself, mortal child."

He looked up suddenly, and there was a new person standing in the throne room. She looked to be young, with pure brown hair, and was dressed in a simple brown robe. Her skin was flawless and smooth, a light brown color, and her eyes looked on him with some mixture of concern and sadness, as if he was lost at sea and floating further from shore. Then he noticed that the queen had stood from her throne, with a shocked look upon her face.

He looked on the new woman again, and she seemed to glow as if lit from within with a pure white light that seemed to brighten the colors of everything it touched. When he looked into her eyes, he seemed to be staring into the infinite depths of ageless space, and he shuddered, turning his face away from that perfect countenance, even as his mind seemed to try to both pull him closer to her and turn him away at the same time.

She looked back at him, and murmured something too softly for most people to hear, but Michelle heard it, and looked at the goddess standing in the throne room before them in shocked, open-mouthed silence. The recitation of her intended fate had swept into her mind like a rising tide that would not be denied, sweeping aside the walls she had erected inside to protect herself from the thoughts about what had happened, and the profound changes she had undergone in the moments when Giltreas had first healed, then resurrected, her. She stared inside herself and accepted at last that she was no longer just Michelle Wilhelm. She was more, she realized. So amazingly, incredibly more.

She embraced everything at last, accepting that she was no longer the same, that she had died and been brought back to life somehow, and she was changed, both inside and out. The acceptance banished all doubts, all fears, all concerns, about her new self at last. With that complete acceptance, her human form began to glow, just as the goddess before her she had never met did in the throne room where she was tending to the crumbling man that had so calmly tried to explain her intended fate at his hands. And as the glow grew, a gentle hum began to emanate from her; a soft, soothing, caressing sound that eased the minds of those good people around her.

The Goddess seemed to notice Michelle at that moment, and turned her head to look at her. Her eyes grew wide in surprise as she saw the human woman that had seemed so different in front of her, and she inclined her head in respect, a gentle smile gracing her flawless lips. A nod, as if realizing what she had been seeing all along, was directed at Michelle. Then she turned back to the slowly disintegrating human man in front of her.

"You have done some terrible things in your life, and yet, I sense inside you a deep well of remorse and guilt. I also see that you are despairing of having a chance to set things right, or at least have a chance at making amends. I commend your change of character, Jack David Mitchell. But you must pay penance for the harm you have caused before you find release from your burden." The incredible voice of the woman seemed to be both just above a whisper and just below a roar at the same time, and everyone who heard it perceived it differently. Some would remember it like the sounds of a gentle brook; others like a gentle rain. Still others would liken it to the sounds of waves on a lakeshore in evening, or perhaps the feeling of a warm gentle summer breeze on their features.

A whirlwind of emotions washed over Jack, and as he stared in awe at the being in front of him, the dam inside holding his emotions deep inside since his teen years burst, and he collapsed at last to the hard stone floor, weeping. Every bit of emotional pain he had experienced, and equally that he had caused, suddenly came over him, overwhelming his conscious mind, and it retreated from consciousness as he convulsed in psychological pain and suffering, curling into a ball and wishing he was dead.

The woman in white bent over him, caressed his brow, and said, "Sleep, child. I will come for you soon, and we will talk." The words were gentle and sad as she said them. Instantly he ceased moving, and seemed to breathe deeper as sleep overtook him, and peace came over him once more as he subconsciously curled up on the floor in the fetal position.

She straightened, and turned to look at Michelle. "Welcome among us, Newest Sister." Then she turned and bowed to Delara, who was still standing, in both surprise and respect.

"Your Majesty, I apologize for interrupting your proceedings. I am Hestia, Goddess of Hearth and Home. I was called by the wailing of this tortured soul. While he has much to answer for, if he passes the trials ahead of him, he will be My Servant, and will learn to heal where he has harmed in the past. He will sleep now for some few days. He will awaken to his new reality, and I shall return when he does."

The three remaining men in the room had shrank back from the incredible presence of the Goddess when she had suddenly appeared in their midst. Aaron turned his head away with a snarl, the blackness and evil in his mind automatically recognizing and reacting to, and rejecting, the goodness of the Goddess's presence. The other two backed away, in awe of her countenance, and in fear. She turned suddenly on them, and they flinched.

"This black-hearted one, he is lost beyond hope. Do with him as you will, or leave him to me, and I will end his mortal existence. One such as he should not be allowed to continue this life. He must go back to the House Between Worlds, and from there, to the Land of the Dead, in the hope that he can atone in his next life for the evil he has spread in this one."

"These other two companions in that foul endeavor show some remorse, but have not proven themselves to be deserving of whatever foul fate awaits that evil one. They may work as slaves as punishment until such time as they have proven they deserve to be free once more."

"Goddess Hestia, I shall do as you say." The queen was relieved to be able to have divine guidance to help sort out this situation, motioning to the guards to take the three men away. Some healers were called, who lifted Jack onto a litter, and carried him off. They did not, Michelle noticed, untie his hands or unshackle his feet.

The Goddess then turned, and looked at Giltreas. "Your Patron has wondered what has become of you." She smiled. "Do not judge him too harshly, child. He is but a piece of the larger whole at play here."

"Do not speak for me, Sister. I am well capable enough to do so myself." An arrogant voice, proud and aloof, filled the throne room. A new presence suddenly was there in front of them all, and this time, Giltreas took a step forward, fell to his knees, and bowed his head to the floor.

The male form in front of them was human from the neck down, but had the head of a dog. In his right hand, he held a staff of gold and silver, with a single blue jewel set at the top. There was a long sword in a sheath at his left hip, as well. He was tall, possibly eight feet or more, and his posture conveyed arrogance aplenty. He wore what Dave, Michelle, and Allison recognized as an ancient Egyptian loincloth, and a robe of some fabric that seemed to be golden in color, and his skin was a deep bronze.

"Where have you been, dog? I have not sensed you these past weeks. I wouldn't think it possible for you to slip your leash, and yet, it appears you have. What trouble have you stirred up that I must now undo?" The contempt of the newcomer bit like a lash, and with the final word of the newcomer's demand, he struck the floor with the foot of his staff, making a sound that thudded through the ears and the chest like the concussion of an explosion.

Giltreas suddenly looked up in confusion. "My Lord? I have consulted you as you have taught me at every turn. I have followed your internal guidance at every action and turn. I have only acted – "

"Shut up, you cur. I must now undo everything you have done, starting with these humans you have aligned yourself with." He looked up at Dave, Michelle, and Allison with disgust, but Dave was not sure if it was directed at them personally. Still, he shuddered inside. Who was this? Why did the form seem so familiar? There was something tugging at the back of his mind, something –

"Stuff it, Anubis. That is your name, right? You certainly are a pompous ass, aren't you?" Dave looked at Michelle in shock as she stepped forward a few paces, standing in a pose that conveyed contempt and a challenge, her hands on her hips.

Anubis also seemed shocked. "No one speaks to the God Anubis that way. You will repent and beg my forgiveness." He loomed over Michelle, and raised the staff as if to hit her.

She just stood there, a look of profound loathing and contempt on her incredibly beautiful features. He swung the staff back, then tried to swing it forward to strike the human woman down, and frowned as it would not move. He turned to glare at the woman in brown, and bared his teeth at her.

"You dare to interfere, Hestia? Know your place, Sister. I have the right to demand respect from mortals!" His tone lashed out at the mortals in the room, and the sounds of his anger was like a volcano erupting against their senses. Most everyone in earshot instinctively stepped back

Hestia glared at him, and spoke, her anger somehow still a part of her gentle countenance. "You would do well to know the focus of your ire, brother. That is no mortal facing you. Are you so blinded by arrogance that you would strike out at a Sister? She named you correctly, 'you pompous ass.'"

He turned back to Michelle, and really looked at her this time, and his eyes widened at what he saw, and the anger dissolved somewhat. Then he turned to Giltreas, and spoke again, anger once again on his face. "What have you done?"

Giltreas was silent with shock at the harsh disapproval of his Patron, unable to find the words to reply. He had followed direction as he always had, listening to the guidance through the Je'Tanna Na that Anubis had always used to speak with him in the past. The staff swept down at an arc and then across, like the swing of a cricket player's bat, impacting from Giltreas' shoulder down to his hip, and throwing him across the room into the stone wall as if he were a child's toy.

Anubis strode towards Giltreas' fallen form, intent on administering more punishment on his erstwhile tool, when Giltreas looked up, a harsh light in his eyes as he healed the injuries from the impact and hitting the wall with a stray thought.

Giltreas had always believed in doing what was just. He had always served Anubis to the best of his abilities, and had always tried to do what he had been told, except when those commands had been too horrific to contemplate. Those times had earned Giltreas the retribution of the Mid-God he had been conceived to serve, a price he was willing to pay. But not this time. His conscience was clear. He had done what he was directed, what Anubis, his patron, had taught him. He stood, and drew his sword, intent on defending himself against injustice, reaching inside himself to those places where his strength came from, and joined himself to everything he was and had become.

Anubis saw the defiance in his tool, and his anger redoubled. He would not be denied by this whelp of his making. He continued forward to continue the lessons the defiant one so desperately needed to remind him of his place, an implacable determination plain on his face, then paused as the defiant one was joined by humans in strange apparel he had noticed near where Giltreas had stepped forward, including the new Sister that had called him that term. They spread out in front of Giltreas, and each had a small black metal thing held in their hands that were pointed at him. He paused as the grim, fearless faces of the humans told him that they would fight on the side of his erstwhile tool against him.

Anubis had not faced determined, defiant humans in over five thousand summers, since the one had stood up to him. A moment of indecision held him, before determination once again made him advance, and now he drew his sword, as well. But a new voice, one that he knew well, stopped him.

"You must not. I might have need of him yet."

Anubis paused, then spoke up in a tone of more respect. "I would not destroy him."

"I wasn't speaking to you. I was telling him that I might yet need you, and that he must not end your existence."

"He would not be able to! What is this?"

"You do not know your tool any longer. He could easily." An uneasy silence came from Anubis as he contemplated what the voice announced to the room at large. Then Anubis spoke again.

"Master Sekur? I do not understand. What place do you have in this discussion? I was correcting my – " Anubis tried to regain control of the situation, but Sekur would have none of it.

"Anubis, Giltreas has been following the words and path of My Will. I have need of him, and his use and connection to you is at an end. He is yours no longer. No one will command him now; he has earned his freedom. And I would not have him end you before your usefulness is no more." The new voice seemed to come out of the very air, and the invisible presence that spoke seemed to be everywhere and nowhere at once. Perceptions of light, depth, and distance altered, warping reality as the newest visitor to the throne room joined the conversation. Anubis stopped stock still.

"You will not alter My Purpose. You may have created the tool Giltreas, and have honed him into the perfect weapon for your judgement against those that have wronged you, and yet, you have never pursued, listened to, nor understood the true reason I have allowed you such latitude in shaping the destiny of this worthy one in front of you. I needed a child born of mortal blood such as Giltreas has to accomplish certain things. The time has come for the Gods to serve the needs of The Plane of the Godless once more.

"This will be held in abeyance no more. The vast numbers of mortal souls waiting in the Lands of the Dead and at the House Between Worlds must be allowed to continue on the Great Path of the Soul. They have completed their journey on my planes, and some have waited millennia for their ascendancy. Raise not your hand against My Purpose, Anubis, or I shall find another who will take up your role, and you will spend an eternity in darkness, isolation, and silence." The words were spoken matter-of-fact, almost without emotion, as if the being speaking them was a well-educated adult lecturing a child.

"I will have the gifts back that I have loaned him, and the skills I have honed in him, before I agree to this. They are not meant for mortal hands, and must be kept away from a child such as he." Anubis's voice sounded faintly desperate and punitive at the same time, but Sekur's voice continued.

"No, you will not. He is no longer a child. They shall remain with him. He has earned the right to them. All of them," the voice added, as Anubis started to speak up. "You will renounce all claims upon him, the gifts he has gained, and his soul. And you will not interfere with him, my work I have set him upon, or any of his companions, at your immortal peril."

Anubis looked both angry and desperate now, as if searching for an avenue to justify his position, but that was quickly turned aside as the presence spoke again.

"Do you wish to question my decision, or challenge my will in this, Anubis?" The voice of Sekur turned dark and dangerous.

Anubis swallowed as he realized that he had no more tokens to play. He had no desire to challenge Sekur. That had never gone well for him in the past, and he saw no reason for it to be any different now. He bowed to no particular direction, and spoke again, much more subdued. "Very well, Master. I shall leave these to you." He vanished in a rush of air.

"Michelle," the voice of Sekur spoke again. "You have been forced down a difficult path; one not of your choosing. No other path would save you. Soon you will be asked to follow an even harder path. Consider well your choice. Seek me when you have questions, and we shall talk. I will never give you a load that you cannot carry, no matter how difficult it may seem at the time. We must all have free will to choose." Then with a rumbling that seemed to come from everything and nothing at the same time, the presence withdrew, and a vast emptiness was felt in the throne room in its absence.

CHAPTER 33

Daniel stood in front of his school locker in the high school hallway, glad it was Friday. While the changes he had undergone in the last month had been profound, maturing him mentally in such a short time, he reflected with an internal smile, he still had to deal with the reality of high school. He was about to turn to speak with his neighbor, when a sudden push from behind slammed him face first into the locker door he had just shut.

The world spun crazily for a moment as he caught himself from falling. He heard the indignation in Rachael's voice in protest of the action, and her hand went to his shoulder to see if he was ok. He cast a quick spell to heal himself from the results of the impact, then turned, even as his mind knew who his assailant was. He smiled at Rachael to assure her he was ok, then that smile disappeared as he started down the hall after the one that had pushed him.

Thomas, as he preferred to be called, was the star linebacker from the football team, and a senior. He was also an inveterate bully, finding a lot of pleasure in pummeling unsuspecting kids. He was laughing with his buddies at his latest efforts in reminding others of his magnificence, when a hand grabbed his arm and threw him through an open door into an empty classroom.

He staggered as he caught his balance, ending up next to the teacher's desk at the head of the room, and turned with his best, most innocent smile on his face, confident that he knew the teacher that had pulled him into the room. Then he paused.

"Danny? What do you want, you punk? Having trouble standing up by yourself?"

Daniel smiled, and waved his hand at the door behind him. The door closed, moving without a cause, clicking closed quietly.

"Thomas, you and I need to talk. And by talk, I mean I will talk, and you will listen. Do you understand me?" The tone of Daniel's voice was soft, but confident and firm.

"I ain't talking to you. Get the hell out of my way before you have another accident." Thomas tried to use his larger size and greater strength to push past the junior, but to his surprise, he was unable to move the boy in front of him.

Daniel let Thomas try to push him for a while, but he had cast a strength spell along with the telekinesis spell before throwing the larger boy into the room, and Thomas had no luck in his efforts. Then he spoke up.

"You are a bully. Bullies are cowards. You pick on and beat up on kids that can't defend themselves from you. You have been doing it for as long as I have known you, since I was in first grade and you were in third. You were even held back a year in junior high because of it. Everyone knows you are an angry, petty, childish, pathetic little person inside who is going to end up in jail because you don't know how to deal with others in a mature way, and you have anger issues."

The calm recitation of Daniel's opinion made Thomas flush with anger, and he acted the way he always knew how: he stepped forward and swung with all his might at Daniel's face with his fist.

Daniel's open hand flashed up and closed around the end of the bigger boy's fist, stopping his swing with speed and brute force. The effort was simple, and was drawn on the skills that Sekur had pounded into him over the training sessions he had put Daniel through. Daniel had wondered out loud to Sekur at the time why he needed to know physical fighting skills when he was a gifted mage, and Sekur had responded with a question. "What happens if someone is able to interrupt your spell casting by hitting you? You need to be able to cast spells, certainly, but you will also find yourself in physical confrontations where using spells and magic to defend yourself will either not be possible or will not be a good idea. Spells can do enormous damage, but when fighting, powerful spells are rarely a sharp, focused tool. And there will be times when the damage a spell can do is not the best solution to the problem you face." A small but significant percentage of time from Daniel's training was dedicated to physical endeavors, both with and without weapons of all kinds. After so many relative years, Daniel felt wary but confident in any confrontation that might get violent. And after so many contrived fights he had been put into under Sekur's training, he had learned how to deal with people like Thomas.

Now Thomas tried to pull his fist back to swing again, but Daniel merely tightened his grip, holding him in place. Then the classroom door opened behind him, and Rachael barged in, followed by Thomas's two team mates with whom he had been laughing just a moment before.

Thomas continued his efforts to pull free, all the while snarling curses and threats at Daniel, who merely ignored him for the moment as he looked over his shoulder at the newcomers to the room.

He rotated in a half circle while keeping Thomas in front of him so that Thomas's back was to the door, to enable him to keep an eye on the bully's two friends. He didn't want to get jumped from behind and have to fight them off as well.

Thomas stopped for a moment to try to catch his breath, and Daniel smiled at him, a cruel smile that was full of condescension, which lashed at Thomas's pride. He doubled up his left fist, and swung that as well, pulling with his right hand to try to catch Daniel coming towards him to increase the damage, but it was a trivial thing to swing his right hand to his right, pushing Thomas to his left and throwing his aim off. Thomas made three more attempts before stopping, but he still was cursing and threatening Daniel.

Daniel tightened his grip on Thomas's fist, and rotated his hand down, forcing the bigger boy down to his knees to prevent his own wrist from being broken while causing a flash of pain that made Thomas gasp out loud.

The two boys started forward at that point, but Daniel held up his left hand in warning, and they subsided, not sure what to do. Then the two boys and Rachael gasped in shock as Daniel yanked the bigger boy to his feet once more. His right hand left Thomas's fist as his left flashed out and grabbed the bigger boy by his shirt, slamming him to Daniel's right and up against the cinderblock wall next to the black board. Then he pulled him back and lifted the boy up, effortlessly slamming him against the wall again, but this time with his feet dangling six inches or more off the floor. Then he turned, and threw the boy away into the aisle between the desks like he was a rag doll.

Thomas sat there stunned on the floor for a moment, wondering what was happening, and how Daniel had been able to get so strong and be able to handle him so easily.

Daniel stepped over to him and bent down, and spoke again.

"You are going to stop being a bully. Do you understand me? You are going to go to the school guidance counselor and get help. Preferably today. Or I am going to beat you to a pulp every day until you do. And if I hear about you, or any of your team mates or friends doing anything to harm anyone else in this school, I am going to beat you, and them, into a quivering mass of snot and drool and broken teeth. Are you understanding me here? Or do I have to start beating on you and your two friends here right now? I will be more than happy to, if you think you don't understand what I am saying."

Thomas nodded quickly, desperate to do anything to get away from Daniel at last, but certain that he would be able to get away with anything he wanted with anyone else.

Daniel read him correctly, though.

"I don't think you believe me. Let me reiterate." He stepped back, and raised his right hand once more. This time, Thomas rose off the floor with a shriek as an invisible hand gripped him. He was swung through the air and dropped next to his friends, whose faces were white with fear at what was happening to their ringleader. Then the door closed once more as Thomas bolted towards it to get out of the room, his friends right behind him. Rachael didn't budge though, he noticed.

Thomas reached the door, but while the knob would turn, the door wouldn't budge. He pulled with all his weight, but it still wouldn't move. Then he heard Daniel's voice behind him once more.

"Do we understand each other?" He turned and nodded, his last vestiges of defiance evaporating like fog in sunlight in the face of his overwhelming fear.

"Good. You can go." The door opened slowly as if to prevent the swinging door from hitting Thomas as Daniel held it tightly in an invisible grip.

Thomas barely made it to the nearest bathroom before fear and adrenalin caused him to throw up all over the floor. His two friends could only stand in white-faced shock and watch him, unsure of what to do.

Rachael looked at Daniel in shock as he turned away and looked out the window, his shoulders hunched slightly as if in defeat.

"What's wrong? You won! Why do you look like you lost?"

He turned back, and she winced at her long-time school mate's facial expression.

"Because I did lose. I lost my temper. I may have done more harm than good."

Rachael was shocked at what Daniel was saying. It sounded more like her dad than a sixteen year old boy talking, and the maturity in his voice was a strange thing in someone so young.

"How did you do all that?" The question burned its way out of her before she could stop it.

He looked at her and smiled, but the smile was tired and strained as he tried to understand the ramifications of what he did with Thomas just a moment ago. "I have discovered some rather interesting abilities some weeks ago."

"What kind of abilities? What can you do?" Her questioning was focused and direct, something he expected from someone of her intelligence. They had known each other for many years, and lived a couple blocks from each other. While not the best of friends, they were social, but not much more.

Rather than answer her question, he asked her one instead.

"Are you going to the search for that missing college girl today after school?"

"I am, why?"

"You will see what I can do then. But you have to promise me to not get involved. Don't talk to the media after. And certainly don't talk to the police. If you are asked, the only thing you should say is that you think my name is Daniel."

Understanding dawned on her as she nodded. Then, "I have to get to my last class. See you later." Rachael hurried out of the room, her mind a whirl. She couldn't pay much attention in class, and was so distracted even the teacher asked her about it, but all she said was she had a lot on her mind.

The teacher accepted the explanation at face value, moving on to the duties at hand.

* * *

Later that afternoon, Rachael saw Daniel in the crowd standing in the parking lot in front of the Sheriff Deputy's car, and saw two news vans parked nearby. Her breath caught in her throat as she took in the scene. There were dozens of law enforcement officers there from several jurisdictions, and the cameras were rolling as the officer heading up the search was holding up a picture of the college girl who had been missing for several weeks.

"…So, based on the most recent information we have, we believe her body is somewhere in this park. We are going to search it from end to end. We seem to have about two hundred searchers here, which will let us cover a good portion of the front half of the park tonight. Remember! If you find something, stop where you are, and call someone with a radio over to have a look at it. Don't touch it, and try not to disturb the ground around it if at all possible! In addition to finding Alana, we also need to collect any evidence of what happened to her, so the guilty party can be charged and convicted."

Rachael nodded. The case had been in the news several times since the beautiful girl's picture had been plastered everywhere by her frantic family. She was not the usual type who conjured up such a response. Alana Monroe was part African American and part Pacific Islander, producing an exotic-looking girl that, while not a super-model, but was still pretty. Rachael had noticed that the efforts to find missing girls seemed to be in direct relation to their beauty, and she was happy that the effort was being expended to find a girl that was more average, and normal, like her.

The crowds started to thin out, and Daniel walked forward part way once more to get a good look at the picture of the missing girl. A couple deputies noticed him looking, and looked at each other. The teen didn't fit the usual pattern of a perpetrator, but they were alert anyways for anyone that was acting suspiciously. They were all aware that perpetrators often took part in the search efforts, for whatever reason. Then they stared at him for a different reason. He began to glow, starting with his eyes.

The bright, clear fall day masked it at first, but then it became more evident as the glow grew brighter.

A reporter had been speaking into the camera that was strategically placed to capture the speech of the officer talking to the crowds, and she stopped as her cameraman started waving frantically and pointing over her shoulder. She turned, and stepped out of the field of view of the camera as she took in the glowing teen boy standing some fifteen feet from the nearest law enforcement officer.

Daniel seemed to hunch slightly, pulling his hands in front of him, then he stood up slightly, his hands going out from his sides, and the glow moved with them, to form a dome that stretched out to a diameter of nearly twelve feet, and over seven feet tall. It shimmered and wavered in the bright sun, but somehow it didn't prevent people from clearly seeing what was happening inside.

Gasps and screams could be heard from the searchers, and especially from the missing girl's family, as more began to happen. Daniel dropped his backpack, and pulled out a blanket from it, tossing it slightly into the air where it began to float.

The officer coordinating the search stared in shock at the event in front of him, not sure what was really happening, or what he was seeing, but the need to investigate was a key part of his makeup, and he stepped forward, two others at his heels. He reached out carefully with one hand to touch the glowing dome for an instant, but didn't feel anything from it. He reached out once more, and touched his little finger on his left hand to it carefully. It felt solid, not harmful in any way, and he placed his entire hand on it. It did feel slightly warm, and it seemed to move slightly, but not because of his actions.

He realized he was being watched, and looked up into the eyes of the boy inside the dome next to the floating blanket. When they made eye contact, the boy nodded once, a slight smile on his face below his glowing eyes, and the officer flushed as the boy conveyed something to him in that nod. Acceptance, or perhaps a look that said, 'ok, I'm going to continue now that you're done.'

Then the boy's face became more serious, and he looked away, his eyes glowing so brightly now that the light was emanating from them, almost obscuring his face.

His arms swung out and straight down at his sides, and a wave of energy flashed out, causing a booming noise as the ground shook briefly, taking everyone by surprise. Those who hadn't been looking at him suddenly turned to find the source of the sound and the vibration in the ground, only to stare at the spectacular event taking place right in front of their incredulous eyes. Then the hands came together, and a light flashed into existence front of him, causing everyone to gasp.

The light disappeared, and body parts came into view floating in mid-air in front of the boy, to the horror of the watching people. A red glow flashed over the parts, followed by a yellow flash, then a green one, then a blue one, and the body was suddenly whole. Alana's family gasped as they recognized their missing family member. The blanket suddenly and quickly flowed around her like water, to protect the modesty of her naked form, and then the no-longer missing girl's body lowered gently to the asphalt of the parking lot, the excess of the blanket piled under her head to gently support her.

Daniel closed his eyes, and prayed to his teacher for his help with the next part. He felt the pulsing energy infuse him, and his entire form glowed with a bright red light that was almost painful to see, intense even in daylight. His hands floated up, then thrust down, and the red light left him to infuse the body wrapped in the blanket at his feet.

Alana woke up on the hard ground, wrapped in a blanket. She opened her eyes, dreading what she would see as her last memory of the man that had assaulted her and hurt her so badly came to her. Instead, she saw a teenage boy standing above her with glowing eyes. She shied back suddenly, realizing that she was naked and wrapped in an unfamiliar blanket, then her eyes widened as she took in the glowing barrier around them. Then she realized she could see perfectly without her glasses.

Daniel spoke quietly, and Alana realized the barrier around them seemed to block the sound from outside from getting in. She had to concentrate on what he was saying.

"Sorry, what did you say?"

"I said its ok, Alana, you're safe now. You're ok. Everything is ok. You've been gone for a while, but you're back now, and everything is ok. Look, there's your family." The soothing tones calmed the chaos in Alana's mind, and when she looked where he pointed, she saw her mother, father, and two sisters pressed up against the barrier, tears in their eyes as they desperately tried to get through the clear, shimmery barrier to her, their missing and now-returned beloved daughter and sister.

Alana scrambled to her feet, trying to hold the blanket around her, and Daniel steadied her as she stood, helping hold the blanket in place. When she was on her feet, he asked, "Are you ready for me to drop the barrier?"

She nodded, and the barrier came down, and with it came the sounds from the parking lot where the search had been headquartered. Everyone seemed to rush into the now-open space at once, and Alana found herself swept up in the arms of her parents and sisters, while Daniel found himself wrestled to the ground and forced into handcuffs. He gave no resistance whatsoever.

When he was stood back up, there was a nasty, bleeding scrape on his face that the now-close television cameras both caught. He winced as the sudden pain made itself known. Then he murmured something, and a green glow came over his face. When it was gone, the gash was gone as if it had never been there before. The reporters both thrust microphones into his face as the deputies and officers tried to wrestle him away from the crowds and into the back of the waiting squad car, slamming the door before anyone else could dive in with him.

A county deputy and a city police officer hopped into the front seat and turned on the sirens and lights, trying to get out of the parking lot with their prisoner before, in their mind, something else really bad happened.

After they'd cleared the lot and pulled out onto the main road, Daniel turned and saw that several cars were following them, from different jurisdictions around the city and county. He was certain it wasn't all of them, though, and was glad that several had stayed behind to take care of Alana and her family. It was not going to be easy for them with the live news feeds capturing and transmitting her return to the living. She would need protection from the crazies that inevitably flocked to supernatural events like what just happened. Daniel was certain that he could take care of himself, but he expected to be unavailable to protect the college girl that had been dead for over a month now.

The silence inside the car was a palpable thing when he broke it by clearing his throat. The deputy driving nearly jumped out of his skin and the squad car swerved briefly before the well-trained instincts of the veteran law enforcement officer righted the car once more.

"What?!? What do you want?" The city police officer knew his voice was a little strained, but it was understandable. His worldview had been turned upside down in mere minutes. He was happy the girl had been found, or whatever what happened was called, but there were so many unanswered questions. Was the kid in back involved? Is that how he knew where to find her? How the HELL had he done what he just did? It was obvious that she had been dead and dismembered, but now she was living. How the hell had that happened? What were those different colored lights that had come from him? What was that barrier he had erected? And how had he shook the ground, and why? The questions were making his head spin, and he drove onwards on instinct, trying to keep his speed down somewhat to give him a better chance to recover in case he lost control.

"I just wanted to say thank you for getting me out of there before the people got unruly. I hope that your fellow officers will protect Alana and her family from the craziness that is about to descend on them. This will not be easy for them, but I am certain that they will be happier in this situation with her than without her." The words were quiet, and sincere, but

310

the deputy glanced at the city officer riding next to him, not saying anything. He had no idea how to proceed with this, and decided to turn the kid over to anyone that would take him as soon as possible. Then he was going to go home and hug his wife and his two sons and his daughter a lot, and probably never let go again.

The ride was quiet and uneventful after that, but the transition to the interview room in the sheriff's station didn't go as well. Several cops were hanging around, some of whom had been at the search and witnessed what he had done. They had parked and hustled into the building first, to be on hand in case something happened that they were needed for. They had stood quietly in the garage along the way from the car to the doorway into the building. It was one thing to think you are ready for a supernatural event, and quite another to be confronted with it when it does.

Daniel stood with the assistance of the deputy as he was pulled from the back of the car, and looked over the officers in the indoor parking area used for the transfer of arrestees. On a whim, he called what Sekur had named his Physicker Sight up, looking over the officers. The resulting glow from his eyes caused more open mouths and some Oohs and the like, startling even the hardened officers.

Daniel winced at what he saw. Several were alcoholics, to be expected in such a challenging and difficult line of work. There was the usual collection of age-related ailments and the like, but one man in particular stood out.

With his hands cuffed behind him, he was unable to point or wave, but he jutted his chin out at the man, and said, "Sir."

The officer looked uneasily around at his fellow officers, before saying, "Me?"

"Yes sir. Can you please come here for a moment? I've had all my shots, and I am completely house-broken. Not to mention I have these lovely bracelets someone graciously gave me. It will be alright. Honest." There was a titter of nervous laughter at that, but the officer drew a deep breath and steeled himself. Then he stepped forward.

"What is it?"

"Have you known about the cancer? It is spreading fast. You don't have much time."

He gaped at the young man.

"How do you know about that?" he demanded oppressively.

"It is one of my abilities. You can see my eyes glow, right? My Physicker Sight is one of the things that lets me see things like that. My teacher told me about it, and why. Do you want me to heal you? Do you all want me to heal all of you?" He looked around at the gathered officers in the immediate area, a gentle smile on his face.

"What do you mean, 'heal us'?" The deputy holding his arm spoke up now, and Daniel turned to look at him. The deputy flinched as those glowing eyes focused on him, but he didn't let go of the young man's arm. He spoke up again.

"What do you mean? What is wrong with me?" He tried to make it sound gruff, but his voice came out strained, and a little high pitched. Those glowing eyes were incredibly distracting.

"You have liver problems, you are missing two teeth, and you have suffered a couple of bad concussions over the years. Your knees are almost completely worn out, and your left hip needs work. And you have abdominal problems, among other things." His eyes turned and looked over the other officers, and no one moved as that unearthly gaze swept over them. He singled out one younger female deputy, and nodded towards her.

"You are unable to have children." Deputy Dee Carlton's eyes filled with tears as he said that. It was the reason she was currently going through a divorce – her husband Brad wanted the kids that she was unable to give him, and he was going to move on from her while he was, in his words, still young enough to be a father. Personally, she thought to herself again, anyone that abandoned their promises that quickly would make a very poor father. Before she could respond to the kid in front of her, though, his gaze swept on.

"Several of you are alcoholics. There are various other things wrong with most of you here. I can remove them all. Here, hold these for a moment." He turned and handed the handcuffs that had been on him to the now-shocked deputy, and took a single step forward. He closed both eyes, which cut off the glow, then swung both hands up in an arc.

A red light flashed from him to wash over all the people in the room, quickly followed by a yellow light, then a green light, and finally a blue light as he moved his arms three more times.

The transformation was quick, and several of the officers found themselves reaching desperately for pants that were suddenly some sizes too large as the extra weight they had been carrying around, some for decades, was suddenly erased as if it had never been there. A few who were holding up their pants to protect their modesty with one hand also had to reach up with the other to remove glasses that were no longer needed.

Daniel looked around and nodded once at his handiwork, and then turned back to the burly deputy who was also holding onto his pants with both hands, his glasses now in one of those hands. He reached out and gently removed the handcuffs from the shocked deputy, then reached behind his back. After a moment, he turned and showed the deputy that the cuffs were back in place, and he was 'restrained' once more. With a smile, he said, "Should we get going? Where am I supposed to be headed again?"

CHAPTER 34

FBI Special Agent in Charge William Nelson looked at the security footage from the station garage once more, unable to understand what had happened. He had arrived from the main office a half hour before, only to find a police station in shambles. Several officers were wearing uniforms much too large for them, for some reason. And everyone had a strained, credulous look on their faces, as if they'd seen a ghost or something. Given that he had seen the live footage from the search scene before leaving the local FBI office to investigate, he could understand that. One of the shocked officers, still holding his pants up with both hands, had stared at him as if he had two heads for a moment. Then he shook himself.

"Sorry, sir, what did you say?"

"I asked you why your uniform doesn't fit. Can you tell me about that?" He asked it gently, trying not to overwhelm the officer, who was clearly on the edge.

"Ah. About that. I seem to have misplaced some fifty, sixty pounds that I woke up with this morning. I mean, it was like, flash-flash-flash-flash, and suddenly my pants are heading south on me. And the kid just stood there, you know?" The officer's head shook once more, and the SAIC just nodded. He would figure it out eventually.

Now, having looked at the excellent quality video image of the event that the officer referred to, he had no idea what had happened. He sighed.

'I guess I need to go talk to the kid,' he thought to himself.

Daniel looked up when the man in the suit entered the interview room. It had been a few hours since he had been left here, and the cuffs were getting uncomfortable. He could, obviously, remove them at any time, just as he had in the garage, but he was going to be respectful until it was no longer a good idea.

The time alone had been well spent, as he'd closed his eyes and communed with Sekur, his teacher. The teacher had no complaints about what he'd done so far, and encouraged him to continue. He still had no complete idea who Sekur was, but he trusted him implicitly. He owed the being for the incredible skills he had trained into and brought out of Daniel in all those nights of endless dreaming.

Now he smiled at the man in the suit, and spoke up. "Can you remove the cuffs? They are getting uncomfortable on me." He twisted slightly to show the cuffs to the agent, who snorted.

"No, I think we will leave them on for now. What's your name?"

"You can call me Daniel. Everyone else does."

"Smart-ass. What's your whole name?"

"I am protecting my family for now."

"Oh, we know all about your family. Your friend Rachael said you were her classmate, and we found your picture in the school records."

"Well, then why did you ask? Do you always ask questions that you already know the answer to?" The tone of voice was innocent, but the question made it anything but.

"Listen, kid – "

"Daniel, please."

"Whatever. Listen, kid," emphasizing the word this time, "I want to know how you are able to do what you've done. And right now, there are several people who are wondering if you were the one who killed that girl, just so you could pull your little stunt out there in the park. So tell me what I want to know, and we won't have to get ugly with this."

"Well, if you know who I am, you also know that I am a minor. I'm sixteen, which means that I have a right to have my mother here when I am questioned. Go fetch her now. Take these handcuffs off. You know that they won't hold me, but I'm trying to be civil about it. And the fact that I am being questioned brings up another subject. Am I being charged with a crime?"

The tone of voice had changed, the agent realized. He was not dealing with a scared, confused teen. He had rarely heard that confident tone of voice in even hardened criminals.

"Who are you? What are you?"

"Ahh. More questions. I refuse to answer until my mother is here. And I want a lawyer as well, since you seem to be making a federal case out of this." The last sentence came out in a perfectly level tone of voice, and Daniel turned his head and closed his eyes, his mind elsewhere.

The agent slammed his hand down on the table, hoping to startle a response out of the young man in front of him, but he didn't open his eyes or even flinch, but the agent didn't stop there.

"Listen, you little..." That was as far as he got before the agent, and the people in the room monitoring the video cameras in the room, jumped in shock.

In less time than it takes to tell, the teen in front of him disappeared, the handcuffs were heard clattering to the floor, and in his place a massive male African lion stood up and put its front paws on the interview table and roared at full volume less than a foot from his face.

The color drained from the agent's face as he suddenly found himself fighting for control of his bladder and bowels. He stumbled back into the chair on the other side of the table, and tried to scrabble further back as the massive form jumped easily up on the table, causing it to creak and groan under the nearly six hundred pound apex predator.

Daniel drew back his lips and roared again, satisfied that he had the agent's attention. Then he cancelled the spell he had used, and jumped lightly off the table, sat back in the chair, crossed his arms, and closed his eyes.

"I said go get my mother. Don't make me repeat myself. And please, don't make me angry." The tone of voice seemed completely calm and level, but there was a slight edge to the words in the last sentence that seemed to make the agent's stomach clench. He stood on suddenly wobbly legs, and walked to the door, his eyes never leaving the teenager sitting quietly in the chair.

The door closed behind him, locking the kid inside, and he slumped against the wall, suddenly realizing he was sweating profusely, drops dripping off his chin as it ran liberally from his face and head.

A deputy turned the corner and looked at him, the look on his face indicating clearly he had been monitoring the scene remotely, and the agent snarled at him. "Well, go get this kid's mother!"

"Right." The deputy vanished, almost like magic, the mentally off-balance FBI agent thought with a hysterical giggle that threatened to break out of even his prodigious self-control.

It was no more than an hour later when the door opened again, and another person was let into the room. The door closed behind her, and she spoke up.

"Daniel? Why are you here? What did you do? The police wouldn't tell me anything about what is going on. That unpleasant FBI agent said you were in a lot of trouble, but he won't tell me any more than that. What is going on?" She was scared, and more than a little angry about being snatched out of her house and driven in a police car at full speed with lights and siren to this place, by a police officer who would only say she was needed to be with her son for questioning. The officer seemed almost to be scared about something. When she had arrived, she had been hustled into the building, then to this room, where she found her son, her only child, sitting alone with his arms crossed and his eyes closed.

Daniel stood up with a smile and walked over to her, hugging her. "Hi, mom. Sorry about this. But, the officers want to know a bunch of things, and I have a right to have you and a lawyer here when they question me. So…" He broke off as the FBI agent opened the door and stepped in again. The smile left Daniel's face, and he stopped talking.

The agent stopped, just looking, then watched as Daniel took the chair from the agent's side of the table and carried it to the other, so that his mother could sit next to him. Then Daniel reached down and picked the fallen handcuffs off the floor, and reached out and handed them to the FBI agent.

"Can you get those back to that nice Sheriff's Deputy they belong to? I am sure he will want them back. Thanks."

Daniel then escorted his mother to one of the chairs, helped her sit politely, and then sat himself. After a moment, he spoke to the agent.

"Can we please move forward? I want to go home."

The agent looked for a moment, then turned and opened the door, only to be handed a chair for him to sit on. Flustered, he brought the chair in, set it down, and sat in it.

"Ok, let's… what is it now?"

"Aren't you forgetting a lawyer? Don't I have a right to have one present if I'm being questioned?"

"You're not being charged with a crime, so you don't need one."

"I still have a right to one, don't I?"

"Well, not…"

"I guess we're done here, then. Mom, shall we go?" He stood and reached out to help his mother to her feet, but she resisted, staying seated.

"Daniel, what is going on here? Why are you here? What did you do?"

"Well, you remember that I was going to help search for that missing girl?" She nodded up at him, confused.

"I found her. They want to know how. I think they believe that since I found her, I had something to do with her disappearance. So, they want to ask me a bunch of questions. I have a right to have you present because I'm a minor, and a lawyer, since it is my constitutional right. This FBI agent is intent on violating those constitutional rights, and is betting that I won't call him on it. I am calling his bluff. We are leaving, or they are going to charge me with a crime. Which won't go over very well."

"Listen, kid, you are going to want to cooperate here, or we will put you in foster care, or better yet, juvenile detention, until you do." The agent was convinced that the kid wouldn't repeat something like his previous act with his mother in the room, unless she already knew about it. Based on her responses, she was most likely in the dark about her son's abilities, which left him on pretty firm ground for the moment.

"Listen you, don't you dare threaten my son!" Mama Bear suddenly made an appearance in the very frightened and very angry mother. She put her arm around Daniel and pulled him close, subconsciously turning him away from the Agent Nelson.

"I'd listen to her. Compared to her, I am just a little kitten. She's the real lioness. Her bite is much worse than her growl." The obvious reference to what happened earlier made him blush, but he tried push his way forward. He pulled out his cell phone and looked down at it as he started to look for a phone number.

"I think that a call to a juvenile court judge I know is in order… gwaaawk!" The agent squawked as the three people, the table, and the three chairs that had been in the interrogation room all appeared on a sandy beach on a beach next to the ocean, under the warm tropical sun.

Daniel's mother gawked at the sights, the pure, pristine beach around them, and the waves of the blue ocean lapping gently at the shore.

The agent stood up, however. The speed and ease, and the complete lack of any sensation, with which the spell had transferred them to this location had stunned him. "Where the hell are we?" The question came out strained, almost in falsetto as he tried to process what had just happened to him.

"Well, someplace where you don't get cell service, that's for sure. In fact, I think the nearest cell tower is, oh, that way," he gestured out over the ocean, "a few thousand miles. But the roaming charges will be killer." The tone was light and innocent, but the look on Daniel's face was anything but. Then he turned to his mother.

"Hey mom, let's go somewhere where we can talk. Want to go for a run with me?" Before she could respond, he cast another spell, and she found herself changed into a tiger. He changed himself to the same thing then ran away some two hundred yards up the beach, his mother in quick pursuit, before cutting away from the water and off the beach into the dense vegetation.

With them both back out of sight from the FBI agent, he cancelled the spells, and his mother's familiar face stared at him with a huge smile at the incredible experience she'd just had warring with confusion for control of her emotions.

"Daniel, what the fuck is going on? How are you doing this?" He almost never heard her swear, and he smiled an apology at her for what was happening. Then he got serious.

"The world is not how it is supposed to be," he started to say, when she interrupted him again, agitation showing plainly on her face.

"What do you mean?" She realized that she was rambling, and shut her mouth abruptly, waving her hand to indicate he should continue.

"Thousands of years ago, at a place the ancient Akkadians called Babel, something happened. I am not really sure exactly what went on there, since I haven't asked about that yet. I have the highlights, though. Basically, the result is the world you see around you. Pain, suffering, disease, racism, hatred, violence, war; none of this is supposed to be happening here."

He paused a moment, and a look of pain came over his face. Sekur had explained a lot about what was going on, during and around his training, but not everything. Some, he was told, he would have to figure out by himself. She waited patiently this time, but with ill-concealed frustration.

"Well, the whole world is going to change. Things are going to be, not necessarily returned to how they were, but set back on a path very similar to how it should have been. I am going to play a big role in what is coming because of what I am capable of doing. I will be helping good people through it, and stopping the bad people from causing problems. For me, it all started several of weeks ago…" He sat down on the ground, waved her over, and when she sat next to him, he told her the whole story.

Back on the beach, the now-completely off balance and terrified FBI SAIC stared frantically at the cell phone in his hand, desperately yet unsuccessfully trying to will it to get any kind of signal so he could call for help.

CHAPTER 35

Allison stepped into the paddock while directed Sadie and Abby to lie down out of the way against the fence, and waved her hand in the "stay" command across the front of her body. Once they were both lying down, she dropped their leashes on the ground next to them in such a way that it wouldn't get in their way if they rolled onto their sides. Both dogs put their heads down and relaxed, knowing that it might be awhile until she came to get them for their turn to train. For once, Allison noted, Sadie didn't say anything. She glanced down at the bigger dog, and saw Sadie looking at her out of the corner of one eye. Then Sadie picked up her head, yawned real big, and settled down, closing her eyes. Abby cuddled up closer to her "big sister", and also settled down. Then Allison heard Sadie speak, a contented "Ah. Nap time," coming from somewhere near her head, as usual. Shaking her head, she led Max into the center of the ring on leash.

Max loved to earn treats. The little black dog with white accent markings, all twenty-three pounds of him, seemed to be wagging his stubby tail so hard that the rest of him moved as a result. His eyes looked up at her the whole time as he anticipated earning a lot of tasty bits of meat that he so enjoyed.

Allison gave the front command, where her right hand went straight out to the side at shoulder level with the palm to the front, and then swung it towards her chest with the palm touching just under her neck. Max walked up to her and stopped right in front of her, looking up at her expectantly.

She followed that with the sit hand signal, which was the right hand down at her right side, palm forward, which was then swept up and forward in an arc, as if she were indicating someone should stand, and Max sat. She gave the heel command, the palm of her left hand down, the fingers pointing straight out to the side, and the arm straight, which she brought forward in a straight line. He came closer, turning to stand next to her left

319

leg, and since she wasn't moving, he sat the way he had been trained. Then she gave the stay signal, also with her right hand, but this time it was held down at her side with the palm back towards her, before sweeping the hand from right to left across her body. Satisfied that Max was not going anywhere at the moment, she reach down and disconnected the leash from his collar. The whole time she was careful to keep him in her field of vision, without making eye contact with him, which was also a form of reward. He hadn't earned any rewards yet, but he would.

She coiled up the leash then stuffed it into her back pocket. She stepped forward ten paces, stopped, and carefully turned back towards Max, still not making eye contact as Max watched everything she did carefully. He was anticipating bounding towards her to get a treat, but he had become much more experienced at this game. He waited, quivering slightly as he tried to sit stock still.

After a fifteen second count, she swept her right hand up, and Max broke out of the stay before she was able to complete the "come" command. Her hand stopped, and she called out, "wrong." Max stopped and stood still while looking and wagging at her. She sighed. This was the one that Max had the most trouble with. Or most fun with, depending on your point of view, she decided.

She stepped forward, and used hand signals to get Max back to the original spot, and in the sitting position once more, before issuing the stay command and stepping back out ten paces.

Three more attempts later, Max finally stayed in place while she completed the come command, and he just sat there. And stayed, staring at her, even after she gave the 'come' command. She gave a slight laugh as she looked away.

Over next to the fence, Sadie opened one eye, looked at Max, and said, "Bad Max. No treat."

Allison laughed a little harder before she got herself under control. "Sadie, that's not helping. Max isn't bad. He is still learning."

"Max is not learning. Max just wants to play, and get treats."

"I know that, but that is part of training. He has to learn to do what I am asking to get the treats. You know this; you learned it a long time ago. Why am I talking to a dog?" She turned back to Max, and spoke up this time.

"Max, come!" She made the statement a command while giving the hand signal once more, and Max ran towards her, wagging his tail. When he got half way to her, she raised her right hand up at the level of her head, palm towards Max, and he dropped to a lay down position, but not without a frustrated "BARK!" that brought a quick burst of laughter to her ears from someone watching from the fence. She gave the "come" and signal once more, and this time Max bounded towards her, stopping right in front of her feet and sitting so nice and pretty as he looked up at her. She took her right hand, and waved it back behind her and around, and Max shot around her legs, coming to a close approximation of the heel position before sitting on his still-wiggling butt. His position was not aligned with her, though, as he was not facing forward as the "come around" command required. His rear end was so far out away from her side that he was almost facing her, which was a no-no.

She took her left hand and gave an adroit little move that Max knew all too well. He scooted his rear closer to her, finally sitting in the correct alignment and position next to her leg. That finally got him a couple of tiny little meat treats. He was young, only two years old, and it was still early in his overall training cycle, but he was smart, eager to please, and picked it all up very quickly. Overall, Allison was pleased with how quickly he was getting to know the commands and what was expected from them. She reached down and gave him a good rub behind his ears, then looked up at her audience today.

The queen's Seneschal stood there at the fence, watching her intently. Seeing her looking at him, he spoke up.

"How are you able to get him to do these things so well? Others have told me how much command you have over your dogs, but I didn't believe it. What makes them do all this for you?"

"Most dogs are motivated by food. If you wave a small bit of food in front of their faces, but don't let them have it, they will start offering behaviors to you to see what will get them the treat. Here, watch."

She turned to Max, and said "All done!" Max bounded up out of his stay position, but his eyes never left her face. She reached into the training pouch at her right hip, and pulled out a training treat. She put it into the palm of her hand, closed her hand over it, and held her hand in front of Max's nose. He didn't immediately get the treat, so he sat. Then he lay down on his belly. That didn't do it, so he stood. Still nothing. So he licked her hand, and nibbled gently at it. Then he sat once again, and raised his paw in a tentative poke at her hand, and she opened her palm and let him have the treat.

She turned back to the Seneschal once again, and his eyes were wide. "I have never seen that before. Are all dogs that way?"

"Every dog I have ever trained that was motivated by food has done something like that, yes. I have heard about dogs that are motivated not by food, but by some special toy that they want to play with, so they will do anything to get it. Every dog is all different, with different personalities and traits and behaviors, just like anyone else, but they will all offer some behaviors to get what they want.

"The important thing is to tie a verbal command or hand signal to the behaviors you want, and then reward them for doing it right with a treat.

For example, here is how you get a dog to sit the first time."

She pulled several treats out of her pouch, and gave them to Max one after another.

"This is called priming him. He gets treats the first time you start training, so that he knows he likes them, and wants more. If he doesn't like them, find other treats. Moist meats with a stronger smell, but that are fresh, cooked, and good for him, work best." Max finished off all but one of the treats and then she closed her hand around the last one. She let Max smell her hand. "He is like every other dog in that their sense of smell is way more sensitive than yours or mine. He knows it is there."

She got Max to stand by pulling her hand back, and he stood up to follow it.

"Now that he is on his feet, watch as I move it in front of his face, then over his head. He will fall back into a sitting position when I do that. As soon as his butt hits the ground, say the word sit, like a gentle command, not a question, and give him the treat." Allison turned her hand over, closed fingers down, and moved her whole hand into Max's face, and back over his head. As the hand with the treat moved over his head and back, his body sank into a sitting position to follow it. As soon as his rear end touched the dirt below him, she said "sit", stopped her hand, turned it over, opened her fingers, and let him take the treat. It was small enough that it disappeared into his stomach after his teeth ground it up.

"Here, you try it." She handed him about five treats, and he fed Max the first four, before closing the last one in his hand. He got Max up on his feet and then did the motion that brought the little dog back to the sitting position, and said "Sit", giving him the treat.

The Seneschal had an amazed look on his face as he got the dog to sit. "Incredible. What can they learn?"

"Sadie is by far the best trained of the three. I've spent the most time with her, mainly because she is the oldest, but she also seems to be the most trainable. Well, she was, before she learned to talk. That improved things considerably.

"But, back before that, everything she knows has both a voice command and a hand signal, so she can respond to both. She will work entirely without treats, mostly because she enjoys working with people. Watch."

For the next few minutes, Allison put Sadie through everything the big dog knew how to do. Sitting, standing, laying down, rolling over, going out, turning for recalls, sitting, heeling around the area, staying while in a standing position, a sitting position, a laying down position, transitioning from one position to the next; everything Sadie knew how to do, she did flawlessly.

At the end, the Seneschal found himself astonished at what Sadie could do. "How long did it take for her to learn all that?"

"It was almost three years of regular, steady work. She is a joy to work with; so eager to please, and very food motivated. After the first year, she stopped learning, and started playing whenever she was off the leash. During recalls, she would bolt off and run around the ring like crazy, with a huge smile on her furry face. It was funny to see, but at the same time, not what we wanted her to do. The obedience instructor and I worked endlessly on getting her to work better. I think it was just a case of her needing to grow up a lot before she was ready to work and be serious. She was barely over a year old at that point."

"So young? I did not know dogs could be trained at all, let alone be trained at that young an age."

"Actually, I started training her when he was just a few months old, when Michelle first got him from the Animal Humane Society. She had to be house-trained, which is teaching her not to poop or pee in the house – only outside, and when she is told it is ok. I don't work for a living since David earns everything we need to live on, and I really love dogs – all animals, really – so I was happy to do it. The best time to start training them is as soon as they are weaned."

Allison paused, using hand signals to get Sadie back to where Abby was and then got her to lie down and stay with two more hand signals.

"You have to be careful in how you train them. I firmly believe that you never hit or abuse an animal – they never deserve it, unlike some humans I have met who only respond to violence. Training a dog is simple, no matter how difficult it is. You reinforce and reward the behaviors you want them to have, and you ignore or entice them away from the behaviors you don't want them doing."

The Seneschal felt his mouth drop open as he contemplated what was being said. He had always looked down at humans with, not so much contempt (he incorrectly believed), but definitely a sense of superiority, although he knew that he had shown some humans derision and disgust. Most of the time, humans were concerned with nothing more than where their next meal was coming from, or who they would be sleeping with next. In all of his very long life, the old elven noble had never found humans to be that interesting or compelling. Perhaps, he thought to himself slowly, it was because he hadn't met these humans from that plane before.

His thoughts turned to what he thought he knew about the Plane of the Godless, and tried to rectify it with what he was learning about Allison. She was incredibly different, and way more complex, than any human he had ever met. She was intelligent, and seemed to understand a great many things, much like a dwarvish scholar might be. But she was capable of acting decisively when the situation called for it, much like an elf, such as when that one evil human had tried to get to Queen Delara in her throne room the first time they had all been brought before Her Majesty.

He had reviewed the single kick she had hit the man with that had so effectively incapacitated that one, Aaron, several times in his mind. Over his nearly three millennia of life, he had never seen the like. He had expected her to be the berserker after that act, and need to be forcibly restrained until she regained her wits about her, as so many humans he had seen before who were so easily given to violent acts, but he had nearly gasped out loud when he realized that she was entirely under control the entire time, and seemed almost to regret her actions. Her respectful bow and apology to Her Majesty had confused him to the point of speechlessness, as had seeing her upset and regretful of her actions immediately afterwards, with Michelle and David.

The complexity of the woman was a difficult thing to contemplate. He had no frame of reference in which to place her actions and makeup to make sense of it all, and that left him off balance and confused. He had quickly realized she was obviously trained beyond anything the elves had ever contemplated before, a realization that was supported by her almost casual approach to training the guard force that followed her daily running and exercise with such fascination.

He had watched from afar as she had demonstrated her training and skills to the guards on one occasion, then expected her to hold it over the men and women she vanquished in quick, brutal fashion, but there had been absolutely none of that. She had simply helped them up and then began to demonstrate what she had done and how she had done it. The guards by now almost fought for the honor of being trained by her, something that was unheard of before – training had always been a necessary, but unwanted, facet of guard life. Now, though, the guards were learning things they had never even known they were capable of, and it was a point of honor to them to see who could progress the furthest.

Allison had made it clear she did not require or expect deference or reward for teaching her abilities and skills to the guards, a selfless act that had astonished him when he learned of it, as had her response when asked why she would put forth such effort for no reward: "I get a lot of enjoyment and satisfaction from seeing others learn, grow, and push themselves to new heights." It was almost as if she felt rewarded by her 'students'' accomplishments, a thought that was reinforced now as he returned to the present and considered her training of the dogs.

"You gain almost as much enjoyment from training these dogs as you do our guard force, do you not?"

"In many ways, even more. Think about it. Dogs are not as intelligent as humans or elves, and have no ability to learn our language, other than Sadie there, thanks to Giltreas' spell." She smiled and shook her head as she remembered the permanent change the spell, cast as a joke, had made in the big dog.

"We take them from the only world they have ever known, their mother and their brothers and sisters, and at a very young age, sometimes just weeks old, expect them to learn dozens of new things from people who aren't even of their species. I am constantly astonished at what dogs are capable of. Even more, I am humbled by how completely and unconditionally they love us, and want nothing more than for us to love them in return. Once you figure that out, you realize how truly special dogs are. You will do anything to ensure you are worthy of that unconditional, selfless love."

The serious tone in her voice conveyed the strength of her convictions about her feelings for dogs, and he blinked as he realized he was impressed with what she was saying about dogs, as well.

Living as long as he had, he was used to introspection and self-assessment. And as he thought about it, he realized that maybe his opinion of humans needed some serious adjustment. Certainly in light of what he was learning about and from Allison, he thought that he needed to be more objective, and not let his past experience cloud his judgment. But he also knew himself, and realized that his automatic reactions were going to be more negative than humans deserved. He sighed internally, as he recognized the task ahead of him to be fairer with others around him in the future.

Allison seemed to sense the Seneschal's emotions somewhat, and looked at him out of the corner of her eye while she worked with Max. The prickly personality she had first seen when they came here seemed to be mellowing, and she was not sure what to make of it. Someone had answered her question as to how old the elven noble was, and it had taken her breath away to realize the elven man next to her was well over two thousand years old, and possibly much more. She supposed that someone that old might get a little set in their ways, she thought with obvious understatement, but he seemed to have the ability to change his opinions and attitudes as he was presented with new perspectives. It was refreshing to see a millennia-old elf be able to do something that she didn't often see even in senior humans from her own world, she thought to herself with an internal smile.

The Seneschal, for his own part, continued to work with Sadie while alongside Allison, learning what she could do and generally having a wonderful time interacting with the well-trained talking dog. Sadie even was able to provide verbal feedback, somewhat, when he didn't do a command right or moved a hand signal the wrong way that she didn't understand.

"Don't know that one. What?"

He took it in good humor, though.

"She is almost training me, isn't she?" He laughed.

"You know, I didn't think of it that way, but it certainly seems like it. When you take a new dog to obedience classes for the first time, if you have a good trainer, you quickly realize that the trainer isn't there to train your dog. He or she is there to teach you how to train your dog. I guess Sadie has really mastered everything I have tried to teach her, and now she is passing that on to you, as best she can," Allison said with a laugh.

He joined in the laughter. "I guess I am in good hands, then, eh, Sadie? How am I doing so far?"

"You do good. And you are much happier now than when we first met. I like you much more now. Especially when you give me treats. More treats, please? What do I have to do to get more?"

They both laughed. "Sadie, you are a shameless moocher, you know that?" Allison reached over to caress Sadie's head.

"That's good, right?" was the response.

CHAPTER 36

Just over an hour later, the FBI agent had been sitting on the beach in one of the chairs from the interview room, wondering what was going to happen next and how he was going to get back to Minnesota, when he heard a voice behind him that startled him into standing up and reaching for his gun.

The gun flew out of his grip and towards Daniel before floating in the air some feet behind him and up in midair.

"We need to come to an understanding, or I will simply leave you here. I'm not the bad guy. I am hoping you don't end up being one, or as much as I will regret needing to, I deal with you as I see fit."

"What do you mean, deal with me? What the hell is going on? How are you able to do all this?"

Daniel sighed. "Let me tell you what is really happening. A very long time ago -"

"I don't have time for fairy tales! Cut to the chase!"

Daniel cast another spell on himself then waved his hand at the annoying FBI agent. Before he could even blink, the senior agent of the entire Minneapolis office of the FBI found himself lifted up and thrown quite far out into the salty ocean water.

"Daniel! What are you doing? Don't hurt him! Bring him back here!" Daniel's mother yelled at him in surprise before she could stop herself, shocked at what her son was not only able to do, but willing to do. In her mind, she persisted in thinking of him as a teenager, and therefore a child, in spite of the very recent memory of her running up the beach of their deserted island in the form of a Bengal tiger, or what he had told her shortly thereafter. It was going to take some significant changes in her thinking before she would think anything else about her only son, and her only immediate family since his father, her husband, had walked out and divorced her when Daniel was only months old.

The agent surfaced, shocked at both being tossed so easily out into the ocean, and finding himself suddenly soaked to the skin in the very warm ocean water. Cursing, he started to swim back towards shore and the teenager that had so casually tossed him out here. But before a moment had gone on, he heard Daniel's mother yelling at the boy, and suddenly he was lifted out of the water again, and his arms and legs seemed to windmill as he was pulled quickly through the air and held above the beach again in midair.

Daniel looked at the middle-aged man he was keeping in the air by the telekinesis spell, wondering what it would take to get through to him. Then he spoke up again.

"Are you going to interrupt me again? If you do, I will take my mother and return back to the police station without you. I assume that you would rather do anything else other than spend the rest of your life on this island wondering if I am going to come back for you?"

The agent finally found his good sense, and just nodded yes, not trusting himself to speak again. Then he found himself being lowered to the sandy beach. He started to shake the water out of his suit, but Daniel spoke a word and waved his hand, and he suddenly found his suit and clothing completely dry. Another word from Daniel and a wave of his hand, and his skin and hair was dry as well. The shocks just keep coming, he said silently to himself inside. Then he nodded his thanks at Daniel, still not trusting himself with speech just yet.

"Good. Thousands of years ago, the humans of this plane and their Gods had a disagreement. The humans told the Gods to stop meddling in their lives and generally treating the mortal humans under their care like pets or pieces on a chess board. Two of the Gods, Anubis of the Egyptian tribes, and Anaradelle the Goddess of Family, Children, and Nature, demanded that the humans build a tower to meet in to discuss humanity's grievances. The Gods felt that if the humans were serious, they would show it by putting in the work to meet their demands. When the tower was built, the Gods and the humans met to discuss how the humans were being treated. After much debate and no agreement, the Gods decided that something needed to be done to show the humans how much they needed the Gods and that they should just submit to Their will, so they decided to leave the humans to their own devices."

Both Agent Nelson now and Daniel's mother Marie earlier were taken aback at the information that Daniel was presenting. The existence of multiple deities went against everything that they and everyone else they knew and had been taught since childhood. Marie was still trying to process everything Daniel told her earlier after their run about his training and abilities. Now, this new information was coming at her from her son, of all people. It was hard to believe it was happening, even as she lived the experience.

"The Gods then told the other intelligent races, the elves, dwarves, halflings, centaurs, minotaurs, among others, that the Gods were going to leave this plane to punish the humans. All the rest of the higher races left this plane, along with every magical creature and being. Then, just before the Gods left, they did two things. They changed every tribe's language so that no one could speak with each other, and then they put up a wall to prevent anyone from using magic on this entire plane. Are you with me so far?"

The FBI agent nodded cautiously, more to acknowledge what was being said, than in agreement, Daniel noted, but that was ok with him. Then he continued.

"The Gods were split into two groups on this. Some of the Gods, such as Odin and his family, felt that it was best to change the languages and put up the wall blocking magic to prevent the different tribes from going to war with each other. The thought was that if they couldn't communicate, they wouldn't be able to have disagreements, which would progress to people killing each other. And they also felt that blocking magic would remove the most powerful tools that people could use in war between the tribes, as a way to limit the damage they could do to each other. So, if anything had to be done, this was for the best. It would keep the peace. Odin also, according to my teacher, didn't agree with what Anubis was doing, but didn't oppose him and those that agreed with him, because he had no other ideas on what should be done."

This was much more than what Daniel had told his mother earlier, and she listened in rapt attention. The story Daniel was telling had such a ring of truth to it that it was almost an audible thing in the air.

"The other group of Gods wanted the humans punished. They felt that the humans deserved the isolation and being deprived of magic, the birthright of every higher race. But regardless of their lack of agreement on the why, the Gods were in agreement about what to do, if for very different reasons."

"Wait, are you talking about the Tower of Babel?" The agent blurted out as realization came to him before he could stop himself.

"Yes, that is what it is called in the Bible. In the ancient Akkadian language, it was called Babel tower as well. Ancient Akkadian is the original human language, by the way. It hasn't been spoken on this plane in several thousand years, since the last Akkadian was killed by a rival tribe. They were most likely targeted first because it was an Akkadian who started the entire rebellion that led to their loosing magic and having their languages changed.

"The Gods decided to have a few of their fellow Gods look in on the tribes of humanity four hundred years later, to see if they were ready to submit to the rule of the Gods once more. If the humans were contrite and more amenable to reason, they would take the wall down, and everything would be as it was before. The language issue would have to be fixed, but that would not be difficult for the Gods to undo. As a group, they fully expected the humans to be repentant and ready to serve the Gods again. Things didn't work out the way.

"What they found was that several of the original tribal structures had been wiped out entirely. War was prevalent. One tribe or another would decide to go to war with a neighbor, and they would fight to the death, the loser's side not just getting wiped out to the last man, woman and child, but also getting entirely erased from history. And as the Gods discovered in horror, the humans created their own false Gods and religions to worship those Gods. The population of this plane had dropped to less than half of what it had been before the Babel incident. Entire civilizations were gone. Very little that the Gods had known was untouched. And everyone and everything left was scarred by conflict.

"Based on what was happening, the Gods thought it was only a matter of time before the population died out. It was decided that the humans here would be left on their own forever. The Gods left, and didn't look back. But there was a problem."

Both the agent and Daniel's mother could only listen in complete silence as Daniel's narrative went on and on. A lot of they thought they knew about ancient human history was wrong, and the shock of how bad things were, and how far off course this world was from what it was supposed to be, was worse than anything they had ever known.

"This plane, which makes up what we like to believe to be the entire physical universe, is one of many that are joined together in a multiverse. There are an unknown number of multiverses that exist. Each multiverse is overseen by what some on other planes call a Greater God, the most powerful deity in that multiverse. This multiverse is the domain of a Greater God that calls himself Sekur, the God of the Wheel. This multiverse is here to teach balance. It is His role in this multiverse is to oversee everything here, in order to create an environment for the souls of mortals to learn and grow in.

"Souls did not come into being in this multiverse originally, but came here from a different multiverse. They 'ascended' to this multiverse from their previous ones. Here they will spend dozens of lives reincarnating in this multiverse, and each time they do, their souls will learn, grow, and evolve. Then when they have learned everything they can from this multiverse, they ascend to the next multiverse, and continue their journey there. This is called the Great Path of the Soul. No one knows where it begins or ends, although Sekur has said he thinks the Great Path is both timeless and endless.

"But back to that problem. When the wall preventing magic from being used was still up, souls couldn't leave this plane and go to the other planes of this multiverse, let alone ascend to the next multiverse and continue their immortal journey. But somehow, souls still ascend to this multiverse, and reincarnate through their lives as they learn and grow. The Land of the Dead for this plane is overwhelmed with souls ready to ascend, who are stuck here until the argument between the Gods and the Humans of this plane is resolved.

"Which brings this back around to me. The wall has come down. Magic has returned. Many of the souls that had been ready to ascend to the next multiverse have continued on to the next part of their journey on the Great Path of the Soul.

"And everyone on this plane now has access to be able to cast spells and perform magic again. And I mean real magic, like I can do, not those sleight of hand tricks that you see on stages and television shows. There are many levels of magical ability that occur naturally in races that can perform magic.

"I am special, because I am able to do so much more than almost everyone else. I apparently have the ability to tap directly into the magic energy of the entire plane to cast spells. There are a few others out there who have, for one reason or another, discovered their abilities on their own. Sekur tells me this ability is exceedingly rare. He trained me endlessly every night while I was asleep for a month of real time. I think the training was the equivalent of around fourteen years or so of dedicated training, six hours a day, five days a week.

"I have sworn to Sekur to only do good things that help people with my abilities, an oath he was more than happy to accept, as it serves His Purpose. But in the process of doing that, it may look from time to time like what I do is evil. I will be called upon to fight others, to stop people who are trying to hurt others. And some of them may die. I will regret that, but I will do it without pause if it serves The Greater Good.

"So you are telling me you will be judge, jury, and executioner in the service of some being I have never met? I don't like the sound of that. What if this... Sekur?" At Daniel's confirming nod, the agent continued, "What if this Sekur isn't what he seems to be? How do I know that he is good? Do I just take your word for it? That is a big leap of faith I am not willing to make right now. You're just a sixteen year old kid. That is not acceptable."

Daniel's mother nodded in somewhat agreement with the FBI agent. "I don't want you doing this. You're just a boy. You have a life ahead of you, and I don't want to see you throw it away on something like this. It is almost more like a fantasy or a good story than anything else. How do you know this is really happening?"

Daniel sighed visibly. Then he spoke once more, but obviously not to either his mother or the FBI agent. "How do I convey this to them, my Teacher?"

There was a rush of sound, and suddenly a man was standing there some few feet away.

"Would it be easier if I explained it in person?"

"Definitely, Teacher." Daniel bowed slightly to the newcomer, who walked up and hugged Daniel, a very fatherly gesture that wasn't lost on either of the other two adults on the beach. Then he straightened up and stepped back.

"I am Sekur. Daniel has been truthful to you about everything he has said. William Morris Nelson, Daniel is my student. He serves The Good. His motives, and his actions, will not be questioned by mortals. He will answer only to me."

Agent Nelson could only stare open-mouthed at the newcomer. The presence of the being was overwhelming, beating in on his senses and his mind like the implacable tide of the ocean. He found he could only look directly at the being for a brief time, before he had to look away. Even when the being was not in his sight at all, his entire being could sense exactly where he was in relation to Sekur. Then that presence was suddenly inside his mind, and voice he had been hearing out loud spoke to him silently.

"You are a good man. A bit arrogant, and willing to use your position to bull your way to a result, but that is understandable, and almost necessary, given your role amongst your fellow mortals. You must work hard to protect Daniel's back from the good ones who will not understand him when his eyes are forward towards evil. He is my sword, and he will accomplish what he needs to do, no matter the cost. You will explain this to those others you work for, and you will be my shield, to protect his ability to do what needs to be done in the service of his oath to me.

"He will do what he must in order to serve the greater good of all. He will pay a price to do so, but will not regret his actions as long as he is true to his oath. Those that he sends beyond the veil to the afterlife will have their chance to reincarnate and make amends in their next life, so all will not be lost for them, but it will still cost Daniel much to do so. He will need his mother most of all, to comfort him and help him bear that burden.

"Which makes your role the most important: you must protect his mother, for that is his one true weakness. I could take her to another plane to protect her, but he needs her here with him as his anchor and fortress of peace and calm. Should something happen to her, he is still very young, and that could threaten his fidelity to his oath, which would be bad for many people.

"The only evil that exists on this plane is in the hearts of mortals, not in some false belief in an evil deity, and Daniel will root out that evil and defend The Good with every ounce of strength and the fullest extent of every ability, magical or physical, that he has. And those abilities are vast."

"Will you protect his back, and protect his mother? Will you serve Daniel's oath to the Good for the souls of Mortals?"

By the time Sekur had finished speaking inside his mind, William had been nodding at certain things as Sekur made his points. He also noticed with a corner of his thoughts that Daniel's mother also appeared to be having her own conversation with the God Sekur. It was not hard to think of Sekur as a God, he realized. The being's presence was utterly overwhelming, but didn't threaten his sanity in any way. It simply made him want to look away, like a man who had lived his entire life in the dark suddenly seeing the sun.

"I will, Sekur." He spoke the words out loud without really having to think about it very much, as the sense of doing the right thing swept over him. Then he realized that Daniel's mother had also said the same thing out loud at the same time, which brought a brief smile to his face as he glanced at her as the imp of the absurd whispered in his ear, 'And by the power invested in me by me, I now pronounce you man and wife. Just kidding.' Or maybe it was Sekur. It certainly sounded like His voice from a few moments ago.

"Good," Sekur spoke out loud again. "As Daniel has said, here are others that also have these abilities. They must be assisted and supported as well, to help them serve the Good. You will recognize them when you see them, should the need arise. Most likely you will not be called upon to help them, but you never know." Then he disappeared in another rush of sound.

Daniel nodded as well. Then the three of them, and the table and chairs from the police station, disappeared from the pristine deserted island beach, and reappeared in the interview room where they had been some hours before.

* * *

"Our top story tonight is what some are calling a modern miracle, and what others are calling the hand of God at work. We should warn you that we are about to show some video footage shot earlier today that is quite graphic, and should not be seen by those that would be upset by it, as well as young children. We have blurred parts of the imagery, but it is not possible blur everything and still convey the story to you. So please have them exit the room, or change the channel for a few minutes.

"An organized search for a missing young college woman, Alana Monroe, took place at a state park to the west of Minneapolis, Minnesota. But what happened next was caught on video by the crews from two local television stations there to cover the event for their newscasts, and in some cases, was broadcast shortly after the events as stations all over the world cut into their regular programming to show the incredible footage. Here is the video footage of the events as they unfolded in the park reserve parking lot."

The scene cut away to show a teenage boy standing in a parking lot several feet in front of two police cars, before he raised his arms and a watery dome going up over him The video camera looked over the shoulder of the reporter who was recording a spoken segment. The camera operator cut away from the reporter in mid-sentence and zoomed in on the boy standing inside the dome, his features only partially obscured by the substance of the dome itself, but not enough to prevent someone from identifying him, however.

Which someone did. "Hey, Darius! Come look at this! Isn't that the kid that fixed your knee the other day?"

Darius Turraine came running into the living room to look at the huge flat screen TV on the expensive stand, and nodded to his brother Donald. "Yeah, that's him! He said his name was Daniel, right? Where is that?"

"They said it is up in Minnesota somewhere. Hey…" Donald Turraine's voice cut off as the events unfolded in front of their very eyes, and all four people in the room stared in awe as Alana Monroe's body parts flashed into existence. Then the body was whole as Daniel healed her. Darius's girlfriend let out a shriek as the dead girl woke up and looked up at Daniel.

"Oh sweet Jesus! Did we just see what I think we saw?" The hushed tone of voice came from Darius and Donald's mother, a devout Christian woman. "Did that girl really just rise from the dead?"

"Shhh!!!" Karen shushed her boyfriend's mother as the news anchor started speaking again.

"Shortly after that happened, the dome, or whatever it was, came down, and Alana was reunited with her previously grieving family, who were obviously overjoyed to have their missing family member back with them.

"But the young man who performed this feat, whom authorities are not identifying right now because he apparently is a minor, was taken into custody, as you can see here, and rushed away from the scene. Numerous requests for information as to what has happened to the teen boy have been ignored, and no information is available about who he is, or how he did what he did. We will get more information out to you as soon as we have it.

"But in the meantime, we have asked two people to come in and give their interpretation of what has happened in Minnesota today, if such a thing is possible. First, we have Cardinal Melvin Anderson, of the Catholic Arch Diocese of Denver. Thank you for joining us, Your Eminence."

"Thank you for having me, Robert." The voice of an experienced public speaker came from the formally dressed member of the clergy as the older man smiled gently and nodded once towards the speaker.

"You're welcome. And we also have Doctor Erik Gulden, department chair of Philosophy at the University of Colorado on the Denver Campus. Thank you for joining us, Doctor."

"It's a pleasure to be here, Robert."

"We'll start with you Your Eminence. What exactly have we seen here? What happened? What do we know?"

"Well, Robert, I want to state from the onset that I am not really sure what we have seen here. It appears to be a miraculous event. Ms. Monroe was missing for over a month, and presumed deceased, as was evident by the state of her physical form when it appeared inside that... dome, I guess it is being called. Her body was healed, and she was resurrected by that flash of bright red light we saw. From a secular standpoint, it appears to be an incredible, unexplainable event.

"But from the perspective of a religious point of view, it appears that God performed a miracle, first by bringing Ms. Monroe's body back from where it had been buried or hidden, healing her, then bringing her back to life." The Archbishop leaned back slightly, his eyes metaphorically glowing with the light of a believer seeing proof of his faith, and his face was transfixed with a look of near euphoria. "I think it is clear. God performed miracles in Minnesota today."

"I see. And Doctor Gulden? What is your opinion of this happening?"

"Well, it is difficult for me to form a firm opinion. First, I would like to say that if you watch the footage in slow motion, as I have had the opportunity to do in your news room, everything seems to be caused by the young man, whose gestures seemed to trigger each specific event. And before the body of Ms. Monroe appears, you can clearly see the young man do something that shakes the ground and makes some noise, apparently to gain everyone's attention before the main event, so to speak. He wanted everyone to be watching him when he did what he did. I don't have a positive reason why, but if I were to speculate, it would be because what he was about to do he wanted or needed to be observed.

"As the events unfolded, it becomes completely obvious that he is the one performing the acts you see, and achieving the results of those acts, not God. While I consider myself a devout Christian man, and religiously, no pun intended, go to church every Sunday, I don't see the hand of God working directly here." The archbishop started to interrupt, but Gulden held up his hand to forestall any interruption on the part of the high-ranking clergyman next to him, and continued on.

"I believe that God may have worked through this young man, giving him extraordinary abilities that enabled him to do what he did. At the point just before Ms. Monroe was brought back to life, you can see his lips moving. Since others reported that no sound was getting in or out of his 'dome', I conclude that he must have been praying to a higher power, in order to help him with what he did next. But I am convinced that God did not play the primary role in what happened. This young man did, with the assistance of the Higher Power that he believes in: his God."

The archbishop sat back, momentarily at a loss as to what to say, and Donald turned to Darius, his eyes still showing his shock at what he had seen. "Man, Darius! You have been touched by something amazing! We knew that somewhat before, but now… Man! I can't believe it! What are you going to do about it?"

"I am not sure. What happened to me was certainly a miracle, but only a minor one, compared to what Daniel did today for that girl. Did you see that?" He was silent for a moment, before speaking up again.

"I'm meeting with the team tomorrow morning. I think that since we saw what happened on TV, I can certainly tell them the truth about what happened, and see how they want to handle it. According to the doctor, there is absolutely nothing in my health that will prevent me from playing right away. I mean, I am in the best condition I have ever been in, including all the way back to when I first started playing football. I will talk to Coach tomorrow and see what he wants to do." The four of them turned back to the TV just in time to see an argument begin to boil between the philosopher and the clergyman.

"I don't believe that God could or would have taken a secondary role in such momentous events. He was the primary being in the situation today," the Archbishop was saying stubbornly, refuting Dr. Gulden's position. "The only real question I have is why these events are happening now. I have been on the phone with His Holiness in The Vatican, and he has said he has seen the footage. I agree with him that this is a miracle of the highest order. He stated that he will discuss it with a special Conclave of Cardinals, and they will pray about what has happened. I personally believe, however that His Holiness will issue a statement confirming the miracle that has occurred, and will have more to say about the event himself in a few days."

"Hey, Donald, you notice that the priest –" Darius started to say, when he was interrupted by his mother.

"Archbishop!"

He continued to speak after a look at his mother, "You notice that the Archbishop seems intent on taking the credit away from Daniel and giving it to God? I wonder why that is? It is obvious to anyone with eyes and more than a single brain cell that Daniel did everything himself. He most likely had help, but he did it. Just like when he healed me."

Donald nodded his head. "Yeah, I see that. I wonder why that is?"

Karen spoke up. "I wonder what will happen if a lot more of these things occur. Will the Catholic Church try to define them based on church doctrine and fit them into a larger agenda based on what they believe or want to happen, regardless of what others can see for themselves? It seems like the Archbishop has gotten instructions on how to portray this. What's going to happen if their agenda doesn't mesh with public perception?"

No one had an answer to that question as they watched the argument build slowly on the TV in front of them.

CHAPTER 37

David smiled to himself as he remembered the end and aftermath of the 'Honorable' Senator Del Monico's "interview". A thoroughly-terrified U.S. senator is not a pretty sight, but the pathetic little shit had had it coming after what he pulled.

Michelle had been, shall we say, less than sufficiently happy with the good Senator. In fact, she had to be restrained from beating the ever loving crap out of the worm of a man. As it was, two broken arms, two black eyes, a broken jaw, a partially torn ear, and a lot of bruises and bloody contusions had shown how she felt about being targeted for assassination, before Giltreas had pulled her off him. He had swept in behind her, his grip pinning her arms to her body as he nearly threw her to David, who had struggled to contain his screaming, cursing, flailing sister. Michelle had surrendered entirely to the violence, even turning on him for a few rounds before she had collapsed against him, the fury giving way to tears. Giltreas had healed the senator, and used a mend spell on his clothing to clean up the damage and the blood. He had also healed David; Michelle had been quite effective in conveying her opinion of The Honorable Senator Del Monico when her brother had stood between her and the elected idiot.

Now, as David sat in the Congresswoman's outer office, he wondered if they would have gotten away with the same snatch and grab as they had with the Senator. Arnold, the Congresswoman's head of her personal security detail, had been less than thrilled to return to the employ of his former boss, but had instead provided David and his team with everything he knew about the powerful senior politician and her dealings.

Arnold had been shocked to learn about what had happened to Michelle, having never been told about what Senator Del Monico had been put up to by Rose Smithson's manipulations and urgings. Apparently she had, wisely as it turns out, kept him out of the loop. If he had known what was really going on in Congresswoman Smithson's office, he would have been the first one to the FBI to blow her figuratively out of office and straight into prison. David found that he liked and admired Arnold. He was intensely honorable, and had served in the U.S. Navy SEALS with distinction, climbing to Master Chief in twenty-two years of military service, before retiring to civilian life.

Arnold had almost demanded to go to the FBI and light up the entire conspiracy, and only the fact that he was not actually on Earth when he made his demand had slowed him down. Some. He was not going to be held off forever, though. But David was able to get a promise from him not to alert Smithson to what was going on. Together they had concocted a story about David getting out of the office before his team had been in place to intercept him, which also had been constructed to cover the disappearance of the Senator from his office for about two hours. Arnold also agreed to not talk about the actions they took after the Senator was spirited out of his office, needing no urging to look the other way. He was disgusted by the acts committed by the elected official.

The Senator had been easier to deal with. Thoroughly terrified out of his mind by the discovery that A) he was no longer on Earth, B) Michelle was not only alive, but transformed and restored to her youth and beauty, and C) he was not really important in one bit in the grand scheme of the universe, he had agreed to do whatever David, Michelle, and Allison asked of him, including lie to the powerful Congresswoman from Ohio. He realized that the recorded confession of him ordering the attack on Michelle using assets of the federal government, knowing full well that she was to be killed, along with David and Allison, and eventually Steven and probably his wife, was the end of everything he had ever worked for, if they decided to use it against him. They had him completely under control, and he knew it.

Steven's wife had been aghast at what she discovered her husband had been swept up in. According to the guards who reported back to Delara, her voice could be heard alternating between very loudly berating her husband and crying uncontrollably. The small room that they had been assigned to in the main building of the Queen's residence had guards stationed outside of it around the clock, in a form of house arrest. Neither protested very much about it, given that there was no place for them to go.

Allison and Michelle had taken to having long conversations with Cora, on topics that ranged widely from what had happened to Michelle, to Allison's background in the military and her volunteering, to the magic skills and spells Allison was learning now.

David's thoughts returned to his present situation. In some ways, it was better than the way Smithson had used Senator Del Monico, but in others it was far, far worse. Smithson had only manipulated him with threats about his reelection, along with the usual liberal dose of verbal abuse employed by bullies the world over, and promises of political power to wield in the Senate as her allies promoted him to better committees, including the chairmanship of a committee yet to be decided. He had gone along with the Congresswoman, because it was easier than crossing her, and he was drawn to the promises like a lion to raw meat.

This new situation, though, would put the Senator in prison for the rest of his life if what he had done ever came to light. Del Monico was somewhat certain that he would not be executed, but that didn't make it any better.

David frowned as he thought about Giltreas. By his own statements, he had been the tool of Anubis, the Mid-God they had met in Delara's throne room, for nearly two hundred and sixty years. David didn't ask him what he had done for Anubis, but it had been fairly obvious, based on what had been said. Anubis had been using Giltreas as an assassin, forced to kill whomever Anubis was upset enough with to go after.

But now, he was suddenly liberated from the role that had been the purpose for most of his entire life. And while David was certain that Giltreas was overjoyed at no longer being forced to kill people, his life now had no direction, no responsibilities, nothing to focus his entire being on. In the days immediately after the monumental happenings in the Elven court, he had wandered around, not really engaged in what was happening around him.

David recognized much the same state of mind in Giltreas that he saw in combat veterans after discharge from the military. Their entire life was regimented, and there was always someone or something there to tell you what to do. You didn't have to think about what came next – the military provided that. Go where you are told, do what you are told, come back and tell someone how it went and what happened.

For returning veterans, there were some resources to help military personnel transition to civilian life. For Giltreas, there was nothing. The team was helping a lot, but none of them were trained to deal with this situation. They kept Giltreas from getting down, gave him things to learn, and challenged him to teach them magic skills and his own style of combat with the 'medieval' weapons that he carried and were used throughout every other plane he had been to except this one.

Giltreas gave every indication of a man without a cause or purpose. He even went to a nearby bar from time to time to have a drink and contemplate what was happening to his life. Usually one of the team went with him, to make sure he was ok. More often than not, it was Jill, a former Army sergeant who was more than a little jaded about life in general, but seemed to take to the former assassin.

Nate had decided to teach Giltreas about firearms, which David had wished he had been there for. But Nate was a qualified marksman and instructor, and Gil had been in good hands. Nate even commended Gil to the team on how quickly he had picked up the skills necessary to load, fire, unload, and clean pistols and rifles, not to mention his marksmanship skills. While not great the first few times, Gil was a fast learner, and his range scores had climbed quickly to an acceptable level, in Nate's estimation. He didn't seem to be able to get much better than above average, but that was ok with Nate and Giltreas both.

The phone on the secretary's desk rang, and he picked it up. After a brief conversation, he had stood and waved David over.

"The congresswoman will see you now, sir. Thank you for your patience."

Inside the woman's office, David was glad they decided not to attempt the snatch this time, mainly because there were three other men in the office, two in the uniform of the Capital Police, and one dressed like an FBI agent. David wondered if his cover had been blown, but then discarded that idea. Giltreas had assured him the illusion spell he had cast would hold for at least two days.

He stepped forward to the huge desk in the office where the woman he was there to see was sitting, and held out his hand.

"Thank you for taking the time to see me, Congresswoman. I hope I'm not interrupting anything important?" he said with a pleasant smile as he shook hands with the person in the world he most wanted to kill at the moment.

"Well, I'm a busy woman, so cut to the point." She stepped back and sat down in her chair, waving him into one of the chairs in front of her oaken monstrosity. Then she waved the three other men out of the office.

"These gentlemen just finished briefing me on a security concern." The law enforcement officers took the sign that this was not the man the Congresswoman had briefed them about, and left the office, closing the door behind them. Once outside, they compared the man they'd just saw to the pictures, and all three agreed it was not David Wilhelm, before heading off to wherever they were needed next.

The congresswoman retook her seat as David found his chair and sat down.

"My secretary told me you are a lobbyist with the Donovan firm? I don't believe I have heard of…"

She paused as she felt something, a tingle or a chill that swept up her arm and through her entire body for a brief moment, then shook her head as if to clear it.

"What were we talking about again?"

"We were talking about that company up in Minnesota you are trying to acquire; MDST Inc., I believe." David got it out calmly enough, given that his nerves were almost vibrating with the tension he was feeling inside. He kept his hands carefully in his lap under the view of the woman across the desk for fear that she would see them shaking. "Why are you trying to get control of it again? I am not quite clear on the reason for that."

Rose considered the person sitting across from her for a moment, then shrugged. "There's really not much to tell, actually. The owner of the company was a nasty bitch who was hoarding a new cryptographic technology that my contacts in the NSA say is a game-changer. We need to bring that technology into the control of the NSA so it can't be used against us. She refused repeated requests to get on board, so we needed to take more direct actions to protect our national interests."

"I see. What did those 'direct actions' include?" It was getting harder to talk about this calmly while simultaneously sitting on the urge to leap over the desk and choke the life out of the woman sitting across from him.

"Well, the plan was pretty simple, actually. Not sure what went wrong with it, but it happens. I'm just glad that we have enough cutouts to keep the trail from leading back to me and the head of the NSA. What we did was…"

* * *

"Borysko, thank you for coming." Kyrylo Yakimchuk waved his subordinate into his office and indicated that he preferred the door to be closed then offered his hand to the man that had made his job so much easier over the years.

"I live to serve, sir." Borysko Yevtukh smiled, shaking his boss's hand. This was the man that let him, and supported him, in the pursuit of his daughter in those moments and days after Svetlana was taken by those men. "What can I do for you today?"

Kyrylo Yakimchuk thought carefully before speaking. "There are reports that your daughter may have certain abilities that certain people in larger offices than this would be very interested to have in our employ." He held up his hand to forestall the outburst he expected, but Borysko simply waited, his guts churning. This was what he was afraid of happening.

"While I disagree with employing a minor in any capacity in our organization, or any other similar place, it is not my opinion that seems to matter here. Certain happenings recently in a nearby country have been whispered into certain ears of the people above us, and those ears are connected to… less than honorable brains, if you understand."

Borysko nodded. "Yes, I understand, my friend. You have children of your own, and I know this kind of thing is offensive to you. How much latitude do I have in this?"

Kyrylo was relieved that he didn't have to deal with an enraged father because of the distasteful thing he was ordered to do. "You have all the latitude in the world. She is a minor, and she is your daughter. In my mind, there is no way that you should be forced to do anything that might put your family at risk. But, if we know about it, you can expect that others with less than good intentions know about it as well. And they may attempt to get control of her and her abilities. It is for that reason that I have been ordered to approach you about this situation."

Borysko nodded. That made sense. While he would never refer to anyone, let alone his daughter, as nothing more than an asset, others would not hesitate to categorize and limit her to nothing more than a tool. And the criminal side of the line would certainly view her as a tool or worse, a weapon to be used until it was broken. When they had their use of her, they would dispose of her and move on. The problem with that was that his daughter was not really just a simple tool. He had seen what she can do, and he was certain that she would never submit. Not now. There was quite a bit different about her. She was confident, calm, and focused. And she was, to put it mildly, imbued with incredible power and abilities.

"I don't think that anyone who tries to force her to work with them would really like the result, regardless of how wrong would be to try that with a fifteen year old girl. Has anyone really taken a moment to think about what they know about her?"

"I don't think they really have done that. I mean, is it true? What they said she can do?" Kyrylo asked the question in an almost breathless fashion.

Borysko paused before answering. "You must understand something first, right? She is my daughter. I don't want any information about what she can do getting back to certain people. We don't want..."

Kyrylo sat back and nodded. "I will not discuss what you tell me with anyone else. But, perhaps it would be better if we didn't have this conversation. That way, if anyone asks, I can honestly say I don't know anything more than what they have told me."

Borysko nodded in relief. "I think that would be best, as well."

"In that case, I need to make sure you understand that no matter what else you or I might want, there are others that desire control of her. She needs to protect herself. And you should make sure she understands that they will try to get to her through her family."

"I understand."

* * *

Craig Sanderson had spent the last two months all but begging his defense attorney to come out to the prison and see him. It was only after he threatened to have family members start calling the media to tell them that he refused to see his client that the lawyer promised to show up when he had free time in his calendar. As it was, it took another eight days before the sergeant of the guard showed up at his cell and informed him he had a visitor.

The sergeant was, by this time, fully on his side, he believed. While the guard would not, in any way, help him so much as jay-walk, he was more than happy to do whatever he could legally, as were the rest of the guard force.

By now, every one of the guards, even the ones that hadn't been working when it happened, had seen the footage of the security cameras from that day. For the most part, Craig had begged the sergeant to keep it out of the news, and leave it locked inside the prison walls. It looked so far like it had stayed that way, too.

The warden had shown up at his cell the next day, with four guards armed with shotguns for an escort. He had stood outside the cell, and talked to Craig through the peep hole, trying to gauge the threat to the other prisoners and the guards, and had left not really satisfied with the answers. Craig had refrained from providing another demonstration of his new abilities, but did mention that there was virtually no way the prison could hold him inside anymore. However, when pressed on whether or not anyone else was in danger, Craig only promised to not be the instigator of trouble, and would as much show restraint as possible in defending himself. He tried, and was convinced he failed, to assured the warden that retaliation was not in his nature.

As the weeks had gone by, and there were no more incidents, the abject fear on the face of most of the guards had faded into something else, a wary sense of truce, which Craig went out of his way to promote. He had no more desire to hurt anyone than the guards themselves wanted to hurt him (for the most part).

His biggest supporter was, by far, the sergeant.

Now, as Craig waited in the interview room for his lawyer, he looked up at the video cameras, and nodded. By prior agreement, he knew the cameras would continue to record what happened when Harold Jameson, Esquire, came to talk to his client, something that generally was never agreed to by the prisoners of virtually every facility across the country.

The door opened, and the handsome man Craig remembered so well entered the room and made his way to the table, the same familiar briefcase in his left hand.

Harold didn't bother holding out his hand to the scumbag in front of him. He only made the trip after the senior partner in the firm told him he was going to go, or be demoted to petty crime and parking tickets. The firm took a dim view of actions that harmed the image of their business, and having the family of an inmate go to the news and tell them that one of their leading criminal defense attorneys refused to see a client in prison after losing the case so spectacularly could be an embarrassment, and the impact of which they didn't want to have to evaluate in the cold light of modern social media and the Internet.

Jameson knew the man was guilty the moment he had set eyes on the guy. There was no other way to explain the feeling he got when he looked at the man, and when the prosecutor had called him for a meeting, he had gone to see what was up.

The prosecutor told Harold over drinks that his client was guilty as sin. The evidence didn't really show it, but he just knew Craig was the one that did it, which brought a silent nod from Harold. He listened as the prosecutor outlined a plan that would put Craig in prison, possibly for life, and allow another of Harold's clients up on a domestic assault charge to plead out to a misdemeanor, and get out of jail with time served.

Harold had agreed to the plan, knowing that if word of it got out, he would be lucky if he only got disbarred. But it was worth it to put Sanderson behind bars. Besides, his other client had a family, and the man was the only source of income for his wife and three kids. They would be homeless if he didn't take the deal.

In retrospect, it wasn't his finest hour. Harold had went and all but threatened the man who thought it was acceptable in the twenty-first century to hit his wife when she got out of line, that if he heard of even one bruise on his wife that couldn't be explained, he knew people that would gladly cut the guy's hands and dick off, and leave him to his own devices. There was no way this was going to come back on him, and the moron had better fly right, or else. Harold had been glad that his visit some weeks later to the man's home had indicated the man was no longer drinking, was holding a job, and the wife had gone all that time without her beloved husband and the father of her children so much as yelling at her. Not that everything stayed that way after Harold stopped coming by. What a waste of space that one turned out to be.

Now he found his seat, and that same uncomfortable feeling inside, shuddered through him again. What was it about this loser that made him feel this way? There was no accounting for it. He sat there and looked at his former client, convinced that he would never represent the man again in court.

"I told you that you are no longer my client. I have nothing more to say to you. But since you got me here, go ahead and have your say." The tone of voice conveyed all the contempt and disgust he felt inside at the crime the man had committed.

Craig sat there for a while, not saying a thing. He just observed the man sitting across from him, waiting.

Harold snorted in disgust, then stood to go, turning towards the door. That was when he heard the voice behind him.

"I have been wondering, ever since everything blew up so completely, what happened and why I am in here. Can you answer that for me?" Craig was calm. He had found that he had no problems controlling his emotions now, not with the new abilities that he knew could get him free almost at will.

"I mean, I had an airtight alibi," he continued. "I had witnesses for my alibi. I had an open and shut case. Even the parents of that murdered boy told the court at my sentencing that they believed that I did not do it. And yet, somehow, you blew that all to hell. I don't remember you even trying to counter the lies the prosecutor told. And he told a lot of them. You didn't even object when the prosecutor moved to have the DNA test results tossed. He will have to answer for what he did, but he's not here right now. You are. So, are you going to answer me?"

Harold ignored Craig, instead walking to the door, and knocked on it sharply. "Guard! I am ready to leave. Guard!"

The sound seemed hollow, and a sinking feeling seemed to slowly build in his gut. He tried again. "Guard!" His briefcase banged into the door this time, making a louder booming sound, but still the door didn't open.

"What the fuck is going on here..." he mumbled to himself.

"I know what is going on here. You sold me out. What did you buy with your thirty pieces of silver, Judas?" The biting tone of his former client lashed at him, and he turned back in fury.

"You fucking loser! I don't know what lies you have been telling people, or yourself, but you are exactly where you are supposed to be. You raped and killed that kid. Everyone knew it. And since everyone knew it, the details didn't matter. All that mattered was justice. And justice is you, in this prison, for the rest of your miserable fucking life. I don't know how you convinced the parents of the victim that you were innocent, but it doesn't matter. I have nothing more to say to you. Goodbye, loser."

Craig didn't even blink at the revelation of how his attorney really felt about him. Time to ratchet things up a bit.

"I know I'm not guilty. I know I didn't kill that kid."

"Well, that makes exactly one person in the entire universe that knows that. Everyone else knows you did it."

"Not everyone. The parents of that boy knew I didn't do it. And, I had an alibi. Heck, anyone with more than two brain cells to rub together for warmth knows I didn't do it. Especially if they look at the evidence objectively. If you hadn't fucked up my case, and then refused to file any appeals for me, I would have never seen the inside of this, or any other, prison."

"You think anyone cares that I didn't file an appeal for you? Who fucking cares?!?" Harold exploded at last, moving forward, and nearly hit the seated prisoner in front of him. At the last minute, his hand slammed down into the table separating them.

"I care. I care about what happened to me. You, obviously, didn't care, and still don't. You had a different agenda. What was it?" A sudden flash of insight hit him, and he spoke before even thinking about it. "What kind of deal did you make to send me to prison? Something with the prosecutor?"

Harold flushed as the accusation hit home. "That's absurd! That doesn't happen! You're out of your mind!" It sounded weak to Harold's ears, though.

Craig knew he was on to something, though, and wasn't about to let it go.

"What kind of deal did the prosecutor make with you to send me away? It had to be something good enough to be worth it. Leniency on another client? That must be it. It couldn't be anything else. Who was it?" Craig suddenly knew he was on the right track as the blood drained completely from Harold's face, and his intensity ramped up as he leaned forward, the shackles holding him to the table clattering as his hands pounded into the table, with entirely different effect from the time that Harold did it.

Harold was at a loss for words. When confronted with the truth of what he had done, he froze up entirely. All he could do was open and close his mouth in a remarkably accurate imitation of a fish out of water, trying to think of anything at all to say that would stop this interrogation. He was suddenly and intensely terrified of the man handcuffed to the table in front of him. His mind chased itself around in circles, before he found what to say.

"Fuck you!" In retrospect, it sounded better in his head, but it seemed to convey the right message, so he said it again, drawing it out for more emphasis. "Fuuuuuck youuuuuu!"

"No, I don't think so. I have already gotten fucked over by you. I think you need to experience a taste of being powerless yourself." A strange smile came over Sanderson's face while Jameson watched, wondering what was going on in his former client's head.

"You know, I used to have a favorite movie a long time ago. Jurassic Park. You know why I loved it? Because of the velociraptors. They were amazing. Incredibly vicious, completely fearless, and entirely lethal killing machines. Probably the most perfect killing machine in history. You know what would make them perfect? If there was a human intellect behind them, and that human brain had absolutely nothing to lose!" He almost roared the last four words, and stood up completely.

Craig shrugged his shoulders, and the shackles fell away from his hands and feet as if they were suddenly much too large, then right before Harold's eyes, and to the astonished eyes of the guards, watching in the security room, Craig wasn't there anymore. But Harold wasn't alone in the room.

In a slight flash of light, Craig changed into a velociraptor, his favorite creature in his favorite movie.

Harold screamed like a little girl as his world suddenly turned into a nightmare of huge teeth and even bigger rage, while losing complete control of his bodily functions. As it was, it turned out to be very fortuitous indeed that he'd visited the restroom before entering the interview room in the prison. If he'd had anything in his bladder or bowels, those noxious compounds would have made its appearance at that time.

Craig hopped up on the table, then over, the massive form leaving indentations in the steel tabletop as he passed. He hoped he was allowing as much of his anger as possible show through the form he changed into, and from the look on the despicable lawyer's face, it looked like he was succeeding.

Harold's eyes bulged out, and he fell back into the wall behind him as the enraged horse-sized dinosaur swarmed over the heavy metal table, leaving deep indentations where his feet landed. He heard a high-pitched screaming noise that seemed to be in time with his breathing, but he had never heard the sound before, and couldn't figure out where it was coming from.

Then all rational thought left him as the angry predator swung its head at high speed into him, throwing him along the wall into the corner, where he crumpled to the floor in pain from the impact of the hard head and the harder steel wall. His vision spun and went grey for a moment, but when it cleared, there was a massive open mouth full of teeth right in front of him. Then the form seemed to hunch back slightly, as if bracing itself for something and he slammed his head back into the hard wall behind him and turned his head to try to get away from it.

That something wasn't long in coming. The velociraptor trumpeted its hunting cry at him at an impossible volume, the sound of an apex predator without equal in the modern world. It seemed to reach deep inside him and turn his guts to water, and he screamed again as the deafening sound hit him with all the concussive force of an explosion.

Nearby in the prison, inmates and guards alike jumped in fear as the impossible sound reached them. Some few seemed to subconsciously recognize that they had heard the sound before, having seen Jurassic Park all those years ago, but none really connected the two together to consciously recognize it. Virtually everyone that did hear that inhuman cry were terrified at the sound, shrinking back into a defensive slouch or putting their hands up in front of their faces.

The guards in the security office looking and listening to the camera feed from the room also jumped like they'd been shocked. Since Sanderson hadn't been very forthcoming with his plans, none had known ahead of time what was going to happen, but all had seen the footage from the 'shower incident' as it was being called. They thought that nothing would surprise them. How wrong they were.

The guards and the sergeant all watched screens in front of them, paralyzed, certain they were going to witness the lawyer they now knew had sent a most-likely innocent man to prison get killed, or even eaten alive, based on the conversation they'd just listened to even as it was being recorded.

"Geez, boss, do we want to pull the P.O.S. out of there before he eats him?" The question came out in a fearful yet humorous almost-whisper, but the sergeant just shook his head.

"I'm not going in there. He's... not in the best of moods right now." The understatement was greeted with some nervous chuckles and laugher from the guards. "Do you want to try to take him down like that? If so, where do you want your remains sent? And besides, didn't you tell me last week that the world has too many lawyers in it?" The sergeant shook his head again. "No way in hell. Just make sure you are recording this. We have to let it play out. I think I know how it's going to end, though."

The massively loud sound abruptly went away, and moments later, hands reached out and yanked Harold to his feet. He opened eyes he hadn't realized he'd shut tight while he'd been expecting to be eaten at any moment. Then a hand flashed up and slapped him, not too hard, but with enough force to get his attention.

"Do you want to tell me the truth, the whole truth, and nothing but the truth now, so help you God, counsellor?"

Harold's mouth opened, and he started babbling uncontrollably. Craig slapped him again.

"Knock it off! Slow down! Make sure I can understand you. Start over. Now, what the hell happened, and why am I here? Speak slowly and loudly. I want to remember this."

And Harold discovered the knowledge that one is to be hanged does, indeed, wonderfully focus the mind, and he allowed his former client to pull him over to the table and into a chair, where he unburdened his troubled soul to Craig, and, unknowingly, to the video cameras recording everything happening in the interview room.

When Harold had said everything he could think of that related to the case, and a whole bunch of other things that really didn't have anything even remotely to do with what he did to Sanderson, the guards all looked at one another in shock. This kind of thing only happened in the movies, or in books, right? Then, as one, they all looked at the sergeant, who gave a sigh. Why did this stuff have to happen when he was on shift? And what the hell did he do about it now?

"Hey, I have an idea." The words came from one of the younger guards.

"And...?" The word came out of the sergeant's mouth slowly, as if he was not going to like what he was about to hear.

The young woman shrugged. "Well, this needs to get out there. So, there's always a chance that our security server gets hacked again and this gets put up on YouTube. It's happened before, right?"

The incident had not been happy for anyone in the prison's I.T. staff, but no one had been fired for it, since the video had only been of a prisoner confessing their guilt for the crime he'd been convicted of to another prisoner. The victim had been overjoyed at the confession, but no one else in any official capacity was really happy about it.

Still, the external audit of the prison's network security that had been released last month had been less than pleasant, with the final report clearly indicating that there was virtually no way to keep anyone with the intelligence of a fourth-grader out of the system to prevent another leak. There was a state task force gearing up to address the issue, blah blah blah. He was certain that the problem would be fixed sometime a decade or more after he retired. Of course, then the current system would be weeks away from replacement, and they would start the whole thing over.

The sergeant looked at the young woman with a beatific look on her face, then turned away.

"I have no idea what you are talking about. Footage from our secure servers got leaked to YouTube? Again? That would be shocking. Shocking!"

She grinned, and her hands flew over the keyboard as her plan began to take shape.

CHAPTER 38

"…And now, the CBS Evening News with Richard Morse."

"Good evening, ladies and gentlemen. We begin tonight with three stories from the Internet; the video sharing website YouTube.com, specifically. For those of you who don't know, YouTube.com is a website where people can share videos of any kind. There are lots of different types of videos on the site: music videos, trailers for movies, self-help videos, how-to videos for everything from working out to fixing things like cars and computers, funny people and animal clips people have recorded; almost anything you can think of is on YouTube.com these days. Most of it is pretty harmless and, usually, entertaining.

"But sometimes, something is posted to YouTube.com that makes the news. There are three such videos that came out in the last twenty four hours. One is a video that certainly looks fake, but may not be, that is of a mythical creature: a unicorn. And it appears that the unicorn can talk. We will have more on that video in a minute.

"The second is a darker video that seems to be of a recording of a defense attorney meeting with his client in prison some three years after his client had been convicted, wrongly and with the collusion of his own attorney along with the prosecutor in the case, it seems. We will also return to that video later.

"But the most shocking video that has hit the Internet in the last twenty four hours is of a senior U.S. Congresswoman, Rose Smithson, a six-term member of the U.S. House of Representatives from the state of Ohio, talking candidly on camera about being involved in a horrific plot to murder a sister and brother, along with the brother's wife, in order for the National Security Agency, commonly referred to by its initials as the N.S.A., to take over the company, all because the company has a new cryptographic technology that the N.S.A. was unable to decrypt or otherwise compromise.

It is unknown whether or not the congresswoman knew she was being recorded.

"In the video, a man, who is off-camera, is asking questions of the congresswoman, who calmly answers the questions candidly, as if she were discussing the latest appropriations bill. Instead, what she is describing is a plot she apparently put in motion to use a black-ops team to murder the owners of the business, a privately-held company named MDST, Inc., which is based in Minneapolis, Minnesota, but also has a second location somewhere in the United Kingdom.

"The public is especially aware of the N.S.A. right now, after the recent revelations by a former N.S.A. contractor, who stole thousands of classified documents before fleeing the country. The documents were eventually given to two British journalists, who met with the NSA contractor in Hong Kong, after which he fled to Russia, where he is currently staying, with the blessings of the Russian Government.

"The congresswoman's office tried to get YouTube.com to take down the video, claiming the congresswoman's words have been taken out of context, but so far, YouTube.com has resisted. An emergency injunction was filed in federal court to compel the website to take down the video, but by now, several websites around the world have received copies of the video, and are hosting it themselves for anyone to view should they wish, so it is unclear what impact would be made by getting the video off of YouTube.com at this time.

"We are joined now by our legal analyst, Ellen DeMarais. Ellen, thank you for joining us."

"Thank you for having me, Richard."

"First of all, have you viewed the video in its entirety? What is your opinion of its legitimacy?"

"Yes, I have viewed it. And I have to say, things are not looking good for the congresswoman. She is clearly not being coerced in any obvious or visible way. The actual video is a composite of three different video sources running simultaneously, with the main video, as you can see here, thank you for bringing that up for me, forming the majority of the screen, with the two insets placed in the upper two corners. The other two video clips were uploaded full size to YouTube.com as well, and the comments for the main video provide links to them for anyone to view separately as well."

"What do we know about the man in the video?"

"Actually, we don't know anything about him at all. None of the camera angles ever reveal his face, and he is not wearing anything that is identifiable. His voice is non-descript, although I understand the FBI is running a voice analysis of the recording to attempt to discover his identity. They really want to talk to him right now."

"Is there anything you can tell me about where the video was shot?"

Morse asked innocently, as if they hadn't discussed the question ahead of time off-air.

"Yes, from what people are saying, that is actually Congresswoman Smithson's office in the capital building."

"So you were saying that the video looks to be legitimate?"

"Yes, it certainly does look that way. When Smithson is talking, you can clearly see, in full High Definition video from the main camera the man must be holding, the congresswoman's lips moving in synchronization with what is being said. And what she is saying is that she ordered a U.S. Government black-ops team to kidnap and kill three private citizens, and possibly two more if necessary, in order for the Government, and specifically the NSA, to gain control of encryption technology that the NSA was unable to break."

"Is there any possibility that the video was faked somehow? That it was cobbled together from several others to manipulate what Smithson was saying?"

"Our own analysts have studied the video since it was posted, and have concluded that if it was cobbled together, it was an incredible job. This level of sophistication would be almost impossible to accomplish by anyone without millions of dollars-worth of editing and rendering equipment. The camera the man is obviously holding, since you do not see it in the other two video streams, is never visible, but it is moving in a seemingly random pattern as the man moves in the chair, causing the congresswoman's image to move around the field of view so that she is not at any predictable point in the clip. That was actually quite brilliant, I must say. It makes aligning two different clips for the purpose of using an editor to string them together seamlessly all but impossible, adding further proof that the video is genuine."

"Where does this case go from here?"

"Well, that is a good question. You can hear in the video that the sister, Michelle Wilhelm, was supposedly murdered, and the team that killed her was waiting to do the same to Michelle's brother, David Wilhelm. That was the last that Congresswoman Smithson heard from the Black Ops team sent to commit these crimes, and no one has seen Michelle Wilhelm since. Allison Wilhelm, David's wife, is also missing, and hasn't been seen since the attack on Michelle several weeks ago. David has been working at MDST, Inc., but has refused all requests for interviews.

"At this point, the Justice Department has announced its intentions to investigate the congresswoman, MDST, Inc., Michelle Wilhelm, David Wilhelm, and Allison Wilhelm, and the possible connection to the National Security Agency. That could take weeks or months at this point. Additionally, the FBI has stated publicly that it will look into the matter, including the disappearance of Michelle Wilhelm and Allison Wilhelm, the use of a black-ops team to commit murder at the orders of a U.S. Congresswoman and the NSA, and the NSA's involvement in all of this."

* * *

"We turn now to the second video posted in the last twenty four hours. This one is about a man in prison for life without parole for the sexual assault and murder of a young boy, nearly four years ago. The man in prison is known as Craig Allan Sanderson, and he is now twenty-eight years old. His lawyer is captured in the video admitting that he made a deal with the prosecutor to let Mr. Sanderson be convicted in exchange for a plea deal for one of his other clients, who was later convicted of armed robbery in a crime that occurred after his plea deal, supposedly to support his drug habit.

"Ellen, what can you tell us about this case?"

"Well, Richard, on the surface, it certainly looks like Mr. Sanderson is guilty. There was an eyewitness for the prosecution, the police had some physical evidence linking Mr. Sanderson to the murder, and it appeared that in every respect, the case was airtight."

"But that wasn't the case, was it?" Richard asked in the effort to direct the conversation.

"Certainly not. It appears that the defense attorney, Harold Jameson, did not cross-examine the eyewitness, never contested the evidence, and generally did nothing to defend his client. We are not sure what caused Jameson to confess, but as everyone saw in the video, he was shaking badly, and sweating. A quick call to his office elicited the expected 'No comment' from the office. We are attempting to get more information for the viewers, including an interview with Craig Sanderson.

"When we called the prison, the person who answered the switchboard said they would pass on the request to the warden. Our producer asked some further questions about the situation, but something in the person's tone of voice seemed guarded or maybe evasive, as if there were more to the story. Not sure what is happening at this point. We did find out from the court jurisdiction that heard the original case that no appeal has ever been filed on Mr. Sanderson's behalf, something we found unusual in a murder case where the defendant was sentenced to life without parole.

"The difficult thing about this situation is that it has just come to light in the last few hours, and on a Thursday evening. We only learned about the case sometime around 2 pm today, and started making calls within about fifteen minutes. We don't expect to hear anything back before Monday at the earliest, but we are sending a team out to the prison to try to get an interview as soon as possible with Sanderson, to see what else there is about the story."

Richard held up a hand for a moment, with his other hand to his earpiece, listening to what is being whispered in his ear, as Ellen watched.

Then he spoke up.

"We understand another video of the incident with Craig Sanderson and his lawyer has surfaced on the Internet, and our producers are asking that we play the clip. I don't know what is on it, but the producer is saying that it is quite incredible. Ellen, watch that monitor there, as we cut away to the video. I am now being told that it is security camera footage of the entire incident from inside the prison where Sanderson is being incarcerated. Watch."

The feed cut away to Sanderson waiting in the interview room, with his hands and feet shackled. His lawyer is led into the room, and a conversation ensues, before the lawyer turns away, and tries to get out of the room. Sanderson never seems to be angry or upset, but the lawyer definitely seems to be getting angrier by the moment. Then the audio feed came up, and everyone could hear the lawyer say he knew his client was guilty, and that he deserved to be in prison.

Sanderson didn't lose his temper, but continued to talk to Jameson, until Jameson turned back and almost struck the shackled inmate, instead directing his hand down on the table in a resounding thud, which didn't startle Sanderson where he sat. Instead Sanderson continued to talk to the lawyer, and as the question was asked what Jameson got out of the deal, gasps were heard from the news room as the lawyer didn't try to refute the allegations. Instead, he seemed almost tongue-tied, and unable to respond. The conversation continued until Sanderson suddenly bellowed out "...absolutely nothing to lose!"

The veteran news anchor and the experienced lawyer both cried out in surprise as Sanderson stood up, and abruptly, in a flash of light, changed into the lethal form of a velociraptor from the movies. Shock held them frozen in place as the huge predator clamored up onto the table, leaving it dented and damaged from the weight of the beast. Harold Jameson screamed in absolute terror as he backed away from the enraged creature, stumbling back into the wall, only to be followed as the beast hopped down from the table and pursued him.

With a bellow, the beast swung its head and bashed the lawyer from the side, throwing him across the wall and into the corner, where he fell in a heap. He looked up just in time to see the velociraptor stop in front of him. Then the lethal prehistoric predator drew back and trumpeted its cry directly in his face, the sound so loud that the microphone on the security camera distorted badly as it was overloaded. When the sound came back, Jameson could still be heard screaming, but the velociraptor disappeared and Sanderson reappeared, back in human form and in his prison jumpsuit. He reached down and pulled the lawyer to his feet, and when Jameson started to babble incoherently, Sanderson slapped him somewhat lightly, which caused him to stop. Sanderson then pulled him over to a chair at the damaged table, sat him in it, and start to speak again. The video they had seen earlier of the confession of the lawyer overlapped at this point, and the producer cut away, and back to the newsroom, where a completely stunned news anchor tried to get his mental footing back while Ellen tried to do the same.

"Wow. Wow! What did we just see? Did that really happen? How did he do that?!?" Ellen spoke up first, no longer sitting back in her chair comfortably, but leaning forward with her hands on the desk surface in front of her, her eyes intent as she stared at the video monitor in shock.

"I don't have any answers for you, Ellen. We will have to see if we can speak with Mr. Sanderson. Certainly, it appears that, if that was a real video, and not a special effects prank on the grandest scale that even Hollywood would envy, Sanderson is not someone to be taken lightly." Williams paused, listening to his earpiece, then spoke up again.

"I am being told that Harold Jameson, the lawyer in the video, was allowed by Sanderson to leave the interview room unharmed," Richard told Ellen and the viewers.

"Really? If I had been found guilty of murder, sentenced to life in prison without parole, and I knew that, as my lawyer, Jameson had colluded with the prosecutor to put me behind bars for something I knew I didn't do, I might not be so charitably inclined towards Mr. Jameson. Interesting." Ellen looked thoughtful as she considered the unreal video they had just shown to the national audience, and possibly the world.

Richard turned to the camera and spoke up once more. "I am being told we need to take a break. We will be right back after this."

He turned to Ellen and they started speaking as the feed dropped, and commercials started to run.

* * *

"Welcome back. The final viral video we are going to show you is a much more light-hearted item. It appears that a mythical creature has made an appearance at a horse ranch somewhere. We say somewhere because we are not sure where this video was filmed. We also have no idea who might have filmed it. According to YouTube.com, the video was uploaded to the site by someone using the anonymizing network, TOR.

"As you may recall, TOR is used by dissidents in foreign countries that are run by oppressive regimes to have secure communications with other dissidents and the outside world. TOR is also used by people who wish to remain anonymous while on the Internet to avoid prosecution. However, in this case, it appears that the people who filmed this clip wish to stay anonymous not for protection from the law, or from an oppressive government, but from the publicity that the video might get them.

"Here is the video for you to see for yourself."

The screen cut away to the footage a unicorn, huge, muscular, with a horn high on its forehead between its eyes, and so pure white it seemed to almost glow from within in the bright morning sun, looking at whoever was holding the video camera, and the viewers could clearly see the unicorn's lips move as it spoke.

The clip was just a few minutes long, and ended as the unicorn turned away from the camera and proclaimed, "…appreciate my company and the refinements of life and love I have to offer."

Once again, Richard Morrison returned to the screen, and spoke up, this time with a smile on his face. "I have seen that video several times, and it makes me laugh each time. If it is a fake, it is an incredible job. Joining us now is the actor and digital special effects specialist Jared Crane, who has appeared on the TV show One Too Many back in 2006, as well as several other notable rolls since. Before that, he also worked for Industrial Light and Magic, the special effects production company that was created to work on the Star Wars movies. Jared, thank you very much for taking the time to join us. Have you seen the video, and if so, what do you think of it? Is it fake?"

"Thank you very much for having me, Richard," Jared replied. "I have seen it several times, the last time on a big high-definition screen and going through it frame by frame. While there are some incredible special effects artists out there, if this is a fake, I can't see it. It is too perfect of an imperfect job."

"What do you mean by 'too perfect of an imperfect job?'" Richard asked.

"Well, in every special effects scene, or CGI, there is a tendency by the person creating it to make it perfect. They do that because it is easier than introducing flaws. A texture might be perfectly smooth, or to have every hair in place and going the same way, for example. But in the real world, textures are not perfectly colored and evenly smooth from one end to the other. People tend to notice this and differentiate computer generated images from the real thing subconsciously, specifically because the real world doesn't look that way. If it is too perfect, it will stand out as not quite right in the mind of the viewer, and the illusion will fail to be believable on an instinctive level. Good production houses will go back and carefully induce well-thought-out flaws in the CGI to make it more believable."

"And you don't see that in this clip?"

"I don't. I am a CGI artist…"

"We should remember that Jared worked on the movie Perfect Storm," Richard Morrison cut in, turning to the camera, before turning back to Jared once more.

"Thank you. I am a CGI artist, and I like to think a pretty good one. I know what to look for, and everything I am looking for, how the hairs on the horse, excuse me, the unicorn, lay, the different gradient textures of skin around the mouth, how the eyes are, you can see that one of them is ever so slightly larger than the other; all these things look to realistic to have come from a CGI artist's rendering.

"While it is possible to have taken a horse, and scanned images of it sufficiently into a rendering engine to use as a basis for this scene, I don't think that happened. Doing that would have left indications in how the unicorn moved to show that it isn't real. It is too good of a rendering to be faked with our current level of technology.

"I think that, as impossible as it may seem, this might be real." Crane shook his head, as if not believing what he was saying. "Of course, now we have the task of figuring out where this happened, going there, and seeing if the unicorn is still there. If he is, maybe we can ask him if he is real or not."

Derrick and Miranda and Katie Hanson all laughed at that from their couch in front of the TV in their living room, as Llellondryn stood behind them watching over their shoulders from behind the couch.

"I think I look real. Do you think I look real?" The huge unicorn preened as he watched the clip of himself and the ensuing debate with pleasure.

"You are real to me, Llellondryn," Derrick spoke up, looking back at the magical being standing behind them. He never thought he would ever allow a horse in the house with them, but then again, Llellondryn was not really a horse, no matter how much he looked like one. And he sure didn't act like one, Derrick thought to himself.

Derrick, Miranda, and Katie had all learned that Llellondryn was easily as intelligent as any of them, and probably much more so. The first time he saw himself on TV during playback of the footage of the camcorder, he had nearly fallen over in surprise, only to mentally bounce back moments later and say, "Was this magical device created specifically to show off my incredibly perfect beauty, grace, and charm?" The statement could have been made in jest, but it was clear Llellondryn was mostly serious, thus cluing them in that, whatever else he was, he was also incredibly vain.

After many lengthy discussions on a huge range of topics, from trucks, to television, the Internet, government, equine birth control, and human girl child rearing, Llellondryn sudden begged Miranda to put the video of him up on YouTube. He craved the attention, he freely admitted. But, not wanting the chaos that Derrick and Miranda Hanson explained would have come with revealing where he was, he agreed that editing the video and hiding the source of the upload was an eminently good idea. It was enough for him to see that it was online, and he was stunned to see it 'go viral' and climb to over four million views in the first day. Now it was up on the national news, and he was over the moon to see his video on TV along with a national news anchor talking about it.

"Well, I would hope so. I mean, I am standing in your magnificent house, after all. Hey, Katie! What do you get when you cross a chicken with a donkey?"

Katie and Llellondryn had become very close friends in the few weeks since the Unicorn had taken up residence in their lives. Both parents had watched in alarm the first time Katie paraded past on the huge white creature's back while he tore past at a dead run, but he had explained, then demonstrated to Miranda, that no one he wanted on his back ever fell off. "It is all a part of the magic that is I!" He had said with his usual panache and flair that came out when he was talking about himself.

The two had become inseparable since that moment, and Llellondryn had surreptitiously moved into the young girl's room, becoming a bulwark against nightmares and a welcomed co-conspirator in getting the exuberant young girl into bed and asleep at night.

"If you don't sleep, sweet Katie, I can't stay here! It would never do to have the other unicorns know that I am the cause of you being tired all the time!" He said that first night, standing at the end of her bed on the hardwood floor, somehow looking aghast and upset.

Derrick had checked the floor for damage as the huge animal moved through the house on the flooring, but none had ever been found. When he asked Llellondryn about it, the unicorn shrugged. "I don't leave tracks unless I really want to. No unicorn does. We are magical beings, and there are those creatures that hunt us, much to their eternal folly. We are not without the means to defend ourselves, magical and otherwise. But they still try sometimes. Your floors are safe, good Derrick. And I will not soil your house. That would be, well, quite rude, don't you think?"

"I dunno, Yondryn, what?" Derrick's thoughts returned to the present as Katie asked her question. Katie loved his jokes. Most were hilarious and ridiculous, and she laughed at every one of them, even the ones she didn't understand. Derrick and Miranda usually laughed as well.

"A Pegasus!"

Derrick and Miranda roared as Katie asked, "What's a Pegasus?"

CHAPTER 39

Allison had finished her morning workout and was walking back to the suite she shared with Michelle as she contemplated how much her life had changed, without any changes happening directly to her. In her mind she was still trying (and, for the most part, failing) to come to grips with the concept that Michelle was now a Goddess. She seemed to be the same person, but she didn't eat anymore, unless something seemed interesting to her, and she didn't seem to sleep, either. Then there were the times she seemed to glow, as if she was made of light or something. It was hard to explain, and even harder to understand. Or accept. Unless Michelle really was a Goddess. Which neatly and perfectly explained everything. And also, absolutely nothing.

Still, Michelle still talked with Allison and Delara every day, and always made time to take care of the three dogs that were ensconced with them in their exile. The Elven queen seemed to be fascinated by Michelle, who still had no idea what she was going to do with herself, especially now that she was immortal. At least, Allison assumed her sister-in-law was immortal. There were very few answers to be had about the situation. She had no idea what was going on anymore, she lamented to herself inside. Not one to be given to long fits of depressed introspection, she didn't dwell on it very long, but once in a while, she did rail against the unfairness of how Michelle's life had been turned upside down, tearing her away from everything she'd ever known.

Allison was also getting frustrated. She had been promised that hers and David's infertility issues were resolved, but David was never able to spend more than a few nights here in the Palace with her so they could attempt to begin their family. The times they spent together were sweet and wonderful, but too few and far in between. They tried to time things right, but that had never been that emotionally comfortable for a couple used to a spontaneous and impulsive physical intimacy.

Allison frowned as she contemplated the enormous strain David seemed to be under. David had brought the video recordings of his 'interview' with Congresswoman Rose Smithson. This time there had been two camcorders on two separate people, both of whom had been hit with both an invisibility spell and a silence spell courtesy of Giltreas, as well as David's cell phone to record the event. The spell had allowed them to follow David into the room without being seen or heard.

Giltreas had also followed him into the room, also covered by a silence spell and an invisibility spell. He had briefly reappeared behind the congresswoman when he had cast the compel truth spell and the other spell he hadn't identified that had lowered her inhibitions while making her not remember the time he was in her office. He had remarked to Giltreas that it seemed to have the same effect as being very drunk, which caused Giltreas to blink, and then nod his head in agreement.

David had brought several company iPads with the video loaded on it, and handed them out to anyone that wanted to see them. Delara had watched it while shaking her head in both anger and sadness at how the humans of Michelle and Allison's plane used people for their own selfish ends. The Seneschal had watched one, and when he was finished, he had looked up at Allison, an unreadable expression on his face. Allison had to explain a lot of the terms used in the video, but he caught the message behind the words themselves. Later, when they had spoken in a more private setting, he told her he found it difficult to reconcile the two different types of humans from her plane. David, Michelle and Allison all seemed to be good people. But Rose Smithson was definitely not a good person. He said one could almost see the taint of evil in her, and certainly sense it in her words. Allison had been hard pressed to explain why someone like Smithson was in a position of power.

The telling point had been when the Seneschal had spoken up. "I don't understand why someone so tainted by evil is not revealed by the simple casting of a spell to detect and reveal evil. Oh my goodness. I so easily forget that your plane has been kept from magic." He had shaken his head then.

"Your people have had to struggle for thousands of years without the simple benefits of magic that we all take for granted." He seemed to stare off into the distance, the sign of someone deep in contemplative thought. Then he sighed once more. "I don't know how I would stand for it. It is not meant to be this way."

She had agreed with him, but neither one knew what to do about it.

Later that morning, she stood in one side of the Elven Throne room, waiting for Giltreas to begin.

David stood there as well, standing behind his wife with his arms around Allison as he held on to them for support. Michelle had joined them as well, dressed in a simple robe and sandals that she had been wearing since she came to Delara's house. Allison thought the items had been provided by Delara herself, but she wasn't sure.

Giltreas had come to David yesterday and said he wished to travel back to see his mother once again, and report on what he had learned about the humans here on David, Michelle, and Allison's home plane. David had jumped at the chance to visit his wife again, and to see Michelle once more. It was a Sunday back home, so he didn't need to be anywhere in particular. The team was at a dead end as far as what to do next, now that they knew who was really behind the attack on Michelle.

After Congresswoman Smithson had revealed her secrets, Michelle had remembered that she had met with two "gentlemen" from the NSA in her office downtown, some eight months before the attack in the woods outside her cottage. They had been there asking about the encryption technology that Michelle's data security team was using on the link between the two data centers in Minneapolis and in London, the site of a smaller company MDST had bought out, mainly just to have a presence in the United Kingdom. The company could afford private links between the two continents, but apparently the NSA must have tapped into the circuits somewhere in between in its holy mission to know everything going on in the world. And it was in one of those taps that the NSA discovered a data stream using a cryptographic technology they had never encountered before.

Michelle had found Mark when he left another company, looking for greener pastures. A brilliant mathematician and budding cryptologist, he had quickly found that he loved the free-flowing, low-pressure work environment at MDST. He approached Michelle about encrypting the intercontinental links shortly before they went live, on the theory that you didn't know who was listening to your traffic, even on private links that no one else was supposed to have access to.

A supposedly private link still had to go through several, if not dozens, of network devices operated by the various telephone/Internet service providers that provided the service. And while it was generally expected that your private data would stay private, there were a couple situations where it did not. Michelle had thought of at least two, at the time: hackers, and official court orders.

Court orders could get complicated when you were dealing with local and national courts in two different jurisdictions. And hackers hell-bent on causing problems and stealing data were simply a wildcard that could not be completely and accurately planned for; one had to just put in the best security processes and procedures, and hope you caught everything in the periodic audits you had conducted.

The NSA had found that a small company in Minnesota was doing something they couldn't compromise. Mark had come up with an encryption technology that no one else had ever discovered, and even with the massive computing power the NSA had on tap, they couldn't make heads or tails of what Mark had created. So they had sent lawyers, to try to bully Michelle into giving them access to the source code, to ensure that no laws were being broken.

Michelle had turned them down flat. First, because she was not selling the encryption technology, and had absolutely zero interest in doing so (knowing the political environment of the time and the fallout that would result), and second, because the U.K. was not on the list of countries to which the Department of Commerce restricted the export strong encryption technologies. She had always considered the second reason to be ridiculous, at best. The US was not the only country creating encryption technologies, and anyone could buy or even get for free sufficiently secure encryption software that would at least slow down most hackers. The stuff coming out of Israel was some of the very best, and available almost everywhere. But the NSA was not most hackers. The NSA contractor had shown the world that.

The attack on Michelle had happened mere months after the NSA contractor had leaked his stolen trove of classified NSA documents to the two U.K. journalists. The NSA had become increasingly frantic to find some way to compromise or co-opt every existing encryption technology ensure the protection of the USA against another terrorist attack. In the rampant culture of extremism that was the norm at the NSA, either you complied with the NSA's not so politely-worded requests (demands, really), which put you squarely in the friends category, or you weren't, in which case you were nothing more than a terrorist yourself, hell-bent on destroying America and everything she stood for.

With that kind of mindset infecting everything you did on a daily basis, it was easy to see the how the line led from Michelle refusing to cooperate with NSA lawyers on a piece of software that, while groundbreaking, was not available to anyone but MDST, Inc., and therefore not threat to Democracy and the Land of the Free and the Home of the Free, to having a black-ops team drag you kicking and screaming out of your cottage in the north woods to be raped and killed, along with the rest of your family as soon as they get around to them.

Delara had been positively ill upon hearing what was going on in Michelle's world. Anaradelle had likewise been horrified when she showed up unexpectedly to watch one of the copies of the video for herself. The Goddess of Children, Fertility, and Nature had embraced her newest sister, overcome with emotion at the first ascendancy in thousands of years.

Delara had looked up at that moment at David, only to see something almost as bad: the look on David's face promised death and worse to his enemies, she realized. And she also realized he had the abilities, and companions (especially in her son, Giltreas), to wreak havoc on those enemies, to the fullest of measures. That did not even consider the heretofore unknown abilities of the recently-ascended Deus in his sister. She had shuddered at that moment, fervently happy that the brother to the newest Goddess in the pantheon was not targeting her. Even without magic, she knew that what an intelligent being absolutely committed to an end could accomplish was nearly limitless. With a Goddess on his side, who was the original target of such evil thoughts and acts, there was no telling what manner of destruction awaited his, and Michelle's, enemies.

Elves for the most part, she explained to David, Michelle, and Allison later, did not take sides in the fighting between the human tribes. Humans were always considered less-sophisticated than the dwarves, elves, and halflings that made up the Four Races. They were more likely to resort to violence, were given to the enthusiastic pursuits of the intimacy of the flesh, and their tribes and clans rarely formed alliances with others, human and non-human alike. Most mages, who made up the intellectual corps of the various races, agreed that it was because the humans were so short-lived, and therefore not blessed with the opportunity to mature sufficiently beyond their almost animalistic instincts and tendencies.

The Gods had ordained that Elves were the caretakers of the other races, and the Elven Throne was the focal point of that role. Elves lived a very long time compared to humans. Most elves made it well past their two thousandth year, and generally, elves over three thousand years old were not all that uncommon. Dwarves and halflings lived somewhere around twelve hundred to fifteen hundred years. The Elven Throne was called upon to mediate disputes, to end bloodshed, and to keep the peace between humans, elves, dwarves, and halflings, as well as to help defend them against the Dark Races of the goblins, orcs and the like. And if the intervention of the Elven Throne was not sufficient, the occupant of the Throne would call upon the Gods and Goddesses of the Pantheon to intervene. That threat alone was sufficient to force everyone to bargain in good faith in order to resolve their differences.

"But as you know, humans are limited to barely over two hundred summers, although some few last until they are two hundred and fifty, or even three hundred from time to time," Delara had told them, expecting a nod or word of understanding, instead of the bald-faced shock that greeted her.

When Allison had explained that the lifespan of humans where they came from was almost always quite a bit less than a hundred years, it was Delara's turn to be shocked, to the point of speechlessness.

Now, David's thoughts returned to the present as Giltreas stepped forward. The Hall of the Throne, as David had learned the room was called, had been filled with mages of the various races, all present to hear about the denizens of the Plane of the Godless, that place of both horror and mystery they only knew about from stories passed down by word of mouth, most of which, they were sure, had grown much worse in the telling.

"Your Majesty. You have set me upon the task to discover the plane of these humans, and report back to you on what I learn and find. I am prepared to do so.

"The humans there are both amazing and terrible, sometimes at the same time. They are capable of amazing feats of selfless courage and compassion, and yet some are capable of horrific crimes that harm entire nations.

"The humans are builders of great works, and wondrous things. I have seen with my own eyes buildings that have more than four floors, and roads wide enough to handle more than six horses abreast. Machines that fly through the air faster than the fastest land animal, and can carry more than twenty people over great distances, sometimes as far as a man with several fast horses can travel in a single day.

"The 'War Wagon', as we have called the black carriage in the stables, is nothing of the sort. It is not much more than what a normal family could afford to purchase for their own usage, should they so desire or require. On a given day, one will see scores and more of machines like that, scurrying to and fro on their incredible roads as they carry people to wherever they need to go.

"And their cities are huge. I have seen, with my own eyes, vast cities that are home to more than a hundred thousand beings."

David at first had no idea why Giltreas was so underselling things, but after some reflection, realized it made sense. Who would believe him if the actual truth were just thrown out there in this environment, without proof. The reality was a massively significant change from what he saw around himself here in one of the largest cities on this plane. While proof was readily at hand (all they had to do was travel to David's home plane to see it for themselves), it was easier to accept in the short term if the things Giltreas was describing were not so different from what they currently knew.

"But, in many ways, the bad is as bad as the good is good. They have weapons of war that may kill hundreds at once, and from a distance as far as the eye can see.

"Many are slothful, decadent, and take joy in the suffering of others. Indeed, some seem to take an evil delight in causing pain and suffering amongst their fellows.

"Some humans there do not care for one another, not sharing what they have to see that none go hungry, nor that everyone has a place to lay their head at night, to be safe from those which hide in the night to steal their things, and even their lives.

"Of those that own great merchant houses, very few seem as kind as David and Michelle towards those who they sell their goods to and those in their employ. Most view their customers as sheep to be fleeced, and their workers as little more than serf, or simply tools, to be discarded when broken or no longer usable.

"Their rulers are no less corrupt. There are some rulers that are above reproach, but they are hard to find, and are easily thrust aside. Indeed, without a spell to detect truth, it is sometimes hard to tell which ones are good, and which are not.

"This is a plane without any save humans themselves. No elves, dwarves, or halflings exist, save in their myths and legends. Certainly no magical creatures, good or evil, lawful or not, are to be found anywhere.

"These humans have many different nations and states that all have their own leaders. Each government is somewhat different, in how the leaders are put in place. Some are monarchies, but many are leaders chosen by their peoples. I have found it matters little how these leaders are chosen, and how they are chosen seems to have no bearing on whether or not those leaders will do good for their peoples. I feel that the lack of rulers not of their race, such as the Elven Throne, causes them great harm.

"The nation of David, Michelle, and Allison, as well as the brigands in your jails, is called The United States of America. It has existed for some two hundred and thirty summers. It came to be out of strife and conflict. Rulers of this nation are elected, a process that has every adult, who has not committed a serious crime, go to a place near their home and cast their votes, a way of telling who they feel should be their rulers, in offices of all kinds for all different types of rulers, from local city mayors to their President, an office that is considered their highest ruler. This is called an election, in which they elect their rulers.

"But each election is never clear of discord. The people who would seek those elected offices, and others who seem to think their thoughts should be heard about those who wish to be elected, make statements that are almost always nothing more than dishonorable statements that cannot be disproven, or they rail against real or perceived flaws, no matter how insignificant, in those they contend with for the same office. I am strongly reminded of pigs rolling in filth, each trying to get the best slops from the trough, or the nicest patch of mud.

"I am saddened to learn that this nation, which is still stricken with corruption and filth, is held as the highest achievement by many others on this plane. Others are much worse.

"As you know, Your Majesty, the Elven Throne in its role as ordained from agreement by the Gods, has always, since the dawn of time and the origin of the higher races, been outside and above the arguments and disagreements that the various races get involved in, both with themselves and with other races. But the Throne is always there to intervene, and to be a place where beings of all races can go to air their disputes and ask for assistance in resolving their differences. And if necessary, the Elven Throne can ask the Gods to intervene, which they are willing to do. But these humans do not have that to help them. The results have been horrible to discover.

"There have been wars innumerable over the thousands of years since the Elven Throne was taken from them. Indeed, there are scores small wars ongoing even now, with no hope of peace for those peoples. And in the last hundred years, there have been two wars so vast they have been called World Wars that stretched over most of the entire plane. And in each of them, many beings have died, both those who went to fight at the urging or demands of their leaders, and those whose only crime was to be living in an area where those forces would meet to fight. And many more beings have been grievously wounded, losing arms, legs, other body parts, eyes, hearing, and even going mad, with sicknesses of the mind that take their intelligence away in a whirl of nightmares and images and memories that overwhelm them and destroy them little by little, day by day, until there is nothing left.

"Even this America has been at war with one or another nation for most of its existence. In the two hundred thirty seven full turnings of its existence, it has known peaceful times without war for only eleven full turnings of the season. It is as if those on this plane have spent their entire existences competing with one another to be the most efficient killers of their enemies.

"For every bad person, though, there seems to be many good ones that have some extra, and mostly, they are willing to share it with those whose lives have been touched by war, foul weather in the extreme, or the violence visited upon them by their fellows. A home burns down, and others will come along and help them rebuild, while others take them in while they wait. It is not perfect, and sometimes, completely getting back to where they were does not happen.

"It is a plane of contradictions, where the highest ideals are spoken of, but rarely do they strive for them wholly. While the humans there seem good singly or in small groups, in mobs they are often brutish and barbaric in their behaviors, falsely feeling protected by being part of the mob. I know not what to make of them most times. They are capable of great compassion and care in one moment, and yet will shock you with horrific acts of cruelty in the next. As individuals, those with whom I have made acquaintances are the best of any, and I would be honored to be known with them. As a people, they are in need of direction, leadership, and compassionate care."

It was not the most polished speech David had ever heard, but it pretty much summed up his own feelings about his version of humanity quite well. He sighed silently. Then he looked up as Giltreas bowed to the queen, the court, and the others who were there to hear his observations.

It was those others David was most curious about. He had noticed several men and women of Elven, Dwarven, and Human ancestry he hadn't met previously standing nearby the raised dais upon which the Elven Throne sat when he had been ushered in to the throne room. They were all standing while facing Giltreas as he spoke. Several times he was certain that he saw disbelief on the various faces at one time or another. He wondered to himself what was going to happen now.

Giltreas simply stood silently, his hands together behind his back, and waited for what was to happen next. His posture was unconcerned without coming across as bored with the happenings, an almost attentive, calm state that David admired. He never felt that he had mastered that during his time in the Corps.

For several heart beats, the assembled men and women simply looked at Giltreas, as if unsure what to say or do next. Then one by one they turned and started talking to each other, in some cases with quite animated and agitated gestures and demeanors. It was obvious to David that a debate was beginning to rage, and he wondered what was the point or points of contention. He didn't have long to wait.

A Dwarf in a belted tunic with his pants tucked into what looked like leather boots turned suddenly back to Giltreas, and barked a question at him.

"I have never heard of any race being able to construct a building with more than four floors. Do you exaggerate to raise these humans up further than they deserve? Everyone knows a building with more than four floors cannot stand. There is no way to make it strong enough to stand on its own, let alone be strong enough to have people walk on it.

"And that machine in the stables is not a war wagon? I have never seen it's like before, and yet you say most people may purchase one if they have the gold? And that there are hundreds like it on the roads where these humans come from?

"You also mention cities of a hundred thousand beings living and working together? There is no way to move enough food or water into a city like that, nor to move offal out of it. Every day wagons by the score bring food to this city, to be sold in the markets, and at that, the Throne limits the numbers of being that live here to ensure that there is plenty for all and that we do not live in a latrine.

"The greatest part of what you have said that I am hard-pressed to accept is that all this has happened without the assistance and leadership of the dwarves. Everyone knows that great works and buildings are the work of Dwarvish hands, not of the Elven, and certainly not of any humans I have ever met.

"I say I must see this plane, to believe what you say is true. Perhaps you have told the truth, yet perhaps not. I must ascertain this for myself. I do not doubt your words, only your untrained observations. You are a warrior and mage, not an engineer. Observing these things is not of your considerable and respected strengths. I mean no disrespect," the dwarf half-bowed an apology towards Giltreas, who merely smiled and returned the half-bow.

"I am not offended, nor do I feel disrespected, old friend. I would be more than happy to bring you to that plane, so you might see for yourself what I have seen, and explain these things to me. As you have so graciously stated, I am not an engineer, and certainly not lucky enough to be a dwarf. I would welcome your observations," Giltreas finished with a half-smile and another half-bow. Then he turned to David.

"David, do you think it acceptable to sojourn to your plane with these good beings that they might tell us what they see of your people?" The innocent look and tone of voice in Giltreas' voice was almost too much for David to bear with a straight face, but years of iron-willed discipline in the Marines and later at the highest level of business enabled him to pull it off, and he nodded gravely to his friend.

"Of course. I would be honored to show them my world, and answer any questions they might have. I would ask them to respect our customs, though. They will cause quite a stir, since they are out of the most ancient myths and legends to my people. Their appearance will be quite shocking to some."

The dwarf nodded towards David, acknowledging his presence for the first time. "Of course. One must be polite; it is the honorable thing to do."

David nodded once, as if that settled it. "Great. Who wishes to come with, and when would this happen?"

A voice spoke up, and David's eyes opened wide, as did Allison and Michelle. Anaradelle suddenly appeared in the throne room, standing off to Giltreas' right side in a slightly open area between the throne and the wall. She stepped forward, and the beings of the various races in the throne room bowed low to the Mid-God that had appeared in front of them.

"I wish to come with you, if I am welcome."

"Goddess, I would welcome you, but it is not my plane, and therefore not my place to do so. The welcome must come from David, Allison, or Michelle." Giltreas swept his arm towards where the three stood, and David and Allison swallowed in the anxious silence that descended on the throne room. Michelle seemed to be the only one who wasn't tongue-tied in the silence.

"I would be happy to have you accompany me to see my world, Sister."

The timbre and tone of Michelle's voice seemed to be changing almost on a day to day basis, as she slowly accepted that she was not merely mortal anymore.

Anaradelle bowed her thanks to the newest Goddess of the multiverse then turned back to the rest of the assemblage in the room, waiting silently for the rest of them to make up their minds.

Delara was the next to speak. "I will accompany you, as will my Seneschal." She turned to the dwarf that had spoken up before. "Gherratt, you will come as well? And you others?" She looked the question over all of the assembled beings who had joined them in the throne room for Giltreas' report, and waited for their responses to her question. Most shook their heads no, but one, whom Allison knew as her teacher in the magical arts nodded yes, smiling at her as he did so. Gherratt the Dwarven engineer also nodded, his gruff voice saying, "Certainly."

Delara nodded. "Very well, it is decided. When shall we do this?"

David thought about it, and after a brief conversation with Michelle and Allison, turned back to Delara. "It would be best to do this in four days, on our Saturday. There are a number of preparations I would like to make, to ensure your safety, among other things."

Delara nodded once more. "It is wise to be prepared. I will talk with my jailer, and he will accompany me as well."

We shall meet back here in the morning in four days to see to this place of such mystery as you have painted for us, Giltreas." She turned and walked back to her throne, then past it to the tapestry-covered doorway, exiting the room.

Anaradelle swept a half-bow to Giltreas, after which she abruptly disappeared once more. Gherratt shook his head at the comings and goings of the Goddess, and turned back to Giltreas once more.

"Giltreas, boy, what aren't you telling us? I could tell you were prevaricating, but I do not know in what. Do you wish it to be a secret?"

"It is better for you to see the sights for yourself for the first time, instead of through my eyes."

"Very well. What will I need in the way of guards? Are there many uncivilized beings there?" The question came out in a delicate tone of voice. Clearly the dwarf was trying not to offend anyone, but David understood the need for safety and security, and he spoke up.

"If you are willing to accept it, I will ensure your safety. I do not expect any significant problems, but Giltreas could pull everyone back through a gate if things become an issue. I will have people that will prevent anyone from following you back to this plane, if there is a problem."

Gherratt bowed to David. "I thank you, human. That is most generous." Then he grinned big. "I am looking forward to seeing these miraculous buildings with more than four floors in them. They must be a sight to see.

Unless the floors are all my height?" The dwarf came barely up to the bottom of David's armpit. David guessed he was all of four feet tall, but that entire four feet was made up of the massive musculature of a being who worked a hard, physical job every day. He was easily as thick as David, and none of it was fat.

Giltreas shook his head, trusting his gesture to be adequate for conveying his message.

* * *

On the morning four days later, the cavalcade was ready to go to David and Allison's world. Michelle was coming back as well, even though David wasn't sure it was really safe for her, but the discussion had been mostly one-sided.

He had argued against it, throwing reason after reason in front of her to slow her down, but she had simply waited for him to run out of ideas then simply said, "I'm coming home with you. I can handle myself now. I am not the same being I was when I was attacked. I am ascended now. And I want to see it again. I have no idea what will happen to me next, or where I will end up."

David had simply given in, then. He had never won arguments with her in the past either, before her ascension. Now, it was simply not even a discussion. She told him what she was going to do, and he really couldn't stop her. He looked at her, and she looked back silently, allowing his scrutiny, wondering what he was thinking, and what he saw when he looked at her.

"Michelle, I don't want to lose you. Even when our parents were not there for us, you were there for me. Now that you are what you have become, I can't stand the thought of not having you around. I hope that fate, or whatever guides you from here out, is kind enough to Allison and I to have you in our lives."

Michelle swept forward and pulled her big younger brother in tight for a hug, burying her face into his shoulder. "I will always be there for you, my Davey D. You are the bright spot in my life that I cherish. Nothing will take you away from me, nor me from you." The words were muffled by his shirt, but he caught them just the same.

Allison stepped forward, unsure if she should reach out to join in to the moment, but Michelle solved that dilemma by reaching for her and pulling her into a three-way embrace. She felt the incredible emotional warmth and welcome of her husband and his sister, and then realized that she could see it, too.

"Michelle, you're glowing again."

"Sorry about that."

"Thanks for the apology, but you're still glowing."

"Deal with it. It's not like I have a light switch up my ass or anything."

Allison laughed then snuggled in closer to the two people she loved more than anyone else in the multiverse.

Yintarin, Allison's magic teacher, looked with wide eyes as he turned and saw the source of the glow that had pervaded the throne room in the brightly-lit afternoon. It was coming from the human female standing in a three-way embrace with David and the other human female, Allison. She had been identified to him as David's mate, which didn't make any sense at the time. Everyone knew that humans didn't take single mates like Dwarves and Halflings did. They were part of small groups of fifty to sixty adults that all seemed to change partners every night in a way he never understood.

Now he looked at the three of them, standing some fifteen feet away, and he could feel the emotional warmth flowing off the one, Michelle. It permeated his senses, and seemed to wash away his concerns and cares, and he sighed happily as the slightly euphoric effect calmed him. Then he shook his head. He didn't understand the tongue they were speaking in, and that surprised him. He considered himself somewhat of an expert in the different tongues that the various races used to communicate, but this one puzzled him. Still, he was a being of almost infinite curiosity, something that stood him well in his field as a mage. He saw a puzzle, and he had to ask the question. He stepped closer.

"Excuse me. I beg your pardon for intruding."

Michelle turned to the dwarf, and smiled at him. "It is ok. What is your question?"

Yintarin was impressed. It was difficult for those taller than him to look down at him without looking down on him, as if is shorter stature made him less important, less intelligent, or simply of lower social standing. It was something that he simply ignored as not significant nor important to deal with. But Michelle accomplished it with an ease that he respected mightily.

"Why do you glow? Are you Deus? I thought I knew most all of the Gods and Goddesses, but I do not know you. I mean no disrespect. But I am curious. It is a failing of all Dwarven mages, I suppose."

"Yes, I am Deus. But I have only been Deus for a few months. And I have only known about it for a few weeks at best."

The bolt of surprise that struck Yintarin at Michelle's words staggered him, and he could only stare back at Michelle in open-mouthed amazement for several moments.

"Why are you so shocked?" The question was gentle, and carefully crafted to put the one being asked at ease.

Yintarin shook himself, as if trying to clear his head.

"You are a new Goddess? Truly?" The dwarf seemed to be having a difficult time catching his breath, and one hand went to his chest as he tried to calm himself.

"What is it? What is wrong? Why is this so… whatever it is?" Michelle seemed to focus all her intensity on the dwarf, who staggered further under the weight of her entire presence. She sensed that she was not making things any better, and closed her eyes, taking calming breaths as she tried to get her emotions under control.

Allison reached out to the dwarf, grasping his arm as he fought to stay upright, and his hand latched on to her arm fiercely, grateful for the support. Allison turned towards Michelle, then saw her with her eyes closed, and as she breathed slowly in and out, the glow faded, and went out entirely. She opened her eyes, then looked at the dwarf, who now seemed to have composed himself. He was looking back up at her, his eyes still somewhat wide, but his mouth was closed.

"Goddess, there has not been a new ascension to Deus in a thousand years on any plane. Scholars who study such things have speculated that there was no need for new Gods and Goddesses, hence the lack of ascensions. Gods and Goddesses have been asked about this before, but none have given a reason. It is thought that they simply do not know themselves. Before that time, there was a few every hundred years or so. It was common for new Gods to ascend from mortals to take roles from Gods who are no longer. But none have needed to be replaced, and none have ascended in millennia."

Michelle paused to consider what the Dwarven mage said to her, then decided she didn't have enough information to determine what was happening. She tried to put it out of her mind, but she kept coming back to what Yintarin said. She was about to ask Yintarin another question, but he bowed, and spoke once more.

"What do you call yourself, Goddess? And what role will you fulfill?"

"What role? I have no idea. I didn't even know I was a... I didn't even know until sometime after it happened. My name is Michelle."

Yintarin's mind was reeling at these revelations. Many things that the Dwarven philosophers thought were true regarding those ascended to Deus seemed to be simply, utterly wrong.

"Goddess Michelle, meeting you has been a shock. Much of what we had assumed to be true, or learned over the millennia, seem to be not the case. It was always known that a new Deus would ascend after a role had been discovered to be unfulfilled, and that the Deus would ascend after being asked to do so, and accepting. The sacrifice one makes to leave the Great Path of the Soul is considerable, and the choice is not made lightly. Forgive me, but I must go communicate with my Elders to tell them of your arrival. Might I take my leave of you?"

Michelle thought about what Yintarin had said, then decided she could find others later to answer the questions that she would inevitably come up with. She looked at the Dwarf, then nodded.

"Thank you very much for your thoughts on what has happened. I greatly appreciate it. Will I be able to call upon you later if I have more questions?"

"Of course. I am at your service, My Lady Michelle." Yintarin bowed so low his beard nearly touched the floor. Then he stood, and walked away out of the throne room.

David turned to Giltreas after the conversation between his sister (if she was that anymore) and the dwarven engineer and said, "We need to go back to prepare the team for the visitors that are coming. Can we go now and come back in a short time?"

"Of course," he said simply, then called the gate back to David's place of business, setting the far end down in the room the team used for its offices. He waved David forward, then stepped through himself. The gates on either end of the connection disappeared from the throne room and the office room shortly after that.

CHAPTER 40

The gate opened up on the main floor in the lobby of the downtown office building that housed the MDST, Inc. headquarters operations. Standing nearby was David's entire team, each one armed with their usual concealed-carry weapon, out of sight in shoulder holsters under matching dark purple lightweight jackets that had MDST, Inc. emblazoned in gold on the back. The various members of the team knew that Michelle had chosen those colors for the company because of her brother's almost fanatical following of the Minnesota Vikings.

The entire lobby area was divided by the centrally located security desk and the glass walls that extended from the desk sideways to either outer wall, forming a straight line that blocked off access to the restricted areas beyond the security desk. Above the glass wall were two levels of balconies, where the upper two floors ended in the lobby area. The edge of the floor overlooking the lobby was marked with a low glass wall, topped with a metal railing that extended the entire length of the wall. At the ends of both balconies, the open area ended at secure doors, that faced each other across the open area of the upper floors, and facing forward to the open space were two elevators on the left, and a stairwell on the right.

The guards manning the front desk had been told to expect the gate that suddenly appeared in their lobby, but they still weren't prepared for it actually materializing in front of them. One actually yelled out briefly in shock, before getting himself under better control. The three guards behind the desk at the moment were still very anxious, seeing something like that for the first time.

The gate itself just stood there for a moment, wavering so very slightly in mid-air like the surface of a lake, before Giltreas stepped through. He turned and nodded to the guards, who relaxed somewhat; Gil Owens had been coming and going the old fashioned way for the better part of two months now, and they had grown accustomed to him quickly. It had helped that he was unfailingly polite to every security guard with whom he interacted. While some had commented on his unusual coloration, he was close enough in appearance to a human being that they could subconsciously accept his differences as simple variations on the human race.

Not so with the next six beings, identically dressed in identical short-sleeved and belted tunics, pants and sandals each carrying a wooden staff that was probably six feet long and two inches in diameter, that stepped through the gate to appear in the lobby, followed quickly by David, then Allison, then an unknown young woman with dark, rich hair that was stunningly beautiful, yet hauntingly familiar just the same.

The six beings, recognizable as guards because of their clothing and behavior, though, were nothing like anyone else they had ever seen, except maybe in a bad movie or something. They looked around, then each nodded to the guards behind the desk respectfully, still trying to take in the impossibly huge room they were in, with the glass wall that looked out on the rest of the downtown city scape, leading to more impossible sights beyond the perfection of the glass itself. It was obvious they had been briefed at least a little on what to expect on the other side of the gate, and they took up positions around the gate in a secure formation, snapping to attention.

But their clothing was not what caused the guards to stare at them, open-mouthed in astonishment. They clearly weren't human, with a pale green-tinged skin, and gentle points that swept back from the tops of their ears, in a graceful, almost aerodynamic way that one guard thought reminded him of a bird of prey in the wind. Still, the two male guards, with their short hair and muscular builds, and the four female guards, with their more slender but still lean muscular forms and long hair braided down one side of their head and back over one shoulder, could still be mistaken, in form at least, as something close to human.

The next being through the gate, though, defied relation to the species of which humans readily identified themselves. Karonashkk had to stoop low to step through the gate, so the guardsmen only saw the top of his steer-horned, red-haired head as he stepped into their world, but the three of them gasped out loud this time as he looked around, then stood back up completely to his eight and a half foot height as he stepped forward once more. He bowed to the guards at the desk, then his eyes widened as he looked around and up at the huge lobby.

"Giltreas, my old friend, your human friends are amazing builders. This palace is incredible. What royal being calls this his home?" The words came out in clear English, in the deep, rich bass to be expected of such a huge form. "And will we get to present ourselves to them in respect?"

Giltreas smiled up at Karonashkk. "This is the building that David and Michelle have their business in. It is not a palace, although from our view, it is grand, is it not? These humans in this country do not have nobles or royalty."

"Truly? I would be amazed to see what they call a palace then. Wait, no nobility? How do they not descend into anarchy?"

Anything Giltreas might have said was lost in the sudden sound of more people coming through the gate. Two more Elven kind came through, these in formal, richly appointed robes, followed by an Elven woman wearing a small, elaborately wrought crown with a single blue jewel set in it, and in an even more richly appointed robe. Then two short men with a long beard and robes to match their shorter stature appeared, and they gawked at the sights in front of him as they tried to look everywhere at once.

Giltreas walked over to where the Dwarven engineer stood, and pulled him gently by the arm away from the front of the gate. The dwarf looked up at Giltreas, an angry look on his face that was betrayed by the humor in his eyes. "You are a capricious one, youngster. I have never seen the like of this building before. But, I see only three floors. Were you, perhaps, unsure of what you were seeing?"

"I tell you truly, I was not. Come, see what is to be seen." Giltreas directed the shorter being over to the windows that were 'behind' the gate, where the engineer hadn't looked yet.

His eyes got very wide as he took in the huge, three story wall of windows, but his mouth fell open as he saw what was on the other side. The downtown skyscraper stretched up only thirty floors or so, but from the restricted viewing angle imposed by the ceiling, one couldn't see more than several floors of windows on the building across the street. As the dwarf got closer and closer to the windows and doors that made up the grand front entrance of the foyer, and his eyes traveled further up the silver and glass expanse of the building out the windows, his eyes and his mouth got wider and wider. Giltreas led him through a door nearly tall enough for Karonashkk to walk through and out into the street, where the diminutive builder could at last look up and see just how far the building went up.

"Maker's Blood! By the stones of my ancestors! Oh, that building is so tall, it makes my balls hurt! How did they make it? And, how did they cover it in metal and glass that way?" The dwarf's voice was hoarse as the impossible sight in front of him took his breath away.

"Come, my friend. I promise we shall learn as much as we may when there is time. But for now, we must return to the Queen and others." Giltreas led the way back through the huge metal and glass doors, another impossible sight that the dwarf didn't see before when he was focused on the impossible building across the street.

Giltreas pulled the dwarven engineer back to the gate, where the last of the group, the queen's seneschal, had come through.

He looked around at the vast, grand foyer, far larger than what he had ever seen for an indoor space, and his eyes were huge and round as he tried to process what he was seeing. Then he turned to look at Giltreas, who was doing an admirable job of looking innocent as he took in the expressions on the faces of those from his home plane.

Delara worked hard to keep a straight face as she took in what she was seeing, and then she turned as Giltreas led the amazed dwarf backwards by one arm back to where his mother stood.

She reached out and yanked her son towards her by one arm, the sudden move startled him into letting go of the dwarf, who simply stopped where he was, continuing to stare out the front wall of windows at the building across the street. Outside, the people continued to walk by as if nothing was out of the ordinary, and the vehicles of all size, color, and configuration seemed to amble past.

"My son, you have not lost your prankish ways, have you? You were clever, now that I think through what you said this morning. Everything was true, wasn't it?" He nodded, clearly fighting a losing battle to keep a smile from breaking out, as she continued. "And yet, none of it was really the full story, was it?" He shook his head, and the smile came out completely as he lost the fight.

"No, my mother."

She waited for him to say more, then sighed. "These humans are so much more than what you said, are they not? I can understand why you did what you did. You wanted us to see for ourselves what they are like. The truth would have been hard for us to swallow, I am guessing."

He simply nodded, without saying a word. Then Anaradelle stepped through the gate.

The powerful Mid-God, who was the Goddess of Children, Fertility, and Nature stopped short once she was clear of the gate, and took in the sights. Even her ancient eyes were wide in shock as she took in the foyer, the upper two floors, and the glass walls that separated the outer area from the inner, secure portion of the grand foyer that was tucked under the overhanging upper floors. She turned to her left, and saw the rock climbing wall, her mouth opening into an "O" of surprise, then closing. She continued turning, stepped around the obscuring presence of the Gate Giltreas had called to bring them to this location, and took in the sights of the downtown area, including the view across the street at the buildings there.

The security guards manning the front desk were somewhat overwhelmed by the presence of the ancient and powerful Deity that had suddenly stepped from the gate and into their midst. She glowed with an internal light that seemed to chase the shadows away from the corners of the room. While they didn't know exactly what she was, the clues were sufficient for them to realize that she was not something, or someone, they had ever encountered before.

A ringing sound was heard coming from something on the desk, but they couldn't, or wouldn't, hear it, and it continued to ring as David looked over at the desk and frowned. He recognized sound as the phone for the drive-up access door to the parking area, and walked over to the revolving access door, flashing his badge at the card reader then pressed the pad of his index finger into the scanner. With a beep indicating he was granted access, the door started to rotate, and he walked through, opening the back door to the security desk. He stepped over to the ringing phone, looked down at the monitor, and picked up the handset.

"Come in, Moira. Don't worry about your pin. You're fine." He pressed the access button, which lifted the crossing arm and opened the door to the parking area. He hung up the phone, then turned back to the guards behind the desk and clapped his hands once to get their attention.

Ian blushed before apologizing. He started moving around behind the desk again, and the others started moving again as well, but still continued to try to sneak peeks at the incredible beings standing in their lobby.

Anaradelle made her way to the outer walls where the double set of glass doors allowed access in and out of the building, her eyes travelling up the side of the brown and glass building across the street. Michelle had followed her to the doors, waiting slightly behind as her new Sister goddess took in the sights and sounds of the downtown business district of the city.

Anaradelle watched the vehicles pass in several moments of contemplation, and the occasional pedestrian walk by before she turned to Michelle.

"This is your world, isn't it, sister? Not just that you are from here, but this is the world you know. A place of huge buildings, and hard ground, and sights that no one not from here could ever contemplate. This is what you know."

"Yes. This is what I know my world to be."

"I wish to see more. Can we go to the top of that building and look out at this place, so I might learn more of it?" The goddess spoke quietly, but there was a yearning in her voice that Michelle didn't understand. She thought for a moment, and then turned to David, who was still behind the desk.

"Hey Dave, do you think William is in his office?" she called across the lobby.

David thought about it for a few moments then nodded, clearly catching the thought behind the question.

"Yeah, he usually works Saturdays these days. Want me to see if he is up for some visitors?" David grinned at the thought of dragging the queen, her elven guards and seneschal, the massive Minotaur, the dwarf, and the Goddess up the elevators to the forty-seventh floor of one of the tallest buildings in Minneapolis tickled his sense of the absurd. Michelle nodded. "Let me give him a ring," he said, pulling out his cell phone.

Karonashkk walked over to the security desk, and half-bowed to the two men and one woman behind the desk, his massive war hammer slung over his head and shoulder on a leather strap that was a good three inches wide.

"I am Karonashkk, body guard to the Queen of the Elven Throne when she travels. I am honored to meet you, guards of Michelle and David's company." The voice came out in the deepest bass tones the three humans had ever heard, and their faces showed their shock as the massive, red-skinned and bull-headed being dressed in a leather kilt that came down to his knees and solid leather sandals, spoke in flawless English to them.

"Uhhnn, yeah, I am honored to meet you as well," Sarah, the guard supervisor spoke back, stuttering briefly before getting her mental feet back under her. "I am Sarah, and this is Bill and Ian."

"Sarah, Bill, and Mark. It is my honor to greet you in my Queen's name." He bowed once more, then turned back to see where his charge had gotten to. Then he walked over to stand around five feet behind her.

Delara had walked to the glass wall, and put her hands on it as she leaned in to look outside that the amazing sights. She heard the heavy footsteps of her bodyguard, and turned to him. "Come look at this place, Karonashkk. See what your friend and my son has discovered."

A young man with very dark skin was walking by at that moment, and saw the strange woman with pointed ears and greenish skin looking out at him from the inside of one of those business buildings downtown. He wasn't sure what he was seeing at first, because the glass distorted color and vision in the afternoon light of the fall day. He slowed, then stopped as she turned away, and looked up at something behind her, her lips moving as she talked to someone. Everything he had seen so far could have just been his imagination, so nothing out of the ordinary was happening. He could tell she was exceptionally beautiful, though.

All thoughts of the beautiful young woman with her hands on the glass went away, along with every other thought, as she turned back to the outside, and someone else stepped up to the glass as well.

"Holy fu---!! What the hell!?!" He whipped out his smart phone and started the camera app to record video. "Gerard ain't gonna believe this! Nobody is gonna believe this. I gotta... got it. Smile for the camera!" He held up the phone and waved to the people (to use the term loosely for these beings) inside the glass.

Karonashkk looked down at the human outside, and smiled, waving back with one massive hand. He had seen Allison's smart phone, so he knew what the young man was doing, but prudence required him to check into it further, to protect his Queen.

DeShay watched as the massive red-skinned dude with the bull head and horns turned and spoke to someone else inside, then looked towards the door to his right. He turned back to DeShay and motioned for him to come to the door, then turned and walked back into the building.

Moments later, DeShay had stepped closer to the entrance to the building, when the huge being stepped out of the door, and turned towards him.

"No way! What are you, dude?"

"I am a Minotaur. I am Karonashkk, Bodyguard to Delara, Queen of the Elven Throne. I am pleased to meet you, human. But I must ask, are you a danger to my Queen?"

DeShay suddenly saw the massive war hammer slung over the Minotaur's back, and shivered for a moment.

"No, man, I ain't no threat. No way. We good, dude. It's all good."

"Then I am pleased to meet you. What do you call yourself?"

"I'm DeShay. DeShay Stallings. Where did you come from?"

"We are from a different plane. I must return to my Queen. Be well, DeShay Stallings."

"Yeah, you too, Minotaur dude. Kairnash." He didn't quite get the name right, but it was close enough, and the Minotaur smiled, then ducked back into the building, the secure door latching behind him.

"Man, I got to post that to my Facebook page." He stopped the recording and brought up his Facebook app, and started to upload the file.

David called but got no answer from William's cell phone. He hung up when it went to voicemail, without leaving a message.

"Nothing, Michelle. Not sure where he is. He didn't answer his cell. What do you want to do?"

"I want to go shopping," Allison piped up. "How about the mall?"

"Which one?" Michelle asked.

"Ridgedale is fine, or M-O-A. That might be more interesting. Besides, I haven't had any ice cream in a while. There is that shop in the Food Court I like, remember?"

David thought about it, but couldn't really come up with a reason why not. Well, maybe the appearance of the guests, but that won't be too much of an issue, right? Besides, Karonashkk is a really nice guy, unless you tick him off.

"Sure, why not. What could possibly go wrong, with this crowd?"

Anaradelle hid a smile as she contemplated the success of the spell she had just cast on the humans from this world. It wasn't something she would have tried on Michelle; a Goddess would detect it, even a Deity as newly ascended as Michelle, and she would most likely resist it by her very nature without knowing. But it seemed to have worked on David and Allison. The spell clouded their mind slightly, and let her influence their decisions, while convincing them that her ideas were harmless. She wanted to see more of this world, and had no desire to explain her reasons to any mortal. They would best be served letting her do what she willed. It was in their best interests, after all. That was her role since time immemorial, and she had always done her best to make sure mortals were directed appropriately.

This plane, and what she sensed from the beings here, was the best example of why she was needed. Pain, strife, discord; all these things she would prevent from this point forward, by giving them something else to focus on and strive for. It was her responsibility to these mortals. They needed her to do this for them, just as the humans of all other planes benefitted from her efforts. All those countless other human mortals lived lives of happiness, simplicity, and peace, because of her. She was proud of her accomplishments with them. And she felt that part of her inside rising to the challenge of what was to come back here. She knew she would succeed. No other option ever occurred to her.

* * *

The Food Courts at the Mall of America are big places. With hundreds of tables, they are the place for hungry shoppers, certainly on a Saturday afternoon in late October, to take a break from walking through the huge mall, and get a bite to eat or something to drink. There are two food courts, both of which overlook the theme park in the center of the immense shopping mall, where rides and games entertained children and adults for hours on end.

Now, a gate opened in the table area. It shimmered and hummed in midair, and stretched up over six feet tall. The bottom didn't touch the tile floor, but hovered just a few inches above. The edge glowed in pale colors, oscillating between blue, yellow, and red, which caused the colors to change to greens, oranges, and other tints as it cycled through the color spectrum. The edge was rounded, and maybe a half inch thick, wavering slightly in place as it rippled as if made from water.

The humming sounds from the magical apparition caused people seated nearby to gasp and begin to move away in shock. But before they could get very far, a plain-looking man in a blue jacket, jeans, and tennis shoes stepped through, followed by several more. They all looked completely normal, and fully human.

While some small percentage of the people in the food court had seen news reports about recent viral videos, or had even seen the videos themselves, most had not. And while the broadcasts, and the videos they had brought to light, had been the talk of water coolers everywhere around the country for days ("Was that unicorn real? No way! Well, maybe?"), nothing in any of the videos had prepared them to witness the gate shimmering into existence in the food court of the huge shopping mall, right in front of them, or to have people come out of it. Or what came next.

Karonashkk stepped through the gate, once again bowing down somewhat to fit his height through, before straightening up slowly while he angled his head to look up to make sure he wouldn't hit his head on the ceiling of the human building. He needn't have bothered. The ceiling of the massive building stretched scores of feet above him, and he gawked much more than he had at the amazing, grand building to which he had come when he first entered this plane. He was only three feet in front of the gate when the next person came through, only to hear some people screaming at the obviously impossible size and appearance of the massive Minotaur.

The next being through was the first of the Elven Guard, and he put his left hand out on Karonashkk's lower back and pushed him forward and to the side, causing the temporarily stunned Minotaur to stumble and nearly fall to one knee as the unexpected pressure caught him by surprise.

Always in good spirits, the massive red-skinned being with long hair laughed out loud as he straightened back up, and walked forward to the railing that kept people from falling from the third story into the rides and games of the amusement park below, his sandaled feet slapping on the cool tile floor. His eyes were wide as he tried to take in the expanse of the inside of the building, then turned back to watch people exit the gate his good friend Giltreas had opened.

People around the strange party reacted differently to the appearance of the Minotaur. Adults clutched their children to them tighter and gathered up their things carefully and quietly in preparation to move away to a safer vantage point, or to exit the area entirely, depending on whether their reaction was curiosity or outright fear.

Officer Connor Brenton of the Bloomington Police Department was standing off to the side of the food court as he monitored the area for problems. He enjoyed being at the Mall of America. It was a chance to walk for exercise, and interact personally with people, instead of being seated in a police cruiser his entire shift, never being up on his feet except when he was out responding to a call, handing out tickets, or on lunch break.

He was some fifty feet away from the center of the eating area, when his head snapped had to his right as the first sounds of distress reached him, automatically assuming some wanna-be gang members were causing trouble again. But when he finished his turn, he gawked at the gate, already reaching for the radio mic connected to the right shoulder lapel of his deep blue uniform shirt as he tentatively stepped towards the thing, whatever it was, that seemed to have appeared from out of nowhere in the middle of his shift.

"Unit 4814, dispatch."

"Go ahead, 4814."

"There is a disturbance in the food court. Not sure what it is. I am going to need some…" Just then, the first human stepped through the gate, and walked forward before turning around and looking back at the next people to exit the gate.

"There are several people coming out of some kind of shiny, glowing thing suspended in midair in the eating area of the food court. Not sure how – OH MY GOD! What is that!?!?"

"Send backup. Some kind of… ahh… I think it's a Minotaur just stepped out of whatever it is that these people are using to get here." Officer Brenton put his hand on his weapon as he started forward carefully as the radio started up again.

"What are you… Holy crap. Where did that come from? How did it get here?" The voice must be looking at the security camera imagery, Brenton thought. Then the massive form stumbled as a… what the heck? Green skin and pointy ears? What is this, a geek convention?

"Additional units, disturbance in the food court. 4814, do you anticipate trouble – wow, they just keep coming out of that thing. We are also getting starting to get 911 calls, and the mall security line is also taking calls. What is happening over there?"

"I am not sure. We need to get this situation assessed and under control before people begin to panic. I am going to need manpower to start get people out of this area, and we need to figure out what to do with these…" He paused as the guards took up a position around the gate, staffs held at their right side as they stood attentively watching the crowds. They had never seen such a massive building before, but they had a job to do, rather than stand around and 'gawk at the dragon'.

The dwarven engineer and the dwarven mage made their entrance, followed by the Seneschal to the Throne. Next, the Elven Queen made her appearance, followed by Giltreas, then finally Anaradelle. Giltreas turned back to the gate, and waved a hand at it, cancelling the spell and causing it to disappear.

Delara gasped as the immensity of the building they were inside suddenly registered. The view over the amusement park was incredible, the ceiling stretched above them a great distance, and the loud sounds from the park and the people shopping pressed in on her.

Anaradelle was likewise nearly overwhelmed by what these humans had built. It was truly amazing, a part of her reflected as she looked upon the peoples around her. As she looked them over, she realized that she would not be able to "see" everyone around her from her vantage point on the floor, and cast a flight spell upon herself that lifted her off gracefully from the floor.

She drifted slowly up into the open air above the food court, then out slightly over the edge of the railing, floating up higher as she went. A glow came from her eyes and from her robes, bright and tangible as it obscured her upper face and body, and she turned left and right to view the human mortals around her.

Then Anaradelle spoke directly into the minds of every mortal on this world, and her voice was as loud as thunder, yet gentle as a light breeze. Everyone awake on the planet suddenly stopped still and listened, as the voice of the Mid-God came to them wherever they were at the time.

"I am Anaradelle, Goddess of Children, Fertility, and Nature. I resume my rightful place as arbiter of all things on this plane for which I am Deus."

The words rolled through everyone's mind everywhere across the entire world. Those who were sleeping at the time would later remember it upon waking. Those who were awake were startled, causing them to jolt upright, or stumble while walking, or physically respond in some startled way. Many people, but not all, who saw their own sudden response to the unexpected event in others began to talk to each other, asking if they heard the same thing. Conversations began all over the world, arguments ensued, and through it all, the strange event produced disagreement as to what happened, and what it meant. No one doubted that the words were spoken. But there was plenty of room to interpret what the sentences meant, and, humans being humans, there was an enormous amount of space between points of view.

People in the food court, both customers and employees of the nearby fast food shops, reacted differently to what was happening. Either they were curious about what was happening, or they were fearful. And of the ones whose first reaction was fear, many opted to call for help.

Emergency dispatchers that answered 911 calls for Bloomington first thought there was some kind of prank happening, as they began to receive calls from people on mobile phones saying that there was something strange happening at the Mall of America. But as the phone lines began to light up with more and more calls, some of them sounding almost panicked and fearful, within five minutes it became obvious that whatever was happening was no prank.

The operators were suddenly overwhelmed with calls, and as the call volume escalated, with each one more unreal than the last. After the initial calls about some strange glowing thing, the calls moved on to a huge red man with a bull's head, to elves, to a glowing woman who was floating in mid-air.

Then the words spoken by Anaradelle crashed through their minds, and a sense of unease swept over the dispatchers. Something was happening, and they were in a position to do something about it. The supervisor started a whiteboard tally of the calls, and when each one came in, he put another mark on the board.

When a known event is witnessed by a high number of people who place many calls, the dispatchers are told to take the report as quickly as possible and clear the line, while assuring the callers that the situation was known and being responded to. The callers were not as sure that something like this could be handled effectively, however. Still, the dispatchers started responding to the calls with, "Are you calling about the Mall of America food court incident? Police are responding. Please move to a safe area, or better yet, please leave the mall and let the police and mall security handle the situation. Thank you."

Likewise, some of the employees of the nearby food shops also called the emergency number that reached the mall's in-house security department, and they began to respond as well, moving first one, then a few of their nearby personnel to the food court to assess what was happening (and to evaluate the sanity of those first callers), while not uncovering the rest of the mall. This would prevent opportunistic crimes committed by people aware enough to know something was going on, while having a larcenous bent to their warped character to take advantage of the situation.

As the calls continued to mount to both the mall security phone number and the 911 dispatch center, higher level employees in both locations reached out to each other smoothly, following the training and planning that had been put in place to respond to significant criminal or even terrorist events. Coordination began with the intent of maximizing the response needed to protect the people and the property there.

David and Allison shook their heads suddenly. The statement from Anaradelle directly to their minds finally caused enough stimuli to their brains that they were able to shake off the spell Anaradelle cast on them back at MDST's downtown office. They both realized that she had manipulated them to bring her here so she could resume her role. David looked at Anaradelle as she lowered back to the floor, and realized what had happened a moment before Allison did, but she was almost as quick.

Anger was plain on his face as he approached the ancient Goddess.

"What did you do to Allison and I? Why did you think you have the right to do that to us?"

Anaradelle was taken aback as she contemplated the angry human mortal in front of her before she glared back and spoke up.

"You have no right to upbraid me in this manner, mortal. I am a Goddess! I will not be spoken to as a mewling child!"

David thought about it for a moment before turning away. He would deal with that later, when he was less angry. As he looked around, he noticed that there were a few police officers present, along with the mall's security officers. Most of them seemed to be involved in moving the shoppers away from the new arrivals, especially the Minotaur, but certainly, the Goddess and the elves were suddenly finding themselves in a more deserted area. One officer had been directing the police and security guards, then looked over at David as he stepped towards them slowly and carefully, his hands in the clear as he closed up the distance slightly.

"Officer, what can I do for you?" David's question came out friendly and calm, hoping to keep the man's nerves from getting the best of him.

"What is going on here? Who are these people? And what is that?" The officer, a sergeant and Officer Brenton's superior, pointed at Karonashkk where he stood attentively behind Delara, the one he was charged with protecting with his entire, formidable skills and abilities, and life, if necessary.

"The Elven woman with the tiara on her head is Delara, the Queen of the Elven Throne. The tall one behind her with the horns and red skin in the kilt is Karonashkk, her chief body guard when she is travelling away from her home city. The six elves with the staffs are her Royal Guard. The man with grey hair and skin, and amber-colored eyes is Giltreas. The elven royal at her other shoulder is her Seneschal. The dwarf on the left is an engineer, Gherratt, who wished to see the buildings and places Giltreas was describing to them. The dwarf in the robe is Yintarin, a mage."

The sergeant looked at David as if he was criminally insane, but the presence of the huge Minotaur said otherwise. He realized that if it were true, and the woman really was an Elven Queen from wherever, he was way out of his league, and really needed to get someone else here who was more qualified to speak with her. He glanced around to evaluate the progress of the personnel attempting to empty the food court area, and noted that some people were not moving much, either to stay and watch what was going on, or because they didn't want to leave their tables. He started to reach for his radio, when his eyes widened as he looked behind David. David glanced over his shoulder at the sound of approaching footsteps, hoping inside it was not Anaradelle.

"David, will you please introduce me to these honorable men? It is important that I speak with them, if nothing more than to put their minds at ease about us."

"Certainly, your Majesty." He looked at the insignias on the on the man's uniform, then spoke up.

"Sergeant…?"

"Sergeant Andrew Bradenton of the Bloomington Police Department," the man spoke formally.

"It is a pleasure to make your acquaintance, Sergeant Bradenton. I am David Wilhelm," David said, then turned and gestured with equal formality to the queen standing beside him, "I present to you Delara, Queen of the Elven Throne. Your Majesty, I present to you Sergeant Andrew Bradenton of the Bloomington Police Department."

Sergeant Bradenton had picked up some basic instruction in how to interact with foreign heads of state over the years, because of the Mall of America itself was an international destination that attracted people from just about every strata of every society. But the good sergeant had never expected to be called upon in a situation like this, and he was very nervous. The ramifications of messing up something like this went beyond thinking. Then there was also the little matter of the "bodyguard" standing watchfully over the queen's shoulder. But he decided to give it his best effort.

"Your Majesty, I am honored to meet you." A respectful half-bow went with the simple statement, and the queen smiled at him.

"And I am honored to meet you as well, Sergeant Andrew Bradenton of the Bloomington Police Department." The queen held out her right hand, palm down, and when he took it, she gracefully directed his hand until her left hand was tucked under the crook of his elbow, with her right resting easily on top of that. She then drew him in to a walk away from the amusement park, to where the noise was somewhat lower. More police officers and security guards had arrived and were directing people away from the group, clearing the path in front of them as they left the food court and moved towards the main hallway. The queen's guards followed along as well, forming an outer circle that watched the crowds carefully for anyone that might be intent on harming their queen.

The queen spoke up when they got to an area that was quieter than the food court.

"I apologize for not sending word ahead that I would be visiting here. Unfortunately, the Elven Throne has not had emissaries to this plane in thousands of your years, not since the years my grandmother was on the throne, so there was no knowledge with which to avail ourselves for that purpose. I understand if you feel you are not the right person for me to be having this conversation with, and wish to summon others to meet here with me." The tone of voice was gentle and graceful, and Sergeant Bradenton looked over at the Queen with whom he was walking.

"Your Majesty, I am certainly not senior enough to be here as the first point of contact with you. I wish to summon the mayor and the chief of police for the city, and they will know much more about how to receive you properly, as well as make contact the right people at the national level who are supposed to be doing this. I do have a question, however, if I may be so impolite?"

"Certainly ask your question, good Sergeant. I will not think it rude of you."

"The woman in white who was floating in the air back there? Who is she?" He tried, and wasn't sure he succeeded, to keep the plaintive tone out of his voice.

"She is Anaradelle. She is a Mid-Goddess, as old as the Higher Races, it is believed."

"Ah. Ok." The answer would require some processing, he decided. "If you will forgive me? I must make a call." He bowed to her, then stepped away, pulling out his cell phone. This was certainly NOT something he wanted to put out on the police radio, especially with all the people with apps on their smart phones listening to everything that was said on those frequencies. Besides, he wasn't sure the person he was calling would be listening to the radio, but he absolutely would have his cell phone on him.

* * *

Anaradelle walked around the food court, looking at the amazing sights that were all around her. Since her pronouncement and formal resumption of her position in this plane's pantheon of Gods, she felt the presence of every human around her, and, distantly as if in the back of her mind, the presence of every human mortal alive on the planet. She saw the stares and looks from the people around her even as the men and women tried to move them away from her and everyone else that had come through the gate together. Some looked upon her in fear, many in awe, all with confusion on their faces or in their minds.

Many of those that had not been moved away yet, or refused to move, held up those "smart phones," as she had learned from Allison Wilhelm, towards her, obviously recording her movements for them to remember her by. She simply nodded to them as she passed them, continuing on without a word.

Something else she saw in the faces around her gave her pause. There were peoples from nearly every human tribe she could think of in this place. That never happened on the other planes where she held sway. Tribes kept to themselves. They rarely ever travelled outside their tribal areas, and because of that, mating between them almost never occurred. But here, she saw evidence of mixing of the tribes nearly everywhere. There was not a single face that was not the product of at least two different tribes of humanity, and some had so much mixed parentage in their faces and bodies that it was a challenge for her to identify them all.

Not that she minded one bit. She always felt the human mortals were so childish in how they kept to their own tribes, rarely joining with those outside of those they lived with. Differences were good, exotic, and challenging to the senses; when those differences were in the ones that one chose with which to spend the pleasures of the body, brought new experiences as well that were to be cherished. Then her eyes focused on one man, an older one, with darker skin and black hair that she was easily able to identify as from the Arabian tribe. He was speaking harshly at a younger woman of childbearing age who was holding the hand of a young man that, to Anaradelle's eyes, seemed to be the son of the older man.

She drew closer, and, with a slight surge of magical strength, gained the ability to understand what was being said.

"There is no God but Allah! You will not listen to the ravings of that Zionist whore. I do not care if she flew, or whatever else she did. She is no Goddess! You will be an obedient daughter-in-law, and do as I say! I will not tolerate your dishonorable tone to me or my son!"

The son spoke up, somewhat timidly, "Father, she means no disrespect. But even you cannot deny what you have seen. She flew! We understood in our own tongue what she said as well any others here…" He broke off speaking as the Goddess approached from over his father's shoulder, and his eyes got wide as he took in her glowing form, and the anger on her face.

"Who has done this to you, my child? Why is your womanhood scarred so?"

The father turned and saw the Goddess and swung his hand at her face as hard and fast as he could, catching her off guard. The slap impacted on her cheek with a loud SMACK. First the glow from her face turned red, then the white glow that emanated from the rest of her turned red as well.

She reached out and grasped the throat of the man that had hit her, and she lifted them both off the floor, floating upward as the man's hands tried in futile effort to break the hold of the hand that was slowly strangling him, his eyes bulging out.

"Gods and Goddesses are forbidden to strike out at mortals," she said with dark malice as the red glow turned so dark it was almost black in her anger. "However, there is one exception to the laws that limit a Deus from meting out punishment. That is when a Deus is struck first. It matters not if your intent was to harm or kill me, or just impertinence. I am freed to respond in any way I feel is just, including ending your life and trapping your soul in the Land of the Dead for all time." The voice of the Goddess penetrated his anger and fear, and it would have caused him to lose control of his bladder and bowels (if he had not relieved himself very recently) even as it caused every fiber of his body to vibrate, and he hung limply in the grasp of the Being that had lifted him so easily some fifty feet in the air.

"Given that there have been no true Gods, be they demigods, mid-gods, or the one true Greater God Sekur, to reach this plane in more than five thousand of your years, you did not know this. However, I can see in your memories that you have spoken these words to many of your fellow humans over the years before murdering them in the service of your religion: ignorance of law is no excuse."

She lowered herself back to the floor, still holding his limp but somewhat still conscious form by one hand. She then turned to the young man and his bride, and spoke to them in their own language.

"Children, attend me. You must give me great reason to allow this worm to stay in your lives any longer, for his mortal life is forfeit for striking me." They drew near, noses wrinkling at the smell of feces and urine that permeated the air surrounding the man.

The legacy of abuse and neglect leaves scars, physical and emotional and psychological. Jaun had the misfortune of being born the son of a powerful, angry man. Jaun's birth had been premature, and he had been small and weak, causing his father to give him a name that meant 'nameless plant' in his native language. The worst part of his life had been the impossible, never successful task of earning his father's respect. Now he looked at the powerful being that literally held his father's life and fate in his hands, and found he had nothing to say.

Zahirah had known Jaun's family for most of her life, and had not been surprised when her mother told her of the arranged marriage to Jaun, to be performed when she turned fifteen years old.

Jaun had been a kind and gracious husband. He didn't seem to have any of his father's anger or bitterness, and was happy to just be with Zahirah. He was three years older, and tried every chance he got to be nice to her. But when his father was not around he had explained to her that he could only protect her if she didn't talk to his father at all, unless he asked a question of her, which never happened. Even this time, Zahirah had not been talking to Saif al Din, only to Jaun. But Saif al Din had returned at that moment and heard her ask what she should believe about Anaradelle.

Saif al Din Al-Hadrami was nothing if not a truly devout Muslim. To him, everyone knew the order of life was God, followed by His Holy Prophet Mohammed, then His True Children (which were those followers of Islam who were devout and chosen by God to cleanse the world of wickedness and sin, such as one Saif Al Din Al-Hadrami, of course), then animals, followed by insects, then worms, below which was dirt, followed by the offal of the world, with infidels several steps below whatever was next. And Anaradelle, no matter her Satan-given magic tricks that fooled weaker, lesser minds, was the greatest infidel he had ever seen. She was nothing more than the manifestation in the flesh of all western excesses and blasphemies.

He saw then that he had failed to sufficiently educate his son's young wife. It was not enough for Jaun to do it; no, in order for her to be worthy of his son, no matter how worthless the boy was, she must be taught what was right by one of The True Children of Allah. He was confident that these fools at this foreign temple to excess and sin built with wealth stolen from the coffers of the Righteous would never raise a hand to him. He was one of the True Children! But it must never do to give Satan an opportunity to thwart his holy and just duty, so he would administer the beating Zahirah so required later, back at the hotel room, with her face covered by a pillow so the screams of her weakness would not pass to the hallway or the other rooms. He would settle for remonstrating her in their native tongue.

Except he lost his temper when the witch herself, that false goddess, walked up on them and interrupted him! The arrogance! He turned, and before he could stop himself, he lashed out at her. And everything he was taught about Allah was forgotten in an instant as she proved that she was no witch, no false Goddess with simple magic tricks meant to fool the weak-minded fools of this land of infidels.

Now, as his mind reeled at the sheer, overwhelming force of her presence, he found no handle with which to grasp rational thought once again, as the terror of his situation consuming his entire mind.

Zahirah spoke up, where her husband could not. "He is a righteous man of God. He is only doing what he must do to make me worthy of his son. I must have his teaching if I am to properly serve my husband, and not bring dishonor to my husband's family and my father-in-law."

Anaradelle was surprised that the one in front of her defended the man who beat her and cowed her with his religion. She had never heard about Stockholm Syndrome before, but as she looked into the mind of the young woman, not much more than a girl, really, she saw that the young woman had been raised from birth to believe that this was her rightful place, as chattel of the son of a fool who worshipped a non-existent God.

It was not enough to save Saif Al Din Al-Hadrami from his fate at the hands of the Goddess he struck, and she opened a gate to the Land of the Dead, before throwing him through it and closing the gate once more.

"Child, I ask you again, who has harmed you so grievously in your womanhood, and why?"

Zahirah hid her face, looking away from that pure visage, glowing white once more that her father-in-law was not here in front of them.

Almost imperceptibly, she spoke once more. "It was my mother. It was done to make me a chaste woman, who would not get trapped by the glories of the flesh and descend into the base desires of a whore, and instead would be a good and faithful wife to my husband."

"I will not let this stand." Anaradelle swept her hand forward, and a glowing green light came from her palm to wash over Zahirah's body, erasing the scars and injuries of a lifetime in a desolate third world country. That act of healing included what was left behind by the act of 'female circumcision' that had been inflicted on one nine-year-old Zahirah by her mother's hand, who received the same treatment from her mother at the same age. The mutilation was erased as if it had never happened before. The shocking act of the Goddess caused the young woman to gasp as every part of her felt like a gentle breeze washed over her. Then the Goddess stood and spoke once more, and her voice carried once again to every human being on the entire planet.

"The peoples of any tribe on this plane that practices barbaric acts on its children in the name of chastity and religion are unworthy of my favor. No children will be born to peoples who do these things for one hundred summers." This pronouncement carried across the entire world as well, and the anger in that voice was clear. The ramifications of the message were not understood until sometime later.

* * *

The call from Sergeant Bradenton, who was a twenty year veteran of the Police Department, and someone that his fellow officers and superiors recognized as being not over emotional nor given to flights of fanciful speculation, caused some initial consternation. An Elven Queen and a Goddess at the country's biggest indoor shopping mall? It was nowhere near Halloween, which brought a somewhat under control laugh from the officer that answered the call. Instead of calling for the boys in the white coats to visit the good Sergeant, he told him he would inform the chief. The chief of police, likewise, briefly considered a call to the psych ward, but the city center was only a short distance away, and the he decided that Bradenton deserved at least the consideration to investigate what was bothering one of his officers, so he walked to the Mayor's office, and leaned in, knocking on the door frame to get the elected official's attention.

"Got a minute, Geoff?"

"Sure, what's up, Mark?" The mayor looked up and smiled. Geoff Smith and Mark Kaminski had developed a working relationship that probably would turn to genuine friendship once the mayor's time in office ended. As such, they talked quite a bit, about everything city and job related, to just how completely they both disliked Green Bay Packers fans.

"Well, Sergeant Bradenton called in and spoke with Captain Masterson, who came to me. Bradenton is out at the Mall right now, and he said he needs both of us to respond to a situation he is in." Mark was not really sure he wanted to repeat what Andrew had said to him, and paused to try to figure out the best way to convey the message without undermining the veteran sergeant in the Mayor's eyes.

Geoff instantly turned his entire attention to his Chief of Police, and his entire body seemed tense and worried. "What's happening over there?"

"Well, I'm not really sure. Bradenton asked for you because he said there is a potential diplomatic situation that needs to be addressed that is above the pay grade of a police officer." He paused again, and Geoff waited for him to continue for a moment, before speaking up.

"We have no information on a high-ranking foreign head of state visiting the Mall, right? Did someone show up unannounced?" Geoff disliked doing dog and pony shows for foreign visitors, but hid that from everyone as much as possible. It would never be good to let everyone know that the Mayor was less than polite and politically correct, but he was pretty sure that Mark had figured it out.

Mark sighed. "Nope, no one is on the schedule. Those usually get worked up in advance. This one, though, has me wondering if Andrew needs a vacation, or something. No, that's not really fair to Bradenton. He's a great officer, and I'm glad to have him under me."

"Well, then what is it?" The question could have come across as impatient, but Geoff wasn't 'that guy', something that made him a very good person to work for, in Mark's opinion.

"He said there is an Elven Queen and a Goddess at the mall, and that he needs someone above him to take point on this. Frankly, I think we should go and see what is going on for ourselves. If Bradenton is having a bad day, we should help the good man out. Are you up for a short road trip?"

Geoff tried not to let his jaw bounce off the desk in front of him, and could only stare for a few moments.

"Do you have concerns about Sergeant Bradenton?" The question came out carefully, and Mark frowned as he considered it, before shaking his head.

"I don't really think so. Bradenton is a retired U.S. Marine, and saw combat on two tours in Afghanistan while in the Reserves. If he was going to come apart even a little bit, it would have happened then. I have seen no indications that he might be leaning in that direction. He is not on the list of people I would expect to be considering taking a break from reality."

"Oh, you have a list? Am I on it?" Geoff smiled slightly.

"You were the reason I started the list, actually," Mark said with a completely straight face, which drew a laugh from the mayor. Then he frowned when his police captain didn't join in the mirth. "Wait, really?"

CHAPTER 41

As these things tend to happen when put together at the last moment, the entrance into the huge shopping mall by the mayor and chief of police of the city in which the mall was located was a hurried affair. Two extra patrol units, with two officers in each, were detailed to assist with any security needs that might arise, along with the already sizeable police presence in the mall itself. A few people here and there in the busy mall recognized the mayor as he and his police chief made their way to the food court to investigate the observations the good sergeant had related about forty minutes earlier, but for the most part, the trip by the two city officials was mostly unnoticed.

The Queen had reacquired her gentle hold on Sergeant Bradenton's arm in the time since he had made his phone call and returned to her to report his superiors were on their way. After an introduction to Karonashkk the Minotaur, she had walked with him to the edge of the floor area that overlooked the amusement park built into the center of the huge building, and had asked him question after question about the place, what the strange metal things were in the park and what they were used for, and many other questions, as quickly as she could think of them.

Anaradelle had not been idle during this time, either. After healing Zahirah and Jaun, she had spoken with them both for a while, as a crowd of people (most with smartphones in hand recording the impossible event) that leaked past the containment the police and security guards were having trouble maintaining, gathered around them. She had no need for protection, and something about her kept the crowd of people from getting too unruly as they watched her move through them. She paused to touch some, murmuring blessings and healings on them as she went, while also stooping to pick up children and hug them, before returning them to their parents.

The crowds were growing larger as word slowly spread throughout the huge mall that something unusual was happening, and people made their way to see what was going on. Before long, she decided, she would need to speak to these people, to tell them about her role in their lives, and what it meant to live in a plane where she was Deus of Life's Mortal Path. First, though, she had much to learn about them, as they were so very different from every other group of humans she had ever found. Just this huge, magnificent building alone was enough to convince her of that. This would take some time on her part before she could start goading them in the right way.

Geoff and Mark saw the gathering of police officers, Elven guards with staffs, and the Minotaur, and headed in that direction. The Queen was simply standing at the railing with her hand in the crook of Bradenton's elbow as they approached.

Mark led the way as they began to get closer, with Geoff standing a bit back to assess what was happening before he would enter the situation. Geoff shifted to his left, and suddenly got a good look at the Elven guardswoman standing there. His mouth dropped open as he looked into the non-human eyes of an elven warrior for the first time in his life, taking in the different eye color and the green-hued skin. Momentarily speechless, he didn't know what to say, before bumping in to what he thought was a huge statue of a Minotaur, although how these people had managed to lug such a massive thing through the crowds to the food court was beyond his thinking—

"Excuse me, good human. I apologize for being in your way." The deep bass voice seemed to come from above him, and he looked up to see what he had just a moment before thought was a statue staring down at him with a smile on its face and humor in its voice. He jumped back quickly, and started to stammer out some nonsensical words, when the massive creature spoke to him again, holding out one huge red-skinned hand.

"I must be polite and introduce myself, good human. I am Karonashkk, protector of Queen Delara, Her Majesty of the Elven Throne. I greet you, and humbly ask your name, so we might be known to each other." The smile continued after Karonashkk stopped speaking, but the hand out in offer of a handshake didn't waver one bit.

"Uhh, I, ahhh, I am Geoff Smith. I am the mayor of the city this mall is located in." He offered his hand gingerly to the hugely muscled being in the kilt, and the minotaur took it in a warrior's clasp forearm to forearm, shaking his hand gently, before letting it go.

"It is an honor to meet a leader of these crafty humans. This place is an amazing thing to a simple protector such as I. How many men and women build this place, and how long did it take them?" He looked around with a huge smile on his face with a sweep of his left arm, before turning his smile back to Mark.

"It took a few years to complete, and I know it took thousands of men and women to build it. This is the largest mall of its kind in this country, although there is a larger one in Canada, the country to the north of us, in Edmonton, Alberta." He winced internally as he lapsed into tour-guide mode. Must be a defensive mechanism, he told himself.

"This place is truly dazzling to me, good Geoff." The conversation carried on for a few minutes as the mayor continued providing answers to the questions that the minotaur asked, amazed inside that he was having such a mundane conversation, the likes of which he had been in dozens of times before, with a being he had never conceived of meeting in his life outside the ancient books of Greece he had read in school a long time ago.

"Sergeant Bradenton," Mark Kalinski spoke up as he got within hearing range of the two people looking over the railing, "Will you introduce me, please?"

Andrew turned somewhat quickly at the familiar voice, relieved that he was finally able to turn the Queen over to someone much higher up in the official political food chain. As he turned, Delara turned with him to face the Chief of the Bloomington police department.

Mark's breath caught in his throat as he looked upon the face of the woman in front of him, and he realized that she was not, in fact, human. The ears were the dead giveaway, he decided. No one would ever be able to make fake ears that perfect. The delicate structure was graceful and unlike anything he had ever imagined. Then he realized that Bradenton was speaking to him, and focused on the officer in front of him.

"… and Chief Mark Kalinski, I present to you Her Majesty, Queen Delara of the Elven Throne." He bowed slightly, then stepped back, getting out of the conversation slightly, but still close enough to be at hand if needed.

"Police Chief Mark Kalinski, it is an honor to meet you. As I have said to your good sergeant, I apologize for not sending word on ahead of my visit, but my people have no representatives here through which to present such notice, and I am young and impetuous enough to simply ignore propriety and rush in. I see now that this has quite possibly caused a stir amongst your peoples, and I apologize for it," the Elven Queen said in a somewhat contrite tone of voice, but the smile on her face showed her good humor at the situation. He was about to speak up, but she continued onwards.

"Your Sergeant Bradenton has been the vision of courtesy and respect. I commend you for the honorable way your guardsman has greeted us. He is to be valued."

"Thank you, Your Majesty." Mark decided to grant her the benefit of the doubt as to her royal status. He had no idea how she got here, or where she was from, but she certainly wasn't human. Everything about her screamed different, even alien, but the whole situation was so far outside his normal realm of experience and expectations that he was having trouble processing what was happening here.

Then he saw who was alongside the Queen, and glanced over at the Mayor, who was engaged in a conversation with the huge, red-skinned non-human. The look on Geoff Smith's face almost caused him to lose his mind with laugher, but he held it together barely. Then he glanced up at the massive minotaur, and swallowed, taking in the fierce bull face and horns, the long red hair braided down one side of his head and over his shoulder, the massive muscles, and, most importantly, the massive war hammer slung on a leather strap over the shoulder of the impossible being.

"Ahh, Your Majesty, is this being behind you with your party?" He was amazed at the level, even tone of voice the question came out in, given that he was almost certain his knees were a little weak and his hands were shaking.

"Yes?" The queen looked over her shoulder, and smiled fondly at her chief bodyguard, then looked back at the human in front of her, who was trying gamely to pull his eyes back to her.

"Yes, this is Karonashkk. He is my personal bodyguard when I travel away from the Elven Throne. When I am back there, he is my chief jailer and the head of the guard force assigned to protect me in my home. He is, well, unless you threaten me or my companions or guards, he is gentle. And he loves children. He will play with them until everyone is tired enough to sleep the night through. And, he is my poet when I am in need of words to express myself."

Karonashkk stepped up and looked down at Mark, who was a good six foot and two inches tall, without looking down on him. His smile was warm and genuine, and he held out a massive hand in greeting.

Mark reached to take it, but before he was able to grasp the hand coming towards him, it reached past his hand and gently grasped his forearm in a warrior's greeting, something he remembered from his time in the Army Special Forces on deployment to such interesting locales all those years ago. He smiled as he returned the gesture, clasping his fingers onto, but not around, the Minotaur's thick forearm in greeting.

"I am honored to meet you, good sir. And I am amazed at this building you humans have made here. I could spend days here, and still not see everything," Karonashkk said with amazement, and Mark smiled.

"We sometimes wonder how many people would be willing to stay here day and night if it was open all the time. It is a pretty great place, but it can be a headache to keep the peace here," Mark said, wondering why he was being so forthcoming. Then that little analytical place in the back of his head told him he was mentally off balance, and he smiled as he tried to center himself.

"I was told there was a Goddess around here as well?" He inquired politely, and the Queen nodded.

"Her name is Anaradelle. She is the Human Goddess of Children, Fertility, and Nature." The queen spoke gently, as if to not cause offense to the deity.

Things were suddenly much clearer to the chief of police. Sometime earlier, he had heard Anaradelle's pronouncement in his mind, and had wondered what his subconscious was coming up with this time. He had errant, random thoughts bubble up into his mind from who knows where from time to time, and he always wondered what was going on with that. It didn't happen all that often, but it did come up once in a while, and had been since he was a teenager. By the time Anaradelle had made her statement, he had become so used to it, he just thought it was his mind up to its usual tricks, and moved on efficiently, as he had so many times in recent memory.

Now, though, he reevaluated that memory, in light of the Queen's statement identifying the deity in question.

The queen continued, "She came through the gate that my son called to bring us to this plane, at the invitation of Michelle Wilhelm, who herself has recently ascended to Deus. I am not certain, but from her actions and mannerisms, Anaradelle may have been here to this plane before."

"She is really a goddess?" Mark's professional skepticism was still stubbornly demanding equal time with his slowly growing sense of wonder at what was happening around him, and it tried to gain control as it forced the question out of him.

"Oh yes. She certainly is that. She is a Mid-Goddess. There are few Mid-Deus more powerful on any plane. We do not know her age, or when she ascended to become a deity. Most deities are much younger, and there are records of when they ascend.

"Anaradelle is ancient, possibly the oldest in any plane. I would advise you be gentle and respectful to her. She brooks no disrespect. She has already dealt harshly here with one mortal who slapped her." The serious tone in Delara's voice almost made him step back as he tried to gage the truth of what was being said to him. He found no indications of any falsehood, and that made him frown in grim concentration.

"There is another here, as well, but she is keeping to herself. I am certain she will reveal herself when she has come to terms with her new nature."

Mark's mind tried to come to terms with what he was being told, but the concept of a female deity was difficult to process. But what to do next was decided for him as a female being with pure white skin and hair, with eyes so pale that their yellow color glowed with internal light that reminded him of the sun, drifted through the air past the police officers and security guards who were trying, with some success, to keep the mall customers away from the commotion. She headed towards the center of the Queen's group of guards, her companions.

She came to land next to the queen herself, off to the chief's left, and the slight, almost delicate form of what could only be the Goddess Anaradelle observed him silently for a short moment. Then she turned to Delara, and spoke to her in a language the chief didn't understand that was full of lilting words and graceful transitions from sound to sound.

Delara noticed Mark's lack of comprehension, and motioned to one of her Elven guardswomen, who stepped closer, and reached into a pouch at her hip. The guardswoman pulled out some brown grasses and a couple small leaves, and closed her hand around them, chanting a brief phrase in that same tongue. The contents of her hand disappeared in a small flash, and the guardswoman held out her hand to the police chief as if in greeting.

When their hands touched, a brief spark left his hand tingling as the guardswoman pulled her hand back, and then Delara held out her hand to Mark, while still facing Anaradelle as she listened to the Goddess speaking to her. He took her hand, and with another tingle, he suddenly could understand everything the Goddess was saying to the queen.

"…and I must leave you here now because of it. I have much to do on this plane to return it to some semblance of how things should be under my guidance. I am, as always, available to you should you have need. Just call to me as you have in the past, and I will come to you as soon as I am able, my child."

Delara bowed her head briefly in acknowledgement, and Anaradelle turned to Mark. She smiled warmly at him for a moment then simply disappeared in an instant. He felt a brief current of air as her physical form vanished and air rushed in to fill the sudden empty space that she left behind.

The crowds watching the impossible event in front of them gasped as the goddess disappeared into thin air, and more people were moving into the area all the time to see for themselves what was being reported by their friends and family members, as social media and Twitter accounts began to fill with reports of the happening. The officers and guards suddenly found themselves trying to hold back the tide in their efforts to evacuate the area, as more people flowed in for every group that agreed to leave. Not many were willing to go, though.

Mark turned to Delara, and asked, "Is she always that way?"

Delara smiled as Mark spoke in the language the Goddess had just been using. Mark's eyes got very wide, and his face went a little pale as he realized he spoke in a language he had never heard until just moments ago.

Geoff looked at his friend in utter shock, unable to say a word as the alien words that had just come from Mark's mouth came to him. He stepped up to Mark, and asked, "What did you just say?"

Mark was still trying to collect his thoughts when the question hit him, and he turned to the mayor of the city and said, "Huh? What?"

Geoff tried to throttle a laugh as his highly intelligent and well-educated police chief was at a loss for words, something he had never seen from the incredibly unflappable man who never seemed to be fazed by anything.

"Mark, you need a moment, pal?"

"No, I think I'm good. Your Majesty, what just happened?" He made sure the question came out in English so that Geoff could follow it this time.

"My guardswoman cast a spell on you, which let you learn the language of the next person you touched," Delara spoke in English. "That next person was me. You now speak my Elven tongue. The mages that study such things say there are limits to it. Your skill in the new language is limited by how much you have learned of your own tongue, and how much I have learned of mine. I am considered to be among the best-spoken of my people, so I am the best choice. But were you not a good and honorable being, I would have not had my guard cast the spell."

The explanation was simple enough, and Mark understood it on the surface, but the deeper implications were impossible to understand in their entirety in the moment. A simple spell could enable someone to learn an entire language, fully to the level of their own abilities and that of the person they touched? Mark's mind spun at the thought.

Then he turned to Delara, and said, "If anyone should have that ability, it should be Geoff Smith, here. Let me introduce you. Delara, I present Geoff Smith. He is mayor of the city in which this shopping center is located. Mister Mayor, may I present to you Her Majesty Delara, Queen of the Elven Throne."

Geoff had some previous experience with greeting visiting nobility, as was required by the presence of the largest shopping mall in the United States of America in his city; it was a requirement of being in the office with which he was elected. Of course, the people from the U.S. State Department had never envisioned a queen of a different intelligent race of beings happening to be one of them, he was fairly certain.

People Who Knew Such Things had always informed him ahead of a critical visit, and at that time told him that he needed to read up on what protocols he was expected to know ahead of time, before such a visit were to take place. Of course, this situation deviated in a couple of significant ways from what would normally happen. For one, he would have been told quite a while in advance that such a visit would be taking place. And two, the visiting dignitary would have been accompanied by someone from the State Department to make introductions. He nearly smiled while in the impossible situation at the thought that the U.S. Secretary of State was not doing a good job this time. Still, he had his manners and his past experience to fall back on.

"Your Majesty, It is an honor to welcome you to our city." He bowed his head and upper body briefly, then straightened up again.

"Please, call me Delara. I am not in my formal throne room, and all these titles simply serve to prop up the ego of a being that has no need of such things." Delara motioned to the guardswoman, who repeated the spell on Geoff. Then the queen reached out her hand, and Geoff, unsure if it was the right thing to do, but not willing to insult the woman in front of him if he refused, took it in a brief shake while a tingle shot up his arm and into his head.

Delara seemed unconcerned about protocol or how things should be done, however. She continued on with the conversation.

"This is a magnificent building we are in, is it not? Your people are indeed master builders and makers. I have seen a Suburban carriage, the offices of Michelle and David's merchant company in the center of your town, and the impossibly tall buildings there. My son has told us some things about this place, and while every bit of it so far has been true, none of it was complete. I shall have to speak at length with my difficult child, and ascertain why he has been so evasive."

The youngster in question stepped forward at that moment, and bowed formally and briefly to his mother, something that earned him a smile and a light slap on the shoulder for his trouble.

"Mother, would you have believed me if I had spoken true? Or would you have simply decided I had spent too much time in my cups, taken with ale?"

A somewhat overly-dramatic, long-suffering sigh escaped the queen. "Ah, my son, you have learned much in your three hundred and more summers of life, but I see the simplest things still escape you. I see I must have my Minotaur chastise you once more, as he did when you were young."

The massive being appeared at Delara's shoulder as if he teleported there, moving so silently that even the elven guards who knew him seemed to be surprised. Karonashkk bent down to Giltreas and glared at him for a moment, then spoke up in English.

"Don't do that again. Behave yourself, child! This is your mother! And your queen! And the woman who once chased you as a child across the breadth of her city for hiding her crown! Don't forget what happened that time." The tone of voice might have been quelling, but the huge smile on Karonashkk's face as he failed to maintain his composure gave away what he was really thinking.

"I seem to recall that working out for everyone, my old friend." The gentle voice was soft, but the smile on the man's face was anything but.

Delara sighed and turned back to Geoff. "I must introduce my offspring, I see. Giltreas, this is Geoff, the mayor of this city. And Geoff, this is my miscreant, idle, lay-about, barbarian son, who never ceases in his efforts to make me fervently wish that I'd had a girl child."

Giltreas simply laughed lightly and held out his hand to Geoff. Geoff tried to keep a straight face as he relaxed inside, shaking hands with the unusual looking man in front of him.

"It is an honor to meet you, Prince Giltreas." Gil shook his head at the greeting.

"I am no prince. I have no titles, nor claim to the Throne, nor any interest in such, and it is best for all concerned that way. I am happy enough to simply be Giltreas, or Gil, if you prefer."

"Gil it is, then. It is an honor to meet you. Did she say that you are over three hundred years old?"

"I have seen three hundred and twenty-six summers. Because of that, I am still considered to be young and impetuous by my mother. She feels that I must reach something closer to her eight hundred and more summers before my judgment is to be trusted. I, of course, have no arguments with my ancient, decrepit progenitor, who may, herself, need to live another thousand summers before she realizes that I am old enough to dress myself without assistance."

Karonashkk leaned forward. "For myself, I am not sure you will ever able to. What are you wearing?" he asked with a smile.

"You should have a care at what you say. I happen to know what you have on under that wrap, my friend."

Karonashkk just laughed. Then he turned and looked at the growing crowd that was gathering around them. The sounds of the mall, previously echoing with the shouts and laugher of children on the rides and the games below them, and the sounds of people walking and talking as they went about their business at the huge facility, were slowly growing more silent as word spread about the strange people and the even stranger being with the head of a bull and dark red skin that accompanied them. The sounds of the crowd gathered to observe the spectacle they were creating, however, was something else. While it was not yet getting ugly, an undercurrent that the Minotaur could not quite identify seemed to be there just below the surface, and it concerned him. He decided that it was not something to act upon yet, but it bore watching, just the same.

One braver young boy, maybe eight years old, broke free from his mother's grip, while she struggled to carry some bags and control a stroller, and ran forward towards him, only to slow as he got closer. The young boy looked up at the huge being who that bent gently down to appear less threatening, before descending carefully to his knees. With his head now just about eye level to the boy, he smiled, without moving forward. He was used to seeing fear in a human's eyes as they saw his race for the first time, which would usually departed when he started to speak, or shortly thereafter. These humans, if Giltreas was to be believed, though, had never seen anyone like him before, and he decided to be very gentle and careful. He had learned a long time ago that it was important to dispel fears, rather than reinforce them.

He looked up at the boy's mother, whose protectiveness of her child overruled her fear of the unknown to reach out to the boy. His smile was somewhat goofy as he tried to be as non-threatening as possible.

"Your boy is very brave, good lady. As are you. What are your names? I am Karonashkk, chief guard to Queen Delara."

"I'm William. This is my mom." The boy spoke up before his mother could stop him, or get a word in first.

"William is a good name. It is good to meet you, William. And William's mother, it is good to meet you as well."

"Uuhh, yeah, thank you. It's good to meet you as well. I'm Elizabeth." The woman seemed unsure of what to do next, but William pressed on.

"Where did you come from? What are you?" William's voice was filled with awe and curiosity.

"William! Don't be rude!" She tried to shush him, but Karonashkk just laughed gently.

"I am not offended, dear lady. I am from the Elven City. I am a Minotaur. I serve the Queen as her chief bodyguard when she travels. When she is in her home, I am the keeper of her jails. I keep bad beings locked up so they cannot hurt good people."

Geoff turned back to Delara and Mark with a smile on his face as the conversation between the boy, his mother and the Minotaur carried on. "What an amazing person. Still, I would hate to see what he could do with that hammer, should he become upset." It was a pointed statement from the mayor, and Delara caught the undercurrent in it.

"I assure you, Karonashkk is not given to violence, or even bad manners. If he were, I would not rely upon him so. Ease your mind." Delara stated lightly, but clearly.

"Forgive me. I have a responsibility to the safety of the public and the property of the city we are in."

"I agree. We shall speak no more of such things, unless need arises."

The improbable conversation between the elven queen and the human mayor continued for a few minutes, before the police chief intervened. "I regret to say this, Your Majesty, but this situation is causing problems for the people who own the stores and shops here in the mall. We have been keeping people away from you to protect both your party and the shoppers here, which is cutting into the business that these people depend on for their livelihood. Is it possible that we might postpone this or take it up somewhere else?"

The queen nodded. "We mustn't harm others, and if my being here is causing harm, we must withdraw. Giltreas, will you please see that everyone that came with us is ready to return to either the throne room or David and Michelle's company building?"

Giltreas nodded, and walked off to round everyone up. He told Karonashkk that they were intending to move back through the gate, and asked his red-skinned friend to help get everyone ready to go.

Karonashkk nodded seriously to his friend, and then reached out to William to clasp arms with the young boy, whose eyes got wide as he experienced the warrior's greeting for the first time. Then Karonashkk did the same to Elizabeth, before standing up to his full height and looked around. His organized mind checked off everyone on the list, excluding Anaradelle who was obviously off on her own and capable of going anywhere and doing anything she wished, until he came to the two dwarves. They were nowhere to be seen.

A quick question to the elven guards came up empty as well. No one had any idea where they had gotten off to. Karonashkk reported this to Giltreas, who relayed it to Delara.

Geoff frowned as he and Mark heard that two non-humans were missing from the unusual group of non-humans. David and Allison heard the report as well, and started looking around. Allison turned to Mark and said, "Can your officers find them? They have no idea where they are, or what kind of trouble they might be able to get into. Here, this is my cell phone number," she said, pulling out a crumpled business card from her pocket and handed it over. "I think we are going to have to leave without them if we can't find them. I need to be notified as soon as you can make contact with them, and we will be back to pick them up."

Mark nodded. "I have no idea what they look like, though. Do you have a picture or something?"

Allison smiled. "Or something. Give me a minute." She dug into one of the small, square-shaped leather pouches that adorned her belt, and pulled out something. Then she held it in both hands, murmured some words, and a glowing image appeared above her hands at eye level.

Mark gasped as the illusion took shape. It was a realistic, three-dimensional representation of the heads and shoulders of two missing dwarves, and he nodded. Then he looked up as Allison spoke up.

"You got a smart phone? Take a picture before the spell wears off."

Mark whipped out his phone and took several shots before the spell faded. Then he pulled Sergeant Bradenton over and showed him the images. "These two are missing from the group. We need to round them up carefully and gently. Remember they are not from around here, so be on your best behavior, as we have no idea how they are capable of responding.

The queen and her main group here are graciously planning to leave right away. As soon as the two wayward ones are found, we need to call Allison's cell number. I will send the pics to your phone, but spread the word quickly to your people. I don't want them to come to any harm, or get in trouble." He glanced at the perimeter and frowned.

"I don't think we will be able to get these people to leave. If I am correct, inform your people and the guards that they will have to hold the perimeter. It shouldn't be much longer before they leave, and that should diffuse the situation and give them nothing to be interested in."

The queen made the decision to move back to the MDST building as soon as possible, and allow Allison to be the point of contact for the police when they found the two wayward dwarves. The police and security guards were now no longer trying to evacuate the food court area, and were forced to simply try to hold everyone back from the queen and her retinue. Some were calling for reinforcements, and more of both guards and officers were slowly trickling in from other parts of the mall to help contain the crowd and prevent them from intermingling with the

Giltreas called up a gate to the lobby back at the downtown MDST building after David called the security desk to warn them, and Delara turned to Geoff.

"Would you wish to come with us and continue our conversation? We will return you to here if you wish when we are done."

Geoff thought about it for a moment, and the once-in-a-lifetime opportunity wasn't lost on him. "I need to take at least one officer with me. Where would we be going?"

Delara nodded. "We are going to the center of this city, where David's business is located. No further, I promise. And your officer is welcome. I promise no harm will come to either of you."

Geoff nodded, and turned to Mark. "Shall we?"

Mark nodded. He had good people here, and trusted them to resolve the situation and locate the two missing dwarves. He turned to Sergeant Bradenton and told him, "I will be reachable by cell or radio, if you need me. They will return me back immediately if I am needed. In the meantime, here are the keys to my cruiser, if you need them. I will be back to get them from you when we are done."

"I need to be back in no more than an hour, though, and I know you do, too."

Geoff nodded in reply. "Agreed." He turned to Delara. "We are ready."

As the last few members of the group trooped through the gate, William broke free from his mother again and bolted past Karonashkk (who was planning on being the last one through as a rear guard) to run through the gate as well, as his mother screamed in shock and fear.

Some in the crowd, who had become disappointed that the show would obviously be over soon, called out as the boy shot past everyone and leaped into the glowing thing and disappeared from view.

The Minotaur surged through the gate and caught up to the young boy, before picking him up gently but quickly and turned to go back through to the mall.

Elizabeth nearly sagged in relief as the huge red-skinned being suddenly appeared, almost as quickly as he had left, back through the gate with the struggling boy in his arms. He set the boy down and held him at arm's length as his mother came up and grabbed the boy by the arm. "What were you thinking?!?" She shrieked as she pulled him close to her.

"Mom! I was just - " He tried to speak up, but she wasn't having any of it.

"You could have been lost! I might never have seen you again! What were you thinking!?!" Her anger and fear coursed through her as tears threatened to break free.

Karonashkk spoke up calmly and quietly. "I would allow no harm to come to your beloved child. He is a normal, curious young boy who made a bad choice. William, you must not do such things to your mother. She cares greatly for you, and her life would be in ruin if anything happened to you. You must think of your mother before doing anything like that ever again."

William looked up at his mother, and saw the pain and fear in her eyes as she glared down at him, and it made him feel awful. He couldn't find the words to say, but instead reached out and wrapped his arms around his mother and held on tight, suddenly aware of just how foolish his act had been.

Elizabeth looked over her son's head at the huge being that had brought her son back to her, and mouthed, "Thank you," her arms still clasped tightly around her only child. Karonashkk merely nodded and smiled, then turned to walk through the gate as the sounds of the crowd being held back by the growing line of police officers and security guards got louder and more unruly. Then an abrupt silence covered the spectators as the Minotaur walked through the gate and it disappeared behind him as if it were never there.

CHAPTER 42

"Svetlana, we need to have a conversation."

"What is it, Poppa?" Svetlana looked up from her book. Her mother had taken her younger brother shopping, and they were alone in their apartment.

Now Svetlana frowned as the serious look on her father's face registered.

"Sveta, I have been told that there are people out there who know what you can do, and they want to gain control of you."

Svetlana nodded. "I imagine both sides of the law want that. This is not unexpected. My teacher has prepared me for this."

Borysko's mouth dropped open. "You know? How do you know?"

"Poppa, I am certain that more than one person recorded what happened outside the police station in Tbilisi that day. Those recordings will find their way to people who have an interest in it."

The calm voice of his daughter was... indescribably calm and serene. But before he could say anything, she spoke up again.

"No one will stop until I tell them to. I need to send a message. Here's what I want to do."

They argued about it for almost two hours before Borysko gave in. Svetlana answered every objection as best she could, and there really wasn't any better, or even any at all, idea that he came up with. There was really no other option. It would take a few days to set up, or longer, but Svetlana was content to wait while preparations were made.

* * *

"Mister President, we have a situation."

"What sort of situation?" President Geoffrey Thomas Morrison had been sitting in the Oval Office, meeting with two U.S. Senators. Senator Malcom Kurtzman from South Dakota, the democratic Majority leader and ranking Democratic member of the U.S. Senate Judicial Committee, was sitting on the right end of the couch, with Senator Brendan Webster, the Republican Minority Leader and ranking Republican member of the Judicial Committee, sitting on the left in some sort of weird juxtaposition at odds with their political affiliation, They were there to discuss the current budgetary standoff with the President, when his chief of staff had opened the door and spoken into the room.

"Sir, there have been some incidents that we need to bring to your attention. The media team has assembled a briefing, and we can show it to you here in the Oval, if you prefer."

"Can it wait? I am meeting with these two fine gentlemen at the moment." He smiled at the two senators, who smiled back, before turning back to his trusted associate.

"Sir, I don't believe so. I think they will want to see this as well."

Nearly an hour later, the President was at a loss for words, having seen the footage from Minnesota of a teenage boy named Daniel resurrecting a college girl, the footage of the unicorn from some unknown location in the country, the entire Sanderson prison footage, which made everyone in the room wince at several points, which came before the footage of Congresswoman Smithson implicating herself as one of the heads of a conspiracy to kidnap and murder the owners of a privately held high-tech corporation in Minneapolis. That was followed by several video clips of a being calling herself the Goddess Anaradelle, which triggered memories of her voice in their minds making some impossible statements.

Finally was the footage from the Mall of America of the exotic woman calling herself the Elven Queen. There were almost a dozen clear, high-definition videos of her in all her glory, including some close-up footage, that had to have been taken with a very good high-definition camcorder with an excellent zoom lens, that was able to show that the green-skinned woman with the pointed ears was not wearing makeup. It was clearly obvious that she really was not human from the footage available to them.

"Man, what is in the water up in Minnesota? Have we been able to confirm any of what we just saw? I don't know where to begin. Let's see, the most immediate thing I am concerned with is Congresswoman Smithson. What do we know about that?"

"We don't have any idea where she is at the moment, or who recorded or uploaded the video. The techs at the FBI, the CIA, and those guys at the NSA are all looking into the video, and the FBI is searching for Smithson, to get her side of the situation. NBC News had an expert in special effects on the news this evening that swears that footage would be all but impossible to fake. We have researched the Wilhelm people and have been unable to find any trace of Michelle Wilhelm and Allison Wilhelm; that's the sister and the wife, respectively."

Senator Kurtzman shook his head. "I can't believe that any member of congress would be stupid enough to talk about their involvement in a plot like that, and with three people in the room holding video cameras. Wow."

"I have to reevaluate my opinion of my colleague in the House, I am afraid. I knew she was ambitious and single-minded, but this is... beyond the pale, should the situation show itself to be as she has said." Senator Webster shook his head as the President nodded. The Republican was laying the groundwork to hedge his bets and distance himself and his party from a rogue member that seemed to be intent on crashing and burning in a singularly spectacular fashion. Not that Kurtzman would have been saying anything fundamentally different were the roles reversed. That was how the game was played.

President Morrison nodded. "This cannot be about containment, because the footage is out on the Internet already. We need to determine what happened in that situation before we have angry mobs storming D.C. We need to get out in front of that, and deal with her directly. With the public's perception of the government as low as it could possibly be because of the entire NSA contractor situation, this is the biggest threat we could have to our democracy right now."

The senators nodded. While they were in creatures of partisan politics, and old hands at the inter-party warfare that was the accepted norm in congress, they both saw the need to preserve the functionality of the government, for obvious reasons.

Just then the door to the Oval Office opened and the head of the FBI hurried in, followed by the Attorney General.

Eric Glickh, the current Attorney General, spoke first. "Good day, Mister President. Your chief of staff told us you were here. I hope you don't mind the intrusion?"

"No, Eric, of course not. You definitely would have been called if you didn't show up. It looks like we are facing a number of situations here that I need to get up to speed on. Have a seat. We were just discussing the Congresswoman Smithson situation. What do either of you know about it?"

Both men found their seats after shaking hands with the two Senators in the room. Then the head of the FBI spoke up.

"To be honest, very little," Harald Kirkpatrick said. "I was notified about the video about ten minutes into the newscast, and I immediately set a team up to locate and interview her. We have to assume that the video is legitimate.

"My analysts tell me the same thing that was said on NBC, that the video would be very difficult to fake. The strange thing is, why would she be so forthcoming in the first place? That is the question I have been asking myself and my entire staff since I saw it. No one is coming up with any answers on that one, so far.

"We also have a team trying to locate Michelle Wilhelm, David Wilhelm, and Allison Wilhelm, although I understand David Wilhelm surfaced at the Mall of America yesterday morning in that incident, or incidents, I should say."

"Why do you say multiple incidents?"

"Well, the videos we are seeing seem to indicate that there are two separate beings we need to focus on.

"First, the Elven Queen and her party. We have a number of very good videos of her and her party. While it might be possible, no matter how difficult, to fake up her appearance, that Minotaur with her would be impossible to fake. We don't know of any people living right now of that height that would be able to fit inside a costume and makeup.

"The tallest known man in the world right now is Sultan Kösen of Turkey, and according to immigration records, he is not in the country at the moment. I don't think he has ever been in the U.S. None of the other men known to be alive today that might be able to fit into a costume like that are on U.S. soil, either. Besides, the videos we have seen show that the facial features of that… being… are fully articulate in a way that is impossible to fake outside of Hollywood special effects in a movie. The queen herself is also covered in lots of different clips that have all appeared on virtually every social media and video sharing website.

"Additionally, if there was only one video, only one source for footage of the… Minotaur, it would be easier to say it was faked. But there are just as many clips of the creature on the Internet, and every one of them is from a different perspective, because they all were shot by different people. Not to mention, footage from multiple cameras from the mall security monitoring system also shows the creature. While not as close up, obviously, the footage from those cameras is completely consistent with the other videos online, and all of it overlaps. The creature is real. And, apparently, is highly intelligent and speaks excellent English."

"Hmmm. Ok, I have no idea what to do with that situation. What about the other being that you are talking about from that same mall?"

"Well, you've seen the footage?" The President nodded.

"I don't have any idea what to make of it, or of her. This Goddess, this Anaradelle, is also some unknown being that we don't have any information about."

"Has anyone done a search to see if the name has been mentioned in anything or anywhere in myth or legend anywhere on the Web?" The President's question was anticipated, and Kirkpatrick nodded.

"I sent requests over to the NSA and the Smithsonian, and they came back saying there was nothing anyone could find anywhere. We sent some people over to the Library of Congress to see if there was anything in any ancient literature, but that will take some time. Usually, we will see something on the Web if there is anything to discover. This Anaradelle seems to be a mystery."

The president started to speak up, when the room began to glow. The glow localized to one area beside the main desk in the room, and when the glow disappeared a brief moment later, the Goddess herself was standing there, looking over the men in the room.

"What place is this? And why have you been speaking about me?" The voice was gentle, and filled the room with the feeling of warmth and comfort.

The four secret service agents stationed in the room were in motion towards the President when the glow appeared, and had just started to pull him aside and towards the nearest door, when Anaradelle spoke.

The President stopped the men from pulling him from the room, and turned to face the newcomer. She was dressed the same way as she had appeared in the video footage they had seen, and her incredibly beautiful face and deepest blue eyes seemed to mesmerize everyone in view.

"Who are you?" The words came from Attorney General Glickh, and he seemed to be speaking before he was aware of it.

"I am Anaradelle, the Goddess of Children, Fertility, and Nature. I am here to restore my order to the peoples of this plane. For thousands of years, your people have had no Gods and no Magic. You have also not had a voice to the Elven Throne to help you resolve your differences with your fellow humans. I am here to restore the Elven Queen as your arbiter as well."

The men of the room all started talking at once, except for the President. His eyes narrowed, and he held up his hand to the other men, without saying a word.

"You are telling me, telling us, that we are supposed to be subjects of the Elven Queen? The one that was seen at the Mall of America earlier today?"

"No, I am saying that you are supposed to have the Elven Throne to help you in your troubles with your fellow men. If you refuse to allow The Elven Throne to help you, then the being on that throne will ask the Gods to sit in judgement of the conflict and decide who shall prevail. Of course, the Gods may resolve your differences in a way of their choosing and disregard mortal counsel, including having your mortal lives ended so you may start anew in the next life, thus giving you a chance to get back on the Path. That is the purpose of this existence here on this plane: to mature mortal souls so that they may ascend to the next plane where you continue your travels on the Great Path of the Soul."

Shocked silence filled the room for a while; then President Morrison spoke up once more.

"We do not believe in you or your Great Path of the Soul. We believe that when we die, if we have been good and followed God's teachings, we ascend to Heaven, where we live out our eternal lives in God's love and grace."

"Your disbelief is childish and blind, and is based in false beliefs in an equally false God that has been dreamed up by leaders desperate to control humans for gold and power. The True Gods are here to make sure you follow the Path. If you do not believe in this life, you obviously need to see the House Between Worlds for yourself, when next you die, and learn what you must before starting over in another mortal life," Anaradelle said matter-of-factly, in a tone of voice that might be used to lecture a wayward child. More than one man in the room bristled at the woman's attitude, but no one had any idea what to do about it. Or about this woman who had appeared in the room when they had said her name.

Anaradelle looked at the mortals in front of her, and sighed internally. She was certain that they did not believe in her. And that wouldn't do. She allowed the full force of her presence to come to the fore, something to which she rarely resorted. To the mortals in the room, it was as if her glow was suddenly as bright as the sun. It could be overwhelming for the weak minded, but this one man in front of her was a leader of his people, no matter how he had come to it. He must know his place in the way of Gods and mortals. It could not be any other way, if her will would be obeyed.

The President, the two senior senators, an aide to the President, and the several Secret Service agents in the room were suddenly overwhelmed as the woman began to glow. Every sense, even every bit of exposed skin suddenly was overloaded with sensory input as the ancient Goddess held nothing back for a moment. The men in front of her cried out, and fell to their knees, then to the floor, just as she held back and restored the hold upon her presence once more.

"My children, you must understand. My Will must be. As a Deus, I have a responsibility to do what is best for you, as you follow your soul's immortal path to reincarnation and ascension. There can be no other way." The men groaned as the pressure abated and they struggled to come to grips with what had just happened.

The doors flew open as other men entered the room, summoned by the sound of people in distress. The President was first back to his feet, followed by the others, and shock at the experience took his voice from him for a time. Then he found it again, and spoke up while half the other occupants of the room turned to the men that had just stormed into the room, waving them off, before turning back to the woman who still glowed, but only at a fraction of before.

"For the moment, I am willing to accept that you are... something more than human. You certainly appear to be a mortal human woman, but that was the most incredible experience I have ever had. But it brings up a question; several, in fact."

"Ask your questions, mortal child. I may answer them."

"What are we to you? Toys? Pawns? Ignorant children who must be led around by the nose until we do what you say?"

"You are impertinent, human. I was old before the first human left his cave to plant seed and herd beasts for food. I am a Deus, and I have been given dominion over mortals so that they might learn and grow. Nothing will turn me aside from that which I know I must do. Each of your mortal lives is simply a brief spark against the light of time. It is only after you live many lives on this plane that your soul begins to have wisdom. Then it is time for your soul to ascend to the next plane on the Great Path of the Soul, and continue onwards once again. Deus such as I are placed in dominion over mortal children to ensure that you follow the Path."

The President thought about it for a moment as his Secret Service detail shifted uneasily, uncomfortable with this strange being in the presence of the man they whose safety was the most important thing in their lives. But it was obvious as they looked around the room at each other that none of them knew what to do. The default position they fell into was to wait and see, while no overt or threatening moves were being made by the strange glowing woman. But they slowly closed up the distance to their President, moving their positions ever closer until they had effectively encircled him. He moved slightly more towards the center of the open space in front of the desk to make their job easier, while they, in turn, moved somewhat subtly to try to place themselves in between their Primary and the strange woman that had somehow invaded one of the most heavily guarded locations in the country, or anywhere on Earth.

Anaradelle saw what they were doing. She understood that these people had no idea what she was, let alone who she was, and responding to it, while logical, was completely pointless. She was an ancient, immortal being of immense power, and nothing they could do would stop her if she was here to harm their leader. And he must be an important leader, indeed, if he was protected in this manner. Most human kings she dealt with, especially on the west side of the bigger continent of Delara's plane, had guards that protected their liege, but not from her. Whether from knowledge of how pointless it truly was, or out of concern at insulting her, she never bothered to determine.

This one, however, and his guards, had no such understanding, and she was amused by it, much like an adult might be amused by watching the antics of very young children. Or young goats.

"What if what we want runs counter to what you think we should be doing?" The question came out calmly, without emotion, much the way one might ask what one thought of the weather.

"You must learn to bend your knee and your will to what I say. I am a Goddess. I know what is best for you. I have directed and shaped your kind for many thousands of years. And I have watched souls come and go to the House Between Worlds, and spend time in the Land of the Dead."

"You would force us to behave the way you want? What about free will? What about having the right to choose our fate, even if it is something that you don't agree with?"

Anger and frustration colored the Goddess's face slightly as she stared at the human in front of her. No mortal had the right to challenge her in this manner.

"You do not have the right to free will, nor the right to choose your fate. Your Path is chosen for you. You must obey that which is told to you. You are a child to me, and children are expected to follow the wishes of those who know best for them!" Her voice raised in anger at the last sentence.

"If we do not have free will, and the right to choose our fate, then anything we do must be what the Gods want us to do, since we are not choosing it for ourselves. So according to your statement, I could go out today and order my military to use weapons of mass destruction on every major city across the globe and kill billions of people, and make every city I destroy unlivable for hundreds of years, and it would be the right thing to do, because we cannot choose a path other than what the Gods have set out for us. Is that what you are saying?"

The words came out calmly, in the tone of voice of a man making a simple statement, and the Goddess was taken aback by the argument and how complex the logic was in the statement. She was about to speak up, to try to form an argument against the horrific statement he had made, but he continued.

"I don't have any way of knowing for sure if what you say about yourself is true, but let's say that you are hundreds of thousands of years old, for the sake of argument. And also, let's just accept for a moment that you are in fact a Goddess. To anyone, especially an immortal such as yourself, any mortal who would live a hundred years would seem like a child to you, even one who lived to be a thousand years.

"But I am not a child to the people of this country who have chosen me to serve them in this office, and to serve the other human mortals living on this planet. I am an adult, and as an adult, I am expected to make choices for myself; to choose my own destiny, to decide my own fate. And I am expected to live with the consequences, both good and bad, of the decisions I make and the actions I take. Moreover, I have been elected to make decisions for the fate of our nation, and the citizens and people that live here, all three hundred and thirty million plus of them.

"You say that you know what is best for us. I disagree. I say that you have no perspective on our lives or anything about us, and therefore have no idea what is the right thing for us to be doing. When was the last time you had anything to do with the people of this planet? How many thousands of years ago was it that you last set foot on this planet, and talked to the people here, to learn what their lives were like? And have you ever asked any mortal what they wanted or needed in their lives?"

Anaradelle had no words to respond to the statements this human was making. It simply was not part of her makeup any longer, if it had ever been, to consider an opposing viewpoint, and because of her humble beginnings and the much simpler nature of mortals when she was ascended to godhood, Anaradelle lacked the mental skillset and experience to work her way through what was being said to her, and to comprehend the messages and the meanings behind them that she was receiving. It had been too long since a mortal had ever challenged her on an intellectual basis, and she was not prepared to fundamentally change enough to have that happen now.

"You will obey the Gods. Or you will suffer your fates." The words were ominous, and as cold as the depths of space.

"If your advice is not in our best interests, we will not obey. If you try to force us, we will fight you. And, if we suffer the fates you make for us, the consequences of that fate will be on your head and the heads of those Gods and Goddesses too arrogant to consider other points of view that clash with their thinking. I will not take ownership of something that I have no control over.

"This country was founded on the right to think for ourselves, and to determine the path our lives will take. We have fought wars against foreign powers and even against ourselves to defend that right for us and for others in this world that were not able to do so for themselves.

"One of our states has a motto: Live Free or Die. It means that I would rather die fighting to be free, than to live for one moment as a slave to someone else who will only tell us how we are expected to behave, and give no consideration to our lives and our desires to be free and choose our own destiny.

"Every man to hold this office in the more than two hundred and thirty years since the founding of this country has taken the same oath when they take up the mantle of responsibility that comes with it: 'I do solemnly swear that I will faithfully execute the Office of President of the United States, and will to the best of my Ability, preserve, protect and defend the Constitution of the United States.' The Constitution of the United States of America is our most sacred document of state. It defines us, and establishes a framework for the Rule of Law, not the Rule of Man, nor the Rule of God. It clearly intends and states that all men, women, and children of this country are subject to those laws in an equal way – no one is above the laws of the land.

"Additionally, this country was founded on the principle of Freedom of Religion, which states that all men shall be free to follow whatever religion they believe in. To ensure that all religions are treated equally, we do not have an official state religion, so that one religion may not be preferred or required over any other. This also means that we do not allow leaders to use religious doctrine to decide the secular fate of our citizens."

The President was finding the entire situation he was in to be impossible, but that did not lessen his belief that what he was saying was right. Before Anaradelle could interject, he continued.

"We raise armies of volunteers from our citizens, train them, and give them the greatest weapons and tools of war this world has ever known, to defend our citizens and our way of life; our right to be the masters of our own fate.

"The Armed Forces of this country also swear an oath when they take up the responsibility of the safety of this country: 'I do solemnly swear that I will support and defend the Constitution of the United States against all enemies, foreign and domestic; that I will bear true faith and allegiance to the same; and that I will obey the orders of the President of the United States and the orders of the officers appointed over me, according to regulations and the Uniform Code of Military Justice, so help me God.'

"Should you attempt to force us to change who we are, or to take away our free will to decide our fate and destiny, you would be an enemy of this country and our way of life, and we will fight you every step of the way. And if we die, we shall die knowing that we have done what is right, just like the millions of young men and women who, in the history of our country, have fought for and died to protect and defend our freedom and our right to self-determination and free will."

The Goddess stood almost in awe of this human, this mortal leader, as he spoke to her in a way she had not heard since the last time she set foot on this plane. He was a child of only a few score summers, and yet he made his arguments as eloquently as any Deus she had ever heard. And some small part inside her was horrified at his statement that hundreds of thousands, and possibly millions, had died to defend this country and the beliefs of those that lived here, at the orders of humans like this one in front of her. A small part of her wondered if it was something about this plane that caused such humans to come into being.

But the message this man made to her confounded her. She could not find the words to refute his statements, and his convictions seemed to be honorable and selfless. Even his aura showed that he was not fundamentally evil. She sighed internally. This was not going well.

"I shall go about into this world and, as is my Divine Right, impose My Will upon these mortals as I see fit, in their best interests. Those that oppose me shall receive none of the blessings I have for them." And she simply vanished as if she was never there in the first place, startling the occupants of the Oval Office once more.

The President looked at the two U.S. Senators, and asked in a strained voice, "Did that really just happen?"

No answers came back to him as the men who were there to witness the happening simply couldn't process the events of the last few minutes. Then Senator Webster spoke up.

"What are we going to do now? If that really was a Goddess, the entire country, hell, the entire world, is going to be turned upside down, inside out, and shaken vigorously. How do we respond to this? Does someone make a statement? Who should do that? What do we say if we do? And if we don't, it is obvious that this will be getting out anyways. From the look of the videos online from the Mall of America, it is already getting out."

"I will have to think about that. What about this Craig Sanderson? Eric?"

The Attorney General was startled by the question, his mind obviously elsewhere. "I apologize, Mr. President. Could you please repeat the question?"

"Of course. What is the situation with this Craig Sanderson person in prison? What do we know about him?"

"I have a team from the Justice department heading there to look into the situation. The information I have at this point is very spotty, but the footage clearly indicates something less than legally justifiable seems to have happened to Sanderson. As to how he was able to change into, whatever that was – "

Kurtzman cut in. "A velociraptor, Mr. Attorney General."

Eric Glickh smiled at the Senator. "Thanks. As to how he was able to change into that velociraptor, I have no information on that. It is telling, though, that if he was in fact guilty of the crime he was convicted of, he would have no compulsion to spare his erstwhile lawyer's life. He was already sentenced to life without parole, and Michigan doesn't have the death penalty. I certainly would not have been as... magnanimous, in his position." A brief, strained laugher from some of the others in the room interrupted him before he continued on.

"A call to the prosecutor's office produced a strong denial that that office would have ever been involved in anything like that, as one might expect. But there is some smoke there, obviously, so we have to find out if there is fire, as well. I should be getting confirmation that my team is in place and starting to work in a few more hours, after they get set up. I will brief you then, if you desire?" He raised his eyebrows at the President, and Morrison nodded.

"Yes, keep me informed. We have to keep out in front of these events, and determine what is going on with them, and what our response will be." He shook his head. "The public is probably not going to be very rational about any of this. Then again, I'm just guessing at that, you understand." Nervous chuckles greeted his statement.

The President was silent for a while; then continued onwards. "What about this teenage boy in Minnesota that did that, whatever it was? Do we know anything about him? Or about the girl he did it to?"

The Attorney General looked thoughtful for a moment. "We really don't have any information about him. We did put in a call to the Hennepin County Sheriff's office, but the information we got back was somewhat confusing. Apparently a senior FBI agent from the Minneapolis office went out to investigate for himself after getting tipped off somehow, and met with the boy in the sheriff's office. He was in there one minute, and the next minute, the boy, his mother, and the FBI agent simply vanished, along with the table and chairs that were in the room.

"The observers said that it was a sudden thing, as well. The boy seemed to move his mouth just before it happened, but that was the only warning. They had been gone for just over two hours when they reappeared back in the interview room, along with the table and chairs.

"The FBI agent hustled the boy and his mother out of the station and into his car, and they drove off. Something happened to the FBI agent while they were, uhh, wherever they were, because he was somewhat more forceful before the incident. But afterwards, the deputies that were there said he was clearly protecting the boy and his mother. Well, more his mother than the boy. Obviously, if the boy did everything that it appears he did, the FBI agent probably felt the boy didn't need protecting."

"What is the boy's name?"

"The police officers at the scene of the event said a school friend of his identified him as Daniel Kevin Laurente. His mother is Marie Anne Laurente."

"And the FBI agent? Who is he?" the President asked.

Harald Kirkpatrick spoke up at that point. "His name is William Morris Nelson, and he is the Senior Special Agent in charge of the Minneapolis FBI office."

"Has he reported in since the incident?"

"I have been trying to reach him, but his cell phone doesn't seem to be working right now. We don't know why. I am certain he will be calling in as soon as he can," Kirkpatrick added.

"Ok. I would like to speak with Agent Nelson as soon as possible. In person, preferably. And I would like to know more about this Laurente boy. But tread lightly. I don't want to set him off. Until we understand more of what he is capable of, and what his motives are in all this, we need to be careful."

The President stopped speaking, and his gaze swept over the other people in the office. Then he spoke up again, his voice taking on a heavier tone.

"It is obvious we are on the cusp of massive changes to our world. Everyone's worldview will be challenged by just what has happened so far, and I am betting that this is not the last of what is coming at us. We need to know what these changes mean for everyone, not just for the people of this nation. We have an opportunity to lead, and I intend to make sure that everyone knows we are doing so. I want teams set up to scour the Internet, and to report back on any possible occurrences that might fall into this new paradigm we are experiencing. We need to catalog these events, and investigate directly when we can, to help understand what is happening, and how we fit into it."

"To what end, Mr. President?" The question was from one of the two Senators, and it echoed strangely into the silence of the Oval Office after George Morrison stopped speaking. In any other situation, it might have come across as political. In the wake of the visitation of the Goddess Anaradelle, it was definitely not, as was the President's response.

"I have no idea." The President seemed at a loss for where to go next.

* * *

The President's words about treading lightly around Daniel Laurente had fallen on fertile ground, but the correct people didn't get the message.

"How are we on plans for acquiring that Daniel kid? Any word on when that will happen?"

"We have everything set up, Assistant Director. At this point we are in a holding pattern. We are waiting for the right time to execute."

The Assistant Director thought about it, and shrugged. "Make sure they don't mess it up. He needs to be in our employ before anyone else grabs him and uses him in ways counter to our National Interests."

"Yes, sir." The men listening heard the 'ethical justification' portion of the message clearly.

CHAPTER 43

Nate walked back into the private area the team used for their cubicles in the MDST building. It was located behind the secured server room on the third floor of the building, and it had its own private bathrooms and break room suitable for eating lunch, as well as a medium-sized lounge area that was used for the team to relax and read, or talk on their cell phones, or just get some solitude. There was also a training room built to handle the entire team of twelve military veterans, as well as a few extra seats for those rare times that others were allowed back there.

The entire area was secured against the rest of the building's occupants, requiring additional access on their employee identification badges. Nate felt fairly secure in walking around this area, because almost no one else ever came back to this part of the building. The regular I.T. employees didn't have badge access to this area.

Most of the work that David's team of veterans performed was on special projects that were chosen to teach the most to the members of the team. In several cases, the actual production projects were implemented by the regular I.T. groups, but David's team also designed and laid out the projects, then studied the documentation of the technology to understand how that technology worked and to learn what was needed to be able to build, maintain, and support the project itself.

In the cases where there was to be a lab or test environment to be built, David's team would build that out, then compare the resulting lab environment to the production environment, and see how things were done differently between the two. In most cases, the lab environment was updated to match production, where there were differences. But once in a while, the lab environment build influenced the production environment, where a better way was found to do something, or the equipment was employed in a way that better matched the business need.

Nate heard Karen talking with Phil as he cleared the doorway, and smiled. Karen was the most direct person he had ever met, and was about as far removed from the philosopher as could be. She was ideally suited to be the Air Force pilot she had become in the military, a tough-minded woman who could be stubborn, but also knew when to accede to someone else's point of view. Now, she was asking Phil to repeat what he just said, so she could process it once more.

"What I said was this: ninety percent or more of how people treat you has nothing to do with you," Phil said in that same calm voice that everyone had come to recognize when Phil was in his training mode.

The team had long recognized Phil as a philosopher, and a very knowledgeable student of human nature into which he had developed during his career in as a military. While some had chosen to give him a little bit of grief over it, all of it in fun, everyone recognized the enormous mental gifts he brought to the team. David had been heard to say once that Phil made the team more successful than David ever would, and no one, after thinking about it sufficiently, could come up with any disagreement, especially David himself.

"Ok, what does that mean? Why does most of how people treat each other have nothing to do with the other person?" Karen posited the question without frustration, having learned very early on that anything Phil wanted to pass on was well worth listening to.

Phil thought about it for a moment as Nate stopped to lean on the cubicle wall next to Karen's desk, nodding to the newcomer as he considered his words next. Then he turned to Nate.

"Nate, you told me once that someone burned a cross on your front yard when you were a kid, right?"

Nate nodded, knowing well where this was going. This was the same argument that Phil had used with Nate when trying to explain the same concept to him, and while he hadn't believed it at first, it had held together the longer that he thought about it.

"Did you know who did it?"

"Not right away, but the police caught them eventually," Nate replied, suddenly unable to find the smile that had been plastered to his face for every moment since his legs had been restored.

"And who were they?"

"Just some idiots I went to high school with."

"How well did you know them?" Phil asked calmly.

"I'd known them all my life. One of the lived a couple blocks away. All three of them had been in the same schools I had attended since kindergarten." It mostly didn't bother him anymore, but there was still that twinge that even close to twenty years hadn't been able to completely erase. He looked up to realize that Giltreas had been listening all along from the doorway of his own cubicle, and wondered how much he would have to explain to the elven man.

"So, how did this incredibly ignorant, stupid, childish, racist act have anything to do with you?"

Karen chose that moment to speak up. "Wait, you had a cross burned on your front lawn when you were a kid? In this day and age? Holy crap! That's insane! Wait, how old are you again?"

Nate laughed at her last question as her smile colored the statement as a joke instead of an insult.

Giltreas joined the conversation. "What is the significance of this burning of a cross? And what is a cross?" The questions came out in that same quiet voice they now easily identified with the non-human member of the team.

Nate and Karen both declined to answer, and instead looked at Phil, who replied, "A cross is a religious symbol. It is a vertical, square post, with a horizontal post attached just below the top. It is said that one society from long ago, the Romans, crucified people on crosses as a horrific way to execute them. It often took more than a day to die that way, and is considered the most painful way to be executed in all of history. It is religious because some believe that the Son of God was crucified on a cross just over two thousand years ago.

"In our history, there have been many periods of time where certain groups of humans were considered less human than others, and were persecuted, robbed, beaten, raped, and even killed because they were different. People who are educated and enlightened consider those who did and still do the persecuting to be ignorant idiots who feared people that were, and are, different than them. It is not something that anyone should be proud of.

"One group of humans, who are white-skinned similar to how I am, has had a history of attacking those with dark skin who are of African-American heritage, such as Nate, here. We refer to them as white-supremacists, because they think that their white skin makes them superior to everyone else, usually with some twisting of the Christian religion thrown in as justification.

"They wore white sheets and pointy hats that doubled as masks, and had a habit of burning crosses in the front yards of people they wanted to terrorize. It was an effective way to convey a message of racist hatred of someone else, and the threat of violence and murder, to them. We have an entire portion of our laws dedicated to what we refer to as hate-crimes, which are crimes based on the hatred of others for things like race or the preferred gender of their life partners. Committing a hate crime will get the perpetrator a much greater sentence when they are caught and convicted."

Phil turned back to Nate, who nodded at Phil's succinct explanation, only to have Giltreas ask another question.

"Am I to understand that humans hate each other because they look different?"

"Yep, pretty much. Pathetic, isn't it?" Nate spoke up in a conversational tone as he looked over at Gil.

Giltreas shrugged his shoulders. "I would tend to agree with you most completely, good Nate."

Phil spoke up once more. "What did those idiots have against you personally, Nate?"

"You and I have talked about this before, and I now tend to agree with you, for the most part. The answer is, 'very little'. If it hadn't been my family, it would have been another black family. They really didn't know me or my family, and when the police questioned them, they admitted that they didn't have anything against me or anyone else in my family personally.

"But even if they had, they were ignorant, racist fools. I had nothing to do with their becoming racist; that was their parents and whoever else they learned that garbage from. I just happened to be the target of their stupidity. It turned out that I didn't know them very well at all, in spite of having gone to school together all those years.

"And they didn't know me. They thought it was a prank that would scare my family. It had exactly the opposite effect. We ended up feeling sorry for them. They had been raised in an environment of hatred and intolerance that had stunted their emotional and psychological growth, which virtually guaranteed that they would never reach their full potential, and that they would always be poorer from a societal perspective, because they would not have the benefit of having those different than themselves, along with their differing points of view and experiences, in their lives, to learn and grow from."

Karen just looked at Nate, then back at Phil. "Wow. That's sick that people still think that way. I guess I can see your point, Phil. I will have to think about that, though." Karen thought about it for a moment, then spoke up again.

"So, what is the other thing you've been saying about human nature?" She asked.

"I believe that somewhere around ninety percent of human behavior, at least in this society and culture, is driven by insecurity. The other ten percent is by guilt or humility."

"Where does pride come into it?" Nate interjected.

Phil turned to look at Nate from where he was sitting. "Pride, as a basis for character and how someone acts, is a shield that we use to disguise and protect our insecurities. Ego is just a greater expression of pride; it is pride taken to the extreme. If you think about it, being proud of some thing or accomplishment about ourselves, especially being excessively proud, is an emotional investment that we make." He paused for a moment.

"Think of it this way," he said. "There are two sides to every intelligent being. The logical, and the emotional. Will-power is the product of the logical side, and is the state of mind that produces change. Stubbornness is the product of emotion, and is the state of mind that resists change. This is getting a little off track – "

"Ya think?" Karen interjected, to the laughter of both Nate and Gil.

"Well, yes, but intelligent beings are complicated. Gil, you will have to decide if this applies to you or not. I don't have any experience with beings like you, or where you are from." Gil nodded casually; then he indicated that Phil should continue.

"Back to it, then. Pride is usually an expression of insecurity, in that we show pride in an accomplishment. This is a stubborn refusal to accept that someone else might know or be capable of something better out there: a better accomplishment, a better result, whatever, that can be pursued. Pride is also the state of mind that says, 'I am better than you simply because I am.'"

"Humility, however, is an acceptance that there is always another level that we can strive to attain, if you will: a willingness to admit to yourself that what you have done is not the best there ever will be at something. Someone might have done it quicker, simpler, better, or taken it further. Or someone else might have done something an entirely different way that produces a better result. Humility is not just knowing, but accepting, that we are not perfect, we don't know everything, and that we all have more to learn.

"Humility also says my rank against my fellow humans doesn't matter, because I am my own greatest opponent. No one will ever come close to holding me back as much as I hold myself back.

"The insecure part of our mind will say, 'I am the best! No one else could possibly be any better!', and stubbornly refuse to admit otherwise. The humble part of our mind will say, 'Someone out there is better than me,' or 'There is a better way, I just haven't been able to pull it off, or even figure out what it might be.' At that point, the humble person will look for a better way, or an entirely new way. The humble person is not afraid to look foolish or incapable by asking someone else for help or advice. Pride doesn't let the insecure mind even admit that it might need help. Humility all but opens that door and shoves us through it, and slams and locks it behind us to keep us from going back there in fear or insecurity about where we find ourselves."

Heads nodded as the crowd around Phil's cube grew. Everyone on the team had recognized Phil's brilliance to be several levels above the norm, and as newcomers on the team saw that many of their more senior co-workers went to Phil to get advice or assistance with one thing or another, they inevitably followed suit. Probably, Phil thought to himself with an inner smile, that it bruised the pride less to see others do it before you.

"Now think about human interaction. Everyone here," he stopped to look up from Karen as he realized that the entire team, David included, had gathered around, "...has had to deal with someone who was arrogant and very prideful. What does this discussion shed light on as the reason for his arrogance? Anyone? Buehler? Buehler? Anyone?" A few chuckles greeted Phil's parroting of the line from that 1980's movie about Ferris Buehler.

Giltreas was the first to speak up. "It speaks to the person being very insecure about something, and hiding that insecurity behind a false shield of arrogance and pride."

"Got it in one. Good job, Gil." Giltreas smiled slightly at the praise as Phil showed his supportive nature for the correct answer. Then Phil continued.

"I would hypothesize that no positive benefits come to us through allowing our insecurities to dominate the basis of our character, which is expressed outwardly as stubbornness and an unwillingness to admit to ourselves that we still have so much to learn. Only through exerting our will-power to overcome our stubbornness, exerting our humility to suppress, undermine, or dissolve our insecurity or insecurities, or to resolve them entirely, and therefore allow our logical side to be more dominant than our emotional side, are we able to grow as human beings, and to affect positive change and bring benefits to those around us."

There was silence in the cubicle farm as the words sunk in. After almost a minute of quiet contemplation, Karen looked up and focused on Phil once more.

"Do you consider yourself to be humble?" The question came out carefully, as if Karen was afraid to offend Phil, but he only chuckled.

"I am as deeply flawed as every other human being I have ever met; perhaps even more so. Or, maybe I am so brutally self-honest that I don't put up with my own internal bullshit as much as others do. Don't forget, lying comes from insecurity. And the first person that we successfully lie to in our entire lives, and the one that we lie to more than all other people combined, is ourselves. Once you decide to stop lying to yourself, and be willing to go back and correct your internal record – the lies you have already told yourself – then you can start building yourself into something greater than the sum of your parts.

"To answer your question, I strive for humility in everything I do. But I fail to achieve it all the time. Think of it this way: aim for the stars. If you fail, at least you are further off the ground than when you started. Who knows, maybe you make it into orbit, and that might be the most amazing thing you ever accomplish. But if you only aimed for the horizon, you will never leave the ground. So, no, I'm not that particularly humble, no matter how much I try to be."

Mark, who had been listening quietly to this point, spoke up darkly. "Maybe if certain elected politicians had heard that speech laid out so eloquently to them as you just did, we might not be facing so much uncertainty in the world right now, especially that Dorkaleptic, pathetic waste of organic material, Congresswoman Rose Smithson. And let's not forget her subhuman spawn of pondscum, Senator Robert Del Monico."

Most of them laughed, but a few newer members of the team hadn't heard the term Mark used to describe the congresswoman, and especially the senator whose 'aides' had approached their CFO about a 'hostile takeover' of MDST.

Mark saw the few confused faces, and decided to elaborate.

"Everyone has heard of Narcolepsy, the condition that causes a sudden, uncontrollable urge to fall asleep? Dorkalepsy is similar, but the effect of it is a sudden, uncontrollable urge to fall stupid," Mark said, as everyone laughed, including Giltreas.

"There are three types of Dorkalepsy. The first is incidental Dorkalepsy. Everyone has this from time to time. We all get a little stupid, just like we all stub our toe once in a while, or say the wrong thing in front of someone who would be the most offended by it.

"The second is chronic Dorkalepsy. You were either born stupid, or you decided to take a heapin' helpin' o' dumb biscuits one day for breakfast, and from then on you are stupid your entire life. These are the people that held the door when God was passing out brains, or got dropped on their heads repeatedly as a baby, or those unfortunate idiots that got beaten with the stupid stick when they were young. This the hundred-forty pound weakling that picks a fight with a Navy Seal, who never even knew that he and his girlfriend were in a Navy bar, after a single wine cooler (this happened to me, by the way – it wasn't pretty for that idiot, but he lived).

"The third is terminal Dorkalepsy. This is when you are so dumb you get your dumb ass killed. People who bring a knife to a gunfight, those who decide to go driving drunk, or those pull a gun on police officers – these are the true modern-day rocket scientists of our society. These are the annual Darwin Awards winners we hear about in the news." At this, Giltreas laughed with everyone else. He had seen a website dedicated to Darwin Award winners, and had marveled at how many ways the humans of this plane tried to, and usually succeeded at, accidentally kill themselves. As sad as the loss of life was to the family and friends of those deceased, the creativity employed in how those unfortunate souls crossed over was entertaining, in a morbid sort of way.

* * *

"Good evening. Today is Tuesday, October 22, 2013. This is ABC World News, and I'm Jane Olson. Making headlines tonight, the stock market has taken a mild, unexpected downturn. Analysts seem unsure of the state of world affairs right now, with the surfacing of several videos on the Internet. Some of those seem to portray what some are calling supernatural events, while one shows Congresswoman Smithson of Ohio outlining a plan using a government black-ops team to kidnap and kill the owners of a business in Minneapolis, Minnesota.

"And now we have some video of a young girl taken in the Republic of Georgia in Eastern Europe that seems to have the ability to turn into a gargoyle of some sort. This is similar to the video that surfaced late last week of the man in prison in Michigan for a murder that he may not have committed, due to the possibly collusion of his defense attorney with the prosecutor in a quid-pro-quo exchange that would have gotten a lighter sentence for another of that lawyer's other clients.

"In that video, a man named Craig Sanderson turned into a velociraptor, which is a carnivorous dinosaur about the size of a large horse, and coaxed a confession out of his lawyer, which just so happened to be recorded on the prison's audio and video surveillance system, and later leaked to the Internet.

"All of these events are making the markets nervous, including the miraculous resurrection of the young woman in Minnesota, who had been missing for several weeks, that was caught on camera during the organized search for her in a county park. Additional reports put the young man who performed that miracle at a doctor's office in Denver, where he healed an NFL football player who was facing a possible career-ending injury, before going on to cure the cancer of the orthopedist who was going to treat the player's knee.

"But the biggest event that is making people nervous is the recent footage from the Mall of America, in Bloomington, Minnesota, of the being calling herself the Anaradelle, the Goddess of children, fertility, and nature. In those videos, she was heard to say that the entire tribes of those people who practice the horrific act of female circumcision will not have children for a hundred years, which was reported to be heard simultaneously in the mind of every person on the planet, including this reporter. We do not have clarity at this time of how those tribal designations will identify where that restriction will be applied, let alone whether or not it will actually happen.

"So far the White House has been silent on these events, not even leaking an unofficial statement to the press through any back channels. It is that silence that is making the markets turn down right now, according to analysts; a failure to have a position on these events that would reassure skittish investors who are still trying to figure out the last of the details of this post Great Recession economy.

"We have sent a team to each of these locations to gather more information. In the case of the young man who performed the miraculous healing and resurrection of Alana Munroe, the missing college student in Minneapolis, we have been able to determine the identity of the young man, but since he is a minor, we will not be releasing his identity until we have been able to investigate further, if at all. We are attempting to get an interview with him for our viewers, though. If we are able to speak with him, we will let you know as soon as possible.

"Additionally, we have interviewed people who were at the Mall of America when the Anaradelle incident occurred, and have been told by them that an additional sighting took place, of a massive being that could only be described as a Minotaur, a mythical creature that is said to have existed thousands of years ago in Greek legend. This Minotaur was in the company of a woman and her companions that appeared to be elves, with green-hued skin and pointed ears, along with what was referred to as two dwarven men."

Footage rolled for several minutes of the beings at the Mall of America, before returning to Jane Olson.

"After the break, we will be speaking with some experts to discover what we may about these events, and to try to place them in a greater discussion about what is happening in our world in these troubling times."

CHAPTER 44

In all the time he had been head of the family that ran things in this part of the world, he had never been arrested. It simply wasn't done. Until now.

The officers of Special Group Alpha had driven up and snatched him in broad daylight, in a daring, audacious raid that had somehow not harmed any of his bodyguards or the bystanders. It was almost like someone had made everyone else around him start moving in slow motion. The men in the black uniforms, however, had been moving at normal speed. Whatever had been done to everyone else hadn't affected him or them, he decided.

The usual hood had been put over his head and his hands had been efficiently secured behind him. Then they pushed him into a van, and off they went. He was hustled into a building and into a room, where he was dropped into a chair. The hood was taken off, and he saw himself in what looked like an interrogation room. He shrugged. Whatever this was, it was a waste of everyone's time. His hands were still tied behind his back in some kind of plastic—

The door opened suddenly, and in walked two men wearing the same gear and balaclavas as the men that snatched him, followed by... a girl in a school uniform? Why would anyone let a little girl in here with him? He was about to ask when she turned and looked at him.

"You are head of the Odessa Mafia." The girl spoke to him in Ukrainian. It was a statement, not a question, he realized.

"What? I have no idea what you are talking about, little girl. Run away and go play with your dolls before you see something you shouldn't," he said with what might be called a grin in some circles.

"I don't want to waste any more of your important criminal time, you walking sack of human feces. So, you need to listen very carefully to what I am about to say."

"You talk awfully nasty for such a sweet-looking little girl. This is not your school, and I am not some schoolboy you can bully into doing what you want. Go away. You can say nothing I want to listen to."

Svetlana sighed and looked down at her hands. Then she glanced up, and a look he didn't recognize came over her face.

"You think I have nothing to say that you would listen to? Maybe you need to hear it said in a different way."

He started to open his mouth to laugh, but he gasped in shock instead as the girl transformed into that creature for which he had his people searching everywhere for the last month.

It was bigger in real life than he thought it would be, a small part of his brain thought. Then most of his mind shut down as the creature darted in close to him. It moved so fast that it seemed to disappear and reappear from one position to the next. He was certain that she was going to rip him apart, but instead it leaned back.

"I am pretty sure you know what I can do, so I think a demonstration of that is not necessary at this point. But, there are a few other things you need to know about me. For instance, you have a son, right?" That voice was incredibly deep and almost guttural, and the words seemed to be formed as if the creature was growling.

All he could do was nod. He realized that the fear of this creature in front of him was seriously affecting his ability to form rational thoughts.

"His name is Hadeon. He is twenty two, and is just finishing up his last year at university in Moscow. He is a handsome young man, no?" Svetlana changed back into a teenage girl once more and waved her hand, and an image appeared of his son, floating in the air. And the image was moving. With a gasp, he realized that it could actually be a projection of what his son was doing right now. At the moment, he should be in class, which the image seemed to show.

"Yes, that is actually happening in your son Hadeon's class. Don't believe me? Here." She waved her hand, and the cuffs holding his hands behind him seemed to disappear, then he heard them hit the floor.

"Your phone is somewhere nearby, probably in the van that brought you here." She waved her hand, and his cell phone appeared on the table in front of him. "There it is." Svetlana waved to the phone on the table in front of him. He stared at it, and then he glanced at the image of his son as Hadeon followed along with the professor, making notes.

"Go ahead, send him a message. Tell him to hold up two fingers for a moment." Svetlana said with a smile.

Valysko stared at the phone in front of him, and then his eyes shot back up to the young girl in front of her. He reached out, and picked up the phone, then sent a text message to his son.

In the projection, his son sat up suddenly, then reached quietly into his pocket and drew out his phone. He read the text, and seemed to be shocked at what it said. Then he looked around, and texted something back.

The phone in Valysko's hand alerted him to an incoming message, and he nearly dropped the phone after reading it. Then he sent a message back again. In the projection, Hadeon's phone vibrated again, and he sent another text message back.

Valysko read the message; then he dropped the phone back on the table. "How are you doing that?" It came out in a shocked whisper.

"I have certain abilities. Magical abilities. I am showing you this because you and I need to come to an understanding about something." She paused, waiting for him to respond.

His response was not unexpected. "You leave my son alone! He has nothing to do with... what I do!"

"I know that. Your son is not in any danger. I would never target YOUR family." The emphasis she put on that sentence indicated that she clearly believed otherwise about Valysko when it came to her loved ones.

"You see, I know that you are looking for me, to try to get me to do 'work' for you. And you and I both know what you mean when I say the word 'work'. You and I also both know that you would have absolutely no scruples about using my family against me." Valysko flushed in embarrassment and anger at the statement.

"What do you think you—!"

Suddenly the gargoyle was back, and she leaned over the table and got directly in his face and roared, a deep, thunderous, and wholly terrifying sound that made his ears ring and caused him to throw up his hands in front of his face and turn away. It didn't stop, though. She reached across the table and picked him up, pulling him in close and roaring in his face again.

"We both know what kind of man you are! If you thought for a single moment that you could use my family against me, you would not hesitate for even the briefest of moments!" The gargoyle's claws were ripping his very expensive suit apart as he tried desperately to get away, but he was completely unsuccessful. His efforts were as ineffective as a young child would be against a professional fighter.

The two black-clad officers started forward to try to stop her, a motion that Valysko saw in a brief moment of hope, but she held Valysko out above the floor at arm's length with one hand while she waved her other hand towards the other men.

"You stay out of this, or I will send you someplace you don't want to be!" She snapped at them. One stopped, but the other continued forward, only to disappear as Svetlana waved her hand once more.

"One, two, three, four, five..." She got to thirty and waved her hand, and the man came back again, and he was sitting uncomfortably on the floor. Only this time, he was red faced and screaming at the top of his lungs, an effect that wasn't lost on Valysko, further heightening his fear.

The man stopped screaming as he saw that he was back in the interrogation room. He took a deep breath, then pulled himself to his feet and ran, still panting in fear, from the room, slamming the door behind him.

Svetlana turned back to Valysko once more after the other man stepped back to the wall with an audible gulp, and pulled him up once more, this time with both hands. His suit and now his expensive tailored shirt shredded further in those razor-sharp talons. Then the talons tore into the very expensive anti-ballistic body armor underneath as if it was so much paper. He gasped in fear as the scalpel-sharp talons lightly scratched his skin, leaving painful, bloody furrows behind.

"Here is the message I need everyone to hear. If anyone so much as thinks about using my family against me in an effort to get me to do anything for them, I will not be pleased. If someone kidnaps any member of my family or anyone else that they think they might be able to use to compel me to work with or for them, I will find whoever is taken in an instant, and get them back, just as I found your son, whom I have never met before, like I did the guard. And if someone harms them or even scares them even the slightest, I will make whomever it was that did it to them look much like what I left behind in that brothel in Tbilisi. I don't care who they are, or who they work for. I will turn them into stew meat. Do you understand me?"

The people watching and listening in front of the security monitor in the other room suddenly looked at each other in shock and dismay. The message she was sending wasn't just for Valysko Goraya, they realized. It was also for them and who they worked for.

Borysko stood in the back of the room, a grim smile fighting for control of his face. He was convinced that the message had been sent to both sides. He got his expression under control once more, just as the two men in front of him turned to glare at him.

"Svetlana wanted me to say something else to you both as well. She will not work for you, because she works for a Higher Power. She will do, on her own, what she knows to be Good and Right, and she will not be stopped or diverted. She explained it to me, and then a Deity came and explained it as well.

"Any actions she takes are hers alone. If you think you can stop her, think again. If you think you can prosecute her, that is also a fool's errand. Keep this in mind: on the one hand, she is a fifteen year old girl. She is a minor. On the other hand, she also has been trained by a Deity of unimaginable power and abilities to do what she can do."

The two men looked at each other, and Ivan Tarasova, the head of the regional office where Borysko was based, turned back to Borysko. "She's your daughter. Can't you just tell her to do what we need her to do? There is no danger to her, only..." Ivan trailed off as Borysko tried, and failed, to keep from laughing briefly before he got himself under control once more.

"She may be my daughter, but she is no longer a child. She told me that she would refuse to listen to me if I tried to get her to do anything for you. And frankly, there is nothing I can do to force her to do something she doesn't want to do. Did you forget already what she did in there just now? Or what that brothel in Tbilisi looked like when she decided not to be meek and play along anymore?"

Ivan shook his head. He definitely wouldn't forget the pictures that Borysko had brought back from his trip following after his kidnapped daughter, courtesy of a certain Georgian homicide detective. "So the reason I let you talk me into pulling that scumbag into the room and letting her talk to him here is because...?"

"Because she said she was going to get to him one way or another to deliver her message, and it was safer for everyone around him, whether they worked for him in the business, or were innocent bystanders who happened to be there when she did what she did just now. Not to mention, she didn't want to throw her capabilities out there where everyone in the world could see what she can do. Not yet. She decided she isn't quite ready for that, and frankly, neither am I or her mother."

Ivan nodded in understanding. Containment was a good idea in this situation. Well, containing information, he amended to himself. There was no way, apparently, that one could contain Svetlana Yevtukh.

"I will continue to work here and uphold and enforce the laws as I always have, if you will have me. But there are limits to all things, and those limits start and end with my daughter and my family." He looked at them for a moment, and when he was positive that they understood his position, he turned back to the monitors watching the interview room.

Svetlana had paused, her magically enhanced hearing in this form bringing the sounds from the monitoring room to her clearly, as she listened to what her father was saying in the other room, before continuing.

"Do you doubt that I can do anything that I have said?"

"Nononono! Please! Let me down!" Valysko screamed, completely terrorized.

"Are you going to leave my family, and everyone else I know, alone? And are you going to convince everyone you can that we are all off limits to you? Remember that I know who you are, and if someone else decides to act, even against your wishes, I might start with you to find retribution!" The last sentence was bellowed at a volume that left his ears ringing.

"Yesyesyes! I will not let anyone in my organization come after you! Please! Let me go! Let me goooo!" For the first time in his adult life, Valysko cried in terror, weeping uncontrollably as he lost control of his bladder and wet himself like a child.

Svetlana looked down at the urine pooling on the floor under Valysko's dangling feet in distaste. She set him back on the floor beyond the wet spot, and flashed back to her human form. Then a series of lights flashed from her upraised hands, washing over the hunched, shaken figure of the crime boss. His trauma ended as the healing spell healed the injury to his psyche, and the mend spell flashed over him, his clothing, and the floor, erasing the evidence that he had lost control of his bodily functions or that she had shredded them in her efforts to reach him and pass on her message.

Valysko realized that his torment had ended, but the message had been delivered, and he looked up from the floor at the girl in front of him. She looked so completely normal and harmless, but that was clearly not the case. He shuddered as she looked in his eyes, her face solemn. It was her eyes, he decided. It was like looking into... He didn't know what. Certainly she was not some normal fifteen year old girl—the thought was a completely absurd understatement, and he tried not to giggle hysterically at it. He was still trying to find his mental balance.

"I will not have my family or friends used against me. Do we understand each other?" Her quiet voice was clear, and not at all hesitant.

"Yes, we understand each other." He said it quietly, and barely a tremor in his voice, which was almost more shocking to him. "I will do what I can with those that I can influence, but you should know that not everyone listens to me. There are other... factions, groups, call them what you will. They most certainly do not listen to me."

Svetlana nodded. She knew exactly of whom Valysko was speaking, and that person would never listen to the man in front of her. Still, it would have to do.

"There are limitations in all things," she said, much to his relief. "I will settle for your... faction leaving me alone. Yours is the largest. Anyone else who comes after me will get what they deserve.

"You might want to consider, as the Americans say, going straight. If I don't come for you, some other magic user will, and you will be powerless to stop them from bringing you to justice, and not the kind that puts you in prison. You might also want to have a long conversation with a Deity to understand exactly what is happening in the world, and what really, actually happens in the afterlife, to see if you can change what is in store for you when you die. The things you have done so far promise that it will not be pleasant for you."

He didn't say anything, finding nothing he could think of that would matter.

"Let me get you back to where you were when this started." He looked up, and nodded his thanks. He picked up his cell phone from the floor where it had fallen as he considered that he had a lot to think about.

Svetlana nodded, and with a wave of her hand, Valysko disappeared, reappearing in the middle of his group of bodyguards. They were startled, but quickly tended to their duties, securing their boss and hustling him out to his car and away to his estate before anything else could happen to him.

Not one of them said a word about his suddenly pure-white hair.

The second officer stepped back into the interview room where Svetlana was still standing while she wondered if she had been successful. She noticed the movement, and smiled at the man she had sent on a little trip earlier.

"Did you enjoy that? You sold it really well."

He smiled. "Definitely. I was a little over dressed for that place, but that helped. It was so peaceful there, in spite of the heat. Where was I? That was an island, right?"

"Yes, my friend Daniel told me about it. It is somewhere deep down south in the Pacific Ocean somewhere. Was that enough time for you to get into character?"

"It worked well." He hesitated for a moment, and Svetlana looked a question at him.

He blushed briefly, but asked, "Is there any chance I could take my family there for a picnic some day?"

She laughed. "I will check with Daniel. It is really his private sanctuary."

He nodded. "Fair enough. Thank you."

"No, thank you. You were perfect." She turned her face towards one of the three cameras that were mounted in the upper corners of the room. "Father, I am ready to go home now."

* * *

Michelle looked out from the top of the MDST building on the downtown Minneapolis skyline. It was just after two in the morning on a Friday night, and she had been unable to sleep lately as she considered what was happening to the world.

In the months since she had been 'raised to Deus', as the Elven and dwarven scholars referred to it, and especially in the two months since she had discovered what had happened to her and how she had changed, everything around her had taken on an unusual appearance to her altered perspective.

Now, the city she was in, and the entire world that recognized such things, should have been happily preparing for the Christmas holiday due to arrive in just four days.

Instead, the entire world was gripped in fear and uncertainty. Wars had broken out everywhere. Conflict was as common as breathing, as everyone formed opinions and took sides on what was happening. And the Gods that had returned were everywhere.

It had come as a massive shock to every religious institution and organization when the Gods and Goddesses of every mythos and legend suddenly returned at once to walk among the mortals of this plane. Gods with names like Loki, Thor, Odin, Apollo, Mercury, Diana, Artemis, Saule, Medeina, Isis, Ra, Anubis, Hathor, Sethlans, Tinia; the list went on and on.

By one website's tally, the list was over nine hundred Mid-Gods and growing rapidly every day, even with the requirement that some form of proof be provided. Video of the Deus in question stating their name and role seemed to be adequate. It also was easily attainable, as the Gods and Goddesses all seemed to share an abundance of ego. It seemed that every God that was ever referred to in ancient myth and legend was, in fact, real, and as eager to learn about this new plane of humans, as most of those same humans were to be left alone by them.

Some scholars were in shock that the Roman Gods, long assumed to be renamed versions of the same Greek Gods, were actually different beings. Not that this was the most important aspect of what was going on right now, Michelle thought to herself.

The Catholic Church had come out swinging, with the Pope making a statement that "we are living in the End Times, a time of False Gods and Pretenders that would lead us astray to damnation and Hell and away from the true teachings of God and His Holy Son Jesus Christ, through whom is the only path to salvation and eternal life."

After that, it seemed that almost every other established religion had come out alongside the statement, decrying the 'False Gods' and reassuring their true believers that nothing had changed on the supernatural level, and that these, as one Islamic cleric stated, "apparitions and ghosts of the sins of a decadent, evil life, must be shunned and turned aside from, lest they lead to death."

Judaism was officially, at least, taking a 'wait and see' attitude, but even there, rabbis were counseling their flocks to 'follow their hearts and faith', something that didn't go over well with everyone in that religion.

Pagans of every sect and variation were jumping out of the woodwork to crow as loudly as possible that because, since the Gods were telling anyone who would listen that they had been gone for over five thousand years, that they alone were right, and had been right all along, and that they were the only true religion. It was mostly met with the dead silence of no one else listening, as always.

And everywhere there was magic. The oddest thing was, everyone seemed to be able to perform at least some minor level of magic. Healing spells were the simplest of the magical skills that everyone was able to perform, to some degree or the other. Everything from scrapes and cuts to outright stabbings and shootings were, if not shrugged off, moved on from with almost a sense of apathy. The videos had helped that quite a lot.

Apparently someone had filmed Giltreas out in the woods somewhere making a new supply of potions for his personal stores. Gee, she wondered who that was. Giltreas had found a campsite and set up a small fire. Then he had identified everything needed, from what type of pot to concoct them in, to what utensils, to exactly how much water and what herbs, plants, and grasses were needed. Most of them were readily available in the forests and on the plains, just lying on the ground waiting to be used. Some were common weeds, and regular grasses that grew wild. The rest were found in supermarkets across the planet. The total cost of the materials needed to make a set of four full potions of each type was generally around five to ten dollars if everything was purchased. It was even less if the components were harvested directly from the field.

From there, he had explained, step by careful step, how to make first a healing potion, then a cure sickness potion, then a cure poison potion, then a cure blindness potion. And then he went over how to know if they succeeded or not. To say it had not gone over well in certain circles was an understatement.

The American Medical Association had come out to strongly criticize and condemn the videos as 'the dangerous and potentially illegal practice of medicine without the oversight and constraints that such critically important things, such as the scientific approach of modern medicine, require to prevent serious injury, impairment, or death from malpractice and malfeasance.'

That dire pronouncement had quickly been followed up by a wheelchair-ridden young man, who had been crippled since birth by Cerebral Palsy, making his own video. In it, he had made his own healing potion, and drank it as soon as it had cooled enough for him to get it down. The dramatic video had been posted only four days later, and the incredible scene of his arms and legs straightening and suddenly becoming fully functional had not been lost on the masses of people who sent Youtube.com into a tailspin trying to see the videos of the life-changing potions and how to make them.

The U.S. Congress had gotten into the act at that point, passing the CHASM Act. The Coordinated Humanity Against Sorcery and Magic Act had been conceived and voted on in less than three days, and it promised severe consequences for anyone caught practicing magic against the specific orders of the American Medical Association. Some people on the Internet were calling it the Completely Hopeless And Soulless Morons Act, which Michelle couldn't argue against, really. Not that she would have.

No provisions in the CHASM Act were allowed for the magic shows and sleight of hand demonstrations that had been a hallmark of the entertainment industry since the origins of Hollywood and Vaudeville, and that had started a class-action lawsuit by entertainers seeking to define the law to exempt what types of magic were acceptable, and what wasn't. But that hadn't been the only aspect of magic that had upset the government and the courts and the local and national law enforcement agencies.

Gun control had been a hot topic of Democratic elected officials for decades, since the attempted assassination of President Ronald Reagan in the early 1980s, and before. Background checks and restrictions had been the path to domestic tranquility and lower crime, according to those who preached that society's ills were cured by keeping guns out of the hands of law-abiding citizens.

Michelle snorted to herself as that bit of logic rubbed her grey matter the wrong way once again. It was a simple equation, to her at least. If someone with a gun was going to rob someone, would he be more likely to rob someone he or she thought might be able to defend themselves, or someone he/she knew was unarmed? And, had no one ever murdered anyone before guns were invented? The silly statement that gun-rights advocates had been throwing about for the longest time came back to her now, too: a gun-control advocate was simply someone who hadn't been robbed at gunpoint yet.

But all that paled in the face of what magic could do. A simple spell that just about anyone could learn to cast, that everyone seemed to decide to call the magic rock spell, had turned the entire gun control discussion on its ear. Why did anyone need to spend the money and expense on a gun and ammunition, not to mention go through the hassle of government red tape for permits and approvals, when you could just learn a simple spell and pick up a small rock the size of your thumb and accomplish the same thing, if not more? A video making the rounds of the firearms websites rocked everyone back on their collective behinds when a magic rock spell cast by someone who seemed to be very familiar and experienced with it, accelerated a half-inch diameter round stone made of granite instantly to a speed of nearly three thousand feet per second. The caster merely had to hold the stone in the palm of his hands, or between two fingers, and cast the spell while visualizing the specific spot on the target that he or she was aiming for. The impact of that much granite at that speed was an explosive combination, to say the least. The wooden post the caster was aiming for, which looked like a leftover section of a telephone pole, ended up with a hole blown clear through it that was over three inches in diameter at the point of exit.

The magic rock spell wasn't the only spell causing law enforcement no end of grief right now, either. No, that was small-scale compared to some of the spells coming out. Someone must have gotten to Youtube.com and convinced them to stop allowing videos depicting magic spells and potion-making, but pretty much everyone with two brain cells to rub together and an Internet connection knew about it anyways. Closing Pandora's Box won't put the evils back in it, she thought to herself. The fireball spell was the worst of the bunch today, until something else came along to take its place tomorrow. Luckily, there were healing and mend spells to be had.

The mend spell was unique in that it fixed or improved any inanimate object. If your clothing was torn, ripped, wet, or worn out, cast a mend spell. It's suddenly dry and perfect again. If a shirt or pair of pants don't fit, cast a mend spell. It was magically altered to fit you, as long as you had that intention firmly in your mind when you cast it.

Intentions were rapidly becoming the new hack for spells. A healing spell could erase years of self-abuse and excess weight, as long as the caster kept that vision or thought in mind.

It could also erase tattoos one no longer wanted, or make new ones. Someone figured out how to make permanent, animated tattoos via a magical spell, and that idea suddenly became the new overnight sensation. Wolves howling, skulls casting evil laughs or having pulsing, glowing eyes, dragons breathing animated fire, beautiful women constantly undressing; the variations were as endless as the minds of those thinking them up.

Dozens if not hundreds of websites around the world were now hosting videos and documents on how to cast spells of all kinds, and what intentions produced the best results. Whenever one was shut down, two more were popping up. The most popular spells, after the obvious healing, cure disease, cure blindness, and cure poison spells (which were being referred to the Four Cardinal Health Spells or Potions) and the mend spell, were the food preservation spell, and the spell people were calling the Obfuscation Spell.

In short, the Obfuscation Spell was a magical version of encryption. Cast it on some data stored in a hard drive, on a book or some other written text, on a video clip or movie stored on a DVD or Blu-Ray disk, or even on a memory card, and only the people you wanted to be able to see, hear, and comprehend it would be able to.

It was possible, if the spell-caster was intelligent enough or forward-thinking enough, to hold in their mind that only a group of people meeting specific criteria would be able to access what was protected by the Obfuscation Spell, even if those people were unknown at the time of the spell casting, or if they hadn't met the criteria yet. No one was quite sure how it worked, but it was obvious that it did work and was fiendishly effective. Of course, Michelle knew how all of it worked, for some reason, but she saw no need to let other people know that, especially not after her fun experiences at the hands of the N.S.A.

Spells of all kinds were popping up on the Internet every day. And people were realizing that defensive spells and spells that healed taxed the spell caster considerably less than offensive spells and spells that harmed.

Michelle shook her head. She had no idea on what to do to fix things in the world; no idea on where to begin. And she wasn't sure if it was her place to step in, or even if she was capable. All she knew was that she felt like she was responsible. If it hadn't been the attack on her that started the whole thing, she thought to herself in quiet sadness and near desperation, none of this would be happening right now.

"Actually, that is not even remotely true. You take more upon yourself than is rightfully yours to bear with that sentiment." A quiet voice came to her from behind herself.

She didn't turn around towards the sound of the voice, but spoke up from where she stood. "That may be true, but it doesn't mean that I don't feel some sense of responsibility. The world's economy is teetering on the edge of total collapse. People are being harmed every day, and in many cases, are being killed by the hundreds or even the thousands. Previously pacifist religious organizations are encouraging their members to pick up weapons and not just defend themselves, but to go out in the world and fight for their 'righteous cause.' What a bunch of bullshit. The religious leaders are still demanding their money and power from their followers, and giving nothing in return. Nothing has changed there.

"And then there are all these Gods and Goddesses wandering around everywhere. I wish I could say they are making things better, but I don't see it. In all likelihood, they are making everything worse as they leave chaos and confusion in their wakes. They have no concept of this world, and no idea how the people of this world feel or think, or what motivates them. I doubt that most of them have the mental capacity to understand how complex everything is, here. This place is not like anyplace else in the multiverse. And it is clear to me that these Deities still think of humans the way Delara's people do – as simple, childish people that only want to eat, sleep, and have as much sex as they possibly can. And how the hell did they get that way?" She asked rhetorically. "That is about as impossibly far on one end of the spectrum as these humans are on the other. Sheesh."

Sekur nodded to himself. He knew he'd made the right choice in her. Now to sell her on his vision.

"All these things you say are true. Every one of them."

She turned to face him at last. "Then why the hell aren't you doing anything about it? Why are you just sitting back and fiddling while my world burns?" Her anger smoked and roiled just below the surface.

He looked at her calmly, with compassion in his eyes. "I am forbidden by the bounds of my existence from doing so. I literally cannot stretch forth my hand and directly interfere. Every being that is on this plane, save me, is both a child of mortal origins, including those Gods that are making such a mess of things right now, and is also possessed of an immortal soul that chains them to the Great Path of the Soul. But there is one thing that is missing." He held out his hand to her, and spoke. "Come, let me show you what it is."

She looked at him cautiously, like he was a used-car salesman in a leisure suit trying to sell her a well-used AMC Gremlin or a beat-up Yugo without a warranty, and he laughed.

"I promise no harm will come to you. You will learn what it is you need to know. And you will be free to make your own decisions. Free will is not just an abstract concept to be debated in a college philosophy class. Every being, on every plane I am over, has free will, and has the joy, or the pain, of their actions as consequence for those choices they make. Come." He held his hand out towards her, and she took it.

In an instant, the world around them became grey, and everything suddenly seemed to be made of shadows. He released her hand and stood calmly as she looked around.

"Where are we? What is this place? Oh! This is the Astral Plane, isn't it?" Recognition dawned as she saw what was around her.

"Yes. There is an Astral plane attached to every Material plane. It is the place where the God of this plane would oversee what happens here, and direct it as he or she saw fit." Her head snapped around to him in surprise at the choice of words he used, and he looked back at her calmly.

"By what you are saying, there IS no God of this material plane. What happened to him or her?"

"Him. His role ended when the wall was put up. He was overruled by the Gods and Goddesses who wanted to punish the mortals here who stood up to Anubis and Anaradelle when they demanded retribution from the mortals they felt were not remembering their place in the Gods' vision of this portion of the Great Path of the Soul. And he felt betrayed by me, when I refused to step in and undo the damage, or even mediate between the Gods and the humans. I released him to ascend to the next multiverse, so he might continue his journey on his own personal Path. There has not been a God over this plane ever since." He looked at her sadly, and anticipated her next question. "Five thousand three hundred or so years ago."

Michelle was stunned by learning this. Then a dawning realization hit her, and she would have fallen over in shock if she was back on the material plane. Her mouth gaped open, and she could only stare at the Greater God as he stood back quietly while he waited for her to work it out for herself.

Minutes went by before she was able to find her voice again. "You told me you were going to offer me a choice. Is it truly my choice? Or are there consequences if I turn it down?"

"There are no consequences in this. I will consider other options and choices of what to do if you say no. You have free will, remember? One cannot call it free will if I punish you for making a choice I don't agree with. I simply cannot unduly influence your choice one way or another. But I can try to convince you with words of the path I wish for you. You must know, however, that it involves some sacrifice on your part."

She nodded. "I would leave the Great Path of the Soul, at least for a time."

He agreed. "Yes. Eventually, you would be able to groom a successor to take over for you. Every role that is needed to serve the needs of the mortal souls may have a successor take over."

A flash of understanding and inspiration hit her. "Most Gods and Goddesses don't do that, do they?"

"No, they don't."

"If I do this, I will have to order all the other Gods to listen to me. Will that be an impossible task? How much will I have to compel them to do what I say? Wait, free will, again. This is a totally thankless job, isn't it?"

Sekur said nothing. She knew enough about it to figure it out on her own. She did have another question, though.

"Why me?" In some people, that would have come across as whiney or plaintive. In Michelle, it was neither. Sekur recognized that she was asking if she was qualified.

"You understand your human mortals. You have leadership experience, training, and skills. You have vision and the ability to turn that vision into action. And, you have suffered, much like others have and will suffer. You have a sympathetic ear, a strong will, a willing, adaptable mind, and a firm hand."

"Wow, interesting inventory there." She laughed. Then she sobered. "Are you really offering this to me? Me? Michelle Wilhelm?"

His one word reply resounded through her. "Yes."

"I have to think about it. I will get back to you." With that, Michelle disappeared from the Astral Plane, and he felt her reappear at her cottage in northern Minnesota where this entire situation all began some months ago. As he watched her there, she waved her hand and Sadie, her ever faithful and vexing canine companion, appeared at Michelle's side. Sadie wagging her tail as she said, "I missed you."

Comprehension that dawned in his eyes and his mind told him that he had made the right choice. She wouldn't rush into this expecting the power to be its own reward. She would take her responsibilities seriously, and work diligently for the betterment of her people. But, while she didn't say no, she didn't say yes, either. For the first time in the billions of years of his entire existence, he knew anxiety, and even a little fear, as he wondered what she would say, and when she would say it. And for the first time ever, he had no idea what would happen next.

To be continued...

ABOUT THE AUTHOR

Peter Hartz lives in Minnesota with his wife and their daughter, as well as two crazy dogs nicknamed Moppet and Floppet. Pete has worked in Information Technology as a network engineer and, recently, as a network architect, for over twenty years.

Peter played Dungeons and Dragons in the late 1980s under the masterful direction of Little John, Alaric, and Elfsong the Dreamweaver, three Dungeon Masters that he met through dial-up bulletin board systems before the Internet was a thing. It was the gaming sessions with Alaric and Elfsong that were the sources of two of the characters in the story.

In 1988 Peter attended the Renaissance Academy for Theatrical Improvisation and started working as a street performer at the Minnesota Renaissance Festival, where he met, pursued, and later fell in love the sweet, wonderful, kind, compassionate, and warm-hearted girl he married.

56649810R00250

Made in the USA
Columbia, SC
29 April 2019